FALLING FOR HIM: PART ONE

BOOKS 1 - 4

THE FALLING SERIES BOXSET

TRACY LORRAINE

FALLING FOR RYAN: PART ONE

FALLING SERIES BOOK #1

To
My biggest fan,
My best supporter,
My biggest inspiration,
My hero,
My best friend,
My mum.

You are missed every day. I wish you were here to see this. x

PROLOGUE

Molly

Eight years ago...

"Mum, I'm going to Becky's sixteenth birthday party tonight, then sleeping at Hannah's," I remind her as I walk into the kitchen where she's sat with her head in an interior design magazine, waving her hands around—presumably trying to dry her nail varnish. I pull out a can of Coke from the fridge before continuing. "I've taken the litre bottle of vodka from the drinks cabinet, and I've got a pack of condoms... you know, just in case." I lean back against the counter and watch for a reaction. *Any* reaction.

"Uh-huh."

"I'm pretty sure some of the boys are bringing ecstasy."

"Hmm..." She hums as she turns a page and studies the room pictured.

"Didn't you only have a manicure yesterday? Why are you painting your nails already?"

Now, that gets her attention. Her head snaps up the moment the words 'nails' and 'manicure' leave my mouth. Surprise, surprise; my mother cares more about that than about alcohol, drugs, sex... and me.

"Yes, I did, but I just couldn't find a thing to wear tonight."

I doubt that's actually true, seeing as she's recently turned my eldest brother's old room into her personal wardrobe after already filling her own walk-in. "So, I went to that little boutique in town this morning and found the most perfect dress. Your dad will love it, but it didn't match the colour I chose for my nails yesterday."

"Wow, what a disaster," I mutter as I leave the room. "I'll be going out in about an hour. *Not that you really care.*" I say the last bit quieter, but I'm not sure why; when I look back, Mum is once again too engrossed in her magazine to acknowledge me.

I let out a huge breath and head back up to my room to finish packing for the party. I'm getting ready with my best friend Hannah and her twin Emma, who live next door. We've all been friends for as long as I can remember. Being twins, Hannah and Emma are really close, but Hannah and I are not far behind. The three of us do almost everything together; their parents have often joked that they have triplets, really.

I always laugh along.

Even though they know what my life is like, I don't think any of them really appreciate how much I wish that were true.

I'm just shoving my fourth outfit choice for the night into my bag when I hear my brother downstairs, greeting Mum. She instantly responds to him, which makes me laugh to myself, although it's anything but funny. One of her golden boys has come to visit. I bet if he needed something, she'd ruin that new nail varnish in an instant. God, I can't wait to get out of this hellhole I call home.

"Is Molly still here?" Daniel asks.

Her reply sounds suspiciously like, "I have no idea."

Walking to the other side of the room, I rest my hands on the windowsill and blow out a long breath as I gaze out over the countryside, trying to calm myself down. I keep telling myself not to get worked up by their actions, but sometimes it's easier said than done.

"Hey, Sis, I'm glad you're still here," Daniel says as he enters my room a few minutes later. My brothers are a lot older than me; I was an unplanned accident fifteen and a half years ago. Daniel is my youngest older brother and, at thirty years old, he's crazy protective of me. Steven is, too, but he now has a serious girlfriend so I'm seeing less of him these days. Daniel is my idol—always has been. He doesn't take life too seriously, does exactly as he pleases, works bloody hard, but always has fun. That's exactly what I want my life to be like, and I plan on making it so—once I get out on my own.

"Hey." I only manage one word because, as soon as I see him, I burst into tears. He pulls me into a tight hug. I hate that Mum and Dad can do this to me. Can make me feel so worthless. It makes me angry every time a tear falls for their actions. I wish I could be stronger.

"What have they done now?" Daniel asks. Both he and Steven know how our parents treat me. Hell, I couldn't count the number of arguments I've overheard about it on both hands and feet, but nothing ever changes. I'm just grateful that I have two amazing older brothers to turn to if I need to. Plus, I have my adopted family next door, who I'm pretty sure would do just about anything for me if I needed it.

"Nothing. I'm fine," I say, pulling away from him and wiping my eyes. I look at him and see the questions in his. "No, really; I'm just being a silly, hormonal teenager."

"Hmm... whatever you say, Molls. You still going to that party tonight?" I don't believe for a second that he buys my lie, but he knows it's easier for me not to discuss it. Nothing he can say is going to make any of it better, anyway.

"Of course, why?"

"I got you something." I watch as he reaches into his coat pocket and pulls out a small bottle of vodka before handing it to me.

"What's this for?" He looks at me and quirks an eyebrow. "I know it's to drink, you fool, but why are you giving it to me?"

"Because I remember what it was like being your age, and I didn't think anyone else would be buying you some. You deserve to act your age, Molly. Let your hair down. You work too damn hard trying to get your grades. But please be sensible. I don't want to be visiting you in the hospital or be an uncle yet. Actually..." He pauses as he reaches into his back pocket and pulls out his wallet.

My eyes widen in embarrassment. "No, no, no... I'm good, you don't need to worry about that."

I hate to admit it, but Daniel is the only one who knows what I've been up to. He let himself into my room one day while I was in my en suite to find an open box of condoms on the bed and, being the protective brother that he is, counted them and realised two were missing. I'm hoping he doesn't want more of an explanation than that, because I really don't want to sit here and explain to my adult brother that I took myself off to the doctors a while ago and got myself on the pill—you know, just in case. Wouldn't that make Mummy and Daddy proud, to be grandparents while their daughter was still a teenager? Imagine the embarrassment.

"Okay, well, have a good time tonight, and ring me if you have any problems, yeah?"

"I promise."

I know I mentioned drugs and alcohol to my mum downstairs, but my group of friends isn't really into all that. I only said it as a way to provoke her in the hopes of getting some kind of reaction. Yes, there are plenty of kids at school who are at it every weekend, but my group actually cares about getting good grades and good jobs. The bottle of vodka Daniel just handed me will probably be it for us tonight.

"See you later then, kid," he says before kissing my forehead and leaving my room.

"That was awesome," Hannah squeals as the three of us stumble into the twins' bedroom sometime in the early hours of Sunday morning. Emma heads straight over to her side of the room and immediately starts replacing her party clothes with her pyjamas, while Hannah and I sit on her bed and reflect on the evening.

"So... come on, spill it... where did you go with Callum?" Hannah pleads.

"Just for a walk in the garden. I told you earlier!"

"I didn't believe you then, and I still don't now. I saw you two getting off with each other in the corner before you disappeared."

Callum is the boy at school that every girl dreams of. He's sporty, clever, funny and, of course, seriously hot, which is exactly why no one expected him to show his face tonight. But he did, and let's just say that I got to know him a little better than I did before. I'm yet to decide if that's a good thing or not.

"Will you two keep it down? I want to get up early tomorrow to do some coursework before we go to Grandma's," Emma complains from her bed.

Okay, so I said before that we work hard to get good grades, but Emma takes it to the extreme. I was actually surprised she gave herself tonight off. She's doing A-level maths already and does Spanish lessons after school to get herself an extra GCSE. I think she's putting too much pressure on herself, but she can't seem to stop in her quest to be the best accountant Oxford has ever seen.

"Sorry," we whisper simultaneously.

"So... come on, Molly, tell me," Hannah says, keeping her voice low.

I let out a frustrated breath and go for it. "Okay, so we went outside and found a quiet corner in the garden behind a bush. He pulled me down to the ground and we kissed for a while and let our hands... roam a little." I look up at Hannah and can see her excitement about what might come next.

"Oh my God, did you have sex with him?" she asks, but says the word *sex* much quieter. I don't know why; it's only Emma who could be listening.

"No, I didn't. I sorta thought we were going to, but by the time I got into his boxers, he was so worked up that he went off like a firework!" I can't help it, I burst out laughing at the memory, earning me another grumble from Emma.

"But I thought Callum's slept with loads of girls?" Hannah asks, confused.

"That's what the rumour mill says... I would be inclined to say that this was his first experience and the rumours are just that: rumours." We fall about giggling like the schoolgirls we are; I guess that vodka hasn't totally worn off yet.

"So, you *were* going to have sex with him, then?"

"Yeah, I guess," I say, shrugging my shoulders.

"But don't you want to wait until you're in love?" she asks innocently.

The only thing I have never told my best friend is that I lost my virginity last year at a party. Hannah has a different outlook on life thanks to her normal, loving family, and I don't want to have to explain my reasons for doing what I did that night—and a few times since. I totally understand her desire to wait until she's in love, and I admire her for it, but what I needed that night—what I *still* need—is to feel wanted by someone. And that first night? That was exactly how I felt.

CHAPTER ONE

Molly

Present

It's midnight, and I've been sat on Ryan's doorstep for nearly an hour. I've already started on one of the bottles of wine. Although it was a scorching summer's day, the heat has now worn off, the clouds have gathered, and it's lumping it down with rain. I'm trying to tuck myself into his little porch to stop from getting so wet, but with the wind direction, it's not doing much good. I'm soaked through. It was a silly idea to pick white t-shirts when I rebranded the coffee shop; thank God for padded bras!

By the time I'd cleaned and locked up, it was just gone ten. I love working at Cocoa's and have done so since I was sixteen. Hannah and Emma's parents own it. Susan started the business after she finished university. She came into some inheritance and, with the money, Cocoa's was born. The place was a huge part of my childhood. Hannah, Emma, and I would go there after school to do homework or just chat about boys, and it pretty much stayed that way until we finished university. We still have a booth in the back corner dedicated to us.

I will forever be grateful for Susan and her husband, Pete, whom she actually met as a customer in Cocoa's. It was love at first sight for them. Not only did they give me a job, but they took me under their wing when I was much younger.

Megan, who works in the evenings, had a phone call from her boyfriend at eight o'clock saying their little boy was really sick. I let her go home to be with him and finished up the rest of the night on my own.

Once I got in my car, all I could think about was having a nice hot bath and snuggling into bed in my tiny one-bed flat with my boyfriend, Max. We've been together on and off for the past three years, but when Hannah, whom I'd lived with above the coffee shop, decided eight months ago that she wanted her own boyfriend to move into the flat, I decided it was time I moved out and left them to it. Max had suggested I move in with him. I wasn't thrilled by the idea, to be honest, but at the time I didn't have the money to find anywhere decent to live. I hate being alone. I would have had to find someone who was renting out a room anyway, so it seemed like a sensible suggestion and a logical step in our relationship.

A week later, we all moved. Me into Max's flat, and Hannah's boyfriend into the one we'd shared for the past six years.

The ten-minute drive to our home seemed to take forever. I pulled up out the front; it was weird to be parking next to Max's car. He had worked nights the whole time I'd known him.

I dragged my body up the stairs to the third floor and let myself in. I shut the door behind me; the only light was coming from the bedroom. My heart dropped into my stomach when I heard voices and strange noises coming from down the hallway. As quietly as I could, I tiptoed toward them.

When I got to the door, I couldn't believe my eyes. Now, I knew Max was no angel, but I was under the impression that we had put the past behind us when we decided to live together and had become a monogamous couple. Yes, the past few months had been a strain, but still.

What was happening before my eyes on our bed showed me how wrong I was.

I numbly slipped back down the hallway and grabbed a couple of pairs of knickers that, luckily for me, were drying on the radiator, and left.

I tried to keep myself together as I made a pit stop at the shop on my way to Ryan's house. I didn't want to be one of those emotional women sobbing in the alcohol aisle, trying to decide which bottle would make me forget.

Once I'd paid for two bottles of my favourite wine and a crate of lager for Ryan, I made my way over to his new house. He'd only moved in two weeks ago, although it was months ago that he made the decision to buy the three-story townhouse in the new development on the outskirts of the city. It was basically a pile of bricks when he took me with him to see it for the first time, but I could see why he'd fallen in love with it. It was modern and spacious, with amazing views across fields from the back. From the front, you could see all the lights from the city in the distance. Because it was yet to be finished, it meant Ryan could choose a lot of the interior to suit his taste, and he didn't have to spend his whole summer redecorating.

Grabbing my phone, I open up my messages to reread the conversation I'd had with him earlier. He said he was going out tonight to celebrate the end of the school year but that he wasn't expecting to be home late. I guess that didn't really go as planned—not that he'd be expecting me to be sitting here waiting for him.

I'm starting to think I should have gone somewhere else. It's not that I don't have any other options, but out of all my friends and family, Ryan knows me the best.

What we've been through this year has made us close. I think I can safely say he's turned into my best friend somewhere in the last six months.

As I wait, images of what was happening on my bed flash through my head. I guess I should have seen it coming, really. A leopard never changes its spots, right?

Eventually, the tears come flooding out. To add to my misery, I now have black mascara streaks running down my cheeks and red puffy eyes.

Finally, I see headlights coming my way and Ryan's white Honda Civic pulling into his drive. At first, he looks shocked to see me. That changes to anger as he strides toward me.

Ryan

As I come to a stop, I can see that there's a very wet Molly huddled in my porch. She looks dreadful. I come to a very quick conclusion that it's because of her dickhead of a boyfriend. I knew it was coming; it was just a matter of when.

"Ryan," Molly sobs as I lift her tiny frame off the ground and into a hug. She shakes from both the cold and the sobs wracking her body.

Tucking her into my side, I grab her bags and let us in. On the ground floor, my townhouse has a large room with French doors looking out to the courtyard garden, and a bathroom. I thought it would make an excellent gym. The middle floor is an open-plan kitchen, living, and dining room with a small cloakroom, and the top floor has three bedrooms, one being the master with en suite and the other a large family bathroom.

I love it.

From the moment I looked at the plans, I just knew it was going to be my little piece of heaven, and I'm still in awe that I was able to buy this place. I'll be forever grateful for the generous gift from Susan and Pete. Nothing will ever make up for what we all lost, but thanks to them, I've been able to attempt to move on with my life.

Currently, there are boxes everywhere. I haven't had much time to unpack with everything I had to do at school to end the year, but my first holiday job is to get this place sorted and looking like a home.

Anger fills my veins as I lead us up to the living room. "It's going to be okay. Let's get you warm and dry and you can tell me what the fucker did." My fists clench. I want to beat the shit out of him for treating her so badly for so long.

"How do you know he's done anything?" Molly asks in a quiet voice.

"I can read you like a book, Molly Carter. Plus, he's a massive dickhead. I think I've mentioned that before. Only Max can make you feel this bad about yourself."

"Why was I so fucking stupid? I had my doubts, everyone had their doubts, but he convinced me that it was what he wanted. I'm not really surprised, but what does shock me is how much it *hurts*."

"Come on, get your arse upstairs and in the shower. I'll find you a t-shirt to wear."

As I root through a suitcase in one of the spare bedrooms, the door to my en suite shuts. I pull out my Oxford Brookes polo and leave it on my bed. I hope my choice will make her smile, remembering happier times.

I knock lightly on the door. "Have you got everything you need?"

There's silence for a few seconds, and I can imagine her checking out all the products in the shower, realising they're all for men. Eventually, I hear a quiet "Yes" from the other side of the door.

"Okay, I'll see you downstairs when you're done. Take your time."

I gather up her wet clothes and take them with me. They may be soaked, but I can still smell her vanilla scent on them. It makes me feel oddly warm inside. She's been my rock for the past six months. I don't know what I would have done without her.

As I put everything in the washing machine, I spot her bra poking out of the pile. "What the fuck do I do with this?" I mutter to myself. Something in me wonders if it needs some kind of special cycle in the machine, but fuck if I know. I decide to shove it all in and just put it on a cool, quick wash.

That shouldn't do it much damage, right?

CHAPTER TWO

Molly

I stand in the giant walk-in shower for a good twenty minutes, letting the hot water from the rainfall showerhead soothe my aching muscles. I could get used to this.

Once I'm finished, I head back into the bedroom and see Ryan's white Oxford Brookes University t-shirt on his bed. I smile for the first time in what feels like forever and pull it over my head. He was wearing this the first night we all met in the student union.

Ryan's also placed my handbag on the bed, obviously knowing from the size of it that there must be something in there I could use, and he would be right. I pull out a hairbrush and try to do something with my hair after not finding any conditioner in the shower. I spritz my favourite perfume and pull on a pair of the knickers I grabbed earlier, feeling very grateful that I don't have to go commando under his t-shirt.

Once I feel almost human again, I head downstairs to where I know there's a big glass of wine waiting for me.

I walk into the open-plan living area to find Ryan leaning his hip against the kitchen worktop with his feet crossed, staring closely at his phone. He's changed since he got in and is now wearing long, slouchy navy shorts that hang low on his hips and a fitted white t-shirt that shows off his wide shoulders, slim waist, and muscled chest and arms to perfection. His dirty blond hair is a mess, as if he's spent the whole time I was in the shower running his hands through it. I've always found Ryan attractive—well, who wouldn't? He's stunning. And his Scouse accent... it's diluted since he first moved to Oxford, but it isn't any less sexy.

But he's not my type; I tend to go for slimmer guys with less muscle, although I still remember trying to hit on him the night we met. I kept trying and trying, making a total fool of myself. I was too drunk to realise he was paying no attention to me but was besotted with my best friend. Good times.

His head comes up as I move toward him and his eyes travel slowly from the top of my head to my toes and back again while his teeth attack his bottom lip.

"Everything all right?" I ask, trying not to smirk.

"Um... yeah... sorry, it's just that it's... um... it's been a while, you know," he stutters as his cheeks turn a little pink.

"Yeah, I know what you mean," I mumble to myself more than him. "Plus, I dare any man not to check out my legs." I'm hoping to lighten the mood; I don't want him to be embarrassed. We both know we can never go there, but a harmless bit of looking is fine.

Ryan mutters something under his breath as he turns around to grab my wine.

"What was that?"

"Fuck... uh... the bloody woman next door is staring again. Look." He gestures to the kitchen window and I just see a flash of red hair as she scarpers.

"She's probably just enjoying her few seconds of man-candy."

He shudders before turning back to me. "Your clothes are on a quick wash. They'll be done soon and we can get them drying. I'm guessing they're the only clothes you have with you?"

I follow Ryan into the living room and curl myself up in the middle of his corner sofa with my wine, making myself comfortable.

"All my stuff is in the flat."

"What happened tonight?" Ryan asks. "Fuck, he wasn't with someone else, was he?"

"It's worse than that." My stomach turns over as I picture it again. Watching Ryan's eyebrows rise in question, I continue. "There was one blonde bimbo riding his cock and another sat on his face."

"I'm going to rip his fucking head off. How could he do that to you? And in your fucking bed? He must have known you were going to be home soon. Fuck, I'm going to fucking kill him. I always told you he wasn't good enough for you. I told you this would happen and that you would get hurt."

He paces back and forth in front of me, his hands alternating between running through his hair and clenching into fists at his sides. The muscles in his neck pulse with anger.

I can't help but think Max should be watching his back, because it's going to fucking hurt when Ryan gets his hands on him.

"What did you do?" he asks through gritted teeth.

"I left."

Draining his can of beer, he's silent before going to get a second.

"Can I have a refill, too?" I ask, realising I've drunk my way through my glass telling that story.

Ryan comes back with the bottle and fills me up before placing it on the coffee table and opening his beer. "So, what are you going to do? I guess he doesn't know he's been caught?"

"I have no idea. All I can think about is how stupid I am. Oh, and how when I decide where I'm going to live, I want a shower like yours."

Ryan doesn't look amused by my comment; his eyes urge me to continue.

"You can stop worrying. I'm not going back to him. I never should have moved in with him in the first place."

"You and Max have never had the type of relationship that would end up being something serious, and you knew it; you were just too scared to get out of it. You don't go from fucking about with Max while screwing others to living together and being in a committed relationship."

"All you had to say was 'I told you so'. I don't need a big lecture," I snap, tears pricking my eyes. Ryan pulls me into his chest, rubbing my back.

"Shit, I'm so sorry. I didn't mean to upset you," he whispers in my ear.

My tears eventually cease and I lift my head off Ryan's chest. Looking up into his blue eyes, all I see is compassion. There's no pity at all, which makes my heart a little happier.

I throw my arms around his shoulders and hug him tight. This was why I came here tonight—for my best friend, who will tell me exactly what I need to hear and exactly what I don't want to hear, to pull me out of the rut I have found myself in.

Ryan

"I hate to break the moment, but I really have to wee," I say into Molly's hair. I feel her shake her head against my neck and it makes me laugh. Standing with her in my arms, I place her back on the sofa before heading out of the room.

When I come back, I find her pulling her clothes out of the washing machine. "You washed my black jeans with my white top and underwear; how is it possible that you've been living on your own for years, yet you still do that?" She has a deadly serious look on her face, making me laugh.

"Sorry. I was more concerned with what I was meant to do with your bra than about separating the colours. It's like an alien creature to me... is it meant to have its own cycle? Extra special treatment or something?" I comment, trying to sound as serious as she had.

It's her turn to start laughing. It warms my heart to see her happiness after all the misery we've been through. She actually laughs so hard that she has to hold on to the worktop for support.

"You're serious, aren't you?"

I just shrug my shoulders and head back into the living room, saying over my shoulder, "It's a dryer as well, but I'll let you handle that."

"Thank you. It's probably safer; I need something to wear tomorrow and I'd prefer if it didn't fit a doll." She smiles.

Following me, she helps herself to my iPad and unlocks it.

"What are you doing?" I ask with a laugh as she settles herself at the coffee table.

"I want to start looking for a place to live. I don't want to cramp your style. You've only just moved in; you don't need me in the way."

The thought of her moving somewhere new on her own doesn't sit well with me. I know she hates solitude and would rather live with someone—which is how she ended up living with dickhead Max, after all.

I make a snap decision, but I know it's the right one.

"Molly..."

"Yeah," she says without looking up from the screen.

"Molly." I try again to make her look up at me. It works this time, and her eyes eventually meet mine.

"Move in here, with me. You can have the room and bathroom downstairs. You'd have your own space, and your snoring won't keep me awake at night from two floors away."

Her eyes widen in shock as she stares at me, processing my words. "Um..."

I sit and wait. The house is so quiet, I can almost hear the cogs turning in her brain as she contemplates what to say next and whether to take me up on my offer. Eventually, I get bored of waiting.

"This house is too big for me, really. It's so quiet here. The rent will be cheaper than a place of your own, and I'll let you decorate your room however you want." God, I hope she won't take me up on that and paint it Barbie pink or anything crazy. She's still silent. "Molly, tell me what you're thinking."

All of a sudden, she's off the floor and practically running for the stairs.

"Shit!" I get up and run after her. "Molly, come back! You can't leave the house wearing that. Molly!" I shout as I chase her down the stairs.

When I reach the bottom, I realise she has no intention of leaving.

She's stood amongst all the boxes and crap in the downstairs room I've just offered her. She looks back at me, tears in her eyes. Great, I've made her cry again.

"Are you sure? This was going to be your gym. I don't want to take that away from you. You bought this house for peace and quiet. It won't be so peaceful with me around, and definitely not quiet. Do you really mean it?"

"If I wasn't sure, I wouldn't have asked. I have two more spare rooms upstairs that could be my gym. What do *you* want? What would make *you* happy, Molly Carter?"

I watch her closely as she studies her hands and nails, trying to work out what she wants. She opens her mouth to speak and, when it comes out, it's so quiet I almost miss it. "I want this."

"I'm sorry, Molly, you'll have to speak up. What did you say?"

This time, she looks up. The tears are still in her eyes, but I can tell the decision has been made. "I want this. I want to move in." With that, she launches herself at me from across the room with such force that I have to take a step back to stop us toppling over when I catch her.

"Thank you so much, Ry. You have no idea how happy this makes me. I'll be the best housemate ever, I promise. This is it... a new start for me from this day forward. I'm going to do things for me, because I want to, not because anyone else wants or expects me to."

We make our way back upstairs, and I start thinking of all the things we need to do to get us both properly moved in. "When do you want to collect your stuff from the flat?" It should be done as soon as possible so she can put Max behind her.

"Well, he's going out for his mate's birthday tomorrow night. Usually, they're out all night, so I could go then."

"I'm not letting you go alone. Firstly, you'll have to do loads of trips in that roller skate of a car you have, and secondly, just no. I'm coming with you."

"Ryan, you don't have to do that. You've already done more than I could ask of you."

"Okay, how about... Shut up; this isn't up for discussion. What time is he going out, and what time should we head over?"

"You know you're a stubborn arse, right?"

Laughing, I shrug my shoulders at her in response.

"If we go over at seven, he should be well gone by then. That will give us plenty of time to make sure I have everything."

We return to the sofa and Molly pulls the blanket over our legs, settling back into the cushions. "How is it that you've hardly unpacked anything yet, but you have a blanket over the back of your sofa?"

Usually, I would agree with her. It is unusual, but it was the first thing Hannah and I bought after we moved in together. We had many amazing nights together sat under this thing, and it might make me sound like a pussy, but I wanted it here with me in my new house. I wanted a little bit of her with me.

"I can tell by that look on your face. It's Hannah's, isn't it?"

"Yes, it is, but tonight, we're not talking about all that. We're being happy and celebrating you moving in."

"That sounds like a plan, Mr. Evans. Chuck the remote over; we need music if we're celebrating."

With that, the sounds of old school hip-hop and R&B fill the room and I groan.

"What?" Molly asks, an innocent look on her face.

"I'd forgotten about your love of this 'music'. Maybe I should have considered that before asking you to move in."

But Molly is already up, dancing around the room with the last of her wine.

In this moment, she looks happy and carefree like all twenty-four-year-olds should. I want her to be like this more. She deserves to be like this more. Hell, we both do after the grief we've been battling for almost six months.

Pain rips through me at the thought of it being that long already. Everything has changed so much and Hannah hasn't been here to experience any of it.

As one song drifts into another, I notice the beat of the songs get more and more sexy—as do Molly's dance moves. She's grinding her hips around and around. I can't help but notice how fucking sexy she is. It's been a long time since I've seen any action and, although my brain knows nothing will ever happen between us, apparently my dick didn't get the message. Thank God for the blanket.

A little bit of guilt washes through me, but I manage to push it to one side.

"Come on, Ry, dance with me." She slurs her words and gives me her 'come hither' look.

Fuck, don't do that. "No, you're okay. I'm fine here, watching."

As the next song comes on, she waves her hands above her head, making my t-shirt rise, revealing the bottom of red lacy knickers that are cut high across her arse—her tight, perky arse.

After another couple of songs with me looking in any direction other than Molly, she starts to stumble around to the point where I think she's going to be on that pretty little arse pretty soon.

"Molly, I think it's time you sat down before you fall down."

"Ooohhh cooome on... dooon't be a spoil sport." She slurs the words as she trips over the coffee table and ends up lying face down on the sofa.

All of a sudden, she flips herself over with a pout, mumbling about how she can't remember when she last had so much fun, got drunk, and danced the night away.

I wasn't going to ruin it by telling her she was only dancing for about thirty minutes, because I can't remember the last time I saw her smile like this.

Eventually, she stops chatting crap and her breathing evens out. I look at the clock and realise it's nearly four in the morning; no wonder she's asleep. I quietly tidy up our mess before scooping her up in my arms and carrying her to my bedroom. Currently, this is the only bed in the house, so until we go shopping, she'll be here with me. I'm not letting her have a bad night's sleep on the sofa.

I tuck her in before stripping down to my boxers and sliding in next to her. I have a super king-sized bed, so it will be easy to sleep together and not even realise there's someone else here.

As soon as my head hits the pillow, I'm out like a light.

CHAPTER THREE

Molly

I wake up with a start, trying to work out where the hell I am. It takes a couple of seconds for the fog to lift before I realise I'm in Ryan's bed. "Shit," I mumble as my hands dive under the covers to see what I'm wearing—if anything.

I'm relieved to find I'm still in his t-shirt and I still have underwear on. I know I shouldn't be concerned—this is Ryan I'm talking about, after all. The last thing I remember is dancing around the living room and wondering why he has such a weird look on his face.

I bolt upright in bed when he appears at the door, smiling and saying, "Good morning," way too loudly. It's then that I realise quite how rough I feel, and I slowly lie back down to try to ease the ache in my head.

"Oh dear, you feeling that good?"

My answer is to glare at him.

"Here, I've brought you water and painkillers. I thought you might need them."

"Thank you," I say in a really croaky voice that makes me laugh to myself. "Why am I in your bed? I don't want you sleeping on the sofa in your own house."

"After you passed out on the sofa, I went to bed, but before I could fall asleep you came in here begging me for sex," he says very seriously.

"Oh God," I say, shaking my head. "You're joking, right? I never did that!" I feel my face get redder and redder and I pull the covers up to hide myself.

"You'll be pleased to know I turned you down. It was tough when you started begging, but I stayed strong."

With that, I totally disappear under the covers, hiding my embarrassment from him. "Oh my God, I'm so sorry. I was really drunk; can you leave the room so I can just sneak out of your house? You'll never have to see me again," I squeak from my hiding place.

"Molly, don't say that."

"Oh, that's fine for you to say. You're not the one mortified by your drunken actions."

"Molly, look at me." He tries to pull the covers from me but I'm clinging to them for dear life. I hear him move to the bottom of the bed and, from there, he peels them back over my head. I immediately cover my face with my hands to hide how embarrassed I am, but I keep my fingers apart enough so I can see him.

After a few seconds of looking at me, he apparently can't contain himself any longer and bursts into laughter. Not just any laughter, but the kind that has him doubling over in pain. Tears fill his eyes, he's laughing so hard, and I make sure to have an unimpressed expression on my face.

Making a grab for a pillow, I launch it at his head, causing him to fall nose-first onto the floor, making his eyes water even more. One hit is not enough for what he just did to me, so I launch a full-on attack.

Eventually, my sense of humour starts to take over, and I'm laughing along with him, and *at* him, seeing as he's now curled up on the carpet, rolling around and holding his nose.

When my side starts hurting, I give up and sit on the end of the bed. He pulls himself up and settles on the floor in front of me. Laughing after everything feels so damn good.

"I'm sorry, it was just too good an opportunity to miss," he says to me, still smirking.

"How long have you been planning that?" I ask him seriously.

"Oh, since I got up about two hours ago."

"You're a dick—you know that, right?"

"I'm sorry." He puts his hands up in surrender. "Now, get your arse in that bathroom and get ready. We've got a lot to do today. I've already put your dry clothes in there so you can get dressed. Meet me in the kitchen—I'll have breakfast ready."

Ryan leaves the room and I make my way into his en suite after taking the painkillers he left for me. It takes me a few minutes to realise what he's done, but when I do, I completely forget about his 'joke' this morning. Not only are my dry clothes in a neat pile on the unit, but there's a new toothbrush and a can of women's deodorant next to them. When I look in the shower, I see new bottles of shampoo and conditioner—nice, girly pink ones. There's also a new shower gel, a pink shower puff, and even a pink razor. My eyes start to fill with tears as I take everything in. He may have been up for a couple of hours, planning how to most embarrass me on our first day as housemates, but he's also done this. I don't think anyone has ever done anything so sweet for me before.

While I'm in the shower, I realise what I need to do. This is my first day putting myself first. I need to ring my friend Shane and call in a favour.

Looking at the time on my phone, I realise that it's already nearly midday on his busiest day of the week. I don't expect him to answer, but as I put my phone to my ear, I'm surprised to hear his voice after the first ring.

"Hey, how's our number one groomsmaid?" Shane asks, making me smile. I first met Chris, now Shane's fiancé, at university. He was studying the same graphic design course that Hannah and I were. We all hit it off straight away and he soon became our gay best friend. Then, not long after, he met Shane and fell crazy in love and, well, as they say, the rest is history.

"I need to call in that favour you owe me. Can you fit me in today? I'll explain everything if you can squeeze me in."

"Lucky for you, my last appointment of the day rang in sick, so I'm free after three o'clock this afternoon."

"Thank you so much. I'll see you then. By the way, we're going for a change."

After Shane hangs up, I do that really embarrassing girly clap and jump up and down thing. I'm grateful no one can see me. I'm so excited that I'm going to start the new me off with a bang.

Once I'm ready, I head downstairs. Ryan must have heard me coming because, when I turn the corner, he takes a teabag out of a mug and slides it across the breakfast bar to me. I ignore the tea for now and go straight to Ryan, throwing my arms around his neck.

"Am I forgiven?" he asks cautiously.

"I can't believe you did all that for me. When did you have time?"

"I woke up early and went for a run. I'm still experimenting with routes around here, but I came across a shop on my way back and thought you could do with some girly shit when you woke up. I also got breakfast," he adds, motioning to the fresh croissants and pains au chocolat on the breakfast bar.

"Yum. I think I'm going to enjoy living here," I say as I round the breakfast bar and perch myself on the stool. "So, what's your plan for the day?" I ask Ryan, hoping that whatever he says doesn't involve me, because I already know what I need to do today, and it needs to be on my own.

"Well, we're going to get your stuff tonight at seven, right?"

"Yes. What about the rest of the day?"

"There isn't that much of it left now, really, is there?" he says sarcastically.

"Just because some of us actually need beauty sleep to look good..."

He smiles before he continues. "I need to get your room cleared out so we have somewhere to put your stuff later. What about you?"

"I've got a few things I need to do."

"Do you have any furniture to move in downstairs?"

That makes me realise how little I do have. "No," I answer sadly.

"Okay. Cancel any plans you have for tomorrow. We're going furniture shopping."

"I've never decorated a room before. I can't wait."

"What? Even when you were a kid?" Ryan asks, sounding shocked.

"No, my mum used to get an interior designer to redo the house every five years or so. It was always the latest fashion at the time. Susan and Pete had the flat above Cocoa's refurbished before we moved in, and Max had been living in his place for a while and liked it the way it was; he didn't want any 'girly shit' around."

"Right, well, here's your chance. You'd better get thinking."

After breakfast, I say goodbye to Ryan and head out, promising I'll be back about six. I'm not looking forward to returning to the flat. Last night already seems like a lifetime ago, but it will be good to close the door on that part of my life and move on.

As I drive down the street I grew up on, I make sure not to slow down in front of my parents' house. It's not like I expect them to be on the lookout. Dad will be working and Mum will be socialising with Oxford's elite somewhere. I have hardly any good memories of that house, and I don't intend on making any now. As I pull into the Morrisons' driveway, however, I begin to smile. I love this house, the people inside, and all the memories I have of growing up here.

"Hello," I shout as I walk in. I'm considered family here, so I haven't knocked on the front door in years.

"In the kitchen," Susan calls back. It's not like I expected them to be anywhere else; they all live in there. They have the homiest house I've ever been in. It's the total opposite of next door. That was like a show home; I always felt like I was making the place untidy by just being there.

"Hey," I say, smiling as I walk into the room. Susan pulls me into a hug, followed by a kiss on the cheek from Pete. Declan and Lilly are back from university and sitting at the table, finishing their lunch. They both wave and smile around their food. Susan and Pete weren't just lucky enough to have one set of fraternal twins, but two. Apparently, it's genetic. Susan's mum was a twin and so was her grandmother. No one ever expected Susan to carry two sets, though. That was a shocking announcement a little over nineteen years ago. The younger twins are now at university. Lilly is close by in Cheltenham, studying interior design, but Declan decided to go further afield to Exeter to study business. They're both back for the summer, and I can tell by the smile on Susan's face that she loves having her babies home. She had serious empty nest syndrome when they first went; she's such a mother hen.

"Do you want anything to eat, angel?" Susan asks me. She's always called her children 'angel' and, from a young age, that included me. That's why, in the end, Hannah and I decided to name our company Angel Designs. We very quickly decided we were not having any obvious imagery: no halos, wings, or fairy-tale stuff. We went for more of an angels-with-dirty-faces approach. Our logo ended up being black and greys with a splash of magenta. The font we chose was edgy, but it worked for us. We loved it—well, I still do.

"No, I'm fine, thank you. A cup of tea wouldn't go amiss, though," I say with a smile. There's always tea in the pot at this house.

"Of course. You sit down and I'll bring it over."

After a few minutes, all five of us are sat around the table, catching up with each other. I love these moments; I never had them with my family.

"So, Molly, how's Max?" Lilly asks me.

"Ah, well, that's sort of one of the reasons I'm here. It's over, I've left—"

"Thank God for that," Susan butts in.

"Susan," Pete scolds.

"Oh, angel, I'm sorry, but I never liked him. He wasn't good enough for you. He didn't treat you well."

"You're right. I knew it was never going to work. I never loved him, and I know I deserve better. And you know what? I'm going to get it. Today is the first day of the rest of my life."

"Good for you, angel," Susan says, putting her arm around my shoulders.

"So, where are you going to live?" Pete chimes in.

"Well, that's another thing, I—"

"I'll go make up the spare room," Susan butts in again. God, I love her; she doesn't even bat an eyelash about taking care of me like one of her own.

"Thank you, but that won't be necessary. Actually, Ryan has asked me if I'll move into his place."

"I think that's a great idea. We know how much you two have helped each other this year. It will be good to have each other close by," Pete says, nodding his head.

"I'm really excited. He's taking me furniture shopping tomorrow and letting me decorate my room however I want. I've never done that before." I try to ignore the slight twinge in my stomach. Am I betraying Hannah by moving into his house? It's easy to put it to one side when her parents are so encouraging of it.

"Good for you," Susan says, smiling.

"Is Emma around?" I ask. Since the accident, Emma seems to have become the opposite of a recluse. She's never home, but no one knows where she is. She's not always at work, because Susan has rung them before now to speak to her. She's only working part-time, but she won't tell us where she goes or what she does, other than work. I've only seen her a few times, and she rarely replies to messages or answers her phone. I can't imagine how hard losing Hannah must have been for her, but we're all worried.

"She went out earlier this morning," Susan says sadly.

"I'll try to catch up with her to let her know I've moved. Thanks for the tea, but I've got to go and sort out 'new Molly'," I explain.

After we've all said our goodbyes, I jump in my car and head to my next destination. It's now nearly two o'clock, so I don't have much time before I need to be at Shane's, but lack of time has never stopped me before. I pull into a parking space behind my favourite department store and head inside.

After only fifty minutes, I return to my car with my arms full of bags. Operation: New Molly is well underway.

After spending a couple of hours being pampered by one of my closest friends, I'm in a great mood.

Shane wasn't at all surprised by what I wanted done; he said he saw it coming. He had texted Chris to say I was going to be there, so not long after I sat down, he arrived to hear the gossip first-hand and to check that I was okay.

I'm now leaving the salon a new woman. Gone are my long blonde locks in favour of shorter, rich chocolate brown waves with a full fringe. I realised after seeing the blonde bimbos last night that Max had managed to influence my appearance. He was always dropping hints about how hot he thought blondes were and how good I looked with blonde hair. It wasn't until I saw myself in the mirror this morning that I realised how much I actually disliked it, and how bad the shape of my hair was after all the bleach. I decided to return to something more natural, have my fringe back, and cut the length to where the swell of my breasts start.

After Shane had finished blow-drying, I asked him if he would put on the make-up I'd bought earlier. As well as getting a couple of new outfits, underwear, shoes, and a couple of other bits for my new room, I'd visited my favourite make-up stand and asked for products for my new look. My old grey eye make-up is no longer, and in its place are palettes of purples, teals, and pastels to make my eyes really stand out under my new fringe. I showed Shane what I was going to change into, seeing as I was still wearing my work uniform from the day before, and he decided on the teal eyeshadow palette to go with the flowers in the loose-fitting sleeveless blouse and the bows on the high-heeled court shoes. Team those with new dark blue skinny jeans and I felt like a million pounds.

I said thank you along with my goodbyes to Chris and Shane, promising I'd be around soon to help with all the wedding planning, and I left. I had one more stop to make before going home.

I t's early evening when I make my way through the front door, dragging everything I've bought with me to find Ryan topless and about to pick up a box from my room. I let out an involuntary moan at the sight. The muscles in his broad shoulders and down his back ripple as he moves.

My moan must have been louder than I thought. Ryan's attention turns to me, revealing the front of his torso in the process. This time, I manage to control myself, but I can't help but rake my eyes over his pecs and ripped six-pack, and then follow the V that disappears into his loose jogging bottoms. The light sheen of sweat on his body only increases the definition he has.

Oh, fuck me slowly, that's one seriously hot body.

When my eyes make it back up to his face, I see his hair is a mess and falling all over his forehead—but what I really notice is how wide his eyes are as he stares at me.

"Holy shit," I hear him say under his breath as he runs his eyes all over my body. I start to tingle from his attention.

I realise I need to say something to break the atmosphere we've managed to create. "So, I take it you like my new look?" I ask, raising an eyebrow. He shouldn't be looking at me like he is right now. A wave of guilt washes through me as reality hits.

"Holy shit," he says again. He shakes his head like he's trying to get control of himself. "You look... I mean... you look... don't get me wrong, you were gorgeous before, but with the new hair, you look stunning. Shit, seriously hot. I hope that dickhead wakes up one day and realises what he's missing without you, Molls."

I don't really know how to respond to that. Ryan and I have always been very open with each other. My relationship with him hasn't been much different to what I have with Chris and Shane in that we knew we'd never end up in bed with each other, so there has never been any awkwardness or sexual tension between us.

Until now.

"Thank you," I say quietly as I break our eye contact. I feel a weird loss as I look away from him and into the room—*my* room—that's practically empty. "Wow, this is much bigger than I thought when all the boxes were in it. I bet you can rent a flat the size of this in the city for silly money. Talking of money, I'm paying half of everything," I say firmly.

"No fucking way. You can just pay half the bills," he argues.

"I can't do that. I'm living in your home, I need to pay my way. How about half the bills and a third of your mortgage each month?"

"I didn't ask you to move in here for my financial gain, Molly. I asked you because I want you here. I couldn't care less if you stay for free."

"I know that, but it isn't happening. You know me better than that, Ry."

"Half the bills and a quarter of the mortgage," he counters.

"Right, fine. Work out how much it is. Do you want it in cash or transferred into your bank account?"

"You're not going to argue? Cash would be good; I can do the food shopping with it."

"That will be split as well, mister."

"Right, okay. Give me cash, and I'll hide it under my mattress for a rainy day. Is that better?" he asks, sounding exasperated.

"Yes, much." Thanks to my parents, I have money, and if I can use it to help him out, I will. I will just have to find subtle ways to do it so he doesn't notice.

Ryan then sees all the bags around my feet, where I dropped them when he turned around. "Wow, you've been busy. New hair, and it looks like a new wardrobe in those bags. What are the suitcases for? You going somewhere?" he asks, eyeing the bright pink and purple flowered cases next to me.

"No, I realised I don't have anything to pack my clothes in, and I thought they would come in handy." God, a holiday would go down so well right about now. Sun, sea, relaxing on a beach. Heaven!

Ryan comes toward me, I guess to grab my bags but, as he gets closer, he stops. "Have you been crying? Your eyes are a little red." Wow, it looks like I won't be keeping any secrets from him; he was right last night about being able to read me like a book.

"I stopped at the graveyard to see Hannah on the way home. Told her about everything," I explain, hoping he understands.

"I get it. I actually went earlier myself." With that, he leans in, kisses my forehead, grabs my stuff, and places it in my room. He gets hold of the last box and heads upstairs. "I'll be ready in fifteen," he says as he disappears.

I stand in the middle of my new room, looking around. I'm so grateful Ryan and I seem to be on the same page for most things. I was dreading him asking me about my visit to Hannah, but he just gets it—so much so that he went as well. I wonder how similar his conversation was to mine.

R yan finds me a little over ten minutes later, sat cross-legged in the middle of my room with a stack of home magazines in my lap. I tried ringing Emma to tell her about leaving Max and moving here, but my call immediately went to voicemail. I shouldn't be surprised, but I hate how she's shut herself off. "What?" I ask when he starts to laugh.

"I just didn't think you'd take this whole decorating thing so seriously."

"I want it to be perfect. I'm thinking shabby chic."

"I'm sorry, shabby what?" he asks, confused.

"Shabby chic. It's a style. Sort of old-fashioned, soft pastel colours and really homey. Here, look, like this." I get up and show him the page I was looking at.

"Right, okay. Come on, Miss Molly, get your shoes on and let's get this over and done with."

Thirty minutes later, we're pulling up in Ryan's car to the flat I shared with dickhead Max, as he's now seemingly called. His car is here, but all the lights are off. "Oh God, I hope he's not at it again," I muse quietly.

"If he is, by the time I've finished with him, he won't be able to do it again," Ryan growls from the driver's seat.

I love the security of having someone defend me like that.

With a reassuring smile, Ryan jumps out of the car and grabs my suitcases before heading toward the flat. He must be able to sense my hesitation because he reassures me that it will be okay.

We've been at the flat for just over an hour, and we have all the rooms but the kitchen cleared of my things. I'm double-checking everything when I hear a crash in the kitchen. I go running in to find Ryan standing there with a murderous look on his face and a hole in the plasterboard. "What the fuck happened?" I question.

"Sorry, it just made me so fucking mad."

"What did?"

"This..." Ryan points to a used condom on the kitchen worktop.

"Oh." Tears start to well in my eyes. If I ever needed proof that Max wasn't faithful, here it is.

"Molly, come here," Ryan says as he pulls me into his arms. Blowing out a slow breath, I try to keep my emotions in check.

After we finish packing my cooking stuff, we leave the flat. I'm confident that we have everything, although Ryan looks a little unsure, as there are only two suitcases and three boxes.

"I thought you loved shopping?" he asks me as we leave. "How come you only have this much stuff?"

"I had a clear-out when I moved in here. This is all I have."

We drive home in silence, Ryan's anger obvious from his white-knuckle grip on the steering wheel. I feel sick after discovering my entire relationship with Max was a joke. It only adds to the grief and guilt I already feel about moving into Ryan's home.

CHAPTER FOUR

Ryan

I hear a moan behind me and turn around. I almost can't believe what I'm seeing. It's Molly, but fucking hell, she looks like every man's wet dream. Her dark brown hair rests just on top of her breasts, and she's wearing a blouse unbuttoned enough to give me a cheeky peek of her cleavage. Her legs and arse are shown off nicely in a pair of skintight dark jeans. And the shoes... fuck me, the shoes are so sexy. When I eventually meet her eyes, their normal chocolate colour is almost black, and the way she's looking at my half-exposed body makes me think she wants to run her tongue over every line and muscle visible. My cock twitches.

"Molly." My voice comes out as a groan as I make my way to stand in front of her. In her high heels, the top of her head comes in line with my chin, not to the middle of my chest like normal. She's staring straight into my eyes, and I can't help but think that she wants this as much as I do. I watch as she slowly leans her head to the side and moves forward until her lips softly brush mine. My dick hardens in response to her simple touch.

Then, it's as if our control snaps at the same time. All of sudden, our mouths crash together and our tongues touch for the first time. Her hands thread through my hair as mine go to her arse to pull her body against mine. She moans as I run my hands up her sides and gently brush the underside of her breasts, causing her to suck on my tongue. God, how I want her to do that to something else. My mouth leaves hers as I trail kisses across her jaw and down her neck.

"Ryan," I hear her whisper. My hands unbutton her blouse as I suck on her earlobe. I'm dying to get a taste of her nipples.

"Ryan," she groans again as I slip her blouse off and my hands go to her back to release her bra. "Ryan." She's getting louder now, and her chest is rising and falling in excitement.

"Oh, Molly." I slide the straps over her shoulders, preparing myself for what's to come. I'm so turned on, I don't want to cum in my pants like a teenager at just the sight of her perfect tits.

"Ryan." My eyes travel from her eyes down to her exposed...

"Ryan!" She shouts my name this time. I suddenly feel my head snap up and my eyes begrudgingly open.

Fuck, it was a dream.

I look toward my bedroom door and see Molly.

"Having a good dream, were we?" she smirks.

"Shit," I say under my breath, but from the raised eyebrow, I guess she heard.

"Breakfast will be ready in fifteen, so get up," she says as she turns to leave. Just before she disappears from my sight, she looks back and says, "I'd have a cold shower if I were you."

"Ugh," I groan as I look at myself. I'm completely exposed, my boxer briefs barely containing my very obvious excitement, and I'm covered in a sheen of sweat.

"Fuck," I mutter as I drag my body out of bed to follow Molly's advice. I wonder, as I brush my teeth, if I need to buy a lock for my bedroom door, or if it's time I got myself laid? That must be it; I wouldn't be thinking about my best friend like that if I were getting some. The image of Hannah's smiling face filters into my mind and I have to reach out to lean on the counter as grief and guilt hit me so strong that my knees start to buckle. Fuck, it's only been six months. I shouldn't be having these thoughts. Or should I? I've no fucking clue what the right thing to be feeling in a situation like this is, and I don't think there are any rules. All I know is that it's been a long six months and the thought of human contact, a little passion, want, and need sounds so good.

<hr>

To my relief, Molly doesn't say anything about my wake-up call when I meet her in the kitchen.

"Smells amazing," I comment as I sit at the breakfast bar next to my waiting coffee. She passes over a plate with toast, scrambled eggs, and bacon.

"Feeling better?" she questions. She focuses on filling her plate, not on me, which I'm relieved about. I'm embarrassed enough; let's move on.

"Much. This is great, thank you. So, I told my mate we would pick his van up sometime before ten," I say, trying to change the topic. It's only now that I take notice of Molly. Her hair is still wet and her face is make-up free. As she steps around the breakfast bar, I notice she's wearing the shortest denim shorts I think I've ever seen, showing off her amazing legs, putting me back into almost as bad a state as I was when I woke up at the sight. She has on a white tank top that's low enough to show the swell of her breasts, and a pale yellow cardigan. It's simple, but seriously fucking hot. I think I've got a problem, and it needs fixing before I do something stupid.

"So, where are we actually going?" Molly questions as we pull away from my mate's drive in his van. It's so big that I'm not hugely confident driving it, but it will fit everything in it that we need to buy.

"Reading."

"Why the hell are we going there? Aren't there enough shops to pick from in Oxford?"

"Yes, I guess there are, but there isn't an IKEA," I reply.

"WHAT?" Molly shouts, scaring the ever-loving shit out of me.

"What? What's wrong?"

"I've always wanted to go to IKEA," she replies. looking at me with a beaming smile that goes all the way to her eyes.

"You've never been?" I ask, laughing at her reaction.

"No. I always hear people talking about it. It sounds awesome. I'm so excited! Eek, it's like an early birthday present for me."

"You never cease to amaze me, Molls." She looks over at me and raises an eyebrow, prompting me to explain. "You've grown up with enough money around you to have anything you could possibly want, but I take you somewhere as everyday as IKEA and you look like I've just made all your dreams come true." And fuck me if I don't love that look on her face right now. I promise myself to put it there as often as possible. I don't really think anyone has bothered to before, and that makes me feel so sad for her.

"Ry, you know I'm not into the whole money thing. I learnt from a young age that I'd rather have no money but loving friends and family around me."

"I do know that. You just take me by surprise with it, sometimes. I used to get dragged around IKEA by my mum and little sisters at least four times a year when I was growing up. It just seems so normal to me." Her bottom lip trembles as she imagines what I've just said. "Molly, don't do that. I want you to be happy. I promise you, you will have a family of your own like that one day. Today is meant to be a happy day." I give her thigh a gentle squeeze to try to break her out of her daydream.

"You're right; today is happy. What was our motto? Live, laugh, love," she says, reminding me of the pact we made together not so long ago.

By one o'clock, we've spent two hours going backwards and forwards around the showroom section while Molly to-and-froed over her choices. At last, we're sat in the café for lunch. I'm stood in the queue, watching Molly sat at a table going through the items on her list against the photos she's taken on her phone. She eventually decided on pale grey furniture for her bedroom—very shabby chic, apparently.

As I walk over to her with a plate of Swedish meatballs each, warmth fills me seeing just how happy she is. We still have the marketplace to go. I'm sure her head is going to explode before we get out of here.

"Wow, they were so good. I need the recipe," she comments, having not come up for air once while demolishing her food. I've never known a woman enjoy her food like Molly does but still manage to keep her amazing figure.

"There's a little food hall by the exit. You can buy all the stuff to make them," I explain.

"Really?" she exclaims. I nod in response. "Wow, this place is awesome. Are you done?"

"Yes, come on, let's go," I say as I clear the table.

"Do you think we need a trolley?" Molly asks as we enter the marketplace.

"You're kidding, right?" I ask, laughing. There's no way we're getting out of here without a full trolley.

"I'll take your laughter as a yes, shall I?"

We have a great time looking at everything. I pick up a few things for the house, but I mostly just enjoy watching Molly take it all in. I'm sure the expression on her face is similar to a child's at DisneyLand.

It's almost three by the time I manage to get her away from the candles and into the section to find and pick up all her furniture. Our trolley is overflowing with all sorts of stuff, and I've nearly taken out about five people with the rug Molly chose for her room that's sticking out just at the right height for other shoppers' heads.

"We need to be quick, or we'll end up getting locked in," I say as Molly leads the way with another empty trolley to put all the flat-packs on.

"Ah, that would be awesome. It would be just like that film where they get locked in a department store. I've always wanted to do that! Oh, over here," she says, pointing down an aisle.

"I'm going to go and take the van back."

We've been home for three hours, and we're in flat-pack hell. I've made her bed so at least she can have somewhere comfortable to sleep tonight, and she's just finishing her second bedside table. The two wardrobes, two chests of drawers, and bathroom cabinets are still leaning up against the wall in the hallway. The end is most definitely not in sight.

"Okay, I'll finish this one, then go and make us some sandwiches for when you get back. Are you still set on getting all this done tonight?"

"Yes! You will have a whole bedroom when you eventually get in that bed tonight."

"Okay, well, hurry then, because I can't do this alone."

I do need to get the van back so my mate can go to work tomorrow, but mostly I need to get away from the sight of Molly leant over a bedside cabinet wearing those shorts with a screwdriver in her hand.

I don't know what's wrong with me. I've never seen Molly in any way but as a platonic friend. Even the first night when we met and she practically threw herself at me, I was just not interested. Maybe it's because that's how she first introduced herself. I've always gone for the quieter girls, the ones who wait to be asked out, not the ones who go after what they want. I guess my type over the years has also been taller, more athletic builds, whereas Molly is shorter and has some seriously sexy curves. We've spent a lot of time together over the past six months, and not once have I had any thoughts that I shouldn't be having about her. I mean, yeah, I did have other things filling my mind, but what's changed so suddenly? She moved in two days ago, and all I can think about is her body, being inside her, and wanting to make her happy.

I think I was right this morning; I seriously need to get laid. *But is it too soon?* a little voice in my head asks, reminding me of everything I've been through.

When I get back an hour later, she has both bedside tables in place and is moving the standing cabinet into the bathroom.

"Wow, you didn't hang around while I was gone," I say, watching her from the doorway.

"I just can't wait to see it all finished. I haven't done the sandwiches, though. I was just going to put this in place, then go make them. I thought you'd be gone longer."

"I did consider staying for a beer and letting you get on with it, but I didn't think that was fair," I explain as I start to open up the packaging for the wardrobes.

I'm tacking the back of the first wardrobe on when Molly reappears with food and drink.

"Picnic on the bed," she says, nodding toward it.

I finish what I'm doing, then go and sit opposite her with the plate between us. "I need to talk to you about something," I say, grabbing my first sandwich.

"You can't kick me out already; the furniture isn't all made yet."

"Very funny. Actually, we won't be talking about it. I've got to tell you something."

"Okaaay, go on," she says, starting to look nervous.

"You know what Tuesday is, right?" I ask, but I know the answer. There's no way she'd forget that it's been six months since she lost her best friend. She nods, looking suddenly sad.

"A couple of months ago, I booked to go away so I wouldn't be home and miserable for the anniversary. Since I booked it, thanks to you and that counsellor you found, I feel totally different about it. I no longer want to disappear for a week and be lonely and miserable. I want to go and celebrate her. Does that make sense?"

"Of course it does. I totally get it. I want to celebrate her, too."

"I want you to come with me. I've already—"

"Ryan, no, I can't just tag along because you don't want to leave me alone. Plus, I've got work and shifts at Cocoa's next week."

"Will you listen to me, woman? If you hadn't so rudely interrupted, you would have heard me explain that I've already spoken to Susan, and Lilly and Dec are going to work your shifts at Cocoa's. I've spoken to the company I booked the holiday with, and there's Wi-Fi so you can take your laptop and work on whatever projects you've got at the moment, and they confirmed that although there's only one bed, there is a daybed and plenty of room for two people to stay."

"Well, you really have thought of everything. Where is it?"

"It's a little beach hut right on the sea in Cornwall. Look." I pass her my phone with the details.

"Wow, it's so cute and peaceful."

"It's a private beach, so there won't be any holiday makers on it other than the ones staying in the huts along with us."

"Sounds perfect."

"So, you're in?"

"Do I actually have a choice?" she laughs.

CHAPTER FIVE

Molly

I was there as soon as the shops opened this morning with a list of what I needed for my week away. I can't wait to get to that little beach hut. I can just see myself sitting in the hot tub overlooking the beach as the sun goes down—complete with a glass of wine. Heaven.

Every time I think about it, butterflies erupt in my stomach, but they never cover the guilt I feel. It shouldn't be *me* excited to go on a holiday with Ryan. I checked the weather forecast when I first woke up this morning. It's going to be amazing all week. Cornwall, here I come.

My full suitcases are on my bed, and I'm double-checking that I have everything. I may have gone a little mad at the shops this morning, which has resulted in me needing both cases, but it's not every day a girl gets taken away.

As well as all the obvious necessities, I ended up with five new bikinis, summer dresses, shorts, vests and t-shirts, a skirt, a pair of flip-flops as well as wedges, new lingerie for the week, and a couple of flowers to go in my hair, Hawaii style.

After crossing off the last items on my list, I zip up my cases and drag them into the hallway. I walk back into my room with a huge smile on my face, just like I have since we finished putting everything together at some ungodly hour this morning. Ryan kept his promise and we didn't stop until everything was together. I knew about it when I got up this morning—every muscle in my body hurt from all the lumping around. I really need to return to my exercise classes once we get back.

Making my way across the room, I grab my laptop and phone and sit on my new chair, putting my feet up on the coffee table that I've set up in front of the French doors leading to the courtyard. I check my emails and to-do lists for the week so I don't fall behind on work. After the accident, I didn't take on as many clients as we had before. Work took a back seat to everything else, but it has started to pick up again—so much so that I'm starting to think I may need to find an office and hire another designer. It's amazing to think that the dream Hannah and I had when we were teenagers might just come true. Dialing on Emma's number, I wait in the hope she'll answer this time. I need to explain all of this to her, but as usual, it rings off and goes to voicemail. Giving up, I shut my laptop down just as I hear Ryan's footsteps down the stairs.

"Two cases? You know we are only going for seven days, right?" He laughs as he pops his head around the door.

"I'm a woman, I can't help it. Don't tell me... you've just got a tiny backpack or something pathetic?" I walk over to the front door, slipping my flip-flops on as I go, and notice I'm not far from wrong; he has a small suitcase which looks miniscule next to mine. I roll my eyes at him. "Whatever," I shrug as I get to him. "I'll carry yours!" I say over my shoulder, as I make my way to his car.

———

The journey has been so much fun. I synced my phone to Ryan's car, much to his delight, and we've been singing along with my favourite old-school songs, as well as playing stupid travelling games and taking the piss out of other drivers. We're now driving through the most picturesque little Cornish village, only ten minutes away from our beach hut, according to the SatNav.

"Wow." As we pull up to our allocated parking space on the edge of the small cliff the beach huts are set in, all we can see is the bay in front of us. "Definitely cannot complain about the view," I say, getting out the car and leaning over the fence at the very edge. "Oh my God, look how cute they are!" I can see the tops of five beach huts from here, with their huge balconies overlooking the bay.

"Come on, grab some stuff," Ryan says from behind me as he unloads the suitcases from the car. "We're in number one, so it's this way, by the looks of it," he says, nodding his head over to a sign. We make our way down the winding path to our little home for the week, and I swear the view keeps getting better.

When we get to our hut, I can't believe my eyes. It has to be the nicest of all the ones we've passed. Its balcony wraps around three sides. There's a section for eating with a white bistro set, and at the front there's a giant outside bed for lounging on as well as wooden sun loungers. The final side has the hot tub. The way it's set into the cliff and right at the end of the path makes it completely secluded. We could go the whole week and not see anyone else if we wanted to.

"Don't just stand there staring; let's go check the place out," Ryan says, opening the little gate.

"I think I'm in love," I say when I get inside. The front wall of the beach hut has sliding glass doors so they can be opened. All the furniture in the open-plan kitchen/diner and living room is white, and all the accessories are bright and multi-coloured, bringing the sunshine inside. The bedroom and bathroom are at the back of the hut and follow the same theme. "I want one," I say, spinning around and taking everything in.

"The internet didn't really do it any justice, did it?" Ryan says, putting the suitcases on the stand in the bedroom.

"Ahh," I sigh as I sink into the warm water of the hot tub. As soon as we put our cases in the hut this afternoon, we went in search of a supermarket. When we got back, I made us grilled salmon and asparagus, and Eton mess for dessert with local strawberries. It was so good. I think I may have embarrassed Ryan a little with the appreciative noises I was making while eating it. Ryan washed up and I put on my first bikini of the week—a 1950s style red and white polka dot number—to test out the hot tub.

With a full plastic wine glass in hand, I sit watching the sky change colour as the sun makes its descent for the night, waiting for Ryan to appear. I was going to wait for him so we could get in together, but he was adamant that I should enjoy myself.

Eventually, he comes out of the hut, wearing a pair of pale blue board shorts that hang deliciously low on his hips, showing off all his defined muscles and his sexy V that had me close to drooling the other day. I try my best to keep my eyes on his face, but it's hard to do. We're here to celebrate Hannah. I shouldn't be feeling this way all of a sudden.

I move over so he has enough space to get in, but he seems to have paused at the steps. "Come on, it's so good in here."

This seems to snap him out of his thoughts, and he hops in.

"Is everything okay?" I ask. He hasn't looked at me yet, the muscles in his shoulders pulled tight, his jaw clenched.

"Yeah, fine. You?" he says unconvincingly.

"Yes, amazing. Thank you so much for sharing this with me. It's heaven."

"No problem," he says, opening a can of beer. "When I booked it, I thought the time alone would be good, but as the months have gone on, I couldn't think of anything worse. I actually thought about cancelling it. So, I guess we should be thanking dickhead Max."

I raise my glass. "To Max screwing me over." Then, I touch it to Ryan's can.

"To Max. His loss is my gain." Ryan quickly looks away. I can't help but notice that his cheeks redden slightly.

"So... I hate to ask, but what's the plan for tomorrow? You said you wanted to celebrate, not be miserable, right?" I question gently, not really wanting to bring the subject up.

"Well, as Jo told me for months after the accident, focus on the good times you had and celebrate what you had together, not on what you've lost. I'm not totally sure how to do that, but I'm sure we'll come up with something," he says, sounding unsure all of a sudden.

Jo was the grief counsellor I found for us after the accident. I cannot believe it's been six months. Six months since I lost my best friend, and Ryan lost his girlfriend. When I think about it, it feels like it could have been last week. Glancing over at him, I feel the weight of whatever's been developing between us press down on my shoulders.

When Ryan phoned me in hysterics in the middle of the night from the hospital and told me to get there as soon as possible, my stomach fell to my feet. When I got there and found out what had actually happened, it felt like my heart left my body. I remember falling into Ryan in floods of tears, and we sobbed together on the floor of the hospital for what felt like hours.

Hannah and Emma had both worked that evening at Cocoa's. When they eventually locked up after a busy night, Emma's car wouldn't start, so Hannah offered to take her back to their parents' house. They weren't far away when Hannah pulled out to cross a junction and a drunk driver flew at them like a bat out of Hell, crashing into the driver's side. According to the medics, Hannah died instantly and wouldn't have been in any pain. Emma, on the other hand, was stuck in the passenger seat with multiple broken bones and bruises. She managed to phone an ambulance and her parents.

Ryan and I seemed to deal with our grief in a similar way. We shut ourselves off from everyone but each other and the Morrisons. Someone recommended Jo to me, and I signed us up for a joint session. We fell in love with her in that first hour. She was straight-talking and didn't do any of the *softly, softly* approach that other people had tried that made my skin crawl. She said it how it was. She would tell us how shitty a situation it was, but that we had to be thankful for the time we did have with her. Celebrate what a wonderful person she was every single day, and relish in the joy she brought to our lives. She told us that we had to continue to live, and we had to find a way to be happy, because that was what Hannah would have wanted for us. We still had lives to live, and they needed to be full of fun and love. Hence our motto: live, laugh, love.

Ryan must have noticed I was taking a trip down memory lane, because at some point he moved next to me and put his arm around my shoulders. I feel his thumb catch a tear I didn't realise had fallen from my eye.

"I'm sorry, we're meant to be celebrating and being happy," I say, leaning my head on his shoulder.

"We are, but that doesn't mean we aren't going to be sad as well sometimes. It's okay, Molls," he whispers in my ear, rubbing his hand up and down my arm in comfort when he feels me crying harder.

Once I pull myself together, I glance over at him and notice his eyes are looking a little wet as well.

"So, the reason I have so much luggage was partly because I overdid the shopping this morning, but also because I brought a few things with me in case we needed them." Ryan raises his eyebrow in question, so I continue. "I brought some of Hannah's favourite DVDs, a couple of photo albums, Twister, and a bottle of Apple Sourz." I can't help but smile at the thought of them and the memories they bring to mind.

"When I said celebrate, I wasn't really thinking I'd have to spend a day watching your favourite girly DVDs, but now that you mention it, I think it's perfect. Thank you for thinking of it, Molly. Why didn't you say anything when I was taking the piss earlier?"

"I didn't want to bring it up before it was necessary. Look what it's done to us!" I laugh, pointing at our smiling yet tear-stained faces. "I don't know how I would have gotten through this without you, Ryan Evans. Thank you," I say, cuddling back into him and looking out to the star-filled sky, hoping Hannah is looking down on us, smiling that we've made it through together.

"You too, Molly," he says, sounding a little choked up.

We spent the rest of the night getting drunk, chatting about everything, and nothing. We did cry some more, but we laughed so much that the happy tears blended with the sad. Ryan was right; we needed to celebrate. She was such an incredible person and filled our lives with so much love and joy that it'll never be possible to forget her.

We eventually turned in, in the early hours of Tuesday morning. Somehow, we managed in our drunken states to figure out that there were electronically-controlled blinds in the ceiling that came down over the sliding doors, so Ryan wouldn't be awake as soon as the sun rose. I argued that I was okay to sleep on the daybed as I was crashing his holiday, but, ever the gentleman, Ryan point-blank refused and practically pushed me into the bedroom. I showered and changed into my new pyjamas that I thought were a suitable mix between cute and sexy for a holiday with my best friend, and fell fast asleep.

I wake the next morning to the sound of my mobile ringing. When it stops, I roll over to go back to sleep, but it starts again immediately. Groaning, I open my eyes and try to locate it. By the time I get to it, it stops again. It's Emma, so I ring her back straight away.

"What the fuck do you think you're doing?" Emma shouts down the line. "How could you?"

"Emma, calm down. What's wrong?" Silly question, really—her twin died six months ago today. What *isn't* wrong? My initial anger at her demanding question dies as my sympathy takes over. I can only imagine how she's feeling today. We all lost so much the day Hannah died, but no one more so than Emma.

"You and Ryan. That didn't take you fucking long, did it? I knew you were after him the whole time he was with Hannah, and as soon as she dies, in you step to take her place. Now you're living with him in the house that Hannah practically paid for, and going away on a holiday with him. How could you Molly, h-how c-c-could you?" She starts to sob uncontrollably. The ball of dread that was sitting heavy in my stomach explodes and I fight to speak around the lump in my throat. I can't help feeling a little guilty even though what she's saying isn't really true, I can't deny the thoughts I've had over the last few days. Her words just confirm how wrong it all is.

"Emma, it's okay. I'm here for you, it's okay." I say in what I hope is a soothing voice as she continues to sob. Eventually, her breathing evens out.

"Molly?"

"Yes, hon?"

"I'm sorry," she says quietly.

"It's okay. You're allowed to be angry, and if that needs to be at me, then that's okay. I'm here for whatever you need." I speak calmly, trying to forget the beginning of our phone call. I know she's only being irrational because she's angry.

"I shouldn't have said that to you. Mum and Dad just said that you came around on Saturday to tell them you've moved in with Ry, and that you were on a holiday with him. I just flipped out, you know? I'm so sorry."

"Em, really, it's fine. I tried to get a hold of you over the weekend to explain everything, but your phone was off. I'll spare you the full details until I see you, but basically, I caught Max cheating, so I went to Ry's. He offered me his downstairs room instead of me finding somewhere of my own. I love it there with him. He's been my rock through this, and I think I've been his. I wasn't expecting to be coming on holiday with him. He booked it for himself months ago, but as he has been dealing with Hannah's death, he realised he didn't want to come here alone like he planned originally. So, he invited me, and we've come to celebrate her. I would never do anything to hurt you, Emma. You know that, don't you? Ryan and I are just friends. He's like my brother, just like he is to you."

"Yeah, I do know that. I'm sorry, I'm just a bit emotional. Hey, he's one seriously hot brother, though, right? How's the beach clothing working out for you?" she says, her normal humour starting to creep in.

"Uh, yeah, not a bad view around here actually, now that you mention it. The bay's pretty nice to look at, too." She laughs.

"Well, I'll let you go and celebrate. Sorry I rang so early, I just needed to shout at you."

"No problem, I'm here for you to abuse anytime you need it. I'll ring you later and make sure you're okay. Keep your bloody phone on."

"Yeah, okay. Talk to you later. Love you."

"Love you too, bye."

I put the phone down and lie back down on the bed. "Wow," I breathe. What a start to the day. That's when the tears come.

Ryan

The sound of Molly's voice wakes me up and I walk over to the door to make sure she's okay. Today is going to be tough for both of us. I put my ear to the door and hear her consoling someone—Emma, I presume.

"Ryan and I are just friends. He's like my brother, just like he is to you," she says, and, for some reason, those words are like a slap to the face.

I walk away from the door and put the blinds up, looking out over the bay, trying to gather my thoughts. I lost my girlfriend six months ago today, the woman I loved more than anything, and here I am, upset because her best friend, now *my* best friend, has just admitted to Emma that I'm like a brother to her. The guilt I've been battling over the past few days hits me once again, but this time it's worse, because I'd told myself she was having similar feelings toward me.

Clearly not.

When my phone also rings and I find my granddad's photo staring back at me, I rush to answer it. Having lost the woman in his life and forced to move on and continue living, he's the only one who really understands what I've been through.

They got together when they were sixteen, were married by the time they were eighteen, and had one kid and another on the way by twenty. They were what most people would probably describe as the perfect couple. They made everything look so easy, and even after all those years together, they were still so in love.

They'd been retired for just over a year when, one morning, my granddad awoke and my gran didn't. She'd suffered a heart attack in her sleep and peacefully drifted off.

My grandad was devastated. He still is.

Their house looks exactly the same as my gran left it before going to bed that night. He hasn't moved a thing.

He's told me how unhealthy it is that he hasn't attempted to move on, but he said that after a lifetime together he's got nothing else to look forward to and that he'd love more than anything to keep her spirit alive.

Since losing Hannah, he's expressed his desire for me not to follow in his footsteps. He's told me time and time again to find the strength to continue with my life. To forge new paths for myself without feeling guilty because it would be what she wanted, too.

Once we hang up, I look out over the sea beyond and try to pull myself together. Walking back over to the bedroom door, I hear Molly saying goodbye. I stand and listen a little longer to make sure she's okay. It's not long before I hear her start crying. Putting all my feelings aside, I knock on the door. No matter how I feel, she's my best friend, and I need to be here for her like she has been for me.

"Yeah," she replies quietly. I open the door, and she's lying on the bed, sobbing into her pillow.

I lie down in front of her and pull her into my arms so she's against my chest. She throws her right arm and leg over my body and clings on while she cries. I try to comfort her by slowly rubbing my hand up and down her back. Eventually, her breathing evens out.

CHAPTER SIX

Molly

I wake up feeling really hot. When I open my eyes, I realise why. My head's on Ryan's naked chest, my arm and leg wrapped tightly around his body. He's holding onto me equally as tight. I spend a few seconds appreciating his sculpted chest before I peer up at his face to see that he's still fast asleep. He looks so young and carefree.

I wish we didn't have to deal with today.

I lie there, looking at him a while longer, before his lips curl up at the corners.

"If you keep staring at me like that, I'll get the wrong idea," he says quietly, his eyes still shut.

I gently smack his chest and lift myself up on my elbow. I hear a thud as my phone slides from the bed, but I don't look away. His eyes open. They're full of love and compassion as he stares back at me. I always know I'm safe when I look into his eyes.

"Thank you for this. I really needed it," I say, looking into his eyes to show him how serious I am. "Emma was on the phone, and she was really upset. Come on, let's get up and have breakfast on that amazing balcony."

I go to move, but his arm around me tightens slightly. "Thank you for everything, Molly. I really mean it," he says, so sincerely it makes my heart hurt. But then, I see the corner of his lips twitch as he says, "The view from the balcony is pretty good, but I'm not sure it can beat the one I've got right now." He looks down at my chest, a suggestive smirk on his face.

I look down and realise I'm giving him an eyeful. I put my hand over my breasts and jump out of his hold and off the bed, scowling at him.

He puts his hands up in defeat. "I only looked once, I promise," he says, still smiling.

I bend down to pick up my phone. "Oh, come on, you're not playing fair." I look back to see him sat on the edge of the bed, staring at my arse. I can't help but notice the obvious bulge in his boxers. Butterflies erupt in my belly at the thought of being able to affect him so easily.

"Do you want me to ring Emma back and tell her you've been checking me out?" I ask as I leave the bedroom.

"Oh, come on," he shouts. "Don't even pretend you didn't get a good look this morning, or from the hot tub last night, or when you came in Saturday evening." He chuckles to himself as he starts walking into the living room, but stops to grab a pair of shorts to cover himself up.

"So, about that dream yesterday morning." I deadpan.

"Touché. What's for breakfast?"

We spend what little is left of the morning sat on the balcony eating fresh fruit, granola, and yoghurt. We must have fallen back to sleep for longer than I thought, but I feel better for it.

"Right, today is the only day I'm not going to work, because we're celebrating. So, what's the plan?" I ask Ryan while we tidy up.

"Let's just chill out here, stick on some of that godawful music Hannah was so obsessed with, and hit the sun loungers."

"Ew, what an awful plan," I say, laughing as I wander through the hut to put on today's bikini—a navy and white striped nautical look. I can't wear the little string bikinis that others do; I need more support than that, so I have to go for the bra-style tops to keep everything in place and under control. Having said that, this one in particular does good things for my cleavage.

"I'll meet you out there. You know the playlist we need on my phone."

I'm just putting my hair up out of the way when the music starts filling the hut. It makes me smile as memories of happier times with Hannah flit through my mind. I grab my Kindle, phone, and suntan lotion before heading out to the balcony.

Ryan's sat on a lounger with his aviators on, sipping a glass of water. I can't help but drop my gaze to check him out; he looks like a bloody model, wearing black shorts with the waistband of his boxers poking out. I'm not sure if it's pleasure or torture, having to look at him.

I can't see his eyes, but I can tell they're roaming over my body. My skin heats under his scrutiny. Grabbing my phone, I open up the camera just in time for his eyes to find mine. There's a wicked glint in them that makes my insides flutter.

"You need to stop doing that," I tell him seriously.

"What? It's not like I'm going to throw you down and have my wicked way with you. I'm merely just appreciating the female form in all its glory." Tingles head south at the image his words create in my head. "Anyway, you're not my type."

And, they're gone.

I don't know why hearing that makes my steps falter and disappointment flood me. I should be happy about this, right?

"Yeah, I guess not. I've got more curves than all the girls you've been with put together." Hannah was a gorgeous, slim, tall build. She wasn't quite straight up and down—she had a cute, pert arse, and I guess you could say her breasts were a small handful. She also had stunning golden blonde long hair and striking blue eyes. I've seen photos of the girls Ryan dated previously, and they pretty much looked the same. I'm the complete opposite with my rounded arse and hips, tiny waist, and double D's. Hannah was almost always quiet, polite, and well-spoken, something Ryan often complimented about her. I, on the other hand, say it like it is... and I swear like a trooper.

My shoulders slouch as I stand in front of him. I hand him the bottle I'm holding and turn around. I must look defeated as I do it because he leans into my ear and whispers, "You're gorgeous, Molly. Don't think for a second I was suggesting you're not."

His words and the warmth of his hands lightly skimming down my sides as he massages in the suntan lotion make my knees slightly weak. The tingles return and descend south. A man has never affected me like this. I've never felt this incredible pull before. I used to thrive on the feeling of men wanting me, but I've never desperately wanted them. Sex for me has always been about being wanted, not because I had to have it right then and there.

I clear my throat. "Th-thank you." Even to my ears, my voice sounds rough as I quickly scurry away from his hands and onto the outside sofa. I lie down on my stomach and keep my face away from him. Why has it got to be him causing these feelings in me? We've known each other for years and been as close as two friends can get over the last six months without me feeling like this, but a few days of living with him, and he's turned me into a frustrated mess. I squeeze my thighs together to try to dull the ache and chant in my head that he's my friend. I can't imagine Hannah would be too pleased about my feelings toward her boyfriend. The thought causes a giant lump to form in my throat and a tear to run down my cheek. This is so wrong. I shouldn't be feeling like this.

"Molls, are you okay?"

"Yeah, fine. You?" I sound anything but, and he knows me well enough to know that.

"Uh-huh, yep, I'm good."

"Hey, do you remember that night we all went bowling?" He laughs, and I turn to look at him.

That did it. We spend the next few hours reminiscing about our memories from university and the following couple of years at work. We had some great times together, and Ryan was right—those times need celebrating. I tell him stories about us growing up and from school, some of which he'd heard before, and some he hadn't.

"Tell me about the first time you met," Ryan says, after a few minutes of silence between us. He already knows this story, but I humour him anyway, because it's comforting to reflect. It's important that, together, we keep her memory alive.

"My first solid memory is from primary school. We must have been four or five. We went over to get our coats and snacks for break time, and someone had put my lunchbox on a shelf that I couldn't reach. This boy came over and said he would get it down for me if I kissed him. I didn't like that, so I shoved my knee straight between his legs and watched him fall to the ground in pain." Ryan flinches, making me laugh. "When I looked up from him rolling around crying, Hannah was stood behind him and had a big smile on her face. She must have seen the whole thing. She reached up and grabbed my lunchbox easily; she was really tall, even then. After that, we spent every day together."

"What happened to him?"

"Um, well. That didn't put him off. He continued chasing me for that kiss. Eventually, he won, and I lost my virginity to him ten years later at a friend's party. But he turned out to be gay in the end."

"Well, I didn't see that coming." Ryan sounds slightly shocked by my honesty.

"It wasn't worth the long wait."

"You lost your virginity at fourteen?" he asks.

"Yeah, unfortunately. I totally regret it, but to be honest, if I'd waited until I found someone special like everyone says to, then I'd still be a virgin now."

"That wouldn't be such a bad thing, Molls. It would mean you wouldn't have had to deal with any of the arseholes you've chosen in the past few years."

"True. It's not like I've had years of awesome sex to make up for them, either. They were all as bad in bed as their personalities."

"Please tell me they all had little dicks as well?"

"Um... not all of them, but as the saying goes, it's not about the size, it's what you do with it."

"I never understood why you got with so many different guys when you could have found a nice one to settle down with. I still had the idea in my head that you were having fun doing it, but you've just ruined that for me. So, if you weren't enjoying it, why *were* you doing it?"

"My parents were pretty shitty. They never wanted me. I learnt from a young age that if you take antibiotics whilst on the pill, they stop it working effectively, so here I am. My parents had already had the two boys they wanted. Steven was sixteen and Daniel was fourteen by the time I was born.

"It was all planned out; they would take over and expand the family business. They decided that I, on the other hand, would grow up, be just like my mum, and provide them with some grandchildren. They decided not to pay for me to go to private school like my brothers, so I went to the local secondary with Hannah and Emma. It was a great school, so I can't complain.

"I had different ideas, though. I wanted a career, and I had no intention of ever joining the family business in any capacity. I wanted to be my own person. My parents told me I wasn't going to sixth form and that I would work for them. I told them that wasn't happening, and that I'd move out, if need be, to enable myself to live my own life. Eventually, they came around to the idea of me staying, but they cut me off. The allowance I used to get was put into a trust fund that I couldn't access until I was twenty-one. I'm sure they only did it to try to stop me from going to university.

"So, I spent my two years at sixth form juggling school work and fitting in as many hours as possible. I was desperate to go to university, and I managed to keep my grades up so I would have a good chance of getting in. But the money was an issue. I would never get any loans or anything with my parents' finances as they were."

"How did you manage it?"

"I applied for every kind of funding there was, and I did manage to get a little bit, but not enough. One day, I got a phone call from my gran, my dad's mum, and she asked to see me. She handed me a cheque that was more than enough to cover my three years at university." Tears well in my eyes as I think back to the determination in her eyes that day. She wanted me to have the world. "She died of a heart attack two months later. I was devastated but determined to make her proud."

"Sorry, I think I'm missing the point. What has this got to do with my original question about all the guys?" Ryan looks confused.

"Other than my gran and the Morrisons, I never felt loved. The two people who were meant to love and support me no matter what didn't care about me. When I started going out with boys, they made me feel special... needed and wanted. At first, it was just hand-holding and kissing, but it wasn't long before I was experimenting with more. All I've ever wanted was to find someone to love me and take care of me, like you did with Hannah. I wanted someone to look at me like I am his reason for living. I was so jealous of you guys." I'm a blubbering mess by the time I've finished, and I find myself wrapped in Ryan's arms again.

"I'm so sorry, I keep crying on you. You must be getting fed up of me," I say once I've calmed down.

"Don't be stupid. I've been wanting to know about your parents for years, but Hannah would never tell me. She said it was your story. I'm so sorry your parents were like that. You deserve them to love you, and I know it's not quite the same, but you know you've got me, right? I'll always take care of you. I love you, Molly. You're my best friend."

"I love you too, Ry."

"Your Prince Charming will come when you least expect him, I promise."

His lips press against my head and warmth races through me. He's right; it's not quite the same, but it's bloody good. I squeeze him a little tighter and try my hardest to ignore the tingles that erupt where our naked skin is touching.

Ryan

I'd guessed most of the things Molly said about her parents from the little bits I'd heard before, but hearing it first-hand still shocks me. I'm so angry they could treat their daughter that way, could try to control her into doing what they wanted. I feel more grateful than ever for my family. Okay, yes, they tried to do something similar, but they accepted my decision in the end and have supported me all the way.

My parents are both very traditional. They always believed that a man should get a 'manly' job like working in construction, find a nice woman, marry her, and make loads of babies together. They believed—a little like Molly's parents, I guess—that the woman should stay home and raise the children while the man worked hard to support his family. This is what they wanted for me: to leave school, get an apprenticeship in a trade, find a job close to home, as well as a nice girlfriend. They never imagined me leaving Liverpool.

I wanted the opposite, just like Molly. I'd wanted to go to college, study sport science, and become a PE teacher from as early as I can remember, and I knew I wanted to leave Liverpool to experience another city. I spent years researching and visiting places I might want to go. I came down to Oxford one weekend with a couple of mates and fell in love with the city. So, Oxford Brookes University it was; all I had to do was get the grades.

My parents have visited me down here a couple of times, but mostly I go up to them. They were not impressed, to say the least, when I decided to stay in Oxford to do my teacher training, and even less impressed when I chose to stay for good. The only bit they liked about it all was Hannah. They loved her.

My parents eased up a little after I moved away. My two younger sisters, Abbi—who is now twenty-one—is about to start her last year of university in Manchester doing primary teaching, and Liv—nineteen—has just finished her first year in Cardiff doing journalism. They didn't seem to get half as much grief as I did when I decided to go away. It always seemed to be the case that I got all the hassle for the decisions I made, but when it came time to make theirs, our parents just seemed to go with it.

"I just wish mine would have come around to the idea like yours did," Molly says quietly.

I've been explaining all about my family to Molly for the last half an hour. It's nice to have someone else who understands what it was like, although my parents were there for me in the end, and still are.

"When was the last time you spoke to your parents?"

"Um... I actually can't remember. I speak to Steven and Daniel quite often. They tend to keep me updated."

"Have you always got along with your brothers?" I've only met her brothers once, at Hannah's funeral. They came to support Molly, which told me they were nice guys, unlike her parents who couldn't possibly leave their holiday a day early. As you can imagine, I didn't get to talk to them at the time, and she hasn't really mentioned them since.

"Yeah, we speak most weeks. We are as close as we can be with such a big age gap. They've always supported my decision to break away from the family business and have never held it against me. They've both told me on separate occasions that they really wanted to be part of it, and really enjoy taking on the renovations and rental side of the estate agency my dad runs. They've started up a sister company and it's doing really well."

"I'm glad you have them to turn to. Your birthday's soon, so you'll hear from your parents then, right?"

"Oh yeah, I'll hear from them."

A

fter spending the afternoon reminiscing, we've somehow managed to drink our way through two pitchers of Pimm's. I don't know about Molly, but I'm starting to feel a little buzzed with the mixture of sun and alcohol.

I watch as she pops the last bit of fruit from her glass into her mouth, and I'm mesmerised by how sexy she looks doing something so simple. When her tongue licks away the juice on her lips, I know I need to get up and do something. "Now that it's cooling down, I think I'll go for a run along the beach." I stand and collect our glasses.

"Okay. I was thinking of heading in for a shower and getting dressed for dinner, anyway. I'm feeling quite cooked."

She's right; she has a lovely glow over her skin, and a bit of a pink nose. I watch as she stands and staggers a little. Yep, it's not just me who's buzzed, then.

I

've been running for a long time. My legs burn and sweat's pouring off me. Once I climbed over the rocks we thought were the end of the beach, I found a long sandy stretch that I ran the entire length of, despite it being more touristy than our secluded piece of heaven next door.

I'm now sat on those rocks, looking over the beach and watching a young family building sandcastles. The little girl can't be more than two years old, and her parents are still in their twenties, I'd say. They're having such fun. I know it's stupid to feel it because I am in no way lonely, but that's how I feel in this moment.

Actually, since I lost Hannah, I've felt lonely.

I loved sharing my life with her. It made me feel complete to wake up to her in the morning and hold her in my arms at night before I fell asleep.

That lonely feeling is soon overtaken by guilt. For the past six months, when I've pictured my future, I was alone. All of a sudden, a change in that vision has taken me by surprise and scared the fuck out of me. I now see Molly—and I don't mean living downstairs. I see Molly everywhere.

"Fuck!" I shout as I run my hands through my hair and feel the tears burning behind my eyes. I promised Hannah I would move on one day. Every time I go to her grave, I tell her I will, because I know that's what she would want for me. I was fine with that happening... one day. But how has that one day come so quickly, and why is it Molly? She made it pretty clear this morning that we're just friends, and she sees me as her brother.

What would Hannah think about Molly and me? Molly was her best friend. Would she think it's weird? What would she want me to do?

I sit there for a while longer, trying to get my head together. I come to the decision that I've got to put my new feelings aside—firstly so I can try to make sense of them, and secondly so I can be the friend she needs me to be. If I force anything, I'm likely to push her away, and I need her. If what I'm feeling is meant to happen, then it will.

With that little pep talk over, I head back to the beach hut. What I find when I get there almost makes me forget everything I've just told myself.

CHAPTER SEVEN

Molly

Ryan's been gone ages. I'm starting to get worried. I called his mobile over half an hour ago, but it rang in the living room. I'm trying to stop myself from worrying by keeping busy. I decided, as we're celebrating tonight, to wear one of the dresses I bought on my holiday shopping trip yesterday. It's a full-length maxi dress with multi-coloured flowers printed all over the thin, sheer fabric. The top is cut low and square across my breasts, showing off my ample cleavage. I've left my hair to dry naturally, tucked a flower behind my ear, and kept my make-up light.

We decided to have Hannah's favourite for dinner. I've prepped all the ingredients, so when Ryan gets back, it's just the beef that needs cooking. I've also made a pitcher of margaritas to go with the tacos, but in the time I've been waiting, I've already had one too many. Add those to the Pimm's from earlier and I might be having an early night.

I've just finished a pint of water to try to dilute it all when I hear footsteps on the balcony.

"Ryan, is that you? I've been worried sick. You should have taken your —" He appears around the corner. *Oh, holy fucking hell.* "Um... your phone... um... taken it... with you. Shit."

He's standing there in the doorway with the setting sun behind him. His body is tanned and glistening where the light is hitting his sweat, his hair sticking up in all directions, and his eyes... shit, his eyes look like they're asking me to devour him. *Um, yes please,* I think as I stand here, close to drooling. I watch as his tongue darts out to wet his lips. Oh God, I want those lips on me. I squeeze my thighs together to try to relieve the ache, but I swear the pressure makes it worse. I feel like I'm about to melt into a puddle on the floor.

Ryan distracts me from my almost orgasmic state. "Holy motherfucking shit."

My eyes go back up to his after getting my fill of his half-naked body. They're roaming all over me before they come to rest on my breasts.

"Are you trying to kill me?"

When I laugh, his eyes come back up to mine. His normally bright blues are darker than I've ever seen them.

"I've pretty much got dinner sorted, so if you want to go have a shower, I'll finish it off," I say as a way to distract both of us.

He's sauntering toward me, an intention in his eyes that I don't want to identify.

"I've already laid the table, so you can meet me outside once..."

He's about an inch away from me. My breasts are so close to rubbing up against his chest, I'm worried I'll go off like a rocket if he so much as touches them. His hand rests on my cheek, and he stares into my eyes.

"I don't know what was wrong with all the guys you've been with before, because your body was designed to be worshipped," he growls before swallowing. The muscles in his neck ripple, distracting me. He leans in and whispers, "For hours."

"Ryan... shower," I manage to croak out, when his face moves closer again. I don't think I've ever felt as conflicted as I am in this moment.

"Ryan," I whisper again, breaking the trance. He flinches before kissing my forehead and leaving the room.

I walk out of the hut and lean against the balcony railing, looking over the beach below. What the hell is going on here? Where did all this sexual tension come from?

After Hannah died, we held each other while we cried. We had nights where we held each other in bed while we slept, but even then, not even a hint of anything sexual was evident. Then, I move in, and suddenly *bam!* He's all I can see and think about.

Nothing can happen between us, though. Just thinking about how Emma reacted when she presumed something was going on is enough to scare me off. How would she react if it actually happened? What about Susan and Pete, or the twins? I could lose them all.

The sudden realisation has me panicking. If something happened between us and it didn't work, I'd lose him as my best friend. There's no way we'd be this close afterwards. The Morrisons might all act like Emma earlier, then I'd not only lose my best friend, but the people I see as my family, too. That cannot happen.

I need to control my feelings where Ryan is concerned. This has to stop. Maybe I need a date, to see someone else. Maybe it's not Ryan I want, but it's my body's way of telling me I'm ready to get out there and find that great guy I've been waiting for.

Instead of going back to dinner, I grab my phone and call Susan to see how she's doing before calling Emma back. I'm glad when she answers. I hope she can start being around a bit more. I really miss her. I also call Lilly and Dec to check up on them. They all sound sad, but they're doing okay.

When Ryan reappears, I've only just started on the beef. "Sorry, I got distracted." I glance over to see him run his hand through his wet hair, leaving it in a sexy mess. I run my eyes over him quickly. He's wearing a black t-shirt stretched across his wide shoulders and chest, paired with tan shorts.

"No problem. We're on holidays, we can do whatever we want."

Dinner was delicious and uneventful, except for the fact that I caught Ryan watching me a number of times. Maybe messy food wasn't a great idea. It felt like every time I licked one of my fingers, his eyes darkened another shade.

As soon as we cleared our plates, I immediately started to clean up—I just couldn't sit there any longer. The tension was killing me.

"I put the DVDs I brought by the TV. Do you want to pick one and put it on? I'm going to get changed." I decided while I was washing up that this situation was somehow the dress's fault, so it's coming off in favour of a tank top and shorts.

When I come out, Ryan is already on the sofa. He's also found the box of chocolate truffles we bought and placed them on the coffee table. As I walk over, I notice which DVD he's chosen. The *Friends with Benefits* box is open with the disc missing. It's like he knows how hot this film makes me. I mean, come on, Justin Timberlake practically naked... who wouldn't get a bit hot?

"Um, why this film?" I try to ask as innocently as possible as I sit on the floor, leaning my back against the sofa in an attempt to keep my distance from him.

"I've never seen it, and you two were always going on about it. Plus, the main actress is fit." He shrugs.

Brilliant, just what we need to add to our sexual tension.

***

We're about halfway into the film and I think it's going okay. I mean, yes, it's awkward as fuck, but if I don't look at Ryan at all, it makes it easier. I'm still sat on the floor and it's really un-fucking-comfortable. I can't feel my arse, and I've got pins and needles in my legs, but I'm adamant that I'm not sitting next to him on that small sofa. He continually tells me to come up, but I keep making excuses.

Eventually, it gets so bad that I'm constantly fidgeting. I feel Ryan get up from behind me and come to stand in front of me.

"What are you doing?"

"I could ask you the same thing," he says, as his hands go to my waist and he lifts me up with no effort at all, practically throwing me on the sofa.

"What the fuck was that for?"

"Just get fucking comfortable. I can't cope with the fidgeting any longer."

I curl myself into the far corner from Ryan, and he looks at me with a raised eyebrow. He's right to think this is weird; we've watched loads of films together and we usually sit quite happily next to each other.

"What the fuck now?"

He narrows his eyes. I just need to act normal. I think I've forgotten what normal is with us, though. I just shrug my shoulders in answer to his question.

"Come here." He grabs me and moves me over until I'm up against his side.

I try to relax, I really do, but I know there's a sex scene coming next and I don't know if I can watch and be this close to Ryan without panting or doing something embarrassing. Being pressed up against his hard body and able to smell him is already hard enough.

"What's wrong? You're as tense as a nun at an Ann Summers party."

"Nothing," I mumble.

"Molls, are you uncomfortable watching this with me?" I know he's smirking. Fucking know-it-all. "Fuck, you *are*. Seriously, we've watched worse than this together before now."

I can feel him laughing, and I know he's thinking of the night his mate left the TV on an adult channel and hid the remote. Admittedly, we were pretty drunk and curiosity got the better of us for about thirty minutes, but that was different. The sexual tension between us wasn't as thick as fog on a winter's morning.

"I know, but after earlier it feels a little weird."

"I know, and I'm sorry. You just took me by surprise, standing there looking all hot and sexy. It won't happen again, I promise. Actually, no, I can't promise that. Just relax—it's not like I'm going to jump you any minute. Molly, you might be my best friend, but you're still seriously hot. I can't help appreciating that."

I relax into him a bit more, and he strokes my arm gently. I may have relaxed, but I'm still stupidly aware of my body. I suddenly realise that, the way I'm lying, I'm giving him a great view of my tits again. I try to discreetly pull my top up, but I stop in my tracks when I hear him laugh, "Are you trying to ruin *all* my fun?"

"Fuck off, Ry." I move back to my side of the sofa, grabbing my drink.

When the film finishes, I get up to put the next one in while Ryan gets us fresh drinks. Surely *Bridget Jones's Diary* is a safer choice than the last one.

By the time the credits come up, we're both well past the point of being tipsy. Luckily, the tension has drained, and it's back to being like it always has been. Ish.

"What are you doing?" I ask Ryan as he gets up and starts to move the coffee table.

"Making some space. You said you brought Twister."

"You're kidding. You actually want to play?"

"You bet your sweet arse I do. Come on, Molls, don't be a spoilsport. It's that or strip poker," he says with a smile.

"I'll go get it, then," I say, sounding less than enthusiastic. There is no way this can be a good idea.

I come back with the game for Ryan to set up, the bottle of Apple Sourz, and a couple of glasses. We have a shot each and get started.

We've been playing for twenty minutes, and so far we've avoided any contact and remained on either side of the mat. I'm thinking I might accidently fall over soon to end the game and stop the inevitable. I have my back facing the floor and am looking up at the ceiling, waiting for Ryan to spin and move. He's sort of on his side next to me, with both hands next to each other, but his foot is between mine.

"Right hand, red."

I breathe a sigh of relief, because this means he can just move his hand one spot to the right from where it is now. Unfortunately, Ryan has other ideas. He moves his hand over my body so that he's hovering over me, his face right above mine. His breath caresses my neck, causing goosebumps to appear on my skin. My chest heaves as my breathing intensifies.

"Are you going to spin, Molls?"

"Yeah, sorry." I reach out for the spinner. "Right leg, green."

Fuck.

I move my leg to the other side of his, so that now I'm totally underneath him. This is exactly why I didn't want to play.

I hear a small moan come from the back of Ryan's throat and I turn to look at him. His eyes are as dark as they were earlier, and he's just less sweaty. His lips are parted where his breathing is coming out in fast pants, and his chest moves dramatically. I look back to his face in time to see his tongue sneak out and wet his bottom lip.

My heart pounds and my temperature is nearly at boiling point. I know that if I don't move, we're going to end up doing something we're going to regret.

I can tell by the determined look in Ryan's eyes that he's not backing down. It's up to me.

I make a snap decision and let my limbs give way so my back hits the floor, and I scramble out from under his body.

CHAPTER EIGHT

Ryan

It's been three days since our game of Twister. What a stupid fucking idea that was. Yeah, I pretty much knew it would be when I mentioned it, but the thought of being that close to her was too much of a pull. Thank God she didn't come back out to the living area after she ran away, because I would have been caught red-handed jacking off after that little episode.

We've had a great few days. Every morning, Molly has worked on designs for different clients. I love watching her sketch. She gets so engrossed in her thoughts and looks really sexy chewing on her pencil. All she needs is a pair of glasses to give her that sexy secretary look. I'm trying really hard to curb my feelings for her, but it's not as easy as I initially thought.

We went for a drive yesterday for a look around. It was a typical Cornish town, and all the people were lovely to chat to. Molly dragged me into nearly every shop we came across and we spent longer than I thought possible inside a little art gallery full of paintings of the surrounding countryside. There was one painting in particular that caught her attention, and she spends an inordinate amount of time considering its smallest details. I'm captivated watching her studying the painting and the way she bites down on her bottom lip and moves her finger gently over the paint as if she's experiencing what the very act of painting it might have been like.

I didn't mind following her around, because it made her happy. She couldn't wipe the smile off her face all day. She came back with a number of bags full of bits and bobs for her bedroom at home, and small souvenirs for the Morrisons and Megan's little boy.

Our time here has been amazing, but it's gone so fast. Tomorrow is our last full day. I'm so glad I asked Molly to come with me, even with the odd awkward moment between us. We've done exactly what I wanted us to do. We've celebrated Hannah, and we've relaxed and enjoyed ourselves. I would have been bored here on my own.

We've decided to go out for a meal at the local pub tonight so we don't have to cook. It's a bit of a walk, but from what the locals have said, it'll be worth it.

Molly is lying on her front on the outdoor sofa, sketching ideas for something on her pad. I walk over with a glass of water and sit next to her.

"What are you working on?" I ask. They look a little suggestive, to say the least.

"A burlesque club—they're doing some bondage-themed nights in a few months and want some promo stuff." I look back down at her sketches, and they start to make sense a bit more now.

"These are amazing, Molls," I tell her honestly. She has hand-drawn a range of bondage items and used the markers to really make them stand out. "I think the whip, blindfold, and the one with the side of a corset on are my favourites."

"I'm going to do one with handcuffs as well, which I think will look quite cool. I'll scan them all in when we get back, edit them further, then add all the text and stuff."

"I can't imagine Hannah working on something like this." Hannah was so sweet; in my head, she and bondage do not go together.

"It would have always been mine to work on, because they liked the hand-drawn elements. Let's be honest, Hannah was a brilliant designer, but she couldn't draw for toffee!" She laughs as she thinks back. "Do you remember when we had to do a life drawing class in our third year? The model was offended by Hannah's sketches."

"Yeah, I remember. She asked me if I would model for her so she could practise, but I didn't want her to knock my self-esteem by drawing some sort of alien thing that was meant to be me."

By the look on her face, Molly's deep in thought.

"What's wrong?"

"Nothing. Just thinking... would you let me draw you?" she asks.

"Um... are you serious? You want to draw me... naked?" I know I've got a pretty good body, but could I really get it all out and lie in front of Molly while she stares at me? All of me?

"I'm serious. I'd love to sketch you and get all these in there." My skin heats as her finger runs over my abs. My dick twitches, ready for action every time her finger touches my skin. "We could put some grapes in front of your manhood if you're worried about how small it is," she deadpans.

"Oh, you'll need more than grapes." I wink at her. "Could you actually take it seriously if I laid out in front of you?"

"It's art—of course I could take it seriously."

"I'll think about it," I mutter, moving back over to my sun lounger. The way she was touching me along with the sweet scent of her perfume is messing with my head as well as my dick. "So, how's work going? I know you took on fewer clients after Hannah died, but it seems it's picking up again,"

"Yeah, it's getting really busy. I'm getting to the point where there's too much for me to do alone, and I need to employ someone else and get an office. But that's such a huge step."

"Molly, you can do anything you set your mind to. If you really think you're at that point, go for it. What's the worst that could happen?"

She smiles and takes a deep breath. "I guess you're right. I'll start looking into stuff when we get back."

"What are we doing for your birthday Saturday night?"

"Megan mentioned us all going out. I just need to text everyone with the details."

"Sounds like a plan; I'm in. Don't make any plans for Friday night, though. You're all mine."

"That sounds a little creepy. What are you going to do with me?"

"Just a little surprise."

I leave Molly looking confused and walk down to the beach with my phone. I've been planning something with Susan and Pete for ages now as a thank you to Molly for everything she's done for all of us these past six months. I wasn't aware up until just now how imminent it could be, but the timing is brilliant for her birthday. Once I've organised everything with Susan, spoken to Emma, and made a few more calls to sort everything out, it's time to get ready for dinner.

"Wow, that food was amazing," Molly says as we walk along the beach after getting back from the pub.

"I don't think I'm going to be able to eat for a week after all that."

"I think I'd drive down here just for a slice of the cheesecake. It was so good."

She's right; the cheesecake was amazing, but she sounded indecent whilst eating it, especially in a packed pub. If people didn't know any better, they'd have thought she was having an orgasm at the dinner table.

We've been walking along slowly for about thirty minutes, carrying our shoes as we step through the shallow seawater. Molly, as always, looks stunning in a strapless white summer dress that's fitted at her waist, then flares out to her knees. The white sets off her new tan well. Her hair is pinned up with a flower in it, exposing her neck. Every time I look at her, all I want to do is put my lips there and taste her skin.

I turn around when I notice she stopped a few seconds ago. She's smiling mischievously. I'm almost scared to ask. Almost. "What?"

"Do you know what we haven't done since we've been here?"

I can think of a number of things we haven't done. "What did you have in mind?" I ask with a smirk.

"We haven't been swimming in the sea. You up for it?"

"Yeah, let's go get changed and come back down," I say as I turn in the direction of the beach hut.

"That's... not exactly what I was thinking." I turn back around to her and find that she's walked up a little from the water and dropped her shoes on the dry sand. She stands so she's facing me and pulls the zip of her dress down. She has a small smile on her face as she watches me watch her.

Shit.

She drops her dress to her feet and stands there, waiting.

Fuck, she's stunning. She's standing there in a white lacy strapless bra and matching tiny knickers that look like they show off most of her arse. I can't move. I'm frozen, staring at her. I'm sure my eyes are bulging out of my head and my mouth is hanging open.

"Ry?"

She walks toward me, slowly, and stops right in front of me.

"Ryan?" she tries again, but it's like I'm dreaming. I'm still immobile as she grasps the top button of my shirt. Agonisingly slowly, it seems, she undoes one at a time, until she's at the bottom. She slips her hands onto my shoulders and pushes my shirt off so it pools on the sand. It's when I feel her hands touch the skin above my waistband that I snap out of my trance. She needs to stop, or she's going to find herself pinned under me in the sand.

"Skinny dipping?" I ask, just to make sure I've understood correctly.

"Well, I don't think going naked is a particularly good idea, so I'm going like this," she laughs.

"You'd be having the same problem if you were stood in my shoes," I say quietly.

She turns and winks at me as she disappears into the sea. "Don't worry, the water's pretty cold. It should sort your problem right out," she says, dropping her gaze to my crotch.

"You're going to regret that, Molly," I say as I drop my shorts and wade into the water in my black boxer briefs as fast as I can, so she can't see exactly how excited I am by this.

She's in up to her neck. I go straight over and pick her up. She wraps her legs around my waist and puts her arms on my shoulders.

"Oh," she says as she wiggles her hips, "I see the cold water didn't work."

"You are in so much trouble, Molly Carter," I scold her, staring straight into her eyes, trying to stare her down and stop her laughing. It doesn't work, but I know what will. I grab her waist and throw her as hard as I can into the water.

"Fuuuuu—" She squeals, but she's cut off as she goes under.

When she resurfaces, she's spluttering and frantically wiping her face. "Do you know how fucking disgusting that tastes, fuckface?" she says, glaring at me.

"No, I wasn't stupid enough to go under like you!" At that, she pushes a wave of water at me, but I see it coming and turn away.

We spend ages messing about in the water like teenagers. It's great to be carefree for a while. Molly is such fun to be around; she doesn't take herself too seriously, and she's quite happy to laugh at herself. I think she's starting to regret winding me up earlier, judging by the number of times she's had to spit out a mouthful of salt water.

I notice that she's started shivering and her teeth are chattering. "I think it's time we got out. You look freezing."

I swim over to where she is and stand close to her.

Time for my revenge.

"Come here," I say as I pull her into my arms and squeeze her tight. "Thanks for this. I like acting like kids again." I kiss her hair, making her look up at me.

"The whole week has been brilliant. Thank you for bringing me. I can't believe it's nearly over, though. I don't feel ready to leave yet."

She makes me laugh as she pouts. "I know, but we still have tomorrow, and then you've got all that new stuff to go in your room when we get back." The thought of that perks her up a little.

I slowly start rubbing my hands up and down her back like I'm warming her up, and I lean forward so I'm whispering in her ear. "Do you know, you're even more gorgeous when you have black make-up running down your face," I tell her softly.

It's completely dark out here but for the light the moon is casting, allowing me to see enough to know I just made goosebumps break out across her skin.

"I don't believe you. No one looks good like that," she replies.

"Believe it."

My hands are still roaming over her back, and I keep pushing them a little closer to her arse or around her sides to her breasts. Her pulse picks up from my touch.

I place a soft kiss under her ear, and I hear her sharp intake of breath at my action. I do it again, and again. Her breaths are coming out fast now, and her pulse pounds against my lips. I move my hands up her back and slip my fingers under the strap of her bra to test the water. She groans and presses her breasts harder into my chest. Her hips slowly start to grind against me, and it takes everything in me not to moan with pleasure. It's now or never, or I'll get carried away. I move my hands around her back one more time as I place another kiss to her neck. This time, I unsnap her bra, pull it away from her, and move toward the shore as quick as I can.

"Ryan, what the fuck?" she squeals from behind me. "Come back, you little fucker!"

I can't help it, I'm crying with laughter as I make my way to our hut with our clothes.

I stand on our balcony overlooking the beach and Molly, who is still in the sea. She looks seriously lost out there alone. I almost feel bad. Almost.

Eventually, she squares her shoulders as though she's made a decision, and she starts to walk out the water, clutching her breasts in her hands.

When she hits the path to our beach hut, I shout down, "Revenge is sweet, Miss Molly." She looks up at me and growls—yes, actually growls.

As she comes toward me, I hold out the towel I got ready for her. See, I'm not a total dick.

"I cannot believe you did that, you fuckwit. I think I hate you a little bit," she says very seriously as she pulls the towel around her, unfortunately managing not to flash me in the process.

When she's sorted, she bursts out laughing. Thank God. She looked so serious, I thought she was about to castrate me right here. I can't help it, and I laugh along with her.

Once she's calmed down, she walks over to the fridge, pulls out the bottle of Apple Sourz, and pours us both a very large shot. "To embarrassing friends," she says with a laugh. I clink her glass and take a drink.

"To revenge," I say, and we repeat the process.

"I actually cannot believe you did that, Ryan. That took more balls than I gave you credit for."

"Don't you go worrying about my balls, Molly. There is most definitely nothing wrong with them."

CHAPTER NINE

Molly

The last day of our holiday was great. We chilled out by the beach hut, reading and enjoying each other's company.

It's now Friday. I've finished setting up my room, and Ryan's put my shelves and mirror up so I could get everything in place.

Going away wasn't the wisest thing to do, but it was worth all the work I've got to catch up with now. Because I've been in my room, the only time Ryan and I have really seen each other has been at dinner. With his extra time during the school holidays, he's been experimenting in his new kitchen and, I have to say, he's not doing a bad job.

Tonight is the night he's reserved for my birthday surprise. I hate surprises, and Ryan knows this, which is why he's been winding me up about it all week. I now feel like a coiled spring with the pressure of it all. He's told me to dress smart-casual, so I guess we are not going somewhere posh.

I decide to wear the black maxi dress with pink flower print that I didn't wear on the holiday; the jersey material clings in all the right places. I've left my make-up light and just added some eyeliner and mascara to make my eyes stand out a little. I grab my flip-flops out of my wardrobe, my handbag off the bed, and head upstairs to see if he's ready.

I find him sat on the sofa, watching the local news. He notices me straight away, turns the TV off, and comes over to me.

"You look amazing as always, Molly."

"You too." He's wearing light blue jeans that hug his arse and muscular thighs in the most delicious way, and a black fitted t-shirt and black Converse. It's simple, but so hot. He has obviously tried to style his hair but, as usual, his dirty blond locks are falling over his forehead in a sexy mess, and he smells out of this world.

"Right, come on. It's nearly time for your surprise."

I groan in response.

He grabs my hand and pulls me out of the house. He stops by the passenger door of his car, opens it, and ushers me in.

"Wow, being a gentleman tonight, are we?" I comment.

"Not likely," he says with a huff, making me laugh. That is, until he leans into me, grabs the seat belt and straps me in. A heated look flickers in his eyes quickly, but it's gone as fast as it appears.

"I am able to do that myself, you know."

"Molls, just be quiet and go with the flow. You're not in control here, I am," he says in his teacher voice.

"Sorry, Mr. Evans," I sing. With that, he pulls something out of his back pocket and moves toward me again. He's so quick that, before I know what's happening, he's tying something around my eyes. Once it's secured, I hear him shut the door and, a couple of seconds later, he gets in the driver's seat and starts the car.

"Is this really necessary?" I growl.

"Just forget that we're going somewhere, and imagine that it's research for that bondage project you were working on last week."

"Um, Ry... I don't think this is quite like that."

"Maybe not, but I thought it might take your mind off it a bit." He smiles. "Have you been to one of the nights you're advertising?" he asks quietly.

"Oh yeah, *all* the time."

He pauses as he considers my words. "You're into all that stuff? You've never talked about it before."

"No, Ry, not really. I've only ever stepped inside for a meeting with the manager."

"Oh, um... what about... um..." He clears his throat. "Bondage in general. Have you done that stuff?"

"Ryan, are you getting embarrassed?"

"I just wondered."

"I've never been with anyone I would have trusted enough to do anything like that. What about you?" I ask, but I'm guessing from his hesitation that he hasn't.

He falls silent once again. I can only imagine he's thinking about Hannah.

"Right, we're here. Stay there and I'll help you out."

"Can't I take it off?" I sulk.

"Nope. Hang on."

A couple of minutes later, Ryan is standing behind me with his hands on my waist, steering me in the right direction.

"Right, we're going upstairs. Lift now... okay, up we go."

"Is it much farther?"

"No, we're almost there. Right, stand here." He brings me to a stop and turns me slightly. "Are you ready?"

With that, he unties me.

"What?" I ask as I look around.

I'm in some sort of office. It takes me a few seconds to register that the work hanging on the walls is what Hannah and I had designed since we started the company. I turn around to look at Ryan. He's not standing alone. Next to him are Susan, Pete, and Emma, and all of them have big smiles on their faces.

It's in that moment that it hits me.

"We're in the flat," I say as they all come toward me, wishing me happy birthday and giving me a hug.

"When Ryan moved into his new house, we got some builders in to revamp the place. We were going to rent it out to students again, but none of us wanted anyone living in the place you'd all spent so much time in. We applied to change its use from a flat to an office. Lilly designed the interior, and we asked your brothers to do the work. Then, it was going to sit here, waiting, until you were ready," Susan explains.

"Until I was ready?" Tears sting my eyes.

"When Ryan rang us last week to say that you were talking about hiring, we had to get our arses into gear and get it finished for you."

"You're telling me that all of this is for the business?"

Susan starts laughing. Apparently, the look on my face is priceless.

"Yes, it's for the business. The business that you and our daughter started. We want you to still be able to live out your dream, and this flat is the perfect way for you to do that. Do you like it?"

"You've already done so much for me... this is just too much."

"Angel, we love you like one of our own. We want to do everything we can to help you. Plus, it's for Hannah as well. She would be so happy to see the business you both dreamed of coming to life."

With that, I throw myself at her and hold her tight as everything she just said settles into my brain. I turn around and give Pete a hug, and then Emma, before I turn and jump into Ryan's arms. I love the Morrisons with all my heart; they're my family, but I never expected them to do something like this for me.

After a few seconds, I realise that no one has said a word. I lift my head out of the crook of Ryan's neck and see Susan, Pete, and Emma staring at us. I suddenly realise how this must look to them and quickly remove myself from Ryan.

"Can I see the rest?" I ask, trying to break the sudden tension.

I'm in awe. The living/dining room is now a large office with two massive desks in it. The bedroom that used to be Hannah's is now a meeting room with a giant table in the centre. Susan said they used her room for this because they wanted her to be involved with the decisions. My old room is now a mini living room with a sofa and TV. Emma's old room is currently empty, and the little kitchen and bathroom are the same as before. Everything is black, grey, and pink, to match our branding, and all the furniture is really modern.

Once I've seen everything, we head downstairs and outside. It's then that I get to take in the massive Angel Designs sign hanging between the two front windows. I love it.

As we get back in Ryan's car, Lilly and Dec join us while Emma chooses to go with Susan and Pete. I can't help but think she's pissed off after my display with Ryan upstairs. She's going to have to get used to us being close, because I can't be without him.

I just get settled in my seat when I feel the blindfold coming back around my eyes from behind me.

"For fuck's sake, not again."

"I'm afraid so," Lilly says. "I'm under strict instructions from Ryan."

I hear him and Dec get in the car and join in with Lilly's laughter at my pouting face.

"We aren't going far, Molls, stop sulking," Ryan says. I fold my arms over my chest and huff my annoyance.

Ryan was lying when he said we weren't going far. I've been sat here in the dark for ages. Eventually, the engine turns off and hear the others get out. They've been talking amongst themselves during the journey, but I didn't join in. I was trying to show them how miserable being blindfolded was making me but, apparently, they didn't care.

Once Ryan has successfully guided me to our destination without letting me fall on my arse, he takes the blindfold off.

We're in our favourite pub, and sitting in front of me are the Morrisons, as well as Steven, his wife Debs, their two little girls, Poppy and Mia, and Daniel.

"Happy birthday, kid," Steven says as he comes over to give me a hug.

A wide smile splits my face at seeing everyone I love in one place.

It's been ages since I've spent time with my brothers. I hug Daniel after Steven has put me down, then Debs and the girls, who are very excited to see me. Poppy is six and Mia is four; they're both the spitting image of their mum, with light blonde hair and pale skin. Poppy has her mum's blue eyes, whereas Mia has her dad's green ones. I can just imagine how much stress they're going to cause my big brother when they're teenagers.

"I can't believe you're here!"

"Ryan phoned us at the beginning of the week to invite us. He told us you were going to see the office. What do you think?" Daniel asks.

"I love it. Thank you so much for helping do it."

"Anything for you, Molly-moo," Daniel says, rubbing his hand on my head, messing up my hair as if I were a little kid again.

We had a brilliant evening. I was surrounded by my family, and I couldn't be happier. I loved them all, and was grateful to have such amazing people in my life.

It's just past midnight, and I'm sat on the sofa with my laptop. As it's now officially my birthday, I have something to check. Ryan puts some music on and sits next to me with a beer in his hand.

"What are you doing?" he questions.

"I just need to check something."

"What's so important that you dived straight for your laptop as soon as you got in?"

"Nothing much," I say, to try to stop him prying. I hate what I'm about to check, but I need to know what it's going to be this year. I know it will make Ryan mad if I tell him the truth. I get the webpage up and log myself in, opening my account. As usual, it's already there. A lump forms in my throat, and my eyes tear up a bit. Every year, I hope it is going to be different and they'll actually do something to show me they care about me. Even a card would mean more to me than this.

"Molly, what's wrong?"

I knew I should have done this when I was on my own. "Nothing. I'm okay."

I go to shut the lid of my laptop, but Ryan is faster and grabs it from me.

"What is this?" he asks, his eyes running over the page. "Why have you had thirty thousand pounds paid into your account with the reference of 'Love'?"

"It's nothing." I feel myself getting more upset as he turns his head to look at me.

"It's from your parents, isn't it? When you said last week that you would hear from them on your birthday, this is what you meant?"

"Yes. I fucking hate it. Every birthday and Christmas, the only contact I have from them is a bank transfer." Saying it out loud makes the dejection only stronger.

"All I've ever wanted from them is their love, to be actual parents to me, but all they do is palm me off with money. I'm sure it's all a tax fiddle or something, because it's a different amount every time—like they just have some money to lose, so gift it to me. Some years they really 'love' me; others not so much. I would be so happy just to receive a handwritten card from them, because at least they would have gone to the effort of writing it themselves and putting a tiny bit of thought into it."

I take the laptop back and move the money out of my current account and into my savings. I log out, and take a big gulp of wine.

The muscle in Ryan's neck starts to pulse. "Have they always done this?"

"Since I graduated."

"What do you do with it? You don't live like someone who's loaded, and I've seen your bank account before now—it looks like a normal working person's."

I blow out a big breath. "Well, I got a big lump when I turned twenty-one. I paid off the debts I'd accumulated as a student, and I gave Susan and Pete the rent I believed I should have been paying for all the years I lived in their flat for free. Then, with my brothers' help, I bought two cheap run-down flats in the city, did them up, and now rent them both out. I wanted to put the money to work, not just blow it on expensive clothes, holidays, and cars, like the other trust fund babies I grew up around. Steven reckons if I sold the flats now, I would easily double my money. I hate that I've used the family business for it, but Steven and Daniel are brilliant at what they do, and I knew I could trust them with it. They're sworn to secrecy. I never want my parents to know.

"I bought my car one year because I needed to meet with clients and taking the bus wasn't cutting it. I paid for the three of us to go to the Caribbean after graduating, too." Hannah and Ryan were together by then, so he would remember that. "I wanted to treat the most important people in my life to an unforgettable holiday. Every year, I give some of it to charity, and I make sure the people I love are looked after—no matter how slyly I have to do it."

Ryan looks thoughtful. "Have you done it to me before?"

"Maybe. I'm not telling you what, though."

"I'm going to let that slide, but I'm watching you, Molly Carter."

I'm woken up Saturday morning by my phone ringing. I begrudgingly open my eyes to see who it is.

"Steven, do you know what time it is?" I grumble. Then, I hear giggling.

"Happy birthday to you, happy birthday to you," my nieces sing to me.

"Aw, thank you, guys. That was lovely. Best birthday present ever."

"Auntie Molly?" Poppy asks.

"Yes, Pops?"

"It's lunchtime. You should be awake by now!" she admonishes me.

"Um, yeah, I guess I should." I hear a commotion in the background as Steven comes on the phone.

"Happy birthday, kid."

We chat for a bit, and I open the present the girls gave me last night. It's my favourite smellies. Debs always picks the best presents. Not long after, I hang up and lie back down, feeling like I could sleep the day away, but my phone goes off again. It's Daniel's turn.

"Happy birthday, Molls."

"Thanks. You sound as bad as I feel," I comment at his sleepy voice.

"I may have gone out after the meal last night," he explains. "Yes, just help yourself," I hear him say away from the phone.

"Got a friend, Daniel?" He's a bit of a player, my youngest big brother.

"Yeah, just some blonde I met last ni— yes, sorry baby, I know you have a name. Is the coffee ready yet?"

"I think I should let you go. If you're up for another night out, we're all going out tonight. Not sure where yet, but I can text you."

"You know me, Molls—can't turn down a night out." My brother may be thirty-seven, but he's still twenty-one at heart. I'm just waiting for the day he meets a woman who knocks him on his arse.

I snuggle back down again into my covers, when I hear a knock at my bedroom door.

"Yeah?" I groan.

"Happy birthday," Ryan chimes as he walks in with a tray of food and a huge bunch of flowers.

"Wow, is that all for me?"

"I thought you could have breakfast in bed." He places the tray down on my bedside table, and I see he's brought me all my favourite pastries, a pot of tea, orange juice, and a huge display of dusky pink flowers of all different types. He stands back and heads to the door.

"Where are you going? I can't eat this all by myself. Come join me."

"I'm just getting your present. Don't worry, I'm not leaving the food!"

He comes back in holding a huge, flat, rectangular gift box. I feel a huge smile break across my face.

"Can I open it now?" I put my arms out like a little kid.

"Of course, birthday girl." I take it from him and rip into the paper to discover what I suspected.

"When did you go back and get this?"

"I didn't. I rang them and had it delivered to Susan and Pete's house."

Tears well in my eyes as I look down at the canvas in my hands. It's a painting looking out over the bay where we stayed. The roofs of the beach huts are showing, and the sun is going down, just like the night I watched it from the hot tub. When I first saw it in the gallery, I couldn't take my eyes off it. The artist had captured the scene perfectly.

"I can't believe you got it for me. Thank you so much. I love it." I crawl over to him so I can say thank you properly, placing a kiss on his cheek and squeezing him tight. It's when my arms touch his bare skin that I realise he's only in pyjama bottoms. A birthday breakfast can't get any better than this.

"Remind me, what's the plan for later?" Ryan asks around a bite of croissant.

"Megan is coming over later this afternoon to get ready with me, then we're meeting everyone at the Indian at eight before drinks. Chris and Shane have it all planned."

"They'd better not take us to the gay clubs again."

"Are you still grumpy about being hit on repeatedly that night?" I can't help but laugh at his unimpressed face. "Oh, come on, you can't blame them. You're hot." He looks up at me through hooded eyes, and my breath catches. Something sizzles between us and I move away, hoping the distance will take the edge off the connection.

CHAPTER TEN

Ryan

Molly and Megan have been downstairs for a couple of hours, getting ready for tonight. I have no idea what takes so long, but they must be having fun because I can hear them laughing over the music from up here.

I'm stood in the kitchen with a towel wrapped around my waist as I look in the fridge for a beer. A noise startles me and, turning my head, I see Molly heading my way, wearing a little vest top and shorts. Her hair is loosely curled and her make-up done. She walks straight to me; I feel her breasts crush against my back as she leans into the fridge with one hand while resting the other low on my hip. She grabs the bottle of wine and slowly pulls back. Her hand moves from my hip, slides up my abs and wraps around the other side as she hugs me. I can feel her nose against my shoulder as she inhales.

"You smell amazing," she whispers against my skin before she walks out of the room, and down the stairs until I hear her bedroom door shut.

What the fuck was that? Tingles warm my skin and my heart races.

"Ladies, it's half past seven, and the taxi is waiting. Hurry the fuck up," I shout through Molly's bedroom door. I have no idea what they've been doing in there all this time, but I'm expecting something awesome. It took me ten minutes flat to be dressed in dark jeans and a polo shirt. I ran some wax through my hair, and I was ready. I've spent the rest of the evening waiting. I haven't been able to shake the feelings Molly ignited in me earlier, and I can't wait to see her.

Suddenly, the door flies open and Megan walks out, ready to go. She looks good in her black skinny jeans and glittery silver top. Her normally tied up hair is hanging straight around her shoulders, and I notice it's a brighter red than the last time I saw her. She's taller than Molly, which isn't hard, and has more curves thanks to her cute little boy.

"Please tell me she is ready," I say to Megan.

"Yes, she's coming, it'll be worth the wait, I promise."

Shit.

I turn away from Megan when I see movement to my left, and Molly appears from her bathroom. My chin drops to the floor as she sashays toward us. Her hair and make-up is the same as I saw earlier, but now she's wearing a tight, deep purple short dress that shows a small amount of cleavage, making me lick my lips. On her feet are glittery silver heels, which make her exposed legs look extraordinary.

"See what I mean?" Megan says beside me.

Molly turns to grab her bag off her bed, revealing the back of the dress—or lack thereof. I suck in a breath at the amount of exposed skin. I can see almost down to the top of her arse. The desire to run my hands across her back is painful—almost as painful as my dick straining against the fabric of my jeans.

"Ry, you okay?" Molly asks as she moves toward me.

I swallow before nodding my head and saying, "Uh-huh," as she walks past me and out the front door. Her scent fills my senses, making my mouth water. I don't think I have ever been as turned on as I am right now, and I haven't even touched her.

"Shit, you've got it bad, haven't you?"

I shake my head. "Sorry, what?"

"Molly. You want her."

What do I say to that?

"She's my best friend, Megan."

With that, I walk out with Megan and lock the door, putting an end to the conversation, but I can tell by the look she's giving me that I haven't convinced her.

———

The others are already seated when we arrive, which is no surprise. We quickly say hello to everyone and get sat down. I don't know whether it's a good thing or not that I'm opposite Molly. I'm not close enough to touch her, but every time I look up, she's all I can see. Shane and Chris are busy filling her in on their wedding plans on one side of me, and Megan and Emma are talking about Cocoa's on the other. All I can do is try to concentrate on not just staring at Molly. The guys have tried dragging me into their conversations, but I wasn't really paying attention to anything. They seem to have given up on me now.

As the meal comes to an end, I go over to the bar to settle the bill. If I'm not quick, Molly will beat me to it, and she's not paying for her own birthday meal.

"Can I settle the bill for the table over there?" I ask, pointing in our table's direction.

"Sorry sir, but it's already been paid for. The lady in the purple dress came up here when you first came in, gave me her card details and told me not to let anyone else pay for this meal."

"I should have known." I look back to the table and see Molly grinning at me. Shaking my head at her, I walk off to the men's room.

I'm washing my hands when Shane walks in.

"She looks hot tonight, doesn't she?"

"Who?"

"Don't pretend you haven't noticed. I've watched you watch her the whole time we've been here."

I say nothing.

"Look, Ryan, if you're into her, then go for it. I want to see you both happy. You deserve that after the year you've had. But I should warn you that whilst you've been drooling over Molly, Emma has been shooting daggers from across the table."

"Nothing will happen between us. She's my best friend. She made it quite clear to Emma the other day, I'm like a brother to her." Shane raises an eyebrow at me. "Yes, I was eavesdropping on their conversation. I wanted to make sure she was okay."

"You've got to understand—she's lost her twin, the other half of her, and she suddenly finds out you've moved Molly in. It must have been a shock.

But even a blind person could see how much you and Molly care about each other. Emma will be able to see that as well, and if something is destined to happen between the two of you, it will all work out."

"I can't risk it, Shane. I'll see you out there," I say, leaving him to it, but I can't deny that his words ring in my ears as I make my way back to the table.

"Was my fiancé trying to turn you gay in there or something? You've both been gone for ages," Chris laughs as I get back to the table.

"Yeah, we had a quickie in one of the cubicles. Not sure what the fuss is all about; you can keep him," I deadpan, as they all turn to me with shocked looks on their faces. I can't help but laugh.

A couple of hours later, we're on the dance floor of one of Oxford's biggest clubs. We're all nicely buzzed, thanks to the shots Shane and Chris ordered for us all.

I've tried my best to stay away from Molly. I don't want to cause any more problems with Emma. I don't want to be the reason they argue.

I watch as a guy who's been eyeing up Molly plucks up the courage to dance with her. I don't like the look of him—he's like the dickheads she would have been with before. He goes up right behind her, puts his hands on her hips, and starts grinding her arse into him. My fists clench at my sides and fire races through my veins as I take in his hands on her body. Looking up, she tries to shrug him off, but he's not having any of it and pulls her tighter to him. I can tell she's getting pissed off, and it makes me want to break the fucker's nose. I move toward them and stand right against her side, removing his hand from her hip.

"Hands off," I growl at him loudly so he can hear me over the music. He looks me up and down and must realise he wouldn't win if he started something with me, then begrudgingly walks off back to his group of mates.

I turn Molly to face me. She puts her arms around my shoulders, leans into me, and whispers in my ear, "Thank you." I grab her hips and pull her against me.

What started out innocent has quite quickly turned into something... not so innocent. Molly turns in my arms so she has her back to my chest and shoves her arse into my groin. She flicks her head around and smiles wickedly at me over her shoulder.

I look up when I feel eyes on me. Shane's smirking in our direction while he dances with Chris, Emma, Megan, and Daniel, who showed up for a drink earlier. He nods at me encouragingly, which catches Emma's attention. She looks our way and her expression hardens. She's really pretty drunk, and she instantly stops moving and looks us up and down. She looks murderous.

She storms over. "What the fuck do you two think you're doing? You promised me nothing was happening," she shouts, waving her arms around in front of us.

"Emma," Molly says, "We're just messing about. Right, Ry?"

Emma turns her attention to me.

"We're just dancing." Listening to myself slur these words to her, I realise just how drunk I actually am.

"You two must think I'm fucking stupid. There's no way you aren't fucking each other."

"Wow, Emma. Chill out. If they say there's nothing going on, then there's nothing going on. Neither Molly nor Ryan would lie to you," Shane shouts above the music.

"But you just saw them! You were *encouraging* it!"

"Emma, they're both drunk. Hell, we all are. We're all just enjoying ourselves."

"You said he was like your brother!" she screams in Molly's direction. "Never in a million years would I dance with Dec like that."

"Emma, if you don't believe us, fine. Go home. We're doing nothing wrong, so get over yourself," Molly growls at her, which shocks me. I've seen her stand her ground with plenty of people before, but I never thought she'd put Emma in her place.

I watch as Emma huffs out a breath and storms off. Daniel comes over, having watched the whole thing, and kisses Molly on the cheek before telling her he's going to make sure Emma gets home okay.

Molly turns to look at me, and I see a single tear fall down her cheek. I know she feels awful about losing her temper. I put my arm around her shoulder. "Do you want to go?" I ask.

"Yes, please."

We say our goodbyes to everyone and apologise for ruining the evening. We're just walking out of the club when Molly's pulled away from me. I look to my right to see the guy who was trying to dance with her.

"What the fuck are you doing?" she shouts.

"Are you ready to dance now?" he snarls, grabbing her and pushing her up against the wall.

"Get the fuck off me!" she screams in his face, forcing me to move.

Slamming my body into his, I watch him stumble to the ground. I turn to make sure Molly's okay before focusing on him.

"He said you'd be a sure thing," he shouts before my fist collides with his jaw.

"Who said that?" I shout at him before taking another shot.

"Me," a familiar voice says from behind me. "I thought maybe she needed a real man for her birthday."

"Max?" Molly whimpers.

I land another punch to the dick on the floor before standing up to face Max. I'm barely at full height when I feel his fist hit my jaw.

"How dare you fucking take her from me," Max growls angrily. "She's mine. You don't get to just move her in with you because you're lonely now your girlfriend's dead." I see red and launch myself at him.

"Ryan, stop!" Molly screams.

Max manages to get a couple more punches in before I have him slumped against the wall, moaning in pain.

"You fucking stay away from her, you cheating piece of shit. I'll finish you next time. I'll fucking finish you." I'm shaking with anger and I stretch my fingers out, my knuckles aching. How *dare* he treat her this way. Molly comes up to my side and puts her arms around me. Still fuelled by too much pent-up anger, I push her away, needing a little space. The look she gives me guts me. Her shoulders drop as she turns and starts walking toward the waiting taxis.

She only makes it a couple of steps before I come to my senses, place my hand on her lower back, and guide her toward a car to take us home.

Molly

Ryan is silent beside me and hasn't said anything since he threatened Max outside the club, but I can feel his body starting to relax against me.

When the car comes to a stop in front of our house, I throw some cash at the driver and pull Ryan out of the car. He stumbles as we make our way up to the front door.

"Steady, Ry, I'm not going to be able to catch you if you fall."

I open the front door. He trips and crashes into the hallway wall. I grab him around the waist as he starts to slide down, pulling him with me into my room. I sit him on the edge of my bed and place my hands on his cheeks, careful of the bruises and cuts on his face.

"Ryan, are you okay?" I ask gently. He still hasn't said anything.

"I'm just so angry about how you're treated by the people who are meant to care about you."

"It's okay, because I've got you. Thank you for what you did tonight, and I'm sorry you got hurt," I say, gently running my thumb over his lip, causing him to suck in a breath. "Sorry," I whisper.

"I'll always fight for you, Molly. Always."

I really don't know how to reply to that, so I stand and get the first aid kit from upstairs, as well as something cold for his face and hand. I'm stood at the sink filling a sandwich bag with ice when a shiver runs down my spine and a feeling that I'm being watched has me on full alert. When I look up, I see the woman next door staring at me through the window. Grimacing at how nosey she is, I release the blind string and cut her off. When I return, Ryan's exactly as I left him but with his head in his hands. As I move closer, he lifts his head to look at me. His lips quirk up at the corners when I smile at him.

"I'm not even going to attempt to get you upstairs and into bed, so you can stay here. Let's get you comfy, and I'll clean you up and put this ice on you to try to reduce some of the bruising. Arms up." He does as he's told, and I carefully pull his polo shirt over his head, minding his cuts and bruises. Leaning down, I remove his shoes and socks, and then I pull the duvet aside, ready for him.

"Right, lie down with your head on the pillow; you're going to have to help me with your jeans." He follows my orders, undoes his fly, and lifts his hips so I can pull them off. I cover him quickly.

I clean his cuts, making him wince before grabbing the ice bags and placing one on his eye and grabbing his left hand to hold it in place. Then, I turn his right hand over and rest a second bag over his knuckles.

"Are you going to be okay while I get changed?"

He groans, so I take that as a yes, grab a pair of pyjamas, and head to the bathroom.

When I emerge ten minutes later, ready for bed, I'm surprised to see him sat up, drinking the water and looking at me. I was sure he was going to pass out as soon as I left the room.

"Hey. How you doing?"

"I'm fine. Come on, get in."

I walk round to the other side of the bed and follow his instructions. I lie on my back, staring at the ceiling for a few minutes, my heart pounding and my skin tingling with awareness. Goosebumps prickle my skin where Ryan's eyes run over me, so I look over to him and smile.

"I really hate him," Ryan says. "And your parents, and Emma a bit right now." His arm comes around my stomach and pulls me to him until he's spooning me.

"Ry, can we not talk about them, please? I just want to forget for tonight. Let's go to sleep." He kisses the top of my head and settles in for the night. I fight to keep the small smile from my lips at how right this feels.

I lie awake in Ryan's arms for ages, but it doesn't take long before his breathing slows. My mind's running around all the events that happened this evening. Emma—she's my biggest problem. Do I try to see her and talk to her, or do I let her stew for a while and hope she comes to the conclusion that she overreacted? What if she tells Susan and Pete, and they're on her side? I don't want to fall out with them, too.

***

At some point, I must have fallen asleep, because I've just woken up with Ryan still wrapped around me. He makes me feel safe, but at the same time it scares the shit out of me. What I'm not so happy about is his morning erection stabbing me in the bum.

I try to sneak out of his hold, carefully lifting his arm and sliding out from under him, but I'm suddenly pulled back.

"No," he grumbles. I find myself in exactly the same position, and my body tenses.

"Are you awake?" I whisper.

"No," he replies, making me smile.

"Really?"

"Go back to sleep."

"I can't."

"You're not going anywhere, I'm too comfortable."

"Well, I should tell you then that I have a problem."

"What now, Molls?"

"There's something stabbing me in the butt. It's not very comfortable."

He grunts. "I see your problem, and I know a number of ways it can be resolved."

Turning my head, I find a huge grin over his face. I pull myself away from him and turn so I'm facing him squarely.

"Not happening, Evans," I say. "Get yourself under control, please."

"Sorry, my body can't help it, especially while it's cuddled around such a hot one."

"Stop it, Ryan."

"Sorry," he pouts. I smack him gently on his chest. I know he's only teasing—well, I think he is—but that doesn't stop my body from reacting in ways it shouldn't.

"I'm warning you now that we will be having a conversation about what's going on here."

"Molls, do I need to give you a sex ed lesson? It's called an erection; men get them when they're turned on, or first thing in the—"

I put my hand over his mouth. "That's not what I am talking about." I wave my hand between us. "I'm talking about what's been going on between us. I need to get my head together, and so do you, because my guess is that you feel like shit this morning."

"I've felt better, and my face is killing me."

"Well, that's what happens when you get into a fight with two dickheads."

He sucks in a breath as if he's remembering. "Max."

"Don't worry—you left them in a worse state than you're in right now. I don't think they'll be bothering me again."

A few hours later, I find myself sat on a bar stool in Cocoa's, chatting to Megan while she finishes up for the day. I spent a couple of hours upstairs making plans for what I need to do this week and looking at the projects I have at the moment, before coming down to get Megan's opinion on my situation with Ryan. I watch as she locks up and comes to join me where her coffee is waiting. She groans as she sits down.

"Long day?"

"Yes, and it's not helped by the hangover which, by the way, you are totally to blame for." She points at me.

"Tell me if I'm wrong, but I'm pretty sure at some point yesterday you told me you wanted to get wasted because you haven't in so long."

She laughs. "So, I have this weird feeling that you're here because you want to talk about someone." Megan tilts her head and raises her eyebrow.

"No need to be so smug." I tell her about the fight she missed after we left, what happened when we got home, and then this morning. She listens to everything and nods in all the right places.

"I think this conversation is going to take longer than I have. James is going out this evening, so I need to be back for Oscar. Do you want to follow me back? We can order a takeaway."

Twenty minutes later, I'm following Megan into the flat she shares with her boyfriend James and their son.

"Mummy!" Oscar screams when he sees her.

She picks him up and kisses him. "Hey, little man. Have you had a good day with Daddy?"

Oscar is the cutest kid I think I've ever seen. He turned three not so long ago. Like his dad, he's pretty tall, but he has his mum's dark hair and eyes. Megan keeps his hair quite long and scruffs it up with a bit of wax to make him a smaller, dark-haired version of his dad.

"Hey, baby," James says, coming over to Megan and kissing her forehead. I'm so jealous of their easy, yet loving, relationship. They've been together for seven years now, and I'm just waiting for an engagement announcement sometime soon.

"Molly, what did you do to my girlfriend last night? She was up half the night, puking."

"Sorry, but that is not my fault. She's a grown woman and should know when to stop," I laugh.

"Have a good night, ladies," he calls from the hallway.

"I'm not a lady," Oscar shouts from his bedroom.

"No, you're not, little man, sorry. See you later, ladies and Oscar," he chuckles as he leaves the flat.

Megan leaves me to order the dinner while she puts Oscar to bed. I ring and place an order for our favourite Chinese dishes and pour us both glasses of water.

"So, Molly. Million-dollar question. Are you going to get under him or over him?" Megan asks as she comes back into the kitchen, trying not to laugh.

"In the back of my mind, I just see it going tits up and then losing him. I would rather fight to keep him as my friend than do something to remove him from my life completely.

"Then there's Emma. Since the accident, she's distanced herself from everyone. She's made her opinion quite clear. I don't want to trash my friendship with her, and I'm yet to find out if Susan and Pete share her feelings. I cannot lose them; I see them as my parents."

"I understand all that, I do, but what if you make a move with Ryan and it's amazing, and it lasts?" she asks, ever the romantic. "What's the alternative?"

"Putting myself back out there and going on some dates, I guess. Finding out if this attraction to Ryan is because of him, or because I need a bloke in my life."

"Are you sure that's what you want?"

"As sure as I can be."

She pauses. "If you're serious, I have someone I could set you up with."

I nod at her. Megan has good taste in men and is a good judge of character, so I'm as hopeful as I can be. "Okay, who?"

"One of James's friends from work. I think you'd get on great. Should I give him your number?"

"Sure. What's the worst that could happen?"

CHAPTER ELEVEN

Ryan

I've spent all day lying on the sofa in front of the TV, thoughts of Molly and everything that has happened over the last couple of weeks floating in and out of my mind.

She said before she left this morning that we were going to talk about what's been happening between us. I've been going backwards and forwards over what I want for hours. After the chat I had with Shane last night, what he said keeps coming back to me. What if he's right? What if this is meant to happen?

I eventually give up waiting for her to come home. I haven't heard from her all day, but she said she needed to get her head straight, so I don't want to interrupt her. It's just before midnight when I hear the front door shut. I wait for her to come upstairs, but she doesn't, instead going straight to bed.

After another hour of lying in bed, not sleeping, my need to see her gets the better of me. Knowing she's downstairs is torture. I quietly make my way down to her room. Luckily, her door is slightly open. I peek around the door frame to see her sound asleep, facing me. A bit of hair has fallen across her face and the rest is lying across her chest. I bite down on my bottom lip and clench my fists. My need to walk over and fix it becomes too much. She's wearing a vest top and tiny shorts, so tiny they don't go anywhere near covering her arse. Her legs are tangled around the duvet at the bottom of the bed. I stand there for a few minutes, just looking at her and listening to her breathing.

It's in that moment that I realise just how much I want her. Just how much I *need* her.

R olling over, I pull my eyelids open. It's already getting on for ten o'clock. Oh, I love the holidays—late nights and even later mornings. Heaven. I jump out of bed and quickly shower and get dressed before heading downstairs, hoping Molly will be there, ready to talk.

When I get to the kitchen, there's no sign of her. I flick the kettle on, then head down to her room to see if she's there. The door is open, but there's still no sign of her. She was obviously up early to get the office set up. I guess my little speech will have to wait.

I end up spending most of the day working out, going for a ridiculously long run, then hitting the weights, trying to keep myself busy.

When I get home, I FaceTime my mum. It's taken me years to get my parents to be able to use it, but I think we've got there at last. I'd totally forgotten about my black eye and busted lip, but one look at me has my mum in a right tizz. It takes me a full ten minutes to calm her down. I explain to her what happened in as little detail as I can. She's made it quite clear in the past that she doesn't really like Molly. It didn't bother me before, but now I could throttle Hannah for telling my mum all about her best friend's antics. I always end up having to defend her to my mum, and I hate it.

After we say goodbye, I decide to see if I can get my sisters on a group chat. We were always really close growing up and, I hate to admit it, but I miss them being so far away. To my surprise, they both answer my call. Neither came home from university this summer, much to my parents' disappointment. Abbi has stayed in the flat she shares with her mate and is working with kids at a summer school. Liv has moved out of halls and into a flat with her mates and landed herself a summer job at a local newspaper.

They don't have quite the reaction to my bruised face as Mum did, but they're still concerned. After I finish telling the story again, both of them have soppy looks on their faces as they stare into the camera.

"What's wrong with you two?" I ask them, confused.

"You love her," they say in unison, smiling dopily at me.

"Yeah, of course. She's my best friend," I say, a bit taken aback.

We spend the next hour chatting about our lives—that is, until I hear the front door close, signalling Molly's return. I quickly make my excuses and say my goodbyes to my sisters.

"Hey," I say as she rounds the corner into the room, carrying a couple of shopping bags.

"How are you feeling? Hangover gone now?" she smirks, placing the bags on the counter and pulling out the contents.

"Yeah, fine now, thanks." My brows draw together at the sudden tension between us. I feel like I've missed something.

"Good. I bought ingredients for a carbonara, if that's okay with you?"

"As long as you're cooking, Molls, anything is good with me."

She laughs and turns to get started. "So, what have you been up to?" she asks over her shoulder.

"Not much. Been to the gym and just talked with my family."

"Oh God," she groans. "I bet your mum loved the look of your face. Please tell me you didn't tell her it was because of me? She already hates me."

"She doesn't hate you, Molly." I'm not sure if that's a lie or not. "I gave her a diluted version of what happened. She understood."

"Yeah, whatever you say, Ry," she says, shaking her head, "How are Abbi and Liv?"

"Both good. They're working hard. I think they're secretly glad they didn't go home this summer. I told them they should come visit. I hope that's okay."

"Of course, it is. It's been ages since I've seen them. And unlike your parents, they actually like me."

Molly continues with dinner while I set the table and pour us both drinks. I sit down and take a sip just as she's plating up.

"Here you go," she says, placing it in front of me.

"Smells amazing, as always. Thank you." Grabbing my knife and fork, I immediately dig in. "So, what have you been doing the last two days?" I ask, curious.

"Well, after I left you yesterday, I went to the office to get a list together for what I need, then I met Megan for coffee. We ended up spending the whole night chatting."

"You spent nearly all day Saturday with her. What the hell did you have to talk about for so long?" Her answer is just to lift her eyebrow at me. I feel my cheeks flush a little, knowing I was their topic of conversation. God, I hope she's come to the same conclusion as me.

"Then, this morning, I got up early to ask my old lecturer if he could give me any names for a potential new employee."

"Did he have any ideas?"

"He gave me a number for a guy who graduated last year. Apparently, our styles would complement each other well."

"Have you spoken to him?"

"I rang him as soon as I left campus. I'm meeting him at Cocoa's in the morning. "

"That's great. I hope he's as good as your lecturer has made him out to be."

I watch as Molly nervously shifts in her seat, looking at me then back down again, like she's building up to saying something.

"Spit it out, Molls."

"I'vegotadateFridaynight," she says at such a speed it takes me a few seconds to decipher what she just said. My heart drops and my mouth opens in surprise.

"What?"

"Megan has set me up with one of James's workmates. His name is Adam, and he's taking me to that new Italian place in town."

"That's good, Molly. You need to try to find your Prince Charming," I just about manage to get out through gritted teeth.

Molly chats away to me some more after that little announcement, but I don't hear any of what she says. I just keep replaying what she said in my head.

I'vegotadateFridaynight.   *I'vegotadateFridaynight.*
I'vegotadateFridaynight.

Molly

Ryan makes his excuses after we finish dinner, and he disappears up to his room with disappointment clouding his eyes.

"Shit," I whisper to myself. He looked like a little kid who had just had his new puppy taken away from him. I feel awful. I didn't want to hurt him. I'd convinced myself that he would agree with my decision, but the look on his face has me thinking that wasn't what he wanted at all.

After going through everything I want to talk to Jackson about in the morning, I head to bed, although sleep eludes me for hours. All I can see every time I close my eyes is the look on Ryan's face. I don't want to be the one who puts it there.

It feels like I've only been asleep for two hours when my alarm clock goes off. "Noooo..." I grumble as I lean over and hit the top of it to shut it up. Dragging my exhausted body to sit up, I wipe the sleep from my eyes before I remember why I'm up so early. I'm meeting my possible first employee. The thought of this gives my body the boost it needs.

<hr>

By nine o'clock, I'm in our booth at Cocoa's, waiting for Jackson to arrive. I gave him a brief description of myself on the phone yesterday, so he finds me easily when he arrives.

"Molly Carter?" he asks.

I look up and am at a loss for words. The guy stood before me is stunning. The first thing I notice are his eyes; they're bright green. His hair is the colour of dark chocolate, hanging long and shaggy around his face. I think it's probably long enough to tie up. He has strong cheekbones and a square-cut jaw. I pull myself together so I can answer.

"Yep, that's me."

He sticks his arm out toward me, and I can't help but let my eyes travel down the length of his forearm, exposed by his rolled-up shirtsleeve. It's pure muscle with strong veins, packaged in a full sleeve of stunning tattoos. It looks like it could do some serious damage.

I realise I'm ogling my potential employee, so I quickly stick my own hand out. "Nice to meet you, Jackson. Have a seat. What can I get you to drink?"

While he gets comfortable, I quickly nip behind the bar and make his coffee. Lilly is working this morning so she doesn't bat an eyelid when I intrude on her.

"Who's that? He is seriously hot," she asks, her eyes roaming over Jackson.

"I'm interviewing him for a job."

"Shit, Molls, you wouldn't get any work done if he was sat opposite you in the office."

"I know, right?"

Jackson must hear us giggling like schoolgirls, because he looks up and smirks at us.

"Fuck," I mutter and make my way back to him with a slightly higher temperature and flushed cheeks.

"Here you go, Jackson," I say, passing his espresso over to him.

"Please, call me Jax. Only my parents call me Jackson. It makes me think I'm in trouble."

"Okay, Jax it is. So, do you want to show me what you've got?" I nod my head toward his portfolio, but instantly flush when he smiles at me and looks down at it on his lap. "I'm dying to see your designs. I've heard great things."

***

"Wow, these are awesome. You've got some serious talent, Jax. How don't you already have a job?" I ask, thumbing through his work.

"I've had a few interviews over the last year, but my style didn't really suit the companies, I guess," he answers with a shrug of his shoulders.

"Well, I hope their loss is my gain."

"Are you serious?"

I look up and give him a wide smile.

We spend the next hour chatting about the company and the work we've done so far, and I explain about Cocoa's and the office upstairs when he asks why I keep helping myself to coffee. I talk about Hannah, albeit briefly, and I'm thankful Jax doesn't ask many questions about her. I get the impression that he understands. We talk money, hours, and all the other nitty-gritty bits that we need to go through, and generally about ourselves. We're going to be spending quite a bit of time together, so it's important that we can get on.

Eventually, I put our mugs in the dishwasher and take Jax upstairs to see the office and the work I've done recently, so he can get a feel for my style.

"Wow, this place is amazing," he says, walking around.

"I know. After meeting you, I'm going shopping for all the equipment we're going to need."

"We?" he asks, his eyebrows raised.

"Yes, if you're up for it. Correct me if you don't agree, but I think we could have a good thing here. Our design styles complement each other's well, but we have different skills to enable us to do a range of jobs, and we seem to get on well enough. So far, anyway."

"I'm really excited about this, Molly. I think we could have something really good."

"Fantastic. Well... welcome to Angel Designs, Jax Parker." I stick my hand out to him and he grabs it, laughing, then pulls me into a tight hug. It reminds me of a Ryan hug with all of the muscle, but Jax is a smaller build. He doesn't engulf me in quite the same way.

"So, I don't want to intrude on your plans, but I'm free for the rest of the day. Do you want company while you kit this place out? I've got a mate who works in one of the computer stores. He owes me a favour. Hopefully, he can do us a good deal."

"Brilliant. I've got a list." I pull my notebook out of my bag and pass it to him as we head out of the office. "See if you think I've missed anything."

We have a great afternoon picking everything we need and getting it all set up in the office, ready for us to start work. I went down to Cocoa's to grab us some lunch that we ate in our new living room. It was weird to think that this was my bedroom for so many years.

During lunch, Jax tells me all about his girlfriend, Lucy. They've only been together a couple of months, but as far as he's concerned, it was love at first sight. She moved in with him last month. It makes me smile, thinking how at odds his appearance is to his romantic heart.

The more we get to know each other, the more I'm confident that we'll get on really well working together. I was pleased when he started talking about his family to find out that, although they own a chain of restaurants across the country, Jax had no intention of working with them. He wanted to do his own thing, like I did. Luckily for him, his family supported his decision wholeheartedly and have been behind him all the way. I got the impression that he couldn't wait to ring them and tell them about this job.

Jax has to give two weeks' notice at the bar he works at, but he's agreed to come in during the afternoons before he starts his shifts to help me get started here and pick up some of my jobs.

Once we say our goodbyes, I head home. I can't wait to tell Ryan about it all, but, to my disappointment, he isn't at home when I get there. Instead, I ring Susan and tell her everything. I can't say I was surprised that, by the time I rang, she had already heard about Jax from Lilly.

"I hear he's quite the hottie," she says with a laugh.

"He's not bad to look at, and his artwork is stunning. I think we're going to make a really good team. The office looks fantastic—you should pop up when you're next at Cocoa's."

"I'm so glad you found someone so soon that you like so much."

"Thank you so much for what you've done for me. I still can't quite believe it. It does feel like Hannah is part of it."

"You're more than welcome, angel." I can hear her start to well up. We chat for a few more minutes, until she has to go and tend to dinner.

I feel a bit lost for what to do. I was hoping to spend the evening with Ryan, but it doesn't look like that's going to be happening. Instead, I grab my sketchpad, settle on the sofa with the TV on, and coming up with some concepts for my next project.

***

I awake with a start at three o'clock from a loud banging on the front door. I scramble out of bed to see what's going on, just as Ryan manages to get his key in the door and comes stumbling through into the hallway. When he sees me, he stops and stares at me. The look he gives me sends a shiver down my spine. I've only ever once seen such a cold look in his eyes, and that was Saturday night, right before he punched the guy who pulled me down the street.

He sways on his feet and stumbles back so he's leaning against the wall for support.

"Come on, Ry. Let's get you up to bed." I go to grab him around the waist to help him up the stairs, but he pushes me away.

"I don't need you, Molly," he growls coldly. I'm taken aback by his tone. He's never been anything but nice, so to hear him snap at me is a real shock.

He turns to face the stairs and starts toward them slowly. "I don't need you." He looks totally defeated with his head down and shoulders slumped.

I stand there, shocked, and watch him climb his way up the stairs. Just as he disappears out of my sight, I feel a single tear run down my cheek. Confusion and hurt engulf me as I stand, staring at the empty space where he just was.

I eventually make my way back to my room and lie back on my bed, staring at the ceiling, wondering what the hell just happened. Needless to say, I have another restless night's sleep.

***

This pattern with Ryan continues for the next three days. I get up every morning, hoping to see him before I go to the office, but he's still in bed. Then, when I get home in the evenings, he's already gone out.

I've texted him a few times but had no response and, when I ring his phone, it goes straight to voicemail.

By the time I get in from work on Friday night to get ready for my date, I'm surprised to find Ryan sat on the sofa, surrounded by empty beer cans and looking a little worse for wear. I really wish I'd had time to talk to him about what's going on, but I've only got an hour before I need to head out to meet Adam.

CHAPTER TWELVE

Ryan

This week has been shit—total shit. Ever since Molly told me about her date, I've been a complete mess, and I can't seem to sort myself out. The only thing that has helped me forget is alcohol. Luckily for me, my mates from school are back and keen to keep up the party lifestyle from their holiday, so we've been out to different bars every night this week. I can't honestly say I remember much of what's happened, but it means I also don't remember thinking or being miserable about Molly.

Tonight is Molly's date, and I made the stupid decision to stay home. I wanted to make sure I was here if she needed me, but at some point during the afternoon, the urge to drown everything out was too strong so I hit the beer—again. Now, I'm not going to be much good if her date goes south.

To say she looked shocked to see me here when she came home would be an understatement. I've missed her so much this week, but the thought of spending time with her at the moment makes my chest hurt. I feel like a complete pussy.

After an amount of time I'm completely unaware of, I hear her coming back up the stairs. When I look up to her, my heart clenches as I see she's wearing the white dress she had on the evening we went out for dinner in Cornwall and ended up in the sea. A giant lump forms in my throat at the memory.

"Well, I'm off. Have a good night, Ryan." The look on her face when she says this is almost as dejected as I feel. She looks at her feet, then turns to walk out. Just before she gets to the door, I find my voice.

"Molly?"

"Yeah?"

"You look gorgeous. I hope he treats you well." I even manage to crack a smile for her.

I must have passed out on the sofa before she got home, because the next thing I know, the room is really bright, and when I open my eyes, Molly's making a cup of tea in the kitchen.

"Morning," she sings cheerfully, making my head hurt.

I just groan back at her.

"Ry, you're not eighteen anymore. Hangovers from week-long binges are going to last much longer than our university days."

I groan again, roll off the sofa onto my hands and knees, and crawl out of the room and up to my bedroom, where I collapse on my bed and fall back to sleep.

By the time I wake up again, it's the afternoon, and I still feel like death. I drag my arse into the shower in the hope it will wake me up, but it does very little to pull me out of the slump I've found myself in.

I head down to the kitchen, hoping coffee might be more successful. I'm grabbing a mug when a note catches my eye.

Ry,
I've gone out with Megan and Oscar, then I'm having dinner tonight with
Jax at The Fat Dog. Maybe lay off the beer today, huh? I'm worried
about you.
Love and hugs,
Molly xx

Red-hot anger flows through me and the mug in my hand goes flying and smashes against the far wall of the living room.

"Who the fuck is Jax?" I growl.

Leaning back against the kitchen worktop, I shut my eyes and try to calm myself down. Molly swore when she moved in here that she was turning over a new leaf with men, and not using them to make herself feel cared for, but here she is, going out with two different guys on two consecutive nights. She might have ruined me at the moment, but I'm sure as hell not going to let her slip back into her old ways.

Molly

"Molly, can I ask you something?" Megan asks sheepishly, which piques my interest.

"Of course. What's up?" She's looking more and more embarrassed by the second. "Megan, why are you blushing?"

"Um... well, J-James has this um... f-fantasy."

"Megan, I love you both, but I'm not having a threesome with you."

"What? No! Sorry, no, that's not it at all." She laughs once she's recovered from the shock.

"Whatever it is you want to ask me can't be as embarrassing as asking that. Out with it."

"He wants me to pole dance for him. It's his birthday in a couple of months, so I looked up classes and the strip club in town has dance studios at the back where they do lessons. Would you come with me? They're on a Monday night at seven o'clock." She huffs out a breath, as if she's relieved she got the words out.

"Oh my God, yes, of course I'll come. I've always wanted to have a go. I've heard it's hard work, though."

We continue chatting about our new hobby while Oscar wears himself out running around the soft play area.

A couple of hours later, I'm sat in the pub with Jax. When he mentioned that he was alone tonight, I invited him out to celebrate his new job. I would have invited Ryan to join us, but I assumed he'd be out like every other night this week.

As usual, conversation is easy between us, and we've been chatting about everything and nothing for ages.

"What's the matter, Molly? You don't seem yourself," he asks, looking concerned.

"It's nothing, sorry. I don't want to ruin your evening."

I hadn't realised the situation with Ryan had got to me so much it was obvious. I guess Megan would have noticed if we hadn't spent our time together getting excited about our new class. In order to keep it a secret from James, we agreed to tell people we were just going to a dance class. I really hope Megan is good at it, because she's so excited to give James the best birthday ever.

"You won't ruin my evening, Molly. If you need to get something off your chest, I'm here to listen. I know we haven't actually known each other long, but it doesn't feel like that. I'm here if you need me, is all I'm trying to say."

Staring at him, I blow out a long breath, tears stinging my eyes as I consider where I should start. Jax reaches his hand across the table and squeezes mine in support.

"It's Ryan. He's acting really weird—going out and getting off his face every night, then coming in late. He was really horrible one night, and he's never acted that way to me before. I'm really worried about him."

Jax knows about me living with Ryan and his relationship with Hannah, but I haven't yet mentioned the chemistry between us.

He opens his mouth to speak, but he's suddenly pulled out of his seat and held up against the wall of the pub. My chair crashes to the floor as I jump to my feet.

"Why the fuck is she crying? What have you done to her?" Ryan hollers in Jax's face, holding him up against the wall by his throat.

"Get the fuck off me," Jax growls, making me jump to action. I start pulling at the arms Ryan has around Jax's throat, pleading for him to let him go.

"Ryan, what the fuck is wrong with you?" I scream in his ear. His hold loosens slightly.

"Wait... you're Ryan?" Jax questions. Ryan just glares at him. "I think you should be asking yourself why Molly's upset," Jax looks Ryan up and down, "Mate," he adds tightly.

At Jax's words, Ryan snaps his head around to me and takes in my tear-stained face. He lets go of Jax and comes to stand in front of me, gently wiping the tears from my face. His features soften and regret fills his eyes.

I spot the manager coming toward us over Ryan's shoulder. "You two go and wait outside whilst I settle the bill—before we have a bigger problem on our hands," I say to them, watching them scurry out of the pub.

Once I've apologised profusely to the manager, paid the bill and left a hefty tip, I make my way out to join Ryan and Jax. They're standing with their backs to the wall, hands in their pockets and staring out over the car park. Both have their jaws set, like they're ready to jump on each other if one of them says the wrong thing. When I see them, I can't help but think what a lucky bitch I am, having two seriously hot men fighting for me. I must have done something right in a previous life.

"Ryan, this is Jax. As in, Jackson Parker, my employee. Jax, this is my idiot best friend, whom I live with." They glance at each other. "I suggest you both make friends, because I'm telling you now that you are both important to me, and I will not have you at each other's throats."

After staring each other down for a few more seconds, Ryan slowly puts his hand out for Jax to shake.

"I'm sorry, mate. I saw red. Molly was upset, and I jumped to conclusions. I'm sure she won't mind me saying she hasn't got the best reputation for picking the good guys."

"Thanks for that, Ry," I say, narrowing my eyes at him.

"It's okay, I understand. I'd probably do the same if she were my girl."

"I'm not his girl," I snap, my frustration at this whole situation growing by the second. "Ryan, I think you've done enough for one night. I suggest you go home."

"Come on, then," he says, and he starts walking away.

"No, I'm not coming with you. I'm way too angry to be anywhere near you right now."

"Where the fuck are you going to go, then?" he asks, looking seriously pissed off.

"Quite honestly, Ryan, it's none of your fucking business. You just go home and calm yourself down before you cause any more damage."

He looks completely deflated by my words. His shoulders slump and he marches to his car. I watch him get in and slam his door, before he punches the steering wheel.

"Wow," Jax says, standing next to me, watching the show and rubbing his neck. "Before I was stopped so abruptly, I was going to say I thought the cause of your problem was that Ryan was into you, but having experienced what I just did, I would say that he's more than just into you, Molly. That guy's got it bad." He turns to look at me with sympathetic eyes.

"Shit."

Twenty minutes later, Jax has dropped me off and I've locked myself into my office for the night. My phone has been going off constantly for the last ten minutes with phone calls and texts from Ryan. I had to put it on silent to save me throwing it at the wall and smashing it to pieces.

I sit down on the edge of the sofa and remove my heels, giving my toes a wiggle to stretch them out after being confined in my shoes for too long. My phone lights up on the coffee table again, displaying Ryan's photo. The one

I took when he was sunbathing on the outside sofa at our beach hut. Thinking of that week makes my heart break a little. Look at us now.

> Molly: I'm fine, but I won't be home tonight. I'm too angry with you to be around you at the moment. I will be at the Morrisons' for dinner tomorrow. Maybe I'll see you there.

Just the thought of going to the Morrisons' tomorrow makes me groan. Not only will I have to see Ryan, but Emma will more than likely be there. It's the only thing Susan and Pete have managed to make her attend since the accident: their monthly family Sunday roasts. I used to love spending the afternoon as part of a real family, but I haven't spoken to Emma since she kicked off last weekend in the club, and I have a feeling I may still be mad at Ryan tomorrow.

After a few moments, my phone lights up again with a reply.

> Ryan: Please forgive me. I was an idiot. x

CHAPTER THIRTEEN

Molly

I walk into Susan and Pete's just after one to find everyone already sat around the table. My plan so far has worked: When I got home, Ryan had already left.

Susan looks up from passing the potatoes around. "Ah, angel, we didn't think you were coming."

"I'm sorry I'm late. I've had a bit of a bad morning, but I'm here now." I smile sweetly at her and she accepts my excuse. Ryan's eyes burn into me, and when I look up, there's an empty chair next to him. I also notice that Emma hasn't taken her eyes off her plate since I walked through the door.

I reluctantly take the seat next to Ryan and try to relax, so it's not obvious to everyone that there's an issue between us. As soon as I settle in, I feel Ryan's hand come to rest on my thigh and he leans over to whisper in my ear.

"I was worried you weren't going to come because of me. I'm so sorry, Molly. Please, I hate fighting with you." His voice has a begging quality to it.

I turn toward him. "I came so no one knows there is a problem. Keep your hands off me," I say, removing it from my leg. "Don't piss me off further, and we might just get away with it." I pull back from him to see Emma glaring at us, shaking her head and tutting.

Susan frowns at her but shakes her head and turns my way when her husband speaks up.

"So, Molly, I hear you've employed a designer already. Quite a handsome chap," Pete says, trying to break the tension.

"Oh yeah, he's a catch, all right," Ryan mutters.

"He's lovely, and he's amazing at what he does. I think we're going to work really well together."

Ryan snorts next to me, and I turn my head and glare at him.

"Don't forget how sexy those tattoos are," Lilly adds dreamily from the other side of the table.

"No daughter of mine is going to be going out with a tattooed thug, Lilly," Pete chimes in.

"Pete, Jax is most definitely not a thug. He comes from a really nice family. They own that chain of steak and grill restaurants you love. He didn't want to go into the family business."

"How unlucky for us," Ryan whispers beside me.

"And just because he has tattoos, doesn't mean he's a thug. It's art. He designed them himself."

Ryan mutters quietly to himself and my anger at his immature behaviour soars.

"Ryan, would you like to share your thoughts with the table?" I ask him politely.

"No, I'm good, thanks." He smirks at me as he says it.

"Then shut the fuck up," I bark back at him, which makes everyone at the table stop eating and look at us. "Sorry," I mumble, returning my focus back to my plate.

"Oh, a lovers' tiff?" Emma asks sarcastically.

"Children, if you can't be nice to each other, please don't say anything at all," Susan says in a motherly tone.

The rest of the meal goes by in uncomfortable silence. As soon as dessert has been finished, I make the excuse of having loads of work to do and leave as quickly as I can. If I hang around, I'll be interrogated by Susan and the whole mess will just come spilling out of my mouth. I feel bad about not helping clean up, especially as somehow Emma managed to run away even faster than I did, but I'll make sure to do more than my fair share next month.

I head back to the office and drag out the case I packed earlier to tide me over for a few days. I hate not going home. I love that house and my room, but I know it's just going to end in an argument with Ryan. After lunch today, it was obvious we both need time to calm down.

I get drawn into my work to pass the time and, before I know it, it's evening. I check my phone—twenty-eight missed calls from Ryan and six texts. I open the first text.

> Ryan: Thanks for leaving me to the wrath of Susan. Coward.

> Ryan: I'm sorry, that was mean. It's just that I was questioned about everything for over an hour.

> Ryan: I should say, I didn't tell her anything about what is going on. I just fobbed her off.

> Ryan: Molly, please come home so we can talk. I know I've been a huge dick. I'm sorry.

> Ryan: Molly, please stop ignoring me. It's killing me, not hearing from you. I hate you being mad at me.

> Ryan: Molly, I'm so, so sorry. Please talk to me. I was just trying to protect you last night. I shouldn't have jumped to conclusions, and I was stupidly childish today. I'm sorry. Please come home. I hate it here without you.

> Molly: Ry, it's obvious we both need time to cool off. I'll be home when I don't think the first thing I want to do is shout at you.

I send my reply, put my phone back in my bag, and get back to work. I just sit down when the doorbell rings. I ignore it, presuming it's Ryan trying to talk to me, but it rings again and again. I'm surprised when I hear a woman's voice shouting my name. As I get closer to the door, I realise it's Susan.

"Molly... Angel, I know you're there, your car is here. Open the door."

"Hi, Susan. What are you doing here?" I ask innocently.

"I think we need a chat, don't you?"

I groan loudly. "Come on in. Do you want tea?"

"Yes, please, angel."

I make the tea, then join Susan in the living room.

"I tried talking to Ryan after both you and Emma ran away, but he just kept fobbing me off with rubbish. Emma has been even more distant than usual over the last week, and she won't talk, either. What the hell is going on with you three?" Wow, Susan must mean business. 'Hell' is a swear word in her book.

"I don't know where to start."

"How about the beginning? That usually works best."

I tell her everything about Ryan and me (leaving out the more X-rated parts), Emma and her opinion about us, Ryan and his binge drinking, and the saga with Jax from last night. She sits and listens throughout the whole thing, but she doesn't say anything. She grabs her cup of tea and drinks it, deep in thought.

"Exactly as I thought," she says, putting her mug back on the coffee table.

"Excuse me?"

"Molly, all you kids think we don't see what's happening under our noses, but we do. Most of the time, we just ignore it, so you can all figure it out yourselves. It's obvious how you and Ryan feel about each other. It's in your eyes when you look at each other, or talk about each other. I'm not going to lie; at first, I wasn't too keen on the idea. But the more I see you both together, the more I see how happy you make each other, and that is all I want for both of you. We have all been through a terrible time, and if out of that you two find each other, then I cannot complain.

"As for Emma, well... we all know how much she has struggled—is still struggling—with losing Hannah. She isn't as strong as you and Ryan, but she will get there. When she does, she will see that what's happening between the two of you is okay. She just needs time."

"What about everyone else?" I ask.

"At the end of the day, angel, we all want you both to be happy, and if that means you're together, that's okay."

Ryan

I've been sitting for hours staring at my phone, hoping I would get something else from Molly, but nothing so far. In the end, I decide to go to bed early and try to catch up on some sleep. I just drift off when I'm awakened by banging. I fly out of bed and down the stairs because, in my sleep-induced haze, I think it could be Molly. When I wake up enough to know it's the front door being hammered on, I realise it isn't going to be her because she has a key and would just let herself in.

I must look really disappointed when I open the door and see Susan, because she takes one look at me and pulls me into her arms for a hug.

"Oh, angel, you were hoping it was Molly, weren't you?" she says quietly to me while she comforts me.

"Am I that obvious?"

"You have no idea. Come on, invite me up. I'm dying for a cup of tea. It's been a long day."

"Sorry, yeah, come on in. I'll just go grab a t-shirt."

"That's a shame, I'm starting to understand what my girls see in you," she says with a cheeky smile.

"Um... thanks?" I don't know what to say to that. I can hear her laughing, though, and it makes me smile.

"You don't need to sound so freaked out, Ryan. I was trying to lighten the mood," she says, still laughing.

When I get back to the living room, I see that Susan has already made a start on the tea.

"So, without meaning to sound rude, what *are* you doing here?"

"I've just been to see Molly." She looks up to see my reaction, although I'm not sure why. "She told me everything you were avoiding telling me earlier."

"Right." I should have seen this coming.

"I've given her my advice on the situation between the two of you. Now, I'm here to do the same with you."

Susan stayed for about an hour while we talked through everything. She refused to tell me what Molly said; that was for her to tell me, really. I admitted something I hadn't realised before. I told Susan that I was in love with Molly. She took this better than I did, especially when I turned into a blubbering mess and apologised to both her and Hannah for falling in love again so soon.

I'm now lying in bed, thinking about everything. "I'm in love with Molly. Shit, when did that happen?" I tell myself I will do everything in my power to show her how serious I am. I fall asleep, happy for the first time in a while, thanks to Susan. She really is an amazing woman.

I wake up late the next morning after a long, deep sleep, feeling refreshed, and I head to the gym.

It's when I'm running on the treadmill that I realise what I need to do. I hang around the gym until I know she'll be home from work, and then head over to the Morrisons' house. Someone must be looking down on me and smiling today, because Emma's car is in the drive, which is an unusual sight these days. I let myself in and head for the kitchen, where I know everyone will be. It's just Susan and Emma in the room, and their heads snap up from the tablet they're both staring at aimlessly.

"Hey," I say, walking over to kiss Susan on the cheek. "I don't know if I said it last night, but thank you."

"My pleasure, angel. I'm glad you're feeling better."

"Emma, could we talk, please?"

Surprise settles on her face.

"I'll leave you both to it," Susan says, scuttling out of the room.

"Um... what's up, Ryan?" she asks suspiciously.

"I need to talk to you, and I need you to listen to me. Can you do that without going off on me?" I say gently.

"I'll do my best."

"Right, here goes, then. I know you're under the impression that there's something going on with Molly and me." She opens her mouth to interrupt me. "Ah, you said you would listen." She closes her mouth and nods. "Well, nothing has actually happened. Yes, we have become really close over the last six months, but it was a completely platonic relationship until she moved in. Something changed. I don't know what it was, and I can't explain it, but there has been this amazing chemistry between us. It scared the shit out of me at first. Molly is my best friend. She's supported me through the worst time of my life, and there I was getting turned on by her doing the simplest things."

Emma screws her face up in disgust. "I said I'd listen, but please spare me the details."

"The thing is, Emma... I want you to know... I'm in love with Molly. No, I didn't ask for it to happen, and I know it's still so soon after Hannah. I do know that, but it just sort of happened. I want you to know that she will never replace Hannah. She will always have a piece of my heart, always, but it's time for me to move on. I know this is hard for you to hear, but I wanted it to be from me."

I look up to see Emma with tears streaming down her cheeks.

"I'm so sorry. I didn't want to upset you, I just wanted you to know everything. You actually know more than Molly does. I haven't told her any of this, and there is a chance that if she doesn't give us a go, then she'll never know, and I'm okay with that, I think. If she doesn't think it's right, then so be it.

"You should know that every time something has nearly happened between us, you're the one who has stopped her. I know you think that we don't care about what you think, but that's not true. Molly misses you terribly."

"Wow," she says, wiping her face with the backs of her hands. "I had no idea you were in love with her."

"Neither did I, until I spoke to your mum yesterday and she made me realise."

"Thank you for being honest with me, Ryan. I really appreciate that. I know I haven't been the easiest person to deal with since the accident, but I'm really trying to move on. It's just so damn hard. I still don't really know how I feel about the two of you, but just know that whatever happens, I'll be there for both of you. You're family to me. Just be warned—if you get together, it may take me some time to come to terms with it. Hannah was my other half, but I know she would want you to move on and be happy, so I need to let that happen."

I pull her into my arms and we sit there holding each other for ages until she calms down.

"Thank you, Emma. If you don't mind, can I suggest something?" She quirks an eyebrow at me. "Could you get in touch with Molly? She really does miss you, and maybe if a conversation about me comes up, you could tell her what you just told me."

"Of course. I don't want to hurt her, and I miss her, too."

After chatting about more general things for a while, the rest of the Morrisons congregate in the kitchen and Susan starts dinner. I end up eating with them again before saying my goodbyes and heading home. The whole drive home, I'm praying that Molly will have come back.

I let out a huge sigh of relief when I turn the corner and see her little Ford outside the house. A wide smile spreads across my face. Unfortunately, it doesn't last long.

I reach into my pocket when my phone starts ringing. I see my mum's name on the screen, press answer, and put it to my ear.

"Mum, what's wrong?" I hear her sobbing into the phone.

"It's your g-grandad. H-he's died," she manages to get out.

Shock envelops me as I attempt to register what she's just said. "Shit. How's Dad?"

"A mess, Ryan. I'm sorry, but we need you up here."

"Of course. I'll be there as soon as I can. Look after each other, and I'll be there soon. I love you."

"Love you t-too, Son. Bye."

I rest my head back on the headrest and process what Mum just told me.

"Fuck!" I shout, slamming my palms down on the steering wheel.

I jump out of the car and run into the house. I head straight for Molly's room; her door is open but she's not there. I turn to leave when I see the bathroom door is shut.

I knock. "Molly, are you in there?"

CHAPTER FOURTEEN

Molly

"Molly?" his voice comes out as a desperate plea.

"Yes, I'm in here. What do you want? I'm in the bath," I don't mean to sound grumpy, but he's ruining my relaxation. I've spent the last two nights sleeping on the sofa at the office, then I put myself through two hours of flinging my body around a pole with Megan. Whoever said pole dancing wasn't hard work underestimated it massively.

"Molly, please, can I come in?"

"Are you serious?" I ask.

"Molly, it's my grandad. He's... dead. Please." I hear a thud on the door and can only imagine it was his head.

"Shit." I quickly look down to make sure I'm covered in bubbles before I reply. "Come in."

The door opens and a very distraught Ryan walks in and sits himself on the closed toilet at the end of the bath. He slumps his body forward and puts his head in his hands.

"I'm so sorry, Ry. I know how much your grandad meant to you."

Ryan has told me countless times about how it was his grandad that got him into all sorts of sports. He used to spend all his weekends and holidays with him, watching whatever was on the TV at the time, and his grandad would explain the rules of each sport to him. When he got old enough to start playing them, his grandad was Ryan's biggest supporter. He was always at the side of the football and rugby pitches, in the stands of the cricket ground—just to name a few. I can only imagine how he must be feeling now.

I move myself in the bath so I'm on my stomach with my head at the end, and I reach out for Ryan. He's away with the fairies, so I don't need to worry about flashing him. I place my soggy hand on his forearm, which makes him turn his head to look at me. My breath catches slightly at the pain darkening his eyes. After Hannah died, I hoped I would never see that look in his eyes again.

"I'm so sorry for everything, Molly. I was an idiot. I'm so glad you're back."

"Indeed, you were, and I'm sorry, too. Even if I wasn't back, you could have come to me. I'm always here for you if you need me."

"Please, will you come to Liverpool with me? I promised Mum I'd get up there as soon as I could."

"Er, well, your parents won't be happy. Are you sure you don't just want to go on your own?"

"No, I need you with me. Please, Molly. My parents will be too distracted by what's going on to notice you." His eyes are begging for me to agree.

"Okay, Ryan. I'll do it for you. I'll get out now and pack some stuff. You go and do the same."

———

A few hours later, we're pulling into Ryan's parents' drive in Liverpool. After a long argument, I eventually persuaded Ryan to let me drive. I didn't really feel like he was in any fit state, so I put my foot down firmly. After hiding his keys.

His mum comes to the door to meet him. I watch as Ryan engulfs her in a hug. I can tell by the movement in her shoulders that she's crying. I stay in the car and give them a moment.

Eventually, she moves away and gestures for him to follow her inside. He puts his hand up to me and waves me in. I hesitantly exit the car and follow behind them into the house. They turn into the living room to join his dad, but I stay in the doorway, slightly out of sight, to give them some space. I hear some banging coming from the kitchen so I head down there in the hope that Abbi and Liv are already here. I'm really pleased when I see both of them stood over the kettle, making a pot of tea.

"How are you both holding up?" I ask when they spot me coming toward them.

"Molly, we didn't know you were coming," they say and give me quick hugs.

"We weren't as close to Grandad as Ryan, being girls and all, but it's still sad," Liv answers.

"I know. He's really upset. He didn't need this after everything else that has happened this year. Your mum seems pretty upset, too, but how's your dad doing?"

Although Ryan's mum and dad have shown their disapproval of me over the years, I actually think they're quite nice people from the stories I've heard, so I do always try to give them the benefit of the doubt.

"Better than we thought. I think he was aware that his dad was getting frail and it wasn't going to be long. Mum seems to be worse than Dad, actually," Abbi explains.

Once everything is on a tray, I follow them to the living room. I hang back by the door again, though. I can't help but feel like I'm intruding on a private family moment. Experiencing their close bond causes a wave of jealousy to wash through me.

They chat for a few minutes while Mrs. Evans pours tea for everyone. I see the moment she notices there is one too many teacups, then watch as her head snaps in my direction and her lips press into a hard line.

I inwardly groan. *Here we go.*

"This is a family matter. I suggest you go home." I feel my eyes pop open and my jaw drops at her words.

A series of voices break me from my shocked state. "Mum!" and "Karen, please!" are shouted by Mr. Evans, Ryan, Abbi, and Liv all at once, mortified by her words.

"No, it's okay. She's right. I don't want to intrude on such a tragic time for you all. Mr. Evans, I'm so sorry to hear about your dad. From what I've heard, he was an amazing guy."

"Thank you, Molly. But please, call me Dave."

"Mum, I asked for Molly to be here. She drove to get me here safely."

"Thank you, Molly," she says unconvincingly.

"You're welcome," I say with my brightest smile.

"But you can go now. Ryan will be fine. He has his family around him." She turns and starts sipping her tea like she's already bored of me.

"Mum, I'm sorry, but Molly's staying. You either need to accept that, or we'll be finding ourselves a hotel for the night."

Mrs. Evans looks like she's been slapped across the face. "Fine, but I suggest she keeps herself scarce. If she were so concerned about family, maybe she should sort her own out."

"Mother, that's enough. I didn't come here to fight. I'll show Molly up to my room so she can get herself settled."

Thank God, I think. *Get me out of here.*

"Ryan, she's not sleeping in your room with you. Have some respect in my house," she scolds.

"Mum, Molly is my friend. She will sleep in my bed—"

"Oh no—" she interrupts.

Ryan throws his mum a death look. "As I was saying, she will sleep in my bed, and I will sleep on the floor. Unless you would prefer we went to that hotel?"

"No, I want *you* here," she says, making it quite clear what she really means.

"Come on, Molly. Let's get our stuff out of the car, and you can get settled upstairs."

***

A few hours later, I'm lying in Ryan's bed in his childhood room that looks like it hasn't been touched since the day he moved out. There are posters of old indie bands on the walls, all his sport trophies and medals, and a few photos of friends and family. I love looking at old pictures of him. He's always been good-looking, but he used to be tall and lanky. His muscles didn't really come in until he was about eighteen. I look down at the floor where Ryan has laid out some bedding for when he comes up later and sigh.

He tried to convince me to come back down, but I refused point-blank. I'd had enough for one day. I just wanted to curl up in bed. The aches and pains from my earlier activity are getting worse by the minute, so I'm lying here trying to sleep, listening to the rumble of the conversation downstairs, whilst being completely covered in the smell of Ryan.

Eventually, I drift off.

Many hours later, I'm aware of Ryan coming in. After he's stripped out of his clothes, he comes over to me, kisses my forehead, and thanks me for coming before apologising again for his mum. His hand caresses my cheek gently and his soft lips press against my head again before he lies down on his makeshift bed.

A few minutes go by as I try to ignore the tingles from his touch, when I suddenly hear a sob fill the room. Opening my eyes, I look down at Ryan.

The moonlight that fills the room allows me to see his back and shoulders shaking. I quickly climb onto the floor with my pillow, get under his covers, and slide myself up behind him. I feel him jump slightly, but he relaxes when he realises it's me. I wrap my arm around his waist and kiss his shoulder before putting my head down next to his. I listen as his sobs eventually fade and his breathing evens out, telling me he's drifted off. After an internal battle, I decide to stay where I am, just in case he wakes up upset. I want to be here for him.

I spend most of the next day in Ryan's room, working. Luckily, the IT guy came to the office yesterday morning and networked our laptops so I can access everything. I do make appearances for breakfast and lunch. Everyone is lovely to me apart from Mrs. Evans, not that I'm surprised. Throughout the day, Ryan comes up to check in on me and brings me drinks. I've heard a lot of coming and going downstairs, but I keep out of the way.

I've spoken to Jax a couple of times this afternoon, as he's sent me some final concepts to approve for a new clothing boutique in the city. He sounds crazy happy on the phone, but I put it down to the fact that I'm pretty miserable.

I just hang up when Ryan comes in. "Hey, you okay?" I ask. He's looking a bit dejected.

"Yeah, some of my grandad's friends just left. We've been chatting about him for ages."

"I bet they have some great memories."

"Yeah, they do. I've come to let you know dinner's ready. I've told Mum to be nice, so it's safe."

Yeah, like that will shut her up.

To my surprise, dinner isn't as dramatic as I expect. Mrs. Evans doesn't even look in my direction, which is fine by me. Everyone else is lovely, though, and we spend the meal catching up on each other's lives.

After, I excuse myself and continue working, just to keep busy. I'm once again lying in his bed, staring at the ceiling. I've heard Abbi and Liv come to bed, and I'm pretty sure Dave has as well.

I've been dying for a drink for ages but have been trying to wait until everyone's come up before I venture out. I cave in the end, but I come to a stop halfway down the stairs when I hear my name mentioned. I bend down to look through the balustrade and into the kitchen where the voices are coming from. I can see Ryan sat opposite his mum with his back to me.

"I just don't understand why you're still friends with her. Why is she still clinging to you?"

"Mu—"

"She is the kind of girl you always said you didn't want. You want a nice, sweet girl to settle down with, like Hannah, God rest her soul. Molly has been around the block a few times, to say the least, from what I've heard." My mouth drops open. "You need to be out there finding a nice girl who will make a good wife and mother to your children, not the local bike who will most probably screw you over with someone else."

"I know. I'm struggling with this enough. I don't need you on my case, too."

Tears sting my eyes. How can he say that? How can he not fight for me?

I make a snap decision. I quietly but quickly make my way back upstairs, shove everything into my bag, and put one of Ryan's hoodies on over my pyjamas. I double-check I've got everything, write a note to leave on his pillow, and sneak back downstairs and out the front door. I throw my stuff in the car, start the engine, and tear out of the drive like a bat out of Hell.

Ryan

I don't know how many times I have to defend Molly to my mum. We've been through this shit numerous times over the years, and almost every time I've spoken to her since Hannah died. It's getting to the point that I just agree to get it over with, because I feel like a fucking parrot, constantly repeating the same conversation and answers to her questions.

"Mum, that's it. I've had enough. Every time we talk, you have something to say about her. You're constantly putting her down, and I'm sick to my back teeth of it. Molly is my best friend. Without her, I don't know how I would have got through this year. Quite frankly, I don't care what you think, because you don't have to be her friend. You just have to be nice to her, because she means so much to me. Who I spend time with is up to me, not you. I am an adult, and I can make my own decisions." I slam my palms on the table and force my chair out behind me as I stand to leave.

Mum stares at me like I've grown two heads. I've never lost my temper with her before, and I very rarely swear around her. I look at her for a few more seconds before striding out of the room. All I can think is how much I want to see the person asleep upstairs.

It's dark when I enter the room, so I don't pay much attention to my surroundings. I do as I did last night, taking my clothes off, then walking over to Molly to kiss her goodnight—but, when I get to the bed, it's empty.

"Molly?" I whisper into the room, but nothing. I check the bathroom but it's empty, too. Starting to panic, I walk toward the hall window to look at the driveway. My heart drops. There's an empty space.

"Shit," I mutter as I run my hands through my hair in frustration. I storm back into my room, putting the light on this time. I pull my clothes back on and stuff my things into my bag before turning to leave the room. It's then that I notice a note on my pillow.

You said you would always fight for me.

"FUUUUUCK!" I shout, running down the stairs. Mum is tidying the kitchen when I round the corner.

"Where are your car keys?" I shout, startling her.

"What?" she questions as she spins around.

"Where are your fucking car keys?" I spit at her.

"Ryan, what's happened?"

"You... _you're_ what's happened. You, slagging her off... and she's fucking gone because of it. She's packed her stuff, got in her car, and left, all because you can't accept her. Give me your keys," I demand, my hand outstretched.

At that moment, my dad comes around the corner with a set of keys hanging between his fingers. He looks half asleep. I must have woken him up with my shouting.

"Thank you. It's good to know someone cares."

I pat my dad on the shoulder as I turn to leave, jump in Mum's car, and race off. She hardly drives the thing, so it splutters a bit at first. I keep reminding myself to keep my speed in check. I won't be worth much to anyone if I'm dead in a ditch.

I go home first—not because I think she's there, because I know she's not, but because I know I have a spare key to my old flat. There's no way she is going to let me in willingly if she's heard what I think she has.

I almost smile to myself when I see her car behind Cocoa's. I go straight to the door to the flat above and shove the key in the lock. Relief floods me when I realise they haven't changed the locks. I take the stairs three at a time, eager to get to her. The place looks deserted, so I guess she must be in her old room.

My pulse hammers around my body as I walk toward her door. It's shut, so I gently push it open to reveal Molly fast asleep on the sofa, the moonlight casting light across her face where she hasn't shut the curtains. A pile of tissues is next to her head, resting on the armrest. The sight breaks my heart.

I run my fingers down her cheek. I want to wake her up gently, not scare the shit out of her.

"Molly," I whisper, kissing her hair.

She groans lightly, and her eyes flicker as she begins to wake.

"Molly, it's just me. I'm so sorry. I came after you as soon as I realised you'd left," I say in a soothing voice, stroking my hand down her hair.

Her eyelids finally open, but as soon as she realises what's going on, her eyes are wide and she sits bolt upright.

"What the fuck are you doing here? How did you get in?" she asks, looking panicked.

"I knew you'd be here, so I stopped at home and got my key. I had a feeling you wouldn't let me in if I knocked."

"I actually hate you right now. I can't believe you just let her go off on me like that. You didn't even try to defend me—you actually agreed with her. You didn't fight for me. You promised."

"It's not how it looked, Molly. I swear it's not."

"That's what they always say."

She tries pushing me away from where I'm crouched in front of her, but I put my arms on her shoulders to hold her in place.

"Just hear me out, please?" I sit back when I feel her relax under my hands.

"No. I want you to leave." She stands up and strides over to the door. "I don't want you here. I don't even want to look at you."

She turns her face away from me, but not before I see a tear fall onto her cheek.

"I'm not going anywhere until you listen to me," I say, walking over until I'm standing right in front of her. The heat from her body warms mine and my fingers twitch to pull her to me.

Reaching out, I gently take her chin in my hand, and move her head until she's looking at me. Her eyes are red and bloodshot, and she has fresh tears running down her cheeks. "Molly, I do not and will never agree with what my mum thinks of you."

"But you did. I heard you. You said you were *struggling* with it. Struggling with... *with me.*"

"Molly, you were right before when you said my mum hates you. Every time I see her or talk to her, she goes off like she did tonight about you. I've defended you so many times, I couldn't possibly count. I'm constantly repeating myself to her, but she never listens. She's formed her own opinions and refuses to change them, no matter what I say. The last few times she's done it, I've found it easier to let her run out of steam before I say anything. Trust me, it makes the whole thing quicker. If you had hung around, you would have heard me defend you. I think I actually scared her a little because I lost it. She has no right to talk about you the way she does, and it really fucking pisses me off." As I explain, my previous anger starts to flow through my veins.

She looks down at the floor again, but I put my hand on her cheek to pull her back.

"You're shaking,"

"I'm so fucking angry. I thought I'd calmed down on the drive here, but remembering it just makes me mad again. You are the most wonderful person, Molly. I don't know how she can't see that, can't see everything you've done for me this year."

"I'm struggling to understand, Ryan."

"I said I was struggling because I am. I'm struggling with what's been going on between us. I know you spoke to Susan the other night, because she came to see me afterwards. Don't pretend like you don't know what I'm talking about, because I know you do. I don't want to ruin what we've already got either, Molly."

"She told you what I said?"

"No, just that you didn't want to ruin our friendship. She would never break your confidence, you know that."

She stares right into my eyes. "I'm not ruining our friendship because we're both lonely." Her eyes are hard as they stare into mine, as if she's trying to make me believe the words she's saying.

Thinking about my response, I pull my bottom lip into my mouth, but the only thing it achieves is getting Molly's attention. Her eyes drop and I watch her pupils dilate as I release it and run my tongue along the length. I can almost hear the argument she's having with herself.

"Molly?" I question, trying to bring her back from her daydream. I step a little closer and rub my thumbs under her eyes to wipe away the tears.

Her eyes bore into mine. They're filled with a desire that causes every muscle in my body to clench as I allow myself to imagine what could be about to happen.

Her gaze drops to my lips once again and I slide one hand so that my fingers are tangling in her hair while the other shifts so I can run my thumb along her bottom lip.

She sucks in a breath and her eyes come back to me. The longing I see reflected in them is exactly what I need to close the small amount of space between us.

Dropping my hand to her hip, I take the leap. When our lips meet, fireworks explode within me.

With our lips pressed together, I lean into her, aligning our bodies perfectly. I run my tongue along the join of Molly's lips, asking for her to open up for me. She hesitates and her body freezes. It's just long enough for me to panic. But, a second later, her lips part and I quickly slide my tongue inside. As soon as it touches hers, another round of fireworks erupts through my body and her taste explodes on my tongue. I swear she's the sweetest thing I've ever fucking tasted. Lifting my arm, I cage her in and press her back harder into the wall. I need her to feel exactly what she does to me.

I've kissed a few girls in my time, but none of them were anything like this. It's fucking unbelievable. My pulse races and my temperature soars as our tongues and bodies continue to dance together. I reluctantly pull my mouth away from hers so I can catch my breath. Placing kisses along her jaw and down her neck, I zero in on that sweet spot under her ear. She moans when I caress it with my tongue, and my cock twitches at the thought of running it over the rest of her body.

I'm just about to move back to her lips when her phone starts ringing, snapping us out of our sexual haze. I have to lean back against the wall to stop myself from falling when she slides out from under me. My whole body's weak just from kissing her.

She's breathless and her chest heaves, but it doesn't stop her from answering the phone. "Hello?" I check my watch; it's nearly four o'clock in the morning. Who the hell is calling at this time? "Adam, hi. Are you having a good holiday?"

Hearing his name brings me down from my high. Wanting to hear as much of the conversation as I can, I move over and sit on the sofa next to Molly.

"Yeah, it's great," I hear him say on the other end. "I can't stop thinking about you, though." If I hadn't already come back to earth with a bang, hearing that definitely finished me off.

"Aw, that's sweet, Adam."

"I fly back in early Saturday morning. Will you meet me for breakfast?"

"Um, won't you be tired?"

"Maybe, but I want to see you."

"Uh, okay then. Text me the details."

My heart drops into my stomach.

"Look, Adam, I don't mean to be rude, but you do know what the time is here, don't you?" she questions him.

"The guys just said it should be the middle of the afternoon. Is that not right?"

"Add on about twelve hours and they would be."

"Hang on," I hear him say, followed by, "Oi, you bunch of shits. Don't fucking run, you pussies!" shouted away from the phone. I can't help but grin. "Sorry about that. I think I may have wound them up talking about you to them all week, and they've just got their own back."

"No problem. Let me know where you want to meet Saturday. Enjoy the rest of your holiday." With that, she hangs up and relaxes back on the sofa.

"Look, Ryan..." She turns to me, and I can tell what's coming next just from the look on her face. "What just happened—" She gestures back toward the wall. "Well, it shouldn't have happened. You're my best friend, and I intend on it staying that way. I'm going out with Adam on Saturday, and I suggest you try and find someone to do the same with so we can put whatever's going on between us to bed."

I just stare at her, open-mouthed, completely lost for words. The only thing going around in my head is, 'I love you', but I don't think this is the best time for that little announcement.

And as for me finding someone else? Yeah, I don't think that's going to be happening anytime soon, either.

CHAPTER FIFTEEN

Molly

I'm staring at my sketchpad the next afternoon. I should be coming up with a logo for a guy starting up a new building company in the city, but all I can think about is last night.

That kiss.

Holy shit, that kiss was like nothing I have ever experienced before. The moment his lips touched mine, my entire body was alight. I'm not exactly lacking experience when it comes to guys, but I can honestly say I've never felt anything like that before. If Adam hadn't chosen to ring at that moment, I can only imagine how far it would have gone, because at the time, I had no intention of stopping, and I got the idea Ryan didn't either, judging how he was grinding his very obvious excitement against my stomach.

"Molly... Molly... earth calling Molly," I hear Jax saying next to me. I snap my eyes up to him and see his brows drawn down in concern. "You've been away with the fairies all day. Are you sure everything's okay?"

"Uh, yeah, sorry," I say, sounding very unconvincing.

"No, I'm not letting you get away with that. Come on, grab your bag. We're going to that wine bar down the street."

I watch Jax walk back from the bar with our third—or fourth?—glass of wine. We've been chatting about all sorts of things since we've been here. He's told me more about Lucy. I'm so jealous of how goofy he looks when he talks about her. I want someone to look like that when they talk about me.

"Does she not mind you being out getting drunk with me?"

"No, she's fine with it. One of her friends has just broken up with her boyfriend; she's been spending a lot of time with her. Apparently, she's a mess. Lucy's friends are really important to her. She's always doing something with one of them. It's one of the things I love—she's so caring of the people who are important to her." There's that goofy face again that makes my insides twist with jealousy.

I look down at my glass and watch the condensation run down the side. I let out a large breath I didn't realise I was holding.

"So, now you're suitably tipsy... what the hell is wrong?"

"Ryan," I say, looking up at him. I go on to explain everything that has happened over the past few days.

"Let me get this right. You only want to be friends with him, even though you feel so strongly about him?"

"Yes, there's too much at stake."

"So, you're going to torture yourself, and him, by the sounds of it, by keeping up the façade that you just want to be friends?"

"I'm not torturing myself. I love being his friend. And he'll find someone like I've got Adam."

"Hmm, yeah, Molly. You keep telling yourself that." I fix him with the dirtiest look I can manage in my drunken state.

We finish our drinks, then Jax finds us a taxi. I tell him that he should be dropped off first because he lives in the city centre, but he refuses and gives the driver my address. He insists that he needs to make sure I'm home safe first. Such a gentleman. I hope Lucy knows just how lucky she is.

I'm at my front door, fumbling around in my giant handbag, trying to find my keys while Jax waits patiently. Eventually, he gives up and rings the doorbell. There are lights on, so Ryan must still be up. I stop hunting and lean against the door, waiting for him to appear and rescue me.

I must have fallen asleep standing up, because the next thing I know, I'm falling into a very naked and slightly damp chest. I open my eyes to find my cheek pressed into Ryan's ripped pec. Looking down at his abs, I see droplets of water running down to soak into the waistband of his boxers. I look lower; it's all he's wearing. My drunken self is very happy with my findings.

I slowly rake my eyes back up his torso until I have my head tipped back so I can look up to his face. I'm shocked by what I see. He's staring straight ahead of him, and his jaw is set like he's about to fight. I turn my head to see he's glaring right at Jax.

"What the fuck have you done to her?" he growls. I feel his hands come around my waist to hold me up.

"What have I done to her? What the fuck, man? We went for a drink after work and got a bit carried away. Molly had some things she needed to get off her chest, and she needed a little Dutch courage to spit it out."

"So, you got her drunk to get what you wanted?"

"What? No! I was being a friend and helping her, listening to her. She's been distracted all day, not been herself at all. Something was obviously seriously bothering her."

"If she needs a friend because she's got an issue, I'm here. She knows I'm always here for her. You can go now. You've done enough, clearly."

I'm listening to their exchange and want to speak, but my mouth won't connect with my brain and work properly.

"She can't talk to you about everything, Ryan. She is allowed other friends."

"Yes, she is, but not ones who are trying to get in her knickers."

"That's rich," Jax bounces back, making me smile. "I've got a girlfriend; I have no interest in Molly's knickers. I suggest you sort out your attitude, ready for when you meet her tomorrow night. I stupidly told Molly to invite you along for dinner with us. I thought it would be good to get to know each other properly, but the more I see of you, the more I'm thinking it's not a good idea. I don't know what she sees in you."

"Likewise."

"Molly, I'll see you at work tomorrow after you've slept off your hangover." I hear Jax walk off, then the car door shutting.

Ryan

Tucking Molly into my side, I push the door closed and gently encourage her toward her bedroom. I should let her sort herself out. It would be the easiest option for me, but her legs are barely holding her upright now.

"Ryan," she moans, as I lower her to the bed. When I stand and look down at her, my breath catches at the determination on her face. "I need you."

I go to step back but I'm not quick enough. Her hands tighten around my waist and she pulls herself back up. Her tits rub against my chest and I have to take a deep breath as I will my body not to react to her. She's drunk off her face and probably won't remember a second of this in the morning. If our time comes, it won't be like this. I want her to remember every single second of it.

Her tiny hands run up over the ridges of my abs and then over my chest before they interlock behind my neck. Even in her shoes, she's not quite tall enough, so she reaches up on her tiptoes. Our lips are barely a breath apart. The scent of the alcohol on her breath hits me and reminds me that I can't allow myself to be swept away like this.

"You shouldn't ever wear clothes, you know? It's even wrong that you're wearing boxers right now," she slurs.

"Molly, you're drunk. Let's get you into bed."

"Umm... good idea. Let's take this to the bed." She releases her hands from behind me, her nails scratching lightly down my back. I can't help the groan that falls from my lips, or the hardening of my cock as she runs her hands over my naked skin.

The moment her fingertips slip under the waistband of my boxers, I know I need to move.

"Come on. Bed," I instruct, gently pushing on her shoulders so she has no choice but to sit back down.

I fall to my knees in front of her and set about undoing her shoes. The clasp is tiny for my giant fingers but, eventually, I drop them both to the floor, ready to get her into bed to sleep off the alcohol coursing through her veins.

"My knight in shining armour," she muses. "Are you sure I can't tempt you?" Her eyes darken and she gives me a salacious smile before her fingers find the bottom of her dress. In one smooth move, she's dropping it to the floor and standing in front of me in the tiniest set of lingerie that I think I've ever laid eyes on. My mouth waters as I run my eyes down the length of her, taking in her dusky pink nipples hiding behind the lace, her tiny waist, and curvaceous legs.

Every muscle in my body is screaming at me to take what I need, but the rational part of me knows that I can't. My cock throbs painfully behind the confines of my boxers, and I breathe a sigh of relief when she takes a step away from me.

"I get it. I get it." Glancing over my shoulder, she winks, her eyes dropping to my crotch. "You just need a little more convincing."

Seeing her hands come up behind her, I panic. The last thing I need is to have any more of her bare skin revealed. Taking a giant step, my fingers encircle her wrists and stop any further movement.

"Molly," I breathe, not quite believing that I'm about to turn her down when she's so clearly willing. "You're drunk, and I know that if you keep going, you're going to regret this in the morning. Believe me when I say that I'd give about anything to have what you're offering, but this isn't the way it's going to happen."

"Just kiss me. Please," she begs, stepping back into me and finding my hands. She brings them around to her smooth stomach and I tense when she tries to encourage them higher.

"This can't happen." Even I can hear the pain in my voice.

"I need you. I need—"

"To sleep this off," I interrupt.

Putting a little more effort in, I manage to lift her and lower her into bed before covering her tempting body with the duvet.

"Come on, Ry. Don't tell me I'm going to have to do it myself." Watching her hand disappear under the duvet is my undoing. I drop a very quick kiss to her forehead and walk out of her room before I'm subjected to more torture.

Closing her bedroom door, I fall back against it and blow out a long, slow breath as I try to calm my racing heart.

I deserve a fucking medal for doing the right thing.

When I hear movement behind me, I quietly push myself away from the door and start the climb up to my own bedroom. I've no idea what she's doing in there, but the last thing I need is evidence that she's finishing the job she suggested starting.

I walk through my bedroom and directly into the shower. Dropping my boxers, I turn the shower on cold and step inside. It has little effect because all I can see is her covered in that tiny amount of lace, begging me to touch her.

CHAPTER SIXTEEN

Molly

I wake up to a pounding in my head. It takes me a few seconds to remember why it hurts so much. Flashbacks from last night flit through my mind. Me telling Jax everything about Ryan whilst drinking too much wine. Jax bringing me home and having a stand-off with Ryan at the front door. Me crushed against Ryan's almost naked body. Just the thought of that makes my temperature rise slightly. I don't remember getting in bed, though. I roll over to look at the time to see it's almost midday. God, I need to get to work. I notice a glass of water and packet of painkillers on the bedside table. They're a very welcome sight. I sit up so I can take them, and it's when the covers slide off me that I realise I'm just in my underwear.

Did Ryan strip me off last night and get me into bed? Oh God, I hope I didn't do anything stupid.

Thirty minutes later, I'm dressed and ready for work. Thankfully, my head is starting to clear, thanks to the tablets Ryan left for me. I head upstairs for breakfast—or lunch, I guess. When I enter the living area, Ryan's sat at the breakfast bar in front of his laptop with a cup of coffee halfway to his mouth. When he hears me coming, he puts it back down and looks over at me with a smirk on his face.

"What's that look for?" I watch him laugh at me. "What?"

"If you don't know, Molly, then I'm not telling you."

"Shit, what did I do last night? The last thing I remember is Jax leaving."

"That's a good thing. You probably wouldn't be facing me right now."

"Speaking of Jax, the four of us are going out for dinner tonight, and you will be nice."

"Why are you dragging me along? I don't want to spend a Friday night with him."

"Because it's important to me. You, Ryan, are my best friend, and Jax is my friend. I want you both to get along because you're both in my life, and neither of you are going anywhere anytime soon. Plus, I'm dying to meet Lucy, but I don't want to be a gooseberry."

"Brilliant," he replies sarcastically.

We meet Jax and Lucy outside The Fat Dog. The second Ryan sees him, he tenses beside me.

"Just chill out, yeah?"

"I'll do my best," he says unconvincingly.

Molly, Ryan, this is Lucy," Jax says excitedly.

"Hi," is all Lucy says as she runs her eyes down the length of me. She soon dismisses us and turns back into Jax's side.

Ryan and I follow behind them as the waiter directs us to our table. His eyes burn into me, and as I look over, I'm not surprised to find the same confused look on his face as is probably on mine.

If I thought Jax looked like a lovesick puppy at work, it's nothing to what he's like with Lucy.

As we take our seats and grab the menus, Lucy fusses about rearranging the table and constantly reaches out to touch Jax. It's as if she's staking her claim.

"You can order for me, baby," Lucy says, smiling up at Jax like he'd just hung the moon.

He nods, and looks at the options while she turns her gaze on me. Her eyes run over my face once again, as if she's sizing me up.

"So Jax said you work as a receptionist?" I ask, trying to break the tension, hoping to find some common ground.

"At the moment, but I'm hoping to give that up soon. Isn't that right, baby?"

"Yep," Jax mutters, still too focused on filling his stomach.

"Can I show them?" He nods, and I narrow my eyes at the two of them.

"Isn't it beautiful? It's almost two carats." She swoons, staring down at the giant rock on her finger. "We're going to have a Christmas wedding, aren't we, baby?" She looks up at Jax with huge puppy dog eyes. I roll my eyes the second I glance at Ryan, who's also noticed her over-the-top behaviour.

"You can have whatever you want. I told you, money's no object." Her eyes light up as she turns and places a kiss to his cheek. "I love you."

"Well, I guess congratulations are in order."

"Thank you," she says sweetly, before suggesting Jax buy a bottle of champagne to celebrate.

Ryan's eyes burn into me. He looks about as confused by the couple in front of us as I am.

We have a nice enough night. Ryan and Jax do a decent job of pretending to get along, but I'm pretty convinced that I never see the real Lucy. I'd like to think that Jax is a better judge of character, so I try to push my concerns to the back of my mind and attempt to start up a friendship with her.

The second Ryan and I are alone, the words tumble from my lips. "I can't believe the size of that engagement ring. It must have cost Jax thousands. I wasn't in a million years expecting him to announce he had asked Lucy to marry him. I mean, they've only been together a couple of months. They barely know each other."

"Yeah, it's fast, but if it's right, it's right, and you just know."

"I guess so. What did you think of Lucy?" I ask. I'm driving us back home after our meal with the happy couple.

"She was... okay," he says, shrugging his shoulders.

"There was something strange about her. She seemed... fake. Like she was constantly trying too hard."

"Yeah. It was like she was doing anything she could to keep Jax happy. It was a bit too much of 'yes, Jax', 'no, Jax', 'whatever you say, Jax' and batting her eyelashes."

"She was not what I imagined at all from the way he talks about her. He loves her and wants to marry her, though, so I guess that's all that matters."

"As long as he isn't trying to get at you, I'm happy."

"Seriously, Ryan, what is your issue with him? He was nothing but nice to you tonight."

"I just don't like him. He was only nice to me because you were there."

"You're talking shit, Ry," I say, pulling up in the drive and getting out.

"I'm going to get changed. If you're going to the kitchen, pour me a glass of wine, please."

"Thank you," I say to Ryan as I settle myself on the sofa in front of a glass of wine he's left for me on the coffee table.

I feel his eyes on me as I take a sip and relax back on the sofa. Looking over, I find I'm right. "What?"

"You could wear a little more, you know."

"Fine, I'll go change. I didn't mean to offend you," I say sarcastically. I can tell by his face that isn't what he meant, but he still refuses to tell me what I did last night, so I think a little payback is in order.

"It... it doesn't offend me, Molly."

I'm stood right in front of him, so I have to tip my head up to look at him. I try to keep an innocent look on my face. It's hard, because I just want to laugh at his embarrassment. "So, what's the issue?" I can't help my face breaking into a smile. I know that what I'm wearing probably isn't all that appropriate, but I'm desperate to know the truth about last night. My white vest is a little on the thin side and my shorts show off the bottom of my arse, but it's summer, and the humidity, even at night, is through the roof right now. Plus, I'm at home. I should be able to dress how I like.

"You're such a fucking tease, you know that?" he says as the corners of his lips start to twitch. "Seeing you like that doesn't offend me one bit," he advises, then moves his head next to mine and whispers in my ear. "It makes me want to rip off what's still covering you and fuck you against the wall." He turns and walks out of the room.

Ryan

Before I know it, it's Tuesday and I'm packing, ready for my much needed break from Molly. After the night in her bedroom and then that damn near see-through vest, I think a little space is just what I need. I'm heading to Liverpool for my Grandad's funeral and then to spend some time with my sisters in both Manchester and Cardiff. I hate the idea of being away from Molly for so long, but I do think it's the right thing to do. The more time I spend with her, the more I'm struggling with my feelings, and it's killing me to watch her go out with Adam. Every time she comes home from being with him, I can tell she likes him more and more. She's been her usual flirty self with me, but she's becoming more distant and we haven't had any more awkward moments since Friday night. She spent practically all weekend with him, and when she's been home, she's been constantly texting him.

"Ry, you up there?"

"Yeah." I hear her walk up the stairs and, in a few seconds, she appears in my doorway.

"You nearly ready to go?"

"Almost. You got much planned while I'm gone?" I don't know why I ask this, because I really don't want to know what she's planning with Adam. I continue folding my clothes as she gets comfortable in the middle of my bed.

"Work, mostly. Adam's coming over for dinner tomorrow night, and I'm going out with Jax and Lucy again on Friday evening. Not sure other than that, but I'd like to see Emma. I thought she might have been in contact by now."

Yeah, I'd hoped that, too. She promised me when I spilled my guts to her that she would get in touch with Molly.

We continue chatting about our plans until I'm totally packed and ready to head out. "Right, I think I'm done and ready to go." I look up and see Molly wince as she goes to move. "You still hurting from your dance class last night?"

"Yes, I didn't realise how unfit I was. Pull me up." She puts her hand out for me and I give her a tug. She moans as she gets to her feet.

"It's only a dance class. How strenuous can it be?"

"You'd be surprised. Come on, let's get you on your way. The sooner you go, the sooner you'll be back. I'm going to miss you."

"I'll miss you, too. Come here." I pull her in for a hug and kiss the top of her head while she's in my arms. She smells so good. Oh how I want to walk back over to the bed and throw her down on it.

Ten minutes later, we've said our goodbyes, and I'm on my way to Liverpool. I hated seeing the tears in Molly's eyes as I pulled away from the house, but my desire to go back and comfort her was just another reminder of why I need this time. I have to sort out my feelings for her so that when I come back, we can be the great friends we were before all this weirdness happened. Surely, I can fall out of love as fast as I fell in it, right?

CHAPTER SEVENTEEN

Molly

"Pull yourself together, woman; he'll be back in just over a week. Get a grip," I say to myself as I walk back into the house, having watched Ryan drive away. I didn't think I would get so upset at the thought of him not being here. I hate the idea of spending the night alone, so I walk over to my bed and grab my phone.

"Molly, how are you doing?" Shane asks when he answers the phone.

"Ryan's just left for a week with his family. I don't want to be alone. Have you two got any plans tonight?"

"No, we're staying in and ordering a takeaway. We were going to plan our stag do—you want to join us?"

The second I hang up, I slip my shoes on, grab my bag, and head out the door.

I love spending time with Shane and Chris. They always make me laugh so much. They don't take life too seriously, and they're constantly taking the piss out of each other. They've told me everything I could possibly need to know about their wedding. It's the last Saturday in November in a hotel on the outskirts of the city.

They have a black, white, and red theme. Apparently, as groomsmaid, I have to wear a little black dress, bow tie, and little top hat. To my surprise, it looks much cuter than the image I had in my mind—thank God.

They've decided to have a joint stag do as nearly all their friends are mutual. They've hired out a VIP section of one of the clubs in the city and are having a 'pimps and hos' theme. We're going to have a meal, then drink and dance the night away. I can't wait. It sounds like it will be a lot of fun—plus, we get to dress up like idiots.

I end up sleeping in their guest room. I miss my bed, but I know the house is going to feel horribly empty without Ryan.

———

I'm stood in my kitchen, piping the lemon meringue pie I've made for dinner tonight with Adam. He should be here in thirty minutes. I really like him—he's a nice guy, but he isn't really doing it for me. He's fun and makes me laugh. I originally thought, with him being a banker, he'd be boring, but he isn't at all. He's a bit of an adrenaline junkie and has done all sorts of crazy things. When I'm with him, it's great, but I can't help wondering what it would be like if it was Ryan sat opposite me instead. I think what's between us is just friendship, but I'm willing to give it a little longer to see if anything sparks.

I put the pie in the oven just as the doorbell rings. I jog downstairs and open the door to let him in.

"Hi," I say, smiling at him. He's wearing light blue jeans and a white t-shirt. He hasn't shaved for a couple of days, making his stubble almost as long as his short, almost-black hair. When I invited him over, I said it was a casual thing, and I'm glad he took that seriously. I'm wearing my boyfriend jeans and a tank top. My hair is in a messy bun on my head, and I've only got a little make-up on.

"Hey, you look good, Molly." He reaches his hand up to my cheek. "You've got flour on your face," he says, wiping it off.

I can't help but feel disappointed. If Ryan did that to me, it would make my pulse rate increase. But I feel nothing.

"Thanks. I always end up covered—I'm a messy cook."

"As long as you're a good cook, that's fine by me." He shuts the door behind him and follows me up the stairs. "Wow, you were right—nice house," he says as we enter the living area.

"I know, I love it here. Can I get you a drink?"

We have a nice evening eating, drinking, and chatting. He's so easy to talk to. The conversation just flows. We never have any awkward silences. He was impressed with my cooking, and he actually went to the extreme of trying to find the packaging I could have hidden because he thought I'd bought it all and was passing it off as mine.

As the night draws to an end, Adam is a perfect gentleman. We have a little kiss at the front door before he leaves, but he doesn't push for anything further.

After tidying upstairs, I get myself settled in bed with my Kindle. I end up reading for hours and, when I eventually decide to go to sleep, it's not my date I drift off thinking about—it's Ryan. This time apart was meant to sort out my head, but I can't stop thinking about him.

When I get home from our dance class Monday night, I immediately run myself a bath and pour in loads of my favourite relaxing bubble bath in the hope that it will make me ache less in the morning. I just get in and comfortable when my phone rings. I lean over to dry my hands and grab it, groaning when I see it's actually Ryan FaceTiming me. I move myself so I'm on my front and balance my phone on the towel on the toilet. I make sure I'm covered in bubbles before I answer.

"You've got to be fucking kidding me," Ryan says as soon as I answer. "I don't see you for almost a week, and when I do, you're naked in the bath."

"Nice to see you, too. How's Cardiff?"

"It's not bad. They talk funny, though. Liv showed us around the place yesterday, but she's got to work this week so Abbi and I just chilled out at her place today, then had a takeaway when she got home. What about you?"

"Just worked, really. We've had so much come in. I went out with Adam again on Saturday night. He took me for a meal and to the cinema, which was nice. Megan and I went to our dance class tonight, hence the bath. Anything to stop it hurting so much in the morning."

"You know I did a massage course when I was at university? I'm sure I could work wonders on your body," Ryan suggests. I watch his eyes darken as he thinks about it. I guess his time away from me has been as effective as mine away from him. The idea of having his hands all over my body has me squeezing my thighs together to try to stop my clit throbbing.

"Uh... I think the bath should do it. Thanks, though."

"Well, if you change your mind, I'm more than willing."

We chat for a few more minutes about what we've been up to, as I try to drag my mind out of the gutter.

"Do you know what day you're going to be home yet?"

"No, we haven't made any decisions. I'm thinking Friday."

"Okay, well, let me know. Enjoy the rest of your week."

"Yeah, you too. Speak soon. Love you, Molls," he says, then hangs up.

"Love you, too," I mutter to myself.

I lie back in the bath and get comfortable again. Between my legs is still pounding, and thinking about that massage only makes it worse. It's been too long since I had an orgasm, I think to myself, while sliding my hand down my stomach to the place that's causing me grief. I rest my head back while my fingers get to work. I can't help my mind going back to that kiss in the office and letting my imagination run wild. I come with his name rolling off my tongue.

I put my phone back down on my desk. I've been trying to get a hold of Emma all week, but my calls just go straight to voicemail. It's really starting to piss me off.

The front door slams just after one o'clock, announcing Jax's arrival. His feet pound up the stairs. When he appears at the top, he looks livid.

"Jax, what's wrong?" I ask, rushing over to him.

"She was fucking playing me. She never fucking loved me, she just wanted to screw me over and take as much money as she could."

"Wait, what?" I ask, a little confused, as I grab his hand and drag him to the living room so we can sit.

"When I got home yesterday, I found her handbag on the side with a load of paperwork spilling out of it. I wouldn't usually look, but a few things haven't added up recently. They were addressed to a Charlotte Smith. I didn't think much of it until I saw a passport, so I grabbed it and opened it to the photo page. There was her picture, next to the name 'Charlotte Smith'. She was fucking playing me."

"What did you do?"

"I waited for her. The look on her face was priceless as I confronted her. She just broke down in tears, telling me how sorry she was. It took a while, but eventually she admitted that her name was Charlotte. She made Lucy up so I couldn't find anything out about her. It turns out everything she'd told me was one big lie. The times I thought she was with her friends, she was actually with her boyfriend, her partner in crime. They had targeted me because of my family's money. She made herself the perfect girlfriend so I would fall for her, and got me to buy her a stupidly expensive ring just so she could pawn it and take the cash. God knows what else they would have done if I hadn't figured it out."

"Fuck, I'm so sorry, Jax."

"I was blinded by how perfect she seemed. I pulled the ring off her finger, made sure I still had the wedding band in my room, and threw her out of the flat, swiftly followed by her stuff. I then called a locksmith to change the locks. I never want to lay eyes on her again. I can't fucking believe how stupid I was. It was all an act." He puts his elbows on his knees and his head in his hands. I pull him into my side and put both my arms around him in comfort.

"I'm so sorry, Jax," I repeat.

We sit, silent for a few minutes while he gets himself together.

"Right. Come on, we've got work to do. I'm not sitting here letting her make me miserable. She can fuck off if she thinks I'm going to waste any more of my time on her from now on."

"Good for you. But we're not working. Come on, we're going for lunch, then I've got something I want you to help me with."

A couple of hours later, Jax is pulling up outside my house, having followed me here after lunch. I give him a quick tour before letting him get comfortable in the living room with a beer. I quickly go downstairs to change and grab my sketchpad.

"After Hannah died, I decided I wanted a tattoo. I wanted something to remind me how short life is, so I've been sketching. I've done loads based on the forget-me-not, different patterns and words... But I think I've got my final design."

"That's so exciting. Your first tattoo. Let me see."

"I was also hoping you could recommend someone—you know, seeing as you have one or two yourself."

He flicks through my sketches. "These are really good, Molly."

"Thanks. It's that one," I say, pointing at one of the designs. "Jax?"

"Yeah."

"What made you get yours? Can I see them?"

"Is that your way of asking me to get naked?" he laughs.

"No, Jackson, it's me asking to see your tats! Now, kit off!"

I watch as he pulls his t-shirt over his head, revealing his toned torso and the tattoos that continue up his chest, ribs, and over his stomach.

"Wow. They're awesome," I say, running my finger over the one on his ribs. Jax goes on to point out each one and why he got it. I'm totally mesmerised by the ink.

"So, where do you want yours?" I stand and run my finger down my side from my bra strap to my waist. "Yeah, that should look good. Have you got any greaseproof paper?"

"Yeah, why?"

"I'm going to trace your design, then we can place it on your skin so we can get an idea of what it'll be like."

"That makes sense," I say, heading over to the kitchen.

I watch as Jax makes quick work of tracing my design with a sharpie. I pass him some scissors when he's done so he can cut it to size.

"Right, ready?" he asks me. I nod and lift the side of my vest.

"You're going to need to take your top off, Molly."

I quirk my eyebrow at him. "Now who's the one trying to get who naked?"

"You won't get the full impact if your top and bra are in the way." My eyes widen and my chin drops at his suggestion. "You can cover your front up still. You haven't got to stand there totally naked, flashing me. Not that I'd complain, of course."

"Shut up, Jax. I'm your boss!"

I turn my back to him and lift my top over my head. I remove my bra and throw it onto the sofa before gathering my top up and holding it in front of the girls, hiding them from view. "Better?" I ask, turning back to him.

"Yes." He grabs the sketch and holds it against my side. "What do you think?"

"I think I love it. You're the only one that I've told about this. I haven't even told Ryan."

"Your secret is safe with me. Can you hold it? I'll take a picture with your phone."

"What the fuck are you doing? Get your fucking hands off her, arsehole!" Ryan's shouting scares the shit out of me. I turn toward the door to see him storming our way, looking murderous. Jax is still holding the paper to my side but he quickly screws it up and puts it in his pocket. Just as he pulls his hand out, Ryan grabs his arm and throws him across the room.

"Ryan, what the fuck? Chill out. Jax wasn't doing anything."

"Then why the fuck are you both stood here half-naked? I fucking told you he wanted in your knickers."

"Dude, that is not what's going on here. Molly's my boss, and like I said before, I want nothing to do with her knickers. I was just helping her out with something."

"What the fuck could you be helping her with that involves both of you being topless?"

Jax looks at me for help. I only just told him Ryan didn't know, but it looks like I'm going to have to tell him now.

"Ryan," I say, walking over to him. "I want to get a tattoo, and I was asking Jax to help me with the design. He's topless because I asked to look at his ink, and I am because he was showing me what my design could look like. That's it."

"You're getting a tattoo? Since when?" Ryan's voice has softened, and his body has visibly relaxed.

"I've been thinking about it for a while. I'll explain later. Right now, I'd like to put my top back on, if you don't mind. Turn around, both of you," I demand, and watch them both do as they're told.

I'm just doing my bra up when I look to my left and see Ryan watching me in the mirror. His eyes meet mine and he quickly turns away, looking embarrassed. I put my top on and turn around just as Abbi walks into the room.

"Abbi, I wasn't expecting you," I say, walking over to her, but she doesn't even look at me. Her focus is solely on Jax. I glance at him and see he's just as transfixed with her. I look back to Abbi to see her cheeks redden and her usually bright blue eyes darken.

I put my arms around Abbi and pull her into a hug. "Close your mouth, Abbi. You'll start drooling in a minute," I whisper in her ear. This seems to snap her out of it.

"Sorry. Who is he? He's seriously hot," she whispers back.

"So, how come you came back early?" I ask Ryan, changing the subject before he blows a fuse at the way his sister's eyeing up Jax.

"Liv had loads of work to do so we decided to come here. Abbi is staying until Saturday, if it's okay with you."

"Of course, it is. Have you guys eaten?"

"No, not yet. We were going to see what you wanted to do. Takeaway?"

"Yes, perfect. Jax, are you staying to eat? If you want to drink, you're more than welcome to stay the night." I see Abbi's eyes light up at this suggestion.

"Uh, as long as Ryan doesn't mind. It's his home, after all," Jax says politely, but I can tell he's dying for him to say yes. I fix Ryan with a glare.

"Of course, no problem with me," he says through gritted teeth.

"Awesome, I'll get the menus."

We decide on Chinese, order a shit load of dishes, and put them in the middle of the table for everyone to have a bit of. I watch Abbi and Jax chat between themselves while we eat. Apart from looking at their plates, they don't take their eyes off each other.

I can feel the tension coming off Ryan in waves. He's clearly unhappy about this. I place my hand on his thigh, making him jump. When I've finished eating, I lean in to whisper in his ear. "Chill out, Ryan. It's not that bad." He just turns and stares at me in total disbelief.

I wait until he's finished eating before I say loudly, "Ryan, could you come downstairs with me a minute? I need you to look at something." I don't know why I said it aloud—Abbi and Jax are so lost in their own world, they wouldn't hear a bomb go off. Ryan doesn't move, so I have to pull him from his seat and out of the room.

"For fuck's sake, Ryan, get a grip."

"Get a grip. Are you fucking serious? Did you not see them?" He gestures above our heads with his hand. "I do not want him lusting after my little sister. He's not good enough for her, and forgive me if I'm wrong, but he's fucking engaged."

"Oh, come on, Ryan. Your little sister is an adult, and Jax is actually a really decent guy. Actually, he is no longer engaged since—"

"They only got engaged two weeks ago! What the fuck happened?" Ryan interrupts me.

"It turns out we were right not to like her. She was playing him for his money. Completely screwed him over."

"I still don't like him." Ryan is actually pouting. I lift my hand and flick his bottom lip, "Hey. Stop being such a pansy about this. Jax is a great guy, and your sister is a great girl. If they get on as well as it looks like they're going to—I mean, sexual tension, *hello*—then we should be happy for them."

"Please do not say the words 'sexual tension' and my sister in the same sentence again."

"Ryan?"

"Yeah?"

"Welcome home. I've missed you," I say, then throw my arms around him and squeeze him tight.

Ryan

Having her body against mine has my dick hardening instantly. I put my arms around her and nuzzle my nose in her hair. God, I've missed her. I breathe in through my nose and take in her usual scent. Her hair smells of toffee from her shampoo, and her skin like sweet vanilla. She smells like home to me. It might be ridiculous, but I'm a little jealous that Molly told Jax about the tattoo before me. I thought I knew everything about her, so it hurts a little. I'm yet to find out what this tattoo is, but I'm dying to know.

If it wasn't clear from my reaction when I first arrived home, it's now really obvious that my time away from her hasn't dampened my feelings at all. I really don't know what to do about it. I want her so bad, but she's still pulling the 'just friends' card. I'm pretty sure she's lying to herself, but I don't know what I have to do to make her throw caution to the wind and give us a go. I just need to be patient.

"Ryan, you need to chill out and let them enjoy this. Imagine if it was the other way around and you found someone you had that kind of chemistry with," Molly says, dragging me back to what's happening upstairs.

I have to bite my tongue to stop me from saying something I could regret.

"Would you want your sister ruining it for you?"

I just look down at my feet.

"No. I didn't think so," she finishes for me. "Let's go to bed and leave them to figure out what *is* between them. Alone."

"Yeah, I guess you're right. I don't like it, but you're right. Let's go to bed. Yours or mine?" I ask cheekily, flashing her a cocky smile.

"How about you go to yours, and I go to mine?" she says with a raised eyebrow.

"If you insist."

"I do. Night, Ryan. I'm glad you're back."

She gives me a kiss on the cheek and I begrudgingly walk away from her once again.

***

I wake up with the sun streaming through the crack in the curtains and a raging hard-on from the dream I was in the middle of about Molly. I can't help but feel total disappointment that it was just a dream. The thought of me coming home yesterday and being ravaged by her as I stepped through the door was much better than the reality.

I drag my sorry arse out of bed, jump in the shower, and set about relieving myself with thoughts of my very vivid dream still in my head. It doesn't take very long before I'm shooting my load over the tiles. I don't feel any better for it, though. My hand just isn't doing it for me these days.

I throw on some clothes after drying off, and I'm making my way downstairs when I stop at the sound of Molly's voice. "You two might want to move before Ryan gets down here. He's having a hard enough time already with what's going on with you two. He doesn't need to see it first-hand."

I groan to myself and scrub my hands across my face. What the fuck am I about to walk into?

I take a deep breath, then finish my descent and enter the living area. When I look up, I see Jax pulling up his jeans and Abbi doing up her shirt. They both look guilty as sin.

"Ugh, my eyes." I grumble as I walk past them toward Molly, who instantly distracts me from the half-dressed couple in my living room. She has on skintight white jeans and a black crop top, showing off her toned stomach.

"Wow, Molly. Those dance classes are doing wonders for your curves." I have to say something. She looks too hot not to.

I hear Jax laugh, then cough to try and hide it. I don't think anything of it because my sister is probably doing something inappropriate behind my back. I run my eyes up and down Molly's body again. My temperature rises and my heartbeat picks up.

"Ryan," she warns in a low voice. "Don't."

I can't help feeling disappointed, like I did when I woke up.

"So," she announces loudly to everyone. "We're all going out tonight. I've text Megan and James, Shane and Chris, and they're all up for it. Oh, and Adam, of course."

Oh, fucking brilliant. I get to meet Adam and potentially watch Molly be all over him.

"I'm not sure I'm up for it, what with school starting next week and all." I try to sound convincing.

"Shut up, old man," Abbi says from behind me. "You're coming; no excuses." I turn around and see Abbi's puppy dog eyes looking back at me.

"Yes, come on, *old man,* it's the last chance you'll get for a while," Molly joins in.

I look back at her to see a similar look on her face that I've just seen on Abbi's. They both know I can't say no to them.

Just over ten hours later, I find myself in a bar in the city, being introduced to Adam.

"It's so good to finally meet you. Molly's always talking about you," he says to me as we shake hands. I don't like him. He could be the nicest guy in the world, but he has what I want.

"Really? Well, I haven't heard much about you."

I know I shouldn't have said it, but I couldn't help myself. Luckily, Megan and James join us and distract him.

"Ryan, if you're anything but nice to him, Molly will never forgive you," Abbi whispers in my ear.

After a good number of drinks, we head down the street to a nightclub. We all go straight onto the dance floor and I instantly feel left out as I watch the couples pair off. I swallow my pride and walk toward the bar to drown my sorrows, but a hand on my arm stops me. I turn to look at who it is; a tall, slender blonde smiles back at me. She was just the type I used to go for before I fell hard for Molly.

She leans in toward me so I can hear her. "You look lonely. Dance with me?"

I glance to where my friends are dancing and see Molly's eyes on me over Adam's shoulder. She quickly diverts them when she sees me looking back. I can't help but think that her watching me dance with another woman might make her realise that it should be her.

"Sure," I say to the blonde. "Come on."

CHAPTER EIGHTEEN

Molly

I've been watching some blonde bimbo grind herself against Ryan's body for the last four songs, and I hate it. She has her hands all over him, and all I can think about is how he would feel, how soft his skin is, how hard his muscles are.

Completely lost in my imagination, I feel myself start dancing with Adam how I would like to dance with Ryan. I shut my eyes and let my body take over. I move so that his leg is between mine and I grind against him to the beat of the music. I run my hands over his body, ignoring the little voice in my mind that says he isn't muscular enough. When he speaks into my ear, I can't help but think his voice isn't deep enough. But the images in my head are turning me on so much that I drown out those thoughts.

Tilting my head up, I capture Adam's lips with my own. His hands slide down to my arse and he pulls me tight against his very obvious erection. His tongue teases the seam of my lips until I open up for him. As soon as I do, he invades my mouth and tangles with mine. That little voice starts again, telling me how he doesn't taste right, how he doesn't set my whole body on fire with his kiss. But again, I try to push those thoughts away and continue.

Adam's chest is rising and falling at such a rate that he has to pull away from my lips so he can catch his breath. He trails kisses across my jaw and down my neck, so I chance a look in Ryan's direction. What I see almost has me pushing Adam off me. He's completely still while the blonde continues to rub herself against him, staring right at me with an empty look in his eyes.

I watch as realisation hits him. He looks me right in the eyes before grabbing the blonde behind her head and crashing her lips to his. She instantly closes her eyes and lets him in. Ryan, on the other hand, still has his eyes locked on me as he practically devours her before my eyes. I feel like someone has just kicked me in the stomach, knocking all the wind out of me.

Adam places a kiss on my lips and continues along the side of my face. "Take me to your place," I say against his ear.

"Are you sure?" he asks with his eyebrows drawn together.

"Yes."

I grab his hand and begin to pull him from the dance floor, but not before looking back at Ryan. He's still watching me with the blonde's lips attached to his neck. I smirk at him as we move and see his eyebrows rise and his head shake from side to side slightly, like he can't believe what I'm doing.

Adam quickly finds us a taxi, and we're soon heading to his flat.

As soon as we're through the front door, he's on me. He carefully guides us into his living room and, in seconds, I feel the sofa hit the backs of my knees. He gently lays me down and kneels between my legs so he can continue kissing me. His hand runs from my ankle up to my waist before slipping under my top and coming to a stop when he's cupping my breast. He lies down harder on top of me and grinds his hard dick against my core.

Trailing his lips across my cheek and down my neck, he breathes me in. "You're so sexy, Molly," he moans as he runs his tongue around the edge of my ear. "I can't wait to feel your skin against mine."

My heart's racing, but it's not for the reason it should be. None of this is right. I shouldn't be here. I shouldn't be with him. My hands tremble as I try to figure out the right thing to do. My arms move of their own accord and run up his back, but it's a slender body, not the ripped, muscular one I desire.

Fuck, what am I doing?

"Adam, I'm sorry. I can't do this." I push at his shoulders, trying desperately to get his weight off me.

I watch as he pulls his head back from my neck, removes his hand from my breast and places it on my cheek.

"It's okay. We don't have to do more than you're happy with. I just thought you were turned on and wanted this."

"I thought I did, but I'm not ready." I close my eyes so he can't see the tears in them or the real reason I called a halt on things. He's just all wrong.

"Come on, let's go to bed." My eyes fly open in shock. "To sleep, Molly. I meant what I said. I really like you. I'm more than happy to take this slow." He stands up and pulls me with him. I bite my lips to stop myself from admitting the truth.

I slip my jeans off while Adam is in the bathroom, then slide into his bed. When he comes back in, he's wearing his boxers and a t-shirt. I roll over so I'm facing the edge of the bed when he climbs in. I can feel him peering down at me, but I keep my eyes shut and stay still.

"Molly?" he whispers.

"Hmm?"

"Can I hold you?" he asks nervously.

"Mm-hmm." It wasn't until my head hit the pillow that I realised just how exhausted I was. Adam releases a breath as he slides his front to my back and gently wraps his arm around my waist.

"Goodnight, Molly," he says next to my ear, then places a kiss to my head.

I drift off to sleep. The last time I was cuddling in bed, it was with Ryan.

"**M**orning, sleepyhead," Adam says as I appear in his living room, probably looking as bad as I feel.

I grunt in response.

"Oh, that good?" he says with a laugh. "Do you want tea or coffee?

"Tea, please," I manage to get out.

"Okay, sit down. I'll be right back."

I sit on the sofa and put my head back on the cushion. I must have had more to drink last night than I realised. I think back over the night's events and instantly feel awful for how I treated Ryan, but he was giving as good as he got with that blonde. I wonder if he took her home. The thought makes me want to empty my stomach right here.

This is crazy. What are we doing to each other? Why can't I be brave enough to just take the jump with him?

I spend the rest of the morning with Adam, and once I'm feeling like I can make the journey without being ill, I ask him to drive me home. When we pull up outside my house, I lean over and give him a quick kiss on the cheek.

"Thank you. I'll speak to you soon."

"No problem. Enjoy the rest of your weekend," he says, before I get out and walk over to the front door to let myself in.

I let myself in and stand and listen to see if I can hear any voices, but it's silent. I go into my room to dump my bag and take my shoes off before I head upstairs to make myself another cup of tea to have with the bath I'm running.

Walking into the living area, the first thing I see is glass smashed all over the kitchen, along with what could be a couple of mugs or a plate; I can't tell with the mess. I scan the rest of the room and see Ryan on the sofa. I'm presuming he's asleep, but I can see worry lines on his face and the tightness of his shoulders. I step a little closer to him. There's dried blood on his fists.

Shit, did he get in a fight last night?

I walk over to the kitchen, trying not to stand on any of the shards while grabbing the dustpan and brush to start cleaning it up. I just bend down to start when I hear shuffling behind me.

"Leave it," Ryan snarls in a harsh voice.

I turn to look at him, and the expression on his face is the same one from the club last night. His eyes are completely empty. His eyebrows are drawn together, a deep line formed between them, and his lips are turned down in what I can only describe as disgust. He hasn't moved, though. He's still on the sofa. Once I've had enough time to study him, he turns away from me to stare ahead.

"I want a cup of tea, and I'm not standing on all of this to get it." I turn back around to start cleaning it up.

"You always get what you want," he says patronisingly behind me.

I'm gobsmacked. I can't find any words to answer that remark, so I choose to ignore it. "What happened here?"

"You ha—"

Just as he starts to spit his answer back at me, the blonde from last night appears in the doorway. She's in the same clothes, but obviously fresh from the shower. I stare at her with wide eyes.

Holy fuck, he did bring her back. A lump climbs up into my throat and tears sting my eyes. I turn around and continue cleaning the mess up so neither of them can see how upset I am.

"You all set, Holly?" Ryan says as he gets up and walks over to her.

"Yes, thank you for letting me have a shower. How are you feeling?"

My back tingles like they're looking at me after that comment, but I'm too scared to turn around and find out.

"Like shit, but you really helped. Thank you."

"My pleasure. You have my number. If you need anything, please call," she says, making me want to be sick again. "My taxi's outside."

"Seriously, thank you. I don't know what I would have done without you," he says quieter, but I still catch it.

After a few more moments, I hear her walking down the stairs, and Ryan flops back on the sofa.

I finish cleaning up and put the kettle on when I can safely reach it.

"So, you were going to tell me what happened. Go on," I prompt.

"It was an accident," he says, shrugging.

"An accident," I repeat. "Multiple smashed glasses and mugs was an accident?"

"Yes. I was drunk."

"Not drunk enough not to spend the night with Holly, though, evidently." I can't help my acidic tone.

"Evidently," he repeats sarcastically before turning away and putting the TV on.

"Okay. Do you want coffee?"

"No," he answers abruptly, so I make my tea and get the hell out of there.

I stay in the bath until it's too cold to sit in any longer, trying to process my thoughts. Ryan brought the blonde home. The thought makes me feel sick to my stomach, but wasn't that what I suggested to him a couple of weeks ago? Except I never really meant it. I didn't want it to happen. I was —still am—too scared to admit my feelings for Ryan.

What if I'm too late?

Ryan

I can't believe Molly pulled him out of the club. She promised me she was going to change, that she was going to wait to make sure the guy was worthy of her. But there she goes—after what, a handful of dates? —home with him. I feel sick just thinking about it.

The woman rubbing herself up against me whispers in my ear, "So, trying to make her jealous didn't work, then?"

I look down to the blonde, confused. "What?"

"I said, trying to make her jealous didn't work, then? That was what you were trying to do, right?" She looks at me, dead serious.

"Uh, I guess, yeah. But why would you…?"

"I came with my friends, like you. Also like you, they're all paired up. I wanted someone to dance with who wouldn't want in my knickers, so when I saw you pining over her, I thought you'd get me what I wanted: a dance with a hot guy. And I might actually help you out in the long run. I'm sorry I didn't." I just stare back at her in disbelief.

"I can't believe you would do that. You don't even know me."

"I'm a good judge of character, and it's telling me you're a good one. I just saw an opportunity to help, so…"

Wow. "Do you want a drink, um…"

"Holly," she adds. "Yes, that would be good."

"I'm Ryan. Come on." I place my hand at the small of her back and guide her to a quiet section of the bar. Once we have drinks, Holly points over to a booth in the corner.

"So, I… uh… sorry, you've just taken me totally by surprise," I say to Holly. "I can't believe you did that."

She shrugs her shoulders in response and has a sip of her drink.

"But you let me kiss you?" I'm still completely baffled by her.

"Was her face as good as I pictured?"

"Uh, yeah, actually, it was pretty good, apart from it made her whisper in her bloke's ear and then drag him out of the club. Didn't quite have the desired effect." I put my elbows on the table and drop my head into my hands.

I end up getting so drunk I can barely walk, so Holly has to escort me home after telling her mates where she's going.

There's a small part of me that's hopeful I'll find Molly asleep in her bed when I get home, so as soon as I stumble into the hallway, I go straight for her room and fling the door open. Nothing.

The image of Molly dancing with Adam won't leave me. I end up pacing the living room, but every time I close my eyes, all I can see is her grinding against him and kissing him.

"Argh!" I growl, before planting my fist into the wall of the living room, then the other one for good measure. The pain takes away my thoughts of them for all of five seconds. I walk over to the kitchen and sweep the glasses and mugs off the draining board, watching them crash to the floor, breaking into shards—just like my heart.

"I fucking love her. Why can't she see that? Why?" I cry.

After showing Holly up to my bed, I get myself settled on the sofa with the blanket Hannah and I bought together. I really don't need those memories, too.

I must have fallen asleep at some point because, the next thing I know, I'm looking up to see Molly's arse as she's bent over, about to sweep up the mess in the kitchen.

"Leave it," I growl at her, a little harsher than I intended.

She turns to look at me and it feels like a knife is pushed right through my heart. She looks like she had a late night. I try my very best not to think about what that entailed.

CHAPTER NINETEEN

Molly

Seven Weeks Later

The last few weeks since Ryan went back to work have been bloody awful. Ryan's done his best to avoid me at all cost and seems to spend way more time at school than he needs to. I miss him terribly; the house is so empty and quiet without him.

Everything else has pretty much continued as normal, and although I've pretty much decided my relationship with Adam isn't going to go anywhere romantically, we've still been hanging out. He's a good guy, and I like spending time with him.

Megan and I are still loving our pole dancing lessons, so much so that we've signed up to a slightly more advanced class. Tonight is the first one, and I'm a little apprehensive. I've also taken up a life drawing class on a Wednesdays at the local college. It's an eight-week course, and next week is the last one. I'm really going to miss it. Ever since talking about it with Ryan when we were on holiday, I kept thinking about giving it a go again. We've had a range of models we sketch throughout the classes, and it's been exhilarating to do something I always loved so much. We can submit any of the sketches we've done in class, or one we've done outside, if we wish, to an end-of-course competition. I know exactly what—or who—I want to submit, but it's just a case of convincing him.

"Oh, come on, please," I beg with my best puppy dog eyes and pouty lips.

"Molly, stop it with the face." He laughs at me.

"I'll buy you anything you want. Well, within reason. I'll ply you with alcohol if it will help, and I'll feed you. Please. You've seen my work; you said yourself that it was good. I promise I won't make you look hideous!"

"I know you're good at it. That's not the point!" he argues, shaking his head.

"Well, what is the point, then? I've spoken to Abbi, and she's totally fine with it as long as she can have a copy!" The connection Abbi and Jax had that very first night is still going strong. He's been spending most of his weekends up in Manchester with her.

"Ugh," Jax groans.

"Why me? Why not Ryan? His body is better than mine."

"Because I'm desperate to sketch those tattoos, and Ryan's still avoiding me. Man up and get naked for me. It's art; you've done it before."

"Let me ask you something. Would you do it for me?"

I answer without hesitation. "Yes. Come on, I've promised already, you can cover up your junk."

"I knew taking this job was a bad idea," he groans, shaking his head.

"Stop being a pussy, Jax."

"Right, fine, but you seriously owe me one."

"Yay!" I say, jumping up and running over to hug him. "Thank you, thank you!"

"You knew I'd cave eventually. I couldn't listen to you anymore. It's all you've spoken about for days."

"Okay, so you're busy tomorrow, right? But can you do Sunday?"

"Yeah, I guess so."

"Brilliant. So, come over to mine in the morning. I'll have everything set up and ready to go, so we can get straight to it."

"At yours? Won't Ryan be about? I don't want him watching. It's bad enough you'll be staring at me."

"He's still keeping out of my way. Plus, he won't want to look at your naked arse. He's still unconvinced about your relationship with his sister. He doesn't need to see what she sees during your dirty weekends."

"He needs to chill out."

"You don't need to tell me that."

I climb my aching body up the stairs in search of a glass of wine after pole dancing. I was right to be apprehensive about it. It was so much harder than our Monday night class. It doesn't help that I landed on my arse a good couple of times, much to Megan's delight.

To my surprise, Ryan's sat in the living room, watching telly. "Are you okay?" he asks, looking concerned.

"Yeah. Megan and I started a more advanced dance class tonight. It was *definitely* more advanced. I need wine and a hot bath. I'm sure I'm not going to be able to move tomorrow."

"Make sure you drink enough water first."

"Yes, Dad!"

"Hey, just looking out for you. I wouldn't want to have to come down and pull your passed out, naked arse from the bath."

"Yeah, you're probably right. If you need me, you know where I'll be." I grab a glass of wine—and water—and head downstairs.

Thirty minutes later, my glass is empty, and I'm overheating. I wrap myself up in my huge fluffy towel and head into my room.

"Shit!" My heart pounds as I find Ryan sitting on the edge of my bed, waiting for me. "Fucking hell, Ry. You could have warned me you'd be there." I place my hand over my racing heart and take a couple of deep breaths to try to calm it whilst pulling my towel tighter around my body.

I look from him to my bedside table that has my bottle of wine, a can of beer, and a bottle of something I don't recognise on it. I place my glass next to the wine bottle and pick up the other bottle. Massage oil.

Oh, fuck no. No, no, no.

"Uh, Ry?" I turn back to him with the oil in my hand.

"Molly, don't look so worried. I'm going to make it better for you. You'll thank me in the morning."

I really doubt that. Having Ryan's hands all over me is going to be torture. I can feel myself getting worked up at the mere thought of it. "I don't think it's a good idea, Ry."

"Oh, shut up. Put a dry towel on the bed, then lie face down on it," he says, like it's the most normal thing in the world.

"I'm not lying naked on my bed for you."

"Okay, put your pyjama shorts on, but you'll need to be topless so I can do your back."

"I can't believe you're making me do this."

"I'm not making you do anything. If you really don't want me to, I won't."

I stand and look at him as I weigh up my options: get seriously turned on by Ryan, or not be able to move in the morning.

"Right, turn around," I demand. I grab a pair of knickers and shorts from my drawers and slide them on under my towel. I go into the bathroom to grab a dry towel and do as he says after pouring myself a large glass of wine and taking a massive gulp.

"Okay, ready," I say, after I've made myself as comfortable as possible in this situation. I hear Ryan's sharp intake of breath as he turns around. I crane my neck to see him but instantly regret it as his eyes darken, running over my body.

"Ryan, get on with it before I change my mind," I say, hoping to snap him out of his perusal.

I watch him grab the oil and pour some in his hands before rubbing them together to warm them up. He goes to the bottom of the bed and starts with my left leg.

"Holy fuck," I moan. "That's so good."

"Told you. Now, just relax."

I try to do just that as he works his way up both of my legs, digging his fingers into my sore muscles, but the higher he gets, the harder it is to relax... and the harder my clit is pounding. I'm trying my best not to make it obvious that I'm turned on, but I'm sure my heavy breathing is a major giveaway. I'm also trying desperately hard not to make any noises, because the couple of times I have, they sounded very suggestive even to my own ears.

"Molly?"

"Uh-huh?"

"I just wanted to apologise for acting like a stroppy teenager since I've gone back to work. I've been stuck in my own head, I'm sorry."

"It's okay... ahh, Ry. I know you've been... ahh, busy." I can't help the appreciative noises that escape as I speak.

"That wasn't really what I meant, but thanks."

I'm just about to ask more, but he moves to my back and totally distracts me.

"Your tattoo is looking good. Does it still hurt?" Ryan asks, running his finger over it.

"No, it's fine now."

Jax went with me and held my hand because it hurt like a bitch, but now the scabs have cleared and the slight swelling and pinkness has gone, I'm really pleased with it. The artist Jax suggested was pure genius; it looks better than I ever could have imagined.

I hadn't told Ryan I was getting it done, and we hadn't spoken about it since the night he found Jax and I planning it and he flew off the handle. When he eventually appeared after work that evening, he found me sitting at the coffee table, leaning over my sketchpad, doing some work. I was so engrossed in what I was doing, I didn't hear him come into the room until he cleared his throat. I looked up at him to see him staring back with desire in his eyes.

"Is everything okay, Ry?" I asked suspiciously.

"I... um... yeah. Molly?"

"Yeah?"

"You need to go and put some more clothes on."

It was only then that I looked down at myself and realised the way I was leaning over the coffee table in my loose top meant that Ryan could practically see everything. Suddenly, the look in his eyes made more sense to me. I put my pencil down and pulled my top up as I stood.

"I had my tattoo done today," I said, pulling up the bottom of my top to show him the giant plaster. "I can't have anything rub against it for a few days." He swallowed hard as he looked at my side.

"Right, but you can wear something bigger than that, right? You can have one of my t-shirts, if you want."

"No, it's okay."

I went to leave the room to change, but not before I caught Ryan adjusting himself as he walked into the kitchen. Even after weeks of barely talking, the effect we have on each other is still the same.

I'm brought back from my daydream with a gasp as Ryan's fingers gently brush the sides of my breasts.

"Sorry," he mutters behind me.

He's sitting across the backs of my thighs, and I can feel the unmistakable shape of his erection pressing into my arse. I really need to put a stop to this, but it feels so good.

"Ry?"

"Yeah?" God, his voice sounds so sexy when he's turned on. It gets gravelly and even deeper than normal.

"I think I'm done," I say regretfully.

"Shit, I'm sorry. I can't help it."

"It's okay, I just think it's time to stop."

"Let me just finish your shoulders."

"Okay."

I lay my head back down and let him continue. After a couple of minutes, I feel his hands come to a stop, but they rest on my lower back as he sits back on his heels and lets out a huge sigh.

Lifting myself up slightly, I turn my head to look at him. His eyes are shut and his head's tipped back toward the ceiling.

"Ry," I whisper. This brings his head down and his eyes open, making me gasp. They're so dark, they're almost black.

After staring at me for a couple of seconds, he moves to get off me. I shift slightly to my other side, and the first thing I see is the huge bulge in his jeans. My mouth waters instantly. How easy would it be to reach out to him? He's only a foot away from me. I raise my eyes until I meet his, and I watch as he runs them over my half-naked body once more before he announces he's going for a shower.

"I've probably used all the hot water."

"I won't need any," he says over his shoulder.

Ryan

I let the cold water run over me, but it does very little to calm me down. The last hour has been both heaven and hell mixed into one. Having my hands all over Molly is something I've dreamt about for so long now, but the reality of it was so much better than I could have ever imagined. Her skin is silky soft and perfect. I love every mole and freckle that I committed to memory during her massage, but having her laid half-naked under me, so close yet so far away at the same time, was pure torture. All I wanted to do was flip her over and kiss her as if my life depended on it.

I've missed her so much over the last few weeks, and I know it's my own fault. I distanced myself from her after the night she stayed at Adam's. I just couldn't take it, watching her get close to him and their relationship develop. She's still seeing him, but she hasn't stayed out all night since.

I've been seeing Holly regularly, but only as friends. Neither of us is interested in anything happening. I'm sure Molly thinks we're dating, and I know I should have said something to correct her, but I just can't bring myself to do it when I know she's seeing Adam.

I take my painfully hard dick in my hand and start stroking it up and down. With thoughts of a half-naked Molly under me and the noises she was making ringing in my ears, it's not long before I feel the familiar warming sensation in my lower back before my balls draw up to my body and my dick twitches in my hand as I come. The relief is welcome, but it only takes the edge off. What I really need is Molly.

"I was just going to come and wake you. I've made breakfast," Molly says as I enter the living area the next morning.

I take in what she's wearing. My life is a little easier now that it's colder. Gone are the little shorts and vest tops in favour of jeans, long sleeved t-shirts, and jumpers. She still looks hot as fuck, though. This morning, she's wearing baggy jeans and a white, long sleeved t-shirt. It's simple but sexy. Her curves are more toned since she's been going to the dance classes, making my hands itch to touch her again. I shove them in my pockets to stop them moving of their own accord.

"How are you feeling?"

"Great—only a little sore. You've got magic fingers."

"You have no idea what I can do with these," I say suggestively, pulling my hands back out and wiggling my fingers at her. I watch her cheeks redden before she turns her attention back to the breakfast.

We spend the day together like we used to. Last night might have been all kinds of painful, but it seems we've had a breakthrough in our relationship, and we're almost back to normal. When I say normal, I don't mean pre-Molly-moving-in platonic friends. I mean post-Molly-moving-in, awkward and full of sexual tension and chemistry. Every time we touch, tingles shoot through my body. Every time she's close and I smell her, my dick twitches. Every time I look at her, I have an internal fight not to reach out and touch her.

Next Saturday is Shane and Chris's stag do, so we spend the day out shopping, trying to decide what the hell we wear to a 'pimps and hos' party. Normally, I hate shopping with women, but today is a different story. Molly's been trying on teeny tiny, slutty outfits. I tried to convince her she needed photographic evidence of each so she could make an informed decision but, for some reason, she didn't want me taking photos. Every time she came out of the dressing room, my dick got a little harder. She went through the entire range of outfits: schoolgirl, French maid, nurse, police officer, soldier. You name it, she tried it on. I was in my fucking element.

I knew my favourite as soon as she came out in it, but I refused to tell her which one it was. She reckons she could tell by my reaction, but is refusing to tell me which one she chose. She made me leave the shop before she bought it. I'm not sure if it will be a good thing or not if she gets the right one. Yes, she will look sexy as hell, and I'll enjoy it immensely, but she's going to the damn party with Adam, so it won't be me who gets to have my hands all over her. It's going to be a torturous night no matter what she's picked.

After getting a lot of stick from Molly for copping out, I decide to just wear my suit with a tank top under it. She did convince me to buy some ghastly chain to wear around my neck, and some godawful, shiny shoes. God, this party's going to suck. I've got to dress like a dick while she walks around like sex on legs.

Once we have everything we need, we head to the supermarket. Molly insisted on cooking a meal for us, so I'm just letting her get on with it while I push the trolley around behind her, trying not to just stare at her arse.

We have a really good night together, chatting and laughing like we used to. It was almost like the last few weeks of awkwardness never happened. Molly talks about work and how busy they are. She tries to tell me about Jax and Abbi, but I put my fingers in my ears and make her stop. I'm still not totally sure about Jax, but I've come to realise over the past few weeks that he's a really good guy, and I think my problem with him is that I'm jealous of how much time he spends with Molly and how well they get on. If anything good can come out of him and my sister, it's that I know he isn't after Molly, which was my initial concern about him. She only ever has good stuff to say about him, so I think I just need to get over myself and be nice.

Once we've eaten, we sit and watch a couple of films together. It doesn't escape my notice that the whole evening, Molly has tried to keep a bit of distance between us. She doesn't come and sit next to me like she used to. Whenever she needs something in the kitchen, she won't lean around me and just grab it; she asks me to move or get it for her. I'm undecided whether her keeping space between us is a good thing or not, but I guess she doesn't want a repeat of last night. As the credits roll up on the second film, Molly announces she's off to bed.

"I've got loads of marking to do tomorrow, so you probably won't see much of me," I say.

"Okay, I've got Jax coming over to work on something, anyway. I'll see you tomorrow. Night." She leans over and kisses my cheek.

"Goodnight, gorgeous." I don't know where it comes from, but I feel as shocked as Molly looks.

I wait for her to leave before tidying up and heading up to bed myself. I can't help but look to the other half of my bed and wish that she were there, not downstairs in her own.

CHAPTER TWENTY

Molly

I quickly check my phone as I sit on the edge of the bed and notice a message from Emma. I still haven't heard from her since my birthday. I've been to two more Morrison Sunday dinners, but she didn't come to either. Ryan keeps asking if I've heard from her like he knows something I don't, but every time I question him, he just shrugs and passes it off.

> Emma: I'm sorry I haven't been around, but I'm ready to talk if you are.

I just stare at my phone in shock.

> Molly: I can only do Thursday night, unless you just want to pop into the office when you're free?

> Emma: I'll meet you in our usual seat at 5. See you there.

What's she going to say? Come to think of it, what am I going to say to her? I'd be lying if I told her nothing has happened, or that I hadn't thought about something happening with Ryan. I have loved every minute of today with him, spending time together like we used to. I'm starting to wonder if maybe us giving something a go wouldn't be such a bad idea. I mean, I pushed so hard for us to just be friends that I basically lost him for the last few weeks. What if we were always meant to be together? Everything happens for a reason, right?

I wake up the next morning to my phone ringing. Picking it up, I see Jax's face smiling back at me.

"Morning," I croak out.

"Okay, that answers my question. I was going to see if you were up and wanted me already?"

I quickly glance at the time. "Jax, it's seven-thirty on a Sunday morning. Why on earth would you think I'd be up? And why are you up, for that matter?"

"Uh... I'm... sortofabitnervous," he says, so fast I almost miss it.

"Hang on—confident and cocky Jackson Parker is so nervous about posing for me that he couldn't sleep?"

"Don't rub it in or I'll cancel and you'll have to find some other mug to get naked."

"Fine, yeah, sorry. Well, I'm awake now if you want to head over. I'll get the garden set up."

"The garden?" he asks nervously. "It's freezing outside. You cannot be serious?" I can't help but laugh.

"You'll be on my bed, don't worry. Hey, I'll even put the heating up for you. Don't want you getting cold while you're naked!"

"Molly, I'm warning you."

"Sorry, you're just making it too easy. Get your arse over here now. I'll be ready."

I can't help but smile to myself as I hang up the phone.

Dragging my sleepy body from bed, I get myself dressed and ready for the day. I go for comfortable and grab a pair of lounge trousers and a tank top. I've just told Jax I'll put the heating up, and I don't want to melt. I pull my hair on top of my head in a messy bun and leave my face clear of make-up. I make my bed and grab the silk fabric I bought for this. I wanted something soft and feminine to contradict Jax's bad boy looks. I've cut a bit off the end so I can drape it over him to cover him up. Then, I shove some cushions under the fabric to give it some definition. I can scrunch it up where it's needed once he arrives and gets in place.

I'm just coming back down the stairs with a tray filled with tea, coffee, and pastries when I hear a quiet knock on the door.

When I open it, I'm shocked by what I see. Jax is standing there, looking back at me, but his face is a little green. He has his hands twisting around each other in front of him, and his foot is bouncing on the ground.

I open the door wider for him to enter before closing it behind him. He turns to look at me with the same scared, deer-in-headlights look. I move over to him and wrap my arms around his shoulders.

"Jax, don't look so scared. It's only me." I rub my hands up and down his back in comfort.

"I know, I just can't stop the nerves. I feel like I'm going to be sick."

"Yeah, you kind of look it. Come on, I've made coffee and breakfast. We don't have to get started straight away. Let's chill for a bit first."

"Yeah, sure... okay."

I grab his hand and pull him into my room. He sits on the side of the bed and sips his coffee. I can see how tense he is, but I don't really know what to do to help him other than get started so he can see it's really not that scary.

Thirty minutes later, Jax is stood in front of me in his boxers. I've just finished faffing about with the silk sheet, and I'm ready for him to get into place.

"Right, you take this." I hand him the smaller bit of fabric. "I'll go in the bathroom while you get yourself sorted, then give me a shout."

"Do I really have to get naked? Can't I just chuck this fabric over me so it covers my boxers?" He looks at me with pleading eyes.

"No, I want as much on show as possible. Come on, Jax, it will be fine." I walk away from him into my bathroom and wait.

"You seriously owe me one for this," Jax mutters before I hear the bed move, but he doesn't say anything else.

"Are you done?"

"Ugh, yes. Let's get this over with, then never speak of it again."

I walk out and look over to him. His face is now bright red with embarrassment.

"Stop looking so worried. You look hot. Abbi is going to love it, and I'm sure her reaction will make this worthwhile for you."

"You'd better be right." I go over to him to adjust the sheet around him. "Careful, pull that any lower and it may as well not be there."

"Chill out. Trust me when I say that I have no intention of seeing your dick, Jax." He still doesn't look convinced. "Trust me," I say again, hoping it might make him relax.

"You know, you could be wearing less," he teases, and I'm pleased when I see his usual cocky grin.

"Uh, no. If you ever take up life drawing, I'll repay the favour, but I need to focus on this."

"Spoilsport."

I just stick my tongue out at him.

The time seems to fly, and before I know it, hours have passed. After drifting off to sleep, Jax is starting to complain he's uncomfortable. I keep telling him to suck it up, but I know I'm being mean. I'm going to have to let him move soon.

I'm so engrossed in my sketch that I don't hear the footsteps coming toward my room. Jax obviously doesn't either, because both our heads shoot to the door when it opens.

"What the fuck?" Ryan asks, taking in the scene before him. "Dude, what the fuck are you doing?" I look over to Jax and see a mixture of shock and embarrassment wash over him.

"You said he was busy upstairs and wouldn't come down," Jax growls at me.

"I said he was busy. I didn't promise anything else." I shrug.

"Molly, why is Jax naked on your bed?"

"I've been doing a life drawing class. I've got to do a final piece, and Jax agreed to be my model."

"I got bullied into it. I didn't agree easily," Jax mutters under his breath.

"How did I not know you were doing a life drawing class?"

"You haven't really been about much. It wasn't a secret. I actually signed up because of that conversation we had on our holiday."

"I'll leave you to it, then," he says, walking away.

"Well, he looked royally pissed off," Jax says once Ryan is upstairs.

"He's trying to like you, Jax, but we do get caught in some compromising positions."

I sketch for another hour before I think I've finished. I've done it in charcoal so it's all black and white. I've managed to capture Jax's ink as I wanted it, and I'm really pleased with the result.

"Right, I'm done." I turn my sketch around to show him.

"Holy fuck, that's good."

"See, I told you to trust me. Right, I'm going to head upstairs so you can get dressed. Thank you so much for doing this for me."

"No problem. It wasn't as bad as I thought it would be, actually."

"Told you so."

The moment I open my bedroom door, the scent of home cooking fills my nose. My stomach rumbles, but when I get upstairs, I head straight for the kettle. I'm dying for a cup of tea. Ryan's sitting at the table, surrounded by folders he's marking, with a deep frown on his face.

"Hey, do you want a coffee?"

"No thanks," he says stroppily.

"Molly, I'm going to head off. I've taken a picture of your drawing and sent it to Abbi. She says she wants it framed," Jax says, shaking his head, a goofy smile appearing at the mention of her.

"No problem, I'll get it sorted for her after I've handed it in. Thanks again, Jax, I really appreciate you doing that for me. I'll see you in the morning."

"Yeah, bye. Bye, Ryan," he adds before he leaves the room, but Ryan just grunts in response.

I make my tea before heading over to him and leaning my hip against the table next to him. "What's wrong?"

"Nothing," he snaps.

"It doesn't look like nothing. Tell me."

"Him," he spits, gesturing to where Jax was just stood.

"What's he done now?"

"You asked him to model for you."

"Are you jealous? Did you want me to ask you?"

Ryan lowers his head as if embarrassed. "You know what? Yes, I am," he says, raising his determined eyes back to mine. "I thought I was your best friend. Not only did I not know you were taking this class, but you also didn't ask me. I hate that we've drifted apart. I miss you."

"You didn't seem too up for modelling when we spoke about it in the summer, so I didn't think you would do it, anyway."

"We were just messing about in the summer. I'd do anything for you, and you know that." He reaches his hand out and grabs my free one, caressing the back with his thumb and sending tingles up my arm—so much so that I have to put my tea down so I don't drop it. "I hate that you've been staring at him practically naked all morning."

Shit, he really is jealous. "It was art, Ry. I was looking at him like I would a bowl of fruit."

"That may be true, but it doesn't help me." He stands in front of me and cups my cheek with his other hand. "I don't want you having some other guy's body in your mind," he says quietly. "How would you feel if the situation was reversed?"

I don't even have to think about it; the thought alone makes me feel sick. "Uh..."

"Exactly." His hand slides around to the back of my head, his fingers thread into my hair, and he pulls me toward him. For a second, I think he's going to kiss me, but at the last minute, he presses his lips to my forehead.

His breath caresses my face and I can't help but close my eyes as I revel in his touch, his closeness.

We both stay still for a few seconds longer before he places his lips against mine for the briefest kiss, before stepping away and walking toward the kitchen.

I stand there and stare, completely confused. I snap myself out of it just in time to see him adjust himself as he comes to a stop in front of the fridge. He pulls out a bottle of wine and pours me a glass. I watch, mesmerised, as he slides it over the counter so it's in front of one of the stools at the breakfast bar, before placing his palms flat on the counter and leaning his hips forward to rest against the worktop.

"Come on, dinner will be ten minutes... I think," he says, nodding to my glass of wine.

I slowly walk over, taking my hoodie off as I go. After that little interaction, I most definitely don't need it on to keep me warm. I throw it on the sofa as I pass and sit myself up on the stool before taking a sip of my wine.

I look up when my skin begins to tingle under his stare. His eyes are glued to the bit of cleavage I've just revealed. His tongue sneaks out and runs over his bottom lip before he swallows, making the muscles in his neck ripple.

"Come and sit down."

"I... uh... I think I need to stay on this side of the counter for a while." His eyes drop to his crotch briefly and I follow them, suddenly realising why he's over there.

"Oh. So, did you get all your work done?" I try to come up with something that might help break the tension surrounding us, but it has little effect.

We chat for a few more minutes before the buzzer goes off on the oven and Ryan dishes up our dinner. I hop off the stool and join him.

The lasagne is delicious, especially for a first attempt, but standing side by side as we clean up from dinner is torture. Every time I brush against him, sparks fly, and I know he's feeling the same because, every time it happens, his eyes snap to mine.

Once we've finished, I excuse myself so I can go downstairs and get changed into something more comfortable. I decide to have a quick shower before getting my PJs on and heading back upstairs.

Ryan is watching some nature programme when I join him on the sofa. He's sat in the middle seat of his corner sofa with his legs stretched out on one side, so I go to sit at the end closest to the kitchen.

"What are you doing?"

"Uh, sitting down?"

"Not over there, you're not. Come here."

I've just placed my glass on the coffee table when his hands firmly grip my hips and pull me backward until I'm sat right up against his side. He settles himself and puts his legs back up on the cushions before pulling me into him so my front is against his side. With one arm around my shoulder, he uses the other one to pull mine around his waist. I tense.

"Relax, Molls. Put your legs up, your head down, and just chill."

I do as he says, placing my legs alongside his and putting my head on his still naked chest. I try to relax but it's hard, pressed up against his smoking hot body. His hand strokes up and down my arm, trying to relax me, and it actually works. I let out a huge sigh and snuggle into him.

"That's it," he says, kissing the top of my head. "I've missed this." He holds me tighter and pulls the blanket over us.

Ryan

"Shit." It's still dark, so it can't be too late. We must have fallen asleep on the sofa after we got comfortable last night.

Molly's lying completely on top of me. How can I be that comfortable? Her arms are on my shoulders, her body flush against mine, and her legs are on either side of me. I shift slightly and realise that my dick is throbbing—not only because I've got Molly cuddled around me, but because her hot centre is right on top of it. The friction is so good that I want to keep moving against her, but I don't think she'll appreciate that wake-up call at the moment.

I stretch my arm out and grab my phone—it's nearly six o'clock—just before my alarm goes off. Putting it back down, I turn my attention to the beauty still fast asleep on top of me.

Leaning down, I press my lips against her hair. "Molly," I whisper. "It's time to wake up." I watch as her eyelids start to flutter. I continue running my hands up and down her back and I'm aware of the moment she's awake and realises what's happening because goosebumps cover her skin. I kiss her head again before I feel her move. Sitting up all of a sudden, my hands slip around so they're on her waist, and I manage to contain the growl that creeps up my throat as she moves against my dick.

"Shit, did we fall asleep? What time is it?" she asks sleepily, looking really cute. Her hair's a mess, her cheeks are pink, and her eyes look like she could be still asleep.

"Yeah, we did, but it's okay. It's not even six yet. Come lie back down. You looked pretty comfy."

She smiles at me, looking embarrassed, but I don't miss her checking out my chest and stomach. She suddenly tenses as she realises what she's straddling. "I... uh... should probably move."

I reach my hand up to her cheek to make her look at me. "Why? Come on, lie down." I give her waist a tug and, after a couple of seconds, she moves herself forward and lies back on my chest with her face turned to look at me.

She must notice me grimace as she moves over me again. "What's wrong? she asks, concerned.

"Nothing. It just, uh, felt good when you moved."

Her eyes widen slightly at this, but to my surprise she stays put. To my utter shock, she actually wiggles her arse, causing a moan to escape my mouth. She just looks at me and laughs.

"Someone's a little horny this morning, are they?"

"You've no idea."

Her arse moves slightly again, as her lips twitch teasingly. Leaning toward her, I whisper in her ear, "If you keep doing that, you could find yourself in a dangerous position." She just shrugs and holds me tighter. She shoves her face into my neck where I feel her breathe me in. It causes a huge smile to break across my face.

We continue to lie like that, just holding each other, until my phone alarm goes off. I move my arms from around Molly's back and place them on her waist to gently push her up.

"Nooooo," she complains as I move her. "Ring in sick and we can stay like this all day."

"As much as I'd love to do that, I really can't." She pouts at me and gives me her puppy dog eyes. "Trust me when I say there is nowhere in the entire world I'd rather be than under you right now, but I have to go to work."

I join her in sitting up, making us chest to chest again. I wrap my arms around her for one last squeeze and kiss her forehead, looking back at her as she stares into my eyes. My heart skips a beat when her eyes drop to focus on my mouth. My chest heaves as my heart rate picks up.

She looks back up to my eyes before leaning forward and pressing her lips to mine.

Neither of us moves. We just sit there, enjoying the closeness. After a few more seconds, she pulls away and opens her eyes. I don't think I've ever seen them so full of hunger. I'm close to throwing caution to the wind and carrying her to my bed for the day so I can have my lips on every part of her body.

To my disappointment, she gets herself up and stretches before heading to the kitchen. "Coffee?"

"Please," I say, following her lead. I may have had the best night's sleep I've had for a long time, but the sofa wasn't the most comfortable of places.

After putting the kettle on, Molly turns around and leans back against the counter. "Ry?"

"Yeah?" I say on a yawn.

"Um... you might want to do something about that," she nods her head toward my very tented trousers, "before you go to school." She can't help herself and bursts into giggles.

The kettle whistles, and she turns around to make our drinks. Walking up behind her, I cage her in with my arms and shove my crotch against her lower back.

"You could offer to help, you know," I say in a low voice, brushing my lips against the smooth skin of her neck.

She shoves her arse back into me. "Not this time, big boy. Go get ready, or you'll be late."

I'm totally distracted all day. All I can think about is how Molly's body lined up perfectly with mine. How she smelled when I held her close. How soft her lips were when they were on mine, and every other tiny thing that happened last night and this morning. We had a meeting after school, but I couldn't tell anyone what it was about.

I drive home with a smile on my face, thinking about what could be in store for us. Molly has a dance class tonight and I'm seriously hoping I get to give her another massage. I'm desperate to have my hands on her again.

I'm on the sofa watching TV when she comes in. She still looks a little hot and sweaty from her class, which has my dick twitching in my jeans. She shrugs her jacket off, revealing a tiny crop top sports bra thing that gives her awesome cleavage and shows off her toned stomach. She's also got skintight leggings on that coordinate with the top.

"Fucking hell, Molly. Are you trying to kill me?" I say, running my eyes up and down her curves.

"I'm hot, sweaty, and minging. Seriously?"

Does she have no idea what she looks like? My eyes are fixed on her as she walks over to the sink and pours a glass of water, giving me a great show of her arse. I can't help but groan at the sight. I walk up behind her and put my hands on her bare waist. She flinches slightly and stops drinking when I touch her.

"You really have no idea how fucking sexy you are, do you?" I can't help running my nose around the edge of her ear. When I breathe out, tiny goosebumps prick her skin. Good, she's just as affected as I am. Placing her glass on the worktop, she turns to look up at me.

"I'm going to have a bath, then I'll be up to make dinner, okay?"

"Sure," I say, following her out of the room.

"What are you doing?"

"Thought you might need a hand." I grin.

"No, I'm all good." She turns and playfully pushes my chest to send me back into the living room, but she's so small, I don't move at all. "I won't be long."

I kiss her forehead before she turns around, and I slap her arse as she walks away. She shakes her head as she descends the stairs.

It feels like the longest thirty minutes of my life before she comes back up. Knowing she's down there in a nice, hot, bubbly bath, naked, is pure hell.

When she appears, she is in her standard lounge trousers, tank top, and zip-up hoodie. Molly looks hot all the time, but I think I prefer her like she is now: relaxed, comfortable, with her hair unstyled in a mess on top of her head, and no make-up on. She's just Molly like this.

My Molly.

She quickly whips up a chicken salad for us before bringing it over to me. She sits on the floor, her plate on the coffee table, and tucks in.

"Was your class good? You don't look to be in as much pain tonight."

"It actually felt easier after doing the more advanced class on Friday. We're thinking about stopping the Monday night one and just doing the harder one from now on."

"So, you're not going to be needing a massage tonight, then? I was looking forward to that."

"I bet you were, you dirty dog."

I just shrug at her and continue eating.

After we've cleared our plates, we stay where we are, chatting about our day and what we have planned this week. Molly has just explained that she's meeting Emma for the first time since her birthday on Thursday. I can't believe it's taken her this long to get in touch with Molly. She really did need some thinking time—I just hope she's come to the right conclusions. Molly tells me about having dinner with Adam tomorrow after work. I can't lie, I feel a little sick knowing she'll be spending the evening with him. After what's gone on between us the last couple of days, I sort of hoped he'd get the boot.

I notice Molly start to roll her shoulders while we're chatting. "You seizing up?" I ask, ever hopeful.

"Yeah, a little. It'll be okay, though."

She must be crazy if she thinks I'm going to pass on a chance to touch her. "Scoot over and come sit in between my legs."

I throw a cushion down for her to sit on and tap the edge of the sofa to encourage her over. It doesn't take much, because she's soon taking off her hoodie and moving toward me. My hands instantly go to her shoulders to try to relieve her discomfort.

"Ahh, that's good," she moans, turning me on more than I wish to admit.

I continue working her shoulders and the top of her back. But it's not long before I start to push my luck, and I slide the straps of her top to the edges of her shoulders. Molly doesn't seem fazed, so I continue. I move down the tops of her arms and then back up again. I keep repeating this, each time pushing her top a little farther down. I can't see the front of her, but it can't be covering too much right now.

Eventually, the pull of her body and her vanilla scent is too much, and I can't stop myself leaning forward and placing a soft kiss just beneath her ear. Her entire body shudders. She tilts her head to the side and I take that as permission to continue. I trail kisses down the side of her neck before following her hairline and working my way up the other side when she moves. Needing more, I sneak my tongue out and caress her skin with each kiss. She tastes incredible. My dick presses painfully against my jeans.

I need to focus. This is about Molly, not me. I need to take this slowly. If she's open to the idea of us, I don't want to rush her and scare her off.

My hands gently brush over her skin while my lips continue exploring her neck and ears. I slide them up her arms, down her back, and up again to her shoulders. When I bring my fingers to the top of her chest, she moans quietly, giving me the confidence to continue. I move them lower toward her breasts. I can feel how heavily she's breathing under my fingertips. As much as I want to continue, I know I can't. I move them back down her arms and follow their movement over her shoulders with my lips.

I feel her head move and, when I open my eyes, she's leaning it right back and is looking at me upside down. The passion in her eyes makes my already ragged breath catch in my throat.

Staring right down at her, I move my eyes from hers down to her mouth, then continue over her neck and down her chest. I was right; her top is barely covering her pebbled nipples. Her chest moves dramatically as her heart races beneath.

I lower my head and rub our noses together, making her lips twitch up at the sides. I need my lips on hers now. I move myself forward and press my mouth to hers. Fireworks fly through my body at the contact. Neither of us moves for a few seconds, but then I feel her tongue run across my lips. I open them and touch my tongue against hers. Our kiss only lasts a short couple of seconds before she moves to the side.

Disappointment floods my body as she stands up, but, to my utter surprise, she turns around and straddles my lap. She stares deep into my eyes like they hold all the secrets in the world, and she places her hands on my cheeks before bringing her mouth back to mine. It takes me a couple of seconds to get into it because I'm so surprised, but when I do, I put my hands on her lower back and pull her flush against me while I tangle my tongue with hers, exploring her mouth.

It's a slow but passionate kiss, and it feels like it goes on forever, but when she eventually pulls back, I realise it wasn't long enough at all. I could live the rest of my life just kissing her and be happy. I look into her brown eyes. They're sparkling with happiness, excitement, and pure lust. She has a small, seductive smile on her lips that makes me want to have them on me again.

"Goodnight, Ryan," she whispers, kissing me quickly one last time and grabbing her top to stop it from completely falling. She stops at the doorway, turns, and gives me a heart-stopping smile before disappearing.

CHAPTER TWENTY-ONE

Molly

I've been in bed for forty minutes and still can't wipe the smile off my face. That was, well, just wow. I don't even know how to describe it other than 'completely-out of-this-world-amazing'. The electric shocks are still going off around my body at the memory of his tongue moving against mine.

When Ryan's lips are on mine, I feel things I never have before. I feel beautiful, sexy, wanted, needed, safe, loved.

Loved.

Holy shit, I'm in love with Ryan. It hits me like an articulated lorry. Fuck.

My heart pounds in my chest as the realisation settles in. I'm in love with Ryan Evans. Not just a little in love—full-blown, earth-shatteringly in love with him.

Needless to say, I don't get much sleep. I spend most of the time tossing and turning, wondering what to do about my situation. Do I tell Ryan how I feel? Will he feel the same? What will everyone think? Will his parents accept me?

"Morning, gorgeous," Ryan says with a huge smile on his face as he walks over to me in the kitchen and wraps his arms around me, pulling me into a bone-crushing hug.

"Morning," I say, muffled by his chest.

"I've got to go. I've got a meeting before school." He presses a quick kiss on my lips before leaving the room. "I'll see you later."

Oh shit, I'd forgotten about my date with Adam. Fuck it, I can't just cancel last minute. He's been really good to me; he deserves better than that. "I, uh... I'm out tonight, remember?"

His face drops. "Oh, you're still going?" he asks, shaking his head. "Sorry, I just thought..." He runs his hands through his hair and turns away from me. "Have a good time." With that, he leaves.

"Fuck." I didn't mean to hurt him, but I need to deal with Adam the right way. He's been a good friend to me.

"Molly, are you okay? You've been really distracted all night." Adam looks concerned.

"I've just got a headache. It's been a long day." It's not a lie. I've spent all day worrying about Ryan. I've texted him a couple of times but have only had short replies. He's really not happy with me.

I give Adam my apologies and make my way home not long after that conversation. He says goodbye but still has a concerned look on his face.

The house is in darkness when I get home, so I presume Ryan has already gone to bed—that, or he doesn't want to talk to me and is hiding in his room. I grab myself a glass of water and a couple of painkillers before getting myself ready for bed.

I'm lying in bed, feeling sorry for Adam and trying to figure out the best way to deal with this whole situation, when I hear my bedroom door open. I'm not surprised. I've noticed Ryan always comes down to check on me after I've been out with Adam.

I keep my eyes shut and stay still, but he doesn't leave. After a few seconds, I feel the bed dip as he sits behind me. He gently sweeps a piece of my hair out of my face and tucks it behind my ear. I have to really focus on my breathing not to allow my heart rate to pick up, giving away that I'm awake.

He sits there a while longer, obviously watching me. I'm dying to open my eyes, but I have a pretty good idea of what will happen if I do, and I'm not in the right frame of mind to be doing anything right now.

The bed dips again and Ryan's lips touch my shoulder with a gentle kiss.

"Goodnight, sweet Molly. I love you," he whispers before getting up, walking out the door and up the stairs.

My eyes are as wide as they can be as soon as I know he can't see me.

***

"Hi, angel. How are you?" Susan asks as I sit myself on a bar stool in Cocoa's.

It's Thursday night, and I'm meant to be meeting Emma in ten minutes. I'm feeling really apprehensive.

I didn't see Ryan last night because I did a late shift here for Susan. He was already in bed when I got in. I didn't need to go and check because I could hear him snoring from the living room.

"I'm good. You?"

"Looking forward to Christmas and having Lilly and Dec back. Emma is still out of the house all the time, and we have no idea where she is or what she's doing."

"I'm meant to be meeting her here in a few minutes."

I watch Susan's eyebrows rise. She knows what's happened between us in the last few months, and she looks as worried as I feel.

"Oh, well, I hope it goes okay. I know you miss her." Just as she says that, Emma walks around the front of the shop and enters. "I'll get your coffees and bring them over," Susan says as she spots her daughter.

"Thank you." I head off toward our usual booth.

She sits down opposite me and we just stare at each other for a few seconds, as if we're both trying to form what we want to say.

"Emma, I..." I try to break the silence, but I still have no idea where to start. I'm more than grateful when she interrupts me.

"Molly, no. Please let me speak, I need to get this out." She lets out a big breath before looking down at her hands, rested on the table. She composes herself before she looks back up at me. "Molly, I'm really sorry. I've been completely out of order. I know it's not an excuse, but this year has been so hard for me. I feel like I've lost the other half of me, and my head's been a total mess. I mean, it still is, but I've been working through things and trying to get everything sorted. I know that I jumped off the deep end with my reaction to thinking there was something going on between you and Ryan, but I just felt like you'd forgotten about Hannah."

I go to say something, but she stops me.

"I know that's not true. I know that some of my feelings have been completely irrational. I know that you both loved her and have spent this year dealing with losing her in your own ways, the same as me. You both seemed to have dealt with it so well. I've been so jealous that, while you two got on with your lives, I've completely fallen apart.

"Molly, I miss you so much, and I'm sorry it's taken me this long to get everything together, but if you'll have me, I want to try to go back to how we used to be. Friends?"

I scoot out from my side of the booth to join Emma on her side. When I get there, I throw my arms around her shoulders, pulling her in for a hug.

"I'm sorry, too. I said some awful things I didn't mean. I know I should have come to talk to you about the situation with Ryan, but you've been so damn hard to get a hold of."

I feel her nod against my shoulder. When I pull back and look at her, tears are shining in her eyes, just like they are in mine.

"I'm in love with him, Emma," I blurt out. "Shit, I wasn't going to say that. It just fell out. I only figured this out the other night, and it's confusing the fuck out of me."

"Have you told him?"

"No, not yet."

"I think you should," she says with a knowing smile.

I go on to explain everything she's missed out on. I tell her about Adam, Holly, Jax, and Abbi. About Ryan avoiding me for what felt like forever, and then about this last week—leaving out any details she won't want to hear.

"Molly, I never in a million years thought I would ever say this, but I think you should go for it. Put the poor boy out of his misery, Molls."

We end up sitting there chatting for so long that Susan brings us some food over. It's almost nine before we say our goodbyes and head home.

R yan's car isn't outside the house when I arrive home. I'm really disappointed. After having my talk with Emma, I was ready to sit down with him and sort this out once and for all.

I put my stuff in my room before heading upstairs to get a drink and slob in front of the TV for a bit. As soon as I enter the kitchen area, I spot a piece of paper on the worktop.

Molly,
I've gone out with Holly. Don't worry about doing me any dinner.
See you later.
Ryan x

I just stand there, staring at his handwriting. I feel like I've just been kicked in the stomach. Now, I understand his reaction to me saying that I was going out with Adam on Tuesday night. I'm sure the look on my face right now is similar to his that morning.

Deciding against sitting in front of the TV and waiting for him to come home, I take myself back downstairs for an early night—not that I'm going to be sleeping anytime soon.

I hear the front door open just before midnight, and his head pops around my door.

"Hey Molls, you awake?"

"Yeah, the front door woke me up," I lie. In reality, I was still thinking about him.

"Sorry, I'll leave you to sleep. Goodnight."

"Night."

I listen to him climb the stairs before going back to not sleeping.

After a long day meeting with clients and many bad nights' sleep this week, I'm feeling ready to go home and spend my Friday evening snuggled down on the sofa with a glass of wine and a good chick flick. But I've just arrived for my pole dancing class with Megan to find out that tonight's class is a two-hour session because the instructor is on holiday next week. Everyone else looks excited by the prospect. I, on the other hand, want to find a corner to hide in and sleep.

"Come on, Molly, look at least a little enthusiastic."

I plaster a smile on my face and do my best to look like I'm enjoying myself for the next two hours.

By the time our instructor does our cooldown routine, I'm really ready to have a hot bath and hit my bed. Megan has to practically drag me from the club to my car. When we usually leave this place on a Monday night, it's pretty dead—in complete contrast to what is going on now. There are drunken men in all directions. Many are shouting and hollering our way. Clearly, they think we're dancers from the club, finishing our shift for the night. We put our heads down, along with the other ladies who leave at the same time as us, and head straight for our cars. I say goodbye to Megan and make quick work of getting home.

I have my music on, hot bath running with bubbles so high they're spilling down the sides, and a glass of wine on the side waiting for me.

I just slip my weary body into the hot, soothing water when a loud bang rattles the house. I sit up so fast the water sloshes all over the floor. My heart thunders in my chest as I wait for something else to happen.

"Molly!" Ryan hollers from the hallway.

"In here," I shout back, but not at the same crazy volume.

The bathroom door flies open with such force, I think it's going to come off the hinges. Ryan looks seriously pissed off. I stare at him in shock.

"What the fuck do you think you're doing, Molly? Why the fuck did you ever think that was a good idea? I mean, for fuck's sake, all those slime balls looking at you. You promised me you'd changed, that you weren't going to be like that anymore. First, you go off and sleep with Adam, and now I find out you've been doing this. What the fuck, Molly? You'd better have some good fucking reasons."

I watch as he rants and throws random questions at me. His hands have been through his hair so many times I've lost count.

"Ryan, calm the fuck down. You're going to have to explain what you're going on about. I'm a little confused."

"I'm fucking livid. I'm so motherfucking angry that you would put yourself in that position."

"I don't know what you are talking about." Then, the penny drops. "Wait. You saw me tonight, didn't you?"

"Yes, I fucking saw you. Care to explain why I saw you leaving a sleazy strip club in your skimpy clothes, looking exhausted? Why the fuck would you want to do that? It's not like you need the money."

"You think I was working at the strip club?" I can't help but laugh at this, but the murderous look on Ryan's face soon stops me.

"Well, what the fuck else would you be doing there on a Friday night? Is that what you've been doing when you said you were going to dance classes? Dancing for arseholes for money?"

"Ry, seriously, calm down. It's not what it looks like. Come here." I put my hand out for him. He steps forward begrudgingly and takes my hand in his. "I am not dancing for scumbags for money, and I do not work at the strip club."

"What have you been doing, then?" he asks, looking thoroughly confused. It's only now he's calmed down a bit that I can tell he's been drinking.

"The club has dance studios at the back. I guess the dancers train there and stuff, but they also rent them out. Megan and I have been going to pole dancing lessons."

"Pole dancing lessons? Why the hell didn't you tell me?" Now, he just looks hurt.

"It was Megan's idea. Apparently, it's one of James's fantasies for her to pole dance for him. She swore me to secrecy because she didn't want him finding out and ruining the surprise."

I watch Ryan as he takes this on board. He drops to his knees in front of me and grabs my other hand.

"I'm sorry, Molly. I just jumped to conclusions. I saw you leaving and there were guys shouting stuff, and I just thought... I just saw red, the thought of guys staring at your body like that. I'm so sorry."

I pull my hand from his and cup his cheek, stroking my thumb gently over his cheekbone. "It's okay. I never thought someone would see us and think that. I should have told you. I'm sorry, too."

I move my hand to the back of his head and pull his lips to mine. He only stays there for a couple of seconds before he pulls away and stands up. "What are you do—" My eyes widen in shock. "Oh."

He pulls his t-shirt over his head before making quick work of the button and zip at his waist. He takes his shoes and socks off, then steps out of his jeans. I can't help my eyes roaming over his perfect body. He's barely touched me but still, his boxers are tented. His hands go to the waistband and I suddenly don't know where to look. He bends slightly and his boxers slide down his legs before he steps out of them. He snaps his eyes to mine. "It's okay, Molls. It's all yours."

I can't help the blush that floods my cheeks at his words. He moves toward me and I break my eye contact and run them down his fine body. My breath catches in my throat as I follow his happy trail to his fully erect cock. I swallow hard and lick my lips. I don't realise I'm doing it until Ryan speaks. "Like what you see, then?" He has such a cocky grin on his face.

"Uh-huh," is all I can get out as he steps into the bath with me. The muscles in his arms bulge as he lowers himself and slides his legs along mine.

I know I'm staring at him with my mouth open, but I can't help it.

When his feet hit my arse, I snap out of my daze. "Please join me, why don't you?" I say, laughing.

"Sorry, but I needed to be close to you. You have no idea how I felt when I thought you were dancing at that club." He places his hands on my shins and slowly rubs up and down.

"I'm sorry I didn't tell you. I should have." I smile at him, feeling comforted by his need to protect me. Maybe I should be pissed that he even thought I could have been a stripper, but the knowledge of how much it angered him to think of other guys looking at me pushes that away.

"Come here." He puts his arms up and slides over to one side of the bath. "I'll keep my hands to myself, I promise."

Ryan

Why the hell did I say that? There's no way that will be possible if she slides her wet, naked body up against mine. This has got to be the stupidest thing I have ever done.

After looking a little reluctant, Molly slides herself next to me. The feel of her naked skin gliding against mine feels incredible. Tingles shoot around my body from the amount of skin-to-skin contact I have with her. When she throws one leg over mine and puts her arm around my waist, I have to shut my eyes and concentrate on breathing for a few seconds. I'm so worked up that if she so much as touches my dick, I'm afraid I'll go off like a rocket.

"Are you okay?" Molly asks. When I open my eyes and glance down at her, she has a confused look on her face.

"Yeah, it's just a bit much, you know? I needed a few seconds to pull myself together."

"I know what you mean. This is crazy, but I sort of like it."

"Really?"

"Yeah. A lot, actually," she says, squeezing me a little tighter against her. I can feel all the soft curves of her body against mine, and it's driving me crazy. "I know you said you'd keep your hands to yourself, but you can hold me."

She tilts her head up from where it's resting on my chest, and I see a little cheeky smile playing on her lips. I wrap my arm around her, gripping her hip with my hand and holding her tight.

We lie like that for the longest time, silent and completely lost in our thoughts, but suddenly I feel Molly tense up next to me.

"What's wrong?"

"Something you said when you came in."

"Which bit?"

"You said I'd slept with Adam. I haven't."

"But you went home with him that night we went out with Abbi and Jax. I watched you two go at it on the dance floor, then you dragged him off like you wanted to eat him alive."

"That was only encouraged by you dancing with Holly. It was just innocent dancing until you two appeared and I had to watch her grind herself against you."

"You did that because of me."

"Yes." She looks embarrassed.

"Well, I was only dancing with Holly because I was watching you two. I was quite set on going to the bar and getting shitfaced until she stopped me and suggested I give you a show in return."

"Whoa, hang on. Holly actually suggested you dance with her? To what? Make me jealous?"

"Yeah, something like that. Apparently, she could tell how miserable I was. I can't believe I'm admitting all this; I feel like a right pussy. I didn't bring her home. She actually had to bring me home because I got so smashed after you left with Adam. All I could picture was you and him, and I needed to drown it out."

Molly slowly props herself up on her arm so she can look at me. "So, you didn't sleep with her?"

"No. What happened that night? You didn't come home."

"When we got in his flat, things did get a little heated, but it just wasn't right. We ended up just going to sleep." She lets out a deep sigh while she contemplates her words. "He wasn't who I wanted him to be. Every time he spoke, touched me, kissed me, it just wasn't right. He wasn't who was in my head."

I have to do it. I have to ask. "Who *was* in your head?"

Her eyes snap straight up to mine. "You."

My heart's beating so fast after hearing that one word, it feels like it's about to break through my chest. I pull her tight with the arm I still have around her so that she falls onto my chest, and I kiss her like she's my lifeline. Having her breasts pressed against my chest while her lips are on mine is the best feeling ever. I grab on to her arse to encourage her to straddle me. When she does, my dick lines right up with her, and I can't help but grind against her. The feeling is out of this world.

"Ry," she says into my mouth, but I can't pull away yet. I've wanted her for so long.

Eventually, she pulls her lips away from me, but I go for her neck instead, needing to have my lips on her.

"Ry, I know what I just said, but it doesn't mean it's going to be happening anytime soon."

"That's fine, as long as I can do this."

I continue kissing and sucking on her neck whilst running my hands from her knees up the backs of her thighs, over her arse, then up her back. I continue to gently rub myself against her. I know she's ready for it, because the heat coming from her is unbelievable.

She pulls herself away from me so she's sitting. Unfortunately, there are so many bubbles in here that I still don't get a look at her tits. I guess good things are worth waiting for. She puts her hands on my chest and looks down at me with heated eyes.

"I'm not going to lie, I've thought and dreamt about this so many times over the last couple of months that I've lost count, but I don't want to rush this. I've spent so long convincing myself that this, us, is a bad idea, that I want to enjoy the build-up. I don't want to jump in head first. Does that make any sense?"

"Yes. I'm happy, as long as I know you're mine."

Molly smiles down at me before settling back down, cuddled against my side.

We both fall silent again.

"Did you end up seeing Emma yesterday?"

"Yeah, I did. We actually spent all night chatting and catching up. It was really nice."

"What did she have to say about this?" I ask, gesturing between us.

"She said the same thing she told you in the summer, apparently."

"One day soon, Molly, I will tell you exactly what I told Emma that day, but only when it's the perfect time." She flashes me a dazzling smile and nods at me. "Shall we get out? The water's cold, and it's probably getting late. We've got the stag do tomorrow, so we're going to need our sleep."

I give her a quick kiss on the lips before jumping out and grabbing a towel. I turn back to look at her before I wrap it around my waist and see her eyes are fixed on my arse.

"Molly, if you keep looking at me like that, neither of us is going to leave this house ever again."

"Sorry," she says, shaking her head. "I can't help it. Plus, I know for a fact that if you'd just watched me jump out of the bath and walk naked to the towels, you would be looking at me in exactly the same way."

She's got me there. I would probably be worse, if I'm honest.

"Here," I say, holding open a large towel I can wrap her in. She just shakes her head at me. "What?"

"Shut your eyes."

"Are you serious?"

"Deadly. I said we were taking this slow."

"Okay, fine." I shut my eyes and hold the towel up again.

I hear the water slosh before she presses against the towel in my hands. I wrap it around her body, then open my eyes and watch as she adjusts it and tucks it in place. She looks up at me with a smile before walking out of the bathroom. I go over and let the water out, turn the music off, and grab her glass of wine, still three quarters full. I think that was forgotten when I suddenly stormed in.

When I enter her bedroom, she's propped up against her headboard, still wrapped in her fluffy towel. I walk straight over to the other side of the bed, put her glass down, and lie next to her, pulling her to me and placing my lips back where they belong: on hers.

I move away from her when things start to get heated again. What I said in the bath was true. I will wait forever, as long as I have her in my arms and against my lips. I roll onto my back and pull her so she's once again tucked into my side. She places her head on my chest, right above my heart.

CHAPTER TWENTY-TWO

Molly

I wake up feeling hot and sticky. My whole body is plastered against Ryan.

I'm completely stark naked and stuck to a similarly naked Ryan. I feel myself tense, my heart rate increase, and I can't help but smile. I've dreamt of waking up like this many times, and now it's actually happening.

I feel Ryan's arm tighten around me, so I tilt my head up to look at him. His eyes are shining bright and he has a smile on his face to rival mine.

"Morning. You look happy to see me," I say, smiling at him.

"You have no idea how much. Especially since you're wrapped around me naked."

"Yeah, about that..."

"Don't look at me. As much as I wanted to rip that towel off your body, I didn't. I only just woke up myself. You must have done it in your sleep."

"What about yours?"

"It must have come undone, because I'm still lying on it."

I run my hand down his stomach and feel his muscles clench as my hand travels lower. Much to his disappointment, I move it to the side and over his hip to feel his towel.

"Oh yeah," I say with a smirk.

"You're going to be the death of me, woman," he says, scowling. I can't help but laugh at him. "Do you want tea?"

"Always."

"Okay, I'll go make it if you promise to still be naked in this bed when I get back."

I pretend to think about it for a few seconds before agreeing. I watch as Ryan drags his sexy body out of my bed, and I can't pull my gaze away from his perfect arse as he walks into my bathroom. After a couple of minutes, he returns, wearing his boxers and clearly showing me how much he loves the idea of me naked in bed.

"Hey, if I've got to be naked, so do you."

"I promise to take them off when I come back, but you know what the woman next door is like for nosing in. The only eyes I want on my naked arse are yours, Miss Molly."

I watch him walk out, then lie back in the bed smiling, listening to him pottering around upstairs.

Before long, he's back, carrying two mugs. He places them on the bedside table before taking his boxers off as promised and slipping back into bed. He pulls the duvet over him, but only so it just covers his lap, leaving his top half uncovered for me to drool over.

He looks at me looking at him. "I love your body," I tell him. I trace my finger between his pecs and over his six-pack before running it over his happy trail and off to the side. I know I'm teasing him, but I just can't help myself.

"So, you get to do that, but I have to wait to see your fit-as-fuck body. Explain to me how that's fair."

"Hey, you decided to get your kit off in front of me; I didn't make you."

"It's worth it to watch you drool over me," he says with a knowing wink.

I just shrug him off while I sit myself up against the headboard and tuck the duvet under my arms to keep me covered. I know it's irrational, but I don't want all the mystery gone after only one day.

We spend hours sat in bed, chatting. Ryan makes regular trips to the kitchen for more drinks and food. He regularly tries lifting the duvet from me while I'm not paying attention, but he only ever gets a peek at my side or my leg. Even that has him licking his lips and swallowing hard. I can only imagine how he'll react when I give in. He makes me feel more beautiful and sexy than I have in my whole life. I feel like I'm on cloud nine right now.

Ryan's happy and playful mood falters a little when I tell him I think we should still go to the party tonight as planned, with Adam and Holly. I also watch his face drop when I explain that I want to keep what is going on between us just between us for a while. I know people are going to judge us, and I want to make sure we're solid before we get hit with any scrutiny. Although Ryan isn't happy about either suggestion, I know he understands. Both Adam and Holly were invited to this party weeks ago, and both have outfits ready. Plus, I need to sit down with Adam and explain, and a stag do isn't the time for that.

Before we know it, it's time to get ready for the party. I usher Ryan out of my room so I can do it alone. I want to surprise him with my outfit.

I've just heard the taxi pull up outside five minutes early, so I do some final touch-ups to my hair and make-up before slipping my shoes on.

"Molls, the taxi's here. Are you ready?" Ryan shouts as he comes down the stairs.

"Yes, two seconds." I do one last check in the mirror before turning around, grabbing my bag and pulling the door open.

"Oh, holy mother of God. You cannot go out like that. I'll end up punching any guy who happens to look in your general direction."

I just smile at him. "I got the right one, then?" I knew instantly that the policewoman outfit was his favourite.

It's a navy blue halter neck, cut quite low. It has a full skirt with a lace petticoat making it puff out, with handcuffs hanging off the belt, a badge on my left breast, and a hat. I've paired it with a pair of black lace-topped hold ups and high black platform heels that have silver chains on the back to match my handcuffs. Even I thought I looked pretty hot when I looked in the mirror.

"Yeah, apparently so—although I'm thinking you shouldn't be allowed out wearing it. It should be banned, for use in the bedroom only."

"Oh, for goodness sake, Ry, everyone there will be dressed in something like this. No one will even look twice."

I give him a onceover. He looks truly edible in his sharp black suit. Even the chain and shiny shoes he complained about look great. I don't think he'll be the only one with some jealousy issues tonight. I just know the amount of attention he's going to receive from looking like that.

"Hmm," he says as he watches me grab my coat. Luckily, it's long enough to cover everything so I won't look too out of place before we get to the club. Adam and Holly are meeting us there as they both live in the city.

"Come on." I grab Ryan's hand and pull him toward the front door. He does not look happy about this at all.

"I'm not going to be able to do anything I want to do to you tonight, because you're going with your 'date'." He sulks next to me in the car.

"That may be true, but you'll be the one I go home with at the end of the night and, if you're a good boy, I might even let you sleep in my bed again."

That perks him up a little. He turns his head and leans in to me. "Naked?" he whispers in my ear, his breath giving me goosebumps.

"Maybe."

I hear him groan next to me.

Before long, we're pulling up outside the club. Ryan pays the driver and we both get out. As soon as we enter the foyer, I spot Adam and Holly talking together in the corner. They must recognise each other from the night at the club.

"Here she is," Adam says as he spots me. He comes racing over to me and goes to give me a kiss, but I quickly turn my head so his lips land on my cheek. I know Ryan's watching, his eyes are burning into the back of my head. Maybe this is going to be harder than I thought. I look over to see Holly watching us, too. Has he already told her something's happened between us? From the way she's scowling at me, I'd say yes.

The four of us walk over to check our coats in. Holly removes hers first to reveal a sexy little nurse outfit. To my surprise, Adam whistles next to me. Holly looks over her shoulder and gives him a sexy little smile. He then looks at me and raises an eyebrow. I feel less confident all of a sudden about showing off the outfit I know Ryan loves so much. I take a deep breath and pull it off my shoulders.

"Fuck," Adam says, looking me up and down.

I fidget, feeling slightly uncomfortable with his perusal. I glance over to Ryan to see his jaw set, the muscle in his neck pulsing, and his fists clenched tightly at his sides. I watch as Holly strokes his arm gently, trying to get him to calm down.

Once I've handed my coat over, I see Adam's hand move like he's going to grab mine, so I quickly lift my arm and scratch my nose. The only man I want touching me from now on is Ryan, so until I can talk to Adam, I'm just going to have to avoid it. He moves his hand to the small of my back instead and guides me to the stairs to join Shane, Chris, and the rest of their guests. Ryan and Holly follow. I can only imagine the look on his face.

Not long after we arrive, they announce it's time for dinner. There are loads of round tables filling the room. Each one has red and black feathers coming out of vases in the centre. It all looks a little burlesque, sexual, and seductive. Those are the last feelings I need to be having with Ryan and my date at the same party.

We find our table and take our seats. I'm sat with Ryan to my left and Adam to my right. This should be interesting.

The dinner is bearable at best. The food and wine are amazing; Shane and Chris did a good job choosing the catering. They look so happy. Every time I glance over to them, they're either staring at each other lovingly or laughing at something the other said. It's so lovely to see.

What isn't so good is Adam constantly trying to spark up a conversation with me. It would be fine, as I've always found him easy to talk to, but under the table, Ryan keeps touching me up. It makes my conversation with Adam a challenge, especially every time his hand gets high enough to touch the edge of my knickers. I gently keep slapping his hand away, but he just keeps putting it back, while his cheeky smirk stays on his lips.

Just before the dessert plates are taken away, Shane and Chris both stand up and clear their throats.

"We know it's not traditional to do speeches at a stag do—hell, it's not traditional to do a joint stag, either, so I don't know what I'm worrying about." People laugh a little. "But we just wanted to say thank you to all of you that could come out, get dressed up, and celebrate our upcoming wedding. We also just wanted to take a minute to think of those who couldn't be here tonight. Just because they aren't in the room, doesn't mean they aren't always in our hearts."

I look at Ryan and he swallows hard. We both know that Hannah would have been here with us right now. She was meant to be a groomsmaid alongside me. I lift my hand up and squeeze his shoulder. He looks over at me and quirks the corner of his mouth up.

"You okay?" I whisper. He nods gently, then looks down.

Emma was also meant to be here, but she decided against it. Even though she told me she was trying to get back to a normal life, she still isn't getting involved with much.

"Now, we know she's going to hate us for doing this without warning her, but what would be the fun in that? Before the drinking and dancing commences, we would like to invite our head groomsmaid to say a few words about how awesome we are." Everyone laughs and a handful of people look at me. *Shit.* "Molly, come on. You're not usually one to be shy!"

I stand slowly, pushing Ryan's hand off my thigh as I go. "Uh... yeah, thanks for this, guys. Um... okay... I just want to say that you two are the most perfect couple I know. From the moment you met, all either of you could see was each other. The love you share is obvious to all of us here for you tonight, and for everyone here who hasn't found that kind of love yet." I look straight into Ryan's eyes as I say this. "You're proof that real love is out there. I hope you have a wonderful night and let the celebrations continue well into your married life." I raise my glass. "To Shane and Chris."

Everyone around me does the same, and I can't help but smile as they lean into each other and go at it for a couple of minutes—too long, considering they're being watched by everyone in the room.

"Come on, it's not your wedding night yet. We've got some dancing to do first," I say, making them pull away from each other.

Shane looks up at me and mouths his thanks. "Right, everyone, let's party."

People start to get up from their tables and follow the happy couple into the bar area and the adjoining room where the music has just started up.

"I just need to go to the toilet," I say to my group. "If you go to the bar, could I have a glass of wine, please?"

"I'll come with you. Same for me, please, boys," Holly says, getting up and walking out with me.

Once we're out of view, she puts her hand on my arm to draw my attention. "Has something happened with Ryan? He is even more distracted by you than usual."

I can't help the smile that breaks out across my face.

"Oh my God, it has. Are you together? Why are you here with Adam?"

I try to work out which question to answer first.

"I guess we're together. I'm with Adam because I'd invited him and didn't want to cancel at the last minute. He's been really good to me, and I want to end it with him the right way."

"Well, you might want to be quick about it."

I start walking toward the toilets before answering. "I know, I know. I don't want anything to ruin the guys' night. I intend on doing it first thing in the morning."

"You think tonight is going to go smoothly enough that he won't know?" Holly asks sceptically.

"I hope so."

We both do what we've got to do, then go and find the boys at the bar. They're standing next to each other, but their body language shows their displeasure. "Oh God," I groan.

"It's starting already. Molly, you're going to have to just do it." I let out a big sigh before joining the boys, grabbing my wine and gulping half of it down.

"Take it easy, Molly. The night's still young," Adam says with a suggestive look on his face. Holly and Ryan snap their heads to me.

Everyone around us is starting to get a little buzzed, and they look to be having a better time than we are. We, on the other hand, are stood with an uncomfortable tension around us. Even people that come over to chat don't stay long.

"Come on, let's go and dance," Adam says with a smile.

If he's hoping for a repeat of the club, then he's going to be bitterly disappointed. I don't want to touch him, let alone grind myself against him.

I finish off my drink before getting dragged to the dance floor. Luckily, the songs are fast, and it's easy to just dance by myself in front of him. The whole time, I can feel Ryan's eyes on me from the bar. Every time I look up, I can see him getting angrier and angrier.

Eventually, the song changes to something with a slower beat. The couples around me get close and dance together. I look up to see Ryan shaking his head at me in warning. Adam reaches out and pulls my body to his, but as soon as I get close enough that he can hear me, I tell him I need to use the toilet.

I let him lead me off the dance floor before escaping to the ladies' room. I lock myself in one of the cubicles, put the lid down, and just sit there.

What the fuck am I doing?

Eventually, I get up and go wash my hands to give myself something to do to waste more time.

When I open the door to the ladies' room, Adam is waiting outside for me. He grabs my hand and pulls me around the corner, out of sight.

"What's up with you tonight? It's like you don't even want to be here. Have I done something to upset you?"

"I'm sorry, I'm just not feeling right."

"Okay. Do you want me to take you home?"

"No, I need to be here for Shane and Chris. I can't just leave."

"Well then, can you at least try to look like you're enjoying yourself?"

"I'm sorry, I jus—" I get interrupted as Adam crashes his lips to mine, taking advantage of my open mouth. I shut my eyes for a second as my slightly drunk brain tries to figure out what the hell is happening.

When I open them, Adam is still attached to my lips, but the only thing I see is Ryan stood behind him, looking mortified. I lift my hands to Adam's chest and push as hard as I can. "Adam, stop," I mumble into his mouth. I eventually manage to push him off.

"Ryan!" I shout. But when I look up, he's gone. I can't help but start to panic. "Ryan!" I shout again, moving so I can look down the hall, but it's empty. *Fuck.*

"Has it always been him, Molly?" I turn to see a very sad looking Adam. "I guess I should have seen this coming. You're always talking about him, checking up on him. I don't know why it didn't register earlier, but you've been practically eye-fucking him all night."

"Adam, I'm so sorry. It just happened. He's been my friend for so long, I didn't really expect it."

"How long?"

I stare at him, silent.

"How long has it been going on, Molly?"

"A couple of days. I was going to tell you tomorrow."

"And you thought coming with me tonight would be okay? You thought that you would be able to act normal while your 'boyfriend' watched?"

"I know it was stupid. I realised that as soon as we arrived."

"Well, it's too late now. I suggest you go find him and sort it out. I always knew I liked you more than you liked me. I just hoped I would grow on you."

"I'm so sorry, Adam." I lean forward and kiss his cheek.

"Go. Be happy. I had fun with you, Molly. Just so you know."

"I did, too. I'm sorry." With that said, I leave him in the hall and jog back to the party.

I spot Holly standing at the bar, but she's alone. "Where is he?" I half shout at her. The panic is obvious in my tone.

"He just left, Molly. He came to tell me he had to go, then he ran out of here like a bat out of Hell."

I grab my phone, find a number for a taxi firm, and put it to my ear. I turn back to wave at Holly just as Adam approaches her. He frowns at me but quickly wipes it off his face as he looks down and smiles at Holly.

The wait for my taxi feels like it takes forever. It's fucking freezing outside, and although I remembered to get my coat, it's not like I'm wearing a lot. After what seems like hours, my taxi arrives and I shout my address at the driver.

The journey takes forever. As soon as he pulls up outside our house, I throw money at him and run to the front door. I'm in such a rush, I drop my key twice before I get it in the lock.

I know he won't be in there, but I quickly check my room first, throwing my bag on the bed and ripping my shoes off my feet before dropping them on the floor. I take off running up the stairs and check the living area—also empty. He must be in his bedroom. I again run up the stairs as fast as my legs will carry me, open his bedroom door, and fly into the room. It's empty, but there's light coming from the half-open en suite. I don't think twice before heading over and walking in.

What I find stops me in my tracks as soon as I enter the room. Ryan is stood under the shower, leaning forward with his palms flat on the tiles and his head hung low between them. He looks completely lost.

I caused that. Pain rips through me at the thought.

I move closer to him and, as if he can sense me behind him, he lifts his head slightly and looks at me. My breath catches in my throat at the look in his empty eyes.

I have to go to him. I need to be close to him.

I start unbuttoning my coat and slide it off my arms, letting it hit the floor. Still, Ryan watches me. I reach behind me, unzip my dress and let it join my coat, keeping eye contact with him the whole time. I slide my hold-ups down my thighs and off my legs before once again reaching behind to unsnap my bra. It hits the floor next to my dress, quickly followed by my knickers.

I walk up behind him and place my hands on his chest, encouraging him to stand straight. I then walk around him so I can look into his eyes. What I see in them scares the shit out of me.

They're cold.

What if he refuses to listen to me, let alone believe what I'm about to tell him?

Keep reading to find out what the future has in store for Molly and Ryan in part two

ACKNOWLEDGMENTS

It's been over three years since I first hit publish on this, my very first book. Reading back through it now, it feels like it was a lifetime ago. So much has changed in that time, but I wouldn't want it any other way.

Not only have I learnt a huge amount about this industry, but I've made some incredible friends along the way. It's really been quite an incredible journey. I never expected to write a book, but as I sit here now, I've got over twenty with my name on them. It blows my mind that my life took this turn, but I'm so grateful that it did because not only do I get to spend my days doing something I love, I also get to be at home with my daughter and watch her grow every single day.

Molly and Ryan changed my life, and I will forever be grateful that they appeared in my dream one night. When I originally started to write their story, I didn't tell anyone—bar my husband, who thought I'd lost my mind. But it wasn't until an unexpected meeting with a carer who was looking after my mum at the time that I found the confidence to admit what I was doing. If it weren't for my mum and the long and painful journey we experienced together, I never would have met Michelle, who is still with me every step of the way today. They say everything happens for a reason, and I truly believe that. I know I wouldn't be here now if I'd never met her.

So, I need to say a huge thank you to my mum, who sadly didn't have a clue about any of this, but as I sat next to her hospital bed, typing, she gave me the strength and determination to chase my dream. I know she is up there supporting me every step of the way.

To Michelle, meeting you totally changed my life, and I can't imagine it any other way now. So, thank you for turning up that day, corrupting me, and introducing me to a world I didn't know existed.

To my husband, who allowed me to chase my crazy dream. I don't think he really expected what was to come, or how many books I would write, but he's supported me the whole way. And now my daughter, too. When I wrote this, I had no idea that I was going to be a mum fairly soon, but she's been the best thing to ever happen to me. She inspires me daily, and I hope that as she grows and sees me doing something that I love, I'll inspire her to do the same.

Evelyn, this book must almost be as big a part of your life as it is mine. I can't thank you enough for all the hours you've put in, polishing it up and making it as perfect as possible. I'll be the first to admit that I didn't know what I was doing when I embarked on this journey with just a crazy idea in my head, and I'm sure you'll quickly agree with me after the amount of editing you've done!

And to you, for taking a chance on me, and Molly and Ryan. You've no idea how much it means to me that you've got this far. I hope you pick up many more of my books and I allow you to escape reality with some hot, sexy men and sassy women.

Until next time,

Tracy xo

FALLING FOR RYAN: PART TWO

FALLING SERIES BOOK #2

To my bump, thank you for giving me some time to feel almost normal again so I could get this published. Better late than never!

FOREWORD

Make sure you have read *Falling For Ryan: Part One* before jumping into this one. You will miss out on all the build-up to their relationship, otherwise.

CHAPTER ONE

Ryan

The moment her bra leaves her body, I stop breathing. She has the most perfect breasts I've ever seen. I mean, I've always known this, but I've never properly seen them before. Her slightly tanned skin is flawless, and her pink, hard nipples are just begging for attention. My dick stands to attention and my heartbeat starts to race. She leans forward slightly so she can drop her knickers to the floor. My knees get a little weak at seeing her naked for the first time.

Looking over my shoulder, I keep my eyes on her as she walks up behind me. When her arms wrap around me and her delicate hands rest on my chest, fireworks ignite around my whole body. She pulls me so I'm standing then sneaks around in front of me. We just stand and stare at each other while the water showers over our bodies. Slowly, Molly rises onto her tiptoes and leans toward my ear, her breath making me shiver. Her breasts press against my chest and all I want to do is touch her...

But I can't. First, I need to hear what she's got to say.

"It wasn't what you thought. I was trying to push him off. I've told him everything. It's over. You're the only man I want. Ever," she whispers into my ear.

We both stay completely still, her waiting for my response, me trying to work it out. Eventually, my restraint snaps. I move my hands to her arse and lift her. Her legs automatically wrap around my waist and I press her back to the wall, pinning her there with my hips. Placing my hands on her cheeks, I stare into her eyes. All I see is her passion and love. "Ever?" I whisper, needing to make sure I heard her right.

"Forever," she says firmly, a seductive smile spreading across her face. That does it. I lean forward and gently press my lips to hers, placing feather-light kisses before running my tongue along their seam, asking for entry. She slowly opens up for me. As soon as our tongues touch, the kiss turns from gentle to heated until we're practically fucking each other's mouths. My hands roam her body of their own accord while hers are gripping my hair, keeping our lips connected. As if I'd be going anywhere. My throbbing dick is lined up perfectly with her entrance, and it takes all my willpower not to plunge into her. I keep reminding myself that she wants to take this slow. I'm okay with that, because when we do get there, it will be earth-shattering.

Eventually, Molly moves her hands to cup my cheeks and pushes me back slightly. I reluctantly remove my lips from hers and look into her hungry eyes. We're both panting hard, and her breath brushes over my face.

"I love you, Ryan."

My breath catches. I'm in complete shock. I just stand still, staring at her.

"Ry?"

Allowing her words to wash through me, I feel a huge smile spread across my face. "I love you, too." I lean into her, kissing and nipping down her neck while trying to turn the shower off. When I manage it, I put one arm under her arse and another around her waist, holding her tight, and walk us out of the shower. I grab the biggest towel I can find when I get to the rail and carefully wrap it around both of us before heading to the bedroom and laying her down.

Resting my forearms on either side of her head, I stare down at her. "I love you so much it actually scares me." Her eyes fill with tears at my words. She nods in understanding. "I know we're taking it slow, but I need you. I need to taste you right now. Is that okay?" Again, she nods, as if she's completely lost in the moment.

Intending to take my time, I start with a long, passionate kiss before descending her body. I nibble on the skin of her neck before placing kisses across her chest. When I reach her breasts, I run my tongue along the underside, and she moans and arches off the bed. I continue licking my way around, teasing her until I get to her nipple. She cries out when I suck it into my mouth, her whole body flinching with the sensation I've created within her. She moans and writhes on the bed like she could come just from this alone. Switching to the other, I give it the same treatment.

She's panting hard by the time I trail kisses across her stomach toward my final prize. My mouth waters just at the thought of what I'm about to do. I've dreamt about it for so long, and already the real thing is a million times better. When I reach the apex of her thighs, I kiss down the left one, slowly pushing it out and teasing my lips along her sensitive skin. I kiss across her pubic bone, sneaking my tongue out to taste her skin. Switching to the other leg, I leave her open and waiting for me. When I eventually pull back and look up, her hair is fanned out across my pillow, her eyes are shut, and she has pink cheeks and a small smile playing on her lips. Her chest heaves, making her hard nipples catch my attention.

Finally, I focus on what's closest to me. She's completely hair-free and fucking perfect. I can already see she's turned on and ready for me. My mouth waters for a taste of her. Leaning forward, I blow across her, watching as she shivers.

"Ryan," she moans. I wish I could tease her longer, but I can't wait. "No one's ever—" I lean forward and lick from her entrance up to her clit.

"Holy fuck."

Her taste explodes on my tongue as she arches off the bed. I move my arm and place it across her stomach to keep her still.

"You've only been with arseholes, baby. Just wait and see how a real man does it."

With that, I go back to what I was doing. I run my tongue around her entrance before sliding one finger inside her while my mouth focuses on her clit, licking, sucking, and biting. In only a few minutes, she's screaming my name and milking my finger for all it's worth. I keep moving gently until she comes back down from her high.

That was so fucking sexy.

When she relaxes, I kiss my way back up her body before lying on my side next to her. She's breathless with rosy cheeks from her intense release. I kiss across her jaw before sliding my tongue into her mouth. A low moan rumbles from the back of her throat as she tastes herself on me. When I pull away and stare into her eyes, they're filled with such intensity. A lump of emotion clogs my throat and I have to fight to swallow.

"Wow," she says with a huge smile. "They really were arseholes," she laughs.

She brushes her hand across my cheek, down my neck and onto my chest before pushing me onto my back. "Time to return the favour," she says, raising her eyebrow.

"No."

Her head snaps up to me, her eyes narrowing like I've completely lost the plot. "No?" she questions.

"No repaying favours. You do it because you want to, not because you owe me. What have I told you about doing things for yourself?"

"I don't think this—you—really counts, Ry."

"Like fuck it doesn't." I slide my arm under her and pull her so she is half lying on me. "I've waited so long to have you like this, and I can wait forever for the other stuff. Tonight is about you, so enjoy it. You're going to fall asleep in my arms like you will every night from now on. We'll take all the other stuff one step at a time. I love you, Molly Carter. More than you could ever know."

"I love you, too, Ryan." She rests her head on my chest and snuggles into me. I breathe in her scent and hold her tight. There was a time I didn't think this was ever going to happen, but here I am with her in my arms.

The love of my life.

Molly

I'm awoken by Ryan's phone. When I try to move, I realise he still has me cuddled tightly into him. Our legs are tangled together and his arm is around my waist, keeping as much of us touching as possible.

My memories of last night have my body ready to continue what we started. I want to give him the immense pleasure he gave me. He's still sleeping when I manage to untangle myself from his body, lying flat on his back with the duvet covering him from the waist down. I can't help admiring his well-defined chest and abs. The beginning of his happy trail and V line are just above the duvet, and the sight makes my mouth water.

Crawling over to him, I place light kisses down the centre of his chest, smiling at the soft moans he makes in his sleep. Before I reach his stomach, I run my tongue back up the way I came, prompting another moan. I lightly tease around each of his nipples. His chest starts moving faster; he's going to wake up soon. I continue to his stomach and use my tongue to trace the lines of his six-pack.

"Molly," Ryan moans quietly, but when I look up, he still seems to be asleep. I carefully pull the duvet lower, revealing more of his delicious V line and slim waist. Swallowing, I take a breath before revealing what I really want to see. I can't help but bite down on my bottom lip when his cock is uncovered. It's already as hard as steel and resting well up onto his stomach, and there's a little moisture escaping from the end. I can't really say I've ever thought of them as something nice to look at, but I'm starting to change my mind. Ryan's dick is as gorgeous as the rest of him, and I can't wait to show my appreciation.

I lower my head to the base of his cock and lick up the vein that runs the length of him. When my tongue touches the head of his dick, he startles. I lift my eyes to see him propped up on his elbows, staring down at me with hunger in his eyes and a smile playing on his lips.

"Well, good morning to you, too, Miss Molly," he says, smiling wider. Moving the covers, I settle myself between Ryan's legs to continue the job I started. Our eyes stay connected the whole time. Once I'm settled in place, I take the base of him in my hand. He sucks in a breath at my contact. The second my lips touch him, he lets out a loud groan. It spurs me on and I run my tongue over his head before taking him as far back as I can.

"Molly, shit," he moans.

After working him in and out of my mouth a few times, I pull back so I can run my tongue up him and tease his thick head. When I see a bit of pre-cum at the tip, I lap it up.

"You look so hot doing that," he breathes, his voice deep and rough, making the ache between my legs almost uncomfortable.

I love watching him come apart under my touch. It makes me feel like the most powerful woman in the world. He's panting hard and I can see a bead of sweat accumulating on his brow. I quickly take him back in my mouth and work him hard and fast simultaneously with my mouth and hand.

"Fuck. Molly that feels... ahh... amazing. Don't stop."

I can tell he's getting close, so I lift my other hand to play with his balls that are starting to draw up toward his body. "Molly... I'm going to... ahh fuck!" His whole body flinches as his orgasm hits him, before his cock twitches as he empties himself down my throat. I continue sucking him gently until he's come back down to earth. Lifting myself off him, I place a quick kiss to the tip of his cock before crawling up his body so I can have his lips on mine. I stop when I'm straddling him and have my weight resting on my forearms on either side of his head.

I touch my nose to his and smile down at him. "Good morning, baby."

"It's a fucking great morning," he says, grabbing the back of my head and crushing my lips to his. His arm wraps around my waist, making me fall onto his chest. Before I know what's going on, I'm on my back with Ryan on top of me.

"Have I told you today yet how gorgeous you are?" he asks when his eyes meet mine again.

"No, you haven't." I answer cheekily.

"Well, you're fucking gorgeous, Molly. I will never get bored of these sexy curves," he says as he runs his hands up and down my sides.

"I don't think looking at you will get old anytime soon, either," I say before biting my bottom lip and running my finger down Ryan's chest and stomach. A groan comes from the back of his throat before his twitching dick catches my eye. I raise an eyebrow at him in question.

He lowers himself on top of me and his lips go to my ear. "If you think one blow job is going to stop me getting turned on by your body, then you've got another think coming," he whispers. A shiver runs down my spine and goosebumps prick my skin.

I'm still smiling when I walk into the kitchen feeling very satisfied quite a while later, but movement at next door's window catches my eye. Tugging at the hem of Ryan's t-shirt, I make sure I'm covered before pulling the blinds down that we left open last night. I don't need her creepy stalker eyes on me.

I return a few minutes later with fresh drinks for us and my phone. After getting myself settled on the bed with my tea, I look up and see a scowl on Ryan's face.

"What's wrong?" I ask, concerned.

"Why are you still wearing that? Clothes are banned on this bed." He tries to say it seriously, but I can see the corners of his mouth twitching.

"Hold this, then." I hand him my mug before pulling his t-shirt back off again. "Better?"

"Sorry, what?" he says with a smirk.

"Tea, please." Holding my hand out, I wait for him to pass it over. I take it from him and take a sip before grabbing my phone.

"What's up?" I didn't realise I groaned loud enough for Ryan to notice.

"I've got a message from Adam. I'm almost scared to open it."

"If the one I had from Holly is anything to go by, I would open it." I look up at him, confused, but he just nods toward my phone so I do as he suggested.

Adam: I guess I should thank you for leaving me last night. Holly's awesome.

My eyes widen as I read the message. I can't help but laugh out loud. It didn't take him long to move on.

"What's funny?" I turn my phone round so Ryan can see the message. He holds his up in return so I can see Holly's.

Holly: OMG, thank you so much for storming off last night, and thanks to Molly for dumping Adam. He is incredible. I think I'm in love. Thank you, thank you, thank you. xxx I hope everything works out with you and Molly.

CHAPTER TWO

Ryan

We've been lying in bed together chatting for almost an hour. The whole time, I've had some kind of contact with her. I can't get enough. We're talking about my plans for my week off when her stomach starts to rumble.

"I think it's time I fed my woman," I say, giving her a brief kiss on the lips before getting up and finding some clean boxers to put on. I watch her grab my t-shirt again and pull it over her head. As soon as she stands up, I move toward her and throw her over my shoulder. She squeals in surprise.

"Ryan, what are you doing?" I watch her hands come up to try to pull my t-shirt down to cover her arse. I slap them away.

"Stop that, you'll ruin my view." She eventually stops fighting me and wraps her arms around my waist, placing kisses to my lower back and squeezing my arse. When we get to the kitchen, I put her down on the kitchen worktop before turning around to open the fridge.

"There should be bacon in there. You could make bacon sandwiches," she suggests from behind me. I'm just pulling it out when the home phone starts ringing. Grabbing it from the base, I pass it to Molly for her to answer it. I presume it will be my mum; hardly anyone else bothers ringing the home phone.

"Chris, hi. I'm so sorry..." I can hear him on the other end but not loud enough to make out what he's saying.

"She said I was drunk and Ryan had to take me home?"

"No, that's not exactly true." I can't stand being this close to her but not having my lips on her, so while she's talking, I lower my head to her neck and place light kisses to her skin.

"Yes, we may have got our shit together." I hear Chris squeal like a girl on the other end of the phone.

"We want to keep it quiet for a bit though, so please ca— ahh... can you keep it to yourselves? Shit." While she's talking, I drop to my knees, pull her to the edge of the worktop, and open her legs before planting kisses along the inside of her thigh, making my way to her pussy.

"No, I'm fine, sorry. Go on." I can hear him talking while her eyes bore into mine. I stick my tongue out and touch it gently to her clit, hearing her suck in a breath.

"Y-yes, we h-had messages from th-them."

"YESSS, I a-agree," she shouts as I suck hard on her clit.

All of a sudden, I hear excitement coming from the phone. "Shane, get here now, I'm totally talking to Molly while Ryan is fucking her, you've got to listen." I can hear him laughing on the other end.

"Fuck, Ryan is not... ahh. Shit, I've got to go. Bye." She hangs up the phone and throws it down on the counter, leaning back on one hand to give me better access and holding me in place with her other in my hair. Seconds later, she screams my name and I can feel her pulsing against my mouth. Once she's finished, I sit back on my heels and wipe my mouth with the back of my hand.

Her eyes are glassy from pleasure, I watch as her focus comes back before she shakes her head at me. "I can't believe you just did that. They totally knew what you were doing." I watch her cheeks redden slightly.

"I know, I heard Chris shout. They were wrong, though. I wasn't fucking you."

"Oh yes, because it would have been so much better if they knew you were eating my pussy while I tried to have a conversation with them!" she says, laughing. "I walked in on Chris giving Shane a blow job once in the bathroom in the flat, so I guess it's only fair they got a preview, too!"

***

M olly's stood at the sink, washing up after we've finished eating. I can't pull my eyes away from her. She's still wearing my t-shirt, but because she's so short, it comes to her mid-thighs. Her hair's still a mess from a night's sleep with wet hair and three orgasms, her face is make-up free, and she looks stunning. I walk up behind her, sweeping her hair around to one side before wrapping my arms around her waist.

"What's the plan for the rest of the day, gorgeous?" I ask between kisses to her neck.

"I was just thinking we could chill out here together. I want you all to myself for the day."

"Mmm, that sounds like a good idea."

I wait until she's finished washing up, which takes her longer than usual because apparently my hands roaming under the t-shirt she's wearing are distracting, before I lift her into my arms and walk out of the room.

"Where are we going now?"

"I want to get you all hot and wet," I say, wiggling my eyebrows at her as we head toward her room.

"It won't take much," she says, nibbling on my earlobe.

"I don't doubt that for a second, but that wasn't what I meant, you dirty bitch!" I walk us into her bathroom before sitting her down on the side of the bath, turning the taps on and pouring some bubbles in.

"Oh," she says, looking embarrassed.

"Hey, stop the blushing. Saying that after I've given you three orgasms in just over twelve hours can't possibly embarrass you." Her cheeks redden even more. I just smile and shake my head at her. She can be so cute sometimes.

After checking the temperature of the water, I walk over to her. "Arms up, Miss Molly." She does as she's told and I pull my t-shirt from her body. I'm still in awe of her curves. "I didn't tell you last night, but watching you strip in front of me when I was in the shower was one of the hottest things I've ever seen."

"Really? I thought you were too pissed off to notice."

"Never. There's nothing in the world that could distract me from your body, Molly. The moment I realised you came after me, I forgot about being pissed, and when you started getting naked, I almost forgot what happened."

She stands up and lifts her hand to cup my cheek, looking into my eyes. "I'm sorry. He just came at me. I was trying to get him to stop."

"It's okay. I know. I knew straight away, really. You never would have had your eyes open to see me if you were into it. I panicked. Please, can we just forget about it? I think the evening ended how we both wanted it to, so let's just move on."

"Oh, it ended better than I could have imagined." She reaches up on her tiptoes and places a kiss against my lips. I take the opportunity to lift her up and gently lower her into the bath. Quickly removing my boxers, I slide in behind her so she can rest back against my chest.

"This would be much more comfortable if your dick wasn't poking me in the back, you know."

"You're just going to have to get used to the fact that, if you're naked, or just in the room, I will be hard." I tighten my arms around her and smile.

She's mine at last.

Molly

After Ryan washes every inch of my body, as well as shampooing and conditioning my hair, he gets out, much to my disappointment. I'm instructed to enjoy the rest of my bath and that he'll meet me upstairs when I'm done.

While I'm lying here, thinking about what he could possibly be doing, it suddenly occurs to me that it's his birthday soon—two weeks, I think. I need to come up with something amazing to show him how much I really do love him. After only a few minutes of thinking, it comes to me—and it's brilliant. Something he'll never forget.

Once I'm back in my bedroom, I smile to myself when I see that Ryan has left me his Oxford Brookes t-shirt, the same one he gave me to wear the first night I stayed here with him. I pull it over my head and slip on a pair of knickers. After towel-drying my hair, I grab my laptop and start looking into hiring the dance studio for an hour next Thursday evening.

Disappointment fills me when I get upstairs and find it empty. I grab myself a drink, settle on the sofa in front of the TV, and find some home improvement show to watch. It's another forty minutes before I hear Ryan coming down the stairs. When he comes into the room, he takes one look at me and a wide smile breaks out across his face. My heart threatens to explode, seeing his happiness. Much to my delight, he's still topless, but he's put on a pair of jogging bottoms.

"What have you been up to?"

"Just arranging a surprise. Nice t-shirt, by the way."

"Thanks, it's my boyfriend's!" I didn't think it was possible, but his smile gets even wider. He looks so happy.

"Say that again," he says with his eyes twinkling.

As soon as the words leave my mouth, he's on me. I'm wrestled so that I'm lying on the sofa with him between my legs, hovering above me with his hands on either side of my head.

"Again," he demands, poking my nose with his.

"Boyfrie—" He crashes his lips to mine before I can even finish the word. His tongue delves into my mouth, kissing me deeply. When he pulls away, we're both panting. Sitting back, he looks down at me. I rake my eyes across his naked skin, enjoying the view, and I raise my eyebrows at his tented trousers.

"Always," he replies to my silent question. Tingles erupt in my stomach knowing I affect him so much just by being close. It makes me feel beautiful and sexy. I watch him put his hand in his pocket and pull my phone out before he places it on my chest. "This has been going crazy."

Grabbing it, I see that I've got ten missed calls from Chris and three voicemails. I groan. Whatever's on those voicemails isn't going to be good, I just know it.

"What's wrong?"

"Three voicemails from Chris. Are you ready?"

"Uh..." I press play and wait.

"Oh Ryan, oh yes," Chris pants. "Oh yeah, just like that. Give it to me, Ryan."

"Oh God," I groan, rolling my eyes before reluctantly pressing play on the next one.

"Oh please, Ryan. Harder Ryan, harder. Fuck me harder," Shane says in a breathy voice.

"Oh Ryan, that's so good. Your cock feels so good inside me. Oh yeah, right there, yeah, right there. Oh, I'm gonna ahhhhhhhhhhhhh!" Chris shouts on the final message.

"I'm going to fucking kill those two."

I realise Ryan hasn't said anything while listening to the messages but, when I look up at him, it's instantly obvious as to why. He's too busy biting his lip, trying not to laugh. "Ryan!" I squeal at him and slap his arm.

"Sorry, sorry." He can't hold it in any longer and ends up clutching his stomach where he's laughing so much. It's infectious. When I've calmed down enough to speak, I grab my phone and put it to my ear.

Chris answers on the second ring. "Hey, what's up?" he says, laughing.

"I was going to be nice, but after that, I've decided my speech at your wedding is going to include you getting caught at it on the hood of your car in the supermarket car park, having to be rescued after a sex swing and handcuff experiment gone wrong, and the time you had to have a butt plug removed at the hospital after Shane got too rough." I watch as Ryan's eyebrows go so high, they almost hit his hairline.

"Molly!" Chris shouts so loud I have to pull the phone away from my ear. "You can't do that. Not all of them are true!"

"Don't care! I've still got a month, I'm sure I can make some others up."

"You wouldn't."

"Watch me, you fuckers," I say, trying to keep the humour out of my voice. "I love you, even though you're both little shits."

"Love you, too, Molly. Enjoy your sexy man."

I look up at Ryan after putting my phone back on the coffee table. He's thinking so hard, I can almost see the cogs turning behind his eyes.

"Which ones are true?" he asks.

"I'll let you think on that. Come here, I want to be in your arms." Moving over, he pulls me into his side.

We spend the rest of the afternoon cuddling and watching TV. I've just got up to decide what to make for dinner when Ryan's iPad starts ringing on the coffee table. Thinking it's probably either Abbi or Liv FaceTiming, he grabs it quickly so he doesn't miss them.

I hear him groan behind me before he starts speaking. "Hi Mum."

I also groan, but I'm careful to keep mine internal. Looking over my shoulder, I make sure I'm out of her sight.

"Ryan, for goodness' sake, put some clothes on. You'll give that girl the wrong idea if you're walking around half-naked." I can't help but roll my eyes at her words.

"Mother!" Ryan admonishes. "Can we please have a conversation where you don't say anything bad about Molly? I don't know how many times I have to tell you how wonderful she is. You'll love her, I know you will."

"As you've said many times, she's your friend, not mine. I just have to put up with her."

I can't help but wonder what she'll say when she finds out we're together. Will she tell Ryan to get rid of me? Shit, will she give him an ultimatum? And if she does, what would he do? I know how important his parents are to him.

"So... How's dad?" Ryan asks to change the subject. I zone out of their conversation while I start to make dinner. I'm almost finished when something Ryan's mum says catches my attention.

"Have you met the guy Abbi is seeing? Doreen said she saw her with some bad boy type in town yesterday. She should know better than that."

I quickly make my way around behind the iPad without being seen by

Ryan's mum and start waving my arms around, trying to tell Ryan not to say anything. I know for a fact that Abbi will not appreciate Ryan gossiping about her and Jax.

"Uh no, sorry, can't help. Abbi's a big girl now, she can make her own decisions. She won't let history repeat itself. She's learnt her lesson."

"I hope you're right, but Doreen said he had tattoos and everything."

"Mum, will you stop? Abbi is her own woman and can make her own decisions," he repeats. "I'm sorry, but I need to go. I'll ring you when I have a bit more time in the week."

"Oh, aren't you coming up here for a few days?" From the sound of her voice, I would put money on her pouting as she said that, trying to guilt him into it.

"No, sorry. I'm busy most of the week."

"With her?"

"If by that you mean Molly, then yes." She huffs at that announcement. "Speak soon, Mum. Bye," Ryan snaps.

"I love you, Son. Bye."

Ryan disconnects the call without saying anything else. Throwing himself back on the sofa, he runs his hands through his hair and leans his head back with his eyes shut. I walk over, sit down next to him, and place my hand on his thigh. He flinches at my contact and looks at me, looking frustrated and disappointed.

CHAPTER THREE

We have Molly's delicious chilli for dinner before spending the rest of the night in front of the TV, watching all kinds of rubbish. It's just after ten when she starts yawning. Sending her up to my bed, I tidy our mess and lock up the house. I'm as quick as I can; knowing Molly's waiting for me in my bed has my already twitching dick standing to attention. I take the stairs three at a time and join her. She looks so tiny curled up in my huge bed. There's a sadness in her eyes when I come to stop next to her that makes my stomach drop. Quickly dropping my trousers, I slide under the covers and pull her body to mine.

"What's wrong, gorgeous?"

She bites down on her bottom lip to stop it from trembling and shakes her head at me.

"No, something is wrong. Please tell me."

"It's nothing, I'm just being silly."

"I don't care how silly it is, if it makes you look like this, then it's important. So, come on, out with it."

She looks down before she opens her mouth. "What if your mum never accepts me? You'll end up ditching me because I don't fit in with your family and your mum's wishes for you."

My chin drops. Is that what she really thinks? Does she really not know how much she means to me? I roll her over onto her back so I can look down at her. She needs to see in my eyes how much I mean what I'm going to say. She refuses to look at me and moves her head to the side. Gently placing my hand on her cheek, I pull her head back so she has no choice.

"Molly," I whisper. "Do you really think that, just because my mum doesn't like you, I would dump you?" She shrugs her shoulders and swallows down her emotion. "You really have no idea how much I love you, do you?

"Shit, Molly, it's all-consuming. I feel like my heart's going to explode at any moment. When I'm with you, I want to be closer. When I'm not with you, you're all I can think about, my body actually aches not being with you." At some point during my little speech, I close my eyes. "I love you so much, Molly. Hell, those words don't even begin to explain how I feel about you. No one is going to be able to get me to give you up. Not my mother, or anyone else who has an opinion about us. She will either learn to love you, or I won't be seeing her very much. My sisters already love you, and I know my dad likes you, even though he has to put up with my mum. We'll win her around and, if we don't, then fuck her. This is my life, not hers, and I will spend my life with the woman I love."

I'm suddenly on my back with Molly straddling me. I've no idea where such a little person gets all her strength from. She places her forehead against mine and looks into my eyes.

"I love you like that, too," she whispers before dropping her lips to mine. It soon turns into something more passionate when she lowers herself and grinds her hotness against me. Grabbing her arse, I encourage her to keep moving. It feels so good. I'm dying to bury myself inside her. "Ryan," she whispers when she pulls away from my mouth. "Make love to me."

I think about it for a few seconds before making a decision I never in a million years thought I would.

"No." It's almost painful to say.

"No?" Her face drops. She looks hurt.

"I promised you we would take it slow, and that's what we're going to do. We're not having our first time after my mother's upset you. When we do, it's going to be perfect, just like you."

"Oh," she says as I watch her lips quirk up to a smile. "Are you sure you're okay waiting?"

"I would wait forever for you."

She puts her face into the crook of my neck, lays her whole body on top of mine and holds me tightly as she places light kisses against my neck and shoulders. Rubbing my arms up and down her back slowly, it's not long before I feel her breath even out. Once again, I drift off to sleep with a smile on my face because I have the most amazing woman in my arms.

<hr>

I wake up the next morning and roll over in search of the body that should be pressed up against mine, but I can't find her. Quickly jumping out of bed, I grab the trousers I took off last night, go into the bathroom to do my stuff, and then head out of my room to find her. As I get to the bottom of the first set of stairs, I hear music coming from her room below. I'm disappointed when I find it empty, but only for a few seconds because I realise there's water running. She's in the shower—perfect! I walk into her en suite to find her stood under the spray of water with her back to me. I stand there for a moment, admiring the water running down her body and over her perky arse. Making my way over and removing my trousers as I go, I walk straight up behind her. She flinches when our skin connects. My hands grip on to her hips before she leans back into me.

"I missed waking up to you, gorgeous, but I'm thinking this might make up for it."

Running one of my hands up her side, I pull her wet hair away from her neck so I can put my lips there. I nibble my way from her shoulder up to her ear while my hands roam around her body. The skin of her neck vibrates as she moans quietly. Finding her pert nipples, I pinch them between my thumb and forefinger, causing her hips to move and her arse to grind against my already throbbing dick. Her chest is starting to rise and fall faster under my hands. "You like that, gorgeous?"

"Mmm."

"What about if I did this?" I say, as my right hand moves from her breast and down her stomach. Her muscles twitch as I run over them. "Will I find you ready for me?"

"Mmm," she groans again.

When my hand reaches the apex of her thighs, I decide against going straight for what we both want in favour of teasing her a little more. Running my fingers gently over her folds, she moans. "Ryan, please," she pants.

Unable to deny her, I slowly slide my finger where she needs it. Her hips buck the moment I find her clit. She falls back against me as I reach lower and plunge two fingers inside her. Wrapping my arm around her waist, I hold her tight as her knees buckle with the pleasure racing through her. I love how responsive she is to my touch. I continue the onslaught until she's shaking in my arms. With the heel of my hand pressing down on her sensitive and swollen clit, I bend my fingers inside her, stretching her open until her walls start rippling, showing the beginnings of her release. She groans as I pick up the pace and suck on the sensitive skin of her neck. In seconds, she's crying out my name as her orgasm takes over her.

She tilts her head back and looks at me with glazed eyes. Smiling down at her, I place my lips on hers. Turning in my arms, her fingers trail down my back, causing goosebumps to prick my skin before she grabs my arse. My cock presses against her stomach and she smiles against my lips.

Stepping back, she pushed me against the tiles before dragging her nails down my stomach and wrapping her hand around me. The sensation of her stroking me has my head falling back with a thud. Reaching up, she trails kisses down my neck and across my chest, while continuing to work my cock.

I watch, enthralled as she moves down my stomach before kneeling on the floor of the shower. Her lips trail kisses down my thighs and my muscles quiver with my need for more.

The sight of her on her knees in front of me already has my balls starting to tingle, ready for release, and her mouth hasn't even touched me yet.

Pulling back, she looks up at me and licks her lips. My cock twitches with anticipation. Smiling when she sees the pre-cum on the tip, my whole length twitches as she gently licks it away. She smiles up at me, clearly knowing how much she affects me. Deciding she's teased me long enough, she leans forward and wraps her hot lips around my length. My head once again falls back against the tiles as I focus on her movements. With my eyes firmly shut, my fingers thread in her hair and grip tightly as she works me.

Taking a deep breath, I prepare to look down again. The sight of her on her knees with my cock in her mouth and desire in her eyes takes my breath away.

I can't help but wonder how I was so lucky to find such an amazing woman who loves me as much as I do her, after already having Hannah in my life. I'm the luckiest bastard in the world.

It only takes her a few minutes of working my dick before tingles run down my spine and my cock pulses in her mouth, shooting my load down her throat. A loud growl rips from me as she milks me for everything I've got.

When she's finished, she leans back on her heels and wipes her mouth with the back of her hand, looking up at me. A cheeky smile plays on her lips. Slowly, she stands, making sure to kiss a trail back up my body. Before she's at full height, I lean down so my lips meet hers.

Grabbing her shampoo, I go about getting her washed for the day. Once her hair is done, I squeeze a large amount of her shower gel on my hands and run them over every inch of her body, taking my time over my favourite parts, making sure they're extra clean. She gasps when my fingers run over her pussy, and I can't help myself. I lower myself to my knees, throw one of her legs over my shoulder, and taste her until she's screaming my name for the second time in thirty minutes.

Molly

"Wow, morning, Molly. You had a good weekend, by the look on your face," Jax says when he arrives at work.

My cheeks heat. "It was good, thanks. How was yours?" I quickly head into the kitchen to make us a drink, mostly to avoid eye contact with him.

"It was brilliant, thank you."

"You've really fallen for her, haven't you?" I ask, happy to shift the focus to his blossoming relationship with Abbi.

"I have, yeah, but she only wants something casual. She's so busy with uni and placements that she doesn't want the added pressure of a relationship." A wave of disappointment washes over his features.

"Oh." I thought they were together, from the way he talks about her. "You're... *exclusively* casual though, right?"

"We're not shagging anyone else, if that's what you mean."

"If it helps, I know she really likes you. I reckon she'll come round to the idea eventually. But she's right—she is crazy busy, by the sound of it."

"I just wish we could be official."

I can't help but feel sorry for Jax. He has such a big heart. "Everything happens for a reason, Jax. It will all work out as it's meant to."

"Yeah, I guess. So... your weekend?"

I go on to tell all about my weekend, explaining about Friday's class and the stag do, leaving out any bits that involve Ryan and I kissing or being naked. When I've finished, he looks at me with a raised eyebrow.

"I don't quite understand why you look as happy as you do if that was your weekend, but I'll let it go for now. Although I should warn you, my imagination is running on overdrive, thinking of all the reasons," he says with a suggestive smirk. I knew I wouldn't be able to keep any secrets from Jax, but I'm glad he's not pushing it. "Right, I'm heading out. I'm meeting a client."

"Oh, who?" Guilt is written all over his face.

"Uh, Mrs. Jones."

"I thought I was meeting her on Thursday?"

"Yeah, she, uh, called this morning to rearrange." Narrowing my eyes at him, I wait for him to elaborate, but it never comes.

"Right..." He grabs a folder that contains the ideas I've been working on for another client I was going to see on Friday. "Why are you taking those?"

"Oh, he couldn't make Friday, so I said I'd stop on the way back from Mrs. Jones later this morning. Right, bye." He practically sprints out of the office, leaving me in his dust, completely confused.

I make the most of my time alone to ring one of Ryan's mates to see if I can get him to help me arrange his birthday surprise next Thursday. I was relieved when I woke up before him this morning—it gave me the opportunity to get a couple of numbers off his phone.

I ring his colleague Will first, and I'm relieved when he says he's willing to help me out and promises to keep his mouth zipped about the whole thing. I've met him a few times over the years and he seemed the most trustworthy of Ryan's friends and colleagues.

Next, I make the call I've really been dreading, but I know I've got to start somewhere.

"Hi Karen, it's Molly, Ryan's friend. I wanted to speak to you about his birthday next week."

"Molly, hello," she says coldly. I'm still feeling slightly positive, because she didn't put the phone down on me.

"Look, I'm not going to beat around the bush. Things between you and Ryan have been strained since I stayed at your house, and although he won't admit it, he misses you. I know you were hoping to see him this week."

"Where are you going with this?" she snaps.

The prospect of spending some time with her only son is obviously enough to endure me, because she soon agrees that she and Dave will come here this weekend. I think it helps that I explain I'm hoping Abbi and Liv will be here, too.

As soon as we say a clipped goodbye, I make a start on inviting everyone else to my celebratory plans.

Rounding the corner into the office after popping downstairs to grab some lunch, I stop dead in my tracks. There, sat on my desk, is a huge bunch of flowers, all in dusky pink like the bunch he got me for my birthday in the summer, only about four times the size. I quickly make my way over to them and pull the card out.

To my gorgeous girl,
I love you with all my heart. xxx

All of a sudden, there's a bang at the bottom of the stairs, then someone's running up. My heart pounds in my chest, thinking it could be Ryan. I can't help feeling disappointed when Jax appears.

"Fucking hell, look at the size of them." His eyes are zeroed in on the flowers behind me. My cheeks heat when he focuses his gaze back on me. "I get that you're not ready to talk about it yet, but let me just say this: I'm so fucking happy you managed to work everything out."

"Thanks. It's just early days, you know?" He nods, accepting my reasons to keep things quiet for now.

Getting the giant bunch of flowers into my tiny car is only the beginning of my challenge of getting home after the damn thing decides not to start. Thankfully, after a few failed attempts, the engine roars to life. I'm halfway home when it hits me that I need to stop and see someone.

Turning the car around, I head toward my new destination. It only takes ten minutes before I'm walking across the car park and down the little pathway before I come to a stop in front of her. As always, the flowers here are fresh. I guess Susan has been recently to replace them. Crouching in front of her, I read what it says for what must be the one-thousandth time in the last nine months.

In loving memory of
Hannah Susan Morrison
A perfect daughter, sister, and friend
14ᵗʰ July 1989 – 15th January 2014

I let out a huge sigh while I think about everything that's happened since the last time I was here.

I once again wonder what she would make of all of this, but I'm more convinced than ever that she'd be happy.

All she ever wanted was for the people she loved to be happy.

I'm just about to walk away when tingles run down my back, and that can only mean one thing. Standing up, I turn around to see Ryan stood a few feet away with a small smile on his face. I rush over and throw my arms around him.

"You coming to see Hannah, too?"

"No. I actually came this morning. When you didn't get home after you messaged to say you were leaving, I got worried, but something told me you'd be here. I wanted to make sure you were okay."

"Ryan, I'm more than okay, and you know what?" He quirks his eyebrow at me in question. "I'm pretty sure Hannah is, too." I turn my head to look in her direction and smile.

CHAPTER FOUR

Ryan

I dropped Molly at work this morning so her car could stay here, and I'm now pacing the living room floor, waiting for the clock to tick around until it's late enough for me to pick her up and explain what I have planned.

I know how much she hates surprises, and I can see how much it's killing her, trying not to ask about it. I told Jax I would pick her up at three o'clock; he's been in on it since I booked it on Sunday morning. He somehow managed to rearrange both of their meetings and clients for the end of the week without getting Molly too suspicious.

As soon as the clock hits two-thirty, I can't wait any longer and set off running down the stairs and lock up the house. I try to drive slowly to her office to waste a little more time, but I still end up getting there early.

"What are you doing here?" Molly asks when I walk into their office.

"I've come to pick you up for your surprise. As soon as you're finished, we can head off." I'm not sure whether she looks excited or nervous.

"Are you going to tell me what it is?"

"I might give you some clues."

"Hey, Ryan," Jax says as he comes out of the kitchen. "Couldn't wait any longer to whisk her away, then?"

"Nope."

"Let me just shut my computer down and we can go."

I help her tidy up and take her dirty mugs to the kitchen. "Ready?"

"Yes, lead the way." I let Molly go ahead of me, then place my hand at the small of her back so I can have some contact with her.

"Why have you got so much stuff? And why have you brought my flowers?" She asks, looking from the car to me with confusion written all over her face. I can't help myself.

"I didn't want them to go to waste at home while we were away."

"You're taking me away?"

"Yes, just the two of us, for four whole days," I say before shutting her door and jogging round to the driver's side.

"Where are we going?"

"I'm not telling you. Now, put some of that music on you love so much and sit back and relax."

"**O**h my God. Are we staying here?" Molly squeals next to me as I bring the car to a stop.

"Yes, we are."

"How do you find the most perfect places? First the beach hut, and now this cute little log cabin in the middle of the forest!"

"Just lucky, I guess. I first thought about going abroad, to Paris or something, but when I got upstairs after leaving you in the bath I realised I had no idea if your passport was in date. So, I just went on Google and stumbled across this." I've barely got my last word out before Molly is getting out of the car and rushing toward the cabin.

"Come on. I want to see inside." She stands by the front door with her hands crossed over her chest, looking impatient as she waits for me to catch up. I walk slowly just to watch her reaction. "For fuck's sake, Ryan, hurry up!"

When I get there, I give her a sweet kiss before putting the key in the lock, opening the door, and gesturing for her to enter. "Oh my God, this is so cute," she calls back to me.

Once she's explored every inch of the place, she heads toward me, launching her tiny body at me. I stumble back against the door and she wraps her legs around my waist, arms around my shoulders, and kisses me until we're both breathless.

When she pulls back and looks at me, the love and lust I see in her eyes make my mouth water.

"You know, if you really want inside me that badly, you could have just asked nicely. I'd probably given it up. You didn't need to do something like this." I can't help but smile at her.

"That isn't what this is about. I told you I would wait as long as you want, and I meant it. This," I gesture around the cabin with one arm while holding her to me with the other, "is about us spending time together. Just the two of us. So, phones are going on silent, and we're disappearing from the rest of the world for a few days."

* * *

It feels like it takes forever to get all our bags in, but that's probably because all I want to do is wrap my arms around Molly and relax. Once we're done, I concentrate on putting all the food away in the kitchen whilst Molly sorts out the bedroom and bathroom. I'm bent over, putting the last few things in the fridge, when I feel her behind me. Standing up, I look over my shoulder to see her leaning her hip against the worktop, her teeth digging into her bottom lip.

"Enjoying the view?" I ask.

"Oh yeah. It's just a shame you're wearing too many clothes."

"I did consider not packing any for either of us and having a naked holiday, but something told me you wouldn't be up for that."

"You're right. There are some times that clothes are a necessity, like when cooking or sitting on someone else's sofa," she says, flicking a glance behind her.

"I'm just going to put dinner in, then I've got something for you."

"Oh, from the present bag?" When Molly went to pull the 'present bag' from the car, I snatched it out of her hands, much to her shock. I wanted to make this weekend special, so I came up with a few different things I knew she'd love, to surprise her with.

"Yes, now go and get comfortable. I made a lasagne this morning, so it only needs to heat up." I watch her eyes go as wide as saucers.

"You made a lasagne this morning?" I grab it from behind me to show her. "Wow, I have the best boyfriend ever!" she squeals, before heading into the bedroom.

Ten minutes later, I'm sat on the sofa with the couple of the presents I've got for her, a bottle of champagne, and two glasses, in the hope that we're about to celebrate. I look up when the bedroom door opens, and my body heats up a few degrees. She's in her usual at-home attire of lounge trousers, a vest, and a zip-up hoodie. Her face is make-up free and her hair is piled in a mess on top of her head. My perusal of her curves has her rooted to the spot, so I get up and walk to her. When I'm inches from her, I place my hands on her hips and look down into her eyes.

"You're always so fucking gorgeous, but you couldn't be any more perfect to me than when you're like this." She looks down, a little embarrassed. Lifting my hand, I tip her head back and capture her lips with mine. I pull back before I want to, take her hand, and drag her over to the sofa. There will be enough time for that later. I sit her down next to me, then turn myself so our knees are touching, and I look her in the eyes.

"Ry, are you okay? You look nervous."

"Yeah, I'm fine. I have something to ask you." I grab the first present I want to give her and hand it over. She looks at me in question.

"Open it, then." I watch as she slides the lid off and looks at the contents, confused.

"A key?" She looks from me back down to the dusky pink key in the box. I grab her free hand in mine to get her attention.

"Molly, will you move in with me?" I watch her eyebrows draw together in confusion.

"I already live with you."

"No, currently you're my housemate. I'm asking you to move in as my girlfriend." She stares at me with a completely blank expression. Panic starts to erupt within me.

"Molly?" My voice snaps her out of it because, before I know it, I've been pushed back against the sofa and she's straddling me, kissing the life out of me. I wrap my arms around her waist and pull her to me so there's no space between us. She eventually moves away from my lips and starts kissing along my jaw and down my neck.

"I. Love. You. So. Much," she says between kisses. "I. Didn't. Think. It. Was. Possible. To. Be. This. Happy." I move my hands and gently grab her cheeks, pushing her face back up so I can see her.

"This is only the beginning," I say before crashing our lips back together.

When my hips start grinding into her warmth, I realise it's probably time we stop before we can't. "Molly," I whisper into her ear as she nibbles on my neck. Placing my hands on her shoulders, I encourage her to sit up.

"What?" she pouts, making me smile.

"I've got more plans for tonight."

"Oh, but you're all ready and raring to go," she says, rubbing herself against my very hard dick.

"I always am when I'm around you. It will be worth the wait, gorgeous."

"Wait. You're serious? You're going to leave me in this state?" I slide my eyes down her body. I removed her hoodie during our little make-out session, which means her heaving chest and pert nipples are very obvious. I sit myself forward and take one into my mouth through the fabric of her top, making her moan, before paying the other one the same attention.

"Yes, that was the plan," I say, just as the buzzer on the oven starts going off. "Dinner's ready. You get the table laid and I'll dish up." I pick her up and place her on her feet, listening to her grumble something about getting laid as she walks off to the kitchen while I rearrange myself in my jeans.

Molly

We've just finished eating, and I can't wait to be lying in his arms while the log burner crackles in front of us, or in the gigantic bath surrounded by bubbles and candles. I'm going to have to see if there's a shop so we can get some, because I doubt he thought about them when he was packing.

"Molly?" Ryan asks, pulling me from my musings.

"Sorry, was in my own little world."

"What were you thinking about?"

"How perfect you are." My cheeks blush a little at my admission, but the smile he rewards me with is worth it.

"So, you never actually answered my earlier question."

"What, you mean me throwing myself at you wasn't enough?"

"It gave me a clue," he teases.

"Yes, I would love to move in with you." I get up and perch myself on his lap so I can place a kiss to his lips. "Dinner was delicious, thank you."

"I learnt from the best."

"So... there's a second present on the coffee table. Do I get that one?"

"Yes." He laughs as I jump off his lap and rush toward it. "I should warn you, it's not as meaningful as the last one. I just thought you would like it." I pick it up, surprised by the weight of it. I carry it back to the table so I can open it with him.

"Oh my God, I was just thinking we needed some of these for when we make use of that huge bath." I can't believe my eyes when I pull the lid off the box and see a selection of different sizes of my favourite vanilla scented candles.

"I know how addicted you are to them."

"Thank you so much. I love you." Moving behind him, I wrap my arms around his shoulders. "Fancy testing that bath out?"

"Maybe later. I thought you might want to do something else first."

"Um, can't think of anything, unless you're going to continue what we started on the sofa earlier." He shifts in his seat at the thought.

"Oh, we will continue, but that wasn't what I was thinking. Pull the curtain back." I'm confused by the request but do as he says.

"We have a hot tub!" He walks up behind me before engulfing me in his arms.

"Yes, we do. Fancy trying it out?"

"Hell yes!" Rushing toward the door, Ryan follows me out. He removes the lid and turns the underwater lights on.

"You get ready while I tidy up the kitchen and pour us some bubbly."

"Okay." Racing off into the bedroom, I rummage through my stuff to find a bikini. I don't remember seeing one when I unpacked, but Ryan seems to have thought of everything.

After a few minutes of hunting, I give up. "Ryan," I shout. Moments later, he's in the doorway.

"What's up, gorgeous?"

"I can't find a bikini. Did you pack one?"

"Oh, damn, I must have forgotten," he says with a shit-eating grin on his face. "Whoops." I place my hands on my hips and glare at him.

"Whoops?" I question.

"Guess we'll just have to go in naked," he shrugs, trying to play it cool.

"Yeah, I guess we will." I pull my top over my head and his eyes darken as he takes in my topless state. I quickly remove my trousers and knickers before grabbing a robe hanging in our wardrobe and draping it over my arm. "Are you just going to stand there staring, or are you going to join me?" I walk past him and out to the decking, making sure my hips swing seductively.

When I get out to the hot tub, he's already put the bottle of champagne on the side in a cooler, and two glasses, along with a couple of cans of beer. I hang my robe up and ease my body into the soothing warm water. I sigh as my muscles relax almost instantly.

I just get settled in one of the moulded seats when Ryan appears in the doorway of the bedroom, completely naked. He stands and stares at me with a smirk on his face. I can't help myself—I move over to the edge of the tub and rest my chin on my hands on the side, appreciating the work of art in front of me. I slowly take him in from head to toe... and maybe back up again. His hair is a total mess from where I was running my hands through it earlier. My eyes skim over his broad shoulders, over his sculpted torso, toward his slim waist. Moisture fills my mouth at the sight of his very obvious excitement, before I make my way down his strong thighs and to his feet. My heart's pounding and my clit throbs as I make my way back up and commit it to memory. When I get to his eyes, they're dark with lust, his teeth attacking his bottom lip.

"Finished?" His lips quirk up in a smirk.

"Never. But I think I need to use my hands to ensure what I'm seeing is real." His eyebrow lifts and he slowly starts making his way in my direction. The closer he gets, the faster my heart beats. "You're perfect."

"Not as perfect as you," he says, before bending down and placing his lips against mine, stopping me from responding.

Once he releases me, I move back and he lowers his body into the water. He pours us both a glass of champagne, then hands me one.

"To us," he says, clinking his glass against mine and taking a sip. I follow suit.

"This is gorgeous. I'm guessing it's not a cheap bottle."

"Only the best for my girl." My heart flips at his words. I put my now empty glass down and look at him.

"The last time we were on holiday, you promised me that my Prince Charming would come when I least expected it. Well, I can honestly say I never expected it to be you." I squeak when he grabs me and places me across his lap.

His lips drop to mine in the sweetest, most passionate kiss I have ever experienced. Goosebumps break out across my skin, my heart pounds harder, and heat pools between my legs. I gasp in shock when he pinches my nipple, putting an end to our kiss. He moves to trail kisses up my neck instead.

"Have you ever had sex underwater?" he whispers in my ear.

I shake my head at him. "No, I haven't."

"One day we will."

"Why not today?" I pant out.

"As amazing as it would be to bury myself inside you right now, I've promised you a perfect first time, and doing it in the hot tub is not that." I don't know whether I'm excited or disappointed by this. "Have you ever had an orgasm underwater?"

"Yes." He pulls back, looking a little shocked by my announcement. "I do it in the bath," I admit after a few seconds.

Ryan groans loudly. "I would pay to see that, Miss Molly," he says, before sucking on my neck as his hand descends toward my centre. "I like firsts with you." His fingers run through my wetness, making my whole body twitch.

"You look so fucking hot when you come for me, Molly. I'll never get bored of watching you," he says, taking my nipple in his mouth as my body comes down from its high. "I love your body. It's so fucking sexy."

"That's weird, because I thought your type was slim blondes," I say, shrugging. I try to keep a straight face, but I can feel my lips twitching.

"I used to think that, but there's only one woman who's my type, and that one woman is you," he says, placing me back in the seat and hovering his body above mine while he kisses me. Reaching out, I grab his length, slowly stroking him up and down. His growl vibrates against my lips as I tease him.

"Sit on the edge," I say against his lips.

"I'm fine here."

"I know, but you'll be even better on the edge." I watch as he follows my instruction. I settle myself in front of him and take him back in my hand while he looks down at me with hooded eyes. "Have you ever had a blow job in a hot tub, Ryan?" He shakes his head. "Good, I like firsts with you, too," I say with a smile.

I begin teasing him, putting my lips everywhere but where he wants them the most. I cover his thighs and lower stomach in kisses while my hand continues to work him slowly. The more I tease him, the more his body begins to tremble.

"Molly, take me in your mouth." I really wish I could deny him, but hearing his deep, gravelly voice leaves me with no choice. I move my hand and run my tongue from the base of him up to the head, before sucking on the tip and lapping up his pre-cum. I love the noises he's making as he watches my every move. His fingers tangle in my hair, encouraging me forward. I slowly let my lips slide down the length of him until I feel him hit the back of my throat.

"Oh, fucking hell, Molly," he groans out. "Yes," he hisses as I start a punishing rhythm. I run my other hand up as high as I can on his stomach, feeling his muscles twitch at my contact before pulling it back down, letting my nails gently scratch his skin. "Argh... shit... yes," he shouts out, just before I feel the first drop of his salty goodness hit the back of my mouth. I continue sucking him until he's dry. He then slides his body back into the water and wraps his arms tightly around me while he catches his breath.

CHAPTER FIVE

Ryan

When Molly starts falling asleep in the hot tub, I decide it's probably time to get out. She's pretty tipsy, having finished off the bottle of champagne herself. We were too busy chatting away to pay much attention to how much we'd drunk or how much time had passed. It's only now when I start to get out that I realise how pruned my skin is.

Scooping Molly up in my arms, I hold her tight against me as I carry her into the huge walk-in shower. I turn it on and wait a few seconds before standing us both under the spray. Molly's eyes stay shut the entire time, even when I place her down on her feet so I can wash the chlorine off us properly.

She starts snoring the moment her head hits the pillow, and I cover her up and head out to the deck to tidy up and cover the hot tub back up for the night. Once I've locked us in, I slide into bed next to her and she immediately lays her head on my chest and wraps an arm and leg around me tightly. Her wet hair is dripping water down my side and arm, but I don't care; she's in my arms, and that's all that matters. She mumbles something I can't make out before she says something that makes my heart hurt for her.

"I have someone at last who loves me." My hold on her tightens and I kiss the top of her head.

"You do. I love you more than you could ever know, and I'm going to show you how amazing you are every single day."

I wake the next morning with Molly still wrapped around my body. I can't help smiling; it's the first time since we got together that she hasn't been up before me. I hold her tightly and enjoy the feeling of her body cuddled against mine, listening to the sound of her breathing. I lie there as long as I can, but eventually I have to go to the toilet. I carefully unhook Molly from around me and slide out of bed. She groans but doesn't wake up.

"Where did you go?" she asks, pouting when I slide up against her.

"Sorry, I needed a wee. I brought you tea, though, to make up for leaving."

"Hmm, good boyfriend," she says, smiling. She opens her eyes and looks at me, causing her smile to widen. "Morning, baby."

"Morning, gorgeous," I say as she moves herself so she's sat up against me and I drop a kiss to the end of her nose.

"Did I see a present in your hand?"

"You don't miss a trick, do you?" She smiles up at me sweetly. "You have a present every day we're here, and seeing as the weather's shit, this is today's." I hand her the gift box full of a range of girly chick flicks for us to spend the day watching.

Molly

I'm woken up the next morning when a large box is placed on my stomach. I prop myself up on my elbows and look between the box and Ryan, who is perched on the edge of the bed, anxiously waiting for me to open it.

"Why do you look nervous about this one?"

"It's just different. I'm not sure if it's something you've ever done before, or want to do."

"Okay, interesting." I pull on the tails of the big bow tied around the box before cautiously lifting the lid and looking in. On the top is a thick, knitted bobble hat. I pull it out and look at Ryan curiously.

"Keep going," he says, nodding toward the box.

By the time all the items are out, I'm pretty sure I know what we're doing today. Lying across the bed now is a pair of walking boots in my size, some thick walking socks, a scarf to match the hat, and some gloves.

"Going hiking, are we?" I ask, looking over at Ryan.

"I thought it would be fun. We won't if you're not up for it, though."

"Of course I'm up for it. I can't read a map for shit, though, so you're going to have to do that bit. I'll just do as I'm told!"

"No problem. I've helped the kids at school out with their Duke of Edinburgh expeditions; it can't be that hard. I'll go make us breakfast, then we can head out. It's nice and sunny so it should be fun."

Hiking isn't something I would choose to do myself, but seeing how excited Ryan is about it makes me think it could be fun. He's obviously done it before.

Once we're both stuffed full with Ryan's fry-up, we wrap up warm, tie our boots, and head out. It might be sunny out, but it's bloody freezing.

"So, the guys who own this place left some maps in the welcome pack," he says, waving one in my face. "This one is five miles, so it should take us two hours at the most." Five miles sounds like a long way to me, but two hours seems doable. We walk around all day, after all. I watch as Ryan studies the map and decides which direction we should be heading before falling into step next to him.

***

"Ryan?"

"Yes, gorgeous?"

"You do know we've been walking for two and a half hours, right?"

"Yeah, I guess we've been going slower than I thought we would. According to the map, we should be nearly back now." I look over at him, once again studying that map, but unlike earlier, I have absolutely no confidence that he has any clue what he's doing. I'm sure we're walking in circles. "I hope you're right, because I'm dying for a wee and I've got blisters."

"Of course I'm right. Come on, keep going," he says, linking his arm around mine and pulling me forward.

"Molly, come on, get up. We will never find our way back if you just sit down," Ryan says grumpily when he turns around to find me sat on the ground.

"I know that, smart-arse, but we have been walking for nearly four hours. I've resorted to weeing in a bush while God-knows-what bit my arse, and my blisters have blisters. I just want to sit down for a few minutes. Maybe it will give you time to figure out how to read a fucking map and get us out of this forest before it gets dark."

Yes, I know I sound like a whiny bitch, but I'm exhausted, sweating even though it's like, minus ten out here, and I'm dying of thirst. And don't even get me started on my feet. I'm sure they're never going to fit in my pretty little heels again.

"Don't get moody with me. It's not my fault the map is wrong."

"Yes, because that is the problem here."

"Fine, blame it all on me. How about you try to figure it out?" he says, shoving the map under my nose.

"I told you before we left I couldn't read a map. It's a shame you didn't realise you couldn't, either. I knew we should have just done the walk marked with the little coloured posts designed for kids."

"Your attitude isn't going to get us out of here, so suck it up and help me figure it out."

I grumble to myself before heaving my aching body off the frozen ground to peer at the map, which is hardly even legible after the surprise rain shower we had earlier.

"Ryan, you can't even see the track clearly now that all the ink has run. You might as well not bother looking at it. Let's just keep going. It won't be long before the sun starts going down. We need to get out of here." Ryan screws the map up and shoves it in his pocket before catching up with me where I've started hobbling my way down the track.

"Look over there—headlights. It must be a road. Come on," I say, grabbing Ryan's hand and practically running in that direction. We've been walking for just over five hours now. The sun has just gone down, and it's drizzling. All I want is a hot bath and a glass of wine... or two. I never want to step foot in a forest ever again. I'm just about to start making my way up the small hill to where I think the road is when I come to an abrupt stop. "Oh, for fuck's sake!" I squeal.

"What's wrong... oh." Ryan says when he comes to a stop next to me in front of the rather large stream. "Um, I'll jump across, then I'll catch you when you jump," he says sceptically.

"You think I can jump that with my little legs?"

"We haven't got much choice, really, have we?"

With that said, he backs up a couple of steps before launching himself across the stream and just making it to the other side. He looks up at me encouragingly. "Your turn."

I walk back a little, muttering about my hatred of hiking and forests and anything related to the two, before I run a couple of steps, shut my eyes, and hope and pray I make it to the other side. My leading foot hits something before I feel Ryan's arms come around me. Cracking my eye open, I look up to him. He's laughing at me but I don't care, because I'm not on my arse in the freezing cold stream.

"You caught me," I say, smiling at him.

"I'll always catch you, gorgeous," he says, kissing my forehead. "Come on, let's find that road."

We walk a few more minutes before we step foot on the first bit of tarmac we've seen for hours. I sigh in relief, knowing that this road will somehow join up to the one we want. When I look up, I can't believe my eyes.

"Oh my God, is that the cabin?" Ryan appears from the trees behind me and looks in the direction I'm pointing.

"Oh, thank fuck for that. I was beginning to think we'd be stuck in the forest forever."

"I knew you believed me and were lying about it all being fine," I say, as we start marching in the direction of our cabin. In only a matter of minutes, Ryan is unlocking the door and I'm pushing past him to lie face-down on the bed. After a few seconds, he crashes around in the kitchen, and I hear the kettle click.

Oh, a cup of tea may go some way to making me feel normal again.

It's not long before I hear his footsteps getting closer. I still haven't moved from my face-down position.

"Molly?" I hear him laugh behind me.

"Go away, I'm dying!" I grumble back at him.

"I've brought you a cup of tea. Roll over." I shake my head at him. It doesn't deter him, though, because his hands are soon on my waist as he flips me over himself. I groan as my muscles pull with the movement. I know he's looking down at me, I can feel his stare burning into my skin, but I refuse to open my eyes. He sighs before he moves and walks out of the room. I worry that I might have pissed him off, but then I hear the most amazing sound: the bath running.

"I thought that might cheer you up," he says when he comes back in and sees the smile on my face. "Now, let's get you out of these wet clothes. You're soaking the bed." He goes to my feet and undoes my boots. I hiss through my teeth when he pulls them off. "Shit, sorry, gorgeous." He carefully pulls off the walking socks, but they feel like they've fused to my skin when he peels them from my blisters. "Bloody hell, no wonder you were complaining. Your blisters really do have blisters."

He stands up and pulls my leggings down, being careful of my feet as he passes. He then grabs my hands and pulls me so that I'm sitting so he can remove my coat, hoodie, and t-shirt. When I'm left in just my underwear, he stands back and has a good look.

"You look fucking hot."

"Shut up. I'm sweaty, my hair is frizzy from the rain, and my feet are about to fall off. There isn't an inch of my body that is looking hot right now."

"You clearly aren't seeing what I am, then, because to me, you've never looked more perfect."

"You're right. What I'm seeing is my boyfriend, who just got me lost in a forest for hours, stood in front of me with way too many clothes on." His eyes run the length of my body once more before he reaches behind him and pulls his t-shirt over his head and drops it on the floor, pushes his joggers from his hips and steps out of them. Crawling onto the bed between my legs, he places his hands on my waist and lifts me higher so I'm resting back against the headboard. He leans over and passes me my cup of tea.

"Drink this, then we're having a bath." He quickly scoots off the bed and walks toward the bathroom. I can't help but watch his perfect arse walk away. "I know you're staring," he says, before looking over his shoulder and giving me a cheeky smile. I shrug at him. I love his body; there's no way I'll stop looking at it.

Once he has the bath ready, he returns to our room to drink his coffee with me.

"Right, gorgeous girl, bath time." Putting his mug down, he leans forward, pressing his lips to mine. His tongue delves into my mouth and I join in. I sigh as his hands tickle down my arms and around my ribs so he can pull my bra from my body. He kisses a trail down my neck and across my breasts, goosebumps erupting in his wake as a throb begins between my legs. Sucking my nipples into his mouth when he reaches them, I moan in pleasure as sparks shoot off around my body. He continues kissing down my body until he's at the bottom of the bed. His fingers hook around the sides of my knickers before he gently pulls them down my legs and lets them drop on the floor. His hands delve behind my knees and I squeal in surprise when he suddenly pulls me down the bed until he can grab onto my arse and lift me. I wrap my legs around his waist and hold on to his neck, revelling in the feeling of his hot skin against mine. When we're in front of the bath, he looks down at me and smiles, his eyes dark with desire.

"What?"

"I'm still wearing too many clothes."

"Put me on my feet and I'll take them off for you," I whisper seductively in his ear. He slowly lowers me and I continue my descent, kissing down his chest, following the waistband of his boxers when I get to them. Gripping the elastic, I pull them down his legs, releasing his hard dick. His eyes are simmering with desire as he stares at me on my knees in front of him. Taking him in my hand, I slowly suck him into my mouth. I give him one long, hard suck before standing back up and smiling at him.

"Fucking tease," he mutters before grabbing me around the waist and lowering us both into the hot, bubbly water. My blisters sting like a bitch for a few seconds but it soon eases. We get ourselves comfortable with me lying between Ryan's legs and my back against his chest. When I say comfortable, I mean as comfortable as I can be with his cock poking me in the back.

We lie in silence for quite a while, just enjoying the warmth of the water and each other, along with the scent the candles are giving off. I'm just starting to doze off when he speaks.

"I had a message on my phone when we got back from Will, telling me to meet him and the guys at the strip club for drinks on Thursday night for my birthday. I'd rather just spend it with you, if I'm honest, so I'm going to tell him I've already got plans." I'm suddenly really glad I have my back to him, because he would be able to see right through me if we were having this conversation face to face.

"Don't be silly, Ry. Go out and have fun. I've booked you in for the weekend. One night apart won't hurt."

"It's not just being away from you, though. Why would I want to go to watch half-naked women dancing when I've got the sexiest woman on the planet at home, waiting for me?"

"You're going to have a laugh with your mates, not to look at strippers. Well, I hope so anyway," I say, laughing. "Plus, I'll be waiting for you naked in our bed when you get home."

"Hmmm, that does make it more appealing."

CHAPTER SIX

Ryan

The last full day of our break has come around too fast. Once we got out of the bath last night, I found an Indian takeaway leaflet in the welcome pack and we ordered ourselves enough food to feed a small family for a week. After walking for so long, we were hungry, but our eyes were definitely bigger than our bellies. We lazed around in front of the TV but ended up going to bed pretty early. We were both exhausted from our excursion. I'm fairly sure Molly will never let me forget about my diabolical map reading skills.

Even though we went to sleep early, we still woke up late this morning and spent until lunchtime cuddled together and rolling around under the duvet. I love having Molly make me come with her hand, and especially her mouth, but I can't help the desire to bury myself in her growing every day. I promised her I would wait, and I will, but it's all I can think about.

We eventually got up and had sandwiches for lunch before jumping in the hot tub and chilling out some more. I haven't told Molly yet, but I've booked us a table at a restaurant in the local village tonight, so we're going to have to get out soon and get ready. Although, having spent all day looking at her naked body, I'm having second thoughts about letting her get dressed. I've got a taxi booked for seven so we can both have a drink.

Leaning over, I grab her hips and pull her over onto my lap.

"Hey," she says, smiling up at me.

"Hey, gorgeous. You ready for today's surprise?"

"Oh yes, what is it?"

"We need to get out and showered, then you can have it."

She narrows her eyes at me and pouts. "Can't I have it now?"

"Nope, come on." I lift her tiny body up and carry her out of the hot tub, through the cabin, and into the shower. I let us get blasted with cold water for a few seconds before it warms up.

"Fuck, that's freezing," she shouts, trying to move from under the spray, but I hold her tight to me. It's the first innocent shower we've had together. It's hard, pun intended, to stop Molly's attempts, but I intend to enjoy her later after our meal.

Once we're done, I get her to sit on the edge of the bed wrapped in her towel while I go and get the biggest gift box I brought with me.

As we walk back into our bedroom, she looks at me with hungry eyes. I'm not sure if they're for me because I only have a towel wrapped around my waist, or if they're for the box I'm carrying.

"Oh my God, it's huge," she squeals, clapping her hands together.

"That's what I've been told," I deadpan, but she just looks at me with raised eyebrows.

"Oh, of course, that, too," she says. "I've got no complaints yet."

"You won't ever have any complaints, Miss Molly. Especially if your past experiences are anything to go by." I can't help feeling smug.

"That's true. If you want to turn it into a competition, you've won hands-down already. The only other person to give me as many orgasms as you have is me!"

"And how I'd love to watch you do that," Just the thought of watching Molly pleasure herself makes my dick twitch under my towel.

"Hmm. Can I open the box now?" she asks excitedly.

As I place it down next to her, she quickly turns so she's sat on her knees, looking down at it, excitement filling her eyes. She slowly pulls the bow open and lifts the lid off. Painfully slowly, she moves the tissue paper to the side and reveals the first items in the box. When she looks up at me, she's got a naughty smile on her lips. My heart pounds and my dick twitches again. The moment I saw the lingerie set in the shop, I just knew it would look stunning on her. She reaches into the box and pulls the bra out. It's a dusky pink, my favourite colour for her, with silver detailing and a bow at the cleavage, and there's a matching thong in the box, too.

"These are gorgeous, and the right size."

"They will look gorgeous on you, you mean. Of course they're the right size. I'm not likely to forget any detail of those perfect tits any time soon."

She places both items on the bed before turning her attention back to the box to unwrap some more. She gasps before pulling out the dress I've chosen for her. She has to get up onto her knees so she can see all of it.

"Did you choose this yourself?"

"Yes, do you like it?"

"I love it." She turns the dress around, holds it against herself and looks down. It's a soft grey colour and has a deep V in the front that's going to do wonders for her cleavage—and my view tonight. It's tight around her waist before it flows loosely to her knees. "Ryan, are you okay? You look a little flushed." I have to clear my throat before answering.

"Yeah, sorry, just imagining what it will look like on the floor later."

"A bit presumptuous, aren't you?"

"Nah, you're a sure thing."

She thinks about it for a few seconds before flashing me a smile. "Yeah, I guess I am where you're concerned."

"There's something else in the box." I nod toward it and she dives in.

"Oh my God. Ryan!" she screams, then jumps at me from the bed. She hits me with such force, I fall back with her on top of me. She doesn't pay any attention to the loud thud that was my arse hitting the carpet, because she's too busy shoving her tongue down my throat. Not that I'm complaining.

Once the shock's worn off, I roll us over so she's on her back and I'm between her legs without breaking our kiss. My fingers automatically go the towel still wrapped around her and pull it open so I can get my hands on her sexy body. She has similar thoughts because she reaches down and pulls my mine open. When she relaxes back down, my throbbing dick lines up perfectly with her very ready entrance. She sucks in a breath when she feels the head of my cock brush her sensitive skin. I can't help but thrust my hips slightly so I'm rubbing against her. It feels so good, and the desire to slide right into her is almost painful.

"Ryan," she moans against my lips.

I pull back and look at her. She's fucking stunning. Her chest is heaving with her increased breathing, her cheeks are flushed, her eyes are bright with lust, and her drying chocolate hair is fanned out around her head on the cream carpet. I can't help but think she looks like an angel. I sit back on my heels and admire her.

"So, you like them?"

"Ryan, they're Louboutins. I fucking love them. They're so expensive, though."

"Only the best for my girl," I repeat my words from the other night.

When she moved in and insisted on paying more than I wanted her to, I promised myself I would somehow give it back, so this is me doing that. She's always helping everyone else out and doing thoughtful things for them. It's now her turn to be well and truly spoilt.

She frowns at me, but I just shake my head at her. "Come on, gorgeous girl, we need to get ready. I want to see if you look as hot as I imagined in the shop in that outfit. The taxi's picking us up at seven, so you've got an hour and no more." I kiss the end of her nose, then get up and go into the bathroom so I can shave and finish getting ready while she faffs about.

"Where are we going?" she shouts through to me.

"Wait and see."

Fifty minutes later, I'm sitting in the living room, catching up with what's been going on in the world while we've been hiding out here. I can't for the life of me understand why it could possibly take Molly so long; she was perfect before she started. I've been sitting here fully dressed and ready to go for over twenty minutes now, trying to figure it out.

I look down at myself. I'm wearing a light blue shirt because it's Molly's favourite—apparently, it brings out my eyes—a black pair of smart trousers, and black lace-up shoes. I hate dressing up. I'd much rather go in jeans and a t-shirt, but I don't think they'd let me in the restaurant dressed like that. I do, however, refuse to wear a tie.

"Are you nearly ready, Molls? The taxi will be here in a minute."

Two seconds after I finish speaking, she appears in the bedroom doorway, and I swear to God I actually stop breathing. I don't think I've ever seen such a beautiful sight. My eyes run down her body from head to toe, taking it all in. She's styled her hair in loose curls that hang around her shoulders. The underwear and dress do unbelievably awesome things to her tits. The dress emphasises her tiny waist before the fabric hangs loosely around her thighs, then shows off her toned calves and her shoes. Fuck me, the shoes are pure gold. I may never let her take them off.

"Do I look okay?" she asks hesitantly, a small smile playing on her lips.

I can't do anything because I'm frozen to the spot. The only things that are moving are my eyes, roaming all over her body, my heart that is beating two million miles an hour, and my dick that is straining so painfully against my trousers that I'm sure it's going to burst through any moment.

"Ryan?" She's staring back at me, concern filling her eyes. Eventually, she hobbles over and crouches in front of me, placing her hands on my knees. "Are you okay?" she whispers.

"I... um... you..." I let out a big breath I didn't realise I was holding and try again. "You just took my breath away. You look stunning, Molly. I can't believe how lucky I am."

"Thank you. And thank you for choosing it for me. I love it and it all fits perfectly. I'm the lucky one."

"I love you, gorgeous." Just as I say that, my phone goes off to alert us that the taxi's outside. "Come on, let's grab our coats."

I look back when Molly isn't right behind me, to see her hobbling my way. "I thought you said everything fit perfectly. You can barely walk in those shoes."

"The shoes are perfect, Ry. It's the bloody blisters!" I hold Molly's coat out for her when she gets close enough before pulling mine on. Turning back to her, I sweep her up in my arms and walk over to the front door.

"Ryan," she squeals. "What are you doing?"

"Carrying you out to the taxi. You can barely walk on a flat surface let alone the stones out there. Can you open the door, please?" She wraps one arm around my neck and reaches the other out to open the door for us. Once we're out, she double-checks it's locked behind us before I walk us quickly to the waiting taxi.

The restaurant I've chosen is just over thirty minutes away. I knew the instant I opened their website that Molly would love it. It's an old thatched building with white rendering and black beams. The photos on the website show it looking really romantic inside, and the reviews of the food are outstanding. I'm looking forward to seeing her face when she takes it all in. She's still demanding I tell her where we're going, but so far I've managed to refuse. I know we're nearly there now, though, and she's about to find out. I look over at her to find her looking down at her lap.

"Are you okay?"

"Yeah, my stomach just feels a bit weird. Probably just hungry." She just shrugs it off like it's nothing, so I think no more of it, especially as I feel the taxi coming to a stop in front of the restaurant. "Oh, please tell me we're going in there," Molly says excitedly.

I knew she'd love it.

Twenty minutes later, we're sat at a little table in the back corner of the restaurant, sipping on glasses of champagne after ordering our starters and main courses. Molly's eyes are still as wide as when we pulled up outside, taking everything in.

"I love this place. It's so cute."

"I knew you'd love it the minute I saw it online."

"Did you see the sign as we came in saying it's in the top ten of the most romantic restaurants in the country?" Of course, I know this, but I don't want to dampen her excitement.

"Is it?" I ask, and she tells me all about it. My heart bursts at her happiness over something as simple as a nice restaurant.

"What's the matter, Ry? You look serious all of a sudden."

"Sorry, I was just thinking."

"About what?"

"It's nothing, really."

"No, go on. You always make me spill."

"I was thinking about how just bringing you to a nice restaurant has made you so happy. It's like no one has done it for you before."

"No one has done it before," she replies sadly. "No one has ever done anything like you have done for me this weekend. I've never been spoilt as much as I have in the last few days."

"I hate that no one has, but I also love it, because it means I get to do it now."

"I love that you get to do it, too. It wouldn't be the same if it were anyone else."

"Are you going to tell me yet what you've got planned for my birthday?"

"Um... nope. You'll have to wait and see. I think you'll be surprised, though."

Before I have a chance to try to convince her to tell me, our starters arrive, looking too good to eat. But as soon as the smell hits my nose, my stomach grumbles, reminding me how long it's been since we ate.

Apparently, Molly's is good, if the noises she's making are anything to go by. It's like I've been transported back to the summer in the pub in Cornwall where she was doing the same thing while unknowingly giving me the bluest balls known to man. At least this time I know that she'll see to my excitement when we get back later. I'm also glad the tables are spaced farther apart here so that every other bloke in the place isn't enjoying her like the last time.

"Oh my God, that was so good," she eventually says when she's cleared her plate and come up for air.

"Yeah, I got that idea. You didn't look up once!"

"Ugh, you must think I'm a right pig."

"No, I love that you enjoy your food. I often wonder why you aren't the size of a horse, though," I say, laughing.

"Yeah, nice. Thanks, Ry."

I just shrug at her as the waitress comes to clear our plates.

Molly eventually stops grilling me about suggesting she should be fat just before the main courses arrive.

Both our dishes are out of this world, and we hardly say a word as we enjoy the incredible flavours.

When our plates have been cleared and we've ordered our desserts, I pluck up the courage to ask her the question that's been eating me for a while. If my thoughts on the subject are correct, I really hope I'm not about to ruin our evening.

"Molly, can I ask you a question?"

Molly

"Uh, yeah sure," I say sceptically.

"Other than your earrings, you never really wear any jewellery. Why is that?"

"Wow, never in a million years did I see that question coming." I can't help but laugh at him a little.

"It's just that I've spent my life surrounded by women: my mum and sisters, and then Hannah, and they all had sentimental bits of jewellery that they never took off because it meant so much to them, but you don't seem to have anything."

"You know the earrings are Hannah's, right?"

"I thought they were familiar."

"They're the only things of hers I took after she died. I wanted a piece of her with me at all times. Susan and Pete bought them for her twenty-first birthday." I'm trying desperately hard to keep myself together. I don't want to ruin an amazing evening.

"Oh," is all he says.

"I don't wear anything else because I haven't got any meaningful pieces."

"That's kind of what I thought. You know, you really have spent time with some worthless shits," he says, gracing me with his megawatt smile before leaning around and reaching for his coat.

"Oh, you haven't, have you?" Smiling slyly, he turns back around and hands me a cream square box with a dusky pink ribbon around it. "What is it with you and dusky pink?"

"I remember it being the main colour in the photo of that interior design magazine you showed me when you tried to explain shabby chic to me," he says, shrugging.

"Ry, you have already spent so much money on me with what I'm wearing. I can't accept anymore."

"You haven't got a choice, Molly. Open it."

I let out a resigned sigh. I know he earns decent money, but I don't want him to spend it all on me. I pull the bow open, then slide the lid off. My breath catches in my throat at the sight of it.

"Oh, it's beautiful." My eyes sting and a lump clogs my throat as I stare at it.

"Hey, it's not meant to upset you," Ryan says softly.

"It's just too much. You've completely overwhelmed me." My chin wobbles as I fight to contain my emotions.

"I just want to show you how much I love you, Molls."

I nod at him, too emotional to speak.

"Do you want to know why I chose it?" I nod again and look up at him through my tear-filled eyes. "It's a heart because you own my heart..." I can't help the happy sob that erupts from my throat at his words. "And it has a little forget-me-not at the end. Look." He points at the necklace. "To remind us of who brought us together."

I cover my face with my hands to try to hide from the other customers around us. Ryan comes up next to me and pulls me into his side. He rubs his hand up and down my back soothingly. "Shh, it's okay," he whispers in my ear. Once I've composed myself, I pull back and look into his eyes.

"Thank you. It's the most amazing gift anyone has ever given me."

"Really?"

"Really. I can't believe you found something so perfect."

"Nor could I. It was in the first shop I went in, like a sign from above or something." I smile at the thought of Hannah sorting him out. "Can I?" he asks, gesturing toward the necklace. I nod, lift my hair, and turn away from him so he can put it on me. "It's platinum, so it won't tarnish easily."

"This must have cost you a bloody fortune, Ryan," I scold.

"Stop going on about money. You're worth every penny I've spent this weekend. Just seeing that smile on your face makes it more than worth it."

"I love you."

"I love you, too."

I'd just about pulled myself together by the time the waitress returned with our desserts. Just like everything else I had eaten tonight, it was out of this world.

We enjoy coffees at the end of the meal before getting a taxi back to the cabin.

We're about ten minutes away, and I can't stop smiling and playing with my new piece of jewellery. Ryan's hand hasn't moved from my thigh and he keeps looking at me every couple of minutes, laughing because I'm still doing the same thing and have the same dopey look on my face. I can't help it; it's just perfect. He's just perfect.

I'm so lost in my thoughts that I don't even notice Ryan pay the driver, then get out of the car. It's not until he opens my door that I'm pulled from my daydream.

"Did you go somewhere nice?" Ryan says, laughing at me.

"Hmm," is all I say as he lifts me out of the taxi so I don't have to attempt walking. He really is the sweetest guy in the world, and he's all mine. Halfway to the cabin, my stomach growls loudly.

"Is your stomach still feeling weird?"

"Yeah, a little, but I have consumed a lot of food and wine today. I'll be fine."

"Good, because I'm dying to peel that dress from your body."

I take the key from Ryan and unlock the door for us. He only stops long enough for me to lock it again before he's whisking me off to the bedroom. Once there, he drops me to my feet and backs me up to the wall. He stares right into my eyes before his hands go to the buttons on my coat. His face is so intense, my knees feel a little weak.

Within seconds, my coat is pulled off my arms and thrown across the room. His lips are immediately on mine and he's kissing me like I'm the air he needs to breathe. The love and desire he pours into it makes me feel like a million dollars, and I pray to God he feels the same depth of emotion in my returning kiss. He breaks away before I'm ready for it to end and starts trailing kisses along my jaw and down my neck. When he gets to the sweet spot under my ear, he grazes his teeth over it, making me shiver with pleasure. He continues his journey down my collarbone and follows the edge of my dress over my cleavage, before dipping his tongue in between my breasts, making me moan. He repeats the actions up the other side of my dress before his hands go to my back and find my zip. When his fingers find the tiny bit of metal, he pulls down so slowly whilst sucking on my neck that I want to scream at him.

Eventually, he has my dress completely undone. He pulls his head back at the same time his hands go to my shoulders and gently push the straps off, and he watches as the fabric floats down to a puddle around my feet. My body heats up as his eyes slowly make their way over my curves and take in the underwear he bought for me. His hands run slowly down my arms, making goosebumps pop up in their wake. Entwining our fingers, he gently tugs me so I step forward, away from the wall and out of my dress.

He stands at arm's length and has another perusal of my body. My thong is soaking wet already, just from having his eyes on me, and my breath is coming out in pants. He lets go of one of my hands, then lifts my other above my head and gestures for me to turn around, which I do willingly. Having my body on show like this should embarrass me, but it's not at all—I'm just totally turned on and I can tell by his straining trousers that he is as well. He growls when he takes in my thong-clad arse, and tingles of excitement run down my spine. Thongs aren't my usual choice, but hearing how much he seems to love it makes me want to throw out all my old underwear and just wear them for him. When we're face to face once again, I'm shocked by the colour of his eyes. They're darker than I've ever seen them.

Reaching my hands up, I start to undo the buttons on his shirt. I lean forward and kiss the bit of skin I reveal each time I open another one, until I hit his waistband. Standing back up, I tug his shirt off his shoulders, watching it fall like he did with my dress.

The moment his shirt hits the floor, his patience snaps. He grabs me roughly and throws me on the bed. I can't help the squeal of shock that rips from my throat when my back hits the mattress. Lifting my head up, I watch as Ryan pulls his shoes and socks off, then his trousers and boxers, before crawling up my body and searching out my lips. We make out like teenagers for what feels like hours, just kissing and exploring each other's bodies. I couldn't imagine anything more perfect. Eventually, Ryan gets fed up with the barriers between us and pulls me on top of him so that he can reach back and undo my bra. As the fabric slides down my arms, I shiver again.

"You're perfect, Molly." I realise neither of us has said anything since we've been inside the cabin.

"So are you," I whisper while I run my hands over the muscles of his stomach and chest before finding his lips again. This time, though, I'm straddling him. I slowly grind myself against his length. I can tell it's getting him close, because he's breathing faster and faster. I can't say I'm too far away, either.

"Molly," he pants. "If you don't stop, I'm going to blow all over my stomach." I take that as my cue to move, so I back up down his legs and settle myself on my knees. I waste no time in grabbing him and sucking him straight to the back of my mouth. Feeling brave, I go a little further than I usually would. "Fucking hell, Molly," he growls, giving me the encouragement I need to continue. It only takes seconds before he twitches in my hand and I feel his cum sliding down my throat while he groans out my name.

When he's finished, I pull back and look at him. He's panting hard and looks completely spent. "That. Was. Amazing," he says between breaths.

Standing in front of him, he reaches out and grabs my hips, kissing and licking my stomach. When he kisses the patch of skin just above the fabric of my thong, a huge rush of heat pools between my legs and my clit throbs harder. I squeeze my thighs together, but it does nothing to relieve it. I need him now.

"Ryan, please."

"If you insist, gorgeous," he says, gently pulling my underwear down my legs. He taps my ankles to indicate that I need to step out.

"You're keeping the shoes on, though." I wasn't intending on taking them off. I saw the way he stared at them earlier. I still cannot believe he bought me Louboutins. They're dusky pink—obviously—platform peep-toe slingbacks, and I fucking love them.

When I'm stood in nothing but my shoes, he leans himself back on his elbows and looks me up and down with a hungry look on his face.

"Come up here," he demands. I crawl up his body until I'm straddling him again and lower my head down toward his. "As much as I love your face, that wasn't what I meant," he says, smiling cheekily at me. "I want to taste you. Now." A rush of butterflies flutters in my stomach at his words and I continue crawling up his body until I'm straddling his face.

"That's more like it," he growls, before licking from my entrance up to my clit in one long sweep, making my whole body flinch. His hands come up to grab my hips and he pulls me down a little more, holding me in place as he starts eating me like he hasn't had a meal in weeks. Feeling too weak to hold myself up, I lean forward and rest my hands on his chest. He releases one of my hips so he can reach up and palm my breasts before pinching my nipples, making me whimper and my entire body shake with my impending release. He pushes his tongue into me as deep as it will go and moves his hand from my breasts to my clit. He pinches it between his thumb and forefinger, and it pushes me over the cliff.

"Ryan!" I scream into the cabin as wave after wave of pleasure crashes through my body. I'm just coming down from my high when my stomach turns over. "Oh God, I'm going to be sick," I say, quickly jumping up and running to the toilet where I empty my stomach. Ryan isn't far behind me. He holds my hair and rubs my back until I have nothing left to throw up. I slump against the wall next to the toilet, too scared to go too far as Ryan wets a flannel for me and wipes my sweaty forehead.

"I'm so sorry, I've totally ruined our night."

"Shut up, Molls, you can't help being ill. You said your stomach's not been right all night. Maybe we shouldn't have... you know," he says, tilting his head in the direction of the bedroom.

"No, that was awesome."

"Yeah, it really was." Ryan walks off then returns a couple of minutes later with a glass of water. He sits down on the bathroom floor with me and passes it over. I take a few sips but regret it instantly as it comes straight back up. When I've finished, I cuddle into Ryan's side and close my eyes, hoping the sick feeling will subside. I must fall asleep there because, the next thing I know, I wake up in Ryan's arms as he carries me to bed.

CHAPTER SEVEN

Ryan

I lie awake, watching Molly sleep for hours. I'd hate to fall asleep and for her to be ill again and I'm not there for her. I feel awful. I should have insisted we just go to bed when we got in after she said her stomach still didn't feel right, but I was selfish.

She looks so beautiful sleeping, so peaceful and relaxed. At some point I must drift off, because the next thing I know I'm being awoken by the sound of Molly heaving again. Quickly getting up, I go to her. She's once again hunched over the toilet as I hold her hair and rub her back like I did last night. I'm not really sure what else to do.

"It's okay, you go back to bed," she says once she's stopped being sick.

She's kidding, right?

"Don't be stupid, I'm staying with you. Even if that means we sleep on the bathroom floor." She smiles sweetly at me for a few seconds before she returns to having her head down the toilet. The rest of the night continues the same. Needless to say, neither of us gets much sleep.

By nine in the morning, she's been asleep for a solid three hours without getting up to be sick. I hate the thought of having to wake her, but we're meant to be out of here by ten at the latest. I decide to go and see if the owners are in to ask if they can give us any longer. I leave a note on my pillow in case Molly wakes up and can't find me, then head out toward the main house.

When I get back ten minutes later, she's in the exact same position she was when I left her, which is a relief. The owners agreed to let us stay until twelve, but we have to be out then as they have another couple coming this afternoon. They were really lovely and even offered us their guest room if Molly is still too unwell to travel. I hope that isn't the case, because I know she would rather be at home than in a stranger's house.

I start packing and loading everything into the car that I can without waking her. I have everything done bar our suitcases and, at eleven o'clock, I decide I can't wait any longer. I take her in a glass of water and a cup of tea just in case she wants either. Sitting up against the headboard, I softly repeat her name until she starts to move. I would normally gently shake her, but I don't want to do anything to upset her stomach.

"Molly," I say one last time just before her eyes open and she looks up at me. She's always going to be beautiful to me, but even I can see that she looks pretty rough this morning.

"Morning, gorgeous. How are you feeling?" She groans in response, so I take that as not good. "I managed to get us a couple more hours here, but we need to be out by twelve. The owners said if you're too unwell to travel, we could stay in one of their guest rooms.

"No, I'll be okay. I'd rather get home. What time is it now?" Molly's voice is all gravelly. Her throat must be killing her.

"It's just gone eleven. I brought you water and tea. Would you like to try either?" She sits herself up carefully and waits to see if anything is going to happen.

"Water, please." I hand it over and watch as she takes tiny little sips every minute or so.

"You stay there. I'm going to pack up the rest of our stuff."

"No, I'll help."

"Like hell you will. You're ill, stay in bed," I say a little more firmly than intended. "Sorry, that came out a little harsh." I walk over and give her a kiss on the forehead and the end of her nose to make up for it.

"It's okay, I know you're only looking after me."

Her eyes follow me around the bedroom and in and out of the bathroom as I pack our things. I leave some comfortable clothes out for her to put on when she gets up, but other than that, everything is away. I help Molly get up and dressed even though she insists she's fine. Once she's had a quick wash and brushed her teeth, I zip up the case and carry it out to the car.

"Are you sure you're going to be okay travelling?"

"There's only one way to find out."

I do one last check of the cabin to make sure we have everything before helping Molly to the car. She puts her chair back a little, leans her head back, and closes her eyes. It only takes ten minutes before I hear her snoring lightly next to me. To my relief, she sleeps all the way home. She wakes up just as we're pulling into the drive.

"Did I sleep all the way here?" she asks, a little confused.

"You sure did. That's a hell of a lot better than puking all the way here, though," I say with a laugh.

I get Molly upstairs and settled on the sofa under the blanket. She's not happy about not helping again, but she doesn't have a choice. I put the TV on for her, then go about unloading the car.

It's mid-afternoon by the time I've got everything sorted, and my stomach is growling.

"Molls, do you want to try eating something?"

"Yeah, okay," she says back over the sofa.

I make her toast with a little bit of butter on, then melt some cheese on mine. I'm just walking back to the living room when I pass the dining table and remember the present I organised for Molly today. Placing our plates on the coffee table in front of her, I go back and grab the present.

"What's that?" she asks when she sees it in my hand.

"Today's present."

"Oh."

I hand it over to her and she pokes at the wrapping paper, looking a little perplexed.

"Open it, then." I'm looking forward to seeing what's inside as much as she is. She rips open the paper then turns it over.

"Oh my God," she gasps, then covers her smiling mouth in shock. I look down at what's in her hand and take in the multi-picture frame I bought before we went away, full with the photos I took of us while we were in the cabin. There are a couple of us in the hot tub—no, not showing any nudity. Some out on our walk, just chilling on the sofa, in bed, and finally at the restaurant last night. It's exactly what I wanted.

"How did you get this done?" she asks.

"I bought the frame last week, then I sent Holly all the photos I took while we were there and she printed them and dropped this off here this morning for you."

"Aw, that's so sweet. I love it."

"I realised we don't have many photos of us together, so I thought this would be a good start."

"It's awesome," she says, putting it down on the sofa next to her.

"Here, try eating some of this," I say, handing over her toast.

The toast stays down for exactly twenty minutes before she starts throwing up again. We both spend the rest of the day lounging in bed so she's close to the toilet. Luckily for both of us, it seems to have subsided by the time evening rolls around. We both fall asleep early as we hardly slept the night before and she was only up twice in the night.

I feel awful going to work the next day and leaving her at home, ill, but I phone Susan on my way to work and ask if she can go around and check on Molly. Obviously, she agrees; she loves looking after people.

Molly seems to be back to normal by Tuesday morning, so it was obviously just a forty-eight-hour bug she picked up somewhere, but I convince her to stay home again just in case. By Wednesday, she's chomping at the bit to get back to the office after almost a week away.

The evening of my birthday is here before I know it. I'm sat at the bar in the strip club waiting for everyone else to arrive. Will didn't say who was coming, but I'm sure there will be a few of us. There usually is when we go out.

But I've now been here for ten minutes and there's no sign of anyone. I feel like a right pervert, sat here on my own with a beer. My heart jumps into my throat as I feel someone come up behind me and wrap something around my eyes.

"What the fuck?" I shout, flinging my arms around, trying to hit whoever just blindfolded me.

"It's Will. Chill out, man."

"What the fuck are you doing?" Just because I now know it is Will, it doesn't mean I'm any less pissed off about being blindfolded.

"I've got a birthday surprise for you—come on." He tugs on my arm and there's nothing I can really do but allow myself to be dragged along behind him, much to my displeasure.

"I swear to God, if you've organised some stripper to rub herself over me, I'm going to be seriously pissed, Will."

"Oh, stop worrying, you pussy."

"Don't call me a fucking pussy. You're not the one blindfolded and being pulled fuck knows where in a strip club. Anything could be about to happen."

"Oh, you have no idea, mate."

Brilliant.

"Stairs," Will says as we start climbing. "Left." We keep walking for another few minutes although it feels like fucking hours because I can't see a bloody thing.

"Right, sit there and don't move. Don't even think about trying to remove the blindfold before someone does it for you. You will be punished if you do it yourself, and it will fucking hurt," Will says before I hear him leave, laughing to himself. "Right, he's all yours. Have fun," I hear him say to someone.

I sit there for what feels like forever with nothing happening. The longer I sit, the faster my heart beats, and the more I'm sweating. I hate not being about to see what's about to happen to me.

For the longest time, the only sound I can hear is that of my own increased breathing. As the time stretches on, so does my patience. I didn't really want to come here tonight as it was. I really had no intention of being locked in a room, blindfolded, waiting for a stripper to come and give me a special birthday present.

I should just leave. What's Will really going to do about it?

I shift in my seat, ready to pull the fabric from my eyes and to make my escape when movement somewhere in the room fills my ears. A Rihanna song begins and then the click of heels has my heart pounding and my fists clenching.

I don't want this. I don't need this.

She moves behind me, and although I can't see shit, I follow the sound of her movements.

My entire body flinches when fingertips run across my shoulder and down my arms.

This is bullshit.

Going to stand, she grabs my upper arms, her nails digging in, and I'm forced to stay put.

Every single muscle in my body pulls tight as she presses herself against me.

I tell myself that all I need to do is sit here. It'll be over before I know it, and I'll avoid the inevitable wrath from my mates if I were to walk out right now.

Her hands run down my arms, making all my hairs stand on end in discomfort. I don't want some random woman touching me. There's only one woman's hands I want on me, and she's at home, waiting for me to return.

Flinching once again when she entwines our fingers, I try pulling away but she's too fast. My arms are pulled back before my hands land on the warm skin of her arse.

"No," I grunt, and I swear her body shakes with laughter.

Her fingers dig into the tense muscles across my shoulders, but it does nothing to relax me.

Thankfully, she releases my hands and I suck in a giant breath—until she throws one leg over my lap and straddles me. Her arse grinds into me. If she's expecting some excitement from me, she's going to be very disappointed. I'm about as far away from being turned on as physically possible right now.

Her hands run up from my stomach and over my chest. Her sweet scent fills my nose and my body screams that it's all wrong. This isn't who I want entwined with my body.

"Fuck," I shout, trying to jump away from her when she grabs my junk.

"That's disappointing," she moans in my ear before her lips land on my neck. I feel dirty.

The relief that fills me when she climbs from my lap is unbelievable.

"Take off the blindfold," she orders. I sigh, thinking it's over.

Very slowly and reluctantly, my hands rise to my head and I slip the fabric off. I keep my eyes shut for a few seconds as I pluck up the courage to see what—or who—is in front of me.

"I'm disappointed in your observational skills, Mr. Evans."

Molly

The look on Ryan's face when he eventually drags his eyelids open is priceless.

"That was you?" he says, eventually gesturing around his body with his hands. "It didn't smell like you."

"That would have made it too easy, now, wouldn't it? Now shut up and enjoy the show. And I seriously hope that by the time I get back over there you're in a... uh... harder state than you were earlier. I've got plans for you tonight, Mr. Evans."

Clad in only the lingerie he bought for me when we were away, I manage to dance for fifteen minutes before the pained look on Ryan's face is too much to bear. I have to go to him. Untwisting my legs from the pole, I get myself back on my feet and slowly saunter over to him, watching as his lips curl up at the corners as I get closer.

"Are you going to willingly touch me this time?"

"Fuck yes," he growls, but before I can get to him he stands and comes to me, quickly lifting me and walking me backwards until I'm up against the wall. I wrap my legs around his waist and groan when his erection rubs my sweet spot through his jeans and my flimsy thong. I was so focused on my moves that I hadn't realised how worked up I was, watching him watching me.

He continues to grind into me and his lips crash down to mine. His hands are all over me like he doesn't know what to touch first. Needing to catch his breath, he moves to kiss my neck.

"Molly," he pants, "that was the sexiest thing I've ever seen. I almost came just watching you."

I can't help but moan at his words. I'm so close. He must realise because he leans back a little, sliding one hand down between us and into the fabric of my thong until his fingers are circling my clit. Within seconds, I'm screaming my release into the room.

While I ride out the waves of my orgasm, Ryan goes back to kissing down my neck and across my chest. Once my tremors subside, he removes his hand and sucks his fingers into his mouth.

"You taste so sweet, gorgeous."

Dropping my legs from around his waist, I let go of his shoulders. He lets me go and I slide down the wall until I'm sat on my haunches in front of him. Palming him through his jeans, I listen to him moan at my touch.

"That's much better," I say with a smile. Leaning his forearms against the wall, he looks down on me with hungry, impatient eyes.

"Only for you, gorgeous girl."

I make quick work of undoing his jeans and push them and his boxers down his thighs just enough to release his cock. I waste no time and slide my lips around him while wrapping my fingers around the base. He's as close as I was just from dry humping me against the wall, so I know this is going to be quick. Pulling back, I run my tongue around the head of his dick before slowly sucking him back into my mouth. It only takes me to repeat this a couple of times before I feel the tell-tale signs that he's about to come. I stroke his balls with my other hand and suck hard.

"Argh, Molly," he groans as his orgasm washes through his body. When he's finished, I sit back and wipe my mouth, feeling pleased with how tonight's turning out.

"Come on, let's get out of here. I've got more plans for you at home, birthday boy." I stand, grab his hand, and drag him over to the door.

"You can't go out there like that," he says in a panic.

"I've got a coat hanging up by the door, you muppet!"

"Thank fuck for that, I don't want anyone else seeing you like that." The possessive tone to his voice has tingles racing to my core. "Hey, what happened to Will?"

"He went home. He was only here to help me get you up here. I rightly thought you wouldn't come willingly."

"Damn right, I wouldn't have."

We make our way out of the club and go to get in my car to head home. I'm just pulling out of the car park when Ryan looks over at me, smiling.

"What's up with you?"

"Just so you know, that's the best birthday present I've ever had."

"It's not over yet, baby."

He smiles again before sitting back in his seat. He's quiet for a while before he speaks, making me jump a little.

"You need to get a new car. I hate the thought of you driving this when it's icy outside. If you have an accident, there's nothing to protect you."

"I've been thinking about getting something bigger." This makes Ryan laugh, so I raise my eyebrow at him in question.

"Well, you could hardly get something smaller!"

"Yeah, yeah, you carry on taking the piss. This little car has done me good, and it's cheap as chips to run."

When we pull up to the house, I'm pleased to see that everything seems to be going to plan.

"Don't go upstairs yet," I call to him when I see him disappear inside. Quickly following him in, I dump my bag by the front door and shrug out of my coat. Ryan's eyes go wide again like he'd forgotten I only had my underwear underneath. I grab his hand and pull him up the stairs behind me. I can feel his eyes burning into my arse as we climb toward the first floor, looking back to make sure I'm right—which I am, of course.

"Enjoying the view?"

"Very much," he replies, without moving his eyes.

He moves like he is going to go into the living room, but I continue pulling him up the next set of stairs. When we get outside our closed bedroom door, I can't help but smile at how Holly did exactly as I asked when I set all this up. Turning around before I get to the door, I put my hands to Ryan's chest and, to his surprise, slam him back into the wall.

He looks down at me with wide eyes.

Running my hands under his t-shirt, I push it up and he gets the hint to remove it. I give him a quick kiss on the lips before moving to his jaw and kissing across his neck and chest, making sure to run my tongue around his nipples. I've noticed it makes him shiver. My fingers skim over his stomach and start undoing his jeans before pushing them down his legs. He takes over by toeing his shoes off and pulling his socks and jeans off.

"Much better. You were way too overdressed." He raises his eyebrow to me in question, but I just grab his hand and pull him toward the door.

He comes up behind me and wraps his arms around my waist as I go to grab the handle. When the door swings open, we both gasp in surprise. Him, because he wasn't expecting it. Me, because it looks more beautiful than I could have imagined.

CHAPTER EIGHT

Ryan

I can't believe my eyes. Our bedroom is glowing with what looks like a hundred candles and there are dusky pink rose petals covering the floor and the bed. Molly leans to the side so she can look up at me, but I can't take my eyes away from the room. It looks like something from a film. I have the sudden urge to get down on one knee or something. I quickly shake that thought out of my head. *One thing at a time, Evans.*

"Are you ready for this?" Molly asks me. I take my gaze away from the room and glance down at her, looking nervously up at me.

"You... um... we..." *Oh, for fuck's sake, pull yourself together, man.*

"Is it perfect enough?"

"You're kidding, right? As long as I'm with you, it's perfect."

Leaning down, I place my lips to hers for a sweet kiss. She turns in my arms, grabs my arms and pulls me into the room. I kick the door shut behind me; I want only this room and us to exist.

Now we've moved into the room, I see there's a bottle of champagne on ice. I laugh to myself when I see a few cans of beer in the ice bucket and a picnic basket next to it.

"Are we having a picnic?"

"If we have time," she says, smiling seductively and walking over to pour us both a glass of bubbly. Handing me a glass, she raises hers for a toast.

"To a very memorable birthday," she says, touching her glass to mine.

"Oh, it's definitely that, gorgeous."

We both have a sip of champagne before she takes my glass from me and places it on the bedside table with hers. Turning back, she grabs my hand once again.

"Are you okay?" she asks, looking a little worried.

I don't know why I'm suddenly nervous. I've had sex plenty of times. I know what I'm doing, and I know I'm good. It's just that it's Molly I'm about to have sex with, and it means everything. I love her so damn much it hurts, and I want every second of it to be perfect. "Yeah. It's crazy, I know, but I'm a little nervous."

"So am I," she whispers. "I've never made love to anyone before."

That does it. I snap out of it, grab Molly, and lift her so she has to wrap her legs around my waist. Her arms instinctively go around my neck, her fingers threading into my hair as she crashes our lips together. I walk us forwards until my legs hit the bed, before I reach up and undo her bra, gently lowering her down. I let go of her and drop her bra on the floor before leaning back over her body and taking her lips on mine. I've been waiting for his moment for what feels like forever and, now it's here, I can't quite believe it.

"I'm going to worship every inch of your body, Molly. When I've finished, it will be like I was the only one here, ever." She groans at my words. We both want to wash away her bad memories. I feel like we've already banished a few, but tonight I'm going to rid her of a few more. I'm going to show her how this should be done and make her feel more loved than she ever thought possible. Putting my lips back to hers, I pour every ounce of love I have for her into it before I trail kisses across her cheek and nibble on her earlobe. Her nails dig into my back, and I haven't even done anything yet. I begin kissing down her neck and listen as her breath comes out in fast pants.

"Ryan, I don't think I can wait for you to take your time," she pants impatiently.

"Well, you're going to have to, gorgeous, because I promised you a perfect first time, and that's exactly what you're going to get."

She groans loudly, turning me on more than I thought possible. I continue down her body, grazing my teeth across her collarbone, then kissing down across her breasts. I run my tongue along the underside, causing her to groan and her hips to buck off the bed before sucking her nipple into my mouth while pinching the other with my thumb and finger.

"You're so beautiful when you're falling apart beneath my hands,

Molly. I could watch you all day," I say before sucking her other pink nipple into my mouth and giving it the same treatment.

I move lower still, running my teeth over her ribs, sucking on the tight skin across her stomach, before dipping my tongue into her belly button. She flinches and giggles.

"Oh God, Ryan, please," she begs as she grabs onto my hair and tries pushing me lower.

"Good things come to those who wait, my gorgeous girl." She just growls at me.

Standing up from the bed, I remove my boxers. I can't cope with the restriction any longer. The prospect of pushing myself deep inside Molly has my dick harder than I think it has ever been in my life. It's actually getting quite painful. I'm torturing myself here just as much as I am Molly, but it'll be worth it. I wrap my fingers in the waistband of her thong and slowly drag it down her legs before I put my hands under her arse and push her tiny body up the bed. Settling myself on my knees between her legs, my dick is resting dangerously close to her entrance. The slight contact makes her whimper. Lifting one of her legs in the air, I work my way down slowly, kissing and licking every bit of skin I can.

"Oh my God, Ryan, you're killing me," she moans, making me smile.

"You and me both, baby," I say, smiling against her thigh.

"Just get on with it."

"Oh, it'll be worth it, you mark my words," I say before putting her left leg down and repeating my actions on the other one while Molly chants for more, getting louder and more demanding.

I think she realises I'm running out of places to kiss by the time I get to the top of her second thigh, because she's panting even harder and I can see a light sheen of sweat starting to cover her body in anticipation.

"Ryan, please, I need your mouth on me. Please."

This time, I do as she asks. I slide down so I am on my front with my face right in front of her pussy. Running a finger through her folds, she almost jumps off the bed, she's so sensitive.

"Fucking hell, Molly, you're soaked."

"That's because I want you so bad," she pants. "Ry, please, I need you now."

With those words said, I slide my hands around under her thighs and grab onto her hips to keep her in place before lowering my mouth down on to her. She cries out when my tongue touches her clit. I tease her and open her up, then tease her some more until she's crying out and writhing on the bed.

I let go of one of her hips and slide two fingers inside her, then I go back to focusing my tongue's effort on her clit. In seconds, she's screaming my name and clutching my hair so tight, I'm worried she's going to pull it out. When she's finished pulsing around my fingers, I slide them out of her, sit up, and wipe my hand across my mouth. Shifting forward, I line myself up with her, but, before I do anything, I lean my body down over hers and kiss her. She moans when she tastes herself on my lips.

"See how sweet you are?" I ask when I pull away. Her cheeks heat and she nods. "Are you ready for this?" I ask, just to make sure.

"More than you'll ever know. Make love to me, Ryan."

Not needing to be asked twice, I sit back up and take myself in my hand, but I stop at the last minute.

"Condom?" I whisper, trying not to ruin the moment. Molly shakes her head and I take it that she's covered, so I go back to the task in hand. I slowly slide myself into her, but I've only got the head in when she gasps and her muscles tense around me.

"Are you okay?"

"Yeah, it's just been a while. Take it slow for a bit, okay?"

"Of course. Just relax."

She nods her head and lets out a deep breath. Leaning down, I kiss her as a distraction as I slide the rest of the way in.

"Fuck, Molly, you feel fucking incredible." I'm glad she needs me to take this slow, because I wouldn't last very long otherwise.

She smiles at me and grinds her hips, telling me she's okay. Pulling out slowly, I quickly thrust back in. Her back arches and a loud moan escapes from the back of her throat. "You okay?"

"Fuck yes," she pants.

I do as I'm told and continue to thrust in and out of her slowly, taking it a bit deeper each time until she's completely filled with me. Molly's panting so hard she's forced to break our kiss, so I sit up a little, taking her at a different angle. Her cries fill the room. "I'm really close, Ry, I want you to come with me."

"No, just let go, Molly." Reaching down, I circle my thumb around her clit.

"Oh my God," she shouts as her muscles tighten around me.

I thrust, harder and deeper, and she snaps. She screams my name as her body convulses around me, her orgasm crashing through her. The tightness as her muscles contract around me is out of this world and almost pushes me over the edge, but I'm determined to give her another before I finish inside her perfect pussy.

Once she's finished twitching around me, I grab her waist and flip us over so she can ride me. And fuck me if the view from down here isn't the best thing in the fucking world. Watching her flushed cheeks, her satisfied smile, and her tits bouncing as she rides my cock is breathtaking. If I were to die right now, I would go one very happy man. Holding onto her hips, I give her a helping hand.

"Molly... fuck. I love you so much," I manage to get out through gritted teeth as she grinds down on me.

My orgasm is fast approaching. I need to make sure she gets off again before I let it take me under.

"I love you, too, baby." It's like she can read my mind, because as soon as she finishes speaking, she runs her hand down her stomach and starts playing with her clit.

"Fuck, I didn't think my view could get any better, but clearly I was wrong. Fuck, you look so hot."

It's not long before her muscles start to tighten again. Luckily, at the same time, tingles run down my spine.

"Come with me, gorgeous."

"I'm there, Ry."

She sits herself down one more time and we both go off together, her screaming my name and me growling hers as we ride out our orgasms.

When she's finished, she flops forward and lies on me, completely spent, out of breath and sweaty. I wrap my arms around her and just enjoy the feeling racing around my body. I'm still buried deep inside her, she's still twitching around me.

"You were right, Ry."

"What's that, gorgeous?"

"It was worth the wait."

We lie in each other's arms while our heartbeats return to normal, enjoying being close.

Molly

If I didn't know so before, I most definitely do now that all my previous experiences were utter shit. That, with Ryan, was fucking mind-blowingly awesome. I can't even describe what that was, but I do know that I want to do it again—a lot, and soon.

I move so my palms are over his chest and rest my chin on them. "Hey."

"Hey, gorgeous. You okay?"

"Amazing. You?"

"What you said," he says, a wide smile stretching across his face.

"You're beautiful, you know that?" He looks at me sceptically. "In a really manly, sexy way, of course."

"Of course," he says, quirking an eyebrow up at me. "You, on the other hand, are fucking gorgeous. Even more so when you're riding my cock." I feel his semi-hard dick twitch inside me as he says that.

"Feels like you're getting yourself ready for round two down there."

"I'm always ready to go when you're around." I smile down at him, enjoying the feel of him laughing beneath me.

"Fancy a shower?"

"Yeah, I think that's a good idea." He rolls us over so my back is on the bed before pulling out of me. A weird sense of loss and emptiness washes through me, but watching his hot arse walking into the bathroom makes up for it, and the rose petals that were on the bed now stuck to his back makes me smile.

"Come on, gorgeous, I don't intend on showering alone." I jump off the bed and rush to join him.

Ryan's already standing under the spray of the shower when I get there. He's facing away from me and the sight of the water pouring down over his broad shoulders, his muscular back, before running over his arse, stops me in my tracks. Just before I start drooling, he looks over his shoulder at me, smirking.

"You going to just stand there looking at my arse, or are you going to join me?"

"Uh." He turns around as I say this, and fuck me. If the back of him was heaven to look at, I can't even describe the front. He lifts his hand up to push his hair off his forehead and I run my eyes down his body, following the trails of water pouring over him. My mouth goes dry. "Do you have any clue how hot you look right now?"

His answer is just to walk out of the shower, pick me up, and carry me in there with him. He places me down right under the spray before crashing his lips to mine and pulling my body tight against his, so I can feel his hardness pressing into my stomach. When he moves his lips away from mine, he's smiling wide as he grinds his length into my belly.

"You ready to go again, birthday boy?"

"You have no idea."

"Oh, I think I do." He looks down at me with one eyebrow lifted. "You should know I've never experienced anything like that before. It was out of this world."

"It was," he says, lowering his lips to my neck and running his hands over my body. Suddenly, I'm backed up against the cold, tiled wall, and lifted so that I have to wrap my legs around his waist. It reminds me of our first time together in this shower nearly two weeks ago. I feel the tip of his dick brushing against my entrance and my hips start to grind against it involuntarily.

We eventually drag our exhausted bodies from the shower once we've actually washed before getting ourselves comfortable on the bed with the picnic basket between us. I filled it with traditional picnic food, little sandwiches, sausages rolls, scotch eggs, et cetera, and for pudding... strawberries and chocolate sauce.

"I can safely say this has been the best birthday I think I've ever had."

"Don't you be thinking the celebrations are over. I have the whole weekend planned out for you."

"Well, I sincerely hope it's that we stay in bed all weekend so I can have you whenever I want."

"Christ, Ry, I'm not your sex slave. Although the job would have its advantages."

"Oh yeah, like what?"

"Looking at your sexy body all day and the multiple orgasms you'll give me while you're at it."

"See, I said you wouldn't have any complaints." He really does have magic fingers... and a magic mouth and cock, come to think of it.

I wake to the sound of Ryan's alarm clock early the next morning. Groaning, I hold on to him tighter to try to stop him from getting up.

"I'm sorry, gorgeous, but I've got to go to work," he says in a sexy husky voice from where he's just woken up. "You can have your way with me all weekend, though," he says with a cheeky smile.

I smile back at him, but I'm suddenly regretting what I have planned for the weekend, because it's going to seriously reduce our alone time.

Eventually, Ryan removes himself from my grip and sits himself on the edge of the bed, looking down at me. "I love you so much, Molly. Thank you for last night. It was perfect." The smile he graces me with melts my heart.

"Yeah, it sort of was, wasn't it? I love you, too." I stretch my body out as he stands, and I can't help the grunt that escapes my lips.

"You okay? Did I hurt you?" he asks, looking concerned.

"Oh, I'm sore, but in a very good way." I love the smirk that stretches across his lips as I say this. I guess going three rounds with Ryan last night after months of celibacy shocked my poor body.

"Good. That means you'll have to think about me every time you move today."

"I'll think about you all day, whether I'm sore from our lovemaking or not. You don't need to ever worry about me forgetting about you, Ry." The wide smile I get in response makes my heart skip a beat.

I stay in bed while Ryan gets ready for work, enjoying the view of him getting dressed. He brings me a cup of tea before he leaves and gives me a knee-weakening kiss, leaving me a little breathless. I've got no time to sit about and think back over our night together, because I've taken the day off to get the house ready for our guests this weekend. Ryan doesn't know it, but he's actually going out with his work colleagues after school so that everyone, bar Will, who will drive him back here, will be waiting for him.

I spend all day cleaning every inch of the house, making all the beds and decorating with birthday banners and balloons. I also spend hours making dishes for tomorrow night's dinner. Never before in my life have I really cared about others' opinions of me, so it's weird to now have a huge desire for Ryan's mum to like and accept me. I want to show her that I can be a good little wife for her son.

CHAPTER NINE

Ryan

Today's been the longest day of my life. I've only had two lessons, which should be great because it gives me a chance to get caught up on other stuff I need to do, but every time I sit down to do something, my thoughts drift back to last night. So, other than being present in two lessons (to describe it as teaching would be a push), I have done absolutely nothing but think about Molly. I'm currently staring at a GCSE folder but not really seeing it, instead reliving my private pole dance from last night, when someone calling my name from behind me distracts me.

"Ryan... Ryan?" I spin in my chair to see Will looking at me with raised eyebrows.

"Sorry, was in a world of my own." His lips twitch at the corners and a knowing look fills his eyes.

"Was last night that good?"

"Mate, you have no idea."

"Glad to hear it. Now, seeing as we didn't get any birthday drinks, we're going after school. You will be at the Red Lion by four o'clock at the latest, and no excuses will work, Mr. Evans. I don't care how much you want to get back to your girl. She had you last night; it's our turn."

I groan in response but nod my head, knowing I won't be able to get out of it. "Fine, but I won't be getting drunk, and I will be going home at a decent hour."

Will holds his hands up in surrender. "Whatever you say."

It's a few minutes after four when I walk into the pub, because I had to get in the middle of a fight on the playground as I tried to escape to my car. Our usual drinking group is already sat around a large table in the back of the bar. Will looks up as I approach. "Mr. Evans, you're late."

"Sorry, the year eleven boys were fighting again. I can't wait for that bunch of dicks to leave. I'm fed up with pulling them off each other." I look at the table. "What's this?"

"This..." Will says, waving his hand. "Is your punishment for being late. And also your birthday present from us." I look up to his face, then back down to the multiple shots of what looks like Jägermeister in front of an empty seat. "Bottoms up, Mr. Evans!"

"What happened to me saying I wasn't getting drunk? I need to be able to drive home."

"I've got it covered, mate, no worries. I'll drive you home, then Ana's going to pick me up from yours. We'll collect my car tomorrow or something. Now, drink up."

Knowing that I'll be able to get home to Molly sometime tonight makes me feel happier, so I grab the first glass and knock it back. I can't help the face I make as it goes down. I really don't like Jäger, but it's too late to complain now.

After a couple of hours, Will puts his phone in his pocket and surprises me by saying he's going to take me home. I was sure this was going to end up being a long night, but I'm more than happy to go home to my gorgeous girl. I sway slightly as we make our way to my car, thanks to the shots and couple of pints I've had in quite a short space of time. I throw Will the keys to my Honda and jump in the passenger seat.

I'm surprised to see the house in darkness when Will pulls up. Molly didn't say she was going out, but I can't see her car, unless she parked it around back. It looks like Ana also isn't here yet, so I ask Will to come up for a drink while he waits for her.

I let us in and, after removing our coats and shoes, we make our way up the stairs. When I flick the light on in the living area, I think I actually have a small heart attack.

"SURPRISE!" everyone shouts. My hand flies to cover my racing heart in the hope that it will help calm it down as I try to catch my breath.

"Happy birthday, Bro," Abbi says as she and Liv come over and each give me a hug and a kiss on the cheek.

I look around the room. Jax, Holly, Adam, Emma, Ana and, of course, Molly are all smiling back at me. I'm grateful, I am, but the only person I really want to spend my night with is busying herself in the kitchen. It's not until I round the counter after greeting everyone that I fully appreciate what she's wearing. Her make-up is light and her hair is wavy but pulled away from her face. Her smoking hot body is covered in a high-neck leather dress, fitted into the waist, with a loose skirt that stops mid-thigh. I continue my journey down her toned legs to take in the sky-high bright red heels. I swallow hard and clench my fists at my sides to stop me from walking over and lying her down on the work surface and taking her in front of our closest friends and family. Shaking my head slightly, I walk over and wrap my arms around her. I'm aware that she still wants to keep what's going on between us quiet, but there's no way I can't touch her.

When my lips are next to her ear, I whisper, "I'm fucking you with those shoes on later."

She groans and her body goes limp in my arms. When she's composed herself, she turns and grabs a glass of water sitting on the side.

"Here, you might want to dilute those shots before you have any more. We've already ordered Indian. It should be here any minute. I got you your favourite. I hope that's okay."

We have a brilliant night. Everyone gets on really well and it turns out Adam's a really cool guy now that he isn't dating the love of my life. We got on like a house on fire. I love having everyone close to me together in one room.

At just after midnight, Will and Ana say their goodbyes, swiftly followed by Emma. She seems more like her old self tonight, which is great to see after so long. The only part of the night I really don't enjoy is that I'm not able to touch Molly as openly as I would like to. That said, I did give it a good go at the dining table while everyone was tucking into their food.

Abbi, Jax, and Liv disappear up to bed, and Molly has headed down with the understanding that she doesn't touch an item of clothing she has on until I'm there to help. I faff around until I'm confident no one will realise I go downstairs instead of up.

When I walk through her bedroom door, my breath catches in my throat. All the lights are off and she's stood at the French doors, looking at the stars. The light from the moon is shining on her, making her look like an angel. I quietly shut the door behind me. She notices and glances over her shoulder with a small smile on her lips. Walking up behind her, I wrap my arms around her waist and rest my chin on her shoulder.

"Thank you for tonight."

"You're welcome, baby. It was good fun."

I nuzzle my nose against her neck, murmuring, "What's the plan for the rest of the weekend?"

"I'm more concerned with the rest of our night than worrying about tomorrow," she says suggestively, rubbing her arse into my groin, making me groan.

"God, I want to be inside you so badly," I say between light bites to her neck and ear. "You've been teasing me all night."

She turns in my arms and looks up at me with heated eyes. "No one's stopping you," she says, smirking, then peppers kisses along my jaw.

I step us backwards until her back hits the doors. She gasps and I make the most of the opportunity by crashing my lips to hers and teasing her tongue with mine. Her hands find their way to the bottom of my t-shirt before running up my sides, making my muscles twitch.

"Off," she demands without breaking our kiss. I oblige. Her lips go to my neck, sucking and biting, while her hands attack my back like she's trying to get us closer, even though every part of our bodies is touching. She trails her lips down to my chest and runs her tongue around my nipples, making me shiver, while her hands travel down my stomach and slide straight into my jogging bottoms and inside my boxers. I have to reach my hands up to the door to steady myself when her hot fingers wrap around my length. I don't think I'll ever get used to this feeling.

"I want you now, Ry. I can't wait." She pushes my trousers and underwear down so they pool around my ankles, and I run my hands up the outside of her thighs and grab on to the sides of her knickers. "Ryan, please," she moans as I slide them down her legs. Lifting one of her legs under her knee, I wrap it around my hip so that she can feel me against her.

"God, I can already feel how wet you are for me, Molly." I put my hands under her arse and lift her against the door before plunging into her. I groan as her head drops back against the glass, showing me she's as affected by this as I am. Her legs clamp around my waist as I start pounding into her with punishing blows. I'll make love to her gently later—right now, I need to fuck her.

Molly

I'm totally spent by the time Ryan has finished with me. After three powerful orgasms, I'm lying in his arms, smiling to myself. His breathing has just evened out, so I turn my head and watch him. He looks so peaceful and perfect in his sleep. His lips are slightly parted and his eyes are fluttering like he's dreaming already. All of a sudden, he makes a groaning noise at the back of his throat, making me jump. Then, he whispers something that makes me melt. "Molly... I love you so much."

A lump forms in my throat as I think of what he could be dreaming about. I return his words before asking him quietly if he's awake. He makes no further noise so I'm guessing he isn't. I lie there for hours, trying to fall asleep, but my heart is pounding like it could explode any minute. That feeling only lasts so long, because banging and shouting filter down from upstairs. I try to strain to hear who it is and what's going on, but they're too far away. It's not until heavy footsteps descend the stairs that I get an idea as to what's going on.

"Jax, that isn't what I meant..." Abbi yells, which makes Ryan start to stir beside me.

Jax shouts back, sounding livid, before Abbi starts begging for him to hear her out. He's not having any of it.

His shouting wakes Ryan up and, before I know what's happening, he's out of bed and grabbing my dressing gown to cover himself up before pulling the door wide open to face the arguing couple in our hallway.

"We do have something good here. Jax, please don't do this," Abbi pleads.

"You should have thought about that before you said what you did upstairs. Goodbye."

Seconds later, our front door slams so hard it makes me jump.

"Abbi..." Ryan says in a soothing voice.

"Don't... just fucking don't." She says it with such venom that Ryan steps back like she slapped him. "Oh, and if you actually want to try to keep the fact that you're fucking Molly a secret, I suggest you at least try to keep it in your trousers when you have guests," she snaps before running up the stairs, leaving the sounds of her sobs in her wake.

Ryan looks back at me with a shocked look on his face. "Should I go and check on her?"

"No. I think she needs to be alone for a while."

I lift the covers so that he can slide back under with me, enough that he gets a peek at my naked body. His eyes run along the length of me before he smiles and drops my pink fluffy dressing gown on the floor, diving in with me.

"I must say… you look pretty cute in pink." He bites down on my nipple in response. "Ow!"

He looks up at me with wild eyes and a cheeky smile.

"Ry, I don't think I can go again." He raises his eyebrow at me in question, then goes about proving me wrong.

Luckily, I remembered to set an alarm for this morning because after all our 'activities' last night, there was no chance either of us would have been awake before Ryan's parents turned up. He still doesn't know they're coming today.

"Really?" Ryan groans when the alarm wakes him up.

"Yep. Plans, remember?"

"Yeah, although I have no idea what they are."

"That's why they're called surprises. Now, get that sexy arse out of bed and get dressed. We've got guests who will expect breakfast."

Ryan pouts at me, making me laugh. "What?"

He peeks down under the covers before glancing at me with a look I'm getting very familiar with in his eyes.

"Uh no, I don't think so. I'm pretty sure I'm going to be walking funny already."

Liv is already waiting for the kettle to boil when I get upstairs. "Morning. Did you sleep okay?"

"Yeah, like a baby, thanks. Do you want tea?"

"Yes, please. Have you seen Abbi this morning?"

"I knocked on her door before I came down but she just grunted at me to fuck off. Did something happen?"

"You mean you didn't hear the blazing row her and Jax had in the middle of the night?"

"No… I fell asleep with my head under my pillow because I couldn't bear to listen to them fucking any longer. I was almost tempted to come down to your room just to get away from all the shouts for God!"

My cheeks heat at the thought of her finding the same shouts coming from my room a lot last night. I turn to get a couple of mugs out so she doesn't notice.

"But once I was out, I didn't know anything until my alarm went off a few minutes ago."

"Morning, Sis," Ryan says, joining us in the kitchen and giving Liv a kiss on the cheek. "Morning, Molls," he quickly adds, flashing me a cheeky smile and a wink.

"Coffee?"

"Of course. Has anyone seen Abbi yet?"

"No. I'm going to take her a cup of tea as a peace offering."

It's over an hour later before Liv comes back down, fully dressed and pulling a depressed-looking Abbi behind her. I immediately get up from the sofa where I was chatting with Ryan to pull her in for a hug. She instantly starts sobbing on my shoulder and saying how stupid she was.

"It'll be okay, Abs. If it's meant to be, then it will all work out," I say, rubbing her back. "You want some breakfast?"

She shakes her head against me. "No, I can't eat anything." She releases me, wipes her eyes and turns to look at Ryan. He's sitting on the sofa looking sheepish like he doesn't know what to do with his sobbing sister. "I'm sorry, Ry," Abbi whispers. "I was angry. I didn't mean it." She gives him a small smile, turning back to me and giving my hand a squeeze before she leaves the room to get dressed.

I look over at Ryan and he just lifts a shoulder at me. I guess that was Abbi's way of saying she'll keep quiet.

Liv and I are tidying up our mess from breakfast when the doorbell rings. "Ry, could you get that, please?" I say over my shoulder, knowing exactly who it is as it's bang on eleven o'clock.

"Sure, are you expecting someone?"

"Just go answer it!" I say with a laugh.

Abbi reappears, looking a little better than before, just after Ryan leaves the room. Her make-up mostly covers the dark circles under her eyes from her lack of sleep, but they're still red and bloodshot from crying. Something tells me her mum will zone straight in on that and presume the tattooed bad boy has broken her heart.

"Oh my God!" we hear Ryan say from downstairs, making us laugh.

"Happy birthday, Son!" Karen and Dave say at the same time. "Are you going to invite us in or just stand there, staring?"

I'm glad Ryan's surprised and that I actually managed to keep all of this a secret from him. A couple of seconds later, we hear them climbing the stairs to join us. I quickly fill the kettle again and put it on as Dave and Karen turn the corner and greet their daughters. Ryan walks around them, comes straight to me and engulfs me in a huge hug.

"You spoke to my mum and organised this?" he asks, a look of disbelief on his face.

"Yeah, I phoned her and she didn't hang up on me," I say quietly with a laugh. "I thought it was time to put what happened in the summer behind us. I know you've missed them, so I wanted you to be able to spend some time with them. The five of you can do whatever you want this afternoon, but you need to be back by seven for dinner. Tomorrow, we're meeting the Morrisons at the Fat Dog. Susan wanted to still cook a roast but, after a lot of convincing, I managed to get her to change her mind. I thought her cooking for ten was crazy!"

Ryan leans back into me and whispers, "I love you so much. Thank you." He gives me an innocent kiss on the cheek, but I can tell by the look in his eyes he wants to do so much more.

"Molly," Dave says, walking over to us with his arms out. He embraces me before thanking me for inviting them to spend the weekend with their kids. Karen isn't quite so forthcoming. She gives me a reluctant kiss on the cheek.

I make them all tea and coffee and put out biscuits for them while they catch up and decide what to do. I excuse myself and head downstairs. I don't want to get in the way of their family bonding time.

CHAPTER TEN

Ryan

I watch Molly leave out of the corner of my eye and my heart drops at how she feels like she isn't a part of this family, and that she feels like she has to leave us alone. I want to follow her and drag her back up here, but I also want to accept her wishes for us to stay quiet. I guess she wants to try to win my mum around as my friend before I introduce her as my girlfriend.

My parents have only been here once before and it was the week I got the keys, so it was pretty much empty. I'm really glad they are now seeing it as my home, not just a house.

We eventually decide that, as the weather is nice, we'll drive into the city and have a wander around. Dad wants to see the university and a couple of our well-known sights in Oxford, whereas Mum, Abbi, and Liv would like to hit the high street. Personally, I'm not bothered what we do; it will just be nice to spend a day together.

I'm hopeful I can convince Molly to join us, so I head down to see her. To my surprise, she's already wearing her coat and is sitting on her bed, pulling her boots on.

"You going out?"

"Yeah, I thought I would go and check on Jax. He sounded pretty upset last night."

"Oh, I was hoping you'd come out with us," I say, sitting down next to her and grabbing her hand.

"No, your mum is already having to put up with me here. I don't want to crash your family day. I'm cooking us all dinner tonight so we can be together then."

"You're my family too, Molly." I watch as her eyes fill with moisture as I say this. "She will never know how amazing you are if she doesn't get to spend any time with you." I rest my forehead against hers when she turns to look at me.

"We will have enough time together before they go back tomorrow. Plus, I think she'll appreciate me giving you guys time." She looks at me with sad eyes. I know she's dying to be part of my family and to be accepted by my mum. I'm just praying that it happens, and soon. I want all the people I love to get on and be able to spend time together.

"Okay," I say, giving in to her. I guess she's right.

"Okay," is all she says in response, but she keeps eye contact with me. "Make sure you're all back by seven. I'm hoping to impress your mum with my cooking skills."

"Aw, you trying to show her what a good wife you'll be?" I say with a laugh, trying to lighten the mood.

"Something like that," she replies sadly. She gives me a quick kiss on the lips before standing, saying that she'll see me later and to enjoy my day.

"Molly?"

She turns to look at me with raised eyebrows.

"You don't think you're getting away with that, do you?" I say as I start walking toward her.

"Wha—"

I cut her off when my lips hit hers. Lifting my hand to the back of her neck, I tilt my head to the side to deepen our kiss. She groans when my tongue slides against hers, and her hands go to my hair, holding tightly. When her hips start grinding against mine, I reluctantly pull away and rest my forehead back against hers while we catch our breaths.

When we've just about got ourselves back together, I give her a quick kiss on her nose before walking to the door. I can't help myself; I have to look back at her before I leave the room. She's leaning against the wall, her chest still heaving, and her eyes are glazed as she stares back at me.

"Tell Jax I say hi and that my sister's an idiot. See you later," I say, taking the stairs two at a time to gather everyone up for our afternoon out.

I get a knowing look off Abbi when I re-enter the living area, but I ignore her probing eyes.

"Where have you been?" Mum asks as I start tidying up their dirty mugs.

"I was just telling Molly our plans for the day."

"Oh, she's coming with us?" Mum says, sounding disappointed.

"No, she's not, and if I'm honest, I don't blame her. It's taken a lot for her to organise this weekend for me. You could at least try to be nice to her. She didn't have to invite you to spend time here. She would like us back before seven because she's cooking dinner for us all."

"Molly is a brilliant cook, Mum. She told me she's doing Italian," Abbi says, trying to fight for her. "So, what's Molly doing today?"

"She's going to see a friend. His girlfriend just broke up with him and she wants to go and see if he's okay," I say, narrowing my eyes at Abbi.

"Oh," is her only response before she darts out of the room to get her shoes.

Suddenly, Mum pipes up again. "Does she have a lot of male friends?" If she carries on like this, I'm going to be asking them to leave before tomorrow gets here.

"No, not really. Jax is her friend, but also her colleague. He's a really good guy and he's hurting. Molly would do anything for the people who are important to her, as you may have noticed. Now, this may be my house, but she lives here too, and if you can't be nice, you'll need to find somewhere else to stay tonight."

Mum scoffs but doesn't say any more, so I'm hoping I may have got through to her.

<hr>

We spend hours walking around, looking at the different architecture and chatting about our lives. Abbi keeps trying to get me alone, but I avoid it. The last thing I need is her asking me questions about Molly, and having Mum overhear. She'll have to wait until we're completely alone. Then, I will tell her whatever she wants to know. Abbi and I don't keep secrets. I'm pretty sure Liv resents how close we are, but she never lets on.

We eventually end up on the high street and the girls drag Dad and me around, shop after shop. We sit together on the stools in various fitting rooms and hope that we make the correct noises when they each appear in different outfits.

We end up in Debenhams. Abbi and Liv promise that this is the last stop, then we can head home. Mum, Liv, and Dad are looking around the jewellery counters, looking for something to go with the dress she just bought, while I'm with Abbi, giving her my opinion on various perfumes.

She glances over to check the others are far enough away before she starts. "So... how long has it been going on?"

I follow her gaze, just to check for myself, and seeing as they're on the other side of the store, I answer her. "A couple of weeks." I can't stop the huge grin breaking across my face.

"At fucking last, Bro," she laughs. "Oh, what about this one?" she says, shoving another little bit of card under my nose. The smell makes goosebumps break out on my skin and I instantly think of Molly.

I look up to see the others walking our way. Before they get too close, I turn back toward Abbi. "It's perfect. Buy that one for me. I'll give you the cash later."

She smiles warmly and nods. "It's so good to see you happy, Ryan. Mum will come around, you'll see."

"I know you're going to hate me for saying it, but you should listen to your own advice there, Abs. Jax is a great guy, and Mum will see that eventually, too."

"I know he is, but do you really think Mum would be able to see past what happened? You know what she's like."

"The only way you'll ever find out is to give it a chance." The cashier comes over and interrupts our conversation.

"What did you buy, Abbi?" Mum asks when she joins us.

"Just some perfume." She grabs the bag off the desk then heads toward the exit. "I don't know about you guys, but I'm starving. Shall we head back so Molly can feed us?"

Everyone agrees and we go in search of the cars. Abbi comes with me and questions me all the way home. I can't wipe the smile off my face the whole way back. Just thinking about Molly makes me so happy. Abbi agrees to keep quiet about us until we decide to tell everyone. I try to convince her to talk to Jax, but I'm pretty sure it falls on deaf ears. My sister can be a stubborn bitch when she wants to be.

The house smells amazing when we let ourselves in. Whatever Molly is cooking upstairs makes my stomach growl.

When I walk into the living area, I can't help a small laugh escaping my throat. Molly is prancing around the kitchen, looking like the perfect little housewife. She's wearing a cute floral dress with an apron over the top, and the dusky pink shoes I bought her. There's food covering all the work surfaces, and the table is laid to look like a restaurant.

"Ah, good, you're all back. When you're ready, come and sit at the table and I'll dish up the starters."

I turn to look back at the others just as Mum's eyebrows lift. I'm not sure if that's because she is impressed or surprised. I'm hoping the former.

Molly

"I never thought I'd say this, Molly, but I think your tiramisu is better than my wife's," Dave says as he scrapes out the bottom of his bowl of seconds.

Liv gasps next to me, making me look up from mumbling a *thank you* to the compliments I received about my dinner. I can't help but think that if looks could kill... well, poor Dave would be six feet under by now from the death glare he's receiving from his wife. He just shrugs at her and continues to lick his spoon. I continue watching their exchange until Karen lets out a huge sigh and rolls her eyes at him.

"It was all amazing, Molly. Thank you," Ryan adds with a cheeky thigh squeeze under the table. He has been remarkably well-behaved at the dinner table compared to last night, when he was constantly trying to touch me up. I guess his stuck-up mother has put him off a little.

"Yes, well... credit where credit's due. That was a delicious meal, Molly," Karen says, almost convincingly.

"Thank you. I'm glad you all enjoyed it."

"Please, could I have the recipe for the ravioli?" Karen asks, shocking the life out of me. My surprise must be written all over my face because she continues with, "If you don't mind, of course."

"No, of course not. It was one of my gran's. I've typed them all up because her writing had started to fade. I'll print you one out after I've cleaned up this lot."

"Oh, I love old recipes. I'd love to have a look at them all."

Wow. Something Karen and I could have in common, after all.

"Sure." I go to stand but Ryan immediately grabs my forearm to stop me.

"Molly, there's no way you're cleaning. You've done enough already. You go relax. I'll do this. Abbi and Liv can help me."

"Can we, now?" Abbi says sarcastically.

"No, Ry, it's your weekend. You enjoy your family being here and leave it to me."

"Molly, shut up and listen to my brother. Go sit down and chill out."

I'm now getting serious looks from all the Evans siblings, so I cave and have another sip of my wine.

"They're right. Let them get on with it, and you can show me these recipes."

I hesitantly grab my glass and stand up with Karen, pointing her in the direction of my room. As I descend the stairs behind her, a weird feeling settles over me that I can't quite put my finger on. I try to shake it off. I should be pleased that I have something to talk to Karen about. A little bonding over some old school recipes might be just what we need.

"Have a seat," I say, gesturing to the chair. "I'll just boot up my laptop." I place my computer on the coffee table and settle myself on my knees on the floor while I wait.

Karen lets out a breath that makes me shudder in apprehension.

"Molly... my son keeps telling me how wonderful you are and... he's usually a pretty good judge of character. But something about you doesn't sit right with me..."

I go to speak, but she continues.

"I have a feeling that something is going on between the two of you. You seem... closer. Plus, a mother never misses those little looks and touches when you think no one is watching..."

"What Ryan needs is a nice woman who's going to treat him right and be by his side all the way. He's already had enough heartache to last a lifetime. After poor Hannah, I do not want him to go through any more. And Molly..." She lets out another breath before continuing with what I fear is coming. "You are going to cause him some serious heartache when you decide he just isn't exciting enough for you. I know about your past. I know you're a little... what shall we say... *free*. I can see it in your eyes that this..." She waves her hands around, gesturing to the house. "...and him, are not what you want long-term. You want the buzz and the excitement."

What the actual fuck?

I sit there on my bedroom floor and just stare at her in complete amazement. I open and close my mouth a number of times because I just can't find the words.

"I think it's best for both of you if you just end this now before too many feelings are involved." I watch as she leans to the side slightly and pulls a piece of paper out of her jeans pocket. She slides the offending piece of paper over to me before she stands up. I have to lean back to be able to look at her, making me feel like I'm at a great disadvantage in this exchange.

"You will take that, and you will find somewhere else to live. You will get out of my son's life. For good." She walks over to the door and looks back over her shoulder. "Needless to say, Ryan doesn't need to know about this. You wouldn't want to break up his family. After all, you know how much it means to him. I'll tell everyone you had a headache. Goodbye, Molly." I stare after her in shock as she disappears back upstairs.

I sit in the same position, looking at the little piece of paper on the coffee table for the longest time. Eventually, my legs go completely dead and I have to move. I scoot over to sit in the chair Karen was in not so long ago, continuing to stare at the paper. I know I need to move, because if I know Ryan at all, he will come down to check on me as soon as he can.

I've just plucked up the courage to look at what's on the paper when I hear him at the top of the stairs. "Grab me another beer, I just want to make sure she's okay."

"Shit." I grab the paper, dive onto my bed, and shove it under my pillow. I lie so I'm facing away from the door and pretend to be asleep.

"Molly?" he whispers before the bed dips. Leaning forward, he moves a strand of hair from my face before placing a kiss to my temple.

I have to really concentrate on keeping my breathing slow because in reality all I want to do is wrap my arms around him and tell him what a massive bitch his mother is. But her words keep repeating in my head.

You wouldn't want to break up his family. After all, you know how much it means to him.

And she's right; I would do anything to keep his family together and around him. I know what it is like not to have one, and I wouldn't wish that on anyone, even a fully grown man. Everyone needs their mum sometimes.

"I love you, gorgeous. I'll be upstairs if you need me," he says softly before getting up and leaving the room.

I let out a huge breath when I hear him get to the top of the stairs. My first tear drops as I contemplate what I'm going to do. Is Karen right? Am I not good enough for him? I've certainly thought it enough over the past few months, but Ryan has always made me feel stupid for thinking such things. What if he isn't aware, though? What if she is right? What if I'm not cut out for this serious relationship thing? It's not like I've done it before.

I turn my head into the pillow when the sobs hit to try to muffle the sound. I don't want to be heard and have people asking questions.

I must cry myself to sleep eventually, because I come around when I feel myself lifted from the bed before being placed back down and the covers pulled over me.

When I wake up the next morning, it's still dark outside. I turn over and see Ryan fast asleep next to me, looking peaceful and content. If only he knew what his mother was up to. I've no idea what time he came to bed last night, but I have a feeling it was late. I get myself comfortable so I can watch him sleep for a while. It's not until I slide my hand under my pillow and hit the piece of paper that my memories from last night resurface. I grab it and gently climb out of bed, collecting a change of clothes on my way to the bathroom.

I t's a bitterly cold, sunny November morning, so I'm really glad I thought to pick up my hat, scarf, and gloves before I snuck out of the house while everyone was still asleep. Once I was dressed, I left a note in the kitchen to say that the table is booked for one o'clock at the Fat Dog, and that I would meet them there. I know that as soon as I see Ryan, he'll be questioning me about where I went, but honestly I had more important things to think about than leaving a plausible note.

I sit myself down in front of Hannah's gravestone after taking the dead flowers to the bin and fiddle with the new ones I brought.

"So... what should I do about Karen, then, Han?" My voice sounds defeated even to my own ears.

I pull the piece of paper I've still refused to look at out of my pocket, let out a massive sigh, then turn it over.

My eyes almost pop out of my head when I see what is written on it. Five thousand fucking pounds. I don't really know what I expected, but I was thinking she'd try to pay me off with a couple hundred. She must really mean business if she's cracked out a four-figure pay-off. I laugh to myself, even though it's anything but funny.

I spend hours talking myself around in circles about what to do with this situation. I know that, no matter what I do, it's going to hurt Ryan. His mum is right about one thing: he has had enough heartache losing Hannah than anyone should have to deal with at such a young age. I guess the question in the end comes down to whether I rip his heart out and do what his mother thinks is best for him, and in turn rip my own out... or tell everything to Ryan about what his mum really thinks of me and rip his family apart.

"Hey, it's me. Can I come up?" A groan comes down the line before I'm buzzed in. I'm hoping the groan is a result of the horrendous hangover he must have rather than my visit.

When I get to the top of the stairs, Jax is nowhere to be seen, but his door is slightly open so I can let myself in. When I get to his living room doorway, I can't help but smile. He's lying on his back on the sofa in only his boxers with a cushion over his head. I'm guessing it's muffling any sound or light entering.

"Jax?" I whisper as I walk over and sit on the edge of the sofa next to him. He groans again, so I gently pry the cushion away from his face.

When he eventually lets go enough that I can get a look at him, I'm shocked. I've never seen him anything less than perfect, but here he is with dark circles under his bloodshot eyes, looking a little green. He looks up at me, compassion filling his features, reminding me that I probably look a little like him from the crying I've been doing.

"Molly?" he questions quietly. His concern makes a sob escape my throat and more tears fill my eyes. "Come here," he says, slowly lifting himself up and wrapping his arms around me. I do the same in return, and I can't help laughing when he jumps from how cold my hands are. Well, I have been sat in a cemetery for most of the morning.

We sit there for ages, comforting each other. Jax is taking this break-up with Abbi much worse than he did when he caught Lucy planning how to rinse him dry. Little does he know that the root of our problems is the same bloody woman.

When he eventually pulls back, I notice the clock on the wall showing it's just gone midday. "Shit, I'm really sorry, but I'm going to have to go. I'll explain everything if you can do me a huge favour in a couple of hours."

"Of course. Anything."

After giving Jax his instructions and attempting to sort my make-up out, I leave to meet everyone at the pub. I check my phone and see that I have multiple calls and texts from Ryan and a couple from Abbi, which doesn't surprise me. From the tone of his texts, I think he's a bit concerned about my disappearing act.

I'm the first one to arrive so I grab myself a drink, sit down at our table, and try to pull myself together enough to get through the next couple of hours. Luckily for me, the Morrisons arrive before the Evans and distract me.

I know the moment Ryan arrives, because his eyes burn into my skin. I look up to see him storming our way with everyone following. I'm sat with Emma on one side and Lilly on the other, so he can't get to me easily, which I think pisses him off further.

"I'm sorry, can I just borrow Molly for a couple of minutes?" is the first thing he says to the Morrisons.

"Oh... of course, angel. Everything okay?" Susan asks, concerned.

"I just need to ask her something quickly."

Ryan practically drags my chair out from under me before grabbing my arm and pulling me back out the way he came in, past a surprised looking Abbi, Liv, and Dave. Karen, on the other hand, just looks smug, and I want to punch her in the face for doing this to us.

Ryan waits until the door's shut before he starts. "What the fuck, Molly? I wake up to find you gone and a vague note, then you ignore all my calls and texts all morning. Where the fuck have you been? I've been going crazy."

"Sorry, I, uh... had to go into work. I forgot to do something urgent for this week. I left my phone in the car, sorry..." I trail off.

Ryan reaches his hand out to cup my cheek and pulls my face so I have to look at him. Concern crinkles the corners of his eyes, but he doesn't question me.

"We'll talk about this later. For now, I'm just glad you're okay. Let's go and enjoy our afternoon, yeah?" I mumble my agreement before following him back into the pub.

CHAPTER ELEVEN

Ryan

The food, as always, is amazing and everyone's getting on really well. Susan and Pete haven't seen my parents since a couple of days after Hannah's funeral, so they have plenty to talk about. Unfortunately, I have to sit at the other end of the table from Molly, but I keep a very good eye on her and notice that she's hardly talking to anyone and just playing with her food. I think Mum knows where my focus is and does everything she can to distract me with another mind-numbing conversation about something her friend Doreen said.

Eventually, though, she does start a conversation up that gets Molly's attention. "Ryan and Abbi, you will never believe who has moved back to Liverpool..." We both just look at her, waiting to fill in the blanks. With our mother, it could be anyone. "Beth and Caleb. Their father's contract in America came to an end and they decided to come back." Beth and Caleb are the same ages as Abbi and I, and we went through school together. Well, that was until their family moved when Beth was sixteen and Caleb was eleven. They lived a couple of houses down from us and we all spent a lot of time together, Beth and I especially. I was gutted when they had to move. For a while I thought she was the one, and I know Abbi was much younger, but she adored Caleb.

"Oh really, that's, uh... good, I guess." I don't really know what to say to this news. It's been so long that I'm sure none of us would have anything in common now.

Mum's eyes light up before she speaks. "Beth asked for your number so you two could catch up. She's single, from what I gather." My blood boils at the thought of her trying to set me up in front of Molly.

"I guess it will be good to speak to her again, but don't get any ideas, Mum, and definitely do not get involved," I beg, and she just gives me a look.

Throughout this whole conversation, I've watched Molly's eyes move back and forth between me and my mum like she's trying to figure something out. Surely, she can see what my mum is doing, but I'm not liking the look on Molly's face. She looks kind of resigned and that worries me. A lot.

Everyone continues to chat apart from Molly again, who's staring down at her hands. Suddenly, everyone's conversations are interrupted when her phone starts ringing. She grabs it quickly, apologises, and then hurries away from the table. I watch her talk briefly with whoever is on the other end before she returns, looking regretful.

"I'm sorry, guys, but I'm going to have to go. That was my brother. Something's going on with his in-laws and they need me to look after my nieces," she explains as she grabs her bag and coat. "The bill's been settled, but if you want any more drinks or anything, then please go for it. They've got my card details. Enjoy the rest of your afternoon." She turns to my parents and sisters. "Have a safe trip back, and I'll see you all soon."

"I'll walk you out," I say, going to stand up.

"No, I'll see you later. Enjoy the time with your family." Abbi and Liv give her quick hugs but then she's out the door before I can blink. We all look at each other, completely bemused, but slowly everyone gets back to their earlier conversations.

Apart from me, because I'm now more concerned than ever about what's going on. I need to get everyone out of here so I can hunt down where her brother lives.

Molly

The look on Ryan's face as I announced I was leaving broke my heart, but it didn't stop me from practically running out of there and away from his interfering mother. I can't believe she's trying to set him up with an old friend. Wait, no, I totally can, especially if she lives in Liverpool. All Karen's dreams could come true at once: Ryan could have a 'nice' girlfriend and move back home. I get a little choked up at the thought. Shaking my head, I focus on driving before I get so distracted, I end up in a ditch.

I pull back up outside Jax's apartment building and let myself in with the keys he gave me earlier. When I get in, Jax is still laid out on the same sofa as he was earlier, but he's wearing a different pair of boxers and his hair's a little damp. At least he's managed a shower.

I take my coat and boots off before throwing myself at the other sofa and lying in the same position as Jax. His living room is laid out with two sofas facing each other with a coffee table in the middle.

"How'd it go?" he asks, looking over at me, getting comfortable.

"Shit. He's so angry with me, and hurt, but I just don't know what to do for the best." Jax raises his eyebrows at me, so I go on to explain all about Karen and her little scheme to get rid of me.

"Wow, what a bitch. You've got to tell him, Molls. He deserves to know what she's really like," he says once I've finished.

"I don't disagree. He does deserve to know, but I just don't know if I can do it to him. His family is so important to him. I don't want to be the one to break it. I'd give anything to have a caring and supportive family like his, even if his mum is a... little misguided."

"Don't you think that's up to him to decide? I would say that you're just as important to him as his family, if not more, Molly. And really, you'd give anything to have a family like that? Have you looked at the people you have around you lately? The Morrisons, your brothers, Megan, Ryan, me," he says, pointing at himself. "Just to name a few. Just because we aren't all blood related doesn't make us care for or support each other any less."

I think for a few minutes about all the people he's just mentioned. "Yeah, you're right. I need to focus on what I have got and not what I haven't, because what I have got is really fucking good. Thank you, Jax."

"You're still not going to tell him though, are you?"

"I don't know. I mean, what if she's right and I'm just not good enough for him? What if I'm not cut out for the committed relationship thing and I'm just going to hurt him anyway? Better to do it sooner rather than later, don't you think?"

"What if you don't hurt him?"

I watch the cogs turning in Jax's head before he jumps up. "I need a drink."

"What about the hangover?"

"The hangover isn't numbing the pain. Alcohol will, though. You with me?"

"Abso-fucking-lutely." I follow Jax into his kitchen where he pulls out a bottle of wine, a couple of beers and a bottle of vodka. He turns and grabs a wine glass and a couple of shot glasses before filling them and handing me my drinks.

"To interfering mothers-in-law who need to keep their fucking noses out of our business and love lives," he says, raising his shot glass.

"To being fucked over by your mother-in-law," I agree, before necking the shot at the same time as Jax.

***

"So where does Ryan think you've gone? Because I'm thinking that if he knew you were here, he would have broken the door down by now, trying to get to you," Jax asks, starting to slur his words slightly.

It's been hours since I left the pub. It's dark out and I'm waiting for that bang on the door. I know that everyone would have headed home by now, and I'm sure Ryan set straight about finding me. I'm not stupid enough to think he won't figure it out.

"I told him Steven needed me to babysit the girls. I'm sure it won't be long before he figures out where I am."

"He doesn't know where I live, though, does he?"

"I don't think so, but I'm sure Abbi will soon tell him." Jax groans and downs another shot at the sound of her name.

"If she means that much to you, you've got to fight for her."

"What, like you're doing for Ryan?" he asks with a quirked eyebrow.

"Shit." I squeal, putting the wine glass and bottle down before trying to wipe off my t-shirt and jeans. If I can't successfully fill my glass back up, it means I'm drunker than I thought. Jax watches me and laughs. "Have you got anything I can change into? These are soaked."

"Yeah, come on," he says, holding his hand out to pull me up. "I'm guessing you're sleeping here tonight?"

"Uh... yeah, I guess. Is that okay?"

"Of course. Here, take this," he says, handing me a t-shirt. "You can have a shower if you like."

"Thank you, Jax," I say, leaning over and kissing him on the cheek. "You're a really good guy, you know that? Abbi is stupid to let you go." He lets out a breath at my words before plodding back toward the living room, leaving me in his bedroom.

CHAPTER TWELVE

Ryan

"And you haven't spoken to her all day?"

"No. Ryan, I'm sorry, but she really isn't here," Steven repeats for about the tenth time since I've been on the phone with him. At first, I thought he was covering for her, but now I'm starting to believe him. "Will you call me when you find her, though? You've got me worried."

"So, she's not there, then?" Abbi confirms when I end the call.

"No, and he hasn't spoken to her all day." It's just gone nine in the evening and I've not heard anything from Molly since her disappearance from the pub earlier this afternoon. My parents and Liv left not long after we got back. Abbi is still here, even though she has to drive back to Manchester tonight. "You need to get going, you've got a long drive."

"No, I've told you I'll stay. I can ring in sick tomorrow if need be. I want to make sure Molly is okay."

"I'm sure she's fine," I try to say in a reassuring voice, but it comes out sounding anything but. "She'll just be at a friend's. I don't want you missing uni because of us. You go, and I promise I'll call you when I've found her."

"You promise?"

"Yes, I promise. Now, get going. It's a long drive in the dark on your own."

"Yes, *Mum*, calm down!"

I carry Abbi's bag downstairs for her and put it in her car before giving her a hug and sending on her way; not before I've promised again to ring her when I've found Molly.

I head back inside and plonk myself on the sofa, trying to decide what to do for the best. She's not at Steven's, which I think I pretty much knew to be the case because I could tell she was lying when she left the pub. Where is she most likely to go to hide?

The office.

Grabbing my keys, I jump in my car before speeding into the city to see if she's there. I'm quite hopeful, because every time she's run before, this is where she's come. As I drive down the road to Cocoa's, butterflies erupt in my stomach, but my heart drops when I see the empty parking spaces around the back.

I can't leave without making sure, so I grab the keys from my glovebox and jog up to the door, letting myself inside to see for myself that she isn't here.

Feeling defeated, I get back in the car and rest my forehead against the wheel while I think about where she could be. If she's not here alone, then it means she has gone to someone. Who would she go to?

Megan.

I shove the key in the ignition and back out of the space.

"Hi, angel. Is everything okay?" Susan asks when she pulls her front door open. It's gone ten o'clock, which is late for Susan and Pete. She's stood there in her dressing gown, looking worried by my late night visit.

"Um... is Molly here, by any chance?"

"No, I haven't seen her since she left the pub. Is everything okay?" she asks as she opens the door wider for me to enter.

Susan looks even more concerned after I finish explaining her weird actions today. She knows as well as I do that it isn't like Molly.

"I was hoping you could give me Megan's phone number. I'm guessing she's most likely gone there."

"Megan had the weekend off, so I don't even know if she's about."

"Still worth a try," I say as I follow Susan into her office.

After a very brief conversation with Megan, I discover she's out of town for the weekend and hasn't heard anything from Molly.

I run my hands through my hair. "Where the hell is she?"

"Which other friends is she likely to go to?" Susan asks.

Susan makes me a coffee while I ring Chris to see if either him or Shane have heard from her, but no such luck. The only thing I'm achieving is getting them worried, which really isn't helping the feeling I have in the pit of my stomach.

"Here you go, angel," Susan says as she passes me a steaming mug. "Any luck?"

"No, no one's heard from her all day. She's been so weird today, but I just can't put my finger on it. She went downstairs with Mum last night and..."

"What is it, Ryan?"

"Jax... she's with Jax. My mum said something to her and she's gone to Jax because he's having the same problem with Abbi, and he'll know how she's feeling." I pace the Morrisons' kitchen floor as all the pieces fall into place.

"What could your mum have said to upset her so much?" Susan asks, looking bemused by the idea.

"Oh, trust me, my mum could have said plenty. She can be vicious."

"Oh," Susan says, looking a bit confused. I guess when you're the world's perfect mum, it's hard to imagine saying something nasty to one of your children's friends. Especially when they know how much they mean to them. "Well, what are you hanging around here for? Go find out," she says, as she stands and gestures toward the door.

"I... I don't know where he lives."

"Well, get on the bloody phone to your sister and find out." Wow, Susan must be more worried by this than I thought if she's throwing swear words around.

I've tried Abbi five times but no answer; she must be driving. This both pleases and frustrates me in equal measures. I'm glad she isn't on the phone while driving, but I'm also desperate for Jax's address. I need to find out what the fuck has happened.

It's a long twenty minutes later when Abbi eventually returns my call. She's very apologetic because she didn't realise her phone was on silent, and it wasn't until she stopped at some services for a caffeine fix that she saw my missed calls.

I quickly say goodbye to Susan, then I'm back in my car and speeding toward the address Abbi has just relayed to me.

Jax lives in the middle of the city, so it's another thirty minutes before I'm pulling up outside his apartment building. I know she's here, because her car's here. I'm just about to press the buzzer to his flat when a drunken couple comes stumbling up to the entrance. I let them go ahead of me but catch the door before it closes. I watch as they enter the lift before turning and taking the stairs two at a time until I'm on the top floor.

I begin hammering on Jax's front door loudly enough that it would wake him if he's asleep. I continue banging for a good few minutes before I hear any movement inside, and a male voice grumbles that he's coming.

"I know she's here. I saw her car," I say, shoving the door after he's cracked it open so hard it ricochets off the wall behind it as I march into Jax's flat.

"Come in, why don't you?" Jax says with a smirk from behind me.

"Where the fuck is she?"

"I think you need to calm down, mate."

"Don't fucking tell me what to do," I say as I poke my head into the kitchen, then the living room, before making my way down the hall toward what I presume is the bedroom. What I see makes my blood boil. "How about instead you explain to me what the fuck is going on?" I shout as I shove his shoulders until I have him backed up against the wall of his bedroom. It doesn't even occur to me that Molly hasn't so much as stirred at my shouting and crashing about.

When Jax doesn't say anything, I get right in his face. "Well?"

Molly

Turning over, I cuddle into the duvet before willing myself back to sleep so I don't have to feel my head pounding and stomach churning. Eventually, I give in, and decide I'm going to have to go in search of painkillers instead.

I gently ease my eyes open and my breath catches in my throat at the sight in front of me. Ryan's staring down at me, looking anguished. I break my stare with him to quickly take in my surroundings, and I'm totally confused when I realise I'm in his bedroom. The last thing I remember was drinking on Jax's sofa. How and when did I get here?

I look back into his concerned eyes. "Ry..." I try speaking, but my throat is so dry that I have to swallow and try again. "Ryan?"

"There are painkillers and water on the side if you need them," he says coldly.

"Thank you," I whisper, slowly pulling my body up enough so that I can take them without upsetting my dodgy stomach.

Once I'm done, I lie myself back down and look over Ryan's features. His eyes are bloodshot with dark circles around them, and his hair is more of a mess than usual. I let my eyes roam down his body, noting that he's still wearing the same clothes as yesterday. "Ryan, what..." I start to ask the first of the many questions that I have, but he interrupts me.

"No, Molly. You need to go first. You have the most explaining to do."

I'm reminded of everything that happened over the last two days, and it makes me want to dive under the covers and hide. I never got to make a decision as to whether I wanted to tell Ryan the truth, but it doesn't look like I have much of a choice now. He must see the internal battle I'm having with myself, because he prompts me to start talking. There never really was a decision to make—I made it a long time ago.

I roll onto my back so I don't have to look at him and let out a huge breath before saying very quietly, "Your mum tried paying me off."

The silence in the room is almost painful as Ryan takes in what I've just said. "So, yesterday was you leaving me?" he asks, making my head snap back to his.

"What? No... Ryan, that wasn't it at all."

"But you ran. You did what my mum wanted and left me." His face is pulled tight with anger. "Was that it? If I didn't find you last night, would we be over now?"

The pain in his voice causes me to scramble out of bed and crawl over to him until I'm on my knees by his feet and holding his trembling hands in mine. "No," I repeat.

"So, what was it?"

"Your mum got me alone under the pretence of looking at some old recipes, but what she actually wanted to do was sit in front of me and tell me all my greatest fears. To hear them spoken back to me and to know someone else thinks the same things about me that I do freaked me out. She warned me about breaking up your family, and I know how much they mean to you, and I didn't—I *don't*—want to be the one who causes issues between you all. Family is too important. I ran, but only because I needed to get my head together. I spent most of the morning with Hannah, but she wasn't much use on the advice front." I quirk the corner of my mouth up when I see a small smile creep onto Ryan's face at my inappropriate joke. "I love you, and I shouldn't care what your mum thinks of me. The only person's opinions I should care about are yours, and I'm just as important to you as your family, if not... more so..." I tail off at the end, just in case I've got this all wrong.

Ryan doesn't say or do anything for a few minutes. I search his blue eyes for any clues as to what he's thinking when he suddenly moves, making me jump. He leans forward, wrapping his fingers around my waist and launches us both to the bed. The sudden movement isn't great for my stomach, but I manage to keep it under control and all is forgotten when Ryan rolls me on my back and presses his lips to mine. He places a few feather-light kisses to my lips before he runs the tip of his tongue along the join, asking for me to open up, which I do instantly. My hands automatically go into his hair so I can hold him closer to me. When I feel the hand on my hip start to move up my waist, I pull away from him and open my eyes. I can't help but laugh at his pouty face. I run the pad of my finger along his bottom lip before kissing his nose.

"Now, Mr. Evans, can you please explain to me how I woke up in your bed?" I lift an eyebrow at him in question.

He leans forward and places his forehead against mine, letting out a breath that tickles down my neck and causes goosebumps.

He closes his eyes before he starts. "You were totally out of it in Jax's bed when I found you. I scooped you up and brought you home with me. I'm sorry, but there was no way you were spending the night in another man's bed, even if you're just friends with him."

His feelings for me shine brightly in his eyes as he stares down at me. How could I ever doubt him?

"I'm sorry. I should have told you right away."

"It's okay. I understand."

"She just said all that stuff, and it's exactly what I worry about. I just freaked. I'm so sorry. I love you so much, Ryan. I'm sorry you thought I left you. I'm sorry for running. I'm j-just s-sorry," I stutter, my emotions getting the better of me. Ryan wraps his arms around me until I've got myself back under control.

He kisses my nose before pulling back and looking into my eyes. "You're it for me, Molly. You need to realise that." He rolls onto his back as he says this, and I cuddle into his side.

The next thing I know, I'm being gently pried from Ryan's body as he tries to sneak out from under me. I groan and go to grab his arm to pull him back.

"I'm sorry, gorgeous, my phone's ringing. I'll be back soon with tea, I promise." This makes me feel better, so I nuzzle into his pillow and breathe in his scent while he's gone.

I listen to his footsteps as he heads toward the living room before his voice makes me jump. "How fucking dare you? I told you not to stick your nose in... no, no, you do not get to explain. I know exactly what you did, and I've had enough. I don't give a flying fuck what you think. I am in love with her and she is the most important thing in my life, and nothing you do will change how I feel about her." Everything goes silent and the only thing I can hear is my heart beating loudly in my chest. I can just imagine her crying and begging for forgiveness on the other end of the phone. "No, I don't care. You say you know her, but what you've done is enough proof that you don't. If you knew Molly at all, you would know she could never be bought off. Her world doesn't revolve around money." It goes quiet again before Ryan raises his voice even louder, shouting that he's done and for her not to contact either one of us for the foreseeable future.

The following silence is almost painful as I consider whether I should go to him or give him some space. All of a sudden, there's a bang, and a loud "Fuck!" I'm just about to put my feet on the floor when his footsteps pound up the stairs.

"Ryan, are you..." The look on his face stops me. He's murderous. His fists are clenched at his sides, his chest is heaving, and I can see the vein in his neck pulsing.

"I'm going for a run." He manages to get out before marching over to his chest of drawers, changing into his running clothes and storming out of the house.

So much for my tea. I sit in bed a while longer, thinking about everything that's happened in the last few minutes, before heading for a shower. It's not until I'm washing my hair that I realise it's Monday, and that both of us should be at work. I quickly finish up and go in search of my phone to call Jax.

Once he's convinced me that he's got everything covered at the office, I agree with his suggestion to stay at home and sort things out properly with Ryan. After hanging up, I make my way down to the kitchen to make us some lunch.

I end up waiting for Ryan to return for so long that I eat my half of the sandwiches. I was intending on taking Jax's advice, but seeing as he's disappeared, I decide to get some work done instead.

My phone rings just after twelve-thirty, and I quickly answer when I see Abbi's name. She's going full throttle trying to convince me—and herself

—why being with Jax is a bad idea, when I hear the front door slam shut, making me jump.

I'm suddenly nervous about the mood Ryan might be in when he appears. After everything both me and his mother have put him through the last two days, I wouldn't be surprised if he's seriously pissed off. When he does round the doorway, my breath catches at the sight of him. My eyes take him in, head to toe. His hair is wet and sticking up in all directions. His skin is covered in a sheen of sweat, making his already tight t-shirt stick to and show off all his well-defined muscles. What really catches my attention, though, are his eyes. The sight of them has me clamping my thighs together, because he only ever has eyes that dark when he's really turned on.

Abbi is still jabbering on in my ear, but I haven't heard a word of it since my eyes landed on Ryan. He throws his water bottle on the kitchen worktop before running his hand through his hair, his eyes never once leaving me. My pulse rate increases with every move he makes, and when he starts slowly sauntering toward me, the pounding in my chest is accompanied by a throbbing lower in my body. When he's in front of where I'm sitting on the sofa, I rise so that my breasts run up his chest. His scent hits me and heat pools between my legs. Ryan slowly reaches his hand up, and I think he's going to cup my cheek, but, to my surprise, he pulls the phone out of my hand and I hear Abbi's voice get quieter as he puts it to his ear.

Our eyes stay locked, but his mouth opening distracts me. "Molly will ring you back later," Ryan says into the phone before throwing it on the sofa behind me.

CHAPTER THIRTEEN

Ryan

It may have been two weeks since I discovered that my mum was trying to control my life, but the anger is still burning within me.

I realised soon after leaving the house that day for a run that the only thing I really needed was Molly. I needed her to know that she truly was the only one I wanted. I needed her, beneath me, writhing and screaming my name. I needed to own her. And that was exactly what I did once I got her up to my bedroom.

The lead-up to Chris and Shane's wedding has thankfully been drama free. No one else has stuck their noses in where they're not wanted.

Every day, I get a phone call from my mum, and every day I ignore it and let it go to voicemail. I listened to the first few messages that consisted of her crying, apologising, and telling me how much she loved me, but I soon got bored, so I've since deleted them as soon as she's left them. She doesn't know Molly, and if she doesn't sort herself out, she never will.

I've decided to stay in Oxford for Christmas and spend it with Molly and the Morrisons. Molly and I are throwing a New Year's Eve party, so I'll get to see my sisters then. Mum put pay to me worrying about not spending the holiday with them when she started meddling in my life.

"I hope the wedding breakfast is as good as the meal last night," Emma says, bringing me out of my daydreams. We've been sitting at the bar in the hotel for well over half an hour, waiting for Shane and Molly to appear. The ceremony is due to start in about fifteen minutes, but with no groom—or groomsmaid, as they've insisted on calling her—to give out instructions, we are all just loitering around. Suddenly, the level of noise in the room lowers and I see Emma look over my shoulder. "About time," she mumbles and waves.

I turn around to see Shane stood in his navy suit like I was expecting. What I wasn't quite expecting though, although I don't know why, is Molly next to him, looking like sex on legs.

"Holy shit," I mumble quietly to myself as I run my eyes all over her. She's wearing a skintight black dress, which has a low-cut square neckline showing off her cleavage perfectly. It makes me want to run over and stick my tongue in it and, from the look of the other men in the room, it's what they want to do as well.

The dress stops just below her knees, showing off her muscular calves which are topped off with some crazily high black strappy shoes which, to be honest, would look right at home with a pair of handcuffs and a blindfold. I shake my head slightly, stopping my inappropriate thoughts, and take in the rest of her. Her hair has been left down but curled loosely, and she has a little top hat perched on the side of her head along with a bow tie around her neck. She'd told me about this outfit, but seeing it is another story. She looks fucking unbelievable. I have to grip on to the inside of my trouser pockets to stop from walking straight over to her and carrying her back upstairs.

I jump when I feel a hand touch my arm. I'd completely forgotten that I was stood with Emma. "Calm down. I can practically see your dirty thoughts running through your mind."

I turn to look at her and she just smiles sweetly back at me, like she didn't just say what she did. "I need a drink," I mutter, turning back to the bar and ordering a Jack Daniels... neat. It's going to be a long day.

Molly

I t's been a beautiful day. Everything has gone exactly to plan—not that I expected otherwise. Shane and Chris have looked on top of the world all day. The moment Shane looked back to see Chris walking in was so intense, I don't think there was a dry eye in the place. The same can be said for when they both said 'I do' and slid each other's rings on their fingers.

Shane looks stunning in his fitted navy suit with a white shirt and red tie, and Chris looks amazing with his matching shirt and tie but dark grey suit. I have to say, after having months worrying about my outfit, even I think I look good. As do Chris's sister, who has the same on minus the top hat, and her six-year-old daughter, who has a slightly more child-friendly version.

We've had a mouth-watering wedding breakfast and, thankfully, my speech went really well. Much to my disappointment, but Shane and Chris's pleasure, I didn't discuss any embarrassing sexual acts that they may or may not have been involved in; I just couldn't do it to them.

Instead, I reminisced about other funny stories from their time together, and wished them well in their marriage. We're now stood in the grounds of the hotel, having our photos taken. I don't know how the boys have kept the wide smiles on their faces all day. My cheeks are already hurting.

"Right, I just want the grooms. Everyone else, go and get a drink," the photographer shouts over to us all after a whole group shot.

I turn to whisper in Ryan's ear after we've all moved away slightly. "Right, it's now or never. Wish me luck." He winks at me before I head toward the happy couple.

"Guys, please, could I have your room key? I left a bag in there."

"Really?" Chris asks with a raised eyebrow.

I lean into him so he's the only one to hear. "Yes, I'm on my period and my tampons are in that bag. So, unless you happen to have some on you that I could use, I need your key."

"Right, okay." He sighs and looks around the room. "Be quick, and don't give it to anyone else. I don't trust anyone with it."

My heart flutters hearing this, but I swallow it down and take the room key, kissing his cheek before heading to the stairwell to meet Ryan.

He looks at me with a questioning expression on his face. I fight my smile, but in only a couple of seconds, I can feel my lips twitching and I can't contain it. Holding up the room key, I wave it in front of him.

"Hook, line and sinker," I say, strutting past him and over to the lift. As we wait for the doors to open, Ryan grabs my hand. With the way he's standing behind me slightly, no one would be able to see, but it still makes my heart rate pick up a little. I know it's irrational, because I'm pretty sure everyone knows there's something going on between us, but I'm enjoying keeping Ryan to myself and having him as my little secret.

When the doors do eventually open, I step forward and pull him in with me. I'm just about to turn and push him up against the wall when another hotel guest waves his hand in front of the closing doors and steps in. I can feel Ryan's eyes on me, so I turn to look up at his smirk. Fucking know-it-all. Despite my best intentions over the past few hours, my need just keeps growing and growing. Tonight cannot come soon enough. I want to get this sexy man into my hotel room and have my wicked way with him.

We head to my room first to grab the supplies before getting back in the lift and heading to the boys' bridal suite. This time, the lift is empty, and Ryan is on me the second the doors shut.

"God, you look so fucking hot. I don't know how I've kept my hands off you," he growls in my ear before running his tongue around the edge and nipping my lobe. He's kissing down my neck when the lift dings, signalling our arrival, and the door opens. Ryan picks up the bag I dropped when his lips touched me, and my hand, and then practically drags me down the corridor to their room.

The corridor is empty so we manage to sneak inside without any witnesses. I kick the door shut behind me and go to walk into the room, but the wind is knocked out of me as I'm slammed back against the door.

"Wha—" I start to question him, but as soon as my mouth is open, his tongue is in it and stroking mine. All thoughts leave my head and I give myself over to him. His hands run up the outside of my thighs, taking the fabric of my dress with them. Once he has the material around my waist, they roam around my arse and waist. He groans into my mouth and I can't help but smile as he kisses me.

"Did you forget something this morning?" he asks, then pulls back to look at me.

"No, I don't think so," I say innocently.

"So, not only have you been walking around teasing me, looking like this all afternoon, but you've also been walking round with no knickers on." He puts his hands behind my thighs and lifts me up against the door. My legs automatically wrap around his waist and my arms around his neck. One of his hands slides from my arse and his finger slips between my folds, making me gasp.

"Oh, Molly, if I'd have known, dinner would have been much more fun," he says, circling my clit. The sensation has my head falling back. When he pushes a finger into me, I can't help the loud moan that escapes my throat. "Fuck, Molly, you've had me walking around rock hard all afternoon. I need you."

"Oh God... Ry, we can't... we can't have sex in someone else's bridal suite." I suck in another breath when he slides another finger in. "S-surely it's bad luck or something."

"I don't give a fuck." He removes his fingers suddenly and walks us toward the bed.

"No," I shout, panicked. "Not the bed." I look round the room quickly. "Over the back of the sofa."

"As you wish."

He changes direction and places me back on my feet before turning me around and bending me harshly over the sofa. He lets out a breath through his teeth as he takes in the sight. "Fucking hell," he says before I hear a thud, and then jump out of my skin as I feel his breath on my core, swiftly followed by his tongue running the length of me.

"Oh God," I moan as he continues to torture me. My orgasm is right there when he suddenly pulls away from me. "Ryan," I complain, before I hear a zip and the rustling of fabric behind me, which fills me with excitement.

Within seconds, the head of his cock presses against my entrance, and before I've even braced myself, he slams balls deep into me in one swift thrust.

"Shit," I shout as my whole body lunges forward in surprise over the sofa. Ryan's hands go to my shoulders to hold me still as he continues his punishing thrusts into my body. Within minutes, I'm lost as my orgasm approaches again as Ryan hits the glorious spot deep inside of me again and again. Suddenly, electric shocks fly around my body as the pleasure radiates through me with one more stroke. My entire body goes limp once I come down off my high, and Ryan has to move his hands to my hips to help hold me up.

His onslaught on my body doesn't falter, and as soon as I'm strong enough again, he moves one hand around so he can tease my clit. "I want you to come with me, Molly," he growls in my ear, bringing me close to the edge again as his fingers pinch me. He does it again as I feel his entire body tense behind me, before I feel the first twitch of his release inside of me and my second orgasm crashes through me.

His body folds over mine, his heart thundering against my back as we return to earth. After a few seconds, he kisses my shoulder, stands up and gently removes himself from me. I hear him shuffle off, but my body is too weak to move. I'm just about to lift myself up when he comes back and I feel him clean me up before carefully pulling the bottom of my dress back down.

"Come on, Molls, we've got a job to do. Stop trying to distract me with sex!" he says, standing me up.

"Addict," I quip back over my shoulder as I head toward my bag of goodies.

It takes longer than I thought to carry out all our devilish plans on the boys' bridal suite, so it's just over an hour after we left the party that we sneak our way to the bar and join Emma for a few drinks. She takes one look at our mischievous faces and we're forced to fill her in...

We loaded their bed with condoms, sachets of lube, rose petals, and wedding confetti, before safety pinning the duvet to the sheet. We've put confetti in every pocket and pouch on their cases, and clothes for them to find later, as well as covering the floor, bed, and filling the basin and bath with rose petals. I'd pre-warned the hotel staff and given them a generous tip to cover the extra cleaning expense tomorrow when the boys head off for their honeymoon.

We're not downstairs long before Chris announces that the disco is starting and the buffet food will be available soon. Slowly, people start heading off for some food and to dance the night away, and before long I find myself at the buffet table.

I'm surprised that I'm hungry after the three-course meal we had earlier, but I end up trying something off nearly every plate while chatting to different guests.

Looking up, I see Ryan in deep conversation with a couple of Shane and Chris's friends, so instead of interrupting them, I look around for Emma. I can't help the wave of sadness that washes over me when I spot her sitting alone, staring at her hands in her lap. I immediately set off in her direction and pull her to the dance floor.

"How are you doing, Em?" I ask while we move in time to the music.

"Better. It's getting easier to get through the day now, but some are harder than others. Especially stuff like this, when it was planned for her to be here with us. It just reminds me of what we've lost, you know?" she says glumly.

"I know," I reply, thinking about how both of them should have been stood beside me today, but Emma decided that, without Hannah, she would just rather hide in the crowd. "I wish you'd been up there with me earlier."

"I don't want everyone looking at me and feeling sorry for me. Plus, can you imagine how I would have looked now in that dress?" She glances down at herself as she says this. Emma was always the curvier twin, but since Hannah's death she's put on a few more pounds with her comfort eating. She's still as stunning as ever, but she's never been able to see it.

"Emma, you're gorgeous, and don't even try to convince me otherwise. I've seen guys checking you out today. You're just too stuck in your own head to notice."

"Molly, I've managed twenty-five years without a man. I neither want nor need one in my life."

"I'm not saying you need one, Em, but I think one would do you a world of good. You know, help you release some tension," I say, nudging her with my elbow.

CHAPTER FOURTEEN

Ryan

"Molly, it's time to get up," I say softly. I've been awake for half an hour. I've showered and dressed already, but as far as I'm aware, Molly hasn't stirred at all with my movement. She was so exhausted last night that I ended up carrying her to bed. She insisted that she had to be last up, ensuring all the wedding guests were sorted for the night, but she could hardly keep her eyes open. I think the stress of the last two days has really taken its toll on her.

I laugh when she groans at me and rolls over to the other side of the bed, pulling the covers over her head. I try to pull them back down but she holds them tightly. "Molly, it's already half past eight, we told everyone we would meet them for breakfast for nine. And don't forget, you've convinced me to spend all day with you, Christmas shopping, once we see Shane and Chris off." This has a bigger effect; as soon as the words come out of my mouth, Molly is sat up in bed.

Apparently, it was a tradition that Hannah and Molly had to start their Christmas shopping on the first of December and, seeing as that's today, I begrudgingly agreed that this year I would be her shopping partner. My feelings are torn about it—on one hand, I'm excited about spending the day with her, but on the other I can remember how much stuff they used to come back with, so I know it's going to be a full-on day of shopping.

And I hate shopping.

I give Molly a kiss on the forehead before she gets up and heads toward the bathroom. She stops just before she gets to the door and grabs the door frame. "Are you okay, Molls?" I question. She's looking a little fragile.

"Yeah, my stomach's just feeling a little delicate."

"You're probably just exhausted. Let's get a fry-up in you, and you'll be all set for my day of torture!" She smirks at me over her shoulder before she disappears into the bathroom.

***

"Oh look, here they are!" Chris shouts above the other wedding guests already seated for breakfast. "So, I guess you two think you're funny, don't you? Do you have any idea how long it took us to unpin our bedding last night so we could actually get some sleep?" I chance a glance at Molly, who's fighting really hard not to laugh.

"I don't know what you're talking about," I say, trying my best to make it sound innocent, but I know I'm failing.

"Yeah, whatever, Evans. She—" he says, pointing at Molly, "—was the only one to have our room key yesterday. I knew I never should have trusted her!" His lips are starting to twitch into a smile as he finishes talking, which causes Molly's laughter to erupt. It soon spreads around the guests, causing everyone else in the hotel restaurant to look our way.

"I would say I'm sorry, but I'm really not," Molly says as she walks over to both of them and gives them a hug and kiss on the cheek.

"You just wait, Molls... we will get our revenge one day!"

"Oh, I don't doubt that." She takes one of the two empty seats next to the happy couple and gestures for me to join her.

Everyone's busy chatting away about the events of the day before, when Emma leans over toward Molly to speak to her. "Where have you been? I knocked on your room door before I came down, but you weren't there." Molly tenses. We both know most people have figured it out, but I think she's more concerned about Emma making a scene.

"I, uh, went to go wake Ryan up. You know what he's like for turning his alarm off and going back to sleep." Molly says unconvincingly.

"Right, okay..." Emma's just about to say something else when Chris distracts her with a question about her work.

Just over an hour later, we've all checked out of our rooms and are saying our goodbyes to the happy couple, wishing them a fantastic honeymoon in the Maldives. As a surprise, Molly had arranged for a limousine to take them to the airport.

"Oh my God! Molly, you're the best!" Chris screeches as they sandwich her in a massive hug.

"So, I'm forgiven?" she asks them both.

"Damn right you're forgiven."

Before long, we've said goodbye to everyone, and I have our luggage loaded into my Honda before heading to the city centre to hit the shops.

"Please can we stop for coffee now?" I plead. We've been shopping for hours. I'm laden down with bags, my feet are aching, and I'm dying for a drink.

"Let me just pick out all the girls' favourite cosmetics and a perfume, then we can go to the coffee shop next door."

"Do you need me for that? I could go get the drinks and grab us a table while you sort all that out," I beg.

Molly shakes her head at me before agreeing. I make quick work of the escalator before heading in the coffee shop and ordering myself a large cup of caffeine to help me through the rest of this trip.

I'm deep in thought about what I can get for Molly when she flops down on the chair in front of me with another two full bags of shopping. "You get everything?'

"Yeah, but on the way out I saw this necklace that I think Liv would love. I wanted to run it by you though, so I thought I'd come get my drink before it got cold, then we can go back."

"I'm sure if you think she'll love it, you're probably right."

"It will be a present mostly from you though, Ry, so it's important you have an input."

"Okay, we'll go back. How much more have we got to do?" I ask, praying that we're nearly there.

"Um... I just want to go to the toy store to get something for Oscar, then I think that's it for the day. I still need to go to the garden centre, but I'll leave that for another day." I try my best not to look relieved, but I don't do a very good job because Molly chastises me for not making the most of something that only happens once a year. How could I have forgotten about her acting like a hyperactive Santa's little helper every year?

Before long, I'm on my feet again and following Molly back to the department store I thought I'd escaped from. I agree that Liv would love the necklace she saw—I mean, of course I was going to agree—Molly has great taste, and it's jewellery. What's not to like? Molly's just paying when I wander over to the watch stands. I'm staring at the Tag Heuers when I feel her come up behind me. "Done?"

"Yes, you planning on buying yourself a present?"

"No, just dreaming. I always told myself that when I got my first teaching job I'd save up and buy myself a Tag, but life has a way of always making sure I have no spare money." I shrug before taking the new bag from Molly and heading to the exit, toward what I hope will be the last shop.

After two laps of the toy store with Molly to-and-froing about what to get Oscar, I eventually convince her that you can never go wrong with Lego. We're heading toward the till when Molly suddenly stops. "What is it?" I ask as she reaches up to touch a teddy bear on the shelf in front of her.

"Oh, nothing," she says, walking off again. "I just had a bear like that when I was a kid. It was my favourite."

"What happened to it?"

She looks down at the ground before answering so quietly I really have to concentrate to hear her. "I got upset one day because I wanted to stay in to work on a school art project. I was about seven, I think, but Mum and Dad had friends coming over for dinner and wanted me out of the house. I ran to my room in tears and was cuddling my bear when they came in behind me and told me I was too old to be cuddling a stupid toy. My dad tried to take it away from me and, when he pulled, he ripped half of his head off.

"A few weeks later, I came home from school to find the builders and interior designer in our house again. My room had had a makeover and all my things were gone. I'd left that teddy bear sat on my bed before I went to school that morning, like I usually did."

By the time Molly has finished telling me this, she's physically shaking. How could parents do that to their child? I drop the bags to the floor before taking a step toward her and wrap my arms around her.

We're cuddled up on the sofa, watching a nature programme, when I think of something. I untangle myself from Molly before telling her I'll be back in a few minutes. I go into the biggest of the spare bedrooms to find the last box that needs unpacking. I shoved it at the back of the wardrobe, out of the way, when the furniture was delivered. I find what I want on the top and grab it before heading back down to Molly.

"What are you hiding?" Molly asks as soon as she sees I have something behind my back. I walk over and sit next to her, before revealing what I went to get.

"This is Bruce," I say, sitting the tatty-looking bear on her lap. "My grandad gave him to me when he came to the hospital just after I was born. He's been everywhere with me. I mean everywhere: every holiday, scout camp, sleepover at a friend's, uni, here. I don't care how much of a pussy it makes me sound, this bear was my best friend as a kid. All my fondest memories have him in it." Molly's lips curl up in a smile as she sits and stares at the bear in her hands. "Now, I expect you to always come to me if you need comforting, but if, for whatever reason, I'm not here when you need it, I'll let you share him," I say with a wink.

It breaks my heart, watching her hug him to her chest. I used to have nightmares as a kid about losing him. I can't imagine how it felt, knowing her parents had thrown her bear away.

She launches herself onto my lap and we hold each other for the longest time with Bruce squashed between us.

Molly eventually falls asleep in my arms and I carry her to bed for the second night on the trot. She needs to relax; she's clearly doing too much.

Luckily, I wasn't covering a lesson during my free period this afternoon, because I planned to sneak off into town so I could get Molly's Christmas presents. I'd put a lot of thought into it over the last few days, and I'm pretty pleased with what I've come up with. It's the first time ever that I've bought anyone's Christmas presents more than a week in advance. I'm feeling very organised, especially as Molly has everyone else sorted. All that's left to do is decorate the house. I promised Molly that we could do it this Saturday to get her into the swing of it before we go to the Morrisons' for their annual family decoration event on Sunday.

I've just finished wrapping them all up and am hiding them under my bed when the doorbell rings. Making sure the bags can't be seen, I jog down to the front door. When I open it, I'm looking at a man and a woman who must be a similar ages to Susan and Pete, but I have no idea who they are. They both stand there, staring. I don't recognise him, but the longer I look at her, I can see something familiar, and then it hits me. They're Molly's parents.

"Can I help you?" I ask politely, although from what I know about these two, I want to be anything but polite.

"We need to see Molly," her mum snaps.

I try to keep my anger in check before replying. "She's on her way home from work. She should only be about ten minutes, if you'd like to come in for a drink." I'm slightly hesitant to invite them in, but I'm not sure what else to do.

Molly's mum peers past my shoulder to look into the house. I have no idea what she sees, but she quickly turns her nose up. "No. Just give her this, will you?" she says, shoving an envelope toward me. She lets her eyes run up and down my body one last time before turning around and tottering back to the car. "Come on, dear," she shouts over her shoulder to her husband. He gives me what I think is an apologetic look before doing what he's told.

Molly

"Hey, I'm home," I sing as I enter the living room. But one look at Ryan and my good mood instantly disappears. "What's wrong?"

"Um... I think you should come and sit down, Molls." His words have my heart beginning to race, but I do as he says.

"What is it?" I whisper, because I don't think I really want to know what has caused him to look so concerned.

"I... um... you..." he stutters.

"Come on, spit it out." The more he's putting this off, the more I'm starting to panic. "Oh my God, is everyone okay? The Morrisons? My brothers?" I ask quickly.

"No, no, everyone's fine. It's nothing like that." He lets out a big breath before turning to look at me, grabbing both of my hands in his. "About fifteen minutes ago, the doorbell rang..."

"Right?"

"It was your parents, Molly."

His words cause my breath to catch. "My parents?" He just nods his head in response. "Well, I'm guessing they didn't actually want to see me, because they'd still be here. What did they want?"

"Well, your mum asked to see you, but she refused to wait and shoved this at me," he says, handing over a blank white envelope.

"Wow, look at that... they haven't even bothered writing my name on it," I say, laughing, but in reality, all I want to do is burst into tears at their constant rejection. You'd think I'd be over it by now. "Right, let's do this," I say, ripping the envelope open and pulling out the contents.

Molly,
We've sold the house and are moving to Spain. Christopher has retired, so the business now belongs to Steven and Daniel. Find a cheque enclosed as your inheritance. It goes without saying that you will no longer receive Christmas or birthday money from us.
Our best wishes for your future.

We both sit, staring at the paper for a full five minutes, stunned into silence. Eventually, Ryan moves, breaking me from my zombie-like state. I watch in slow motion as he leans forward, picks up the envelope from my lap, and pulls out another, much smaller piece of paper. I hear him suck in a breath when he turns it around and looks at it. "Shit," he breathes.

Looking over, my blood boils when I see the figure on the cheque. "Are they fucking joking?" I shout. "This has to be a fucking joke. They tell me they're leaving the country with a fucking note, and they don't even bother to tell me where in Spain they're moving to? But it's all okay, because they've left me with half a million pounds so they can't feel fucking guilty. If they actually cared, they w-wouldn't d-do this." My rant eventually subsides as my sobs take over. It's not sad tears; it's pure anger. Ryan pulls me onto his lap and rubs my back, the whole time whispering softly in my ear that he loves me.

A thought hits me, and I jump off Ryan and head toward my bag. "What are you doing?"

I ignore his question and continue putting my phone to my ear. "Voicemail, what a fucking surprise," I mutter to myself. I fume as I listen to Steven's message. When I eventually hear the beep, my anger's got the better of me. "What the actual fuck is going on?" I shout into the phone. "You'd better ring me as soon as you get this to explain yourself."

When I put my phone down, I realise Ryan has gone. "Fucking brilliant," I mutter, pacing up and down the living room, trying to get myself together. How is this actually happening? Surely, I'm dreaming? I pinch myself, but it only proves to me that, yes, this is real life. I continue pacing, completely lost in my own thoughts, until I hit something hard in front of me. I raise my head to see Ryan looking down at me with sympathetic eyes.

"Come on," he says, grabbing my hand and pulling me downstairs behind him.

"What are you doing?" I question, but he doesn't answer, he just keeps going, pulling me to my old room, then into the bathroom, where I can't quite believe what's in front of me. "You are the best boyfriend ever, you know that, right?" While I was pacing upstairs, Ryan had been down here, running me a nice bubble bath, complete with soft music, scented candles, and a large glass of wine. I must have been completely out of it.

He pulls me so I'm standing in front of him, wrapping his arm around my waist. "You need to relax," he whispers in my ear before kissing my neck gently. "Arms up," he instructs, and goes about undressing me before tapping me on the arse once he's done, sending me in the direction of the tub. When I look back his naked body greets me as he drops his trousers to the floor and moves over to me. The sight of him causes tingles to erupt in my nether regions. My tongue sneaks out of its own accord to wet my bottom lip as my eyes run over every inch of his bare skin. "You keep looking at me like that, and we'll be doing anything but relaxing. Now, come on, get in."

We get ourselves settled so that I'm lying with my back to his front. Ryan holds me tightly around the waist and kisses the top of my head every few minutes. We're lost in our own thoughts for the longest time, but eventually Ryan breaks it by whispering, "How are you doing, Molls?"

"I think I may have overreacted earlier. I mean, what did I really expect from them?"

"So, you're not angry?"

"I'm just disappointed, I guess. I know I shouldn't, but the thought is always there that one day they might do something to surprise me. At every turn, they just do shit like this. With them out of the country, at least I can put them behind me."

"They don't deserve you, Molly. You're way too good for them."

I just hum in response as all the things I've done over the years that disappointed them run through my head. "Molly." Ryan's warning tone pulls me from my memories. "I can practically see the thoughts running through your mind. You're so much more than them, and I promise to prove that to you every day."

"You already do."

We both return to our own thoughts for a few more minutes before Ryan once again breaks the silence. "What are you going to do with the money?"

"Um... I don't know. Part of me really wants to rip it up and post it back to them like we did to your mum's one last week, but as I don't have their address, I guess I'll just bung it in a savings account. It might come in useful one day. Everything happens for a reason, so I guess the reason will show itself."

"Maybe it will put our kids through university," Ryan muses quietly.

"One thing at a time, Ry. We haven't even told everyone we're together yet!"

"Yeah, about that..."

"Christmas. I want to tell everyone at Christmas," I blurt out, surprising myself.

"That sounds perfect. You can be my Christmas present," Ryan says as he gently sits me up. "Turn around, I want to see your face." I do as I'm told, careful not to slosh water all over the floor. When I get there, I settle myself across Ryan's lap, feeling content with his arms around me.

Ryan insisted we had an early night last night, and I have to say I do feel better for it today. I've been so tired recently. I'm sure I'm coming down with something. I'm looking forward to spending a quiet Christmas with Ryan and the Morrisons. I've told Jax we're going to have the whole Christmas off, and he was more than happy to put in a bit more work now to allow that to happen. I glance up when he puts a fresh cup of tea down on my desk for me. We've worked together seamlessly over the past few months. I couldn't have asked for a better first employee.

"Why are you looking at me weird?" Jax asks as he sits down at his desk.

"I was just thinking how well us working together has panned out. I was lucky to find you."

"Aw, Molly, are you getting all sappy on me?" he teases.

Our conversation is interrupted when my phone dings with a text. I quickly grab it and open up the message from Ryan.

> Ryan: Do you trust me?

> Molly: Completely.

> Ryan: Good. When you get in tonight, go into your old room and put on what's on the bed. Then wait for me. Love you. x

I can't help the wide smile and butterflies. I wonder what he has planned.

"Oh God, Ryan's sexting you, isn't he?" Jax groans from behind me.

"No, he's not. He is planning something, though."

When I pull up to the house, it's in darkness, but Ryan's car is parked out front so I know he's here somewhere. The butterflies in my stomach have only increased since receiving that message earlier. I'm so excited to see what he's done.

I let myself in and go straight to my old room, flicking the light on before looking straight at the bed. My breath catches and the butterflies triple at what's waiting for me. There, laid out, are the shoes I wore for the wedding, a blindfold, and a pair of handcuffs. As I said to Ryan back in the summer, I've never experimented with bondage, but that's not because I'm not curious. It's because I've been with some untrustworthy arseholes. Ryan is a completely different story. I trust him with my life.

Ten minutes later, I'm lying on my bed in just my heels and a blindfold. I didn't do anything with the handcuffs as I soon realised I needed another pair of hands. I've been waiting for a couple of minutes already, and I'm starting to wonder how long I'm going to have to wait. I've heard some noises from upstairs, so I know he's here and is torturing me. The longer I'm lying here, the more excited and impatient I'm getting. I want his hands on me now.

I get to the point where I'm about to go and find him when I hear the door creak open. When did he come downstairs?

"Shit, Molly. I think I could come just looking at you," he says with a husky voice.

My body squirms, knowing that his eyes are focused on my naked skin. Suddenly, the mattress dips by my feet, then I jump when Ryan grabs one foot and places a kiss to my ankle before making his way up my leg.

When he gets close to where I want him the most, my hands go to tangle in his hair. "I don't think so," he grumbles, quickly moving higher and grabbing one of my hands. My heart's already pounding, but when I hear the jingle of the handcuffs, it really starts to race inside my chest. My right wrist is attached to the metal post on the headboard, quickly followed by my left. I give them a tug but realise I'm not going anywhere. My skin heats where his eyes touch. I'm aware that the position I'm in is making my breasts stand proud, but when I feel Ryan blow gently on my nipples, I'm more aware of them than ever. Just that simple action has my back arching off the bed.

"Fuck, Molly, you've never looked as sexy as you are now, lying there, waiting for my touch. I hope you didn't have any plans for tonight, because I'm not letting you up any time soon."

I moan in response. The longer he's sat there not touching me, the wetter I can feel myself getting. "Ryan, please," I groan, getting impatient.

"All in good time, Miss Molly," he says as the bed dips again.

His lips land on my wrist, placing light kisses, nips and licks all the way to my armpit. I feel like I should shy away when I feel his tongue there but, surprisingly, it turns me on more. He moves across my chest and kisses my collarbone, but doesn't touch my breasts, which are begging for his attention. He gives my other arm the same treatment. The throbbing in my clit is so strong that I rub my thighs together to try to release some of the pressure. Ryan notices, though. "I'm the only one allowed to get you off," he says, moving so he's sat between my legs, stopping me.

"You're killing me, Ry. Please touch me," I say, lifting my hips and offering myself to him, but he places his hands on my hips and pushes them back down, grumbling about restraining my ankles next time.

He leans forward again, but he surprises me by placing his lips against mine. I instantly part my lips and run my tongue along his bottom lip. "So impatient," he says before responding to my kiss. When he pulls back, I can hear him panting as much as I am. He kisses down my neck before descending between my breasts, kissing and licking all around them but keeping away from my nipples that are practically screaming to be sucked on.

"Ryan... ahh..." I moan, as his tongue starts to circle dangerously close to where I want it. "Please..." I feel him pull back from me before he teases the very tip of me with the end of his tongue. "Oh God, please." I must have pushed past his self-control because, all of a sudden, my nipple is being sucked harshly into his hot mouth. I arch and writhe on the bed. He teases the other between his thumb and forefinger, making me moan. "Oh yes... fuck, Ry." His mouth releases me with a pop before he swaps over. My breaths are coming out in short, sharp pants, and my body is covered in a sheen of sweat. "Shit, Ry, I'm so close, and you haven't even touched me yet," I say between pants as he continues his ministrations on my breasts.

Releasing me, he starts to move down my body. Pushing my legs wide open with his shoulders, I'm forced to wait for him to touch me. When he does, it's not what I'm expecting. His hands come back to my breasts and continue with their pinching and pulling. I'm instantly squirming again, so close to falling over the edge, then he blows against my very ready pussy and I fall apart as shockwaves shoot around my body, causing fireworks to go off behind my eyes.

"Ryan!" I shout as wave after wave of my orgasm flows through me.

"Holy shit."

As soon as I come down from my high, I realise Ryan has filled me with his fingers and is slowly fucking me. Once he notices I'm back with him, his mouth zeros in on my clit until my second orgasm flows through me.

"Fuck, I can't wait any longer," Ryan says as he moves about on the bed and, within seconds, I feel the head of his dick pushing at my entrance.

I'm expecting him to slide in slowly, but my eyes fly open when he thrusts forward and fills me to the hilt in one movement. "Yes..." Ryan hisses through gritted teeth as he pulls out.

I didn't think I could be on the edge of an orgasm again so soon after the last two, but it feels like it's only seconds before I'm there again, and I can tell by Ryan's almost painful grip on my hips that he's close, too. Ryan's cock twitches once, and I'm just about to fall into my third orgasm when I hear loud banging on the front door.

"Fuck, Molly," Ryan groans and thrusts forward one last time, hitting that sweet spot and sending me over. I shout his name out as I come before he flops down onto my chest.

"God, that sounded hot, but can you come and answer the door now, please?" a voice says from the front door, reminding me that someone was knocking.

Ryan instantly sits up and pulls the blindfold from my eyes. "Was that...?"

"I don't think I can cope listening to that again. Don't go for another round. Ouch!"

"That's our baby sister you're talking about," another voice says.

"Shit, my brothers!"

CHAPTER FIFTEEN

Ryan

Walking back into the living room, having put some clothes on, I find Molly making coffee for her brothers, who are now sat at the dining room table. I can't help but notice how embarrassed Steven looks in comparison to his younger brother, who is smiling at me like I've just won the lottery.

I try to shake thoughts of our earlier encounter from my head as I walk over to Molly. "I'll finish those. You go and talk to your brothers," I say, pushing her in their direction. She eventually goes over, shouting their orders to me.

"Molly, I know you're angry..." Steven starts, but quickly gets cut off.

"No, I was angry when I first read their note, but I soon realised that I really shouldn't have expected anything different, and I know I went off on you a bit, but once I calmed down, I figured out that you two would have told me if you knew. I'm sorry for shouting," Molly says, trying to explain herself.

"You don't need to apologise. You had every right to feel that way—hell, you still do. We had a feeling something was up, but you know what Mum and Dad are like. It could have been anything. They asked us both over for a meeting last night, which I assume was after they came here. It was only then that they explained to us that they were moving and handing the business over. I can't say I'm shocked. They've talked about going abroad for years, but I didn't think they'd do it quite like this," Steven explains.

"They're flying out tomorrow," Daniel adds. "They moved out of the house this morning. They've had the stuff they want shipped over and the rest cleared out. Dad has taken his retirement out of the business and left it to us."

"I'm pleased he's given you two control. You deserve it after all the work you've put in over the years. Plus, I would much rather see you enjoy the money it brings in than them," Molly says spitefully.

"Right, well," Steven says, looking sheepish. "This is really why we want to talk to you."

Molly stares between the two of them for a few seconds, as if she's trying to read their minds. "Go on," she says sceptically.

"We want you with us. This company is the family's, and you are as much a part of that as we are. You should reap the rewards as well," Steven says softly, trying to gauge Molly's reaction.

As his words settle in, her eyes widen and she slowly stands, pushing her chair out behind her. "Oh no... no... no. I've always stayed as far away from the business as possible. I don't want anything to do with it, you both know that. Why would you even suggest it?" She paces back and forth in front of her chair.

"We get that, Molly, we really do, but you were distancing yourself from it because you wanted distance from our parents, not the actual business. They're out of the picture now, and we want it to be the three of us. We don't, and never have, wanted you to be the forgotten sibling in this family. We want you with us all the way." The emotion in Steven's voice must get through to Molly, because she comes to a stop in front of him and just stares at him for a solid minute. "Just hear us out. What do you say?" he adds to try to get her to respond.

"Do they know you're asking me this?" she eventually says.

"No. They told us they want nothing more to do with the business, and it is completely ours to do what we want with. So, this is our first order of business. We want you to be a Managing Director of the company with us. We're happy for you to be a silent partner; you don't have to have anything to do with the day-to-day business at all. There is only one thing we would ask from you."

"And that is?"

"We want everything rebranded. Something new, modern, and fresh to reflect a new start."

"So, let me get this straight," Molly starts. "You both want me to be an equal partner in the family business that I hate, so that I can get the money out of it as well, and the only thing you want is for me to do some designs?"

"Yes, that's pretty much it," Daniel agrees.

"But that means the two of you will earn less for working stupidly hard."

"Well, when you say it like that, I guess it makes us look stupid," Steven says with a laugh. "But you're forgetting we already take good wages out of the business. The extra money will be profit that we will share. And we will share that not because of the amount of work we've each done, but because it's a family business and we, Molly, are family. And you deserve every penny for the way they've treated you over the years. You enjoy that money. Go blow it on a stupidly expensive car to replace that toy one you've got."

I have to add my agreement to this.

"I guess," Molly mumbles as she sits back down. All three of us watch as she pushes the sleeves of her hoodie up her forearms and rests her head in her hands, clearly thinking about what has just been proposed.

I look away from her and see Daniel's eyes light up. "Fuck, are those...?" He points to the red marks on Molly's wrists. "Dude, that's so fucking hot," he says, turning to me and putting his fist out for me. My eyes widen, and I'm sure my chin is close to hitting the floor. No way am I fist-bumping him for having dirty sex with his sister.

His words break through Molly's thoughts because her head snaps up and the three of us stare at Daniel, completely dumbfounded.

"You know you're heading toward forty, not twenty, right?" Molly asks.

"I don't think it matters how old you are. Playing with handcuffs is always hot, right?" he asks, looking between Steven and me.

"You seriously need a woman to whip you into shape, Bro," is Steven's only response.

"Hey, now, the only one doing the whipping when there is a woman involved is me, thank you very much."

"Okay... so, ignoring our sex-crazed brother, what do you say, Molls. You in?" Steven asks.

The three of them spend the next hour debating the issue. Molly eventually agrees to be involved, but she's adamant that she wants a smaller share. Her brothers aren't really up for this, but Molly holds her ground until they don't really have much choice. Once they come to an arrangement, they agree to sleep on it over the weekend and talk early next week.

Molly's just walking them toward the stairs when Steven stops and turns back. "I didn't say it earlier, but I'm happy you two have finally figured out that you should be together. You look after our baby sister, Ryan. She's really quite special." When I meet his eyes, it's clear as day how much he cares for Molly, and I can't help but think again how lucky she is to have brothers like them when her parents are worth shit.

"I intend to, don't worry. See you both soon," I say, before heading to the kitchen with the mugs.

When Molly reappears after saying goodbye, she has a box in her arms and a huge smile on her face.

"What's that?"

"My Christmas decorations," she says, smiling, looking like the stress with her parents the last two days hasn't happened.

"Oh."

"What?" she asks, her eyebrows drawn together.

"Sorry, I just assumed you didn't have any. You didn't have a lot of stuff when you moved in, so I just assumed..." I trail off, feeling like an idiot.

"Hey, it's all right," she says, putting her hand on my thigh. "I would have thought the same. These," she says, going back to the box and opening it up, "are the baubles my gran bought me. She used to get me one every year. Mum hated them and refused to put them on our 'designer' Christmas tree, so my gran bought me a small tree to go in my room so I could put them all up. When I moved out, I made sure I had them with me. They mean a lot and hold some really good memories. After my gran died, Hannah would get me one every year instead. I guess this year will be my first without one," she says sadly, but she's soon distracted by a cupcake tree decoration.

It looks like I need to get another present for Molly.

"She would somehow always find out what day we would put the decorations up, and she would come around with my new one. I used to get so excited," she explains.

Shit, if I'm going to keep up that tradition, I need to get organised, seeing as we're putting the tree up tomorrow.

While I think about how and what I'm going to get, Molly pulls each decoration out one by one and explains its importance. I love listening to her happy stories from her childhood. I'm so used to hearing bad ones that it makes a nice change.

Molly

I walk back into the living area after my bath, and the sight in front of me takes my breath away. There are candles everywhere, and spread out in front of the tree Ryan and I spent the evening putting up is a blanket with loads of pillows, Ryan laid out across it in only his boxers. My mouth waters as ideas start to play out in my mind for what I want to do with him.

"Come here, baby," he says, holding his arm out for me.

I quickly walk over and grab his hand as he gently pulls me down to him. My knees are just about to hit the floor when I see the little box in front of him. I look back at him, smiling. "Is that for me?"

"It sure is. Go on," he says, pushing it over to me once I'm settled, pressed up against his side.

I turn the tag over and read what it says aloud. "Happy first Christmas."

"Open it."

I slowly pull the paper away, then slide the lid off, revealing what's inside.

"It's a beach hut," I squeal, pulling it out and hanging it off my finger, admiring the clear glass globe that encloses a little hut surrounded by sand and shells. I feel myself tear up as I stare at it, and Ryan makes me jump when he wipes a tear off my cheek with his thumb that I didn't realise had dropped. "You made out last night that you didn't know about my decorations, but you had this already," I say quietly, because I'm totally amazed.

"When you fell asleep last night, I went online, and by some miracle I found this at the garden centre. I got it on the way to the gym this morning. I couldn't let you miss a year."

Ryan lowers us so that we're lying on the blanket with me straddling him. I lean forward and pour everything I feel for him into my kiss. When I need to breathe, I trail kisses across his jaw. The feel of his stubble scratching my lips makes me squeeze my thighs together with memories of them being scratched by that stubble. I whisper, "I love you so much, Ryan. Thank you," in his ear, before going to get off him.

His eyes fly open as he grips on to my thighs tightly. "Where are you going?"

"To put my new bauble pride in place. I'll come back, I promise," I say, blowing him a kiss when he releases his death grip.

"Come back naked," he says in a deep, sexy voice that makes a shiver run down my spine. "I want to make love to you in front of our first Christmas tree."

I quickly hang up my decoration before practically ripping the clothes from my body and lying back down so that every inch possible is touching Ryan's body. He doesn't waste any time in rolling us over so he's hovering above me before letting me have the single most passionate, loving, and sensual experience of my life.

"Hi, angels. How are you both?" Susan chimes as we walk into her kitchen, ready to start a full day of decorating the house for Christmas.

"We're good," Ryan answers, guiding me over to one of the stools with a hand at the small of my back. "You guys all okay?"

"Yes, I'm just disappointed Dec isn't coming up for this. All of us should be here, you know?"

"I'm sure he would if he could. He must be really busy to miss it," I say, trying to lessen her disappointment, but I can't help but agree. This is the family's first Christmas without Hannah. I really thought he'd have made every effort to be here.

"Yeah, I'm sure. Tea? Coffee?" Susan asks, looking between us.

"Of course," I laugh.

An hour later, we're all stuck in. Pete and Ryan are outside, putting up the lights around the house and garage, and Susan, Emma, Lilly, and I are in the living room, finishing off the first of three trees this house has during the festive season.

I flop back on the sofa after putting the last decoration on the tree and let out a big breath. "Are you okay, Molly? You look exhausted," Susan asks, sounding concerned.

"Yeah, I think I'm fighting something off. I've been tired for a few days. I'll be fine."

"If you want to watch, we don't mind," Lilly adds.

"No, no, I'm good. Let's go get started on the dining room."

We've just got the branches straightened out when the rumble of a motorbike brings my head up to look out the window. "Who do you know who rides a bike, Lilly?" I ask, only because I've never seen anyone on a bike here.

"Um... oh my God!" she shouts, then takes off, running. I keep my eyes on the driveway, waiting to see who it is, but it's not long before I get my answer because Lilly launches herself at the leather-clad body just as he pulls the helmet off his head.

"What's going on?" I hear Susan ask as she appears at the front door. "Declan!" she says cheerily, walking over to him for a hug. "Wait... why is my baby driving a death trap?" He shakes his head at her and pulls her in for a tight squeeze and a kiss on the head. I can't help but smile when I think of the scrawny little boy he used to be, compared to the built six-foot-something man he's grown into.

It's another couple of hours before we've all finished our jobs, and we're gathering around the dining table for dinner. The smell of Susan's roast has had my stomach growling for hours. It got so bad that I had to sneak into the kitchen and raid the biscuit tin when no one was looking.

"So, were you lying when you said you couldn't come?" I ask Dec.

"Yeah, pretty much. I'm really busy, so there was a chance I wouldn't make it. I managed to get everything done over the last few days because I knew I'd never hear the end of it if I missed today," he says, looking at Susan, who gives him an innocent look, which makes everyone laugh.

"So..." Susan starts, and I can practically feel all her children groan, wondering what's coming next. "Who was that girl I heard on the phone the other day? A girlfriend?" she asks hopefully.

"No Mum. Just a... friend." Dec looks a little uncomfortable.

Susan lets out a breath before saying, "I knew from the day you were born you'd have the girls chasing you, angel, but can't you just pick a nice one to settle down with? Not... well, you know..." She trails off, letting us fill in the blanks. Yes, it turns out Susan's precious little boy is a bit of a player. Pete thinks it's great, and encourages him all the way, but Susan doesn't like how he treats women, even though Dec insists they go into it knowing nothing serious will happen between them. "If only you could get over—"

"Mum, enough," Dec snaps.

"Oh, Susan, leave the boy alone. He's just enjoying his youth," Pete says, sounding bored.

"Thanks, Dad."

We all look at each other but quickly change the subject to try to break the tension.

When dinner's finished, I'm made to sit down while everyone else tidies up. *I must really look like crap if they don't want my help,* I think to myself. I eventually get bored on my own in the living room and go to see if I can do something.

"Where's Susan?" I ask, noticing she's been gone for quite a while.

"She... uh... had to make a phone call," Ryan stutters, making me wonder what the hell is going on, but in the end, I decide Christmas is only around the corner, so it's probably something to do with that.

"Who's here so early?" I ask Ryan as the sound of our doorbell rings through the living area. He just shrugs his shoulders at me whilst mumbling for me to go and see around a mouthful of Shreddies.

"Morning, angel," Susan sings when I open the door. She comes marching in with Emma and Lilly behind her.

"W-what are you guys doing here?" I stutter with surprise.

"No time for questions, angel," Susan says hurriedly. "Now go get dressed in something comfortable, pack a bikini, and get your butt upstairs in ten minutes. We'll be waiting," she says, pushing me into what she thinks is my bedroom. Luckily for me, most of my clothes are still down here.

"But I've got work," I say, as she physically starts shoving me toward my old room.

"It's all sorted, now do as you're told."

I stand in the middle of the room for a couple of seconds as I listen to them head upstairs and greet Ryan before I step into action. I had already showered but had put my pyjamas back on so I could see Ryan before he left, instead of missing him while I got ready. I'm pretty glad I did now, because it looks like it would have been a waste of time.

Within eight minutes, I'm upstairs with a bag in my hand, ready to go as instructed, even though I have no clue what's going on.

"Right, I'm off to work. You girls have a good day," Ryan says, giving Susan a quick hug and kiss on the cheek before doing the same to me.

"Come on, we're going, too," Emma says, grabbing my hand and tugging me back toward the stairs.

We're all settled in the taxi that was idling outside our house before I manage to get any answers.

"I'm sorry, but what the hell is going on?" I ask, looking at all three of them.

"Well..." Susan starts. "I was worried about you yesterday. You looked exhausted. And when I mentioned it to Ryan, he said he was concerned you were doing too much, so I organised us a last-minute day at the spa. Megan is meeting us there as Oscar is at nursery today, and the five of us are going to have a day of being pampered."

God, that sounds so awesome.

We're ushered toward the changing rooms once we get to the hotel and told to put our swimming costumes on and get dressed in huge fluffy white robes, before being shown to a private relaxation room. It has six chaise lounges, candles everywhere, soft music playing, and the biggest continental breakfast I have ever seen. It has every kind of fresh fruit imaginable, as well as all sorts of pastries. The smell has my stomach growling loudly, making the girls laugh.

"I'll be back in a few minutes with drinks. Buck's Fizz okay with you all?" the beauty therapist asks, and we nod enthusiastically. "Please help yourself to food, it's all yours."

"You were right, Susan, I really do need this." I say, once we are alone again.

"You don't need to thank us, Molly. We're more than happy to help, eh, girls?" she asks the others, who all nod while stuffing their faces with all the goodies. "Anyway, you should be thanking Ryan. It was his idea."

"So, how are you two getting on, living together?" Emma asks once she is settled with a mountain of food piled on her plate.

"Yeah, good, thanks. I think we've adjusted pretty well."

I hear Lilly mutter something like, "Yeah, I bet you have," whilst chewing on a pastry, which makes me change the subject. I decided I wanted to tell everyone at Christmas, and that is what I'm going to do. "Is Dec back for Christmas now?"

"He decided to stay, but he's going straight back after New Year's. He's got something going on, but he won't share. It's frustrating. But you know what he's like—always wheeling and dealing," Lilly explains. Ever since Dec understood how to make money, he's always been doing something, even if it was selling sweets—or fags, as he got older in school. God only knows what he's up to down in Devon.

CHAPTER SIXTEEN

Ryan

Molly seemed to perk up a bit after her day at the spa. She was glowing that night when I came home. It was good to see her so relaxed after how hard she's been working and the stress our families have caused—not to mention her quest for Christmas perfection. I swear watching her wrap a present is like watching an artist at work. I'm going to be embarrassed, handing my pathetic excuse for present wrapping to her when the big day eventually gets here.

Tonight's the night of our Christmas party. I finished school at one o'clock, which gave me time to go shopping and get all the food and drink, as well as helping Molly make sure the house is tidy and the guest rooms are set up. I invited my sisters, but Abbi is still doing anything she can to avoid Jax, and Liv has already headed up to Liverpool—both have promised to be here for our New Year's party. I'm pretty sure Abbi has started something up again with Caleb, her childhood boyfriend, as she's mentioned him a lot recently. I've told Molly about it and she has sworn me to secrecy, because she knows Jax will be crushed.

"Are you nearly ready, Molls? They'll be arriving any minute," I call through to the en suite where Molly is still faffing around. I've been ready for nearly an hour. I've done my first lap of the buffet and had two cans whilst I've been waiting for her.

"Yes, stop getting your knickers in a twist," she calls back with a laugh. "Right, what do you think?" she asks as she appears in the doorway.

My heart pounds when I look up and see her in a dress so fitted, it looks like a second skin. It's flesh coloured with black floral patterns over it and gold sequins. The top has thin straps and the neckline is shaped around the curve of her perfect breasts, showing off the cleavage I want to bury my face in. I run my eyes down over her tiny waist and curved hips to where the dress stops just shy of her knees, then continue my descent to her glittery gold fuck-me heels. Eventually, my eyes make it back up to hers and she raises an eyebrow at me, reminding me that she asked me a question. "I think it's going to be a long night," I say in a deep and gravelly voice.

Her lips twitch up at the corners and she slowly saunters toward me. She doesn't stop until her body is flush against mine. When she feels my arousal pressing against her stomach, she tilts her head to the side and flashes me a wide smile. "I presume you like the dress, Mr. Evans," she says as she gently rubs herself against me.

Leaning forward, I whisper in her ear, "You look incredible, but if you don't stop what you're doing, tonight is going to turn into a private party for the two of us." I place my lips against the sweet spot under her ear and goosebumps prick her skin. I sneak my tongue out and gently run it along her skin, causing her whole body to shiver in my arms, but before I can tease her some more, the doorbell rings, ending our moment. "You'd better go and answer that... I need a few minutes before greeting our guests."

Molly stares me in the eyes for a couple of seconds before standing back and looking down at the obvious bulge I'm sporting in my jeans. I haven't dressed up as much as Molly tonight, but I have put on my smartest jeans and layered a shirt over my t-shirt. My hair is in its usual styled mess and I have my slightly smarter boots on instead of my very worn yet very comfortable ones, or my standard Converse. I thought I looked okay, but the heat in Molly's eyes when she first saw me earlier told me everything I needed to know. I'm going to have to spend the whole night trying to keep my hands off her, even though the majority of people who are coming tonight already know about us.

***

"We have a game for us all to play," Chris announces when there's a lull in the conversations around the room. Everyone has been here for a good few hours now, and those of us who are drinking are nicely buzzed. We've had a great time so far listening to

Shane and Chris's honeymoon tales, and generally catching up with everyone.

A series of groans sound out around the room at his announcement. Those of us who have known him for a number of years know his games can be somewhat on the embarrassing side.

"Go on then, what is it?" Molly asks from the other end of the sofa. I've had to resort to keeping as much distance between us as possible, or the need to touch her is overpowering.

"Truth or dare."

Well, that sounds too normal for one of Chris's games.

Molly is obviously thinking the same, because I watch her eyebrows draw together in thought before she asks, "What's the catch?"

"What makes you think there's a catch?" Shane asks, trying to look innocent.

"Because we know you two better than you think we do."

"Well, let's just say we've already planned the truths and dares," Chris says with a wink, which makes Emma jump up from her seat next to Molly.

"Right, I think that's my cue to leave. I promised Mum I'd open Cocoa's for her in the morning, so I need to get to bed."

"Oh, come on, Em, don't be a spoilsport," Chris pouts.

"Sorry, guys, but I'm done. I'll see you two next week," she says, looking between Molly and me. "Enjoy the rest of your evening."

"Hang on, I'll come out with you," Megan says, grabbing her bag. "I promised James I wouldn't be late. We've got to travel up north to visit his side of the family this weekend... yay!" she says, pretending to look excited but sounding anything but.

Once we've said our goodbyes, Chris and Shane get us sat around the coffee table before deciding that Jax should go first because he's the only single one.

After nearly an hour into the game, we've discovered that Jax gets turned on by sexy lingerie and that he prefers the girl to be on top and take control, both of which I tried really hard not to take on board because I just know he's picturing my sister as he says them. Ana looked completely embarrassed by the whole thing, I thought she was going to combust when Will confessed to everyone that for their anniversary one year, she surprised him by turning up at school with the intention of taking him to his favourite restaurant, but before they went anywhere, they ended up having sex on his desk in his department office. She hasn't been able to look at me since, knowing that I will, sometime in the near future, go in that office. It turns out that even though Holly and Adam are the newest couple in the room, they're also the wildest. They have described, in detail, their last online order for 'supplies', and we've had to endure listening to Holly explain how Adam is the biggest she's ever had.

Why exactly did I agree to play this game?

We have also watched Shane lick and suck every inch of Chris's feet, which made me feel pretty sick, if I'm honest, and I have just discovered that it was the story about them getting caught at it on the bonnet of Chris's car that was the true story Molly was threatening to put in her groomsmaid speech all those weeks ago.

"Right, I think everyone should do a truth and say the most exciting place they've had sex now that you know about us," Chris says, looking to each of us.

"That isn't the rules of Truth Or Dare," Ana says. "Plus, you know ours already."

"I don't care about the traditional 'rules'; this is my game. So... Jax, you first."

"Hang on, I think you should go first. You've told us about the car, but you told everyone to explain the most exciting place they've had sex, so both of you must confess something," Molly pipes up.

"Okay, that's easy... in our friend's bed when we snuck into their flat because it was closer to the university than where we were living." Chris's eyes don't leave Molly's when he explains this.

Molly's mouth hangs wide open before she points at herself. Chris doesn't even look embarrassed when he nods.

"I could have you done for breaking and entering," Molly says, making everyone laugh.

"We used the spare key, so there was no breaking anything!" Chris says. "Jax, go on, your turn."

"Uh... on my desk," he says quietly, but not quietly enough for Molly not to hear him.

"What?" she squeals.

"Sorry," he says, looking between the two of us sheepishly, knowing that not only is it Molly's office he did it in, but it was with my sister.

"Brilliant," I mutter under my breath. "Can we move on, please? Holly?"

We all watch as Holly and Adam look at each other.

"Oh, I know... in the changing room of my favourite clothes shop," Holly says excitedly.

"Mmm... yeah, that was hot, but what about that time in that café by my work in the disabled toilets?" Adam adds.

"And the woman in the wheelchair from the next table spent the whole time we were in there banging on the door. I tell you what, though," Holly says, looking around at us all, "those handles are fucking useful!" I can't help but laugh. What I'm hearing from Holly tonight is so at odds with the sweet, caring woman I've come to know over the past couple of months. I guess a good man can do that.

"Will, it's your turn," Jax says before Holly starts going into much more detail.

"It's not very original, but I guess the toilets of a nightclub."

"Who the hell with? Because it certainly wasn't with me. I like to think I have a bit more class than that," Ana says, pissed off with his confession.

"Sorry, baby, but I was young, horny, and stupid," he says while smiling at her sweetly.

"So, what's changed?" she spits out.

"Um... I'm not young anymore," Will replies, trying to look cute so he'll be forgiven.

"Ryan?" Chris asks, trying to take the focus away from Will and Ana.

"Hot tub," I answer.

Molly immediately goes to correct me. "But we didn't—" She quickly realises what she's saying and shuts her mouth. I know full well we didn't actually have sex, but it's the best I have other than admitting we did it in Chris and Shane's bridal suite.

"Interesting," Shane mumbles, looking between the two of us, while Chris and Jax sit there with smirks on their faces. Will and Ana don't pay any attention because he's still trying to sweeten her up.

"Okay, so Molly, your turn." Shane prompts.

I look over at her, wondering what she is going to say, because we haven't had this kind of conversation before. I watch as a wide smile spreads across her face and I can't help but dread what is going to come out of her drunken mouth. "I've had sex in someone else's bridal suite."

And there it is.

I look around the room as every head snaps up to look at her in total disbelief. Maybe I should have listened to her that day when she said it was wrong.

"Oh my God, you had sex in our hotel room on the day of our wedding?" Chris says in total shock.

"Now... I didn't say that, did I? I've been to plenty of weddings over the years. It could have been any one of those."

"Name one," Chris demands.

"Uh... Steven's?" Molly says, but it comes out as a question.

"Yeah, whatever you say, you dirty slut!" Chris says with a smile.

Other than that, Molly and I have managed to get away quite lightly. I've had to explain the disaster that was my first time, and Molly, so far, has only had to confess that, yes, she has kissed another woman, which came as no surprise to Chris, Shane, and me because we watched Hannah and Molly do it a few years ago during another of Chris's stupid games. We got very drunk that night but I have never forgotten that part, and I don't think I ever will. I have a fear though, from the looks that Shane and Chris keep giving each other, that they have got it in for us, and I am equally excited and dreading what's coming next.

"Right, Molly, you're next... truth or dare?"

We all watch as she finishes her drink before slamming it down haphazardly and shouting, "Dare."

Chris's eyes sparkle as he looks at the card in his hand before reaching behind him and pulling something out of a bag. He glances between the two of us before placing what I now see is a can of whipped cream on the coffee table. "You, Molly, are to lick this off Ryan's chest."

I turn to Molly and see a huge grin break across her face. "Oh, hell yeah!" she squeals, before launching herself at me, and pulling my shirt from my shoulders. I can tell by her eagerness that she's more than a little drunk.

Seven sets of intrigued eyes burn into us, all of them obviously wondering how this is going to play out. I look back to Molly when I feel her start to lift the bottom of my t-shirt. I take pity on her lack of coordination and help her pull it over my head.

Ana gasps from the other side of the room, saying, "If you two go to the gym together, why don't you look like that?" as she turns her stare on Will.

"He puts in way more effort than I do. Sorry, baby, but this is as good as it gets," Will tells her, patting his toned stomach before pulling her on his lap for a kiss.

"I need a close-up, so I'm doing the cream," Chris announces seriously, walking over and instructing me to lie back on the sofa.

Chris really goes to town with the cream, squirting it over every line and indentation on my chest and stomach. My eyes are locked on Molly the entire time, watching hers get darker and darker as they run over my exposed skin. This whole situation is turning me on way more than I'm sure it should, seeing as we are surrounded by our friends.

"Okay, I think I'm done. All yours, Molly, you lucky bitch," Chris says, giving her an evil look.

Molly pulls her skirt up her thighs and throws one leg over me to straddle my body. I'm quite grateful for the move because it shields me slightly from the prying eyes of everyone watching my torture. It also provides a great view straight down the front of her dress.

She starts at my neck, and her moans of pleasure when she tastes the cream on my skin shoot straight to my dick, making it twitch.

Fuck, this is going to be hell.

Making her way slowly down to my pecs, she spends her time licking around my nipples, teasing me. Her eyes stay on mine the entire time, and I can see everything she's feeling in her depths. I know for a fact that if I wanted to, I'd be able to slide into her tight little body instantly. The thought causes my dick to press against the tight confines of my jeans, making it even more uncomfortable. I try to give myself a talking to about letting my thoughts wander, but they're too hard to control in a situation like this.

I'm pulled from my thoughts when Molly's tongue circles my left nipple, making me shiver, like always. She smiles up at me playfully before giving the other one the same treatment, then begins to lick up the cream covering all the lines of my stomach. Every time her tongue touches me, my muscles flinch, and she smiles wickedly, showing me how much she's enjoying this. Fuck, how I wish we were alone and she could continue her descent until she has her mouth where I truly want it.

Trying desperately hard to keep my breathing in check, I watch until Molly has completely cleaned me of the cream. I expect her to sit up, but she surprises me with one last swipe of her tongue. She starts at my hip, placing her tongue against the skin just above the line of my boxers, before very slowly licking across to the other side. By the time she's halfway across, she's managed to get her tongue under the fabric and I can't stop a groan that rumbles up my throat.

I'm so fucking turned on, it's painful.

Shutting my eyes, I try to keep myself together. As if this whole thing isn't embarrassing enough, I really don't need to shoot my load in my boxers in front of everyone like a little schoolboy.

When she's done, she shifts herself back up until she's straddling across my crotch, lining up her scorching heat with my throbbing dick. I press my head back into the sofa and keep my eyes squeezed shut. Everyone's silent, and I can feel their eyes on me the longer I lie here, not moving.

Ana eventually breaks the silence by announcing that they're taking the remainder of the can to bed with them, then breaks into a fit of giggles. She's obviously now drunk so much she's no longer embarrassed. I hear Will groan in response, before I presume he does something inappropriate, because Chris and Shane start telling them to get a room. Good, that means I'm no longer their entertainment. I open my eyes to find Molly's heated gaze staring right back at me, making me wish I'd kept them closed.

Molly

Fucking hell, if that wasn't the hottest thing I've ever done. The alcohol buzzing around my system mixed with the taste of the cream and the manly sexy scent that is uniquely Ryan has my entire body ignited and begging for attention.

Ryan is still lying completely rigid underneath me. From the rate his chest is heaving up and down, and the feeling of his rock-hard erection beneath me, I'm guessing he's trying to rein his body back in as well. If he's feeling half as turned on as I am right now, it's going to take a few minutes.

Luckily, everyone is distracted, but I'm completely focused on the pained expression on Ryan's face and all the inches of perfection that are before me to pay them any attention.

Slowly, Ryan reveals his stunning eyes to me. A dark navy has replaced their usual bright blue. The sight of them makes my breath catch in my throat.

He looks like he wants to say something, so I lean forward and he whispers in my ear, "Are you trying to kill me?" I can't help but laugh, which brings everyone's eyes back to us.

"Ah, Ryan, you're back with us!" Jax laughs. "Did you enjoy that?" he asks with a quirked eyebrow.

"Fuck off," is Ryan's only response.

"Okay, Ryan, you're having a dare, I've decided," Chris states.

"Brilliant!" Ryan mutters as he sits himself up properly after I've removed myself from his lap.

"I dare you to do a body shot off Molly," Chris says with way too much excitement, making Ryan groan next to me.

"Fine," he says, as if he's trying to sound totally unaffected by the whole thing. But his voice comes out as a deep rumble, so if that was what he was going for he's failed. Miserably.

"Right, put Molly on the worktop." Chris then looks at me before saying, "You're going to need to unzip your dress so we have some skin to work with, Molls." I nod at him before Ryan stands and scoops me up in his arms, carrying me toward the kitchen, where he places me on the edge of the worktop. His hands go to the zip at the back of my dress, but he looks down at me before he moves it, getting my approval. I'm drunk enough that I don't really care about getting half-naked in the kitchen with our friends watching.

Chris appears at our side with a bottle of tequila and a saltshaker. I'm starting to get the impression this has been well planned.

"Right, Molly, lie back." I do as he says, now that the top of my dress is around my waist, revealing my gold, strapless bra. Chris places a lemon wedge between my lips before wetting his finger with a little tequila and running it up the line of my cleavage. I can't help but giggle when I hear Ryan growl as he watches Chris touch me. He looks murderous for a few seconds before I guess it registers that Chris is very much gay and no threat at all. Chris then shakes salt on the trail and gets ready to pour some liquid in my belly button. "Okay, so once I've poured some, Ryan, I want you to lick the salt, lap up the tequila, then take the lemon. You ready?"

Chris's preparation and explanation seem to take forever. All I want is Ryan's mouth on me. The longer I lie here waiting, the more impatient and turned on I'm getting.

After what feels like hours, Chris eventually pours a little of the cold liquid onto my belly, making me flinch. He tells Ryan to go, but his face is already well toward my tits before the words leave his mouth, showing Ryan's impatience.

"Oh God," I moan when I feel his tongue run slowly between my breasts, making my already peaked nipples press against the confines of my bra. When he moves south and starts lapping at the tequila sitting in my belly button, I press my legs together in an attempt to stop the throbbing that has now increased to a seriously uncomfortable level. When he's happy he's got it all, I feel him move, and then his lips brush mine as he bites into the lemon.

To my surprise, he doesn't move away from my lips. Instead, he takes the lemon, spits it to the floor and crashes his lips to mine for a scorching kiss. Whoops and hollers sound out around the room, but I barely hear them.

Eventually he pulls back, but only enough so his nose rests against mine. He looks straight into my eyes before he says, "I'm sorry, guys, you all know where you're sleeping, so I'm sure you can sort yourselves out." Before I have a chance to realise what he means, he has me in his arms and is racing toward the stairs. I hear more cheers behind us as we start to climb the stairs and everyone disappears from my sight.

When we get to our room, Ryan carries me straight over to the bed and drops me onto it before following me down and laying his body on top of mine. His lips instantly find mine and he continues to kiss me with the same all-consuming passion, only this time we don't have any spectators. One of his hands tangles in my hair and holds me tight to him, while the other runs up and down my side, settling on my breast. My hands move of their own accord all over his smooth, perfect skin, and come to a rest, tangled in his hair.

I'm completely lost in his kiss and don't realise he's moved until he sits himself on his heels between my legs and looks down at me while he catches his breath. He's still topless so I can easily see how fast his chest is heaving. I rake my eyes down his abs before slowly letting them crawl back up his perfect chest and run over his face, taking in his lust-filled eyes, his slightly pink cheeks, his swollen red lips, and his messy I've-just-been-fucked-to-heaven-and-back hair. He takes my breath away. "I love you so much," I tell him when I meet his eyes again.

"I'm sorry," he whispers as he lowers his head, breaking our eye contact.

"Hey," I say, sitting myself up so I can grab his cheek and pull his eyes back to me. "What's wrong?"

"That," he says waving his arm toward the door, "was just too much. My restraint snapped and I had to have you alone. I need to be inside you and feel you coming around my cock so badly that I couldn't think. I know you didn't want them to know." He tries to look away again, like he's ashamed of his actions, but I tense my arm and stop him from turning his head.

"Ryan, don't be stupid. Let's be honest, everyone downstairs already knew we had something going on. We're telling everyone on Tuesday anyway, and it's not like they'll spread the news before we get to it. Now," I say in a slightly sterner voice. "Don't you ever apologise for wanting me. I'm with you all the way; I want it just as badly as you do, so can we please stop this and get to what we both want?" Before I've even finished the sentence, Ryan's off the bed and pulling my dress down my legs.

"Fuck me," he groans when he stands back and looks at me. I bought a new set of gold lace underwear for tonight, which I kept hidden from him, but I've also added sheer hold-ups with gold lace at the top. Finish that off with my gold heels, and I feel like a fucking goddess, lying here under Ryan's heated, appreciative gaze. I lean back on my elbows and let him get his fill.

After a full minute, he pulls his phone out of his pocket. "Can I?" he asks.

"Just one." Wow, I really have drunk too much.

"I'm pretty sure I'll never forget this sight, but just in case…" He shrugs his shoulders.

It's not the first time I've been asked to have my photo taken, but it is most definitely the first time I've agreed. I know without a doubt that the photo is for Ryan's eyes only. I trust him implicitly. I watch him as he takes the picture, then puts his phone on the unit, before stripping out of his clothes. I can't take my eyes off him as he reveals more of his perfect body for me to gawk at.

Once his boxer briefs hit the floor, he looks back at me and smirks. "You like my body, don't you, Molly?" he asks quietly.

"You have no idea. I'd like it better if I could touch it, though," I say as I reach out to him, but he doesn't move.

"What is it exactly that you want to touch?" The more he talks, the lower and sexier his voice gets, making my mouth go dry. I watch as he slowly lifts one hand toward his head. "Do you want to be running your hands through my hair like this?" he asks as he brings his hand to rest on the back of his neck. "Or would you rather be doing this?" His hand slowly runs across his chest and down his stomach toward his straining dick. I can't help the groan that comes from me as I watch the show. "Or is it here that you want to touch?" he asks, wrapping his hand around himself and slowly moving it up and down his length. The sight of him pleasuring himself in front of me sends an electric bolt straight through me.

"Oh God, that's hot," I groan.

"Show me how ready you are for me, Molly. Spread your legs and touch yourself," he demands, and I do it instantly. When my fingers touch my sensitive flesh, my moan of pleasure is drowned out by Ryan's growl and, before I know it, my fingers have been replaced by his and I'm once again flat on my back with him hovering above me.

My orgasm is about to rip through me, but Ryan pulls his fingers away at the last minute. "No," I complain.

"I want you coming around my cock, Molly," he says, as he lines himself up with my entrance.

He slides into me painfully slowly until he's balls deep and whispers in my ear, "This isn't going to be gentle. Are you ready?"

"Yes," I breathe. I'm more than ready for what he's about to give me.

He pulls out almost all the way and I see his muscles tense as he prepares to slam back into me, when both of our heads snap toward the bedroom door at the sound of Tenacious D's 'Fuck Her Gently' booming through. Ryan looks back at me and we both burst out laughing.

"I love our friends," I say, once my laughter has died down.

"Mmm... I love you more." Those words are all it takes for the song and everything else to be forgotten, and we lose ourselves in each other for hours.

I stretch my body out the next morning when I wake up, and all my muscles pull from our late-night activities. I haven't been to a pole-dancing lesson for a few weeks because I haven't been feeling up to it, and the lack of exercise is starting to show.

Ryan's still sleeping next to me if his soft snores are anything to go by, so I carefully roll over and go to get up. The moment I stand, my stomach turns over and I have to run to the en suite.

I sit back on my heels after emptying my stomach and realise I feel much better for it. I'm just about to stand when I hear Ryan walk up behind me.

"Did I just hear you being sick, Molls? Are you okay?" he asks, the concern clear in his tone.

"Yeah, I'm fine now. I guess it was just too much food, wine, and excitement last night," I say with a shrug of my shoulders as I go to the sink to brush my teeth.

We walk down to the living area hand in hand thirty minutes later. No one else is awake yet, so we quietly go into the kitchen and put the kettle on so we don't wake Jax, who's asleep on the sofa. I didn't hear anyone go to bed last night. I'm unsure if that was because I'd fallen asleep or if I was still being thoroughly distracted by Ryan. I'm sure if it's the latter, someone will say something about it, because we were not quiet—I remember that much.

"Coffee, please, lovebirds," I hear Jax say from the sofa when the kettle pings.

"Morning," I say, smiling at him when his head pokes up over the back of the sofa.

"I understand why you both look so happy, but how do you look like you've had a full night's sleep? We all know that wasn't the case."

"Sleep is overrated," Ryan mutters as he pulls the milk from the fridge.

"God, I miss sex," Jax complains as he gets up and pulls his jeans on.

Everyone else appears over the next couple of hours, most looking the worse for wear. I understand why when I pick up the empty tequila bottle and shot glasses from the coffee table later that day.

Needless to say, Ryan and I get no end of grief about our performance last night—and well into the early hours this morning, if what they all told us is anything to go by.

It's late afternoon before everyone starts heading off. My brothers pull up outside the house as Ryan and I say our goodbyes to Jax, who is the last to leave. "No peace for the wicked," I mutter to myself.

"Hey, good to see we aren't interrupting anything this time," Daniel says with a laugh.

"Nah, they wore themselves out last night," Jax shouts over to us from his car.

Daniel barks with laughter while Steven looks mortified at having to be part of yet another conversation about my sex life.

"Jax," I shout back, making him look up at me. "You're fired!"

"Yeah, whatever. You couldn't cope without me now, and you know it," he shoots back, jumping in his car and heading off.

When we get upstairs, I notice that Steven is carrying an envelope. "Are those the papers I have to sign?"

"Yes, it's all as you requested."

"Great," I say sarcastically, because I'm still not completely happy about getting involved with the business, but at least I got my way with having a smaller share than my brothers.

They don't stay very long, which I'm relieved about. It's not that I don't want to spend time with them, because I do, but right now I'd much rather be cuddling with Ryan on the sofa in front of soppy Christmas films.

CHAPTER SEVENTEEN

Molly

Christmas Eve is my favourite day of the year. I can't help it—I feel like a child again. I'm going to be spending tomorrow with all my favourite people, including my amazing boyfriend. I still can't believe I have everything I have ever wanted, and that the person who has given it all to me is Ryan.

"What are you smiling about?"

"Just excited about spending Christmas with you."

"I'm so glad we managed to get out of spending tonight at the Morrisons'. I don't think they'd have been too happy about being in the same house as us with the things I have planned for you tonight," Ryan says as he walks back over to the sofa with our drinks in hand. He places them on the coffee table before lying down in front of me and pulling me against his body. His lips find mine and, within seconds, his tongue is exploring my mouth.

After a few minutes, his phone starts ringing on the coffee table. Groaning into his mouth, I go to pull away from him, but he mumbles to ignore it and continues kissing me.

No sooner has his phone rang off than it starts again. Eventually, I manage to detach Ryan's lips from mine to get him to answer it.

"Ugh, it's my mum," he says, putting it on silent and placing it back on the coffee table, but it lights up again before he gets to put it down.

I can see from the photo on the screen that it's Abbi this time. "Just answer it."

He grumbles as he sits himself up before swiping the screen and putting it to his ear.

"Abbi, what's—" He's cut off by something she says, but I can't make her out. "Shit, he's okay though, right?" Hearing him say that gets my heart beating faster. "Are you sure she isn't just using this as a good excuse to get me there, if he's okay?"

I continue listening for a few minutes before he agrees to whatever it is they're talking about and hangs up. When he turns to look at me, a wave of disappointment washes over me, because I know what's coming from what I overheard.

"My dad's had a heart attack." I suck in a breath. "He's fine—it was mild and he's recovering well, but they want me there. I'm so sorry, but I've got to go."

"It's okay, I understand. They're your family—you need to be with them."

"You could come?" he asks tentatively.

"No. I'm sorry, but it's Christmas, and I really don't want to see your mum. Not yet, anyway."

"It's fine, I shouldn't have asked. I'll be back as soon as I can, I promise."

"Yeah, I know," I say sadly. "You'd better go and pack some stuff."

I can't believe how, in the space of two minutes, all my earlier excitement has completely vanished, and I now feel empty, knowing I'm going to be spending Christmas without Ryan.

He seems to be packed and ready to leave in no time. All I want to do is cling onto him and beg him not to go, but I know that it's irrational, unfair, and selfish. His dad is in the hospital; he needs to be there for him and his family.

"I want you to take these with you and open them in the morning," I say as he zips up his suitcase, his Christmas presents in my hands.

"We could open each other's now, before I go," he suggests.

"No, I want you to open them tomorrow, whether I'm with you or not."

He walks over to his wardrobe and pulls out a bag. "You have to open yours in the morning, then," he says as he hands it over, and I swallow down the lump in my throat I've been trying to fight. My eyes sting and I pray I can hold them off until he leaves. "Oh, Molls, please don't get upset. You know I'd rather stay here with you, don't you?"

I just nod at him, my first tear falling. I need him to get going now, because I can't cope with drawing this goodbye out. I need to fall apart on my own and not make him feel guilty. I wipe my tears and square my shoulders in an attempt to pull myself together. "Right... are you ready?"

"Yeah, I think so," he answers sadly.

"Come on... the sooner you get gone, the sooner you can be coming back to me."

"I'm really sorry about this."

"Ryan, stop apologising. This is not your fault, and you're doing the right thing."

"Okay," he says as he pulls me in for a hug. "I'll be back as soon as I can. I love you.".

"I love you, too. Send Abbi and Liv my love."

"I will."

With one final kiss, he walks out of our bedroom and out of the house. I can't bear to watch him walk away from what was supposed to be my best Christmas ever.

It takes a good ten minutes for my sobs to subside enough for me to make my way back down to the living room and the glass of wine and DVD of The Holiday that's waiting for me. I curl myself up under the blanket and try to forget about everything as I let Cameron Diaz and Kate Winslet distract me from my misery.

The film is nearly over when I hear a noise coming from downstairs and the door slam shut. My heart pounds, thinking that he's come back. I sit up straight on the sofa as I hear footsteps heading my way. My heart feels like it breaks in two when the person that comes into view isn't Ryan. I immediately burst into tears and run at Susan, who holds her arms out for me.

"Oh, Molly," is all she says as she leads us back to the sofa.

I pull my face from her shoulder and look into her kind eyes. "Ryan won't be here for Christmas," I tell her in a steadier voice than I am expecting.

"I know, angel," she says softly and wipes a tear off my cheek. "He rang and asked me to come and make sure you were okay. He told me I wasn't allowed to leave you here alone and that you were to come back with me." I just nod at her, because the lump in my throat is stopping any words from coming out.

Ryan

A couple of hours later, I'm pulling up in the driveway of my childhood home. Abbi rang thirty minutes ago to say they'd been kicked out of the hospital because visiting hours were over, and that they would meet me at home.

When I get there, Abbi explains everything about Dad's condition. Everything is positive; he should make a full recovery, but he needs to make a few lifestyle changes once he's discharged. Mum's already fast asleep in bed. Today has really taken its toll on her.

I wake up the next morning to the sounds of Mum crashing around in the kitchen like I used to as a kid. When I eventually join her, I see that Abbi and Liv are already there and Mum is just dishing up our traditional Christmas breakfast of pancakes. It's always been one of our favourite parts of Christmas. Okay, maybe not when we were children, but as the three of us got older, we appreciated it more and more. My stomach's been grumbling the whole time I've been getting ready, knowing what's happening downstairs.

"Ryan," Mum squeals when I appear in the room. She walks over and holds on to me tightly. "I'm so glad you're here... I've missed you so much." Her voice cracks and she quietly starts sobbing in my arms. As much as I hate her actions toward Molly, she's still my mum, and she's upset, so I soothe her as much as I can.

Once we've eaten, Mum instructs us to pack up the presents from under the tree so we can take them to open with Dad.

I feel really bad as I watch my sisters leave the house with bags of presents, because I haven't bought Mum and Dad anything, and what Molly and I did get for my sisters is still at home. I didn't think of grabbing them before I left. The only presents I can take with me are the ones Molly packed in my bag yesterday.

I wait as Mum pokes her head around Dad's door to see if he's awake. "Merry Christmas, darling," she sings, pushing the door wider and gesturing for us to follow.

"Merry Christmas, Dad," the three of us say as we enter the room.

"Ryan. What are you doing here, Son?"

"You're in the hospital, in case you've forgotten. I needed to be here for you, old man."

"Enough of that, please. Come here," he says, holding his arms out to me. I walk over and gently give him a hug. The others follow suit.

We're chatting away when a nurse comes in and asks us to leave for a few minutes while they do some tests.

"We're going to get coffee. Want one?"' Abbi asks as we step out into the corridor.

"Ryan," Mum says after Abbi and Liv have turned a corner away from us. "Come and sit. I want to talk to you."

I do as she says, but I'm apprehensive about what she's about to come out with. If she's going to say anything about Molly, I think I may just get up and leave. I already hate that I'm spending today without her. I don't need Mum slagging her off as well.

"Ryan... I'm sorry about what I did. It was selfish of me to try to run your life the way I think it should be. I never should have done it, but at least I know that she's serious now. I'm sorry to say it, but I thought she'd take it and run. I—"

"You saying that just shows me how little you actually know about her, and what you're basing your opinions on. She's not like that at all."

"I see that now. Let me just say this." She looks down and holds one of my hands in both of hers. She takes a deep breath before looking back up into my eyes. "I had the shock of my life yesterday. I cannot imagine my life without your dad. He is the other half of me. It suddenly hit me that that could be what I've been trying to keep you from having. Okay, so Molly may not have been my ideal woman for you—" I go to interrupt but am stopped by the look on her face."—but as you've said before, that's not for me to decide, and if she's your other half, I need to be happy for you. If she makes you even half as happy as your dad has me over the years, then it's worth fighting for."

I reach up and wipe a tear that's fallen from Mum's cheek while I think about her words.

"Mum... I... I'm completely in love with her. She's my everything. We've been together for a couple of months, and I can honestly say I've never been happier." I can't help the smile that spreads across my face, actually telling someone that.

"Then you need to make damn sure you are her everything, too, Son. I want nothing more than for you to be happy, and if Molly does that, then... I can't wait to meet her... the *real* her."

Wrapping my arms around my mum's tiny frame, I whisper, "Thank you," in her ear.

A few seconds later, the nurse appears from Dad's room, saying we can go back in. We barely sit down before Abbi and Liv reappear with our coffees.

"Did I see you bring presents?" Dad asks us.

"Yes. Girls, do you want to start handing them out?"

I stop them before they make a dive for the bags. "Um... I'm really sorry, but I haven't got anything for you guys. Mum, I was so annoyed with you that I haven't actually got you anything... sorry," I say with a grimace. "And I left yours at home," I say to my sisters.

"You're here, and that's all that matters... and I'm hoping I'm forgiven?"

"As long as you do as you just said, then yes." I feel three sets of eyes staring between us.

Eventually, Dad breaks the silence by telling Mum he's proud of her and, just because I can't hold it in any longer, seeing as today is the day we were going to tell everyone, the words just come spilling out of my mouth. "I'm in love with Molly, and we've been together secretly for a while now," I say in a rush.

"Secretly, my arse!" Abbi says, laughing.

"Does this mean we can all admit that we already knew?" Liv asks.

"Yes, shut up, smart-arse. I know we weren't actually very secretive, but we knew people would have opinions, so we needed to make sure it was serious first."

"I'm happy for you, Son. She's a good girl," Dad says with a smile on his face.

"Yes, she is."

We've been handing out presents around the room for about twenty minutes. I've got the standard socks and pants from Mum and Dad as well as a family photo for my house, a couple of cookbooks, and a rather large voucher for a garden centre to buy myself a set of garden furniture. I've also opened a t-shirt from my sisters and all kinds of smellies. They've also given me a bag to take home for Molly. Guilt hangs heavy at not being able to give anything in return—that is, until my mum squeals on the other side of Dad's bed.

"What is it?" we ask her at the same time.

She gets up and comes running toward me with some paperwork in her hand before hugging me tightly. "You said you didn't get us anything, you liar!" she says, laughing. Her delight is clear on her face.

"Mum, I wasn't lying. I really haven't bought anything."

She stands back and looks at me before passing the paper over. My eyes go wide as I read what it says.

"Holy shit."

"What is it?" Liv asks.

"It's a voucher for a holiday in Paris in Mum and Dad's name... from me and... Molly. She did this," I say, looking up to Mum. "Molly has done this... I had no idea."

"Why would she do that after what I did to her?" Mum asks, confused.

"Because this is who she is, Mum, not whoever you had in your head. I told her I wasn't getting you anything because of what happened, but she wasn't happy about it."

"We were talking about wanting to go to Paris that weekend at yours over dinner. She must have been listening."

"See? This is who she is," I say again, just to make sure she knows.

The surprises don't end there. Before long, Abbi and Liv are handed similar looking envelopes.

"What has she done now?" I ask, laughing.

"She's booked for the three of us to go to London to watch a show we were talking about for a weekend later in the year," they explain, showing me the paperwork.

Well, shit... if my girlfriend isn't the most caring woman in the world, then I don't know who is. I just wish she were here to see the excited looks on their faces. She would love it.

"Ryan, are you going to open those?" Mum asks, pulling me out of my thoughts.

When I look up, she's nodding toward the presents on my lap. The last ones in the room to be opened. I've been holding off because, after seeing what she got my family, I'm kind of scared to find out what she got me.

The first couple I open are fine—more boxers, some t-shirts and jeans. There's a photograph of the two of us that I took in bed one night. I look down at the last box and slowly start to pull the paper away. My heart hammers and my hands start to sweat a little because, if I know Molly like I think I do, then whatever is in here is going to knock me on my arse.

"Fuck," is all I can say when the box emerges from the paper. I slowly open it up and there, gleaming at me, is the most stunning timepiece I have ever seen.

"Holy shit... do you know how much that costs?" Abbi says next to me in a slightly higher voice than usual. All I can do is nod as I pull the watch out of the box. Something tells me to turn it over and, when I do, I see that I was right. There, inscribed on the back, are Molly's words.

All of my love.
Forever.
Molly x

The memory of us in the shower the night of the stag do hits me at full force, remembering when she said those words for the first time. I feel myself tear up and Abbi's hand comes to rest on my shoulder in comfort.

After staring at it for a few minutes with the room in silence, I slide the watch into place on my wrist before standing up and looking at everyone's slightly choked up faces.

"I'm sorry, but there's somewhere I need to be."

CHAPTER EIGHTEEN

Molly

When I woke this morning, it took me a few seconds to place where I was. I stretched my arm out across the bed to find Ryan, but he wasn't there. It wasn't until the unmistakable smell of Susan's homemade waffles hit my nose that I remembered where I was, that Ryan wasn't here with me, and that I was spending another Christmas alone.

"Good morning, angel. Merry Christmas," Susan sings from her spot in front of the oven as I join the rest of the family around the table.

As soon as my arse hits the chair, Susan is placing a plate of hot waffles and a mug of steaming hot tea in front of me. I instantly reach for the mug and hold it in both hands.

"Is this new?" Susan asks, lifting my wrist up.

"It was a Christmas present from Ryan. I opened it before I came down."

I look at the charm bracelet I'm now proudly wearing. I can't help smiling, but at the same time my eyes water at Ryan's thoughtfulness. There are two charms currently on my bracelet: one is an angel, and the other is two interlocked rose gold hearts.

Susan looks up from inspecting the two charms when I sniff. She smiles at me with her eyes full of sympathy. "He'll be back before you know it," she whispers to me before going back to making sure we're all full to bursting with breakfast.

"Mum, how long until dinner's ready?" Dec asks after we've finished opening the presents quite a while later.

"Two hours yet, angel."

"How are you hungry already?" Lilly asks, bemused. "You had, like, twenty waffles this morning!"

"An engine this perfect needs good fuel, Lil," Dec says, lifting his shirt to show off his abs just to prove his point.

"Oh, put it away, no one wants to see your body," Lilly says, throwing a cushion at him.

"Huh, my abs usually get a different reaction from women," he deadpans, returning the cushion, which hits Lilly square on the head.

I decide to get up before they start properly fighting. "I'm going to tidy this up, if you want to help," I say, looking around the room at all the scrunched up wrapping paper. "Then I'm going for a lie down, if that's okay?"

Susan, as always, got everyone perfect presents. I love sitting and watching them all enjoy opening what they've got. I don't need presents; watching the happiness around me is enough, even if it's tinged with a little sadness with the loss of Hannah. No one has mentioned her yet, so I'm guessing everyone is just trying to get through the day in one piece. I can't imagine she's far from anyone's minds.

"Of course, don't worry about this. Tweedle Dee and Tweedle Dum here can get it," Susan says, pointing at the twins.

I make my way up to the guest bedroom I slept in last night. When I look in the mirror, all I can see is my sad, tired eyes. No wonder everyone's been acting strangely around me. I look like I could break down at any moment. My skin is unusually pale, my eyes have dark rings around them, and they're rimmed in red from either tiredness or crying after opening my presents from Ryan earlier, I'm not really sure which.

Leaning back against the bedroom door as soon as the latch clicks closed, I let out a huge sigh. I glance around the room and, the moment my eyes land on the teddy bear Ryan bought for me lying in the middle of the bed, a sob erupts from me without warning.

My back slides down the door until my arse hits the floor. I put my head on my knees and give myself over to my tears.

The stress of the last few weeks with work being crazy, Ryan's mum, my parents and brothers has taken its toll, and I'm completely exhausted. I love Ryan with everything I am, but hiding our relationship for the past couple of months has been hard. I know it was the right thing to do, but keeping secrets from the people closest to me has caused more stress than I thought it would. I'm done hiding. I hoped that we would be together when we told everyone our news, but that obviously isn't how fate intended it to happen.

Once I've pulled myself together, I get myself up off the floor and slump down on the edge of the bed. I pull my phone out of my jeans pocket before lying back on the pillow and putting it to my ear after pressing *Call* on Ryan's name.

It rings until it goes to voicemail—again. I drop the phone next to me, grab the teddy bear, and hold it close to my chest.

I know it's not Ryan's fault. His dad his ill, for fuck's sake, but I can't stop feeling like I've been abandoned. I know that's not true. I could tell by the look in his eyes when we parted yesterday. He didn't want to leave just as much as I didn't want him to go.

I'm trying my best not to get annoyed with him because he's probably in the hospital, but it's not that easy. It's Christmas day, and I haven't spoken to my boyfriend.

I come around feeling really hot. At some point, I'd managed to get myself under the covers whilst still being fully clothed. I flip them off and turn over, keeping the bear tight to my chest. I've no idea how long I've been asleep, but I feel like I could do with some more. I'm just fading away again when a shiver runs down my spine.

I crack open one eye to put my mind at rest. I mean, I'm in the Morrisons' guest room—who the hell would be watching me sleep?

I have to blink a couple of times, because what I'm seeing cannot be right. I must be dreaming. I open them both this time just to check, but he's still there and it's not my imagination playing tricks on me.

Standing, leaning back against the door, is Ryan. The corners of his lips curl up when he sees me awake. I run my eyes all over him, because if this is a dream, I need to make the most of it. I run my eyes up his thick thighs to where his jeans are resting low on his hips, giving me a hint of what he's wearing underneath. I continue my journey, taking in his thick knit jumper stretched over his broad chest and shoulders. I run my eyes up his neck. I take in his stubble-covered jaw, up past his eyes, and to his head, covered in a grey knit beanie hat. It's sitting so far back on his head, I have no idea how it's staying put, but he looks edible with his messy dirty blond hair sticking out the front and falling over his eyes.

I'm pulled from my thoughts when he moves toward me. He lowers himself so that he's sitting on the edge of the mattress and looks down at me while running his knuckles down my cheek.

"Am I dreaming?"

"No, gorgeous," he says, toeing his boots off and lying down next to me. "I came back for you. I couldn't cope being away from you any longer."

He places his hand on my cheek and wipes away the few tears that have fallen, when I notice the watch is on his wrist. "Do you like it?"

"Are you kidding? I love it. Thank you so much. Have you opened yours?"

I look down at the bear now squashed between our chests, and Ryan laughs as he follows my eyes.

"I guess you have, then. Did you like the bracelet?"

Before I answer, I shove at Ryan's chest as hard as I can. He must take pity on me because he rolls onto his back easily, allowing me to straddle his waist. Leaning forward so my lips are just touching his, I whisper, "I love it, but I love you more..." I take a breath to carry on telling him how glad I am that he's here and how badly I've missed him, but Ryan can't wait any longer, because he presses his lips hard to mine and his tongue passes my open lips. His arms come around my back and he holds me tight to him while he kisses me like he hasn't seen me in months, not hours.

Our kiss soon turns into something much more heated as we explore every inch of each other's mouths. Ryan's hands creep up under my top and his fingers pinch my peaked nipples through my bra while I grind against his length.

I pull my lips from his so I can try to catch my breath. "I can't believe you came back. Are you sure I'm not dreaming?"

"I'm sure, gorgeous. God, I want to be inside you so badly," he groans in my ear before he starts kissing and nibbling down my neck.

Fuck, I want that, too. Why couldn't we be at home alone right now, not at the Morrisons'? And from the smell now wafting through the room, I'd say dinner is nearly ready. "Ryan, please," I'm so close already, I'm sure Ryan has some magic power over me.

"Molly... you're killing me. We can't, Susan said dinner was almost ready before I came up here."

I'm moved off Ryan and rolled onto my side so we're facing each other again.

"It would have been quick," I say, pouting.

"That may well be true, but I'm not having all them listening when you scream my name. Plus, I want to take my time with you."

I'm just about to respond when I hear Susan's voice. "Molly, Ryan, dinner is ready."

"See," Ryan says with a smirk as he gets up and adjusts himself in his jeans before heading toward the door.

"Ry," I say before he grabs the handle.

"Yes, gorgeous?"

"Thank you for coming back."

"There isn't anywhere I'd rather be." He grabs my hand and pulls me along toward the stairs but, as we enter the Morrison's dining room, I feel him go to pull his hand from mine. I hold on tight and, together, we walk up to the table. All eyes turn our way.

"Ah, angel, you look so much better," Susan comments when she sees me.

"Thank you. I needed that." I know I'm implying the sleep I had, but what I really needed was the person stood next to me.

"I... uh... we..." I look up to Ryan and he just smiles back at me encouragingly. I take a deep breath and start again. "We have an announcement to make..." I look around at the faces of my adopted family, and I can't help but laugh when Susan starts excitedly bouncing in her seat. "Ryan and I are together. I know that—"

"Don't even think about going there," Susan interrupts. "We're all so happy for you both, and we are ever so thankful that we don't need to pretend we don't know anymore."

Ryan

We just get seated when Emma clears her throat at the other side of the table from Molly and I, making everyone look up. "Okay, so as we're making announcements, I'd like to say something."

The silence is deafening as we wait. I cannot begin to imagine what's running through her head right now. Molly squeezes my hand tighter.

"So..." Emma begins, "I know you've all been worried about me these past few months, and I'm sorry that I've caused that, but I've been trying my hardest to deal with losing Hannah. I feel like I'm now at a point where I want to share some things with you and ask for some help."

"Go on," Susan encourages when Emma looks like she's about to bolt from the room.

"Okay, so... it all started when I wanted somewhere quiet to go to think. I started going to the village where Gran and Grandad used to live, sitting down by the river. I used to spend hours there, thinking about Hannah. Eventually, I ran out of thoughts, and once I got past the guilt of not being able to remember anything else, I started thinking about what could have been. All these thoughts just started flowing around in my head, so, one day I took my laptop with me and I started writing. To cut a long story short... I've written a book."

"Oh, angel, that's wonderful," Susan says.

"I need to make a huge apology. Ryan... I may have killed you off. The story is about Hannah rebuilding her life and moving on."

The look on Emma's face as she says this tells me all I need to know about how scared she has been to tell me this. "Emma, it's—"

"No, let me finish." I nod at her to continue. "I'm sorry, but I think you should be thanking me because it was writing about Hannah moving on and finding someone new that helped me understand what's been going on with you two, and it's what Hannah would want. She loved you both and would want you to be happy. And if that's together, then so be it."

"I don't know what to say... thank you, I guess."

"Can I read it?" Molly chips in excitedly. I know she's as big a reader as Emma is, so I'm not surprised by her enthusiasm.

"I was hoping you would. I've only just finished typing the story, so it's going to need quite a bit of editing. I can only imagine how many errors will be in it. But I was also hoping you'd help me with a cover design and with promotion when it's done."

"Of course I will," Molly squeals as she gets up and runs around the table to hug Emma.

A thought hits me. He may not thank me for it later, but I'm sure he'll be willing to help. "I've got a mate who's an English teacher. I'm sure he'd read it for you to help edit it."

"That would be amazing, thank you. And thank you all for understanding and being patient with me this year. I truly couldn't have done it without you."

Everyone has just about finished consoling Emma, who seems to be a bit overwhelmed after confessing what she's been up to, when Dec pipes up. "While we're at it, I've got news, too."

"Are we ever going to get to the turkey?" Dave complains lightheartedly.

"Don't worry, old man, you're not going to starve to death anytime soon," Dec deadpans as he waves his hand in the direction of his dad's rather round belly. "So, as you know, I like to make money." Lilly groans. "Thanks for the support, Lills! Anyway, I've started up my own surf school. Someone from uni introduced us to this little bay about an hour away from campus. It's really up and coming with tourists, and the surf is insane. It's early days, but it seems to be doing well."

"My goodness, when did all our children become so successful?" Susan chimes in, looking like she could burst with pride.

Eventually, there's enough of a break in the conversation that we can actually start dishing out the dinner. Dave makes a really touching speech for Hannah which has us all sobbing into our gravy, but soon the conversation resumes around Emma's book and Dec's business.

"Lilly, have you got anything to announce while we're here?" Dave asks.

"Uh, no, I don't think so."

"What about that new boyfriend of yours? When do we get to meet him?" Susan has been trying to get an invitation to meet this mysterious man of Lilly's for a while now, but she keeps putting her off.

"He's not my boyfriend, Mum. We're just... friends?" It comes out more like a question.

Susan mumbles her disapproval quietly and the heat is soon taken off Lilly, much to her relief.

Once we've finished eating, Molly and I are given the task of washing up and drying everything that won't fit in the dishwasher. We're alone for the first time since we were upstairs. The electricity between us hasn't lessened. My body is still aching for her, and every time she so much as brushes my skin, fireworks go off around my body. Molly is acting like everything's normal, but I can tell by her eyes that she is just as affected as I am.

I put the last tray away before coming up behind her at the sink and wrapping my arms around her waist. She shivers when my breath whips past her ears and she leans back into my body.

"We are not staying here tonight," I growl in her ear.

Her breath picks up and she shakes her head. "No, we're not."

"Let's finish up in here, then make our excuses. I want you alone and naked, and that's not happening while we're under this roof. I think it's time we celebrate Christmas our own way, don't you?" I ask as I run my hands up her stomach and squeeze her breasts. The moan that comes from her almost makes me forget where we are. I continue teasing her and kissing down her neck, but we're soon interrupted.

"Dude, seriously, just take her home already," Dec says with a laugh.

Molly's instantly out of my arms and looking panicked. "W-we want to be here," she stutters.

Dec comes over and wraps his arm around her shoulder. "I was joking, Molls. You two deserve some time alone today. Plus, with you gone, I'm a dead cert for winning Monopoly."

CHAPTER NINETEEN

Molly

I know I'm only torturing myself, but since we walked through the front door, I've found little jobs to keep myself busy, just to see how far I can push Ryan. I've unpacked my overnight bag, had a shower and dried my hair—very slowly, I might add. Ryan's come up every ten minutes or so to see if I'm ready yet, and each time, I have to try to hold my laughter in.

"Hurry the fuck up and get your arse downstairs on the sofa with me, Molls," he grumbles when he comes back up to find me still faffing around.

"Yeah, I'll be there in, like, two minutes."

"I'm bored of waiting." He walks toward me. "Nothing you're doing can be as important as what I've got planned." That thought alone gets my blood pumping. As soon as he's standing in front of me, he grabs me by my thighs and throws me over his shoulder before marching us downstairs. I'm thrown onto the sofa, and I have to quickly cover what I'm wearing under my dressing gown.

That's a surprise for later.

Once I'm sorted, I look up to see a glass of wine for me on the coffee table next to a wrapped present. "Are you sorted now?" he asks with a smirk.

"Yep, I think so...what's that?"

"That, Miss Molly, is your last Christmas present. Go ahead... open it."

I grab it off the table as the sofa dips next to me. The heat of Ryan's body engulfs my tiny one. I start pulling the wrapping paper and his eyes stay on me the entire time.

"I wish I'd been there to see you open the others this morning. I was desperate to see your face," he mumbles.

"Me too, Ry. Wait... what is this?" I ask, looking down at the new sketchpad, pencils, and charcoal sitting on my lap.

"I promised myself something a couple of months ago, that I would do something for you."

I look back into Ryan's eyes and watch them darken the longer I stare into the blue depths. Suddenly, he stands up, making me jump where I was so lost in my own thoughts. "Where are you g—" I'm completely distracted from what I'm saying when Ryan pulls his jumper over his head, revealing perfect, defined skin. I run my eyes over his chest and lick my lips in preparation for what I hope is to come. His hand moves to his belt and I'm totally mesmerised by his slow, seductive movements.

Before long, Ryan is standing before me, completely bare, and all I can do is lean back on the sofa and take in the view. Fuck, if he hasn't got the most perfect body I've ever seen. "I could get used to this," I mutter as I continue roaming my gaze over him.

"Where do you want me?" he asks, trying to look completely relaxed with the situation, but I can see the gentle pulsing of the muscle in his neck as well as the most obvious sign that he's excited about whatever is about to happen.

"As long as it involves you being closer to me than you are now, I really don't care."

"That's not going to work. You're going to have to be far enough away so I can't touch you, or we'll both end up distracted."

I look up into his eyes as I try to understand. After a couple of seconds, it hits me. The sketchpad and a very naked Ryan. "You want me to draw you?"

"I do. I promised myself the day you sketched Jax that I would let you do it, and I thought today would be as good as any. "So, where do you want me?"

I think about this for a few minutes. The bed would be the obvious choice, but I'm not convinced by how much drawing I'd actually get done. The sofa? Yep, probably the same problem. Oh, I could draw him in the shower with water running down his... nope, bad idea. "The kitchen," I blurt out.

"The kitchen... why?"

"Because I think it's the safest place."

"The safest place?" he asks, confused.

"Yes. I have all these ideas running around in my head, but all of them will probably result in me not doing much sketching, and us getting very distracted. Just so you know, I'm totally going to get you in those places, but maybe after we haven't been apart for a while."

I watch the muscles in his neck flex as he swallows. "I didn't think this through properly... we should have done it tomorrow."

"We're at Steven's all day tomorrow." I've spent Boxing Day at my brother's since he moved in with Debs and our parents decided to spend their Christmases in different exotic places on holiday.

"God, this is going to be torture," he mutters as he heads toward the kitchen. I sit here a little longer than necessary, watching his arse.

I get him standing with his back and hands leant against the worktop behind him. He leans forward slightly with his head down but his eyes looking up at me. When I first stand back and take him in, a shiver runs around my body. He looks insanely sexy with his come-fuck-me eyes and messy hair. I really don't know if I'm going to be able to see this through.

I get myself settled on the counter opposite with the sketchpad on my lap and work as quickly as I can.

"Are you okay?" I ask, after about forty-five minutes. I'm really impressed; I did not think he would stay there that long.

"Not really, I need you. Now," he growls.

I put the final touches to my sketch but don't let him see that I've finished, so I can tease him a bit. "Not much longer now. Are you hot?" He just raises his eyebrows at my question. "I'll take that as a yes, then, shall I?" I say, hopping off the side. "Well, I am." I begin untying the knot around my waist. Turning my back to Ryan, I slowly slide the satin fabric off my shoulders and down my back. His breathing gets heavier behind me as I reveal more of what I'm wearing.

"Molly," Ryan warns in a very deep, gravelly voice.

Looking over my shoulder, I give him what I hope is a sexy smile. I must have nailed it because he growls, but, to my surprise, he hasn't moved from his place. I know he has a great view of the back of the dusky pink sheer halter-neck babydoll I'm wearing. He can see my bare back all the way down to the top of my arse, where the fabric covers the tiny thong. Slowly, I turn to reveal the front. It has a deep V showing off my cleavage, and a bow under my breasts, before the fabric flows to the tops of my thighs. It's so sheer that nothing is hidden at all. My temperature reaches new heights as Ryan's eyes roam all over my body.

Doing my best to pretend that I'm unaffected by the situation, I slowly walk back and sit myself where I was before and once again grabbing the sketchpad. I pretend to add some more marks before I look up.

Ryan's jaw is set tight and his lips are pressed into a thin line. His eyes are smouldering and his entire body is vibrating with need. "Are you done?" he growls in a low, almost menacing voice.

Ryan

I can see from here that she's only pretending to sketch, and without a second thought, I push myself from the counter.

Before she knows what's happening, I've pulled the sketchpad from her hands and placed it on the side before grabbing her knees and spreading her thighs so I can stand between them. My hands land on her lower back, pushing so her arse is hanging over the worktop. "I need you now," I growl in her ear.

Her answering shiver and groan tell me she needs exactly what I'm about to give her. I slide one hand between her legs and roughly pull the fabric of her thong out of the way before thrusting into her. In one swift move, I'm balls deep in her hot, wet pussy, exactly where I need to be.

She flinches at my intrusion and I will my body to still while she gets used to my size. When she relaxes under my hands, I start moving, slowly at first, but before long, Molly's raking her nails down my back and I'm slamming into her body with forceful thrusts.

The pain of her nails digging into my skin only increases my tempo, as do her moans of pleasure. "Ryan, God yes... deeper." I pull her further off the side so I can get as deep as possible. "Oh yes, that's it... fuck."

"I want to feel you milking my cock, baby. I want to feel you coming around me." My words are the last encouragement she needs, because her entire body stills before it quakes as pleasure rips through her. As soon as I feel her squeeze me tight, I'm falling with her and growling my release into the crook of her neck as she shouts my name.

I continue thrusting my hips as her orgasm subsides and watch her return to earth.

"Fucking hell, Ry, that was something else," she pants as she goes to lean back on the counter. I watch as a look of horror fills her face as she takes in the blood under her fingernails. She looks up at me with shocked eyes. "Fuck, I'm so sorry."

"It's okay, it was fucking hot, feeling your nails dragging down my skin."

She pulls herself off me and moves so she's sitting back on the side. "Turn around," she demands, and I do as I'm told. Her quick intake of breath tells me all I need to know. "Shit, you have actual scratch marks and blood running down your back. I'm so sorry."

"It's fine, honestly. It doesn't even hurt."

"I need to get it cleaned up. What if it scars?"

"Well, then we will have a reminder of hot sex in the kitchen. Molly, I really couldn't give a fuck. That was... incredible. I'd do it again a thousand times over."

"Really?" she questions, sounding more inquisitive than sorry all of a sudden.

"Yes, really. Now mop me up, woman, and then I'm taking you to our bed to make love to you. I may have said this before, but this body deserves to be worshipped. For hours."

I have no idea how long it takes me to fulfil my promise, but it's now past ten o'clock and Molly's passed out from exhaustion next to me after what must be a record number of orgasms. She did her fair share of worshipping, though. I think she must have traced every single line, ridge, and mole on my body.

I've been lying next to her for about twenty minutes, just watching her sleep. Thoughts of the time we've spent together have been running around my head, as well as what the future holds for us. I haven't broached the subject with her yet, but before I left the hospital earlier, Mum asked if I would bring her up for a couple of days before New Year's, so she could make things right. I'd really like to spend some more time with my family and make sure Dad is okay before I have to go back to work.

Eventually, I can't lie here any longer, and I get up to use the toilet and clean up. I have a quick shower before heading downstairs to tidy up our mess and clean the kitchen counter. When I get there, Molly's sketch of me stops me in my tracks. I knew it would be good because she's seriously talented, but for how quickly she did it, the accuracy of her drawing takes my breath away. No one would ever be able to doubt that was me standing there. She's even captured the heat in my eyes. I close the sketchpad and place it on the coffee table so it's safe, wondering what I should do with it.

Part of me wants to get it framed, but another part of me is well aware that it's my naked body, and I don't really want everyone seeing it. What I am sure of, though, is that we will be doing that again. Whatever Molly was thinking about when she was trying to decide where she wanted me to model for her, I intend on fulfilling those fantasies in the near future.

CHAPTER TWENTY

Molly

This week has flown by. It seems like one minute I was packing up presents to take to Steven's house for Boxing Day, and the next I was getting the house sorted for our New Year's Eve party.

Before we headed over to Steven's Boxing morning, Ryan gently broached the subject of spending a few days in Liverpool with his family before New Year's. I was apprehensive about spending time with his mum, but I couldn't use that as an excuse not to go. She promised to both Ryan and I that our relationship was starting afresh, so I have to give her the benefit of the doubt.

We spent three days with his family, and it was just as heart-warming as the time with the Morrisons. His dad was discharged the day after Boxing Day, and he was enjoying the hell out of being treated like a king by his wife and children. On the second day we were there, Karen organised for just us girls to have a day out, so we hit the sales and had afternoon tea in a fancy hotel in the city centre. To say I was dubious before we left the house would be an understatement, but the day was amazing.

I never thought I'd say it, but I was actually a little sad to leave. We were going to be seeing Abbi and Liv as well as Beth and Caleb, who I met one evening, at our house for New Year's, but we didn't make any plans as to when we would see Karen and Dave again—although I'm pretty sure we will be talking regularly from now on.

"Molly, did you buy crisps?" Ryan asks, distracting me from my thoughts while I'm setting out the buffet food for our party tonight.

"Yeah... maybe I left them downstairs." I check the clock before heading down—people will be arriving any minute, and I still have things to organise. Shit.

When I round the corner at the bottom of the stairs, I see two bags that I must have forgotten to bring up after I went shopping this afternoon, both full of different varieties of crisps. I smile to myself when I hear laughter coming from my old room where Abbi, Liv, and Beth are getting ready for tonight.

I'm just about to head up again when the doorbell rings.

"Hey, come on in," I say to Jax when I open the door. I'm actually amazed that he agreed to come. It took some serious convincing on my part.

"Hey, mate," Ryan says, greeting Jax once we get upstairs. "I'm glad our begging didn't go unheard."

I quickly continue setting out the food while Ryan arranges the drinks in the kitchen.

"Jax, do you want a beer?"

"Please," he calls, before turning his attention back to me. "You look amazing, Molly. That dress really suits you."

"Thank you. You know, you don't scrub up too bad, either."

"Here you go," Ryan says, handing over his drink before standing behind me and wrapping his arms around my waist. "She does look gorgeous, and please tell her she's not fat at all."

"Ryan," I chide, slapping his arm gently. He doesn't need to go around telling everyone about my insecurity. I've eaten way too much this Christmas, and I'm so bloated. I'm glad I chose a maxi dress for this evening, as it's loose and flowing. Bring on Friday, so Megan and I can get back to our pole dancing lessons.

"Is she here?" Jax whispers to me after Ryan has gone back to bartending duties.

"She's downstairs, getting ready. It will be fine, Jax. There will be loads of people here to distract you, and if you need to get away, just use our room. But please stay."

"Okay, I'll tr—"

Jax is interrupted as Caleb walks over to us. "You must be Jax. I'm Caleb," he says, sticking his hand out. "You look just as Abbi described. It's good to meet you at last."

I watch as the two shake hands and confusion washes over Jax's face. "You too. She... talks about me?"

"Yeah, all the time. I've been looking forward to meeting you. Right, I'm going to go and see if they're ready yet. They've been down there for hours," he announces, striding back out the way he came in. He's right, they have been a long time, but then I did insist on a formal dress code tonight, much to Ryan's displeasure. Women must be in dresses, and men in suits.

I have to say I'm very pleased with my suggestion, because Ryan is smoking hot in his black suit and white shirt. It still has the top few buttons undone, because he refuses to wear a tie. I cannot wait to peel the fabric from his body later.

Caleb, on the other hand, looks like he's just fallen out of work with his perfect cut slim-fit grey suit with a skinny red tie. His mousy brown hair has been gelled within an inch of its life, and he's clean-shaven. Unlike Ryan, who has recently been forgoing his daily shave after I showed my appreciation on Christmas day. I love the feel of it under my fingers and... other parts of my body.

"So, that's Caleb, huh?" Jax still looks completely confused. "I'm sorry to ask, but how does she go from me to him?" He asks, pointing in the direction he just left. "I mean, we're like night and day."

Jax is right. To say I was a little surprised when I met him for the first time a few days ago would be an understatement. "Abbi doesn't look at him like she does you. Plus," I drop my voice to a whisper because Ryan got a little mad when I made this suggestion to him. "I get some serious gay vibes off him."

Jax goes to reply but is stopped by the appearance of Liv and Beth. They come straight over and Liv introduces him to Beth. They both look amazing. Liv is wearing a turquoise prom dress and Beth has on a red cocktail dress with glittery heels.

Once Jax has said his hellos, his eyes immediately go to the door, waiting for the last two people to appear from downstairs. He doesn't have to wait long, because in a matter of seconds, Caleb walks through the door with Abbi's hand in his. Jax groans in pain as his eyes run up and down her body, clad in a fitted red floor-length dress. It shows off all her sexy curves to perfection. Her blonde hair has been curled, then piled on top of her head. Her eye make-up is dark and her lips as red as her dress.

"Sweet mother of Jesus. Is she trying to torture me?" Jax mutters.

Her eyes latch on to his the instant she walks in the room, as if she knew exactly where he was standing. She gives him a once-over before nodding slightly and walking over to talk to her sister and Beth, who are waiting in the corner of the room with drinks for them.

I turn to Jax and take in his deer-in-the-headlights look. "Are you okay?" I ask tentatively.

"I... uh... need something stronger than his beer."

"Coming right up," Ryan says from behind us, making us jump. He must have been watching the show, too.

Thankfully, Chris and Shane are the next to arrive, and they immediately distract Jax with their stupid stories, which I'm grateful for.

"How's he doing?" Ryan asks once I've managed to get away from Jax.

"I think he's pretty much in hell. I mean, you've seen your sister, right?"

"Yeah. When exactly did my little sister turn into... well... that?"

"I'm sorry, Ry, but your sister's hot. Just be grateful we're not going out tonight, because she'd have guys lining up for her." I feel a little bad for saying it when he groans. "Sorry," I wince. I'm only telling the truth.

"Angel, you look beautiful. Did you both have a good time in Liverpool?" Susan asks as she passes me a huge bunch of flowers and a bottle of champagne to celebrate the New Year, followed by hugs from Pete and Emma.

"It was brilliant, thank you. You look lovely as well. Drink?" I ask.

"Don't be silly, I'll sort us out. You enjoy yourself." With that, I'm shooed out of the way and Susan takes over the kitchen. She just can't help herself.

Behind Susan and Pete are Lilly and her roommate, Taylor. They met at uni and now live together in the flat Susan and Pete organised for them. Taylor's lovely; he's also hilarious. He can have an entire room laughing in seconds with his stories.

Half an hour later, all our guests are here. Our living area is packed and everyone's chatter fills the house. My nieces and Oscar are playing on the Wii and getting in everyone's way, but no one seems to mind. Everyone is enjoying themselves too much to pay much attention to them—well, everyone apart from Jax, who looks like he could claw his eyes out at any minute.

It seems like Daniel has taken a shine to Beth and has her pinned in a corner—not that she looks like she wants to escape. Shane and Chris have been laughing with Taylor and Lilly very loudly, but what has caught my attention most are the looks I've seen pass between Taylor and Caleb. If I'm not mistaken, I would say there's some chemistry there. I'm now surer than ever that Caleb's gay.

Before I know it, it's eleven-thirty. "Ryan, can you come and help me get the champagne glasses down, please?" I ask, because they're on the top shelf.

I stand next to him as he passes me the glasses and I put them on the side. Unfortunately, the little bit of skin that Ryan reveals when he stretches up distracts me, and I miss the worktop entirely. The glass smashes on the tiled floor and shards shoot off in all directions. "Fuck."

Bending down, I start to pick bits up, but I'm stopped by Ryan. "Let me do that—you get the dustpan and brush. I don't want you cutting yourself. Bollocks!" Just as he says this, a drop of blood hits the floor. I quickly grab the kitchen roll for him and wrap it around his finger when he stands up.

"Hold this, I think I've got some plasters downstairs. Hang on." I quickly hurry out of the room, minding the glass. I go charging through my old room and fling the bathroom door open, not thinking anything of it as I head straight for the cabinet, but I'm rooted to the spot when someone calling my name makes me look up.

There, on the counter, is Abbi with her dress around her waist, her legs wrapped around Jax's hips, and her heels digging into his arse. His trousers are pooled at his feet, exposing his very naked behind. They both stare at me with wide eyes and a look of horror on their faces.

"Shit. Sorry, I wasn't... uh... yeah," I stutter as I head for the door. I've regained some of my thoughts by the time I get there. "Jax?" I shout over my shoulder.

"Uh-huh?" is all I get.

"I never knew your tattoo went all the way down to your thigh."

"Fuck. Off," he grunts.

I quickly close the door and head back upstairs.

"Are you okay? You look a little flushed," Ryan asks.

"Yeah, fine." I would tell him the truth, but Susan and Pete are fussing around him, trying to pick up all the glass. "I couldn't find them, sorry."

"I think I've got one in my handbag. I put it on your bed, angel, if you could grab it for me." Susan calls from her kneeling position on the kitchen floor.

I just turn the corner at the top of the stairs and am about to open our bedroom door when two figures catch my attention at the other end of the hall.

I quickly jump into our bedroom before I'm seen and close it quietly behind me. "What the fuck is up with people tonight?" I mutter quietly to myself, shaking my head. First, I catch Jax and Abbi going at it downstairs, and now I've just found Caleb and Taylor making out like teenagers, hiding at the end of the hallway.

I make use of our en suite while I'm here before heading back down with Susan's handbag. The hallway is empty when I open the door, so I hurry back to the party, aware that it's nearly midnight.

When I walk in the living area, the first thing I see is Caleb and Abbi laughing with each other with a glass of champagne in their hands like nothing's happened. I search out Jax to find him with Shane and Chris again, and Taylor's whispering in Lilly's ear. I wonder if he's giving her the details of his little rendezvous.

"Molly," Ryan shouts, getting my attention. I hurry over, passing Susan her bag in the process. "Are you okay? he asks again when I'm closer.

Checking no one is in earshot, I lean into him. "You would not believe what I have seen in the last ten minutes." I pull back to look at him and he raises his eyebrows in question, so I continue whispering. I give him a quick rundown of the events I've witnessed as I wrap a plaster around his finger.

He looks around the room to the four people I mentioned. "Are you sure? They all look pretty normal now."

"Yes, I'm sure..." I go to say more but everyone starts counting down. I quickly pull Ryan into the living area with everyone else, just as Big Ben chimes. I stretch up on my toes and crash my lips to his. He deepens the kiss and slides his tongue deep into my mouth, pulling my body painfully tight against his. Everything and everyone around me disappears, and the only thing I focus on is the amazing man in my arms and on my lips. He means everything to me. The past year has been hard, but out of all that pain, I've found something that has made me happier than I have ever been in my life.

Love, pure and simple.

Eventually, my senses come back and I realise everyone in the room is cheering. Ryan pulls away from me, and I open my eyes to see that it is at us. My face heats and I shove it in Ryan's chest to hide from everyone.

"We were hoping you'd pick her up and carry her out of the room like the last time we were here," Shane pipes up.

"Shut up and drink your champagne!" Ryan quips, making everyone laugh and return to their previous conversations, thankfully ignoring us.

Ryan places his fingers under my chin and forces my head up, so I look at him. "This is going to be a good year, Molly, I can feel it."

Ryan

It's been just over a week since our New Year's Eve party. It took us a few days but we eventually got the house back in order after our guests left looking the worse for wear at some point the next day.

Getting back to work was hard after such a brilliant two weeks off. Molly and I hadn't spent more than a couple of hours apart since my trip to Liverpool on Christmas Eve, and it was harder than I imagined. She's still not feeling herself—so much so she actually cancelled on Megan on Friday night for their pole dancing class.

"Mate, I think I'm dying," Jax says between pants.

I look over to see him bring his treadmill to a stop and rest his head forward on his arms as he tries to catch his breath. Jax has been coming to the gym with me for a few weeks now. We've actually become quite good friends. He was pathetic in the first couple of weeks, but he's starting to build up his stamina.

"How many miles?"

"Three!" he gasps back.

"I'll let that slide. You've spent a lot of time on the weights today," I say to him like I would one of my students.

"Why, thank you, Mr. Evans!"

"I want to do a few more miles. If you want to head off, I'll meet you in the sauna in a bit, yeah?"

"Yeah, okay. Try not to make me look too bad."

Shaking my head at him, I put my speed back up. Jax walks out and I can't help feeling a little sorry for him. I didn't quite believe what Molly said she saw on New Year's Eve, but the moment I looked into his eyes that night, I could see a sparkle in them. Unfortunately, Abbi blew all that to shit when she got up before anyone else the next morning and left with only a note for Jax, saying she was sorry.

Almost an hour later, I also give up and head in the direction of the sauna. When I open the door, I see that Jax is the only one in there, sitting on the bottom bench with his head tipped back, deep in thought.

"You okay?" I ask as I hop up onto the top bench. He lets out a huge sigh. "We really are trying to do everything we can to help."

"It just feels like a sinking ship."

I couldn't agree more. Currently, Abbi is refusing to answer the phone to either me or Molly. She must sense what we want to say to her. I only know she's okay because I've had to ask Liv.

"Hey, Molly's out babysitting tonight, if you want to come back for a beer?"

"Seriously, you want to spend all your night with me? Even I know how miserable I am!"

Jax eventually heads for home just after nine, the snow that was falling lightly when we left the gym now starting to get heavier.

Molly's out babysitting Oscar because it's Megan and James's anniversary. They promised her they wouldn't be late, so I'm hoping to get a text from her soon to say she's heading home. I'm already feeling anxious about her driving home as the snow's starting to settle. That car of hers gives me nightmares as it is; I do not need snow on top of that.

Just after ten, I get the text I've been waiting for. On a good day, it would take her twenty minutes, but in the snow it's probably going to be more like forty, so I decide to head upstairs so I can be waiting for her in bed. I'm already getting tingles at the thought of her eyes darkening and her cheeks flushing when she finds me ready and waiting for her. God, I cannot get enough of her.

I must fall asleep, because my phone ringing wakes me. I quickly sit up and see that it's already eleven o'clock. I look to the other side of the bed—it's empty. My heart races as the panic sets in. I grab my phone and answer it without checking the caller ID.

"Molly?" I shout into the phone.

"Ryan, it's Susan. We're two minutes away—get dressed now," she says in a menacingly low voice.

I pull the phone away from my ear and just stare down at it. Please, God, no, don't let what I'm thinking be true.

"Now, Ryan!"

CHAPTER TWENTY-ONE

Ryan

Somehow, I manage to pull some clothes on and get out of the house. I'm standing at the front door when a taxi pulls up and Susan jumps out the back. One look at her and I know, I just *know*.

My world implodes around me.

This cannot be happening again.

Susan pulls me from my dark thoughts, grabs my hand, and drags me toward the idling taxi. Tears are pouring down her face, but I feel like I'm in a complete trance. It's like aliens have taken over and are controlling my body.

This cannot be real.

"Ryan," I hear someone say in the distance, but I let it wash over me.

"Ryan... Ryan."

A hand on my thigh brings me back around and I look at Susan's concerned face as she studies me.

"Ryan, I don't know anything. I must still be Molly's emergency contact because I had a call to tell me that she was in the hospital after a car crash."

I rest my head back and look up to the stars through the sunroof of the taxi, sending up silent prayers that my girl is going to be okay.

Please, let her be okay.

Not many minutes later, the three of us are running to the reception desk of A&E in our local hospital.

"Molly Carter," I say, in a much calmer voice than I am expecting. "She came in by ambulance, from a car accident." My voice cracks at the end.

"Her ambulance came in a while ago. Sir, I'm going to have to ask you to wait until we know what that situation is. I'll tell the doctors she has relatives here already, so one will come and see you as soon as they can. You *are* relatives, yes?" the receptionist asks.

"Uh..."

"He's her husband," Susan quickly pipes up from behind me.

"Okay, well, Mr. Carter, if you'd like to take a seat, someone will be with you shortly."

"It's Evans, Ryan Evans."

"She hasn't changed her name yet. It was only a few weeks ago," Susan adds.

We find seats for what turns out to be the most horrific wait of my life. No one comes out to say anything. We have no idea if she's alive, although judging by the fact that no one has told us otherwise, I'd like to assume she is. I just need to know what the hell is happening.

Eventually, the receptionist pointing over at me catches my eye, and someone I presume is a doctor walks our way.

"Mr. Evans, I'm Dr. John. I've been taking care of your wife. If you'd like to follow me, I'll explain what's happening."

"Can I see her?"

"The nurses are just getting her tidied up. They won't be long."

We sit in the relatives' room with the doctor for ten minutes while he explains that Molly suffered a major blow to the head when she crashed. She has a broken collarbone and arm that will be casted shortly, and that she's very bruised and battered, but most of that is superficial. The only major concern is the swelling of her brain. They're monitoring it, but it could be critical if it increases, so they may have to operate. The next twenty-four to forty-eight hours are crucial, and he keeps repeating that it's serious. Every time he says it, my fists clench. I know how fucking serious this is; he does not need to keep telling me.

"Can I see her, please?"

"Yes, they should be done by now. I'm sorry," he says, looking over at Susan and Pete, "Only one visitor at a time."

"Ryan, you go. We'll be here if you need us, but Molly needs you the most. Go."

"Follow me, Mr. Evans." I follow the doctor through the maze of hallways until he comes to a stop outside a door. "Mr. Evans, your wife is in intensive care while we monitor her condition. You will need to buzz in here to be allowed entry in the future." I nod my head at him and he unlocks the door. "We have her sedated at the moment while we monitor her."

The moment he opens the next door I see her. I practically push the doctor aside in my haste to be with her. She looks so broken, laid out on the hospital bed with wires and tubes coming from her. Tears pour down my face and the lump in my throat feels like the size of a football. I take her tiny hand in mine and pray once again for her to pull through.

Moments later, I'm distracted by a nurse placing a chair down behind me. I turn to look at her, instantly grateful.

She gently places her hand on my forearm and encourages me to sit down. "This must have been a terrible shock for you. You need to rest," she says as I lower myself down.

"You've got a fighter on your hands there," she says, smiling over to Molly. "My name's Hannah, and I'll be your wife's nurse for the night. If there's anything I can get either of you, please ask." I just about manage to hold my sob in until she walks back over to the nurses' station. Hannah—of course. I can't help but smile slightly.

The doctor comes back at some point. I've completely lost all concept of time, so it could have been minutes or hours, I have no idea. He checks the machines before looking at her notes at the end of the bed. Once he's happy, he pulls a chair over and sits in front of me.

"I don't want you to get your hopes up too much, but things seem to be looking like they're going in the right direction. As I said earlier, these first few hours are crucial, but so far, the signs are good." I let out a huge breath at his words. "Now, I need to ask you something." He looks over at Molly, then back at me. The look on his face has me dreading what is going to come next. "Did you know your wife is pregnant?"

I just stare at him with an open mouth and wide eyes. Molly's pregnant.

"Mr. Evans?" he says, trying to bring me back to Earth.

"She hasn't been feeling well for a few weeks, but no, I didn't know that. I'm pretty sure she didn't know, either." I think back to her drinking over the last few weeks. I know Molly well enough to know she wouldn't do that if she knew.

"Well, our tests show that she's about nine weeks pregnant. I obviously don't need to tell you that there is an increased risk of her miscarrying with what her body has been through, and still is going through, but I wanted to make you aware. We will scan her later to check everything, but the heartbeat is strong."

I slump back in the chair as I try to process everything.

"I'll leave you to your thoughts," the doctor says. I watch him walk over to the nurse and say something, making her smile kindly at me and nod her head.

I turn back to Molly. I hold her hand softly in one of mine and place my other gently on her stomach. Finding out that she's pregnant should be one of the happiest moments of my life, but here I am, scared out of my mind.

———

She ends up spending four days in intensive care. The longest four days of my life. Just like Hannah, the nurse, said, she's a fighter. She's making good progress, and the swelling has reduced massively. She's almost out of danger, but they've kept her sedated longer than originally planned to give her body as long as possible to heal. I haven't told anyone about the baby yet, because I want Molly to know before anyone else, but also because I'm scared that if I admit it, it's not going to happen.

I'm more desperate than ever for her to wake up, to see her eyes, to see her smile, to tell her I love her and to know that she can hear me. I've barely left her side. The farthest I've been is the toilets and the canteen when no one else was around to get something for me. The doctors and nurses have tried to send me home to get some rest along with all the Morrisons, my family, and our friends. They've all been here at some point over the last four days, even though they were only allowed in for a few minutes.

I stand aside as the nurses finish off getting Molly settled in her new room. They managed to get her a side room, which will be nice and quiet, although I'm not sure if it's for Molly or just so they don't have to fight with me to leave because of the other patients she would be on the ward with.

"Darling, please come home and have a shower and a good night's sleep," my mum says gently from the chair next to me. Now that Molly is in a room of her own and is getting stronger, they've let up on visitors.

"I'm not leaving her. There's a perfectly good shower there," I nod my head to the adjoining bathroom. "If I want one."

"Baby, I don't think it's a case of you *wanting* one," she says, squeezing my hand gently.

Yes, I know how I look and how I must smell, but I'm not leaving Molly, especially now they're reducing her sedation. She could wake up at any minute, and I want to be there when she opens her eyes.

"Okay, well, when your dad gets back with some food for you, we're going to head to yours. We'll be back tomorrow, but ring if you need anything."

"I will, Mum. Thank you."

Susan and Pete rang my parents from the hospital the night Molly was brought in, and they drove straight down to be with us. They've been here ever since. Her brothers appeared a couple of hours after we did, looking panic-stricken. I managed to let them have some time with her. Abbi and Liv were here all weekend, but they both had to go back. They've promised they'll be here if I need them. Molly might have the shittiest parents ever, but everyone else around her who loves her makes up for them.

Not long after Mum and Dad leave, Susan walks in.

"Ryan, I'm not taking no for an answer. Take this, and get in that bloody shower. When Molly wakes up, she does not want to be looking at such a mess. I promise I will knock if she so much as twitches, but please, for all our sakes, have a wash," she demands, handing me a bag full of toiletries.

"But..."

"No buts. Get in there, now."

***

The next morning, I wake up with the same stiff neck as every time I wake up in this damn chair. I grab my phone to check the time, but what I see first makes me stop dead in my tracks. It's the 15th of January. Shit. I look back up at Molly and wonder if this day is going to be cursed forever more.

I spend the morning between nurses' and doctors' visits, talking to Molly about Hannah and about the things we did together. I try to keep it as light as possible, because I don't think I can cope with any more misery, and I know that if Molly can hear me, she will feel the same.

It's just after lunchtime when the Morrisons appear. I stand and give them a hug before offering Susan my chair. I watch from the corner as they all say hello to Molly in the hope she can hear them. I listen to them explain what they're doing tonight to celebrate Hannah's memory, and they try to convince me to come, but I think they already know my answer. As harsh as it sounds, I need to focus on my future, and my future is still lying fast asleep on that bed.

The Morrisons leave not long after, and the afternoon is a train of visitors. Jax sits with us for over an hour before Steven and Daniel show up after work, shortly followed by Shane and Chris, then finally Megan, after she's put Oscar to bed. By the time she's left, I'm completely exhausted.

It's just gone half past eight when I feel it. I had slightly dozed off, but

I'm sure I didn't imagine it. I sit myself up straighter and wait to see if it happens again.

Five minutes later, it does. Molly gently squeezes my hand.

I scoot my chair closer to her and patiently wait to see if anything else is going to happen. I lift her hand to my lips and pepper her knuckles with light kisses. "Come on, Molly. Come back to me, gorgeous," I whisper between kisses.

As I wait, the little squeezes of my hand get tighter until I eventually start to see her eyes flickering.

Molly

The voices slowly start to make sense to me at the same time the pounding in my head increases. Where am I?

"Are you sure you won't come? A good meal would really do you some good," says a voice I recognise but can't quite place.

"You're probably right, but I'm not leaving."

Ryan. *Wherever I am, he's here, so it must be okay*, is the last thing I remember thinking before the blackness faded back in.

"Has Abbi been back?" a male voice says.

"No. She rings every day, but I haven't seen her since she ran away from you on Sunday."

Ryan's still here.

"Hey, bro, how's our girl doing?"

That's Daniel's voice. I'd recognise it anywhere.

"No change. They say that's to be expected, though," Ryan says. The sound of his voice makes my heart beat a little faster.

Who are they talking about?

"This waiting sucks," Daniel says before everything fades again.

It's quiet. It's the first time I've not heard anyone talking. Am I alone?

It takes all my strength but I manage to move my fingers slightly and realise I'm not. He's holding my hand.

I fight the darkness claiming me this time. I need to see him. I manage to move my hand slightly again before I feel myself drift off, but only for a couple of minutes, I think, because my arm being moved wakes me. I feel his lips touch the back of my hand and, like always, tingles shoot up my arm. He's here.

"Come on, Molly. Come back to me," he whispers.

Come back? Where have I been?

I try desperately hard to open my eyes, but they feel like they weigh a tonne. After a while, I give up and fade away again.

I wake with a start and, this time, my eyes fly open. My heart is racing. The room is dark apart from the moonlight that is coming through the gaps in the blinds. I sweep my eyes around and it suddenly dawns on me that I'm in the hospital.

Instantly, the memories of the accident hit me, a bit like the car did that night. I close my eyes and shake my head to try to rid myself of the image, but the pain that pierces my skull as I move is like nothing I have ever felt.

I look down and see the cast that's all the way up my right arm before the figure on the other side comes into view. Ryan is sat on a chair next to my bed, but he's leaning forward and has his head resting on his hand that's clinging onto mine. His other hand is resting gently on my stomach. He's facing me and I can see his hair falling into his eyes. I desperately want to brush it out of the way. He's much paler than usual. The rings around his eyes are dark, and it looks like he hasn't shaved in days.

I lick my lips and find my mouth is really dry. God, I need a drink. I swallow slowly before trying to speak.

"Ry," I whisper, my voice coming out rough and gravelly.

I squeeze his hand in mine, say his name again, and watch as his eyes flicker. When they do open and see me, my breath catches at the pain reflected in them. It's almost instantly gone, as what I think is hope appears when he realises I'm looking back at him.

"Molly," he whispers.

"Hey."

"Hey. How are you?"

"I've been better, you?"

"A million times better, now that you're awake." He stands up and moves toward me so he can place his lips to mine. "Fuck, Molly, you have no idea how scary that was," he says quietly, and I can feel his lips trembling against mine.

"I'm sorry."

"Hey, it's not your fault. I need to tell the nurse you're awake," he says, going to move.

"Not yet. Please would you just hold me?" I shift as much as I can to the side, so Ryan can squeeze on the bed next to me.

"I don't want to hurt you."

"You won't."

We lay there for what feels like hours. There was a moment when I saw that car coming at me that I didn't think I'd ever get to be in his arms again, and the thought of leaving him was far scarier than anything that could happen to me. I wonder if that was how Hannah felt at that moment.

"Ry," I whisper, because I'm not sure if he's fallen asleep.

"Yes, gorgeous?"

"What's the time and date?"

"It's... uh... eleven-thirty on the 15th of January. Why?" he asks.

I don't answer straight away because it takes me a few seconds to pull myself together. "Hannah. It's exactly a year. Exactly a year ago that she died and I woke up."

Ryan doesn't get a chance to comment, because a nurse pokes her head in to check on me. "Hey, what are you doing up there, mister?" she asks before her eyes widen slightly when she sees me looking back at her. "Molly, you're awake."

"Sorry, I asked him up here," I say as she makes her way to my side.

"Don't worry, love, I'd want him up next to me as well," she says with a wink, making Ryan blush as he gets off the bed. "I'm Maggie. I've been looking after you on this ward. How are you feeling?"

"Fine, apart from my head. And I need a drink." Before she has a chance to do anything, Ryan is there next to me with a cup of water and a straw, apologising because he should have offered me some as soon as I woke up. Maggie disappears to find me some more painkillers, leaving us alone again.

"Are you really okay?" Ryan asks, sitting himself back on the side of my bed.

"My head is fucking killing me, but other than that I think I'm okay. I'm guessing I've broken my arm."

"I'll leave out the details until you're a bit stronger, but yeah, you've broken your arm and collarbone. You'll be in a cast for a few weeks."

"Oh well... it could have been worse."

"Do not go there, Molly." I watch tears fill his eyes and he looks away from me, lost in thought.

"Hey, look at me. I'm here, and I'm mostly fine, I promise."

After Maggie reappears with painkillers, Ryan sneaks back up on my bed and we fall fast asleep. Apparently, even though I've been asleep for days, I still need more.

The next thing we know, we're being woken by a different nurse doing the morning medication round.

"Good morning. Molly, it's so good to see you awake," she says cheerfully as she grabs my notes from the end of the bed. "The doctor is on his way to come and see you. He shouldn't be long."

Only a few minutes after the nurse leaves, a doctor walks in. He explains everything to me about what I've been through, and when he explains how close I was to not being here right now, I feel awful about my comment to Ryan last night about how it could have been worse.

The news now seems pretty positive, though. The swelling on my brain has reduced so much that they aren't worried, and my arm just needs to be in a cast for six weeks, then I should be good as new. I will need some follow-up appointments to check everything, but I should be discharged in a few days, as long I stay stable.

"Okay, well, unless you have any questions, I'll go get the ultrasound now that you're awake. I'm sure you're dying to see." Before I have a chance to say anything, he's out of the room.

"Uh... what was that about?"

I watch Ryan's face split into a huge smile before he says anything. "You know how you've been feeling a little off recently?"

"Yeah."

"Well, it turns out there's a reason for that." I raise my eyebrows at him in question. "Molly... you're pregnant."

"I'm... um... what?"

"You're pregnant."

I think back over the last few weeks, being sick, being tired, feeling bloated and having painful boobs. Yeah, I guess that would make sense.

"I... um... when?" It may be true, but I'm stunned.

"Well, they think you're about nine or ten weeks, so I'm thinking it was my birthday."

"But I'm on the pill. How? I haven't missed my period, so..."

"You were sick when we were away."

"When did you work all this out?"

"Molly, I've been sat here for days, waiting for you to wake up. I've had plenty of time to think."

"Sorry," I whisper. "Are they sure it's okay?"

"They've scanned you a couple of times to check, and the heartbeat is really strong."

"Have you seen it?"

"I refused to look until we could do it together. I've heard its heartbeat, though. It's amazing." I watch his eyes fill as he talks. I swear he hasn't stopped smiling through this whole conversation.

"I'm guessing you're happy about this, even though it wasn't planned?"

"You're kidding, right? I couldn't be happier. We're having a baby!"

I can't help but laugh at his excitement. He leans over to kiss me and places his hand on my belly. I cover his with mine as I smile against his lips.

Three days later and I'm packed and ready to head home at last. It turns out I'm not a very good patient. I'm too independent to have to rely on people to look after me. I'm not under any illusion that it's going to be any different when I get home, what with Ryan, his parents, the Morrisons, and our friends fussing around me.

We told everyone about the baby the day after we had the scan. I needed a day to get used to the idea. To say it was a shock was an understatement. Everyone, as expected, was over the moon for us. I'm pretty sure both Susan and Karen have already started shopping for the new arrival, even though we still have months before it's due.

I managed to convince Ryan to go home to sleep now that I'm awake, which he did begrudgingly, but he does look better for it. He has still spent every waking moment here with me. I wouldn't have it any other way.

To my surprise, Karen comes walking into my room a few minutes later with a huge smile on her face.

"Are you ready to head home?" she asks, going to grab one of my bags.

"Uh... yeah. Sorry, but where's Ryan?" I ask, trying not to sound too disappointed.

"He's had to go into work to sort something out to do with his time off. He'll be back as soon as he can."

Karen drops my bag and comes over to give me a hug. "Come on, let's get you home."

My heart brightens a bit when she pulls up outside our house and I see that Ryan's car is here. At least I won't have to sit and wait for him to come back. I watch as Karen takes my bags from the boot and places them in the hallway before coming back to help me out and into the house. She stands behind me as I climb the stairs in case I fall, but as soon as I'm at the top, she announces that she needs to head off and asks quickly if I'll be okay. She takes me completely by surprise, so I give her my thanks for bringing me home and watch as she scurries out of the house.

As I head over to the living room door, which is weirdly closed, I can't help but think how strange it is that I can hear Ed Sheeran singing about loving until he's seventy. I'm used to hearing Ryan's indie rock filling the house. I push the thought aside and open the door to the room.

CHAPTER TWENTY-TWO

Ryan

Every surface is covered in candles, their flames filling the room with a warm glow as the sun sets outside. I quickly press play on the iPod and triple-check that the little black box is still sitting on the coffee table where I left it.

After a few minutes, I hear footsteps climbing the stairs, before my mum tells Molly that she's got to leave. I let out a huge breath to try to calm my nerves before the door handle turns.

Time seems to stand still as I wait for her to appear, but when she does, the look on her face takes my breath away. She still has purple and green bruises down one side of her face, and her arm is in the cast, but she looks as perfect as ever to me.

Once her eyes have taken in the candles, they find me. They're already full of unshed tears. I hold my hand out to her and, very slowly, she moves toward me and grabs it in her own trembling hand.

I slowly lower myself onto one knee and grab the open box on the table. Her eyes widen to the size of saucers as I do it.

"Molly, I'm so glad that life is unpredictable, because I never would have believed that we could have found what we have with each other. I never thought the best friend I could ever ask for could also own my heart in the way you do. You amaze and inspire me every day, and I would like to spend the rest of my life trying to do the same for you. I love you more than I ever thought possible, and I never want to spend a day of my life without you by my side." I take a deep breath and blink back the threatening tears before I continue. "So, Molly, you're my best friend, and the love of my life. Will you do me the pleasure of being my wife?"

She instantly nods her head and through her tears manages a very shaky yes.

I let go of her hand so I can pull the ring out of the box and slide it on her finger. Both of our hands are shaking so much that it's a challenge, but we manage it. I stand, ready to carefully pull her to me, but she surprises me by jumping into my arms and sobbing into the crook of my neck. Tears fall down my face as well. The stress of the last week and the contentment that she's now home, in my arms, and wearing my ring, is just a little too much to take. Movement outside the kitchen window catches my eye, and when I look up I find our nosey neighbour watching us with a wide smile on her face. Nodding at her, I turn my attention back to my fiancée.

I lower us to the sofa and we hold each other for long minutes.

Eventually, Molly releases her death grip and leans back so she can look at me. "I love you so much, Ryan."

"I love you too, soon-to-be Mrs. Evans." Her face breaks into a wide smile and she pulls her hand in front of her so she can look at the ring—the ring I'd seen back in the summer in Cardiff with Abbi and Liv. When I decided what I was going to do, I had to send Liv out on an emergency shopping trip. The main ring is white gold, but the setting of the diamond is rose gold. Molly's colour.

EPILOGUE

Molly

It's been four weeks since I came home from the hospital and had the shock of my life. Well, I guess the second shock of my life, after finding out I was pregnant a couple of days before that. Ryan did say on New Year's Eve that this was going to be a good year!

My follow-up appointments have been good, and I've not had any headaches at all. We've got a baby to look forward to, and a wedding to plan. I can't help but smile every time my ring catches my eye.

Jax has been working his arse off, trying to make up for me not being there. I think he's grateful for the distraction, because Abbi is still doing everything she can to avoid him—so much so that he's actually decided not to come tonight.

"Molly, come on, people will be here in a minute," Ryan hollers up the stairs. "I'm sure you look perfect, so stop fussing." I can help but smile at myself in the mirror. Never in my life did I think I could be this happy.

I head downstairs to find my fiancé and get ready to celebrate our engagement with our closest friends and family.

"See, I said you'd look perfect," he says as I enter the living area. I've got on a floral fitted maxi dress that shows off my tiny bump. It may still seem small, but I'm going to have to go clothes shopping soon.

Ryan comes walking straight over to me, pulls me to him, and gives me a sweet yet knee-weakening kiss.

"Is that really necessary?" Abbi shouts from the dining room table.

"Yes," Ryan answers once he has had his fill of me. He sticks his finger up at her when he sees the disgusted look she has on her face.

Everyone arrives not long later. It feels like New Year's again, with us celebrating a new chapter in our lives.

"Molly, your phone," Ryan says, handing it to me. I look down to see a message on the screen.

> Jax: I'm sorry I can't be there tonight. I'm thinking of you both. Xx

I feel myself get a little choked up at the thought of him sat at home on his own. Bloody hormones.

"You okay, gorgeous?" Ryan asks, looking concerned.

"Yeah, it was just from Jax. I'm so sad he felt like he couldn't be here."

I look over to Abbi and can't help but think that she probably only looks marginally happier than Jax probably does right about now.

The next few hours fly past and, before we know it, people are starting to head off home. I'm just saying goodnight to Steven, Debs, and the girls when my phone ringing distracts me. I quickly grab it off the side. It's Abbi—why is she ringing when she's still here. I excuse myself to answer the call.

"Abbi, what's wrong?"

"I'm in the bathroom downstairs. Please come now," she sobs.

"Shit," I whisper when I enter the room and see Abbi sat on the floor by the toilet with blood everywhere. I quickly drop to my knees next to her and grab her hand. "Abbi, what's—"

"I'm having a miscarriage, Molly."

Want to know more about Abbi and Jax's relationship?
Keep reading for *Falling for Jax*!

ACKNOWLEDGMENTS

A huge thank you once again to Pam for helping me with Molly. I couldn't have released either book without your help.

To everyone who was brave enough to take a chance on Part One and love it enough to read Part Two and get this far—thank you for taking the time to try out this new author. I hope you have enjoyed Molly and Ryan's story and are still up for what is yet to come from the others.

It took me six months to release Part Two of Molly and Ryan's story thanks to my ever-growing bump who decided spending most of my time either throwing up or sleeping was a better idea.

I want to thank everyone who's giving me and my first book baby a chance. Molly and Ryan's story has totally changed my life and they will forever hold a special part of my heart. I hope you continue through the series and find out everyone's stories. I've loved every minute of discovering both existing characters and the ones you are yet to meet.

I need to say a massive thank you to my husband, who's supported me through this, and of course my gorgeous daughter who allows me time to continue writing every day.

Molly and Ryan were the start of something I never expected, but three years after their initial release, I can't imagine myself doing anything else. I love spending my days creating these incredible characters—when I'm not chasing a toddler, of course. I hope there are many, many more to come.

Until next time,

Tracy xo

FALLING FOR JAX

FALLING SERIES BOOK #3

FOREWORD

I would advise reading Falling for Jax after reading both parts of Falling for Ryan, so you have a better understanding of the characters and their history.

CHAPTER ONE

Jax

Bang, bang, bang.

Argh, fuck off and let me be miserable in peace, I think as I neck the shot I just poured. I've lost count of what number that was. Tonight is the night of my two best friends' engagement party, and here I am, sat at home, nursing a bottle of Jack Daniels. Alone.

Bang, bang, bang.

I should be there celebrating with them. They deserve it after everything they've been through in the last year, but I can't bring myself to see *her*.

It's all her fault.

They're the two best friends I've had in years, and she's stopping me from being there with them. Unbeknown to them, they've managed to pull me out of the rut I found myself in after years of pure hell, and I can't be there for them on such a big day. I want to see her more than anything, but I've found that caving in to that need only hurts more in the long run. It's better if I stay away. She's made her decision—she doesn't want me.

Bang, bang, bang.

"FUCK OFF!" I shout, much more aggressively than I was intending.

"Jax, mate, it's Ryan. Open the door, man!"

Why the hell is Ryan here? He should be at his engagement party.

"Jax, for fuck's sake, open the door. NOW!" he shouts again.

I pour myself another shot of Jack and stumble my way toward the shouting in the hope that I can get rid of him.

When I pull the door open, I'm slightly taken aback by the look on Ryan's face.

"James Blunt? Really?" he deadpans as he pushes his way into my flat and removes the shot glass from my hand.

I go to say something, but I'm quickly shut up when Ryan forcefully pushes me in the direction of my bedroom.

"You need to go and get dressed now, Jax," Ryan demands.

"I've already told you, I'm not coming to your party," I slur as I bounce off the wall. Okay, yep, I think it's safe to say that Jack and I have become very good friends tonight.

"It's not that," Ryan says, sounding defeated. "Abbi needs you. She's on her way to the hospital with Molly."

"Fuck," I turn around far too quickly, making the room spin way too fast for my liking. It's only now that I see the worry etched into every feature of Ryan's face. "What's happened?"

"I'll explain in the car. Right now, you need to put some clothes on—unless you want to turn up at the hospital in just your underwear. You've got two minutes, or I'm taking you with me like that."

It's weird. The moment I look at Ryan's face and his words settle themselves properly into my brain, my alcohol-infused thoughts completely disappear.

Abbi needs me.

I race down to my room and throw on the first items of clothing I find. Within seconds, I'm running behind Ryan, out of my building and straight into his car.

"What's happened?" I ask with a shaky voice.

"I don't really know. It was all a bit mad, but there was so much blood. It was fucking scar—"

"What the fuck has she done?" I ask, starting to feel myself panicking. "Oh fuck, did she slit her wrists? Shit, fuck, this is all my fault. I should have been there. I'm fucking cursed; this is all my fault," I continue rambling to myself, but I have no idea if I'm actually saying the words out loud. The roaring in my ears and the pounding of my heart have taken over. Fuck, I haven't had a panic attack in months.

Ryan calmly saying my name eventually breaks through my haze. "Jax... Jax... breathe, Jax... breathe. Abbi's okay. She's going to be okay."

I do as he says and concentrate on controlling my breathing. My hands are shaking, and I can feel the sweat pouring off me, but eventually I feel myself start to calm down and the attack subsides.

Breathe in... breathe out... breathe in... breathe out...

"Are you back with me, or do I need to pull over?" Ryan asks, sounding a little panicked himself from the driver's seat.

I shake my head at him but realise he's driving so he probably can't see me. "No," I croak out.

"Okay, just keep breathing. We're nearly there."

I nod my head before leaning my elbows on my knees and resting my head in my hands while I continue to concentrate on staying calm.

"She didn't do anything like that, Jax. Why the hell would you think that?"

"It's nothing," I whisper, hoping he'll let this go.

"That wasn't nothing. Do you have panic attacks often?"

"I haven't had one for months."

"Do you want to talk about it?" I lift my head up and look at Ryan. He quickly glances over at me and can obviously see the answer to his question in my eyes. "You're right, now isn't the time. We need to get to Abbi."

"Is there a reason you're skirting around what's wrong with her?" I ask as Ryan pulls into a parking space outside the hospital.

He turns to look at me and I can see pain and compassion fill his eyes before he opens his mouth to speak. "I think she was having a miscarriage, Jax." My world completely shatters, my heart aching more than I've ever experienced before. He looks down at his lap for a couple of seconds while I try to process what he just said. "I think it was yours." He looks back up and puts his hand on my shoulder, showing his support. "She didn't say it exactly, but she said she needed you, so..." he tails off, letting me fill the gaps.

Ten minutes later, I find myself pacing the floor of the A&E waiting area while Ryan and Molly watch me from their seats.

"How long can it take, seriously?" I snap at them.

"They said someone would come and talk to us as soon as possible. Just try to be patient. They know what they're doing," Molly says softly.

She can try to convince me all she wants that everything's okay, but I saw the fear in her eyes when we found her pacing this very floor waiting for us to arrive. Being pregnant herself, I can only imagine how scared she must be right now. It hasn't escaped my notice that she hasn't stopped rubbing her belly the whole time we've been here.

"I'm going to get you a coffee. I'm sure the Jack flowing through your system right now isn't helping. Do you want anything, gorgeous?" Ryan asks, turning to Molly.

"Just water, please."

I watch as he kisses her forehead before he gets up and heads for the vending machine. Jealousy twists my stomach. They have everything I want. For some reason, finding what they have seems to elude me at every corner.

I think I've found the one, but then she ends up either moving abroad with her work because it's more important, cheating, trying to rinse me of everything I have... or, like Abbi, they just don't want me, plain and simple. What the hell is wrong with me?

Half an hour later and we still have no news about Abbi's condition, but a commotion at the entrance distracts us and we see Liv running in, followed by Beth and—oh, fucking great—Caleb.

"Everyone has left yours apart from Susan, Pete and Emma, who insisted on clearing up. I tried to make them go home, but Susan insisted that she wanted to do something to help," Liv says to Molly and Ryan.

"Of course she did," Molly mutters, shaking her head.

"Any news?"

"No. We're still waiting. They'd better hurry up though, because Mr. Impatient here will wear a hole in their floor."

"Fuck off, Ry," I snap. Does he need reminding of what he was like when Molly was in the hospital?

Caleb starts to laugh, but I stop him with a glare that has him swallowing and looking away pretty quickly. Molly can tell me all she likes that she thinks he's gay, but that doesn't explain why he's always hanging around Abbi like a bad smell.

"Abigail Evans' family?" a nurse asks as she walks over to us.

"Yes," we all answer at once.

"All of you?" she frowns. If she even thinks for one second that she isn't going to tell us what's going on, she has another think coming.

"Yes," we all say again.

"I'm her older brother, this is my fiancée, these are my younger siblings, and this is the father. Now please, will you tell us how she is?" Ryan states very matter-of-factly.

The nurse looks a little sheepish after his outburst but goes on to explain to us that Abbi's okay. She's had a miscarriage and has lost a lot of blood, but she's going to be fine after a good few days of rest. They currently have her on strong pain medication, so she's asleep and will be for some time yet.

"Can we see her now?" I ask impatiently.

"You can, but only one at a time, please. She needs her rest. And so do you, by the looks of it," she directs at Molly, who's yawning and curled into Ryan's side. "I would suggest you leave her to rest and come back tomorrow."

"If it's okay with you, I'd like to just pop in and see her for my own peace of mind. Then I'll take Molly home," Ryan says to the nurse.

"We'll all come back tomorrow," Liv says, speaking for Beth and Caleb, "now we know she's okay."

"I'm not going anywhere. I want to be here when she wakes up," I say quietly.

The nurse is about to argue, but she soon stops when her eyes meet mine. She just nods and indicates for Ryan and I to follow her.

Within seconds, we're outside a bay, waiting for the nurse to pull back the curtain so we can see Abbi. When she does and Abbi comes into view, I have to fight to swallow around the lump that's formed in my throat. She's curled up on her side, facing us. Her hair, usually bright blonde, looks dark and limp, hanging around her shoulders and across the pillow. Her skin is unusually pale and the circles around her eyes are a stark contrast with their darkness.

"Thank you," Ryan says to the nurse before she turns to leave and closes the curtain behind her.

I watch from the corner of the cubicle as Ryan walks up to her bedside and gently sweeps the hair away that has fallen across her face. I see him tear up a little as he looks down at her.

"Don't do something like that again, Abs. It was proper scary," he whispers so quietly I almost miss it. My heart bleeds a little for this man in front of me. He's had to deal with so much in the last year or so, yet he's as strong as ever. "Jax is here. He's going to look after you. I'll see you tomorrow. Love you," he says, placing a light kiss to her temple.

He just about manages to hide his emotions by the time he comes back over to me, but I can tell he's been more affected by this than he's letting on.

"You okay, mate?" he asks me.

"Yeah. I'm sorry about earlier." I look away, embarrassed that he had a front row seat to my breakdown.

"Don't," he warns. "Anytime you want to talk, I'm here for you. Molly, too." I just nod at him, unable to speak with the emotion choking me. "Okay, I'll see you tomorrow. Try to get some sleep, yeah? And ring if you need anything," he says as he squeezes my shoulder and quietly leaves me alone with Abbi.

I grab the chair in the corner and carefully move it next to her bed. I sit myself down and gently hold her hand in mine. Her eyes flicker open at my contact, and her lips twitch at the corner, giving me a hint of the smile I love so much. I watch a single tear escape and soak into the pillow she's lying on before her eyes close again.

"Baby, it's okay. I'm here." She squeezes my hand—I guess to tell me she can hear me—before the sounds of her light snores fill the room. I lean forward and place a soft kiss to her forehead before trying to get myself comfortable for the night.

Abbi

I feel myself come to slightly when he holds my hand. He still causes the same reaction in my body, even when I'm doped up on pain meds. I drag my eyes open so I can see him. When my eyes eventually focus enough to make him out, my heart breaks a little more in my chest. I caused that look on his face; I caused that pain. One of the tears I have been fighting to keep in escapes, and I watch him as he watches it fall. I want to say something. I want to apologise but I'm too weak; instead, my eyes close and I drift off to sleep again.

I've had a great week with Ryan in Manchester, then with Liv for the last couple of days in Cardiff. I look in my rear-view mirror and see him singing along with whatever he has playing in the car as we come off the motorway, heading toward his house in Oxford. For as long as I can remember, I've idolised my big brother. Even now, as an adult, he amazes me. His strength and determination despite everything he's been through this year alone are awe-inspiring. He may be my big brother, and he may be four years older than me, but he always has been and always will be my best friend. I hate that we're currently so far apart, but, if my last year at uni goes all right, I plan on applying for jobs down here so we can be closer.

Talking of Ryan's friends, I've been on his case about Molly all week. He might not want to admit it to me, but I can see in his eyes every time one of us has mentioned her name that he's fallen madly in love with her. I can't blame him; she's gorgeous, and the sweetest person ever. I think the only problem may be that she was Hannah's best friend. I wouldn't be surprised if Ryan is struggling a bit with that. Well, I'm sure he potentially won't be the only one struggling with that if something was to happen between them. I mean, getting with your dead girlfriend's best friend could cause some drama. Especially where our mother is concerned. She has made it quite clear on many occasions how she feels about Molly. Only two weeks ago she ran her out of our childhood home with her over the top opinions of her. Ah, never a dull day in the Evans family!

When we arrive at Ryan's house, we both have to drive around the back because Molly is parked out the front, but there is also another car blocking her in. I could tell by the look on Ryan's face behind me what he was thinking, and if he's right and the car belongs to the guy Molly is seeing, then good luck to him because he's about to encounter my very jealous brother's unexpected appearance. Oh, this could seriously get interesting.

We both jump out of our cars at the same time, and I can see that Ryan is barely holding himself together with the excitement of coming home early in the hope of surprising Molly, but now also probably with fear of catching her doing something he never wants to see.

"You go. I'll get our bags in."

"No, it's okay."

"Ryan, please, go put yourself out of your misery," I say, attempting to push him in the general direction of his front door but, seeing as he is built like a brick shithouse, I'm not very successful. What happened to that scrawny little boy I used to chase around with my make-up? I wonder, smiling to myself as he walks off with his usual swagger.

It's ten-minutes later by the time I have our bags in and am heading up the stairs to see what's going on. I'm pretty sure I heard Ryan shouting a few minutes ago. I swear, if he caught this guy fucking Molly on the sofa or something, then I could be about to walk into a murder scene!

The moment I walk around the corner into the living area though, my surroundings completely disappear as I lock eyes with the most stunning looking guy I think I have ever seen. I'm aware that both Molly and Ryan are in the room and that Molly has said something, but I am completely fixated on the Sex God in front of me. I know I'm staring, but I can't help it. I let my eyes roam over every inch of him. His hair is very dark brown and is long and shaggy hanging around his face. It's just begging for me to run my hands through it. His eyes are the brightest emerald green I think I have ever seen, and his square jaw and full lips are just asking to be kissed, licked and nipped. The more I take in, the faster my heart and clit start pounding. My eyes run down his neck that has a silver chain around it, and attempt to take in all the ink that is covering inches of his perfect skin. I continue moving south down his smooth stomach and I follow his happy trail and the slight V that disappears into the waistband of his boxers, then his slim-fit jeans. I make my way down to his feet that are clad in black engineer boots, before slowly climbing back up.

At some point during my perusal of this fine specimen of a man, Molly made her way over. She startles me when she throws her arms around me.

"Close your mouth, Abbi, you'll start drooling in a minute," she whispers in my ear.

"Sorry. Who is he? He's seriously hot," I whisper back in her ear, praying I actually said it quietly enough that he can't hear me, whoever he is.

"Come with me and I'll explain," she says, before grabbing my hand and dragging me down the stairs while shouting over her shoulder for Ryan to get us drinks.

"Molly, you need to tell me who the fuck that is right now. If you tell me he is the guy you are seeing, then you are seriously gonna have to dump him, cos I need that, like... badly," I say, hoping it didn't sound as desperate to her as it did to me. I can't help it, though. It has been so long since I've had a good seeing to. My taste in men, as displayed upstairs, is the bad boy fuck-you-hard-and-fast-but-leave-you-heartbroken-harder-and-faster type. I've been trying desperately hard to be a good little girl and do what Mummy says and find a nice guy. Let me tell you, nice guys are all well and good when they take you out for a meal and for a walk in the park, but in bed... I'm sorry, but they ain't worth toffee. You want a screaming orgasm, then you go find yourself a bad boy. Just make sure you have plenty of tissues, wine and chocolate at home for when he leaves you high and dry.

"No, Abs, that's not the guy I'm seeing. Jax works for me. If you want him, he's all yours!"

"Jax... fuck, that's hot!" I swoon.

"It's short for Jackson and yeah, he is pretty hot. I should warn you though, Ryan doesn't like him very much, and probably even less now after what he caught us doing when he came in."

"But you just said..."

Molly goes on to explain all about the tattoo she wants in memory of

Hannah, and how Jax was helping her out with it when Ryan walked in and pretty much caught them both topless. I can only imagine how Ryan reacted to that. No wonder I heard him shouting from outside.

By the time we get back upstairs, I'm disappointed to say that Jax has put his shirt back on. Luckily for me though, the rest of him is still pretty droolworthy. I had to really bite my tongue when Molly suggested he stay for dinner and then to get drunk and stay the night.

As the night drags on, it's becoming more and more obvious that Jax and I are making Ryan very uncomfortable. I can't help it though, the pull I feel to him is indescribable; it's like we are two magnets drawn to one another, and I am only happy when a part of me is touching him.

S omeone snoring wakes me up from reliving my first meeting with Jax. Things were much simpler then, before I had the chance to royally fuck everything up.

The loud snore comes again from my right, and I shoot daggers at the curtain to whoever the woman is on the other side for disturbing me before I got to the really good bit. When I look back, Jax catches my attention. He's still here. I was worried when Molly told me Ryan was going to go and get him that he would refuse to come to me. I couldn't really blame him if he did, mind you.

I know I shouldn't let it happen, because in the morning, when he knows I'm okay, he'll leave me after all the pain I've caused him, but my heart is a little lighter, knowing he's by my side. The pain of losing our baby still hurts like a motherfucker, but at least he's here with me.

The rhinoceros of a woman in the next bed lets out another almighty snore that makes Jax sit bolt upright in the chair he's in, and his eyes fly wide open. I watch him for a few seconds as he takes in his surroundings and remembers where he is. The moment it all settles, he looks straight to me. I have to bite down on my bottom lip, because the hurt pouring from his eyes as he looks at me makes me want to cry. What's the point in crying? What's done is done. Crying isn't going to help anyone.

"Abbi, baby, are you okay?" he asks in the softest voice, which is so at odds with his appearance to the world.

I just nod at him as I continue to hold everything in. Me breaking down is only going to make him feel worse. He continues watching me closely as he leans forward and takes both of my hands in his. He lifts them both to his mouth and I watch as he kisses the knuckles. He keeps eye contact with me the entire time; it's like he's waiting for me to do something.

When he lowers them, I know it's time to pull up my big girl knickers and say what I need to say. I take in a huge breath, hoping that with it I'll suck in some strength to be able to say what I need to say.

"Jax..." I croak out. He raises his eyebrows and waits for me to continue. "I'm so sorry." I have to close my eyes to hold in the tears. So much for sucking in some strength—well done, Abigail!

He's at my side instantly, pulling me into his arms, and I can't hold it any longer. Weeks of keeping secrets from everyone, months of keeping the man I love more than anything at arm's length, then finally the pain of losing the one thing I had of him is just too much. I burst into tears and wail as my body trembles in his arms. I'm so loud in those first few minutes that I even manage to drown out my noisy neighbour. The whole time, Jax whispers soothing things in my ear and gently rubs my back. I don't need to look at him to tell that he's crying along with me; I can hear it in his voice, and it only makes me cry harder. I've reduced this amazing man to tears. He shouldn't be here supporting me; he should be at home, hating me for what I've put him through.

My sobs eventually subside, and I can feel myself falling asleep again. Jax must feel me getting heavier in his arms, because he shifts us so we're both lying on the bed and I'm curled up into his side while he holds me tight.

CHAPTER TWO

Jax

Her bright blonde hair and sparkling blue eyes lit up the room from the moment she entered. Her cheeks were blushing a dusky pink and her red lips were parted as she continued her perusal of my body. My dick twitched in my trousers as I watched her tongue sneak out and wet her bottom lip.

Fucking hell, I wanted those full lips on me. I moved down her slim neck to her shoulders that were covered in a blue and white checked shirt. The first few buttons were open, showing me a little cleavage and giving me a hint of what was hiding underneath. I followed the swell of her breasts down to her waist, then took in her denim-covered hips. Thankfully, the skirt she was wearing was short enough to show nearly all of her long, toned and tanned legs.

Fuck me, I'd died and gone to heaven.

She had the perfect girl next-door thing going on, and fuck me slowly if I didn't want to find out just how innocent she may be. Unfortunately, Molly walking straight in front of her blocked my view before she dragged her down the stairs and away from me. In hindsight, that was probably a good thing, because I could have jumped her then and there without caring if anyone was watching.

"Uh... who was that?" I ask Ryan once they've disappeared from sight. My voice sounds deep and gravelly, even to me.

"That was my eldest little sister, Abbi," Ryan snaps, interrupting my inappropriate thoughts. He already doesn't like me; I really don't need to be pissing him off further by eye-fucking his sister.

Fuck. My. Life.

"She's... um... pretty." Sexy, gorgeous, stunning, perfect. I keep the last few to myself, not wanting to overdo it. I'm well aware that he could kick me out at any minute, and, more than anything, I want a little time to get to know the knockout who just went off with Molly. Fuck, I'm in serious trouble here.

Thankfully, Molly got involved when they both reappeared, and practically insisted I stay not only for dinner but the night. I'm counting my lucky stars as we speak.

The entire evening, although amazing, has been fucking torturous. All I want is to get her on her own, but every time I so much as look at her, I have Ryan giving me the death stare. She either hasn't noticed her brother's reaction to me or just doesn't care, because she's ramped up her flirting to dangerous levels over the last few hours. I'm dying to get my hands on her, but I get the feeling that Ryan is never going to leave us alone.

We've been sat on the sofa chatting for a while, and Abbi is practically sitting on my lap when Molly obviously gets bored of Ryan's attitude and all but forces him out of the room and up to bed. He doesn't leave without giving me one final stare before turning his back on us, though.

I don't get a chance to relax, because as soon as I've heard Ryan's bedroom door shut, Abbi is pulling her already short skirt higher and throwing her leg over mine so she's straddling me and looking straight into my eyes with a mischievous smile tugging at the corners of her delectable mouth.

"Thank fuck they've gone," she says in a low voice before she crashes her lips to mine and all but forces her tongue into my mouth. Now, don't get me wrong—it's not that I'm not willing, I'm just completely dumfounded at the forwardness of this amazing woman now rubbing herself against my rock-hard cock as she fucks my mouth. In a matter of seconds, I get with the programme and kiss her back with the same intensity.

My hands go into her hair, loving the silky smoothness of it as it runs through my fingers. I drag my hands down her sides, gently caressing her breasts with my thumbs, making her groan in my mouth. When my hands get to her thighs, I push them under her skirt and lift it around her waist. I grab her hips and pull her down as hard as I can, which causes me to be the one moaning. With her skirt out of the way, I have easy access to the part of her I want the most, so I join in with her and grind my hips up. I line my cock up with her clit and hold her tight as she begins to squirm against me.

"Oh my God, Jax, make me come," she says as she pulls her lips away from mine so she can catch her breath. My eyes lock with hers, and what used to be bright blue eyes are now deep and full of fire. I let go of her hips briefly so I can undo the buttons on her shirt and rip it from her body.

"Fuck, baby," I groan as I take in her white lace bra. It's so sheer that I can see her perfect pink pebbled nipples through it. My mouth waters at the thought of sucking on them. She arches her back, pushing them toward me as if she knows what I'm thinking. Before I do exactly that, though, I reach behind me and pull my shirt over my head. Her hands instantly go to my chest and her nails scratch downwards, making my entire body flinch.

Fuck, this woman is going to kill me.

I place my hands back on her hips and pull her down with such force that I'm sure I'll leave bruises, before I lean forward and pull one of her nipples into my mouth. The moment my tongue flicks her tip, I feel her body still before she flinches violently in my hands as her orgasm takes over. She leans forward, bites my neck and screams as her body continues to ride her seemingly never-ending pleasure.

When she's back, she removes her teeth from my neck and sits back to look at me. Her eyes are bright and glistening, her cheeks are flushed, and her lips are parted as she pants to catch her breath.

"Fuck, that was the hottest thing I've ever seen," I say, more to myself than her, but the smile she graces me with makes my heart turn over in my chest in a way I've never experienced before. Fuck, is this it? Is she the one I've been waiting for?

I watch as she slowly and elegantly gets off my lap. A little bit of panic creeps in that she's going to leave me here, but the moment I see her hands reach for the button on her skirt, I relax. Her fingers pop it open efficiently, and I watch, mesmerised, as she wiggles her hips and pushes the skirt to the floor. I can't help the loud groan that escapes as I look at her, standing there in her white lace bra and tiny thong. I was right earlier—I really have died and gone to heaven.

"God... I've wanted you since the moment I walked through the door earlier. I've already fucked you six ways from Sunday in my head. I bet my imagination pales to the real thing, though."

"Holy fucking shit," I groan. "Where have you been all my life?"

"Waiting, baby. But, luckily for you, the wait is over," she says as she lowers herself to her knees between my legs.

Fuck, please don't let me embarrass myself by coming the moment she touches me. I'm so close to the edge right now that it's a real possibility.

She leans forward and runs her tongue around my nipple before biting down on it.

"Oh, fuck."

She pops the buttons on my jeans with as much ease as she did her own, and, within seconds, I'm lifting my hips to allow her to pull them and my boxer briefs down. She slides them down my legs but leaves them gathered around my ankles. Apparently, she's too impatient to remove them completely, because she's back up and grasping me in her tiny fist almost instantly. My head drops back against the sofa at the sensation, and I have to grind my teeth together in an attempt to reign my body in.

The moment I feel her tongue touch the tip, my hips are off the sofa. "Whoa, easy, soldier," she says, looking up at me through her eyelashes. "You gonna be able to handle this, big boy?" she challenges.

"I guess there's only one way to find ouuuuuuuuttttttttt," I groan, as she takes all of me in her mouth in one fell swoop. "Hooooooly fuuuuuuck, babyyyyyyyyyyy." My hands go to her hair and I hold gently as she sucks me into her hot mouth again and again. She must feel the moment just before I'm about to come, because she sits back on her heels and removes all contact from me.

"What are you doing?" I pant out as she stands.

"Now... Jackson," she says, turning around and looking over her shoulder at me. "I don't usually fuck a guy I've just met," she continues as her hands come behind her back and unsnap her bra, "but you... there's something about you." She stretches her arm out and drops her bra to the floor while she continues to look at me. "And I can't describe what it is, but fuck, I need you inside me... badly." My heart is racing at such a pace that I'm sure I could be about to have a heart attack, right here in front of this goddess, on my boss's sofa. The thought of Molly and Ryan being in the house is a fleeting one, because Abbi slides her thumbs inside the waistband of her thong and slowly starts pulling it down her legs, bending over to give me one seriously impressive view. "Is that okay with you, Jackson?" Fuck, I love it when she says my name.

"Uh..." What?

"Is it okay if I fuck you?"

"Uh-huh... yeah." Fuck, is that my voice?

Suddenly, she turns around and slowly, very slowly, walks my way. My fists clench at my sides as I try to resist the urge to reach out, grab her and *impale her on top of me. She comes to a stop in front of me and runs her eyes over every inch of my skin, as if committing it to memory.*

"Condom?"

It takes a few seconds for her words to register in my lust-filled brain, but when they do, I whisper, "Wallet... pocket," and point in the general direction of my jeans that are still around my ankles.

Once she's found it, she rips it open with her teeth and pulls it out. I'm just about to reach up and take it off her when she takes my cock in her hands and rolls it on in one smooth motion like an expert. Once she's happy, she lets go and settles herself, once again straddling my lap. Her lips come down to mine and my hands go to her hair. As our tongues collide, we both groan into each other's mouths. She begins rubbing herself against me and I can't take it any longer. She got me so close to the edge earlier; I need to be inside her too badly. I reach down and hold my cock up for her. She lines herself up with me before ever so slowly dropping down until she's seated to the hilt.

"Fuck, baby, you're so fucking tight."

"It's been a while," she whispers as she nips my ear, "and it's been even longer since it's been done properly."

Challenge heard loud and clear, Abigail Evans!

My hands go to her hips and help support her as she begins to move. She lifts up until I'm almost out of her before slamming back down. It makes my breath catch in my throat with surprise. She wasn't joking when she said she wanted to fuck me. There's nothing gentle about this!

Within minutes, she's contracting around me, and I know her release is close. I circle my hips when I'm deep inside of her and I know I've hit the spot because she sucks a breath in through her teeth.

"Oh yeah, right there, oh yeah." I reach up and cover her mouth with my hand, the last thing we need is to be caught. With one more thrust of my hips, she goes off, and the feeling of her muscles clenching tightly around me sends me over with her. I try to swallow down my groan, but it's a challenge. It feels like all my limbs are about to blow off with the intensity of my release.

Abbi flops her limp body forward onto me, and we lie there, panting, as we come down from that incredible high. Now, I thought I'd had good sex, but fuck me, sex with this woman is like nothing I've ever had before. It's fucking electric.

The sound of someone moving around upstairs gets us jumping into action. I quickly take the condom off and pull my boxers up before ridding myself of my socks and jeans. I don't care whose house I'm in; I'm not sleeping in my jeans. Abbi grabs my shirt and pulls it over her head, excusing herself and heading toward the cloakroom to clean herself up.

After disposing of the condom—discreetly, I hope—I lay myself out under the blanket on the sofa, anxiously awaiting her return. Fuck, I hope it's not awkward.

Abbi

I wake up again to the sound of Jax groaning next to me. I suddenly realise why when he thrusts his crotch up into my hand that seems to be cupping his hard dick—whoops! Luckily, I move it seconds before a nurse pops her head around the curtain.

"He shouldn't be up there with you," she chastises.

"Sorry, I was upset in the night. We must have fallen asleep," I whisper, trying not to wake him.

The nurse has other ideas, because she practically shouts back, "That's okay, dear, but I think it's time he got off, don't you?" with a raise of her eyebrow. Maybe me moving my hand didn't really matter, because the huge bulge he's currently sporting is apparently very obvious. "I'll be back in a few minutes to check your vitals. Perhaps you could wake Sleeping Beauty before then?" She gives me a wicked smile before disappearing behind the curtain.

"Jax," I say, gently shoving his shoulder. "Jax."

"Mmm, Abbi," he groans.

"For fuck's sake, stop having dirty dreams. We're in a hospital! Wake up," I hiss again, shoving him more forcefully.

"Yeah, what?" he asks, suddenly wide awake.

"Having a nice dream, were we?" He looks over at me and actually blushes, bless him.

"Umm... yeah, very nice," he says with a naughty smile. "How are you feeling, baby?"

"I've got the most horrific period pains known to man, but other than that, just tired. The nurse is coming back any minute. She wants you off the bed and, I think, a little less... excited," I say, flicking my eyes down to his manhood.

"Brilliant," is all he says as he flings his legs off the bed, stands up and stretches, making his t-shirt rise up.

"Whoa... hang on a minute, is that a six-pack I see there, Mr. Parker? Has someone been working out?" I can't help teasing him, or the smile that splits my face. I'm sure that in the state I'm in, my body shouldn't be able to get worked up, but this man in front of me is like my drug. No matter how much I try, I'm totally addicted to him.

"Well, I've had to do something to blow off steam," he says sadly, and I know him well enough to know exactly what he means.

"I'm sorry, Jax. I thought it was for the best."

"You thought, as in, in the past? What do you think now, then?"

I'm just about to answer when the bloody nurse comes back in and faffs around. "I'm sorry, sir, but we need to check Ms. Evans over. She'll be moved to the ward later. Visiting hours start at two. I suggest you return then. That will give you a chance to go home, shower and... you know..."

Okay, well, that was kind of inappropriate!

"Okay... well, I guess I'll see you later then, Abs. I'll let the others know you're moving. I'm sure they'll be here before long to check you're okay. I'll... uh... come back later," he says, looking completely torn about having to leave me.

He leans forward and places a kiss to my forehead, which makes me want to burst into tears for some reason.

I manage to choke out, "Okay," before he disappears behind the curtain. When I can no longer hear his footsteps, the dam breaks once again, and tears start pouring down my cheeks.

"Oh dear, it's going to be okay. He'll be back later. I'm guessing he's your," I watch her look down at my finger before continuing, "boyfriend?"

"Yes... no... I don't know. It's a mess," I get out between sobs.

The nurse, Anne, stays with me until I calm down, then she goes about getting me sorted for the day. Apparently, there isn't any rest for the wicked, because she has me up and in the shower in no time. She does let me sit in it, though, which I'm grateful for. I'd be lying if I said I felt strong enough to stand for more than a minute or two.

I do feel better after a shower; I didn't quite appreciate just how grimy I was after everything yesterday.

It's no longer than an hour after I've been moved to the ward that I hear a very familiar voice arguing with the woman at the nurse's station about seeing me. She's really quite adamant that he's not allowed in until visiting hours, but he's not having any of it.

I pull on all the strength I have and slowly waddle my way over to the entrance to the bay I'm in.

"Abs, you should be in bed," Ryan admonishes.

"I thought I'd better come and rescue the nurse who was trying to deal with you." The nurse in question does look rather relieved, which makes me smile.

"I promise we'll be quiet and pull the curtain around." I smile sweetly at her before turning and walking back toward my bed. I only make it two steps before Ryan has his arms around my waist and is helping me.

Once he has me back safely in bed, he sits himself in the chair and grabs my hand. "How are you doing?"

"Okay, I guess. The painkillers are working wonders, thank God, but I've got all sorts of gunk falling out of me." I can't help but laugh at the expression on his face. "Oh, Bro, you've got all this to come. Just you wait until Molly goes into labour."

"Seriously though, are you okay?"

"I don't think it's really hit me yet, to be honest, but then again, being pregnant hadn't either. I'd only known a couple of days and... oh, I don't know," I say glumly.

I can see in his eyes that he wants to ask me loads of questions, but thankfully he holds them back. I don't really want to talk about what's going on right now.

"Is Jax okay? He was... um... a bit of a mess when I got him last night," he asks quietly.

"Yeah, I think so... why?"

"Well... he had this panic attack in my car. It was proper scary. He just kept ranting about you slitting your wrists and how it was all his fault, how he made you do it and all this other crazy stuff. I've never seen him like that. I didn't really know what to do."

I'm at a loss for words. I've never seen that side of Jax, either. He's always been so strong and, well... stable, I guess. "He seems okay. He stayed with me all night. I think he would still have been here now if the nurse hadn't kicked him out this morning."

"Are you going to put him out of his misery anytime soon?" Ryan asks, looking down and rubbing the back of his neck as if he's trying to relieve the tension there.

"I'm i-i-i-i-in love w-w-w-w-with him, Ry," I sob.

"I know you are," he says, before pulling me into his arms. What the fuck is it with the water works? I've never been a crier. This is ridiculous. Fucking hormones!

Thankfully, lunch arriving interrupts us, so I don't get to answer the question that I've been asking myself for... oh... months now. I do know that everyone around me is right and that I should go for it, but it's been ingrained in me for a long time to listen to my bloody mother, and if I'm honest with myself, I am scared that history will repeat itself. I know it's stupid, because Jax is nothing like that, but fears are irrational, as they say.

Ryan stays a while longer and finishes off the lunch that I can't manage, which is most of it. "Abs, you need to eat," he says, looking concerned.

"I know, I'm just really not feeling it."

He can obviously see my eyes getting heavy, so before long, he's saying his goodbyes and I watch him quietly sneak out behind the curtain.

I only manage about half an hour's sleep before my next visitors appear. Liv comes bounding up to me and pulls me into a bone-crushing hug before she moves to the side to allow Beth and Caleb to see me. Luckily, they're slightly gentler.

I don't talk much while they're there. I'm so tired that it's as much as I can do to stay awake and listen to them chat amongst themselves. Beth talks nonstop about Daniel, Molly's older brother, and everything they've been up to.

Caleb doesn't say a lot. He just listens to his sister and grimaces at the thought of her with an older man. The only time I see any interest from him is when Liv innocently recollects something that Taylor, Lilly's best friend, said to her last night. I swear I see his eyes sparkle at the mere mention of his name. Interesting.

I'm the only one who knows for sure about Caleb's preferences in life, but that's only because I'm the only one who has been brave enough to ask. Everyone else seems to pussyfoot around the subject. I really wish he would just come out—he's never going to find a nice guy if he's hiding himself away from the world.

My eyes are closed and I'm just listening to the happy chatter around me when everything goes deadly silent. I crack my eyes open slightly to see what's stopping them to find that Jax has reappeared and is staring straight at Caleb like he wants to kill him. It's in that moment that I realise he's holding my hand. I release Caleb's and mouth to him that it's okay. To say he looks a little intimidated by Jax's glare would be an understatement.

I look back to Jax and my breath catches. "What have you done?" I whisper.

Gone are his long brown locks, in favour of a short buzz cut. I didn't think it was possible, but it actually makes him look even better than before. His square jaw and strong cheekbones are even more prominent. When I run my eyes down his body, I see a white plaster poking out from under the sleeve of his t-shirt.

"Have you had another tat?" I ask, looking back up to him, but he's motionless, just staring at me.

"We're gonna go," Liv says, getting up from her seat. "I'm so glad you're okay, Sis. I'll see you soon, yeah?" She squeezes my hand and gestures for the others to follow her.

Jax and I just stare at each other until they've left the ward. "Jax?" I question.

Very slowly, he moves over and sits himself on the side of my bed and gently grabs my hand. He keeps his head lowered as he quietly says, "I don't like him, and I really don't like him touching you."

I know it's stupid, because I know he still cares about me—hell, he wouldn't be here if he didn't—but hearing that he's jealous makes my heart do a little happy dance. "You're jealous of Caleb?" I ask, just to make sure.

"Yes," he states.

I sit up and reach out my other arm to grasp his cheek and lift his head up so I can look at him. "You really don't need to be jealous of him. You can't say anything to anyone because I'm the only one he's trusted with it, but he's gay." I watch him let out a huge breath before he pulls me into him and holds me tightly.

"Thank fuck for that," he whispers in my ear. "I seriously thought I was gonna lose my shit when I saw him holding your hand."

"It's okay, he really isn't a threat. I'm sorry I've made it look that way recently, but we're just good friends."

"So, nothing has ever happened between you?"

"Well, I wouldn't say that, exactly." I grimace as I say it, and he physically flinches in my arms. I quickly continue. "A few years ago, before I knew, they'd come home for a few weeks and I tried to begin something with him, but it was a bit of a non-starter. He just wasn't interested in what I had to offer, if you know what I mean. I never wanted him, though; I was just in a bad place and thought he'd fit the bill perfectly."

Jax pulls back and looks at me. "Fit the bill?" he asks with his brows drawn together.

"Don't worry. Now's not the time." It's not because I don't want to tell him what happened before; it's more that it's never really come up. Now is definitely not the time or the place, though. I can see that he's about to push the subject, but he quickly changes his mind and pulls me to him once again.

I must have fallen asleep in his arms again, because the next thing I know, I'm being woken by someone growling my name.

"Abigail Mary Evans, what the hell are you doing?" I don't need to open my eyes to see who it is and what the look on her face must be like. This is the moment I've been trying to avoid, more for Jax's sake than my own.

"Mum, Dad," I say as I open my eyes to see them standing at the entrance to my cubicle. "You should both be in Paris."

"We organised an earlier flight when Ryan rang and said you were in hospital. Do you think we could have some privacy?"

I follow her eyes as they move across to the man who is once again lying on my bed with me, with his arms wrapped tightly around my waist. I'm surprised the death stare he's receiving from my mother hasn't woken him.

I lean over, rest my hand on his cheek and whisper his name.

CHAPTER THREE

"Jax... Jax, baby, you need to wake up." I wake to her soothing tone, but the moment I open my eyes and see the look in hers, I start to panic.

"Baby, what—" A throat clearing by the entrance stops me in my tracks, and I turn to look at the two people standing there. There's no question as to who they are, because the lady is just an older version of the woman I'm desperately in love with. If what I've heard is true, then this should be fun.

"Some privacy with my daughter, please," she snaps at me when she sees that I'm awake.

I look back at Abbi and try to give her a smile, but I'm not fooling anyone. I place a kiss on her forehead before I go to get up, ignoring the huffing and the "Is that necessary?" coming from the end of the bed.

"I'll just be outside," I whisper to Abbi. I can see from the look in her eyes that she doesn't want me to leave, but this moment has been a long time in the making. She needs to talk to her parents about me.

This is it. Make or break, I think to myself.

I know she still cares about me. I feel awful about it, but I didn't leave immediately this morning. I sat outside the bay for ages—well, until I heard them talk about moving her. I decided that was my cue to use what was left of the morning. Ryan then texted to say he was on his way, so I was happy that she wouldn't be alone for too long. It broke my heart, listening to her break down with the nurse after I left. I was desperate to go back in there and hold her, but, at the same time, it told me everything I needed to know about how she's feeling.

I sit myself down on the chair behind her curtain and wait for what's about to come. Surely it can't be that bad? Can it?

"Abbi, before I even get on to *that*," her mum snaps, "I think you need to explain to us why you're in hospital, don't you?"

"I've had a miscarriage."

"You've had a miscarriage?" There's silence for a few seconds, and I can practically hear Mrs. Evans thinking from here. "Who was the... do not tell me that *he*..." she spits. "Abigail, what were you *thinking*? Has your past taught you *nothing*? You do not spend time with men like him. They're bad news, and you know too damn well just how bad. I cannot believe you would be so stupid." I hear her heels tapping, telling me she's pacing as she rants at her daughter.

"Oh, it all makes sense now. That was who Doreen saw you with months ago, wasn't it? That is the bad boy with the tattoos? For goodness' sake, Abigail, I cannot believe that you've put us all in this position again. You told us we could trust you after everything that happened, but you've just gone and found yourself another thug, and *yet again* you seem to find yourself in a hospital bed because of it. What is wrong with you? Are you just plain stupid?"

The moment I hear a sob from Abbi, I know that I've heard enough. I stand and pull the curtain back with such force that I actually pull it off some of its runners.

"That's enough. I will not stand here and listen to you talk to your daughter like that. She's suffering enough right now; she doesn't need you making it any worse." I walk straight over to Abbi and wrap my arm around her in comfort.

"Excuse me, but this is none of your business. Who exactly are you?" she snaps as she looks me up and down in disgust.

"I'm the *thug* who's in love with your daughter, and I will not let anyone, even her own mother, talk to her in that way," I say, desperately trying to keep a lid on my anger and emotions and not shout so loud that we all get kicked out of the hospital. The gasps that come from the three of them as I say I love her, and the following silence, are almost deafening.

"You love me?" comes a quiet voice to my left.

"Yeah, baby, I love you so much it hurts," I say, staring into her eyes so she can see just how serious I am.

Her eyes immediately start filling with tears again and, as she blinks, one falls down onto her cheek. I lift my hand and brush my thumb over her soft skin to wipe it away. I leave my hand there and she leans into my touch. "I love you, too," she whispers, so quietly I almost miss it.

"You've got to be fucking kidding me," Mrs. Evans shouts at the end of the bed.

"Karen," Mr. Evans snaps. It's the first thing he's said the whole time he's been here.

"I'm sorry, but this is crazy. Abigail, you cannot love him. I mean, *look* at him. What would everyone think? Look at all those tattoos," she says, waving her arm up and down. "And it looks like there's a new one. For goodness' sake, Abigail."

"You're right, Mrs. Evans, there is a new one," I say as I reach up to pull the plaster off. Most of my artwork is just that, artwork, but tucked within are different personal reminders, memories and treasures that I hold dear. I pull the plaster off and lift my arm to show Abbi. There's no point in her parents looking; they won't understand the significance.

I watch her face as she studies my new ink for a few moments. Mrs. Evans is still huffing, but I ignore her completely as I wait for Abbi to work out what the Roman numerals stand for. I see her counting in her head before her hand comes up to her mouth and more tears fill her eyes. "It's the date we met," she says as her hand comes up to touch the sensitive skin around my new tat. "Twenty eight, eight, fourteen," she says with a shaky voice.

"Oh well, that's just great. A tattoo of the date you met is meant to prove to me how you feel about my daughter, is it?"

I snap. I can't help it. In a low voice, I say, "I don't care about proving anything to you. The only thing I care about is the woman lying in this bed that you, quite frankly, are being cruel to."

Mrs. Evans opens her mouth to say something, but Abbi beats her to it. "I think it's time you left."

I feel my heart drop out of my chest at her words. She cannot be serious. After all of that, she's kicking me out? I turn to look at her to argue but, to my surprise, I see her glaring daggers at her mother.

"I'm sorry I made you leave your holiday early, but if you can't support me and my decisions, then I don't want you anywhere near me," she says in such a strong voice that pride for her oozes from my every pore. She's done what she's been trying to avoid all these months—having to basically choose between her parents and me.

We both watch in silence as her dad puts his arm around her mum's shoulders and all but pulls her out of the bay. He turns around and mouths an apology before heading off down the corridor until they're out of our sight.

I turn to look at Abbi at the same time she turns her head to me. "Jax, I'm so—" she starts, but I cut her off by lowering my lips to hers. It only takes her a couple of seconds, but it feels like forever as I wait for her to catch up and open up for me. When she does, the fireworks that ignite around my body are no different to that first kiss on Ryan's sofa.

Abbi

When he eventually pulls his lips from mine, my lungs are burning from lack of air, but I don't care. I could think of much worse ways to go than being kissed to death by Jackson Parker. Just one touch of his lips and my knees go weak. He only pulls back enough to rest his forehead against mine and looks straight into my eyes. A shiver runs through my body, because it feels like he stares straight into my soul. He's the only person I've ever met who truly gets me and loves me, despite all my slightly rough edges. I'll be the first person to admit that I'm not always easy to put up with, but he seems to take it all in his stride.

"No wonder you've kept me well away from her," he says, trying to make me laugh, but I can see that his smile doesn't reach his eyes. He's still very unsure of what I'm going to do next, I think.

"Jax..." I try to swallow down my emotions; I'd like to get out what I need to say without more tears. "I'm so sorry for everything I've done. It was so selfish of me, I know that, I do, but I just knew how she'd react to you, and I didn't want that for either of us. I know I shouldn't care what she thinks, but she's my mum, and I can't help wanting to make her happy. I've always been such a disappointment to her that I just want her to be proud of me." I feel my chin start to tremble.

"I know, baby," Jax says, kissing the end of my nose. "How about you take a minute, then tell me everything from the beginning, I want to know everything."

"Okay," I whisper, but I suddenly remember something. "I think you have some explaining to do as well." His brow creases as he thinks about what I've said. "Well firstly, there's the hair. I'm not sure how I feel about it, if I'm honest," I smile, which feels so good after all the crying and stress. "But more importantly, Ryan told me what happened with you last night."

"Of course he did," Jax says, shaking his head slightly.

"Hey, he's just worried about you, baby, and rightly so by the sounds of it. So how about I tell you everything and you do the same? Just, not right now. I'm exhausted. Please will you just hold me?"

"I'd do that forever, baby," he says, kissing my nose again before wrapping me in his arms. I let out a huge breath and relax into him.

Our peace only lasts a few minutes, because my phone vibrates on the bed. When Ryan came earlier, he brought me the bag I'd packed to spend a few days at his house, so at least I have clean underwear and pyjamas to wear now. I grab it and pull it up in front of me.

> Ryan: Mum and Dad have appeared at the house. Are you okay?

> Me: We're fine. x

> Ryan: We?? By the way, Molly is on her way. She won't take my word for it that you're okay!

> Me: Yes 'we'! Love you, bro. x

"Are we okay, Abs?" Jax asks, startling me.

"If you'll put up with me, then yeah, I think so. I've been so stupid. I understand if you don't want me or can't forgive me, but I'm in love with you and I don't want to be without you again. I've been nothing without you." And here come the tears again.

"Oh, baby, I'll always want you. Don't ever think that I don't. I love you, too, if you'll have me."

His lips come back to mine when I start nodding at him—and that's how Molly finds us a few minutes later.

"I don't think that kind of thing is allowed in here!" she says with a laugh, making us break apart. "I was coming to see for myself that you're okay, but I don't think it was necessary, really. It looks like Jax has your care covered. Mate, loving the new look. What's that about?"

"New start and all that," is all he says as he shrugs his shoulders before kissing my cheek.

Molly walks over to where we're lying together on the bed and throws her arms around both of us. "I'm so glad you've sorted everything out." When she pulls back, she looks between us both before saying, "Coming from someone who Karen truly hated for quite a while, I can honestly say that, given time, she will come around. She will see what a lovely person you are, Jax, and she will accept you. Mind you, saying that, I'm back in her bad books at the moment, because she found out I'm the reason you two met... oops!"

I go to apologise to her, but she stops me, "Don't you dare. It's fine, I distracted her with this cute little outfit I picked up for the baby. Talk of her first grandchild soon distracted her." She must see my eyes tear up a bit at the mention of her baby, because she grabs my hand, saying, "Oh, Abs, I'm so sorry."

"I'm gonna give you two a few minutes," Jax says, obviously sensing that we need some time together. "I'm going to get a coffee. Do either of you want anything?" We both say no and watch him leave.

"I'm so sorry, Abs, I don't want to upset you," Molly says, trying to rub her growing belly discreetly.

"Molly, don't. I don't want you to hide my new niece or nephew from me because of this," I say, reaching out and placing my hand on her tiny bump. "I'm so sorry if I scared you last night. I just knew you wouldn't panic and would know what to do."

"I'm here, whatever you need. Are you really okay, though?"

By the time Jax reappears ten minutes later, we both have tears running down our faces, but we're also laughing. He looks between us, confused for a few seconds, before muttering something about hormonal women while sitting himself back down next to me.

"Right, Ms. Evans, I've come to discharge you," a doctor says as he walks in with a clipboard. "We're just waiting for your prescription to come up from the pharmacy, then you should be all good to go."

"The spare room is all set up for you, Abs," Molly says, squeezing my hand.

"I don't think so," a stubborn male voice barks from next to me, making Molly snap her head around to look at him. "She's coming home with me."

Molly knows Jax well enough by now to know that she will never win, so she just nods at him while looking at me to check if I'm happy with that. I just smile at her while the doctor goes on about my medication and how I should be resting for at least five days, but he's going to give me a note to have two weeks off work. Shit... school and uni. I'm so close to the end that I really don't want to cock it up now. Fuck, I'm going to have to ring my tutor as soon as I can to sort it out.

Molly stays until I'm free to leave so she can help Jax escort both me and my bags to his car. She gives me a tight squeeze, making me promise to ring her if I need anything. Once she's spoken to Jax, I see her wave and start to head over to what I now see is Ryan's car. It's only now that I realise that someone must have brought her, because she still can't drive with her cast on.

"Why didn't he come up?" I shout.

"He dropped me off so I could have some time alone with you and went to do some shopping. I'll see you soon," she says with a wave and heads toward my smiling brother. Will he ever lose the lovesick puppy look around Molly?

"What are you smiling about?"

"That sappy look on my brother's face when he looks at Molly."

"Huh…"

"What?"

"He says I look like that when I look at or talk about you," he says with a shrug of his shoulders, like it's nothing.

"Really?" I say as a wide smile spreads across my face. Jax briefly looks over at me in question as he reverses out of the space. "I've always wanted someone to look at me like I'm their everything."

"You are my everything, baby." He grabs my hand and brings it to his lips. God, I wish those lips were on mine.

I rest my head back and look at him with a small smile on my face as I take in his stunning profile as he drives. And to think, I nearly threw this away.

<hr>

When I walk back from the toilet, I see that Jax has got himself settled on the sofa. I may have only just had two earth-shattering orgasms, but I can't help the tingles that erupt in my lower belly as I take him in. When he notices me, his face splits into a heart-melting smile. Fuck, how I want a guy to look at me like that every day. When I get close to him, he lifts the blanket for me to join him, but I'm rooted to the spot as I once again run my eyes over every inch of him. I just can't get enough of him. It's like I'm scared that this is all a dream and he's going to disappear the minute I wake up.

"You can touch as well as stare, if you'd like," he says as his previous smile turns in to a knicker-melting one, and fuck it all to hell, they would have melted if I had any on!

"Now there's an offer I don't think I can refuse," I say, lowering myself down next to him. "Your ink is stunning." I run my fingers over his shoulder and down his arm, taking in the intricate patterns.

"*Thanks. I designed them all myself.*"

"*Wow, really? Do they have meanings?*" *He thinks for a few seconds.* "*Shit, I'm sorry, that was really personal. You don't have to answer that.*"

"*It's okay. The main patterns are just designs that I've developed over the years, but hidden within are personal things... like here,*" *he says, pointing at his ribs.* "*That's the date of my mum and dad's wedding day. And here,*" *he says, lowering the waistband of his boxers to reveal his hip, making my mouth water,* "*is a copy of my degree certificate. I got the tattoo the day I graduated.*"

I can't help it—I reach down and run my finger over his skin and, without realising what I'm doing, I move down slightly to get a better look. "*Wow, that is tiny but perfect. The artist must be seriously talented,*" *I say as I continue to mindlessly trace the different lines of his tattoo.*

"*Uh... talented... yeah,*" *Jax groans, which snaps me back to what I'm doing.*

"*Shit!*" *I suddenly realise I've pulled his boxers down even further, and my face is practically in his crotch as I take in his stunning artwork.* "*Um...*" *I say, slowly removing myself from my compromising position.* "*Sorry!*"

"*Don't be. You can hang out down there as much as you want, baby,*" *he says with a sexy smirk. It didn't escape my attention that he seemed to get a little excited during my perusal of his nether regions, and his boxer briefs look pretty uncomfortable right now.*

I run my eyes slowly up his stomach and chest, trying to hunt out other hidden meanings in his tattoos. A small laugh escapes me when I find a little pink teddy bear with 'Chloe' and a date written on its belly. My finger once again has a mind of its own and traces the edges of the small bear.

"*That's for my niece. I got it the day she was born.*"

"*It's so... cute?*" *I say with a laugh. This bad boy has a tattoo of a pink teddy bear... It tells me so much about the person he is.*

My eyes continue their journey until I meet his. They're so green, they take my breath away, and the hunger in them is off the charts. "*What is it about you?*"

"*I was going to ask you the same thing.*"

"**B**aby... we're home." Jax's words filter into my sleepy head, and I can't help but think how right his words are. We're together; as long as he's with me, I am home. "You look happy," he says as he unstraps me.

"I love you. I'm always happy when I'm with you."

"Ah... I love you, too, baby. Now let's get you up to bed so you can sleep properly."

I'm aware of him carrying me up to his flat and getting me in his bed, but as soon as my head hits his soft pillow, I'm fast asleep. The couple of times I wake up, he's right there next to me. Without even knowing it, he makes me feel safe just by being with me. Ryan has always been my hero, but from the moment I laid eyes on Jax, he's given new meaning to the word.

I wake up the next morning to the smell of frying bacon, making my stomach growl loudly. It makes me realise that I barely ate anything yesterday. When I look up, I see Jax walking down the hallway toward me with a tray in his hands, but what really catches my attention is the fact that he's only in his boxers. I loved his body before, but his time at the gym with Ryan has both bulked him out and toned him up. Fuck, if I don't want to run my tongue along the ridges of his new six-pack and deeper V lines right now.

"Stop looking at me like that, baby," he warns as he places the tray down on the bed and gets himself sat next to me.

"I'm sorry... it's just... fuck." I reach out and run my fingers over his stomach.

"Shit, baby, you can't do that. This is hard enough as it is."

I glance down at his crotch and can't help but laugh. "You don't say!" When I look back up to his face, he's just glaring at me.

"Eat your breakfast, you pain in the arse!"

He doesn't need to ask me twice. I grab one of the plates of grease he brought in and wolf it down.

"God, I needed that!" I say, looking over to his plate to see that he's only just over halfway through.

I look up to his face, then back down to his plate again. He can see exactly what I'm thinking. "Go on," he says, smiling at me. I reach my hand out and grab a hash brown, taking a bite. I can't help but groan. I love them but only allow myself the indulgence every so often. "Fuck, Abs, really?" Jax actually sounds like he's in pain. "I've got to let your body recover; stop teasing me." I just shrug at him and continue eating his hash brown as quietly as possible.

CHAPTER FOUR

Jax

"Jax, I really want a shower," Abbi says as I walk into the bedroom with a drink for each of us.

"You know where it is, baby. Help yourself." When she doesn't say anything, I turn to face her. "What?"

"I'm not confident that I'll be able to hold myself up long enough." I can see her trying not to smile as she says this. The corners of her mouth are twitching.

"I can run you a bath instead."

"No, that will take too long. I just want a quick wash. Will you help me?" Her smile breaks with that.

"Are you doing this to torture me?"

"No, I'm serious about wanting help. That's just an added bonus."

I let out a huff, resigning myself to the pain this is going to cause me. "Now?"

"Please," she says, smiling sweetly.

I get up off the bed and head into the en suite to get the shower warmed up for her and a couple of big, fluffy towels ready. I put all her toiletries in here yesterday when I unpacked her stuff, so I grab everything she may need and place it in the shower. I turn around to get her, only to find that she's already here. She's leaning up against the door frame, watching me intently.

"I was just coming to get you."

"I'm already here."

"I can see that! Come on, the shower's ready."

I take a big breath before I begin helping her out of her pyjamas. The moment I pull her top over her head and reveal her perfect tits, my already hardening cock from just the thought of being naked with her jumps straight to attention. I try to focus my efforts on helping her remove her trousers and underwear while she leans on my shoulders for balance.

"Fuck, you're even more perfect than I remember," I whisper when I stand in front of her.

"Jax, this is painful for me as well, you know. I want you just as badly."

I just groan at her words before stripping off my boxers and walking us both into the shower.

I make quick work of washing her, mainly so I can get this over with for both our sakes, but also because I can see her fading fast. My girl is still exhausted. She should be resting, not turning me on in the shower with her naked body. Once I'm done, I carefully pull her out of the shower, wrap her in a towel, and lift her into my arms so I can carry her to the bedroom. She wraps one arm around my neck and rests her head on my shoulder. I love how content she makes me feel in that moment. I think I fall a little more in love with her right then.

I place her down on the bed, then put her bag next to her so she can sort herself out with minimal effort.

"Shit, can you pass me my phone, please?"

"Sure," I say, handing it to her. "What's up, baby?"

"I need to text Molly to get me a few things." I must look offended that she hasn't asked me to do it, so she goes on to explain. "I've only got tiny knickers left," she says, dangling a tiny red thong off her finger, making me swallow a groan at the thought of her wearing it. "And I need something a little more... uh... fuck it, more granny pants style to cope with the size of the sanitary towels I've got to wear. I need more of them, too..." I can't help it—the look of disgust on her face as she says granny pants has me bent over, laughing. "Oh yeah, laugh it up!" she mutters as she texts.

"Why are you still laughing at me?" she asks with a pout when she puts her phone back down and looks up to my amused face. "They're not exactly sexy, are they?" she says, making me want to laugh again, but I just about manage to hold it in.

"Baby, you look sexy to me in anything. You could wear the biggest knickers on the planet, and I'd still want you." I'm still stood with just a towel around my waist, so there's no mistaking what the thought of her—even in her granny pants, as she calls them—does to me.

"Jax?" she says, looking up through her lashes at me.

"Yes, baby?"

"Will you do something for me?"

"Anything, you know that."

As I wait for her to tell me what she needs, I watch her slide her underwear on and lie back on the bed. Her eyes are full of passion and her nipples are pointing straight at me, just begging for my attention, but I know I need to let her rest. Fuck, this is pure hell. Her gaze wanders over my exposed skin before she looks up from under her lashes at me and wets her lips slowly.

"Touch yourself. Show me how you bring yourself pleasure when I'm not around," she says in a low, sexy voice.

"Fuck, baby."

"I want you so bad, but I can barely do more than keep my eyes open right now, so I want to watch. I want to watch your body come apart while you think about me."

I bring my hand up to my neck as the words register in my lust-filled brain. What the fuck did I do to deserve a woman like her? She's pure magic. I let my eyes run down her body before locking them on to hers. Who am I to refuse a lady what she wants?

I slowly let my hand move down my chest and abs until it finally hits the towel around my waist. The further my hand descends, the faster Abbi's breathing becomes. I swear I could explode with one touch of my hand if I'm not careful. It's been way too long since we've been together. Her eyes break from mine as the towel trails to the floor and gathers at my feet. She sucks in a breath as her eyes focus in on my rock-hard cock. I grasp it in my hand and slowly work it up and down, desperately trying to keep my eyes open to look at her laid out before me.

"Come here," she whispers in a deep, gravelly voice.

I walk over to the side of the bed and stand next to her, but that obviously wasn't what she had in mind, because she gestures for me to straddle her legs, which I do willingly. Anything to be able to touch her. As soon as I'm settled, her hands come to my thighs and push me that much closer to my release. I know she's close from just watching me, because I can feel her rocking her hips and squeezing her legs together. Fuck, it would be so hot if I could make her come this way.

Abbi

I knew it would be hot, but fuck me gently, this is something else. I'm half tempted to grab my phone and record it for when I go back home on my own. I'd never need porn again.

I watch his hand stroke his cock with such force that all the muscles in his body are pulled tight. The veins in his arms are standing proud, making me want to lick my way up each of them.

He's got me so worked up that I think a single touch from him would set me off. My clit is throbbing and my body is prickling with desire. My hips move of their own accord, trying to get some friction to give my body the release it so needs.

"Fuck, baby... fuck, I've missed you so much," he grates out between gritted teeth.

"God, me too. I'm so sorry, Jax. I love you," I say, as I run my nails down his strong thighs. It's obviously just that little extra push that he needed, because he throws his head back as his whole body flinches, then stills, before he comes hard and shoots his load all over my tits and stomach.

"Fuck, that was hot!" I say to him when he looks back down at me with a smirk.

"Like that, did you? Did it turn you on to watch me get myself off?"

"Uh-huh," is all I can manage.

"I thought so. Your body is begging for me, Abbi. It's calling out for my touch, for my attention. How close are you to coming, baby? Do you think I could do it by barely touching you?"

"Oh God," I groan and nod my head at him.

"I think so, too," he says, before reaching both hands forward and pinching my nipples hard. Before I know what's happening, my orgasm is taking over and my body is pulsating at the pleasure radiating through me.

"Holy shit," Jax says with a shit-eating grin on his face. "I didn't think it would be that easy!"

After Jax has cleaned me up and made us new drinks, he sits himself on the bed next to me with his laptop to get some work done. I feel awful because he's rearranged a couple of meetings so that he could stay home and look after me today. I assured him I'd be fine, but he insisted. Plus, he's pretty exhausted himself after everything that's happened.

He barely gets his document open when the buzzer goes off. He gives me a kiss on the head before getting up and leaving the room, still topless. I love watching the muscles in his back flex as he moves.

Moments later, he's back with Ryan and Molly in tow. "Hey, Sis, how you doing?" Ryan asks as soon as he steps through the doorway.

"Fine, just exhausted."

"He'd better be looking after you properly," he says, looking in Jax's direction.

The image of what we were up to not so long ago pops into my head. "Oh yeah, he's looking after me all right," I mutter with a smile that makes Molly smirk at me knowingly, and Ryan growl.

"Do you two want a drink?" Jax asks, trying to change the subject.

"Have you got decaf tea?" Molly asks.

"Uh no, sorry. Might have some fruit tea, though."

"Yeah, that'll do. Ryan, go help him and give us girls some peace, yeah?"

"I think we're being kicked out," Ryan mutters to Jax as they both turn to leave.

"Here you go—sexy knickers, as you requested."

"Ugh, this sucks!" I complain as I pull them out of the bag.

"How are you doing? I take it everything is okay with Jax."

"I'm doing okay. Everything happens for a reason, right? The baby was never meant to be, and I'm okay with that. I mean, it's not like I'm in the right place in my life right now to have one, and weirdly it has pulled me out of the pit of misery I found myself in. It's given me a good slap around the face, and showed me what is really important in life. I've got the man I love back by my side, and I couldn't be happier about that. I was stupid to think that what we had wasn't good enough, because, in all honesty, it's amazing, and he is everything to me. Mum will just have to get over it. I know she will because she loves me, but I've come to realise over the past two days that it's her issue to deal with, not mine. This is my life, and I will live it as I see fit. I love him with everything I am, and no one, not even my mother, is going to ruin that for me. I deserve happiness," I finish proudly, then look up to see that Molly has tears streaming down her face. "Shit, I didn't mean to upset you. Here," I say, passing her a tissue from the box I've needed to have on hand the last couple of days.

"Sorry, I'm just so proud of you, Abs. We've been trying to tell you this for months, but being a stubborn witch you haven't listened to a word. You've finally figured it out," she says, wiping her eyes.

"Thanks, I think," I say with a laugh.

"What is it with you two and the laughing slash crying thing you seem to have going on?"

"Hormones," Molly, Ryan and I all say at the same time, causing more laughter.

"Women!" Jax huffs as he places my mug down next to me.

"Jax, I'm sorry to ask, but is there any chance you could be at work tomorrow afternoon? I've got something I want to run by you. Say, two o'clock? Abbi, you're more than welcome to come, too, if you need a change of scenery," Molly says.

"Uh yeah, sure. You could just tell me now, though!"

"No, I've got a few things to figure out first."

After we've finished our drinks, Molly clears away all our mugs and does the washing up, completely ignoring Jax's telling off about her doing it.

"Right, come on, let's leave these lovebirds in peace," she announces as she walks back into the bedroom. "Jax, make sure she rests," she adds with a wink, causing me to laugh and Ryan to groan once again. I know it's evil to wind him up, but it's too damn funny not to.

Once Jax has seen our visitors out, he comes back and settles down next to me again with his laptop. He tells me to get some rest, but I can't help but watch him work. His talent blows me away. Within minutes, what was a blank page looks stunning. I wish I had just a fraction of his creativity. My artistic skills really are limited to that of a primary classroom. Hell, even some of the kids I've taught have been miles better than me. It's embarrassing, really. I'm in complete awe of the work he and Molly create. I wake up every morning, looking at the drawing of Jax that Molly did months ago. It is by far my favourite possession, closely followed by my hair straighteners! Being able to look at his sexy body in such detail has always made me feel closer to him, even with the miles that have been between us, both physically and emotionally, over the past months.

Yesterday was Ryan's birthday and, to celebrate, Molly organised a surprise weekend for him. She has actually organised for our mum and dad to come down tomorrow to spend the weekend with him. Things have been a little strained in our family since Mum made Molly run away from our house in Liverpool after she overheard Mum telling Ryan what she thought of her. Ryan is refusing to forgive Mum for what she said, which I totally understand. It's one of the reasons I don't want her meeting

Jax. I don't know the ins and outs of Molly's family, but I know she doesn't talk to her parents and she's keen to keep our family together, so she stuck her neck out last week and actually rang our mum. And, much to Liv's and my utter shock, she actually agreed to spend the weekend in Oxford with us all. Liv and I are heading to theirs today for a night in, then they're joining us tomorrow morning. As far as I know, we've all managed to keep it secret from Ryan, so he's not expecting any of us.

I spoke to Molly earlier, and she told me she was having the day off work so she could get the house ready for guests. She happened to mention that Jax is in the office all day on his own, so that's where I'm heading now. I had a lecture this morning, and as soon as we were dismissed, I ran straight for my car and headed south. We haven't seen each other since last weekend, when he booked us a surprise break at a boutique hotel in Yorkshire due to me being so busy with uni and school work, so I'm dying to see him. I miss him so much. He knows I'm coming, but I told him I wouldn't be there until early evening. I cannot wait to surprise him.

It's just after three o'clock when I pull up in the car park behind Cocoa's coffee shop, which is below the office Jax works in. I check my reflection in the sun visor mirror and change my shoes before making quick work of getting out the car and heading toward the door. It's unlocked like I was expecting, so I quietly open it then lock it behind me, before I start sneaking up the stairs as quietly as I can. When I turn the corner at the top, my eyes instantly lock on to Jax's back. He looks to be totally engrossed in what he's doing on his computer. I watch him work for a few seconds before I continue over to him until I'm standing right behind him.

I lean forward and run my hands down his shoulders and chest before whispering in his ear, "You shouldn't leave the door unlocked; anyone could walk in and try to have their way with you." He jumps and goes to move away from my touch, but he almost instantly relaxes when he realises it's me.

"You're here," he says as I start to kiss his neck.

"I wanted to surprise you."

"You did that, baby," he says, spinning round on his chair and pulling me onto his lap so he can kiss me.

"Fuck, I've missed you," he says between pants when he pulls back. His chest is rising and falling harshly, and I can feel his hard cock against my arse already.

"So I see." I grind my arse into him, making him groan.

"I thought you had uni today."

"I did this morning, then I headed straight down to you. I wanted to spend as much time with you as possible before my parents come tomorrow,"

and I make an excuse as to why you can't meet them. *I keep the last bit to myself. I'm yet to work out how I'm going to convince him to disappear without hurting his feelings. I just know it will all end badly and ruin the weekend Molly has planned for Ryan if I allow my mum to meet him. I shiver at the thought of what her response to meeting him could be. Eh, it doesn't bear thinking about.*

"Umm, I'm up for that," he says before lowering his lips to mine again.

When we have to come up for air, I quickly hop off his lap so I can give him his next surprise. "I've got something for you," I say as I step out of his reach slightly with what I hope is a sexy smirk on my face.

"Oh yeah," he says, looking very intrigued. I watch as his eyes run the length of me. My usually straight blonde hair is in soft waves around my shoulders. I have smoky-grey eyes and red lips, which I know he loves. I'm covered in my black mac with full skirt, and my feet are encased in stilettos that are as red as my lips. Jax bites down on his bottom lip as he takes it all in.

"Finished?" I ask with a quirk of an eyebrow.

"I could look at you forever and it would never be enough," he says, making my insides turn to mush. *Fuck, I've fallen badly for this guy. It's gonna hurt like hell when he realises he's too good for me.*

"Do you want some more to look at?"

"Oh God, what are you wearing under that coat?" I see his eyes sparkle as realisation dawns on him.

"Would you like to see?"

I watch the muscles in his neck flex as he swallows before saying, "Yes," in a very deep, gravelly voice that makes liquid pool between my legs.

I lift my hands and slowly undo the knot in the belt around my waist. I keep my eyes on Jax as he begins to squirm in his seat. I love the power I have over him like this; it makes me feel like a goddess.

"Fuck, baby, you're killing me," he groans when I reach up to undo the buttons down the front.

I swear his eyes get a darker shade of green with every button I open, and with every inch of skin I reveal.

"I've died and gone to heaven," Jax says, when my coat eventually hits the floor and his eyes roam over everything I've just revealed. I'm wearing a black and red set of lacy lingerie. The bra cups are so small and see through that they might as well not be there; I'm practically spilling out of them. The tiny thong barely covers my newly waxed mound, and the garter belt around my waist holds up the sheer black stockings that are covering my legs. I think it's safe to say that Jax approves of my outfit.

Once he's happy he's taken in every inch of me, he gets out of the chair, sending it off into the room with his force, and pulls his t-shirt over his head and drops it to the floor with my coat. He walks straight up to me and lifts me into his arms. His hands immediately go to my arse and squeeze as his lips crash to mine again. He walks us backwards toward his desk and, just like in the movies, swipes all the paperwork off before lowering me down on it.

"Wow, that was even hotter than I could have imagined," I manage to get out before he's back on me. He's like a man possessed, and I fucking love it. His kisses are wet and dirty, and his hands are stroking and pinching whatever he can get hold of.

"You're. Fucking. Amazing," he says between kisses as he descends down my neck and onto my breasts, before sucking one of my nipples into his hot mouth after lowering the cups of my bra. He continues his descent, and, when he gets to my hips, he wraps his fingers around the waistband of the thong and ever so slowly drags it down my legs before bringing it up to his face and breathing it in. The sight alone has me squirming with need.

"Jax, please." He doesn't disappoint. He drops straight to his knees and has his mouth on me in seconds. He zeroes in on my clit and sucks on it, making me squeal before grazing it with his teeth.

"Oh fuck, Jax... Yesssssss," I shout, my heels digging into his back. He continues his onslaught on my clit and adds two fingers inside me. "Oh God, oh God, oh God," I chant as my release gets closer and closer. I haven't got myself off since I last saw him, and I need this like I need my next breath. I feel his fingers brush over that magic place, and it sends me over the edge. "JAAAAX," I shout as my body twitches uncontrollably as wave after wave of pure pleasure rolls though it.

I don't even realise Jax has moved until I feel his cock pressing against my entrance. He slams into me in one single thrust, barely giving me the chance to adjust before he starts pounding into me with such force that I can feel the desk moving under me. His hands are holding on to my hips so tightly that I know I'll have a Jax brand tomorrow.

CHAPTER FIVE

Jax

I was making good progress with the project, but, after being asleep for nearly two hours, Abbi has started moaning and squirming next to me. There's only one thing she can be dreaming about, and shit if I don't want all the details. If she hadn't just miscarried our baby, then the ending to this particular dream would be very different to what is going to happen in reality. How I would love to find out how wet she is right now, and to give her the release her body is seeking even in its sleep. As is usually the case whenever I'm around this insanely sexy woman, my dick is hard and throbbing at just the thought of being inside her. Fuck, fuck, fuck!

I'm looking down at her when her eyes fly open, revealing dark, shiny blue irises.

"You having a good dream, baby?" My usually confident and forthright woman actually blushes. "Oh, that good?" I probe.

"Your office desk," is all she says before gracing me with her winning smile.

"Oh yeah, that was damn good. Best surprise I think I've ever had. Well, other than finding you in Ryan's doorway last summer. It was like all my prayers had been answered when I looked at you that day."

Thinking that I really need to change the subject to something a little safer, I put my laptop on my bedside table before turning to look at Abbi. "How are you feeling?"

"Better, actually. I don't feel as tired," she says as she props herself up against the headboard, looking a mixture of cute and sexy in her frilly pyjamas with her bright eyes and messed up hair. She has some colour back in her cheeks.

"That's good. Are you ready to have that chat now?" I ask gently, not wanting to push the issue too much, but at the same time trying to make it obvious that it has to happen sooner or later.

"Let me go use the toilet and get a drink, then I'll tell you everything you want to know."

"Coffee?"

"Please," she says, before disappearing into the en suite and shutting the door behind her.

When I get back, I find her sat cross-legged in the middle of the bed, waiting for me with a look of apprehension on her face. I sit up against the headboard and grab her hand in mine while I wait for her to begin.

"I should warn you that this is probably going to make you angry—like, really angry." I think I already expected that from how whatever it is has affected her mother.

"Okay, I'd like to say I'm prepared, but seeing as I really have no clue as to what you're about to tell me, I can't."

I watch her nod her head before she looks down at her lap and begins. "I met him through a friend of a friend's brother. We were at a party and they crashed it; unbeknown to us at the time, they spiked all the drinks when they got there and set about enjoying the effects the vodka had on a bunch of fourteen-year-olds." I clench my fists at my sides to try to stop myself from interrupting her.

"I remembered them from school. They were a couple of years older than us but a year younger than Ryan. The one we all used to fancy when he was at school—Charlie, although everyone called him Spike—took a liking to me straight away. I thought it was great, because he was the one all the girls wanted, and there he was with me. He was different from when he was at school, because he was now well and truly inked up. He was covered in what I now consider menacing tattoos—you know, the skulls and imagery of death sort of things." I just nod at her encouragingly, even though I already want to go and rip this guy's head off without even knowing what it was exactly that he did.

"He was really sweet. He was for months, actually. He would take me out to the cinema, McDonald's, bowling... that sort of thing, or we would just sit somewhere and chat for hours. He'd tell me about college and the courses he was taking, as well as asking me about school. He seemed to really care. Mum and Dad knew I was hanging around with him, because they'd seen us together, but they thought we were going out as a group. He never came into the house, though; he only ever picked me up from the door. I wasn't brave enough to let Mum, Dad, or, more importantly, Ryan, anywhere near him. Ryan was seriously unimpressed with my friendship with him; he had an idea as to what he was like, but he didn't fully understand it. Plus, he was so busy trying to get into uni that he wasn't paying as much attention to what I was doing.

"He started taking me to more and more parties, plying me with drink. Everyone was doing it, so I thought it was normal. I was fifteen by then, and getting drunk was what everyone at school was talking about, so I just went with it. There were many, many mornings I would wake up with no recollection of what happened the night before." The more she says, the more I can feel my heart rate quicken and my anger start to flow through me. I'm trying to keep my cool for her sake, because the last thing she needs is for me to lose my shit over this.

"I knew they were doing other stuff, but I thought it was just weed and turned a blind eye to it, always refusing to do it myself. He got me to trust him more and more. I thought the sun shone out of his arse and would do anything he said. Well, it got to the stage where he was telling me that his mate wouldn't give us any booze unless we made it worth his while. He'd had me giving him blow jobs and hand jobs for months, and he used to tell me how amazing I was at it and how he wanted his mates to know how good I was." I'm now struggling to sit still; every muscle in my body wants to get up and move, punch something, but I need to stay with her. She's clinging on to my hand—I can only guess for strength to help her get through this.

"So when he suggested I do it for his mate in exchange for drink, although internally knowing it was wrong, I did it." She looks up at me briefly, and I can see fear and disgust in her eyes. But more than that, I can see her begging me for understanding. I somehow manage to nod and twitch my lip at her in encouragement.

"It continued like that for a while, but soon he was asking for me to do more and more. I hadn't slept with him, but I could sense it was coming. He continued being so sweet to me, and I kept lapping up the attention. Well, it went as I expected, and he got me drunk one night at a party before telling me that he wanted to make love to me." I feel her shudder as she says it. "He told me how much he loved me, and if I loved him, I'd do it. So, being the naïve little girl I was, I did. It was fucking awful, hurt like hell, but he didn't care; he was getting what he wanted." She's shaking so much that I pull her onto my lap and start rubbing her back comfortingly.

"I'm sorry, you shouldn't have to listen to this." I just hold her tighter, scared of what might come out of my mouth if I open it.

She takes a big breath and continues. "This continued, and I just got used to it, I guess.

"It was Ryan's nineteenth birthday and he'd come back from uni for the weekend. I had promised him and my parents that I'd be back in time for breakfast on the Saturday morning before spending the day with them. They thought, as they usually did, that I was spending the night at a friend's, so they didn't really bat an eyelid. Well that night, from what I can remember, was... extreme. There were so many people at this party, most of whom I didn't know. We started drinking, and him doing whatever else he did that I tried to ignore. As the night went on, the more drinks we had, the wilder people got. He'd already had sex with me in someone's bed, but that wasn't all he had in mind that night. He came back up from getting drinks with another guy in tow and told me he wanted me to let him have sex with me. I refused, because that was just too much. I begrudgingly did other stuff with his 'mates', but I was drawing a line. I don't really remember anything else of that night.

"The next thing I knew, I was waking up in hospital with my parents and Ryan sat around my bed, looking distraught."

"Fucking hell, Abbi." I turn her around so she's straddling me and hold her as tight as I can without hurting her while she cries.

When her tears subside, she pulls back to look at me. Her hand comes up to my cheek and, as she wipes it, I realise I have tears running down my cheeks as well. "I'm so sorry, Jax. Please don't hate me."

"Oh, baby, what I feel for you is not in question here; it never will be. I love you, no matter what, okay?"

I feel her square her shoulders and swallow down some strength. "I only know what happened from what Ryan has since told me." She takes another deep breath. "Apparently, me saying no wasn't really an option, because they spiked my drink and did what they wanted anyway. When I was over an hour late for breakfast the next morning, the alarm bells started ringing, especially when Mum rang my friend's house and they explained that I'd never been there.

"Ryan knew instantly that I was with him, so he got online and started looking at people's profiles that he knew socialised with him. It didn't take him long to come across where the party was the night before. He called some of his mates and they came to find me. Apparently, the house was completely trashed and there were people passed out everywhere. They found me in one of the bedrooms, totally out of it. They rang the emergency services, wrapped me up in the duvet, and Ryan carried me out while waiting for the paramedics. They'd really gone to town; I was covered in bruises and scratches, and everything hurt like hell when I came to. Worst of it was, though, they'd done blood tests while I was out and it turned out I was pregnant; only a few weeks, but I was."

"Motherfucker," I say under my breath, but it's enough for Abbi to start trying to comfort me instead of the other way around.

"As you can imagine, I wasn't in the right state of mind to be making any decisions, but Mum went on and on until I eventually caved and had the pregnancy aborted a few days later. I was a nightmare after that, because once I'd come to terms with what had happened, I resented my mum for making me kill my baby. Now, I'm not saying I would have kept it, but I wasn't allowed the time to make my own decision. I completely fucked up what time I had left at school, and then I had to retake everything at college the year after, which is why I'm a year behind graduating."

"Fucking hell, Abs... that's... fuck..." I'm so overwhelmed that I don't really know what to say.

"So, I guess it's all karma, really. I killed that baby's chance of life without a second thought, and now I've lost one that I wanted," she says quietly.

"Wait... what? You cannot actually believe that. Whatever the reason for your miscarriage, your past decisions are not to blame. It just wasn't meant to be this time."

"It doesn't really matter, Jax; it's all in the past now. I don't want to dwell on it. I've moved on, and I am not that person anymore."

"Abs, you are by far the strongest person I know; I had no idea something like that had happened to you. You're so... normal." She raises her eyebrows in question to that comment. "Okay, well, maybe *normal* isn't the right word," I say with a laugh. Christ, I would never have thought I could laugh so soon after her telling me that, but this woman in front of me is fucking magic. She absolutely astounds me.

"I'm sorry to ask, but what happened to him?"

"Well, turns out he was a heroin addict, and that night he was trying to buy some off the guy he wanted me to have sex with. Well, once he got hold of some, they both took a shitload but it was cut with a load of stuff it really shouldn't have been. They were both dead before the sun came up that morning," she says with a shrug.

"Fuck." I let her words settle before saying, "Now, right there is your karma."

Abbi

Jax spent a long time just holding me after my revelations. I can't blame him; he didn't see that coming at all, and it's more than a little bit shocking. Talking about it all now feels like it happened in another life; that, or I'm describing something that happened to someone else. It took me a good few years and a number of professionals to deal with it all, but I can say without doubt that I'm over it now. Some would say that something like that should scar you for life—and yes, it's always going to be there, but it doesn't take up my thoughts or nightmares anymore. I have so many good things in my life, Jax being front and centre, and I allow myself to focus on those things instead. Yes, there have been moments over the past few months when I tried to leave him behind that it's haunted me and dragged me down, but now I've got a second chance with him, all my time and effort is going to him, to prove that I'm worthy of him despite all my previous bad decisions.

"No wonder your mum hates me!" he eventually says, releasing his hold on me slightly.

I pull back to look at him. I'm still straddling his lap, and I see some of the stress and anger leave his features. I don't want this to weigh him down, either. I want us to move forward together.

"She can't hate you, Jax; she doesn't know you. But she'll come around eventually, and she will love you because you're the kindest, sweetest, gentlest and most loving person I have ever met, and you make me so happy, Jackson Parker. Happier than I ever thought possible. Promise me you won't let this affect us or bring you down. It's so in the past, and I want it left there."

"I'm probably going to be angry for a while, but I promise to let it go. I need to worry about you right now and focus on the future. You're right: the past is the past, and there's nothing we can do to change it or the decisions we, or others, made."

I feel like I've lost him in some other world as he says the last bit. Something inside me says it's going to lead on to the reason for his panic attacks.

Jax lays us down but keeps me on top of him. His hands continue caressing my back, almost as if he's in some kind of trance. He stays quiet for long minutes, and I start to think he isn't going to say anything, but eventually I feel him suck in a deep breath before he begins to tell me his own story.

"My family's always had money. The restaurants that have been passed down have made sure of that. My sister and I have never wanted for anything; we had a private education, had all the brands, gadgets and latest fashion crazes. She loved it; she used to flounce around school like she owned the place with all the other rich girls that had Daddy wrapped around their little finger. I, on the other hand, hated it with a passion. I hated all the stuck up little twats I had to go to school with. Everything was about money. If there was a disagreement or a fight, you could guarantee that the cause of it was money in some way. Needless to say, I didn't really have any friends at school. Thank fuck Mum and Dad didn't make us board; if they had, I'm pretty sure I'd have found myself expelled just so I could get out of there. Luckily, as you know, my parents are amazing. They just wanted us to have the best education possible. They weren't like the parents of some of the other kids at school, who would swan off on their exotic holidays while they left their kids behind with a stash of money to do with as they pleased. I used to count down the hours before I could get home and just be me.

"Suzi and I were never really that close with her being a few years older and... well, generally acting like the kids at school that I hated. I used to spend all my time with my cousin, who lived in the housing estate behind our house. We were the same age and were practically like brothers. My aunt and uncle, my mum's brother, were lovely and always welcomed me in their home in the same way Ben was at ours. I idolised my uncle; he was an artist, the same as my auntie, and at one point he had artwork all around the city. It was insane how good he was. People commissioned him to do all sorts. One of my favourite things to do as a kid was to just sit and watch him work. His skill amazed me." I understand that, because I do that exact same thing to him. I keep still on top of Jax and just listen to him, occasionally placing a soft kiss to his neck where my head is nestled.

"They never had money like we did, though, with them both being self-employed, so Ben went to the local secondary school where I dreamed of going with the normal kids. He was also really talented, and he wanted to be an illustrator. My life outside of school was great; we used to have great times as a family. My mum and aunt were really close friends, so we were all together often, had some holidays together and that sort of thing." Jax clears his throat, and I take the opportunity to sit up so I can see him and offer my support for what's going to come next. I place my hands on his cheeks to force his eyes to mine. I mouth 'I love you' at him, and his lips twitch slightly at the corners, but he's obviously too lost in his memories to properly focus on me. He takes my hands in his and looks at something over my shoulder before continuing.

"It all started going south when my nan and gramp, my mum and uncle's parents, died in quick succession. My uncle took it really badly; he started locking himself in his studio for hours. He wouldn't see or talk to anyone. He wasn't working, so my auntie started struggling to support the family with just her income. We didn't know this at the time—they were both proud people and would never admit they were having money problems. If only they'd asked for help. This went on for a while, and he got worse and worse. It was obvious he was depressed, but he wasn't surfacing for long enough or was sober enough to talk to anyone about it. He must have known about the money situation, which probably made it worse.

"Anyway, it was my mum and dad's wedding anniversary, and we were all having a meal at our house to celebrate. Everyone was there apart from my uncle. I said I'd go and find him while Mum dished up, so I jogged to their house. It was deserted, so I guessed he was in his studio, which was basically a posh shed in the garden. The door wasn't locked, so I let myself in and found..." I watch as a single tear escapes and runs down his temple. My heart breaks for my man as I see the pain and heartbreak take over his features. I squeeze his hands in mine for encouragement, knowing that it gets easier once it's out. "He was hanging from the rafters," he whispers in a wobbly voice.

"Oh, Jax," I say, before I lie back down on top of him to comfort him as he starts to cry.

Eventually, his sobs subside and I roll on to my side next to him. I place my hand on his cheek so I can turn his head and place my lips to his. He returns my kiss, but only briefly, because he's soon lying on his back and carrying on from where he left off.

"It was fucking awful. Everyone was a mess, but Ben took it the worst. He just couldn't understand why his dad would leave him and his mum like that. He went completely off the rails, and as I started sixth form, he dropped out and spent his days bumming around. It was like a switch had flipped in him; one day he was his usual self, then the next he was this manic-depressive who hated the world. My aunt couldn't deal with him. She was beside herself. We all tried, we did everything we could think of, but at the end of the day, it wasn't enough. When she found him, he was surrounded by packets of pills and a note saying he wanted to be with his dad."

"Holy shit, Jax. I'm so sorry." As I hold him tight to me, I can tell he's trying to keep control of his breathing.

"That's when the panic attacks started," he says quietly. "Having both of them kill themselves just freaked me out, and I was petrified that everyone else I loved was going to do it as well. I knew at the time it was irrational, but I couldn't help it. So when Ryan told me they'd found you and there was loads of blood, I just flipped. The thought of losing you, Abbi... well, I can't even..."

"Hey, Jax, it's okay. Don't go there. I'm fine; everything is fine. I'm not going anywhere." I lean toward him and give him a kiss that I hope tells him everything I feel for him. I feel his hand come to the back of my head, and we stay like that on the bed for what feels like hours, just kissing and supporting each other after the pain of revealing our pasts.

We had a pretty quiet night after that. We spent ages lying in bed, holding each other, but eventually we both got up once my stomach started growling. Jax tried to insist that he bring food to me, but I was more than ready to start getting back to normal life, so instead we had a little picnic on the sofa of anything we could find in his kitchen. Neither of us went to put the TV or any music on. We were both so lost in our own thoughts and happy for it to be quiet around us.

Jax did confess to me that he's worried that he might have the depressive gene in him that both his uncle and cousin had, and that he's petrified to be like that. I tried to reassure him that, with everything he has been through, it would have showed itself by now if it were there. He seemed happy with my answer, but I could still see the worry in his eyes and I wished more than anything that I could take that and all his pain away. When I started yawning again, Jax pulled me down to his bedroom and we fell fast asleep in each other's arms.

CHAPTER SIX

Jax

To describe the last few days as emotional would be putting it lightly. I'm still reeling from Abbi's confession about her past, and I can't believe how something so horrifying hasn't stopped her from being... well... amazing. I'm in awe of her strength and her ability to bounce back from something like that. I can still feel my own anxiety just bubbling under the surface from telling her about my uncle and cousin. I never talk about what happened, even with my family. It's just too hard to think about, and I don't want to have to deal with any more panic attacks than necessary. After it happened, they used to be a daily thing, but as time went on and I managed to cope with it better, they started getting more irregular. It wasn't until I met Abbi that they practically disappeared; so did the nightmares. My sleeping hours had been taken over by dreams about her, not the horror of my past, and I welcomed that with open arms. She mentioned earlier about her own nightmares, but with all the nights I've been with her, she's never shown any signs of it. I wonder if I stopped hers as well. I really hope so.

She's been asleep in my arms for hours, but I just can't shut my brain off. Too many thoughts are running rampant.

Today has been amazing. I'd been anxious all morning, knowing Abbi was coming this evening so she could spend the weekend here for Ryan's birthday surprise, but having her surprise me early at the office, wearing the sexiest outfit I think I've ever seen, was like all my dreams had come true. I'm sure Molly would kill me if she ever found out we had sex over the desk.

We've had a great night at Ryan's. The look on his face when he came home slightly worse for wear and found everyone here was brilliant. I can't believe everyone managed to actually keep it all a secret from him. Tomorrow, Molly has arranged for his parents to come, which everyone is shocked about because Ryan's mum hates Molly. I'm really looking forward to meeting the woman. From the little I've heard about her, she sounds... interesting. Abbi met my parents a few weeks ago for my birthday. They loved her from the second she walked through the door. Now, every time my mum rings, she seems more interested about Abbi than she is me—not that I care, because it shows that they love her as much as I do.

"So, what's the plan for tomorrow, baby?" I ask Abbi as I look down at her. We've just attempted to have quiet sex due to the fact that her little sister is asleep on the other side of the wall, and her protective big brother, who still doesn't really like me, is just down the hall, but I'm not entirely sure how successful we were. I tend to lose all control when we're together, and I know for a fact that Abbi does as well. I love watching her come apart under my hands.

"I don't know. We'll probably just do boring family stuff. I wouldn't want to force it on you. You go and do whatever you need to do, meet some friends or something. I'll try to sneak off at some point to spend some time with you," she says, looking a little nervous.

"Time with you is never boring, Abbi. Whatever your family decides to do will be fine. The only plans I've got this weekend are to spend as much time with you as possible."

"No, really, it'll be boring. You go, and I'll just see you in the afternoon."

"Do you not want me meeting your family or something, Abbi?" I've had my concerns about this for a few weeks, but I kept pushing it away. Then, a couple of weekends ago, we went to Liverpool so Abbi could show me where she grew up. We were walking down the high street when all of a sudden she dragged me into a shop in a panic. When I asked her what the problem was, she said she'd seen one of her mum's friends and that she really wasn't in the mood to get stuck talking to her for ages, so she hid. I'm starting to think that maybe I was the reason...

"No, it's not that, it's just…" she trails off, looking unsure of herself.

"Just what, Abbi? Because from where I'm sitting, it sure looks that way. You've gone out of your way to stop me meeting your parents," I say, remembering how that same weekend I suggested we go out for a meal with her parents so I could meet them, but she came up with some excuse about them having friends round for dinner and that they'd be busy, even on the Sunday morning.

"No, they just… wouldn't understand. Mum wouldn't understand."

"Understand what?" I'm starting to get really pissed off now. I'm not into this cryptic shit.

"She wouldn't understand us… you," she says in a quiet voice.

Now I really am pissed. "She wouldn't understand me?" I jump out of bed and make a grab for my clothes.

"No, you're just not what she'll want." She can't even look at me, now.

"I thought I was with you, not your mother." With that, I pull my top over my head and storm toward the door.

"Jax, no, please don't go."

"Why not, Abbi? Come on, tell me I'm wrong. TELL ME!" I roar, starting to lose control of my anger. The woman I love more than anything is basically telling me I'm not good enough. That what we have isn't good enough to introduce me to her bloody mother.

I storm down the stairs with her hot on my tail. I need to get away from her and calm down before I say something I really don't mean.

"Jax, that isn't what I meant…" Abbi screams from behind me as my feet hit the hallway floor.

I head toward the front door as I say, "Yes, it fucking was. You're ashamed of me. I've been trying to tell myself for weeks now that it's all in my head, but you just confirmed all my fears. You don't think I'm good enough." My voice sounds menacing, even to my own ears.

"No… Jax, please," she begs, starting to cry.

"I'm done with this bullshit. I thought we had something good here, but clearly only one of us thinks that. Was I just an easy fuck for you? Was that it?" I snap back as I hear Molly's bedroom door open, but I don't look back.

"We do have something good here. Jax, please don't do this."

"You should have thought about that before you said what you did upstairs. Goodbye." I say, before I pull the door open and storm out of the house, listening to Abbi shout at me to come back through her sobs.

Something brings me from my sleep. My heart is racing and I'm sweating slightly. Thinking it must just be the panic caused from dreaming about the night I left Abbi, I try to fight it and get back to sleep. I sat in my car for hours after I left the house that night. I had one hell of a panic attack as what I'd just done settled in. I'd left her, the love of my life. What the fuck was I thinking? Why should I care what her mother thought? I knew I was too drunk to drive home, so I just sat there with my car running with the heater on full blast while I tried to calm down and think about what to do.

"Nooo," Abbi moans from my left, scaring the shit out of me. "Nooo please, no," she shrieks and begins sobbing.

Shit, it must have been Abbi that woke me up. I turn to look at her to see her thrashing around with tears running down her face. "Baby, it's okay," I say gently, trying to wake her, but it does nothing. I grab her shoulders and shake her gently. "Abbi, baby... wake up, you're having a nightmare."

Suddenly, her eyes pop open and she looks scared shitless. I pull her sweaty body to mine and hold her tight, whispering in her ear that everything's okay and that I love her.

"I'm sorry, I haven't had a nightmare like that in years. Talking about it must have dragged it up."

"It's okay, baby." I lie us both back down and hold her until we doze off again.

When I wake up the next morning, the bed is cold and she isn't there. The panic I felt when I woke up in the night resurfaces as I try to get my sleep-addled brain to function.

Abbi

I managed to sleep for a few more hours after my nightmare, but eventually I got fed up and pulled myself away from Jax, trying desperately not to wake him.

I sit myself at his breakfast bar with a coffee and my phone. I heard it go off when we were talking yesterday, but I completely forgot. I've got messages from Liv and Caleb asking if I'm okay. Caleb is also apologising for causing any issues with Jax. I reply to both and reassure Caleb that it's all fine, but have to apologise myself for telling Jax his secret.

When I feel like it's late enough, I find my tutor's number and hit the call button.

Once I have all the information I need, I make myself another cup of coffee before ringing Ryan to find out if he'll be at the office with Molly later, because I need his help.

"Hey, baby, I missed waking up next to you," Jax says as he wraps his arms around my shoulders and kisses my head.

"Sorry, I couldn't sleep any longer. I think I've had my fill over the last few days."

"What have you been doing? I heard you talking."

"I rang my tutor to try to sort everything out with me being off."

"Will it all be okay?"

"Yeah, it'll be fine." I don't go into detail because I don't know if what I'm planning will be a possibility yet, and I don't want to get his hopes up. "Don't forget, I've got an appointment before your meeting with Molly later."

"Yeah, I know. Do you want some breakfast?"

The appointment was fine; everything looks okay, apparently. I just need to rest, and after a week or two I should be as good as new.

The others are already at the office by the time we get there, and to our surprise it's not just Molly and Ryan—their friend Chris is there, too.

"I hear congratulations are in order," he says, as we all greet each other. All eyes snap to him, and he suddenly looks panicked. "What? You're back together, aren't you?" he says, looking between Jax and me while everyone else lets out a breath.

"Yeah, we are," Jax says, giving my shoulders a squeeze.

"Right. Jax, Chris, we've got some stuff to talk about, come on. You two can have the sofa," she says to Ryan and me.

It turns out that Chris approached Molly after her accident and basically told her if she had enough work and needed another designer, he'd hand his notice in and work for her. Molly, although a little hesitant at first, eventually came around to the idea with a little help from my brother. It means she can relax a little more and prepare for the baby's arrival in a few months.

Ryan was happy to try to help me out with my plan for my final uni placement and said he would get some emails out as soon as he got home and let me know if anything came up.

Before I know it, it's the weekend, and although I'm still a bit tired, I know I need to get back up to Manchester. My tutor has told me I can change my placement as long as I have enough lesson observations completed from my current one and hand my assignment in. The sooner I can have all that done, the sooner I can move. Things are looking promising this end as well, thanks to my amazing big brother, but I'm keeping it under wraps at the moment, because I don't want to have to disappoint Jax if it all falls through. I'm also yet to tell him I'm going back before my sick note ends. This could get interesting.

"Jax?"

He's in the kitchen, sorting us out some lunch before we head over to Ryan and Molly's for the afternoon. Molly and I are leaving the boys to it so I can get my limp locks sorted out. Since things ended with Jax, I haven't really cared enough to keep up with looking my best, so my usually bright blonde hair is looking a little sad. Molly also wants to hit some of the baby shops in town now that she has her cast off and can drive herself. She was hesitant to ask me, but, as I've told her numerous times, I'm totally fine with it and am happy to be excited with her about my new niece or nephew. Our baby wasn't meant to be, but it brought us back together. We have plenty of time in our future for babies.

"I've decided that I'm heading back to Manchester tomorrow, so I can get back to school. The quicker I get all my observations and teaching hours done, the sooner I can be finished." Well, that's sort of true. Ish.

"I don't think so, Abbi," he growls as he places the plates on the coffee table in front of me. "The doctor said you should have two weeks off to rest."

"I know, but I feel fine," Also true. Ish. "Jax, I can't sit round wasting days. I'll have all of the Easter and summer holidays to do that. I need to get back to normal life."

"I'm not going to win here, am I?" he asks, a little defeated.

"I'm sorry, Jax. It's not that I don't want to be here with you, because I do more than anything, but I need to get uni finished." I also need to start looking for a job, but I don't mention that because it will lead to the location of said job.

"I don't like it one bit, but I do understand. Just promise me you'll look after yourself and rest as much as you can. I know what you're like."

It's like I blink; the weekend is gone, and I'm trying to say goodbye to Jax but my sobs kind of interfere.

"Baby, if you're not ready don't go, stay with me," he says as he holds me.

"No, I need to go." I know that the sooner I go and get everything sorted, the sooner I can be back in his arms.

I square my shoulders and take a deep breath. "I'm okay. I love you, Jax. I promise to ring you as soon as I get there, and I'll see you as soon as I can, yeah?" I take a step away from him and give him one last kiss before I get into my car. I have to bite down on my cheeks to try to keep from breaking down again in front of him.

"I love you, too, baby, more than you could ever know."

I feel a sob rising so I just nod, unable to speak, and pull away, leaving him looking completely lost on the path outside his flat. The moment I turn the corner out of sight, the tears start. They eventually dry up for a few minutes, but as soon as I think of him, they start again. He's been amazing this week. He's looked after me better than I could have ever asked for. He's been supportive, sweet, and so gentle with me. We haven't had sex again yet—actually, other than the day after getting back from the hospital, we haven't done anything. We were both just content being with each other, enjoying being in each other's arms again and really getting to know each other. I have no doubt that when we do reconnect, it is going to be electric. My body is physically aching for him.

The minute I enter my flat, my best friend and flatmate, Sarah, is on me, along with our friend Eve. I once again break down in tears in her arms. They pull me over to the sofa and sit me down while waiting patiently for me to calm down.

"Has that fucker broken your heart again?" Sarah asks. I'd text her to say I was staying in Oxford longer than originally planned, but she has no clue about the rest of it, so I spend the next hour explaining to both of them about the miscarriage, getting back with Jax, and my plan for uni. They both listen intently and save any questions they have until I finish.

"So, you're leaving?"

"That's what I'm hoping, but I need to wait and see if it's possible first.

Don't worry, I'll pay up my share of the rent. I'm hoping for some free lodgings in Oxford, whether it be with Ryan or Jax."

"Don't be stupid, I couldn't care less about the money, and it's not that I want you to go, but the timing is pretty good, actually." She looks over at Eve, who I now notice looks a little glum. "Fuck face cheated on her, and she's been sleeping on our sofa. If you go, she could have your room." Wow, this all seems to be working out well; I just pray the rest of it continues that way. "I'm gonna miss you, though."

"I know, I'll miss you, too," I say, pulling Sarah in for a hug. We've pretty much been inseparable since the day we started uni together, but I guess all good things have to come to an end. The fact that I've got a sexy as fuck guy waiting for me at the other end softens the blow for me slightly.

I'm exhausted when I get into bed that night. After my session with the girls, I spent hours on the phone to Jax, trying to convince him that I'm okay.

The minute my head hits my pillow, I'm out like a light.

CHAPTER SEVEN

Jax

My heart feels like it's being pulled out of my chest as I watch her drive away from me. I hate that she's decided to leave early. I told her I understand her reasons, and I do, but it doesn't mean it hurts any less. She could have spent two weeks here with me, but she's gone after only one. I lift my hands up and go to run them through my hair, only to find that it's gone and I have nothing to pull on... which was the reason for cutting it in the first place. That night at the hospital with Abbi, I spent practically the whole time pulling at it, to the point that I was annoying myself. The first thing I did when I left the next morning was find a barber to get rid of it. Soon after, I headed to the tattoo studio to get my new ink. I'd been planning to have it before everything kicked off with Abbi, and, like the pussy I am, had the design I wanted folded up carefully in my wallet. I knew I needed to get it done. Even if things didn't sort themselves out between us, I needed a reminder on my skin of what we did have, because I'm pretty damn sure I'd never find something like that ever again. I think Abbi unknowingly ruined me for anyone else from that first evening of meeting her. Hell, I'm pretty sure I fell in love with her the moment my eyes locked with hers that day.

When I realise that I'm still standing on the path outside my flat, looking like a loser, I hang my head and trudge back. It's going to be cold and empty without her.

My heart warms a little when I see a note pinned to my fridge. I instantly recognise her writing and pull it off to look at it.

My sexy man,
I'm sorry I had to leave, but trust me. I have my reasons and will explain all soon.
I love you with all my heart. Thank you for everything you've done for me this week.
I'll see you soon, I promise.
All my love,
Abbi x

I pin it back up on the fridge so I can look at it. God, I'm seriously whipped. My phone rings somewhere in the flat, distracting me, and when I eventually find it it's stopped ringing, but I call Ryan straight back.

"Hey dude, Abs just text to say she was headed home. You okay?"

"Yeah, I guess."

"We're having Sunday lunch at the Morrisons', but we'll be home by six at the latest. Come round, we'll have a few beers, yeah?"

"Yeah okay," I agree. I'm not really feeling like it, but being out of my empty flat will probably do me some good.

I sit down on the arm of the sofa and think about what Ryan just said before finding my car keys and heading out to go see my parents.

"Jackson, you should have told us you were coming. I'd have plated you up dinner," Mum says the moment I enter the dining room to find everyone there looking back at me.

"Dax," my niece, Chloe, squeals from her high chair next to my sister. She puts her arms straight up in the air for me to go and get her, but she instantly gets chastised by Suzi.

"It's fine, Mum, it was a last-minute thing."

"I've got enough for another portion in the kitchen. Sit down, and I'll go get you some."

"Thanks," I call after her.

After dinner, I join my mum and Suzi in the kitchen to help clean up, while my dad and brother-in-law head straight for the TV with Chloe following close behind on very unsteady legs.

"What's up, baby boy? You look sad," Mum comments.

"It's Abbi."

"Still?" my sister questions.

"We're back together."

"And you look sad about that, why?" Mum asks, looking confused.

I explain the whole story to them and about how she's gone back up to Manchester, making me feel lost without her.

"Firstly, fuck her mother," my sister says, earning the evil eye from our mum. "Secondly, it sounds like she loves you as much as you do her. Bite the bullet, baby brother, and make her yours."

"I would have put it slightly differently, but I agree," my mum chips in. "She's amazing and absolutely perfect for you. Do you want to risk losing her again?"

"Don't you think it's a bit soon for all this?"

"She was going to have your baby, Jax," Suzi says, squeezing my forearm.

I think about everything my mum and sister said on the drive over to Ryan and Molly's. I can't help but think they're totally crazy. I mean, we may have known each other since last summer, but we spent most of that apart. Yes, she was going to have my baby, but it was conceived as a drunken spur of the moment thing in my friends' bathroom; not exactly what romance novels are made of. I love her more than I thought possible. I know she's the one I've been waiting for, and that I want to spend the rest of my life with her, but I'm sure me doing it now will just totally freak her out. She's so busy trying to finish uni, then she's going to need to get a job. It's totally crazy, right?

As I continue driving, my mind wanders back to New Year's Eve.

It took a lot of convincing on both Molly and Ryan's part to actually get me to turn up to this damn party. I was quite happy at home with my bottle of Jack, and maybe even a glass, depending on how I felt at the time, but here I am, ringing their fucking doorbell.

I know she's already here, because I've just seen her car. I also know he's here, too, because Molly warned me. Fucking great.

After greeting Molly and Ryan, thankfully he fills my hand with a drink, so I can start my mission of getting off my head to try to numb the pain that this night is surely going to cause.

It's only a few minutes later when a guy I've never met comes walking straight over to me like he knows me.

"You must be Jax. I'm Caleb," he says, sticking his hand out. "You look just as Abbi described. It's good to meet you at last." I'm startled for a few seconds.

"You too. She... uh... talks about me?"

"Yeah, all the time. I've been looking forward to meeting you. Right, I'm going to go and see if they're ready yet; they've been down there for hours," he says before turning and leaving the room. I watch him go with what must be a look of pure shock on my face.

I turn to Molly, who is still stood next to me, and say, "So that's Caleb, huh? I'm sorry to ask, but how does she go from me to him?" I point in the direction he just left. "I mean, we're like day and night opposites." I'm a tattooed bad boy, apparently, and he's just a pretty boy.

Molly goes on to tell me that Abbi doesn't look at him like she does me and explains how she thinks Caleb might be gay. I can't help but cross every part of my body with hope for that to be true. The thought of him touching her makes me feel murderous, but if that's true, he hasn't, so I can relax a little.

It's not long before Liv and Beth appear, looking amazing, but as soon as I see them enter the room, my eyes are fixed to the door because I know she'll be next. And I'm not disappointed, because seconds later she appears with her arm through Caleb's, and fuck me sideways if she does not look out of this fucking world hot. She's wearing a tight-fitting, floor-length red dress that hugs every insanely sexy curve she has and drops a little low at the front to give a hint of her cleavage. My dick instantly starts hardening at the sight of her. Her red lips are practically calling me to walk over and plant mine on them. Fuck. My. Life. I knew coming was a bad idea, and she's just proved me right.

"Sweet mother of Jesus. Is she trying to torture me?" I mutter to myself, but Molly hears and agrees with me before I tell her I need a stronger drink.

Molly has just walked off when Abbi raises her eyes to mine. Our contact holds for a few seconds too long, making something crackle between us, before she drops her eyes and gives me a once over like she did when she first saw me.

Shane and Chris try to distract me from a long night of pining after Abbi. They're great guys and very funny together, but I only half listen to the conversation they're trying to hold with me. Most of my attention is on Abbi, who's facing me while talking to her sister and Caleb. I've caught her looking at me about the same number of times she's caught me. She, unlike me, looks away, as if she's been burned. I couldn't care less if she knows I want her. The last few weeks without her have been pure hell.

This back and forth between us continues for the next few hours, until I get so fucked off with the whole thing that I walk straight up to her once I've made sure everyone is distracted with their own conversations.

"We need to talk," I say in her ear, not missing the fact that goosebumps erupt across her skin. I grab her hand and gently but firmly pull her from the room and down the stairs. I want to be as far away from everyone upstairs, so I'm not content to just be in the bedroom where she's sleeping. I continue to pull her into the bathroom so there are more doors between us and everyone else.

I pull her to stand in front of me. Her chest rises and falls rapidly and her red lips are parted as she breathes through them. We both just stand and stare at each other for what feels like ages, but in reality is probably just seconds, before she practically throws herself at me. My back hits the wall with the force of her coming at me. My gasp of shock works to her advantage, because she shoves her tongue straight in my mouth and strokes mine, bringing me out of my trance. My hands instantly go to her arse and I grind my rigid cock into her stomach while we fuck each other's mouths with no finesse at all. We're all tongues, teeth and lips in our wet and dirty kiss.

"Fucking hell, I've missed you," I groan as I begin to kiss down her neck and nibble on her collarbone.

I allow enough space between us for her to begin undoing the buttons on my shirt. When she has it open, she immediately runs her hands up my stomach to my shoulders so she can remove it. It falls on the floor somewhere as I start moving her backwards until she bumps into the vanity unit behind her. I drop to my knees in front of her and lift her skirt up around her waist. She grabs on to the fabric and holds it there. I lean back on my heels for a few seconds to appreciate the sight in front of me. She's wearing a tiny little black and red lace thong that barely covers her, and black fuck-me heels. It's almost like she knew this was going to happen and dressed up for me. I don't waste any time in ridding her of her underwear. I don't care how pretty they are, I need what's underneath. I wrap my fingers around the thin lace and pull until it rips and I can pull them from her body. I throw them over my shoulder as she groans out about how hot that was and begs me to touch her. With pleasure, baby.

I lean forward and run my nose through her folds. Ah, I'm home, I think as I smell her sweet scent. I shove her legs a little farther apart with my shoulders before I begin teasing her clit with my tongue.

"Ah, fucking shit... ah, Jax... fuck," she starts muttering incoherently above me.

I reach my hand up and slide two fingers into her. I reach up until I hit that spot inside that I know makes her scream my name. Fuck if I don't need to hear that right now, and I couldn't give a rat's arse if anyone hears. Fuck, Ryan could walk in right this second and I wouldn't bat an eyelid about continuing. I need this woman fiercely.

I reach up a little higher and I feel her twitch, telling me I've hit the spot, so I up the pressure on her clit as I feel her whole body start to tremble. That's it, baby, let go.

"JACKSON! FUUUUUUCK!" she shouts, and I feel like a fucking god.

I stand up as I wipe my mouth before grabbing the back of Abbi's head and slamming her lips to mine. Her hands go to my trousers and we continue to kiss. Within seconds, they're falling around my ankles and her hand is wrapped around my dick. My eyes roll back in my head at the sensation. I grab the backs of her thighs and lift her on to the unit without breaking our kiss. Once I have her balancing on the edge, I waste no time in lining myself up at her entrance. It registers in my head for all of about two seconds that I don't have a condom, but I rationalise that I'm clean, I trust her with my life, and that she's on the pill.

I slide all the way into her in one thrust, revelling in the feeling of her skin on skin. I've never gone bareback before. Fuck, it feels so good. I feel her stiffen in my arms and I hold still for a few seconds so she can adjust, but I can only wait so long. I reach out and wrap her legs around my waist and begin to pound into her.

I have to break our kiss because I'm panting so hard and I want to watch her fall apart.

"Fuck, I've missed you, baby," I grunt out between my pants, and she says similar things between her moans of pleasure.

I just start to feel the signs of my approaching release when the bathroom door flies open. I look over my shoulder to see Molly stood there, frozen on the spot.

"Molly," I say, trying to bring her out of her daze.

I watch her eyes focus before she says, "Shit! Sorry I wasn't... uh... yeah..." She turns and goes to leave the room, but before she does, she says my name.

"Uh-huh," is all I manage to get out.

"I never knew your tattoo went all the way down to your thigh. That's hot," she says, amusement in her voice.

"Fuck. Off," I manage to grunt at her before she closes the door behind her, leaving us alone once again.

I look up to Abbi to see what she's going to do. I swear, if she stops this now, my balls will explode. But I should know her better than that, because what she actually says is music to my ears.

"Fuck me, Jax."

So I do as I'm told and continue where I left off. Within seconds, we're both sweating and riding out the waves of our orgasms together. Abbi throws her head back and screams my name. I will never get used to the feeling I get when she does that. I feel ten feet tall and like I'm on top of the world.

I pull up outside Ryan and Molly's house and have to sit there for a few minutes as I get myself under control from my vivid recollection of that night. If only Abbi didn't run the next morning... we could have sorted things out so much sooner. I don't dwell on it, though, because we're together again now, and the only thing that could make me happier was if she was here, not nearly two hundred miles away.

An hour later, I'm sat on Ryan and Molly's sofa with a beer. I think I've depressed them enough, chatting about how much I miss Abbi already, but they're both sympathetic and listen to me go on.

I'm just about to try to change the subject because I am well aware of what a pussy I sound like, when Ryan pulls out a box from under the coffee table.

"This came yesterday. To say I was shocked by it was an understatement, but Mum likes to keep us all on our toes," he says as he hands it over to me.

I look up at him with my brows drawn together. "What?" I ask, but he just nods for me to open it. I open the top to find an envelope and a load of tissue paper underneath. My name is on the front of the envelope, so I pull it open and read what is inside the card.

Jackson,

If you love her as much as you say you do, then you need to prove it. If you treat her like the princess she is, then we will get on just fine. But until I know I can trust you with her, I will continue to think the worst of you.
Please prove me wrong. I beg of you.

Karen

"What the fuck?" I ask, passing Ryan the card.

"Keep going," is all he says, again nodding toward the box.

I shake my head at him and this craziness but begin to pull the tissue paper away to reveal a box... a ring box. What the fuck is wrong with everyone today? Is it national proposal day or something? I can't help but laugh.

"What's wrong?" Molly asks.

"Nothing, it's just that this isn't the first time today this has come up." They snap their eyes to mine from where they were reading the card in question. "My mum and sister were suggesting a couple of hours ago that I do the exact same thing."

I pull the lid open on the box and my eyes practically pop out of my head. "Fuck me!"

"She must like you more than she lets on, Jax, because that's her grandma's ring. It's Cartier. It's worth a fucking fortune. She clearly thinks more of you than she does of me, because I didn't get it," Molly says with a laugh.

"My grandma put in her will that it was to go to Abbi, because she always loved it," Ryan adds.

"Fuck," I say again, trying to take it all in. "So even though your mother hates me—I now know why, by the way," I add, looking at Ryan. He just nods at me in understanding. "She thinks I should propose to Abbi?"

"My mum has some fucked-up logic at times, but I actually think I can see where she's going with this. She thinks that if you really are serious, you'll prove it by marrying Abbi. If you were just messing her about, then you'd be running scared right about now. It's a test, but I totally understand whatever you decide to do next with this." Throughout his little speech, Molly looks more and more confused.

"Ryan, I know it's not for me to say, but would you please fill your fiancée in with what happened? I don't think it's fair for her to be entering your family without knowing."

"You're right." So Ryan goes on to explain everything to a very shocked Molly. I don't get any less angry hearing the story for the second time, but it is interesting hearing Ryan's side of it. He really is very protective of his sister. I suddenly feel very grateful to have his support with my relationship with Abbi.

I get up to leave a few hours later with the priceless Evans heirloom in my hand. Ryan stops me before I get to the door.

"Jax, just so you know, I'm totally behind whatever you decide to do. You're good for her, and I know you want what's best for her. She's lucky to have you, mate." I can't help it, I get a little choked at his announcement. It took quite a long time for Ryan to accept me as a part of Molly's life, let alone his sister's, so I'm relieved to hear him say that.

"Thanks mate, I love her a lot." I can't help the soppy look that I know appears on my face at that statement. "I'll see you soon. See you tomorrow, Molls." I shout over Ryan's shoulder.

I spend hours when I get home staring at the bloody emerald, trying to get some inspiration. Me asking Abbi to marry me is not in question, but how I make my proposal worthy of her is.

Abbi

That thirty minutes in that bathroom was out of this world, especially if I forget about Molly interrupting us. Thank God it wasn't Ryan... that could have been messy.

Jax had always given me strong orgasms, but the two that night were something else. Maybe it was our time apart, but fuck, I thought my head was going to blow off when both of them crashed through my body.

It wasn't until Jax had cleaned us both up and left me alone so we didn't reappear together that it hit me as to what we'd just done. The hunger and passion of the moment completely blocked any of my brain signals registering with me. I stumbled toward the bed on wobbly post-awesome-orgasm legs and put my head in my hands. I stopped taking my pill because I ran out, and I decided that if I couldn't have Jax, then I wasn't going to be shagging anyone, so it was pointless. But I'd just had Jax, and I let him in without a condom. Fuck, shit, fuck. What are the chances though? People try for babies for months if not years—what are the chances?

Fuck.

I eventually headed back up not long before midnight to celebrate the New Year with my friends and family. I kept as far away from him as possible for the rest of the night, and as soon as the first person left, I disappeared to bed. I just didn't know what to do or what to think.

I woke up early the next morning and decided he didn't need my bullshit, and if our one night of passion turned into something, then I would deal with that when the time came, but for now he was still better off without me. I scrawled out a note and snuck upstairs with it so I could leave it for him. He was asleep on the sofa; he looked so peaceful, like he didn't have a care in the world. I walked over to him and placed a gentle kiss on his forehead, leaving the note on the coffee table before I changed my mind, and got the hell out of there. I then cried all the way home and for most of New Year's Day, locked in my bedroom with my phone turned off.

I wake to the sound of my alarm the next morning, reminding me that I made the decision to go back to school this week. It's more painful than normal to drag my exhausted body out of bed to get ready. I eventually leave the house only five minutes later than I usually do, which surprises me because I feel like I've been moving in slow motion.

I'm feeling much better by lunchtime, but that could just be because I've had a call from my tutor who had found a school in Oxford willing to offer me a placement. The best thing about it is that they're happy for me to start as soon as possible.

By the end of the day, I had everything organised, and I would be starting at my new school on Monday after having two lesson observations this week. It does mean the assignment that was due in two weeks now needs to be in by the end of this week, but I figure that it's going to get me back to Jax sooner, so it's all worth it.

The only thing I have left to arrange is Ryan and Jax. I've decided I'm not going to tell Jax—I want it to be a surprise—but I need a back-up just in case he doesn't want me living with him. I mean, we've only been back together for just over a week. Just because I'm ready to commit to spending the rest of my days with him, doesn't mean he's quite there yet.

It's ten to four on Friday when I finally submit my assignment. I flop back in the chair with a huge smile on my face. I've done it. I've completed my essay and, amazingly, I'm actually really happy with it. I feel awful that I haven't really been able to speak to Jax much this week with the amount of work I've had to do, plus the added job of packing my stuff up, but I'm hoping his face when he arrives later will be well worth it. I've just about managed to keep a lid on my plan, and he's currently driving here to spend the weekend with me... or so he thinks. What's actually going to happen is that we're going to load his car up, just like mine will be in a few minutes, and we're going to head straight back down to Oxford to start my new life. Sarah and Eve have gone out to give us some privacy. They're packing up Eve's stuff for her to move in when

I've gone. The three of us had a meal together last night to say goodbye. It won't be the end for us, though—they are too important to me to leave them behind.

An hour later, and I have as much stuff squeezed into my car as I can. I move it down the street so he can't see the boxes inside. The rest is going to have to go in Jax's. It's only now as I pace the floor of the living room that the nerves start to flutter around my stomach. What if I've made a mistake? What if he doesn't want me in Oxford? What if he's changed his mind about us?

It's nearly eight o'clock when I see the lights of Jax's car pull up on the drive. I stand at the window and watch him look at the empty space with a concerned look. He must think I've gone out. I continue watching as he steps out of his car and stretches after his long drive. Maybe the plan to drive back tonight was crazy. He probably just wants to crash. Shit.

The buzzer going off pulls me from my worrying, and I head over to let him in. The minute I see him, all my earlier concerns fly straight out the window. He grabs me and pulls me into him for a heart-stopping kiss.

"I know it's only been five days, but I feel like I haven't seen you in forever. I hate you being so far away from me," he says when he's finished kissing me half to death.

"I know, I've missed you, too."

"I'm surprised you've had time with how busy you've been." I would be worried I've pissed him off, but he says it with a smile.

"Come with me, I have a surprise for you," I say, grabbing his hand and leading him to my bedroom.

"Does it involve handcuffs?" he asks in a slightly deeper voice than a few seconds ago, making me squeeze my thighs together. *Not yet, Abigail. You have a plan, remember? And fucking him isn't part of it... yet!*

I bring us to a stop outside my closed bedroom door. I don't know what he's expecting, but from how fast his chest is rising and falling, I'm thinking it's definitely not what he's going to find.

I swing the door open and Jax looks around the room before turning to look at me. "What?" he asks, looking confused, then looking at my empty room again. His eyes land on the boxes at the end of the bed when I pull him in.

"Are you... moving, Abs?"

"I am. I haven't told you, because I didn't want to disappoint you if I couldn't make it happen, but..." I trail off as I pull him over to sit on the edge of my bed. "When I spoke to my tutor last week at your place, I asked him if there was any chance I could change my placement. I explained the situation, and he said he'd look into it. I also asked Ryan to put the feelers out with some of the primary schools he's in contact with and—"

"You're coming to Oxford?" Jax interrupts. He looks like a little kid bouncing with excitement on the edge of the bed. I can't help but laugh at him.

"I am," I say, but end up screaming the last bit as Jax launches himself at me and holds me in a death grip.

"Oh my God, I love you, Abbi. I love you. I love you. This is amazing. I can't believe it." He pulls back and places both his hands on my cheeks and looks into my eyes. "You're being serious, right? This isn't a joke?"

"I'm serious."

The look in his eyes right now melts my heart. I don't think I've ever seen him look so happy.

"Marry me?" he says, then instantly looks panicked by his question. "Shit, that wasn't meant to happen like that. I'm sorry," he says, looking down at his lap. "Fuck."

"Jax."

"No," he says, getting up and pacing the floor. "Shit, that wasn't meant to come out. Can you just forget I said that? It's not that I don't want to ask you, but it's meant to be perfect, and I just royally fucked it up."

He continues mumbling incoherently as he starts wearing a hole in the carpet. I sit frozen on the spot as what he said settles into my brain. Something tells me I should be feeling panicked about this. I mean, we've only been back together a week, but I'm not—I actually feel ecstatically happy. It was only a few hours ago that I was thinking about wanting to spend my life with this amazing man, and he's asked me to do just that. I lift my eyes up to him and watch. He's wearing a black hoodie with the sleeves pushed up and slim tan chinos tucked into his boots. His hands would be running through his hair at a rate of knots, but seeing as he hasn't got any now, he's just rubbing his head. His face clearly shows all his frustration with himself for what he's just done. He's frowning, his mouth is slightly downturned, and he's still muttering quietly. It's really quite amusing when I think about it.

I stand up and get in his way. Unfortunately, he doesn't stop until he crashes into me. His arms come around my waist to hold me up and stop me falling on my arse.

I lift my hands up to his face, loving the feel of his stubble under my palms. "Have you finished?"

"I'm so sorry, Abbi, that wasn't supposed to happen. I've been planning all this stuff and—"

I cut him off before he starts rambling again. I look straight into his green eyes before saying, "No, that probably wasn't the best proposal of all time, but I couldn't care less, Jax. I love you more than anything and want to be by your side forever. It doesn't matter how you ask me. My answer would always have been the same. Yes."

"Yes?" he whispers, looking confused. "But I... that was—"

"Yes, Jax," I repeat.

"But I haven't even got the ring." I can't stop thoughts of my grandmother's ring flitting through my mind. That's never going to happen; Mum would never give it to Jax. Not that it matters, because I'll have the most incredible man on my arm and whatever he has chosen for me will be perfect, because it's from him. "I'm going to do this again properly. I promise."

I go to argue, but I can see from the look on his face that there's no point. He's clearly disappointed in himself, and he obviously wants it to be perfect, so I'll let him have his moment.

"Okay... shall we get this stuff in your car and head home?"

"We're going now?"

"Yeah, I thought it would be better to get there as soon as possible. I've arranged with Ryan that I can stay there if you—"

"Hang on, you're moving to Oxford but staying with your brother?"

"No, I just organised that in case you weren't ready for me to move in with you. As I was surprising you, I didn't want to force you into having me."

"Are you fucking serious?" he asks, frowning again. "Do you really think I'd let you live at Ryan's?"

"Well no, not really, but I needed a back-up plan," I shrug.

"God, I love you. Come on, the sooner we get all this crammed into my car, the sooner we can be home." He goes to grab a box but stops and looks back at me. "Hang on, you're telling me I've got to drive back for over three hours, alone?"

"Uh yeah, but when we get there, I won't be leaving again!"

"Yeah okay, it's worth it. Come on."

***

The minute we both pull away with our cars loaded down with my stuff, my phone rings. I smile to myself when I see who it is and hit the answer button on my steering wheel.

"Hey baby, I miss you."

"You just left me like, two minutes ago."

"I know."

It continues all the way home. In a way, it's like we're in the same car. He tells me about his week, and I tell him about mine now I can reveal exactly what I've been doing. I tell him about my new school, and he continuously tells me how much he loves me and how lucky he is. By the time we pull up at his building, my cheeks actually hurt from smiling so much.

It's well past midnight by the time we have all my boxes inside Jax's flat. Thank God for the lift! I sit myself down on the sofa while I wait for him to get us some drinks.

My eyes widen when he walks in with a very expensive bottle of champagne and two glasses.

"So, you just happened to have that chilling?" I ask with a laugh.

"Actually, yeah. I was hoping to need it in the near future, so when I bought it I shoved it straight in the wine cooler."

My heart turns over in my chest when it hits me that he was actually going to propose, and it wasn't just a spur of the moment thing. My heart then starts pounding when I see him reach into his hoodie pocket and pull out a box I recognise. No, it can't be. Can it?

He slowly lowers himself on one knee in front of me and pulls the lid open. I gasp in shock. There in his hand is my grandmother's ring. How the fuck did he do that? Tears instantly start pouring down my cheeks. I look from the ring up to Jax's eyes—they're the same colour. This ring was meant for us.

"Abbi," he says, bringing me from my thoughts. "I've been waiting for you all my life. You make my heart beat faster when you're in the room, and you make me feel like you've taken it with you when you leave. I've never met someone I can be myself with completely, and have you love me the way I am. I never want to spend a day without you in my life, or my bed, again. You are my everything. Abigail Evans, will you marry me?"

"Yes," I squeal before dropping down on my knees with him and crashing my lips to his. When I pull back, I see that his eyes are almost as wet as mine, but they're sparkling with happiness.

He reaches down and grabs my left hand before pulling the ring from its box and sliding it on to my ring finger.

"Jax, how did you get this?" I ask once I've calmed down slightly.

"Your mum sent it down for me via Ryan. It's sort of a long story, which I will explain, but right now I want to make love to my fiancée."

CHAPTER EIGHT

Jax

I'm still shocked by the turn of events that led to this. The night after I was given the ring, I decided to bite the bullet and ring her parents. Her dad answered, so I thanked him for the ring and explained that I was already planning how to best pop the question to her without their interfering, but I was grateful that I was now able to give her the ring she'd been dreaming of. Much to my relief, he told me that he fully supported us, and that he would explain all this to his wife when she got home. When my phone rang just over an hour later with the same number, I was surprised to find Abbi's mum at the other end in tears. She apologised and explained how scared she'd been for Abbi, knowing she'd been seeing me but not being able to meet me. I understand her concerns, as this was how it had all started before. We had a very long chat, and although I doubt we'll ever get along like a house on fire, I think we'll be okay.

I scoop Abbi up in my arms. It makes me smile when I look down at her, because it looks like I'm practising carrying her over the threshold on our wedding night. God, I hope she doesn't want to have a long engagement, because I cannot wait for her to have my name and be my wife.

I place her on her feet at the end of the bed, pull her jumper over her head, and slide her jeans down her legs so she's standing before me in just her sexy lace underwear.

"I've got a present for you to unwrap." She looks at me, confused, but soon gets the idea when I nod down to myself.

She wraps her fingers around the bottom of my hoodie and I lift my arms up for her, bending at the knees to help her. Once she's exposed my chest, I hear her gasp, so I know she's revealed her surprise. She quickly rids me of my hoodie and I look down to see her tracing a line with her finger around the plaster stuck to my left pec. Just the simple touch from her has my skin breaking out in goosebumps.

"What have you done, Jax?"

"My dad only has one tattoo. It's my mum's name and their wedding date right over his heart. When I was old enough to appreciate its meaning, I decided that one day I would do the same. Did you never notice that it was pretty much the only naked bit of skin?" She nods but doesn't say anything. If the tears in her eyes are anything to go by, I'd say she's too choked up. "Pull it off. Gently," I remind her—these things hurt like a bitch.

Slowly, she picks enough at the corner to grab and starts to reveal what's beneath. The moment she sees it, her hand goes to cover her mouth and her tears break free.

"Oh my God," she says. Her hand drops and she leans closer to get a better look. It's still a bit pink and puffy, but it's clear to see.

"Jax... it's... amazing."

There, permanently etched into my skin, is Abbi's name in an intricate script with patterns and emeralds around it.

"All I need now is to add our wedding date."

I place my fingers under her chin and lift her face up to me. She eventually breaks her gaze away from the tattoo and looks into my eyes. "I love you, Abbi."

"I love you, too," she says quietly, reaching up and placing her lips to mine. Very slowly, I set about making love to my future wife.

EPILOGUE

Abbi

"**D**id you know his tattoo artist is a fucking woman? A hot one at that!"

"Of course I did; she did mine, remember? She's seriously talented," Molly says with a shrug of her shoulders, not seeing what my issue is.

"Her talent isn't in question, Molls. She's had her fucking hands all over my man. She's done all of them, even the one you've seen that goes down his leg. He'd have been lying there practically naked for her to enjoy."

"Jealous much, Abs?"

"Fucking right, I wanted to stab the bitch in the eye with her own tattoo gun. She looked so fucking smug, and the way she looked at him, I swear I nearly lost my shit. He's gonna have to find a new one."

"I think you're blowing this a little out of proportion. Just chill out. Let me see what she did." I carefully pick the plaster off from around my wrist and show Molly my first and only tattoo. It is exactly the same as the one that lies over Jax's heart, but instead of my name it's his, and it's on the inside of my wrist.

"It's stunning, now stop bitching and enjoy your night." I look around at all my favourite ladies together, having a good time celebrating my hen night. Next weekend is our wedding, only five weeks after Jax popped the question. We both quickly realised that we didn't want to wait, so we just went for it. We originally were going to wait till the summer but realised Molly and Ryan's baby was due then, and we wanted them there for us so we brought it forward.

My four bridesmaids, Liv, Sarah, Eve and Molly, all worked together to organise it, and until about an hour ago, I had no clue as to what we were doing, but here I am in a private room of the strip club in town where Molly used to do pole dancing lessons, watching a couple of hot guys prance around said poles. They're quite entertaining to watch, but I'm not sure I want to look at a naked male body other than my fiancé's. I mean, let's face it, his is perfect, so no matter who steps up on the stage, they won't hold a candle to him.

The boys are out at the bar Jax used to work in. He wanted a quiet night with his few close friends and family. Our night looks like it is going to end up being much wilder than theirs.

Suddenly, the music changes and a spotlight showcases a chair in the middle of the stage. Four pairs of hands grab onto me, pulling and lifting me onto it before some guy dressed in a very skimpy army uniform comes and starts dancing around me. I look around at my ladies and see everyone enjoying themselves, at my expense, as I sit here trying not to get a face full of arse or dick. I notice my mum and Emma looking very sheepish over in a booth on the far side of the room. Now, I totally get why my mum is hiding, but why isn't Emma with Molly, Liv and Susan, shouting and screaming?

Once all the fun and games are over, and the now naked dancer is getting groped by a number of my hen party, I sneak off, grab a drink and go and sit with Emma, who's now alone.

"Hey, what's up? You never seen a naked man before?" I ask with a laugh, but the blush that creeps up Emma's face tells me everything I need to know. "Oh!"

"Abbi, don't start, I don't need a man. I'm quite fine as I am," she protests.

"Fine isn't good enough, Emma. A good man will make you feel great, trust me." I say, wiggling my eyebrows at her.

Molly comes over to join us, and we watch as she tries to squeeze herself and her bump into the booth.

"Molly, we're going to find Emma a sexy man," I announce, and ignore Emma groaning next to me.

"Amen!"

Keep reading for Falling For Ruben

ACKNOWLEDGMENTS

I firstly want to say a huge thank you to my amazing ARC readers for *Ryan*. I was so scared to let people read it after working on both novels for nearly two years, but the messages of support you sent me while you were reading them and the amazing reviews you have written have given me such a confidence boost. I cannot thank you all enough for giving me a chance and for falling in love with Molly and Ryan like I did.

It became clear to me pretty early on in writing Ryan that Abbi and Jax would need a story of their own, and I'm so glad that you all felt the same. I hope you enjoyed finding out more about my feisty blonde bombshell and lovable bad boy!

And of course, my amazing husband for supporting me through this unknown journey and encouraging me when it's needed. I love you x

FALLING FOR RUBEN

FALLING SERIES BOOK #4

To the two most important people in my life: my amazing husband and our gorgeous baby girl. I love you both so much. <3

Emma

I've been at this damn party for ten minutes now, and I really wish I hadn't bothered. A night at home with my coursework would have been more fun. Why do I have to be such a pushover where my twin sister is concerned?

"Come on, you deserve a night off. It'll be fun. Come on, please, Emmie," she pleaded until I caved.

So here I am, sat like an invisible guest at this party, in the corner of the living room. I don't even know the girl whose birthday it is that well.

I look out at all our school friends dancing and laughing, and I can't help but feel like I really don't belong here. If I had a way of getting home, I'm pretty sure I would have left already.

Mum's comments from earlier are still echoing in my head. I'm used to hearing such things, but they still sting. I know they love us all equally, and that I'm just as important to them as Hannah and the other two, but I can't help feeling like I'm the black sheep of the family.

"Ah, angels, you look absolutely gorgeous," Mum said as Hannah and Molly entered the kitchen before we left for the party. I followed by a few seconds. "Oh, Emma, you look... lovely. When did my babies grow into young women?" she said with tears in her eyes.

The worst bit about what she unknowingly said is that it's true. My twin Hannah and her best friend Molly are gorgeous. Hannah has long, golden locks that hang straight down her back. She's tall and has a figure I'd kill for. Molly is much shorter, but she already has a perfect hourglass figure. The boys fall over themselves just to talk to both of them. Me, though... I'm invisible. I'm a whole head shorter than my supermodel looking twin, I have a pear-shaped body, and my thighs and arse are huge. That doesn't mean my boobs are small, though, because they aren't, but I hate them as well. My sister looks so elegant with her tiny frame and flat belly. Mine, on the other hand, sticks out. In some clothes, I swear I look pregnant. No one has said anything about it yet, but I'm just waiting for the slip-up to happen.

So tonight, we're all dolled up to attend this sixteenth birthday party for someone at school. Hannah has on the most awesome pair of flares. They're skintight until they hit her knees, and she's paired them with a cute little crop top, showing off that previously mentioned stomach. Molly looks equally as good in a denim skirt I would be more inclined to describe as a belt, and a long-sleeved crop top. I, however, don't dare wear stuff like that. I swear it would give people nightmares for weeks. I have on a pair of baggy jeans—well, they aren't really baggy, but compared to my sister's skintight ones they are—and a long flowing top to cover my belly, hips and arse. My very average mousy brown hair, in contrast to theirs is, as usual, doing its own thing. It's neither straight nor curly and refuses to let me do either to it.

I feel Hannah turn to look at me and I see sympathy in her dazzling blue eyes as they meet mine. They're the one of two things we have in common. The other is our mouths. We have the same smile and the same full lips. I'd say Hannah's are kissable; I doubt anyone will get close enough to mine to find out.

To put it simply, I feel like a frump compared to them. I love them both dearly, but I'm jealous as hell.

As well as being stunning, Hannah is confident, funny, artistic, clever, and the sweetest person you could ever meet. In contrast, my only positive attribute is that I'm intelligent and good with numbers, which is why I want to be an accountant.

The front door to where the party is being held suddenly slams shut, and everyone turns to look. I can't see anything because I've tucked myself into the corner, but all the girls suddenly go all doe-eyed. I understand why in a matter of seconds when I see Callum round the corner and my body temperature increases, my face turning a bright shade of red at just being in the same room as him.

Oh. My. God. Callum is... well, Callum is a god. He is by far the most popular boy in our school. He's the captain of the football team, and he's fit.

And I don't just mean fit... I mean F.I.T! He's in all the top sets and gets the best grades, and, in case you didn't guess already, he belongs on the front of a magazine. I mean, the boy is stunning. Dark, messy hair, dark eyes you could drown in, dimples... damn, he has it all.

And all the girls want a piece of him.

His only downside is that, apparently, he's let quite a number have that piece. He's already started turning into one of those man whores I read about in my books. It should make him less attractive, but let me tell you—it doesn't.

I watch as he and his crew descend on the dance floor, and I really shouldn't be surprised when he pulls Molly in front of him and starts dancing with her.

I continue watching them but get distracted when Hannah walks up. "Come on, Emmie, at least try to look like you're enjoying yourself."

"I am," I say unconvincingly.

She raises an eyebrow at me knowingly. "Come dance with me?"

Now, I love dancing. Like, *love* it. But there's no way I'm dancing for everyone to see. Nope, that's only for when I'm in my bedroom alone.

One of our friends comes and drags Hannah off, leaving me once again alone. I glance up at Molly and Callum to see that they have their tongues down each other's throats, so I decide to venture to the kitchen for a drink.

When I reappear a while later after chatting with a couple of friends, Molly and Callum are disappearing through the French doors. After a few minutes of watching everyone else, curiosity gets the better of me and I follow them outside.

It's not hard to know where they are. I can hear them moaning and groaning on the other side of the bush. I can hear Callum telling Molly how sexy she is and what he wants to do to her. It makes my stomach turn; it's not what he's saying or doing to her, it's the fact that I'm pretty sure no one will ever say any of those things to me.

I leave them in peace and wander back into the house to find somewhere else to hide until it's all over.

The minute I close our bedroom door, Hannah and Molly start gossiping and giggling like little girls. I guess that small bottle of vodka they had between them earlier is still coursing through their systems.

All I want to do is fall fast asleep and forget this night ever happened.

Forget that the boy I fancy, but have absolutely zero chance of getting, made a beeline for Molly, and did God knows what to her in the garden.

"Soooo... come on, spill it... where did you go with Callum?" I hear Hannah plead.

I desperately don't need to know the answer, so I shove my pillow over my head and try to drown them out. It doesn't work; I can still hear them mumbling and the word sex being mentioned more than once.

Neither of them listens to my complaining about wanting to get some sleep so I can do some work in the morning, so I'm forced to fall asleep listening to them gossiping about something I'm never going to know anything about. No boy is ever going to look twice at me.

CHAPTER ONE

Emma

Present...

"I cannot believe you own Rose Cottage. You've wanted to live in that place since you were like, four!" Molly exclaims when we sit at our table. "And what you've done to it is amazing, Em. No wonder you can't wait to move in."

Two months ago, I collected the keys to my very first home, and I've had builders and decorators in ever since, totally refurbishing it. I never thought I would ever actually own it, But after my twin, Hannah, died in a car accident last year, I started spending time in the village our grandparents used to live in to bring me happy memories, and I started to think about getting my own place. I walked past Rose Cottage every time I came here, and, every time, the memories of us as children warmed my heart.

I had no idea what had happened to the sweet old couple who lived in it, and I hadn't seen them since my return, but one morning, when I walked past, there was an estate agent putting up a *For Sale* sign. Butterflies immediately erupted in my stomach, and my hands got a little clammy at the thought of actually owning the cottage. I marched straight to the café we're sat in now, found the estate agent's number, and demanded a viewing that day. I had no idea how much it was on the market for, but I had to have the chance to look around. It might have been the only opportunity I'd get.

Well, it turned out that the old couple passed away in quick succession just before Christmas. They only had one child and she now lives in America with her husband and two children, so she wanted a quick sale. When the estate agent handed me the paperwork for it later that afternoon, I could not believe my eyes at the price, but that wasn't the only thing I fell in love with that day; not only was the outside a picturesque chocolate box English cottage, the inside, although very dated, was just as stunning with cosy rooms, low windows and open fires—everything I'd dreamed it would be. Something about it made me feel at home instantly, and that was something to be said after a year of feeling completely lost without my twin by my side.

I made another unexpected spur-of-the-moment, completely out of character decision that day. I put an offer in then and there. I was the first and only person to view Rose Cottage. My timing was perfect.

After a quick trip to the bank to sort out the money I would need for a mortgage, as well as what I had as inheritance from my grandparents and what I'd saved myself over the years, the ball started moving and it was only five weeks later that I got the keys.

I don't think I've ever felt more alive than I did that day. It was like I was taking a step forward in my life after months of misery and despair. This house was my saving grace; it was going to help me find myself again.

As soon as the keys were in my hand, I got the builders organised and they started two weeks later. The entire inside of the cottage was ripped out and started from scratch. Now, all that's left is for the flooring to be laid, and a few finishing touches. Then, I'll be moving into my new sanctuary, and I cannot wait. I'm quite happy living with Mum and Dad, but the thought of waking up in that house and looking out over the little garden and the fields beyond has me bouncing my knee with excitement.

"Emma, did you hear a word I just said?" Molly asks loudly, pulling me from my thoughts.

"Huh... sorry, no," I say apologetically.

I look up to see both Molly and Abbi with smiles on their faces. Today was the first time they've seen the cottage since it's been done up. Molly had decided I'd been working too hard, so she organised a day out. We went baby shopping this morning and Abbi and I watched as she bought anything that was remaining in the shop that she and her fiancé, Ryan, Abbi's big brother, didn't already own. Sprout has only six weeks until his— I say his, but we don't know the sex—due date, and the soon-to-be parents are desperate for everything to be perfect and ready for his arrival.

After seeing my house, Molly looked like she was seriously flagging in the heat, so I brought them to the coffee shop I've spent many hours in over the last few months.

"I was saying that I finished your manuscript last night, and I love it. Hannah would be so proud of you," she adds, making my eyes water and causing me to swallow down a huge lump in my throat. She pushes a pile of paper across the table that I didn't see before. "I've highlighted a few edits; nothing much, though. We need to get this published, Emma. The world needs to read it."

So, yeah, I've written a book!

I came to this village after Hannah died to try to remember her, but when I realised there were only so many memories, I decided to write her a future. I'd always been an avid reader, and over the years I've attended many creative writing classes and written a few things just for myself.

But as this story progressed, something inside me said it was good enough.

———

It didn't take me long to write the story, but it has taken me months of editing to feel happy giving it to Molly to read through. I felt sick to my stomach when I handed it over two days ago, but she's put my mind at rest by constantly texting me whilst she worked through it, telling me how much she's enjoying it and wanting to know what's going to happen.

"You're not just saying that to be nice? You really think it's good enough?" Okay, so maybe I'm not totally confident in my new adventure.

"Yes, Emma, how many times do I need to say it? It's as good as my favourite books. Your characters have real depth. They're funny and sexy, and the twists in the storyline keep you gripped right to the end. There is no way this won't do well. We just need to make sure we market it right. I need to discuss ideas for the cover with you and..."

"Sorry for the wait, guys, I'm run off my feet," says the waitress as she places a tray down on the table. I think she must own the place, because in all the hours I've spent here writing, there have only been a couple of times that she wasn't here.

"No problem, thank you," Abbi says as she helps grab the mugs and plates off the tray. As soon as the millionaire's shortbread hits the table, Molly makes a grab for it, making us all laugh.

"What? Sprout wants it," she says with a shrug.

"I brought you extra to apologise for the wait," the waitress says as she also puts a plate in front of Abbi and me.

"She seems nice," Molly says when the waitress has walked off and she's swallowed her mouthful.

"Yeah," I agree.

"You mean you've never spoken to her? You've practically lived in this place for months. You really should put yourself out there to make some new friends, Em."

"I've got plenty of friends," I mumble, before having a sip of my coffee and hoping Molly changes the subject.

Thankfully, she does, going back to discussing my new home before making us both put our hands on her belly to feel Sprout kicking.

"I think it's time Sprout and I headed home for a nap, ladies," Molly eventually announces, yawning.

"I want to be home before Jax, so that's perfect," Abbi adds with a naughty glint in her eye.

Abbi and Jax got married just over a month ago. I have to say it was the nicest wedding I have ever been to. It was small and intimate, with only twenty guests. They got married in the registry office, and then we all went to an Italian restaurant. It was understated, relaxed, and perfect. I have never seen two people more in love than them that day. It almost made me jealous—almost. I am perfectly happy as I am, no matter how much others nag me about finding a man. I know what I want from life, and I can achieve all of that single, thank you very much. From looking at the glint in her eye, I would definitely say that Abbi and Jax are still in that lovey-dovey honeymoon stage. It's almost sickening to see them together.

The waitress comes back looking a little harassed just after Molly's announcement to clear our table for others.

"You know... if you need some help, Emma's mum," Molly says to the waitress while nodding at me, "owns a coffee shop. I'm sure Emma would love to help you out." I see Molly wink at me as she says this; interfering little witch!

"Oh my God, that would be awesome. My part-time girl didn't turn up again, and with the weather being so nice, it's crazy. Are you sure you wouldn't mind?"

I shoot Molly a death glare while thinking about how to answer that question. After all, I can hardly say no, can I? "Uh... yeah... sure."

"Thank you so, so much, Emma. Come over when you've said goodbye to your friends. You don't know how much I appreciate the offer."

Molly and Abbi collect their handbags, but something catches Molly's attention and she walks up to the counter. "Wow, Connie's boyfriend is hot!" she exclaims, pointing at a photo frame behind the counter. Abbi agrees, before they both kiss me on the cheek and disappear out of the door. Now, I have to admit that the photo Molly has just pointed out has caught my eye a number of times. I'd like to say that's because it's the only photo in the whole coffee shop, which is true, but I think it has more to do with the guy Connie's stood next to. As Molly said... he's hot. Now, I very rarely say that about any guy, but there's just something about him. It's his mystical dark eyes, I think, that call to me every time I'm here.

Someone complaining about how long they've been waiting for coffee pulls me from my daydream about the gorgeous stranger and back to what I should be doing.

***

It's just after eight o'clock when Connie locks the door to the coffee shop. I flop down onto the worn leather sofa in front of the large window that looks out over the village green and, after slipping off my flip-flops, place my feet on the coffee table. Connie looks over at me, and I immediately feel guilty about putting my sweaty feet up on the table where her customers eat.

"I'm so sorry," I say, hurriedly putting my feet back down.

"Don't. I was just thinking how comfortable that looked. I don't think I've sat down since getting out of bed this morning; my feet are killing me," she says, as she slumps down beside me and copies my pose once she's pulled her phone out. "Ugh," she complains after tapping the screen for a few seconds. "I should have known."

"Everything okay?" I ask, although I don't feel like I really know her enough to pry.

"Yeah, the guy I'm seeing has bailed on me again tonight. I should have seen it coming. Hey, let me buy you dinner to say thank you for helping me out today; I don't know what I would have done without you."

"You don't need to do that. I actually enjoyed myself. All your customers are so sweet here."

"Yeah, they are, especially the regulars. But I need to say thank you, so I'm not taking no for an answer. I'm not thinking anything flash, mind you, I'm too exhausted. How do you feel about finishing up here, then stopping off at the chip shop? I've already got a bottle of wine chilling in my fridge."

"You really don't have to," I say again, but over the last few crazy hours I've kinda warmed to Connie and would quite like the opportunity to get to know her a little better. From what I can tell so far, I think we're going to get on well. I hate to admit it, but Molly could well be right; I could do with some more friends. I've hidden myself away since the accident and just kept my family and closest friends around me. Moving here is a new start for me, and maybe a new friend is just what I need. "But I could totally eat fish and chips right about now!" I tag on, because I don't want her changing her mind if I refuse too much.

It only takes us an hour to finish up and to be pulling into Connie's driveway with our dinner. Her parents own an old farmhouse on the edge of the village, and Connie lives in a converted barn on the grounds. She explains to me how her dad's building company did the work a few years ago when they were quiet. Her brother moved into it first, then she did a few years later. She briefly gives me a tour of the downstairs. It's stunning with its exposed beams and highly contemporary decoration. I don't get to explore upstairs, because that's her brother's domain, apparently.

Once Connie has retrieved the wine, she joins me, sitting on the opposite huge, soft, brown sofa to me. God, I could lose hours on this thing with a good book. We both curl our legs up under us and get stuck in our food.

"That was amazing, but I really need to start being good," I say after licking my fingers free of salt and grease. Having sat back after putting my plate on the coffee table, my protruding belly catches my eye and reminds me of the weight I've gained over the last few months. I've always been on the larger side. I guess if you were being nice, you'd call me curvy, but my comfort eating has pushed that to a whole new level. My usual snug-fitting size twelves have turned into size sixteens. I know I should have done something about it before it got this far, but I've been so lost that I just didn't care. But I want to be happy again. New home, new life, new me. It is definitely time.

"It's okay to be bad every now and then," Connie says, trying to make me feel better.

"Yeah, but the problem is I've been bad every time recently!"

"Oh!"

"You can get away with it," I say, looking her over. Connie has some great curves, exactly what I crave, and I bet the guys fall over themselves trying to get at her. She's also quirky as hell, with her inverted blonde and pink bob that sits just above her shoulders, and her rock chick ripped jeans and band t-shirt that she changed into when we arrived. She has way more style than me. I feel like her frumpy older sister in my bog standard a-little-too-tight bootleg jeans, and a navy polo shirt that doesn't cover my muffin top like it used to.

That's how I always used to feel, growing up with a twin as stunning and elegant as Hannah.

The memory of her chokes me up a little, so I change the subject to something safer. The last thing I want to have to do is explain my reason for being upset. "So, won't your brother mind that I'm here?" I see Connie look at me quizzically before deciding to answer my question.

"No, he's in Australia. Has been for five months now. I can't wait for him to come home; I miss him so bad." I see her glance across at a photo on the sideboard of her and a blond-haired, good-looking guy. What is it about everyone I know being surrounded by good-looking men? I mean, first there was Ryan, followed by Jax, but now Connie has both the guy she's seeing and her brother, who also look like they could grace the cover of a magazine and not look an inch out of place.

Connie goes on to explain that Ruben, her brother, and his best friend have gone on a six month 'gap year', surfing in Australia. She tells me all about how they both work for her dad, but once Ruben is back he'll be taking over the reins of the company so their dad can semi-retire.

Before we know it, it's gone midnight. The second bottle of wine is almost empty, and we've watched at least four old episodes of *Sex and the City* while chatting away. I've never met someone I've instantly connected with like this. It's like we've known each other forever.

"So, tell me about your boyfriend," I say to Connie as I take a sip of my newly filled wine glass.

"I wouldn't call him my boyfriend. We're just... keeping each other company when we need it." I'm not sure I totally believe this, after seeing the photo of them together in the coffee shop. They looked really happy and comfortable with each other.

"Connie... just call a spade a spade. You're telling me you're friends with benefits. I was under the impression it was more than that, from the little bits you've said."

"No, not really. We hang out every now and then, but it isn't, and never will be, anything serious. Plus, I'll have to put an end to it before Ruben comes back, because he hates Elliot."

"Surely that's none of his business." I say this, but if I spin the situation around and it was either me or my little sister Lilly dating someone Dec hated, then I can only imagine his reaction. Dec may be the youngest, but, being the only boy, he is fiercely protective of us, and I get the impression that Ruben may be the same with Connie.

"They've hated each other for years—since primary school, I think. They went through school being rivals for everything: best grades, football captain, most popular... you know what school is like," she says, reminding me of all the things I hated there. All the competition to be the best, the most perfect and popular. I guess that's how it goes when you're that good-looking. It was certainly the case at our school. "And now they have rival companies. Elliot's family are also builders, so they're always competing for jobs. If it's not that, then it's girls. Ruben would kill me if he found out I'd been sleeping with him."

"When's he due back?"

"Just over a month. I've still got time," she says with a wink. "So... boyfriend?"

"No, not unless you count fictional ones."

"Fictional?"

"Yeah, as in book boyfriends. I'm a bit of a romance book whore," I admit.

"Huh... I've read a few romance books, but I've never fallen for any of the characters," Connie says, looking completely perplexed.

"Sounds like you've read romance books... not *romance* books." I go on to give her some suggestions, but when she looks totally overwhelmed I ask her to grab me some paper and proceed to put down some of my favourites. "You've got a Kindle, right?" I ask as I pass my list over to her.

"Uh..."

"Bloody hell, woman." I grab my phone out of my bag and have one ordered for her in minutes. "What's the coffee shop address?" She rattles it off to me and I type it in for the delivery. "There, it will be here Monday. You just need to stock that baby up." I know, I know, talking about books gets me a little overexcited.

I end up sleeping on Connie's sofa after we give up chatting sometime around three AM. It's been great to chat the night away; it reminds me of my days in university when I lived with Molly and Hannah. We often used to stay up half the night setting the world to rights. It's amazing the number of things I find I miss that I had totally forgotten about.

CHAPTER TWO

Emma

It's been a month since the first day Connie and I started chatting, but it feels like I've known her all my life. Instead of coming into the coffee shop, ignoring everyone and hiding in the corner, I now sit up on the stools at the bar and chat away to her while she serves customers and I edit my manuscript. I've even let her start to read it when it's quiet, although she has no idea where the idea came from. I'm still not ready to talk about that. Well, that's when she can pull herself away from the Kindle. I think I've got her hooked!

I've helped out more and more at the coffee shop, seeing as her part-timer never reappeared and I moved into my new place two weeks ago, which is only a short walk from here. I make sure I walk to the high street at least once a day as part of my new healthy eating and exercise programme. I think I'm doing okay; I've lost a little weight since that night with the fish and chips, but more than that, I feel better. With Connie's help, I've been eating really well. Apparently, her brother is a health nut, so she's picked up some dishes from him. Most nights we eat together, either she'll come to me or I'll go to her. I've found a back way to hers through some fields, so I get even more exercise on the days I go there. I've even started trying to run it! I thought I was dying the first couple of times I tried it, but it's slowly getting easier. I need to make the most of it, though, because I will not be trekking through the fields once the summer is over.

As I grab a chocolate muffin for a customer, I look at the *Emma, keep out!* sign taped to the back of the display stand as a reminder to me to stay away. I glance at the bowl of fruit Connie keeps stocked up next to it and laugh to myself. She may not have been in my life very long, but I'm already not sure how I would cope without her. I'm starting to feel like a new me, and she has a lot to do with that. Her happy, cheeky personality would lift anyone's spirits, and I've never known someone to smile as much as she does.

I've been in the coffee shop all morning while Connie is at the hairdresser's. I see a flash of purple and blue as she comes rushing in, shouting her apologies for how long she's been, before promising she'll be back and disappearing into the office. I just look back from the door she went through when the hairs on the back of my neck stand on end and a shiver runs through my body.

When I look up, I lock on to a very familiar set of dark eyes. My breath instantly catches in my throat, and my body freezes.

I watch as he runs his hand through his dark brown hair as he looks back at me. It's much longer than in the photo, showing just how old it really is. Not only does Connie have long, mousy brown hair—not the sleek, colourful style she has now—but his hair is now falling in a shaggy mess around his face and onto his neck, not cut into a neat style. He also has pretty long scruff on his face, like he hasn't shaved for some time. If it wasn't for the eyes that I feel follow me around this place whenever I'm here, I don't think I would recognise him.

My brain starts to work the closer he gets, and I start to wonder why he's here. Connie was meant to have broken up with him because her brother is due back tomorrow. She will not be impressed with him turning up like this. It's weird, because with all the time I've spent here and with Connie in the last month, I have never seen him in person. I was starting to think he was a myth.

Before he gets to the counter, I run my eyes down his body. Something happens in that moment that I have never experienced before. My heart starts to pound, and I start to sweat. Yeah, I've been nervous before, but never has just the sight of another person caused this reaction in me. Not even when I fancied the pants off Callum in school.

He's wearing a very loose-fitting black vest that hangs so low on the sides that he might as well not be wearing it. It shows off way too much bronzed skin and sculpted muscle. I continue down to see a pair of long khaki board shorts, and, finally a pair of flip-flops on his feet.

Sweet Jesus, even his feet are hot.

Wait, what the hell is wrong with me? I never, ever have thoughts like this. I sound like a girl in one of my books, standing here drooling over the guy my friend has been sleeping with. I don't even notice that what he's wearing doesn't at all match the miserable grey and rainy weather outside. My thoughts are too jumbled up by his hotness.

"Is... uh... Connie about?" he asks in a deep, sexy voice. Nothing he says registers, and the only reaction I have is to snap my eyes back up to his magical ones. Now he's closer, I can see that they're the same colour as the espresso here but with flecks of gold which catch the light and really soften his face, making him seem a little less intimidating with his perfect nose, square jaw and sharp cheekbones.

I bite down on my bottom lip and continue to stare at him. The old me is screaming at me to get a grip, but the new me is enjoying the feelings this guy is giving me.

So this is what it feels like, I think to myself as I continue to stare. He doesn't look away, either, although there's nothing about me to look at. I'm wearing a denim skirt that's long enough and loose enough to cover all my now slightly smaller lumps and bumps, and a white 'Connie's Coffee and Cake' t-shirt that I managed to throw chocolate powder over a couple of hours ago. When I see his eyes flick down and focus in one place, I shouldn't be surprised. If I were watching this play out with any other man and woman, and the woman was wearing a t-shirt that had a slightly too low V-neck for her oversized boobs, I would expect him to stare. But this is me we're talking about: the overweight, frumpy, less than average looking girl who is currently covered in chocolate and smells like coffee.

I feel my face heat the longer he stares. The flush hits my cheeks before it travels down my neck and onto my chest. I see his tongue sneak out to wet his bottom lip, before his mouth opens like he's going to say something, but we both get distracted by high-pitched screaming from across the room.

"OH MY GOD!" Connie squeals, as she runs and launches herself at him. He just about gets his senses back as she flies through the air at his body. She clings on to his neck and wraps her legs around his waist. He holds on to her just as tightly. My brow quirks in question.

It's not until Connie pulls away from him with tears spilling down her face and her bottom lip trembling that I realise something isn't right here.

"I didn't think you were back until tomorrow," she says, looking at him like he's a god.

"I lied to surprise you," he says in his sexy voice that makes my knees a little weak. "Surprised?"

"Oh my God, yes. It's so good to see you. And I've been dying to introduce you to Emma. Emma, this is Ruben, my big brother," Connie says, smiling up at him like he's the most amazing person in the world, so she misses whatever odd and shocked expression must pass across my face. Ruben spots it, though, and looks at me questioningly.

"Nice to meet you," he says, returning his focus to me. He stares straight into my eyes, and it renders me motionless for a few seconds. This is not good.

"I've... uh... got to go... I've had a call from work. It's uh... urgent."

Connie barely hears my words, because she's still staring at Ruben like he could disappear at any moment. I swear I see disappointment wash over his face as he continues looking at me. Maybe it's just the bit of cleavage I have on display. I mean, he's spent months with bikini-clad girls, then twenty-four hours on a plane; maybe he's missed looking at it!

I watch as Ruben gives Connie a shove and nod in my direction before she thanks me for the morning and promises to ring me later.

As I grab my stuff to leave, I listen to the siblings' conversation behind me.

"Where's Fin?" Connie asks, sounding slightly disappointed after her earlier excitement.

"He went straight home to see his dad," Ruben responds, but when I glance back I see that he's not at all focused on Connie. His eyes are actually locked on where my arse was bent over to get my bag out of the cupboard. *It's definitely time I got out of here*, I think as I say my goodbye to Connie, nod at Ruben, and practically run from the coffee shop like a lunatic.

When I get home, I realise I've jogged all the way without having to stop for a breather. My chest swells with pride and achievement, maybe I can do this.

I enter my cottage through the back door, grab myself a glass of water, and sit on one of the stools at my breakfast bar.

What the fuck was that?

I feel like I've just acted out a scene from a book that I didn't quite believe ever really happened in real life—just like I don't really believe that men can be quite so fiercely in love with their women that makes them act the way they do in a book. I mean, it's just fiction. Fantasy. It's what women want to read about: the perfect man, the white knight ready to ride off into the sunset with.

I gulp down my water and think about all the reasons the feelings I just experienced are very, very wrong. Firstly, I do not, never have, and never will want a man. I am, and always have been, happy on my own. Secondly, that was Connie's brother, not 'friend', who I was lusting over. She has told me all about him and his ways with women, and the competition he has with Elliot over them. I don't want to be involved with that or with him.

I spend the afternoon at my desk, looking out over my little garden and working on my manuscript, but I can't really concentrate. I keep relating anything that happens in the story between the guy and girl back to Ruben and me this morning.

"ARGH... this is not helping," I shout, as I push myself back from the desk in a huff.

Maybe I should have just gone to work like I told Connie. I've got plenty I could do there, but I've already done my hours for this week. I've loved working part-time over the last few months; it's allowed me time to get the house sorted, but also to make good progress on my book. But right now, being at the office all the hours God sends like I used to seems like a good distraction.

I need to do something about my pent-up energy so I decide to have a go at another run. I change into my running clothes, making sure my boobs are securely fastened into my sports bra, grab a bottle of water and my iPod, and head off.

Ruben

All I want to do is sleep for a week, I think as I strip down to my boxer briefs and slide into my bed. Ah, there's nothing like your own bed! The last six months have been nothing short of amazing —a once in a lifetime experience. But I am so ready to be home and back to normal life again. After non-stop partying the last two weeks, then the long flight home, all I want to do is sleep. I would have done that as soon as I got back a couple of hours ago, but I knew Connie would never forgive me, so after dumping my stuff, I headed straight to her coffee shop.

She was the one thing I worried about when I left. After all her friends left the village for bigger lives after they graduated, Connie has been kinda lonely, although she'd never admit it. She clung on to me—and Fin, which I was not happy about—when they all left. Don't get me wrong, it's not that I mind; I love my sister dearly, and other than Fin, I'm not ashamed to say she's my best friend. There's nothing we don't share. Well, almost. There are some things siblings don't need to know about each other's lives.

I made sure I video call her at least once a week so I could check up on her, and she always seemed to be doing okay. A little sad, but okay. It wasn't until a month ago that I saw a real change in her. She explained to me all about meeting Emma, and I was thrilled she had someone to spend time with again and to do all the kinds of stuff girls do together.

Although I'd never met Emma, I felt like I'd known her for years with the detail Connie would go into, telling me about her new friend. I know about her job, the book she's writing, and the diet and exercise regime Connie has started helping her with. I've also seen pictures, and it's those pictures that have helped with me wanting to come home. One look at her cornflower blue eyes, contrasting golden skin and dark hair, mixed with her sweet smile, and I was enthralled. I can't explain it, but something about her spoke to me, even in a photograph that was thousands of miles away.

I could see from the photos Connie sent why Emma is set on losing some weight. Now, don't get me wrong, I'm a guy who loves—and I mean loves—a curvy girl. But from living with Connie, I can see how she might be self-conscious. To me, her body is banging. Everyone says that you are either an arse or boob man; call me greedy, but I'm both. I'd have a girl with a great rack and an insane booty any day over those stick thin, nothing to grab onto girls that Fin goes for. Okay, so granted it's kinda hard to see her curves under the baggy clothes she always seems to wear, but that's what I'm imagining, and I've been dying to see if I'm right.

What I wasn't expecting was that Emma would be the first person I would see on my arrival home. I saw her behind the counter of my sister's coffee shop the moment I walked in front of the window. I watched her for a second as she stared at the display of cakes with longing in her eyes. She's obviously still dieting, then!

I couldn't take my eyes off her from the minute I walked through the door. Much to my delight, she was exactly what I was imagining. Well, her top half anyway, because she was behind the counter. Her dark hair was pulled back from her face, showing her flawless skin. Her eyes were bright as she looked back at me, and the moment she bit down on her plump bottom lip, I instantly got a semi.

I made my way down her neck to see exactly what I was hoping for: a great rack. No, great probably doesn't begin to explain how fucking awesome her tits are. And what was even better was that the t-shirt she was wearing was a little on the tight side—and a lot on the low side—so I got a great view of her cleavage. I knew I was still very obviously checking her out as I walked up to the counter and asked where Connie was, but I couldn't help it; I couldn't get enough of her. As I got closer, I saw that she was covered in chocolate powder. It covered one side of her boob and was sprinkled across her cleavage. Good God, how badly did I want to lick that off? I leaned my hips against the counter when I got there, because I felt like I had no control of my body around her. I really didn't need to introduce myself to my sister's stunning friend with an obvious raging hard-on.

I got distracted by my sister when she came running at me. She looked so different from when I left. It was only a matter of weeks before her long brown hair was gone in favour of short bleach blonde locks with alternating crazy colours. It seems that it's purple and blue this week. I was worried about her sudden image change when I left, but it seems to have helped her find herself. She has an identity now, and she's morphed into an independent adult—not that she wasn't pretty independent before, seeing as she had her own business by the age of twenty-two. To say I'm proud of what my little sister has achieved would be an understatement.

"What was that about?" I asked Connie after Emma gave some excuse about work and all but ran away. I guess she was running away from me, if her deer-caught-in-headlights look was anything to go by.

"Don't know. I'll check in with her later and make sure she's okay. So, come on, take a seat. I want to hear everything."

"I've spoken to you every week since I've been gone. You already know everything," I said, laughing.

"Yeah, but it's not the same as you telling me when you're actually here, in front of me."

I finally managed to get away from Connie's incessant questions just over an hour later. I walked up to our front door, thinking that I should probably pop into the main house to see Mum and Dad, but I was exhausted. I'm sure they'll understand. I'm going to see them later, as Connie has already rung them and organised a family meal for tonight to celebrate my homecoming.

I only get a couple of hours' sleep. My messed-up sleep pattern combined with the memory of those cornflower blue eyes have me tossing and turning until I give up and get up, shower and dress. I try sitting and watching the TV while I wait for Connie to get home, but I can't settle, so I grab my running shoes and head out. I usually run every day, and being cooped up on an aeroplane has my muscles twitching for some exercise. I head off on my usual ten mile route and instantly feel better. I head out the back of our parents' land and into the fields beyond, until I hit the pavement at one end of the high street and make my way through the tourists taking in the sights. I continue, and I'm about to head back into the fields on my return journey when the sight of a familiar arse bent over while its owner heaves for breath stops me in my tracks. I can't help but stop and stare, even though she's obviously suffering. She's wearing skintight leggings with a baggy white t-shirt over the top, but it's currently hitched up, giving me my awesome view. As I get closer, I see that she has her hands on her knees and her eyes are shut as she tries to regulate her breathing. She's beetroot red, and the sweat is pouring off her, thanks to the break in the clouds and some summer sun streaming down.

"You okay?" I ask, leaning down slightly so I can see into her eyes when she opens them. She startles and screams at my words. "Shit, sorry. I didn't mean to scare you."

I didn't think it possible, but when she does look at me, her cheeks blush even redder with embarrassment. "Don't worry, I was just trying to... uh... not die. I'm fine though, you carry on."

"You've only just started running, right?"

"Is it that obvious?" she asks, flashing me a cute smile.

"Yeah! I could help you train, if you'd like. Show you the ropes and some good places to run around here."

"Uh..." She looks very unsure of herself all of a sudden. "It's okay, you don't need to put yourself out like that."

"Don't be silly. I run every day, and it can get lonely sometimes." Okay, so this is a total lie. One of the reasons I like running so much is because I get to be alone with my thoughts, but the pull of being able to spend some time with Emma is too much. *Ruben, what the hell is wrong with you? Did you leave your balls in Aus?* "Did you do any stretches before you started?"

"Um... no."

"Okay, let's do some now while you catch your breath. They'll help you ache less tomorrow if you do them properly."

CHAPTER THREE

Emma

I use the handrail up the stairs to help pull my exhausted body toward the bathroom. I begin stripping off as I make my way to the shower and turn it on once I'm there. As soon as the water is warm, I stand under and let it soothe my aching muscles. I'd been out with Ruben for just over an hour, and he seriously put me through my paces. I should be embarrassed by my pathetic level of fitness, but I'm so knackered right now that I really don't care. Plus, his support should really help with my weight loss. I feel like I could have lost a stone already with the amount of exercise he made me do.

I can still feel his hands skimming up my legs when I was stretching. He was pointing out where I should be feeling the pull, but all I could feel were the tingles running up my legs and awakening places in me that I didn't know were asleep—or existed.

For some reason that I'm still unaware of, I've agreed to meet him again tomorrow afternoon for another session. I'm not entirely sure how I went from not wanting to be near him after meeting him for the first time and discovering he was Connie's older brother, to agreeing to spend more time with him tomorrow. I rationalise that I'm only doing it because I want to lose weight and he can help me with that, and that it's got nothing at all to do with the pull I feel toward him, which has only got worse now I've met him in real life. Nothing to do with that at all.

When I get out and dressed, I check my phone and see that I've got a missed call from Connie. I'm surprised she remembered; I thought she'd be too distracted by Ruben's arrival.

"Hey, how are you doing? I heard you spent the last hour training with Ruben. He can be a tyrant when it comes to exercise."

"He definitely pushed me to my limit," I say, but I don't think Connie understands quite how badly that was—and not just with the exercise. Having him so close, sweaty and smelling amazing was challenging to say the least.

"You okay? You sound weird."

"Um... yeah... no, I'm fine. Just knackered," I say, very unsuccessfully.

"Right," she says but luckily changes the subject. "So, Mum and Dad are doing a barbeque to celebrate Ruben being home. Do you want to come?" In all the time we've spent together this month, I am still yet to meet Connie's parents. I'm thinking tonight isn't the time, though; with their son having been away for so long, they won't want some randomer there.

"No, not tonight. I'm just going to chill out on the sofa with a book. Maybe next time, yeah?"

"Awesome, so you'll come to ours for a meal tomorrow night, then. I'm cooking Ruben's favourite. Come round after your workout with him."

Wow, I totally walked right into that one. "Yeah, okay," I agree, because there isn't much else I can do at this point. I mean, spending more time with him than I've already agreed to won't be that bad, surely? All my messed up feelings are just in my head, anyway. It's not like he's thinking the same things, so I should be able to just give myself a good talking to and get on with my life. My normal, ordinary life, where men don't exist and I am more than happy.

I do some cleaning, albeit slowly with my sore legs, and make myself some dinner, but I can't shift the thoughts of Ruben running around my head. I need to talk to someone. Usually that person would be my dad. While my siblings always went running to our mum, I, on the other hand, went straight for my daddy. The problem is, this isn't really a situation I want to discuss with him, and they're also on their once-in-a-lifetime dream cruise that they've been talking about forever. In the end, I pick up the phone and call the one person who I just know is going to have a field day with this.

"Em, you okay?" Molly questions when she answers the phone. I guess she has a right to be concerned; it's not like I've been the best of friends since Hannah died. I really should make more of an effort.

"Uh... yeah. How are you and Sprout doing? Not long to go now," I say, trying to put a little joy into my voice so she doesn't sense that something is up.

"What's wrong?" That worked well, then.

"Nothing, just rang for a chat."

"About anything specific? Has something happened?"

"Um... no not really. It's just... oh it's nothing, I'm just being silly. Come on, tell me about Sprout."

"I'm coming over. Something's up."

"NO!" I shout, a little louder than expected. "Sorry, it's just that you're weeks off giving birth; you don't need to be dragging your backside over here. I'm fine, I just wanted to talk to someone."

"I've already got my shoes on and my keys in my hand. Won't be long," she says, before hanging up on me.

That didn't quite go as I'd planned.

I'm glad to say that things between Molly and me are pretty much back to normal now. I wouldn't blame her if she didn't have time for me after how I treated her at the beginning of her and Ryan's relationship. Hannah and Ryan had been together for years; it was obvious that one day we'd all be attending their wedding and cuddling their babies. I was a bitch to Molly —that's the only way to describe it—when I grew suspicious of them last year. I don't think anyone could blame me, though. It had only been six months since Hannah had died, and it was clear as day that things were heating up with her and Ryan after she moved in with him.

I was a mess.

There is no other way to describe my state of mind back then. I was blind to the fact that they were struggling with the development in their relationship almost as much as I was. They didn't see it coming, either.

An hour later, and Molly is sat on my sofa with a lemonade while I sip the wine she brought, trying to work out what to say. She's been sat there staring at me for a couple of minutes, obviously trying to work out what's going on.

"There's something different about you," she says eventually, looking me up and down. "I mean, there's the obvious weight loss, which looks amazing by the way, but there's more. I just can't put my finger on it."

She continues to stare at me until I snap. "That guy in the photograph at Connie's isn't her boyfriend. It's her brother."

It's all I have to say, because Molly's eyes go wide as saucers before she scares the shit out of me by screaming, "AT FUCKING LAST! WOOHOO!"

I put my glass down before putting my head in my hands and shaking it gently, while I feel the blush spread across my face and down my neck. After a couple of seconds, I feel Molly's arms come around me and listen to her apologise for getting a little excited.

When she moves back, she hands me my wine and tells me to down it before asking me to explain all.

I have to say, I do feel better, having got it all out. Molly just smiles like a Cheshire cat the whole way through. Of everyone over the last few years, it's Molly who has really been on my case about finding a man, but I think even she had resigned herself to the fact that it wasn't going to happen.

"You've seen him though, Molls. There's no way he's going to be interested in me. Ow," I say, as I rub the sore spot on the back of my head where she just slapped me. "What was that for?"

"Every time you put yourself down, I'm going to hit you. Emma, you are gorgeous." She starts at the top. "You've got awesome thick hair, a complexion most women would die for, and stunning blue eyes. Your body, yes, is a little curvier than it was in the past, but it's no less sexy. You've got an awesome set of tits on you that I know for a fact men love, and you've got an arse like Beyoncé—even more so with the exercise you've been doing. Top that off with a little waist and good, shapely legs... you're the whole package. You seem to think all men want tall, skinny, blonde women." I see her cringe a little at the description, because that's exactly what my mum and Lilly are, and what Hannah was. She knows as well as I do that I've spent my whole life comparing myself to them, and hating that I got my dad's genes in the body and hair department. The only things we all have the same are our eyes and mouths, which I am grateful for; otherwise I'd feel even more like the black sheep of the family. "You said it yourself a minute ago that you caught him checking out your tits and arse. You might be his perfect woman, Em, you just don't know. When are you seeing him next?"

"I'm meeting him tomorrow afternoon for a workout, then I'm going to Connie's for a meal. She said she was cooking his favourite, so I guess he'll be there."

I watch her think for a minute before she says, "Okay, perfect. That gives us enough time."

Oh God. "Enough time for what?" I ask with trepidation.

"To go shopping and get you something kick-arse to wear tomorrow night."

I put my hands up in defence. "No, no, no, I'll just go in jeans and a t-shirt. It's only a casual thing, I think, so it won't matter."

"Yes, it bloody well matters. If you want him to notice you, then you've got to make an effort. I'm not suggesting you dress formally, but a nice casual dress that shows off your best assets will not hurt." As she says this, she waves her hands in front of my chest. Okay, yes, I can't argue; she does have a point, and she is right. He was definitely checking out my boobs this morning.

"Molly, I am not wearing this," I shout through the curtain of the dressing room she's put me in with a wardrobe full of dresses. "I don't even think tit tape would make it work!"

"Show me," she shouts back from her perch on the sofa outside.

I feel like I've been cooped up in the little room for a week while Molly and the shop assistant pass dress after dress through the curtain to me. Molly has enjoyed telling the shop assistant, who looks no more than seventeen, all about my situation, as well as every minute of my complaining about this whole disaster.

"No, I feel like I'm totally exposed."

All of a sudden, the curtain is whipped back to reveal Molly, stood with her hands on her hips, looking at my very uncovered chest. I instantly move my hands up to cover them, but she growls at me and pulls them back to my sides.

"Wow," is all she says.

She has me in a mostly black maxi dress covered in exotic, brightly coloured flowers. The fabric is a little bright for my usual choice of clothing, but it's really nice. The problem, however, is the top half. It has wide straps, but the neckline plunges right down to the little bow on my bra, showing off way too much boob in my opinion. Molly could wear this dress and look stunning, but I feel like I might as well be walking about topless.

"Molly, I am not wearing this out in public. I feel like I'm too naked for even you to be looking at me."

"Emma, seriously, you're covered in fabric down to the floor. All you've got is a little bit of cleavage on show; it's nothing. And let me tell you... Ruben will think he's died and gone to heaven when he sees you in this," she says with a wide smile and twinkling eyes. She's enjoying this way too much.

"Holy cow," the shop assistant says when she walks past. "That is definitely the winner. You look incredible."

"See," Molly says with a raised eyebrow.

"I'm sorry, but it's too much. All I'm doing is going to a friend's house for dinner, not a bloody night out."

"Okay, how about we compromise," she says before disappearing.

I look back at myself in the mirror and can't help but think that I do look like a completely different person to the one I did a few months ago. It's like I've got life back in my eyes, and it's clear to see in this figure-hugging dress how much weight I have actually lost. My saggy, wobbly bits are looking much tighter and smoother. Having to send Molly back out for smaller sizes didn't hurt, either.

I eventually caved on the dress when Molly reappeared a few minutes later with a black lace cami in hand. As she said, it covered me up enough to be less self-conscious, but, to her delight, still showed off my tits. Great!

That wasn't the only thing I had to cave on before being able to escape the department store. When we left, my purse was almost four hundred pounds lighter, and I was weighed down with bags containing the dress and cami, along with new workout clothes, a couple of other summer dresses, a skirt and a top. Apparently, this new development in my life needed celebrating with new, sexier clothing, according to Molly. What she doesn't know is that most of this stuff I'll be returning in the next few days. I do not need a whole new wardrobe just to impress a man. I am who I am, and you either like it or lump it.

Well, that thought lasted all of a few hours.

I was so nervous by the time the clock ticked around to an hour before meeting Ruben for our run that the added confidence that went with the new workout clothes actually made me feel that little bit better. I'm waiting for a knock at the door in my new understated black leggings, with a black tank top that looks pretty plain... but turn around and the back is open and exposing my fire engine red sports bra that has some funky strapping across the back. And because it's as supportive as possible to keep my boobs in place, it holds them tight and shows them off nicely just above the top of the low neckline. I would usually feel exposed in this, but after that dress earlier I almost feel like I'm covered top to toe. Plus, I only realise the back is open when I feel a draft, so I can mostly ignore that bit of skin.

I take one last look in the mirror in my hallway before I answer the door to him, and I can't help but wonder what the hell is going on with me. I shrug it off when the door knocks again and go to answer it.

"Wow, you look good, Emma," he says, flashing me a genuine smile that makes a dimple pop up on his left cheek. My heart skips a beat when my eyes first land on him, but I soon snap out of it. I will not be one of those women; I'm not even sure I want to be the one I'm acting like now, to be honest. I give him a once-over before pulling the door shut behind me. He's once again wearing a skintight white t-shirt, but this time his shorts are a little shorter, showing me thighs that are made of pure muscle. Holy hell, this guy is hot. I shake my head and follow him, jogging down my garden path.

———

I can't lie, I feel like a million dollars once I'm ready to head to Ruben and Connie's for dinner. I have the dress on we bought earlier with the cami. It does the job perfectly. I've added a simple pair of flip-flops and straightened my hair, as per Molly's instructions. I'm amazed by how long it is; it's been forever since I've bothered doing anything with it. It's now a long way from its original bob and is resting well down onto my boobs. I refuse to put any make-up on, though. I only very rarely do that, and I know that Connie would see right through me if I turned up wearing it. As Molly said yesterday, I'm lucky with my skin. I very rarely get spots, and with all the outside exercise I've been doing, I've got a nice glow that brings out some of my freckles.

When I walk into Connie's a while later, I find her and the blond-haired guy I recognise from some of the photos in this place sat at her breakfast bar deep in conversation. I'm presuming from chatting to Ruben that this guy is Fin, his best friend. I also get the impression from the very few things that Connie has said about him that there could be some history between them, and looking at how close they're sat chatting doesn't alleviate any of my suspicions. I end up having to clear my throat to get their attention.

"Oh, hey, Em. Wow, you look awesome," Connie says quickly, backing away from Fin and coming over to give me a hug. "This is Fin, Ruben's best mate. Fin, this is Emma, who I've been telling you about."

We say our hellos and Connie is just getting me a drink when the atmosphere in the room changes. I don't need to look behind me to know he's standing there. Not only did I hear his footsteps, but the hairs on the back of my neck have been standing on end for a few seconds. I watch Connie and Fin look back and forth between the two of us, but I'm frozen in position. No one says anything, and it's the most awkward few seconds of my life.

After what feels like an eternity, Ruben's rough voice finally breaks the silence, "Chuck us a beer, Con." It does nothing for my statue-like body, because I feel his breath blow through my hair and onto my neck before he grabs a lock and runs his fingers through it while making a low growling noise in his throat. Everything goes back to being silent as he comes to stand in front of me, my hair still in his hand. His dark eyes quickly scan over my face before locking on to my boobs, exactly as Molly had planned. I watch him lick his lips and wait for him to say what he looks like he's building up to.

"Christ, babe," is all he says before turning, taking the beer out of Connie's hand and downing it in one. We all watch him with our mouths hanging open. Now, I don't know Ruben that well, but I'm guessing from Connie and Fin's reaction that that wasn't a normal thing for him to do.

Ruben

What the fuck was that? I've seen plenty of hot chicks before. Hell, I've done much more than look at them, but why does this one have such an effect on me? Why the fuck could I not control any part of my body when I walked into the kitchen to see her dressed like that? Why the hell did I have to run my fingers through her hair like a complete pussy? And why couldn't I just acknowledge her and say hello like any other normal human being?

I've been sat on the sofa for two minutes with my second beer, after having downed the first one that Connie gave me in the hope that it would sort me the fuck out. I mean, I knew she was stunning—that's why I already can't get her out of my head—but that dress. Fuck me, that dress. And that hair. Christ, I don't know what to do with myself. I rearrange myself in my jeans and run my sweaty palms down the denim on my thighs as Fin walks into the room and drops down on the sofa next to me.

"Well, those photos Connie sent through didn't really do her any justice, did they? She's smoking hot. I bet she's—"

"Not interested," I finish for him. There is no way I'm sitting here and listening to him talk about banging her. Any other chick is fair game, but not her.

"Ooooh, you're a little touchy. Want her for yourself, do ya? I shouldn't be surprised, she's so your type. Maybe a little more average than your normal conquests, but hot all the same. And she looks so innocent, I bet she's—" he tries again, but one look at the scowl on my face shuts him up.

He puts his hands up in surrender. "Okay, okay, she's all yours. Not my type, anyway," he says, looking back toward the kitchen where both Emma and Connie are in our line of sight. Why do you think I chose this seat, after all?

"How about we make this interesting," he says, after being quiet for a few seconds too long, which means he's scheming.

"What?" I grumble, because he's distracting me from watching her.

"I bet you can't get her in your bed by the end of the month." I raise my eyebrow at his suggestion, because I have no interest in this bullshit. "Okay, yeah, you're right, she's way too sweet. How about we say by your parents' anniversary party at the end of June. That gives you almost a month to break her down. That's totally doable."

"Fuck off, Fin. We're not eighteen anymore. I'm not making stupid bets with you."

"Pussy. You're just scared she'll reject you and your small cock."

"Fuck off," I growl again.

"How about I sweeten you up with a reward. Other than her sweet, sweet pussy, of course." I just look at him, seriously losing the will to live with this conversation. I have no intention of making Emma a bet. "I know that your mum has already agreed with Danni that you'll take part in the fashion show this year. You weren't here to defend yourself, so she said yes on your behalf. I have also seen what she's expecting you to wear, and it's just too fucking funny, dude."

Danni is a girl we both went to school with. Although a year younger, she did fashion at uni and now lectures at the college. Every year, they put on a charity fashion show to raise money for a local children's charity. Every year, she asks Fin and me to get involved. And every year, we say no. There are many reasons for this. Firstly, I have no intention of being perved on, wearing next to nothing on a runway. I can't think of anything more humiliating. But also because she's a Scott—Elliot Scott's little sister. We have this long-running rivalry, and I want nothing to do with anything that family does. Now, I mostly find this easy, unless he comes looking for trouble, but I find it harder where his sister is concerned. I hate to admit it, because when it first happened, my only motivation was to piss Elliot off, but I took her virginity when she was fifteen, and I have the scars to prove it. But since then, she's always been my go-to girl. I know I shouldn't, but she makes it too easy. She wants the same from me as I do from her, and that's it. We never talk otherwise, and for both our sakes, we stay out of each other's way.

"I am not fucking doing that. She can fuck off."

"It's done, dude, and it's the weekend after your parents' anniversary. Your mum has promised you'll do it."

"Fuck."

"I know a way you can try to get out of it, though. You bang her," he says, looking over his shoulder, "before the party—which you totally won't be able to do; I mean, look at her, she's obviously been sent to tease you, not fuck you," he says, laughing and taunting me, "and I'll do the fashion show for you. I might even get myself a taste of Danni, seeing as you've been keeping her to yourself all these years."

"Guys, dinner's ready," Connie shouts.

"For fuck's sake. Right, fine," I say to Fin, before getting up and joining the girls in the kitchen.

The rest of that evening was pretty torturous for me. I had to listen to Fin tell the girls about my conquests in Australia. I'm guessing it was for Emma's benefit. As much as he thinks she isn't going to sleep with me, he's going to make me look like the biggest dick on the planet to really put her off. During all this, I was sat opposite Emma, trying not to spend the whole night staring at her rack. It was a serious fucking challenge. When Fin's stories got even more exaggerated and ridiculous, I knocked her leg under the table to get her attention so I could shake my head at her to try to let her know that he was being a dick. I'm not sure whether she meant to or not, but I swear, after she gave me a small smile, she ran her foot down my leg softly. It could just be my imagination getting the better of me, though.

Connie and Fin both disappeared into the living room after dinner, leaving me to wash up. Emma was adamant that she was going to help, and I wasn't going to stop her. It used to bother me when Connie and Fin spent time alone together, but those days are long gone. Thankfully, they're just friends, and I don't need to worry about his womanising ways affecting my sister.

I offered to drive Emma back later on in the evening but was disappointed when she said she'd driven and was fine to get back okay. I kinda liked the idea of it being just the two of us in the car and walking her to her door. Could have been an excuse for a little kiss, even if it was on the cheek.

I manage to get a couple of short workout sessions in with Emma over the weekend, but my dad keeps me busy going through everything for the business. I'm meant to be taking over gradually, so he can work part-time. By the time Sunday night rolls around, I think I know what jobs we have on and where all the men are working, including Fin, over the coming weeks, and I have a to-do list from Dad as long as my arm. I'm not sure how I feel about this change so early on in my career. I love being out on building sites and getting my hands dirty. Having to be on the phone and behind a desk most of the time isn't really me, and if he thinks I'm going to be wearing a shirt and tie, then he can fuck right off.

Monday is hectic. I end up working right through until midnight. Thankfully, my mum brings me food to the office, which is another barn on their land, so I don't have to worry about trying to fit in eating alongside everything else I'm trying to get my head around. My dad is great at running the company, but he's a little outdated. It's time to bring Foster and Son into the twenty-first century. I've set up social media accounts for the company, as well as upgrading the website and our company email accounts. Dad looks a little perplexed by the whole thing, but he trusts me and knows I'm right.

I texted Emma during the day to let her know, after Connie gave me her number.

> Ruben: I'm really sorry babe, but I'm going to have to cancel the run tonight. Too busy at work.

She replied almost instantly.

> Emma: No worries, I'll just have to do it alone. Maybe tomorrow?

Why do I get the feeling that she has no idea how that sounded in my head!

By Friday, I am fed the fuck up. I have only managed a couple of fifteen minute runs first thing in the morning, and then I've spent all day sat on my arse in the office. I haven't seen Emma all week, even though I know she's been at my place, because Connie has mentioned cooking dinner for her and Fin a couple of times.

Needless to say, my mood with the men when they ring up is not good.

"Ru, man, what the fuck is up with you?" Fin asks when he rings just after one.

"I'm fed up of being stuck in here all hours. I want to get out and do something."

"Or do you mean some*one*?" he asks with a laugh.

Yeah, that would probably relieve some tension, but at this point in time I'd be quite happy just to spend some time with her. "Fin, cut it out and do some work."

"All right, pipe down, boss. Why don't you knock off early? You've worked some crazy hours this week. Let your dad deal with the last couple."

I take his advice a while later and head home to change, ready for a serious run—hopefully with Emma, if she's about.

I'm opening her back gate and letting myself in, like she told me to do last time I came here, in no time. The run here helped me lose some of my frustration, but I'm hoping seeing her will sort me right out. What I don't expect is quite how she will make me forget about everything that has happened this week instantly.

The house is quiet when I enter, but her car was out the front and the door was unlocked, so I'm guessing she's here somewhere.

"Em, you home?" I shout as I head toward the living room. I get no response, but what I find has every muscle in my body locked tight. She's in the middle of her living room, already in her running clothes, minus the tank top, which makes me happy, but what makes me even happier is the pose she's in. I glance at the screen and see she's following a yoga DVD, and she's currently stood with her legs wide apart, completely bent at the waist with her hands and head on the floor. The view is incredible. I lean myself against the door frame and watch for a while longer. I know it's totally pervy and creepy, but I can't help myself. That arse, argh!

After a while, she must open her eyes. She lets out the most earth-shattering scream when she sees me and falls straight over onto the hearth of her fireplace.

"Ah, fuck!" she shouts and pulls her earbuds out. That was obviously why she didn't hear me, although I kinda liked the idea that she knew I was there and watching her. Yep, as I said, pervy and creepy!

"Jesus, Ruben, you could have warned me you were there," she says, trying to right herself. I watch intently as she rearranges her sports bra, ever hopeful for a flash of something good, but no luck. "Are you just gonna stand there staring, or are you gonna help me up?"

"Yeah, sorry." I quickly go over, grab her under her arms and pull her up.

"Ouch," she complains on the way up. Once she's standing, she looks at her side at the same time I do, and we both see a bright red, bleeding scratch from where she landed on the stone. "Brilliant."

"Where's your first aid kit? I'll clean it up for you."

I come back to find her sat on the edge of the sofa. "Sorry, I didn't mean to shout. You just scared me and I was all light-headed from being upside down. I'm not always this clumsy."

"It was my fault," I say, but can't help myself and add, "I was too distracted by your arse up in the air like that." She looks away from me, embarrassed, while I grab the antiseptic spray to clean her up. "Can you lift your top a little?" I ask, having cleaned everything I can see. She looks back at me over her shoulder and raises an eyebrow. "I just want to make sure I got it all. Just a little bit... or I could make you take it off completely," I add with a wink.

"I doubt that," she snaps, giving me a death stare.

"One day," I add, before tidying everything up and taking it all back to the kitchen. When I return, she's still staring at the same spot on the wall as when I left. I think I'm getting to her.

We grab our bottles and head out into the fields. I'm impressed with Emma's improvement in just a week; she's obviously been out without me the last few days.

"You okay?" I ask when we come to a stop.

"Yeah, I actually am. It's getting easier."

"Good, that means we're doing it right. Let's stop here for a few and do some stretches."

"Okay, but we're gonna have to head back soon. Look over there," she says, pointing to a very black sky creeping up behind us. It's been a scorching hot day, but it looks like that's about to change with one hell of a storm.

"We'll do this then head back, yeah?"

We're about halfway back when the first crack of thunder sounds. "You're gonna have to go quicker, babe," I call behind me.

"I can't," she cries, just as I feel the first fat raindrop fall on my head.

I stop and reach for her hand when she gets close to me. "Come on," I say, dragging her along as the rain starts to pound down on us.

"I can't," she heaves over the sound of the rain, "I can't go any further." I stop pulling her and slow us down so she can catch her breath. The rain hasn't slowed at all. We're soaked to the bone, and the thunder and lightning are right on us.

"We're almost back; you can do it," I say encouragingly.

"No, you go and I'll meet you back at mine."

"Shut up, I'm not leaving you out here. Jump on," I say, turning my back to her and lowering slightly. She doesn't do anything for a few seconds, so I look back to find her biting her lip in thought. She looks sexy with her hair stuck to her face and rain pouring over her. "Em, come on."

"You won't be able to carry me," she says quietly.

CHAPTER FOUR

Emma

I really don't want to show all my insecurities, but there's no way he can carry me all the way back. I know he's strong and fit, but that's crazy.

"Of course I will. I backpacked around Australia with a bag that probably only weighed a little less than you do."

"That was probably just the weight of my arse. I'm too fat and heavy for you to carry, so—"

"Don't," he warns. "Don't ever let me hear you say that about yourself again, do you hear me?" he snaps as he steps up in front of me, so I have no choice but to tip my head back to look at him.

I'm shocked by the tone of his voice, and embarrassingly I feel my eyes pool with water.

"Now listen to me, and I mean really listen." If it's possible, the rain gets even heavier in this moment, so he has to shout it at me. "You are not fat or heavy. You are a stunning, curvy woman, with an awesome arse and a pretty insane rack. I'd have thought you'd have realised this by now, with the number of times you've caught me staring. I'm not helping you do this so you can lose loads of weight and be all stick thin, I'm helping because I want you to be happy and confident with how you look. You're hot as you are, and any man would be lucky to have you."

I can't stop the tears that spill over my eyes and mingle with the rainwater already pouring down my face.

"Ah, babe, come here," he says, before he pulls me into his arms. I'm shocked by his affection and don't really know what to do for the first few seconds. It's not very often I get held like this. I never knew how good it could feel. Eventually, I relax into it and put my own arms around Ruben's back. He's well over a head taller than me, and he completely renders me speechless when I feel him kiss the top of my head.

To my disappointment, he pulls back after that. "Okay?" he asks.

I just nod my head at him and wipe my cheeks with the backs of my already soggy hands. He turns around again, and this time I do as I'm told and jump on. His hands instantly come to hold on to my thighs, very close to my arse that he just said he's rather keen on. The thought makes me blush, and I'm grateful he can't see me. After adjusting me so it's comfortable for him, he tells me to wrap my arms around him and, after doing so, he takes off jogging. I can't help the laugh that comes from me at the utter ridiculousness of the situation.

"You all right?" he shouts up to me.

"Yeah, this is just insane. Are you okay?"

"Yep, just hold on tight."

It feels like hardly any time later that Ruben's putting me down outside my house, and I let us in. We go straight into the kitchen so we can drip over the tiled floor. I still can't wipe the smile off my face. I don't know if it's the fact that we're both soaking wet, or what Ruben said to me out in the field. His words are still ringing in my ears. I didn't realise how much I needed to hear someone say them, other than my family and friends.

Ruben looks at me with raised eyebrows but soon begins to laugh along with me. "Wait here, I'll just be a few minutes," I say before heading upstairs.

I peel my wet clothes off, which is easier said than done when they're skintight. Then, I quickly jump in the shower before throwing on a pair of jogging bottoms and a vest. I'm aware that Ruben is still creating a puddle down in my kitchen, so I grab two towels, one for my hair and one for him, and head back down.

What I find when I get there gives me the shock of my life.

Ruben is standing at the sink, pouring himself a glass of water, in only his black boxer briefs. I see the muscles ripple down his back as he turns the tap off and goes to turn around.

"I... uh..."

"Ah I didn't think you were coming back. Here, have a drink." He reaches his hand out with a full glass for me, but all I can do is stare at his practically naked body. Oh my God. He's all taut skin and muscle, but it's his legs that really set my pulse racing. His thighs are like steel.

"Em?"

I do catch his eyes drifting down to my tits at this point and realise that he can quite clearly see my nipples through the fabric now. That hidden support isn't up to much. Shit, shit, shit.

"Yeah, here I... uh... got you a towel to uh... dry off."

"Sorry, I hope you don't mind, I used your tumble dryer."

"No, yeah, that's fine, help yourself." *To me*, I think, but manage not to say out loud.

"Thanks."

I continue to stand gawping like a lemon while he rubs the towel over his hair and across his shoulders, before I watch him wrap it around his waist and go about removing his boxers and adding them to the tumble dryer.

There's a naked man in my kitchen.

"Shall we go and sit down? They won't take long," he says, striding past me and into my living room.

I lean myself back against the worktop and will my body back under control while I sip the glass of water he gave me. What is wrong with me? I have this huge urge to go and jump on him.

"Are you going to stay in the kitchen all night, or are you coming to join me?" he shouts, sounding amused.

I slowly move myself and head into the living room to weigh up my options. I've got a two-seater sofa and a chair. The chair is placed almost opposite the sofa, and I'm thinking that's not a good idea with Ruben sat relaxing in a towel with his legs parted, so I opt to climb between his legs and coffee table and sit next to him. What I don't plan for is tripping over his legs and ending up sprawled across his lap. My face burns red with mortification.

"Shit, sorry."

"I thought you said you weren't always clumsy?"

"Yeah, well, I'm not. It just seems to be around you."

"I'll take that as a compliment," he says with a huge grin on his face. The sight of his dimple popping up doesn't help matters, either.

I put the TV on to distract us from whatever the hell is going on here, but it's obvious that neither of us is watching it. I continue to keep my eyes focused on it, because I can feel his stare burning into me and I'm scared to turn around and look at all his naked skin.

"Em?"

"Uh-huh?"

"I didn't have you down for a Jeremy Kyle fan."

"What? Oh... uh... I'm not. I wasn't actually..."

"I know. You're just avoiding me. Do I really make you that nervous?"

"It's just that... you're sat there... well... like that," I say eventually, turning to him and motioning to his nakedness with my hands. "It's not exactly a normal thing to me," I say, instantly wishing I hadn't.

"Well, I'd certainly hope you don't have strange naked men sat on your sofa often. I like to think I'm the exception," he says with a laugh.

"Yes, you definitely are."

"You know, I meant what I said out in the field earlier. You really don't need to change anything about this body," he says, running his fingers up and down my arm, giving me goosebumps.

I look away, embarrassed by his comment. Maybe one day I'll be able to take a compliment.

"Hey," he says, reaching his hand out to cup my cheek and turn my head back to look at him. "I love how shy you are. It's really endearing."

We continue to stare at each other for a long time before he breaks eye contact by looking down at my lips. I panic when I see him start to move toward me. My heart starts racing and my palms sweat. I jump up from the sofa, telling him that I'm going to make dinner. I quickly scurry out of the room, but not before I notice the slight tenting of Ruben's towel. He clears his throat before saying that he'll join me in a few minutes.

Dinner was seriously awkward. Ruben put his dry clothes back on after joining me in the kitchen, making me feel slightly less on edge about his nakedness but no more confident about the situation I've found myself in.

After we've eaten the chicken salad I made, I leave Ruben in the kitchen washing up while I grab a hoodie. I sit myself down on the edge of my bed and take a few deep breaths, trying to get myself together. The picture frame on my bedside table catches my eye, and I look at the photograph of Hannah and me from a few years ago. We were on holiday with Molly after we graduated, and we were all on a night out. We've got glowing tans, and Hannah looks even more stunning than ever with her sun-kissed blonde hair and slinky dress. My heart hurts when I look at the happiness shining from our eyes. Yes, I've managed to deal with the pain that losing her caused last year, but in no way has it got any easier, looking at the most important person in my life. She was literally the other half of me, and she was ripped from me the night of the accident. I'm sure I'll always feel like I'm missing a huge part of myself.

I promised myself after she died that I would never allow myself to get close enough to anyone else to feel even a tiny amount of the pain I felt when I lost her. I've let my guard down with Connie, but I've been very careful to keep many of my walls built high. I don't think she knows it, but there are many secrets between us that I have no intention of revealing. But Ruben... Ruben is another story entirely. In the short few days I've known him, I can feel the bricks slowly crumbling around my feet. I can't let that happen. He admits himself that he uses women and doesn't stick around after he gets what he wants. Those stories Fin was spewing the other night show just how true that is. Even though he was exaggerating most of them, I know there's truth in there.

If I allow myself to let him in, he's going to rip my heart out, and I have no intention of anyone doing anything to my heart. I need to put some space between us.

I square my shoulders and head back down to the kitchen.

"Sorry, but I couldn't find where these go," he says, pointing to some utensils he's dried up.

I grab them and turn my back to him while I put them away. I know I'm being a coward, but I can't look at him while I do this.

"You need to leave," I mutter quietly, but I know he hears because I hear his sharp intake of breath.

"What, why?"

"I just need you to leave. Please," I say, still turned away from him.

"But—"

"Ruben," I warn. I stand tall, so he can see that my mind is set and he has no argument.

"Fine," he says sternly, before I hear heavy footsteps and my back door slam so hard it resonates through the whole house.

I turn so my back is to the worktops and slide down until my arse hits the floor and I put my head on my knees. When I was upstairs looking at Hannah, I was sure that was the right thing to do; but why do I now feel like a huge bitch? And, more importantly, why does my heart ache?

I keep myself locked in my house, working on my manuscript all day Saturday. My phone goes off, but I don't even look to see who it is. I'm too scared that it might be Ruben trying to call me out on my bullshit yesterday. I don't have an excuse for my behaviour that I want to talk about. I end up putting my manuscript to one side in favour of starting on a new idea I've had for a book.

Before I know it, it's gone midnight, and I have a seriously numb arse from how long I've been sitting in the same position. My phone has gone off a few more times over the last couple of hours, but again, I ignore it in fear.

I wake the next morning to my phone ringing incessantly. As soon as it rings off, it starts again. I begrudgingly pull the covers off and go in search of the irritating device. When I see that it's Connie, I answer.

"Morning," I say groggily.

"This is late for you. I thought you'd have been up hours ago." She's right, I'm usually an early riser. I guess working so late last night meant I got to have a lie in. "Anyway, do you want to come for breakfast? I got a load of food for Ru and Fin after their night out, but they left to go and play football instead. They won't be back until late; they'll end up in the pub with their mates, and now I'm lonely!"

I was still planning on avoiding Ruben after the disaster that was Friday night, but I guess it's safe if Connie is saying they'll be out all day.

"Please, Em. You can even come in your PJ's. I'm not planning on changing out of mine anytime soon. Please," she begs, obviously sensing my reluctance.

"Yeah, okay. Let me just get changed quickly, and I'll run over."

"Wow, you really are taking this seriously. Don't be long, I'm starving."

I put my phone back down without looking at any messages and quickly swap my pyjamas for my running clothes and head out of the house. It's still relatively early, yet the sun is already starting to burn the bit of skin I don't usually reveal on my back. Luckily, I see Connie's front door ahead just as I start to feel sweat beginning to run down my skin. I let myself in, relieved by the coolness as I enter the kitchen and slip off my shoes.

Connie has her back to me, slicing up something on the worktop when I enter. To say I'm not disappointed about the lack of frying bacon smell right now would be a huge lie—although I should have known better than to expect a full-on fry up. I already know they all eat healthily, and Connie has made sure to never eat anything naughty in front of me since I started my diet. Normally I love that she's so considerate of my weight loss, but this morning a little bit of grease would have hit the spot.

"So... go on then, what happened with Ruben? Did he try it on or something?" she asks, continuing what she's doing.

"What makes you say that?"

"Well, he came back from yours in a hell of a mood on Friday night and locked himself away with his music blaring until God knows what time. Then, he moped about yesterday and went out drinking with Fin at the earliest opportunity. Luckily for me, they brought the party back here in the early hours. I was awake most of the night, listening to the antics going on in the living room. I've spent most of the morning since they left cleaning every surface with Dettol."

"Why?" I ask naïvely, but as soon as the word is out of my mouth, I regret it.

"Because I can only imagine what they were doing in there with the girls they brought back. The noises... urgh!"

The thought of Ruben being with other women makes my stomach turn over, although I'm pissed off with myself for having that reaction, because I should not like him. What pisses me off even more than that, though, is the wave of jealousy that washes through me. I try to shake the images from my head.

When I look up, Connie is looking right at me. "Em, are you okay? You've gone kinda pale."

"Yeah, I'm fine. Do they do that often?" *For fuck's sake, shut your mouth, Emma!*

"Every now and then, but I've learnt to just let them get on with it. I once stormed out to try to shut them up and kick them out, but the image of what I walked in on that night will forever be burned into my brain, so I tend to just stick my head under my pillow and try to ignore it. Anyway... you didn't answer my question. Did something happen between you two?"

"Oh, nothing, we just had a disagreement," I say, trying to play it down so she doesn't dig too deep.

"So, he didn't try anything with you?"

"No." I'm not sure if that's a lie or not, because technically, I guess he didn't do anything.

"Good, because I told him I'd cut it off in his sleep if he did. Although I do think you need a man, he is definitely not what you need. He's a whore; you need a nice guy."

I couldn't have said it better myself.

Connie starts bringing everything over to the breakfast bar, and I can't believe my eyes. I know she said she'd bought a load of food, but this is crazy. By the time she's finished, the surface is covered in every kind of fruit I can imagine, bagels, cream cheese, smoked salmon, granola, and a variety of yoghurts, just to name a few. "Christ, Con, you planning on feeding the five thousand?"

"You have no idea how much two grown men can eat after a night out," is all she says, before she comes back over with a huge jug of orange juice.

It's only now I get a good look at her. She's wearing an oversized t-shirt that's so big the neck hangs off one of her shoulders, and it's long enough to just cover her arse. I can't help but notice it's a little thin and see through, but she doesn't seem to care, and it's not like we're out in public. I envy Connie's body confidence. She has her hair pulled back with a headband, and it's clear how much sleep she missed out on last night with her dark eyes. What really stands out to me, though, is the bright red mark on her neck.

"So, it looks like the boys weren't the only ones to see some action last night," I say mockingly to her.

"What?" she questions as she walks over to the mirror in the hallway. "Oh, for fuck's sake. How am I meant to hide that from Ru?"

I guess I don't need to ask who it was who came over last night. "I thought you'd finished that?"

"Yeah, well, I didn't get invited out for drinks, and I wanted a bit of fun. I knew he wouldn't refuse," she says with a wink. I don't mention that her chest also seems to be covered in marks in varying shades of red. She's going to have to do something about that before Ruben gets back.

Ruben

I've been in a constant state of pissed off since I was sent away from Emma's house on Friday night. I don't know what's wrong with me. I shouldn't care. Normally, having a woman send me away is a blessing. It saves me the trouble of making it clear that nothing further will ever happen between us. I'm not a complete bastard, though. I know how they must feel when I wake up and kick them out without a second thought. Having said that, it was a bit of a shock to the system, having it happen to me.

I kept myself locked away from Connie on Friday night. I didn't want her probing into my mood. She's warned me to keep my hands off Emma, and I fully intended to keep the promise I made to her for all of about two minutes after the words left my mouth. I don't know what it is about Emma; she has this ability to draw me to her like a fucking moth to a flame. I thought she was with me on Friday night. Yes, she was embarrassed and nervous, especially when I was practically naked, but I wasn't expecting her to send me away like that.

I moped around all day Saturday with the same thoughts running on repeat. I tried to go and do some work, but my head wasn't really in it. I've never wanted a girlfriend—well, not since I was a kid, anyway. I've always taken what I've wanted and tossed them aside, no matter how much they begged for me to keep them around, but the one girl I want keeps pushing me aside like a piece of rubbish. I'm sure I've seen want and desire in her eyes when she looks at me. I know she hasn't got a boyfriend, so what is it that's stopping her? Her body is screaming at me to touch her, to do all the things I want to do to her, but she keeps putting up this barrier.

Maybe she's been hurt by an ex in the past. The thought of someone being with her, let alone hurting her, makes me want to punch the wall. No man deserves her, let alone get close enough to hurt her.

The second Fin suggested we head into town for some drinks, I was on board. Getting a little buzzed and finding some girls to take my mind off Emma was exactly what I needed.

I got the buzzed bit down, although, I'd more describe myself as well and truly trashed. The problem was that no girls interested me. No matter what they looked like, what they were wearing, how much boob they had on show—that was my usual poison—I just wasn't interested. And I was even more pissed off that the reason none of them interested me was because they weren't her. What the fuck was wrong with me?

"Dude, what the fuck, man? Look at her, she totally wants you," Fin says, pointing at a girl in a stupidly tight purple dress that she's about to fall out of. "You'd usually have your face straight in those tits," he adds, making me cringe.

Yeah, I know my behaviour with women isn't something I should be proud of. That's exactly why Emma is doing the right thing by pushing me as far away as she can.

"Not tonight," is all I say back to him. But he doesn't care; he has his tongue down some blonde's throat before I even finish speaking.

It's no surprise to me when we eventually leave the club in the early hours that Fin drags two girls along with him. Somewhere over the last few years, it seemed to have turned into a tradition that after a night out we would bring a couple, or a handful, of girls back to my place to carry on the party. This started before Connie moved in, and I really should have put a stop to it when she did, but one thing led to another and here we are, still doing it. I always feel awful about it afterwards and ensure I make it up to her, because no little sister should have to put up with that, but she lets us get on with it. I'm not sure how I would feel if the situation were reversed, mind you. I'd kill any fucker I found with their hands on her. I know she's not a virgin, but I try to convince myself that she doesn't get up to, or know about, any of the stuff the girls Fin and I spend time with do.

I leave Fin and his girls to it not long after we get back. I have no intention of watching the three of them get it on in my living room. I usually turn a blind eye when I've got company of my own, but tonight's different. Instead, I head up to my bedroom and rub one out on my own, with thoughts of Emma's smoking body running through my mind.

I'm woken by my alarm blaring a few hours later, reminding me that I agreed to play football with the lads, seeing as we haven't seen them since we've been back. I haul my hungover arse to the shower to try to wash away the stench of last night's alcohol. Once I'm feeling a little more alive, I venture downstairs to see what mess I'm going to find my living room in.

The scene is pretty much what I thought it would be. Gone are the girls from last night, and left behind in their wake is a very naked Fin, starfished on the sofa, surrounded by wrappers and used condoms. The image makes me cringe, and a thought suddenly hits me.

Fuck, when did I grow up?

I used to find myself in that situation most weekends and didn't bat an eyelid. Why, all of a sudden, do I feel like what I'm seeing in front of me is just wrong? What freaks me out even more is that the vision I'm seeing instead is of waking up next to Emma every morning and being able to look at her naked body, not my best friend snoring butt naked on the sofa. Fuck me, I'm turning into a right pussy.

I grab the cushion closest to me and launch it at Fin. "For fuck's sake, cover your junk," I say when I see his eyes pop open, "and tidy the fuck up."

I walk back toward the kitchen and see that Connie's door is open slightly, but when I call through, there's no answer. Great, she must have seen the state of our living room as well, then. I don't think I need to be worrying about the fact that she's seen Fin in all his glory when the evidence of his activities last night are all around him. That should be off-putting enough for her.

"It's too fucking hot for this, dude," Fin complains, bent over with his hands on his knees.

He's right. We've been out playing for nearly an hour, and it's fucking baking hot. All of us are beetroot red from the sun, and the sweat is pouring off us.

Someone else obviously feels the same and shouts over, "Shall we call it a day? This is ridiculous."

Before Fin and I went away, the usual routine was to play for a couple of hours then head to the pub for a few cold ones, but it seems that in the six months we've been gone, everyone has been pussy-whipped and isn't allowed out to play after the football.

"I guess we should head back, then," I say to Fin as I grab my t-shirt from the sideline and tuck it into the waistband of my shorts. "With a bit of luck, Connie will have been food shopping."

I know she's there the minute I walk through the front door. It's like my body knows when she's close. I can feel the buzz.

We walk into the kitchen to find Connie and Emma sat around the breakfast bar full of food. Fin takes one look at it, exclaims his delight and begins to tuck in immediately; he's completely unaware of the shocked looks on the girls' faces.

We move everything over to the dining table so we can all sit around. Connie is fast to sit away from me, which is weird behaviour for her, and Emma also tries to be as far away from me as possible, but I'm not up for that, so when she sits opposite Connie, I take the chair next to her.

We spend a few minutes chatting awkwardly, until Connie brings up her birthday next weekend. "Apparently, the heatwave is going to continue, so I want to spend Saturday around the pool chilling out with Emma, if that's okay?"

"You have a pool?" is the only thing Emma says, looking shocked.

"Well, our parents do. You up for it?"

"I guess."

"You two are welcome, if you haven't got anything else to do. Then, I want us all to go out to that new cocktail bar in the evening. You all in?"

We all agree and continue eating.

"Have you got any Marmite, Con?" Fin asks.

She says yes, and gets up to grab it for him. The three of us watch her move over into the kitchen and reach up to the top shelf to grab it. I wasn't overly impressed with the practically see-through t-shirt she was wearing. I don't want Fin seeing any more of her than he has to, but as she reaches up, it's clear to all of us quite how tiny her underwear is as we get a full shot of her arse.

"Fuck's sake, Con, can't you put some more clothes on?" I grumble, looking down at my food.

"I'm in my own house; I'll do as I damn well please, thank you very much. You know me. I'd quite happily sit here in less, but you wouldn't have it."

This comment makes me look up to show her how unimpressed I am with the suggestion. I'm well aware that Connie has no issues about getting her body out; she's been that way since she was a kid. I just sorta hoped she would grow out of it. It's only now, as she places the Marmite down for Fin, that I get a look at her left side.

"What the fuck is that?"

Her hand instantly flies up to cover the bright red love bite on her neck, and she mutters, "Fuck," under her breath.

"I thought you stayed in last night?" I question.

She just shrugs at me, which pisses me off. But what pisses me off even more are Fin's comments about her getting some last night. I do not want to think about it, thank you very much. She's my little sister.

"Wait a minute," he says, reaching out toward the neck of her t-shirt, "Is that some more?" he asks, as he reveals the tops of her breasts to us.

"Fuck's sake, dude. Don't touch her," I snap.

I'm grateful in that moment, because Connie's phone starts ringing in her bedroom. It's already pinged with a few texts that she's ignored, so I stand up to go and get it.

"Where are you going?" she asks in a panic, but it's too late; I'm already in her doorway.

Other than having a naked man sprawled out, the scene in front of me isn't all that different to what I walked into in the living room this morning. There are condoms strewn around the place, but there's also a bottle of lube leaking on the wooden floor, and a couple of sex toys on the bed.

I put my hands up on the door frame and hang my head as I try to rein in my temper, because there's no use being angry. My sister is twenty-six next week. She's an adult and free to do all the things that I do. Telling myself this doesn't make it any easier to see, though.

"Ruben... it's..." she doesn't get to finish, because a loud male voice booms through the house and sets my blood on fire.

"Beautiful, I left my wallet... oh. Hey, Fin."

I see red. I turn on my heel and fly straight at Elliot, knocking him into the kitchen wall. I pull my arm back and throw my fist straight in his face. He's shocked by my attack, so I get a few good punches in before he starts to retaliate.

"You fucking arsehole," I repeat as I hit him.

Things obviously start to make sense in Fin's head, because before long, he's there with me, holding Elliot back so I can continue to hit him. For all Fin's flaws, he's loyal to the core and will always have mine and Connie's backs.

"How long did you fucking leave it before my flight took off, you fucking bastard? I bet you were right here waiting to fucking pounce, to have what wasn't fucking yours."

My rant goes on and on, but eventually I start to hear female shouting and screaming enter my hazy brain. I feel Connie start to pull at one of my arms to make me stop, but I'm too lost to my anger. I pull my other arm back, vaguely aware that my elbow connects with something, before plunging it into Elliot's stomach, causing him to bend over, heaving.

I'm just about to kick him when a piercing scream stops me. I spin around to see Emma bent over and clutching the side of her face with both hands.

"You fucking idiot; now look what you've done," Connie shouts at me as she heads toward Emma.

Oh no she fucking doesn't. I barge past her and scoop Emma up in my arms while demanding that Connie goes and gets some ice.

I take the bag of peas from her as I pass and head toward the stairs with a sobbing Emma still in my arms.

"He'd better have fucking gone when I get back down. If I ever fucking see him again, it will be too fucking soon."

CHAPTER FIVE

Emma

I knew I should have stayed out of it, but I couldn't let Ruben continue to beat the shit out of Elliot. He stood no chance, with Ruben hitting him and Fin holding him back. Connie started pulling at Ruben's arm, so I felt like I should do something to try to help the situation.

I feel Ruben sit down. He clutches me tighter to his body and rocks me back and forth, I presume willing me to calm down, as I'm still sobbing loudly. He continues to apologise softly in my ear, and he kisses the top of my head, but I keep my hands locked firmly over my eye, in fear of my face falling off from the pain throbbing through it.

"Em, babe, please move your hands. You need something cold on it to stop it swelling too much. I'm so sorry, I didn't know you were there," he repeats for the millionth time.

I know it's not his fault. I do know that, but it doesn't stop me being angry at him for acting like a moron and flying off the handle at Elliot.

Eventually, he manages to pry my hands away from my face so he can look at me. I see the lines of worry etched into his face with the one eye I can open. He looks distraught. As he should, I guess.

"Fuck, I'm so sorry, so sorry. I didn't know, I'm so sorry. I would never..." he tails off as he places soft kisses around my eye and down my cheek, gently wiping my tears away. Once he's finished, he wraps the bag of peas in a t-shirt he has lying on the floor and gently presses it to my eye. I can only guess from how big it feels and from his reaction that it's pretty bad. I've never had anything to do with fights, and I've never been hit, so I don't really know what to expect.

Ruben sits us back against his headboard and continues to hold me tightly to him. Neither of us says anything for the longest time. Even though it feels like my face is broken, I find it oddly soothing to be in his arms and plastered against his naked chest. The only time either of us moves is when he leans forward slightly to kiss my head or to rub his hand down my arm in comfort.

There's more shouting and screaming going on downstairs, but Ruben must block it out just like I do, and eventually I feel his heart rate start to slow and his body start to relax as the fight leaves him.

"Are you okay?" I eventually whisper. He hasn't moved for a while, and I wonder if he's fallen asleep.

"Shhh," he whispers back. "Don't worry about me. Are you okay?"

I look up at him and take in his swollen eye and cut lip. I reach up to wipe the little stream of blood running down his chin, making him wince. "Sorry."

I'm not entirely sure why I do what I do next. I guess it's concussion or something, but I turn myself so that I'm sat astride Ruben's lap. His hands come to rest high up on my thighs, and I grab one at a time to inspect the damage. Both are covered in dried blood and are red and swollen. I lift each one gently up to my lips and press a light kiss to them, just like he did to my eye. He watches me intently as I do this, and once I've finished, I hold his eye contact. My heart—that's only just begun to slow its pace thanks to the adrenalin pumping around my body—picks up speed again the longer we sit and stare at each other.

I hate to say it, but he only looks hotter with a busted up face, whereas I dread to think what I currently look like. I carefully remove the bag of peas, which makes me wince and him to look like he's about to apologise again, but I stop him in his tracks by placing it over his swollen eye. His hand comes up to cover mine where I'm holding it in place on his face, and we continue to sit deadly still.

I feel myself lean toward him, and, before I know it, I've got my lips next to his cut lip. I feel him suck in a breath at my contact, but other than that, we stay connected.

I pull back a couple of seconds later. "Thank you for looking after me," I whisper.

He sits himself forward slightly and moves his hands so they cup my cheeks. He's careful not to touch my eye, though. "Always," he states, "but you shouldn't have needed looking after. I'm sorry." The apology is said so quietly that I practically have to lip-read it. He shifts a little closer again, before pressing his lips directly to mine. My heartbeat picks up pace again and I feel myself start to sweat as panic washes over me.

I'm both relieved and disappointed when he pulls back and looks at me again. "Promise me something," he says, leaning back. I nod at him so he continues. "Don't go anywhere. I need to have a shower. I stink, and I'm covered in blood. But please don't go." He moves his hand around the back of my neck and slides his fingers into my hair. He gives me a gentle nudge until I nod, agreeing that I'll wait. He continues to stare at me a little longer, but what he sees obviously makes him happy, because he soon lifts me off him and places me down on his bed.

When he's standing, he leans back over me again and presses his lips to mine in the gentlest of kisses before standing and heading toward the en suite. He pauses before he gets to the door, and I think he's going to say something further, but instead he just looks over his shoulder at me and gives me a heart-stopping smile. Then, as if I haven't had enough shocks already today, he shoves his thumbs in the waistbands of his shorts and boxers, pushes them down, and steps out, giving me an incredible view of his backside and thighs before continuing, slowly, into the en suite.

I smile to myself. He knows exactly what he's doing. He knows his assets, and he's using them to his advantage.

My smile falters somewhat when I consider that if I were more outgoing like Molly or Connie, I would have the confidence to strip off and follow him in there. But that isn't who I am, and the mere thought of it has me on the edge of a panic attack. That's the kind of woman Ruben deserves, though: someone who is confident and knows how to use their body to their advantage, just like he did to me.

I'm up off the bed instantly, and in a split second I'm charging down the stairs. I grab my keys and pull my shoes on, before running for the front door. Connie and Fin are somewhere down here, but they don't notice me. They're still too busy arguing about something.

My eye pounds as I run. Every time my feet hit the pavement, it's like Ruben's elbow is connecting with me again and again. I clutch the bag of peas to my face, willing them to make a difference. I would walk, but I know that he'll be after me the minute he realises that I've gone, and I want to get home and lock myself in.

Ruben

I walk into the en suite, smiling to myself. I know I should be anything but happy with everything that has happened, but Emma kissed me. She kissed me! Okay, so it was the sweetest, most innocent kiss I think I've received in my life, but it was a kiss.

God, I feel like a pansy! I might as well just hand my balls over to her now.

I knew I might have been pushing it a little with the kissing, but I couldn't help it; to see her in so much pain because of me was pure hell. I would have done anything I could to make it better, to ease her pain.

I was raging when I heard his voice boom through our house. A place that his voice doesn't belong, ever. I just lost my shit. I know my behaviour was totally unforgivable and utterly hypocritical, but I just saw red at the thought of Elliot preying on my sister the minute I left for Australia. The thought of him having his greasy, scumbag hands on her. Ugh, even the thought makes me want to go and find him and start round two. Absolute arsehole.

I know it takes two to tango, and believe me, I'm almost as pissed off with Connie as I am with Elliot. I mean, what was she thinking? She knows about all the shit that has gone down between us over the years. Why the fuck would she go there, and did she really think I would never find out? She was fucking him in the house we share, for fuck's sake. Did she think it would all be okay if we happened to bump into each other having breakfast one morning?

I don't even know what to say to her right now. I think her best bet is to steer well clear of me until I've properly calmed down. Fin can deal with her; I know he's just as pissed off with her, if their shouting is anything to go by.

I step under the hot spray and let it soothe my muscles. My whole body is tense and ready to fight. Emma helped calm me, but now I've stepped away from her and thought about the situation, I can feel myself getting het up again.

I miss her. I only left her a few seconds ago, but I wish she were in here with me. The thought of turning around in the shower to find her standing there, naked and ready to join me, has my dick throbbing for her. I know that isn't who she is, though, and I wouldn't change her for the world. I just hope that I get the chance to make her see how sexy she is and to encourage her to be confident in her own skin, so she could do things like that with me. *Only* with me.

I make quick work of washing before stepping out and wrapping a towel around my waist. I ignore my hard-on. Emma is so close that the only person I want touching it is her, even though I know the chance of that happening is slim to none.

I walk out of the en suite to find what I feared.

She's gone.

I throw on the first clothes I find and rush out of the house.

"Ru, where are you going? Where's Emma?" Connie shouts after me from her seat on the sofa. Fin is scowling at her while she's sat with her arms curled around herself and tears still streaming down her face.

"Out," is the only thing I say, because I really don't want to talk to her and I need to find Emma.

I jump in my car and head in the direction of Emma's house. I'm presuming she hasn't gone through the fields to get back to the village, because that's by far the longer route.

A few minutes later, I find that I'm right when I see her slowly jogging in the direction of her house. I pull up next to her and wind down the window. "Emma, get in."

"No," she says defiantly, her chin raised in the air.

"Emma," I warn, "get in the car."

She ignores me completely this time and picks up her pace. I pull up at the curb a little ahead of her, get out, pick her up, and place her in the passenger seat.

"Get the fuck off me," she shouts, and goes to get out when I step away.

"Don't even think about it. I'm taking you home," I growl, slamming the door. I jog around to the driver's side, praying she stays put and I don't have to chase her again.

She does as she's told. I guess she's too exhausted to fight.

We drive the rest of the way to her house in silence. She's pouting next to me with her arms folded across her chest, showing me that she's completely closed herself off to me. It hurts after what happened between us earlier that she can build her walls back up again and push me away so quickly. She's going to have to realise at some point that I'm just going to keep pushing back, harder and more insistent, until she breaks.

I pull up on her drive and we both continue to sit for a while in silence, staring at the rose beds outside her cottage.

"Why did you run?" I eventually ask.

"I can't do this," is her only response.

"Can't do what?"

"This. All of this," she says, waving her arms around. "I'm not who you think I am. I'm not what you want, or what you need. Just leave me be and get on with your life. Carry on bringing random girls home from clubs and whoring yourself out around the village. That's who you are, and I don't fit into that. I'm done."

I'd almost believe her, if her words didn't crack at the end. I ignore her spiteful comments about me, because, well... let's face it, they're true.

I jump out the car and follow her to her door. "Emma, please wait."

I hear her sob before she looks back at me with tears running down her face. "No. Just leave, Ruben." I'm stopped in my tracks by the look on her face, and she takes the opportunity to get inside and lock the door behind her.

I hammer on the door for a good twenty minutes before it's clear that she meant what she said. So, with my head hung, I trudge back to my car. I sit there for a while, just looking at her house, hoping I'll see her at the window, showing me that she didn't actually mean what she just said, but there's no movement from inside. Eventually, I reverse off her drive and leave.

***

I decide to drive about for a bit as I don't feel in any state to deal with Connie, or even Fin, for that matter. When I enter the house, it is completely quiet. If it weren't for their cars outside, I would think they'd gone out. The kitchen is in the same mess as when I left it, with blood splattered up the wall, reminding me of what happened not so long ago.

The minute I step foot in the living room, my earlier anger resurfaces. Both Connie and Fin are laid out on the sofa. He has her tightly curled to his chest, spooning her. This wouldn't usually bother me as much as it does right now, but Fin is still topless and Connie is still wearing that fucking see-though t-shirt that's now hitched up around her waist, showing off the tiny bit of elastic she calls underwear, and Fin's hand has disappeared under it.

I don't know what's wrong with me today, but I storm over and pull Connie out of his arms and push her onto the other sofa.

"Ruben, what the fuck are you doing?" she challenges.

"Shut up, Con. You've already done enough," I tell her in an eerily calm voice. Fin, on the other hand, I bellow at. Full volume. "Get the fuck out, right now."

"What the fuck, dude?" he says, coming around from his sleep.

"Get. Out," I repeat.

"We were just asleep, man. Chill the fuck out."

"I saw exactly what you were doing. Now. Get. Out."

He eventually gets the hint, gets up from the sofa, giving Connie a sympathetic look, and leaves the room, swiftly followed by the house.

I wait a beat before turning around to face Connie.

"Oh no you don't. Do not give me that face," she says, standing up. "I am an adult. I make my own choices, and I do not need you fighting my battles for me." She goes to leave the room but turns back at the last minute. "The kitchen is a shithole. I suggest you clean it up. And while I'm at it, can I also suggest you start apologising to everyone you've hurt today? I'm having a bath. Do not interrupt me," she seethes.

I do as she suggested and set about cleaning the kitchen. The blood is a bitch to get off the matte paint on the wall and takes me way longer than I expected. I organise for a huge bunch of flowers to be delivered to Emma tomorrow, as the texts and phone calls go unanswered. I smooth things over with Fin and thank him for having my back earlier with Elliot. Men are easy to deal with. We apologise and move on. Women, on the other hand, are a completely different ball game. They're stubborn fuckers and make you work for forgiveness.

I start off with a peace offering. I knock gently on the bathroom door, as I don't really know what to expect.

"What?" she snaps.

"I brought you wine."

"And a big fat apology?"

"Yes."

"Good, come in then. But you should know it's only because I want the wine."

I go in, place her wine on the side of the bath, kiss her forehead, and take a seat on the closed toilet lid, keeping my eyes closed the entire time, feeling awkward as fuck.

By the time I leave the bathroom, we've talked it all through, and I think we're okay again. Well, that's not entirely true... I'm still mortified about the fact that she's been sleeping with Elliot, but what can I do about it now?

CHAPTER SIX

Emma

My phone ringing wakes me up sometime later. I grab it off the side and see that I've missed loads of calls and texts from Ruben over the last two hours, but thankfully it's Connie's name that comes up this time.

I answer and convince her that I'm fine, that she doesn't need to come round to look after me. She tells me what happened after Ruben disappeared with me and about him going crazy when he came back. She probes and probes, trying to get me to fully explain what happened with Ruben, and why he came back almost as savage as he was with Elliot. I don't think she believes me when I say that I just wanted to be in my own home, but that's all she's getting out of me.

I get up to get some painkillers for my aching face when I put the phone down, I pad through to the bathroom, inspect the damage caused to my eye then grab the pills. I'm pleasantly surprised that it's just red and swollen, but I'm not stupid enough to think that's how it's going to stay! When the bruising hits tomorrow, I'm sure it will be really attractive.

After I find some painkillers, I do something really pathetic. Something that, if you asked me a couple of months ago, I would adamantly swear I would never, ever do. But here I am now, having met Ruben with his mysterious eyes and thighs of steel, and I'm another one of those pathetic women I hate. I find the t-shirt that was wrapped around the peas and hold it to my nose to smell. Although cold, it smells just like him, with a hint of aftershave. I quickly shake it out and pull it over my head, before heading back up to bed, wondering what the fuck has possessed my body since meeting Ruben bloody Foster.

I'm wide awake at six the next morning after God knows how many hours' sleep. To my pure delight, one look in the mirror tells me I was right to think my eye was going to get worse. It's a lovely shade of red and purple; very attractive.

After making myself a cup of coffee, I curl myself up on my chair and edit what I wrote on Saturday. I have to cave to my hated glasses, because there's no way I'm sticking contact lenses in my eye with how swollen it is. Trying to get it out yesterday was challenge enough.

I'm so engrossed in what I'm doing that I jump out of my skin when there's a knock on my front door. I sit stock-still for a while, thinking it's probably Ruben seeing if I'll talk to him before work. Predictably, there's another knock, but this time it's followed by a key in the lock, so I know it can't be him. Only my parents and Molly have a key, and seeing as they're still on holiday, it's not a surprise who it is. I jump up to go and unlock the door from the inside, knowing a key won't get her very far after locking myself in last night.

"I knew you'd be awake already. So... I've been up since five because Sprout was kickboxing in there, so I... wow... Emma, what the fuck?" she says, having only just glanced up at me. She grabs my chin in her hand and carefully pulls my glasses off so she can see the damage.

"It was Ruben. Come and have a seat and I'll explain."

"It was Ruben?" she asks, astonished. "Why the fuck would he hit you?" I watch as she grabs her phone out of her bag. "I'm calling Ryan, he'll come beat the shit out of him for you. I can't believe he fucking hit you." She starts pacing up and down my kitchen before clutching her belly as if in pain. "Shit."

"Oh my God, please don't give birth in my kitchen," I say, as I grab her arm and pull her to the bar stool to sit down.

"I'm fine," she says, still rubbing her belly. "It's just Braxton Hicks, I've been getting them for a few days now. Hopefully it's a sign that Sprout will be appearing soon. So, back to what I was saying, I'll ring Ry and—"

"Chill out, Molls. Ruben does not need beating up. He didn't mean to hit me; I was just in the way." She looks at me like I'm talking another language, so I go on to explain.

"And you sent him away, just like that?" she asks incredulously.

"Yeah. He's a man whore, Molls. He spent the night before shagging some random girls in his living room with his best mate, while his sister slept in the room next door. Not the sort of guy I should be interested in."

"Do you actually know that he was involved? You said that Connie didn't come out of her room, and from what you've said to me about Ruben, he seems pretty smitten with you."

"Smitten? Really? No, he just wants a quick fuck, but he's barking up the wrong tree here, and the sooner he realises that, the better it will be for both of us."

We eventually get on to the reason Molly was here so early this morning. She has been working on all the promotional stuff for my book. The cover has been finalised, and I love it. It's genius. She's made a load of teasers with the quotes we both picked out and has found me a company to host my release and get it out there. Oh, and I should mention she's also opened Facebook, Instagram and Twitter accounts under my author name.

"I can just about use Facebook, but I have no idea about Twitter. You're gonna have to show me what to do."

"It's easy, Em, you'll be fine. Plus, I've made myself an admin on your page and written down all your usernames and passwords, so I can do some of it while I'm not working to keep me busy. That way, you can just focus on writing and working."

We continue chatting about it all until the door's knocked again. Molly must see the colour drain from my face, because she offers to answer it for me and send him away, if that is who it is.

The only thing I hear when she opens the door is a loud, "Oh my God!" I get up to go and see what's going on to find a deliveryman placing the biggest bunch of flowers on the kitchen side that I think I've ever seen. Molly sees the guy out while I just stand and stare.

"See, I told you. Smitten!" I glare at her until she prompts me to open the card.

Emma,
I'm so sorry. Please forgive me.
Ruben x

She comes to look over my shoulder so she can read the card. When she does, she spells out the word *smitten* in a very smug voice. I abandon her and the flowers in the kitchen and return to my earlier seat, trying not to think about them and what they mean. Maybe he's just sorry for hitting me, and that's all there is to it.

Molly is still with me later that afternoon when we hear someone let themselves in. Once again, she's up and at the door to see who it is before I'm even out of the chair. How she does that, being heavily pregnant, I have no idea.

"Hey, Molly. How are you doing?" I hear Connie ask.

"Getting impatient."

Relieved, I get up to go and greet her. "Wow, that's turned into a real shiner," she says when I show my face. "Hey, I didn't know you wore glasses."

"I don't very often. I hate them. I normally have contacts in, but I didn't think that was a good idea."

"Guess not. They suit you, though."

"No they don't. I look like a right geek."

I see a look pass between Molly and Connie before she says, "Okaaaay. So, Ruben is still in a right pissy."

"Look what he sent," Molly says excitedly, pointing at the huge bouquet.

"Ruben sent you flowers. Well, fuck me, has Hell frozen over?"

I guess sending flowers obviously isn't something Ruben does often.

"I can't believe you've broken him," Connie says once we've sat down with drinks.

"I think you'll find he broke me," I say, pointing to my face.

"Yeah, okay, but that's not what I meant and you know it. He's got it bad for you, Em, and he has never, literally never, acted like this before. He had a couple of girlfriends when we were at school, but since we were teenagers, he hasn't been interested. I think Mum and Dad put him off or something."

"But your mum and dad are happily married; how would they put him off?"

"It hasn't always been that way." It's obvious she doesn't want to add any more.

"I'm not interested though, Con. You've said yourself: he's a whore and he uses women. I don't want to be one in a long line of hook-ups for him. I will not be like those girls the other night."

"What if that isn't what he wants?"

"What else can he want?" She raises her eyebrows at me. "You just said he doesn't do girlfriends. Why are you changing your tune so suddenly?"

"I did say that, but I also said I've never seen him act like this. Maybe you're different. Maybe you're the one who will make him see sense and grow up a little."

"Says the one who's been shagging his arch-enemy," I say, sarcastically, but the look she shoots me has me apologising immediately.

Molly eventually heads home and I cook dinner for Connie, just like the old times, before Ruben appeared and sent my world into a tailspin.

"I never thought I'd say this, but maybe you should give it a go, Em. You could be just what each other needs," Connie tries again before she leaves for the night, and I once again sweep her comment under the carpet.

The week drags as I sit at home and wait for the bruising and swelling to go down. I ring in sick to work because I can't turn up to the office looking like this, and I refuse to do any shifts for Connie. I feel bad about it, but I think she knows that my black eye does stem from her stupidity, so she doesn't say anything about my refusal.

Every day, I receive a different present from Ruben. I've had an Amazon gift card as well as paperbacks of one of my favourite series. And this morning, to my sheer delight—and horror—I received a rather large gift card to my favourite underwear store. I can only hope that Connie has brought up in some innocent conversation that I shop there, because I hate the thought of him knowing I have an obsession with fancy underwear. Just because I never show them off to anyone, doesn't mean they don't make me feel better about myself. And because I'm that obsessed, I dig out some concealer from the depths of my make-up bag to attempt to cover what's left of my bruise and head into town to buy myself some new undies. I rationalise that I've managed to lose quite a bit of weight, so I might just need a different size!

Connie stops in on Friday night with ingredients. I'm not sure if she actually wants to have dinner here, or if she just wants to know what I was sent today from Ruben—although when I see her face, it's clear that she already knows.

"You told him, didn't you?" I demand the minute I see the expression on her face.

"Don't know what you're talking about," she says, trying to play innocent, but she digs straight into the bag sat on the counter full of my new goodies. "Wow, that's sexy; he'd love that."

"Shut up."

"I mean it, he has a thing for—"

"Shut up, or you're going home to eat alone!"

"Sorry, just saying."

Before she leaves, I'm instructed to be at her house no later than eleven in the morning for our day around the pool, followed by a night out. Connie has told me that both Ruben and Fin are working all day tomorrow, so it's just us during the day, which means I only have to see him in the evening, and I'm sure he'll be too busy with all the women that will surround him to pay much attention to me.

I arrive in plenty of time the next morning, with enough stuff for a weekend away. I've got a bag for the day, a bag for tonight, and a third full of stuff for Connie for her birthday. I heave it all into her kitchen and shout for her. She appears seconds later, still doing up the top on the tiniest black bikini I have ever seen. She looks stunning in it, but it's tiny, the bandeau top just about covers her boobs, and the bottoms are cut so small that I can only imagine how much of her arse is out on show. I would never be seen dead in it.

"Happy birthday," I say, giving her a hug when she's finished faffing with her boobs.

"Thanks. You moving in?"

"This is for you," I say, handing her the bag with her presents in.

She immediately dives in and starts pulling the contents out. There's a huge range of things I bought, as well as her actual presents, including a huge bottle of Pimm's and all the accompaniments, her favourite biscuits, ice creams that need to go straight in the freezer, and a bottle of pink champagne. I bought her some of my favourite series in paperback, and a gift card for her favourite shop to spoil herself with. I wasn't confident enough actually picking the clothes out for her, so I cheated.

"Awesome, thank you."

"I made you a cake as well. I tried to make it a little healthy, so it's a beetroot and chocolate cake." I wasn't sure about the sound of it when I saw the recipe, but surprisingly, it tastes really good.

"I love that. Thank you. Come on, let's get you changed and head over to the pool. I've got the sunbeds all set up, the fridge is packed."

I head into her bedroom and pull out my swimming costume and towel before removing my shoes and cardigan.

"Just as I thought," Connie says, as she comes behind me and lifts my swimming costume between her thumb and forefinger like it's a dead animal. Okay, so it's not the most attractive of costumes, but it covers as much skin as possible and it draws no attention to itself, or me.

The costume is suddenly launched across the room, and a bag is placed down in its space. "Here, try this one."

I tentatively open the bag and unwrap the tissue paper to reveal a siren red swimming costume. "I knew you wouldn't go for a bikini, so..." Connie mutters in the background. I hang up the scrap of fabric in front of me and inspect what little there is of it. It's a halterneck with a very low-cut front. The only saving grace is that the cups actually have some support in them. There's a strap around the back that can be undone before it plunges—I would imagine almost to your arse crack—and covers about a third of your actual arse.

"I am not wearing this," I say, turning to look at Connie, who is grinning wickedly at me.

"That's where you are mistaken, Emma, because you are. It'll just be the two of us. No one else will see you; it's my birthday, and I want you to start embracing your curves. This will look fucking awesome on you, trust me."

I go to argue but get cut off by her telling me that I don't have a choice and pushing me into the bathroom. Once the door is shut, I just stand and stare at the costume. Connie can obviously guess what I'm doing, because before long, I hear her shout that she hasn't got all day. I eventually decide I'm just going to have to man up and get on with it. She's right, I guess; it is only she who will see me, and she won't judge me.

I manage to get it on, and I'm surprised by how supportive it is. I feel nicely sucked in in the stomach department, and my boobs are held nice and firmly, exactly where they're meant to be, and covered enough so I don't feel like they're about to pop out at any moment. And if I do say so myself, they actually look pretty good. Shit, I just gave myself a compliment. Maybe Connie was right the other day—Hell has indeed frozen over.

It's all going relatively well until I catch sight of my thighs as I turn to leave. There are way too many stretch marks, and way too much cellulite on display. I fucking despise my thighs, hips and arse. I have done since I was a teenager, and they grew too quick for my skin, causing these disgusting stretch marks. They're the reason I'll never be seen in short skirts or shorts.

"You better be ready, because I'm coming in," Connie announces, a second before the door swings open.

My first instinct is to try to cover my thighs with my hands, so Connie finds me kinda slouched over.

"I knew that would look amazing on you. Stand up straight." I do as I'm told because I don't have much choice. "Fuck me, Em, your tits look insane in that. Ruben would have an aneurism," she says, as she jiggles the straps about a bit and tightens it up further to give me even more cleavage. "Not that he'll get to see, of course," she says with a wink, making me question the truth in her words.

I decide to make life a little easier on myself and go for a compromise. "I'll wear it as long as I can cover my thighs."

"Why, what's wrong with your thighs?"

"Are you joking? They're all bumpy and scarred."

"No they're not. They are perfectly good shapely legs. Thousands of women would die for legs like yours. But because I'm such a good friend and saw this coming, I bought you something else."

She disappears from the room before reappearing with a short black wrap I can tie around my waist. I breathe a sigh of relief as she hands it to me and immediately put it in place to cover my thighs. I look back at myself in the mirror and actually smile at my reflection.

"See, you look hot," Connie says, as she grabs my hand and starts pulling me out of the bathroom. "We're not going to get tans in here."

"Wow, it's like I slept through the flight and woke up on holiday," I comment as we approach the pool. As she said earlier, the loungers are out, there are umbrellas up, and a couple of inflatable beds are sat by the edge of the pool. To my surprise, there's even a bar in the corner. The pool is huge. I'm not sure what I was expecting, but it was not this long, rectangular, perfectly blue pool with a round Jacuzzi at one end and a waterfall letting the water into the larger pool.

"How have you never mentioned this to me before?"

"I don't know, I guess it's just normal to me. Dad had it built when I was a teenager. He and Mum do laps every morning. We don't often use it for the glamorous stuff. Today is different, though. I've banned my parents from coming down, so it's just us, the sun, and the water. Oh, and some alcohol," she says with a wink, heading to the bar.

An hour later, we're covered in suntan lotion, lying on the sunbeds with glasses of Pimm's in hand. "This is the life," Connie says as she takes the last sip of her drink and stabs the fruit with her straw. "You mind if I go topless?"

I don't know why I'm surprised. Connie is a bit of an exhibitionist when it comes to her body. She's quite happy to wander around in her underwear, or less, not caring what anyone thinks of her.

"Sure, go for it."

"Join me?"

"You must be kidding, you only just about got me out here wearing this," I say with a laugh.

"True. You do need to undo the back strap if you're gonna lie on your front like that, though."

"Why?"

"Because the strap on the dress you'll be wearing later is smaller, and you don't want tan lines."

"What do you mean, the dress I'll be wearing tonight? I brought one with me."

"I've got you a better one."

"Aren't I meant to be the one giving you presents today?"

"Oh, what I've given you today isn't from me," she says with a wicked smile. "I just chose it all."

"Ruben."

"Yes, and it will continue until you forgive him and talk to him."

"I don't need to forgive him. He hasn't done anything wrong."

"Why won't you talk to him then?"

"Because I don't want to get sucked into something. He's no good for me."

"What if he is, though? I bet he could work wonders on you," she says, looking me up and down suggestively.

"That's your brother you're talking about."

"I'm well aware. I'm also well aware that he has mad skills where a woman's body is concerned, I've heard enough over the years. I think it might do you some good."

I eventually get her to change the subject, and after another hour or two of turning over so we bake evenly, a couple of cool-off dips in the pool, and picking at some lunch, we both fall asleep under the warmth of the sun. Connie's on her back, showing the world her assets, and I'm on my front with my strap undone as I was told—or should I say, as Connie left it when she last walked past me.

CHAPTER SEVEN

Ruben

Well, this week has been all sorts of weird. I've done things I never in a million years thought I would do. Even though I've been totally shunned by Emma after dropping her off on Sunday afternoon, I still felt awful about giving her a black eye, so I decided I needed to do something to at least try to make it up to her. Let's be honest, though, hitting a woman is totally inexcusable and unforgivable, so I wouldn't blame her if she never spoke to me again.

The first thing I did was to ring up the florist in the village to order her some flowers. Having never done it before, I wasn't expecting the amount of questions I got about what sort of arrangement I wanted and what flowers I wanted in it. My answer of something pretty that a woman would love didn't really get me very far with the florist. I ended up finding myself describing Emma's cottage so they could put together something in keeping with the style of her home. It was all going relatively well, or so I thought, for my first time, until the lady on the phone told me how much they were going to cost. I nearly had a bloody heart attack, but I soon came around when she asked if the woman they were for was worth it. I think my response was something inappropriate like 'Fuck yeah she is'. That earned me an inappropriate grunt from what I can only presume was the prim and proper, slightly elderly lady at the other end of the phone.

Once I got over the initial shock of the price, I realised that the lady on the phone was right. I can only presume she knew that I was apologising for something. I mean, why else would a guy order a girl flowers? Although one, albeit huge and expensive, bunch of flowers didn't go anywhere near showing how sorry I was for what I did. So with the help of my lovely little sister, we came up with some other things that might help to make Emma talk to me again. We ordered her a set of books that are apparently some of her favourites, along with a rather large gift card so she could buy more. I didn't realise what a bookworm Emma is until Connie started explaining to me. I hadn't seen any books in her cottage, but apparently they are still packed in a number of boxes in her spare room, waiting for a bookcase. Then, to my pure delight Connie suggested we head into town to buy Emma an outfit for Saturday night; something that would enhance her awesome curves in a way that she doesn't do herself very often. Now, shopping with my sister isn't new to me, but shopping where I get to have the final say on what we get is definitely new. I don't know much about women's clothes to really have much of an opinion. But eventually, we found a dress that we both agreed would look amazing on her—also one that she wouldn't point blank refuse to wear, like some of the ones we looked at.

I then discovered something very interesting about shy, innocent little Emma. It seems that she has a penchant for very sexy lingerie. When Connie started walking into the underwear shop, I pulled her back and refused to help her shop for underwear. It's bad enough that she leaves it around the house drying and occasionally wanders around wearing it. I did not need to be there when she chose it. I was soon informed, however, that it wasn't for her, and that we were buying for Emma. I can't lie, my temperature did rise a little as we walked through the shop to the cashier at the thought of her wearing some of the sets that were hanging up. I came back down to earth with a bump when Connie suggested that it would definitely help Emma forgive me if I got her a sizeable gift card. I was completely in my own world, imagining her parading about in all this lace, and totally forgetting that I have no chance in hell of that ever coming true after what I've done. After everything I have sent her so far this week, and the hundreds of apology texts I've sent and voicemails I've left, she hasn't even replied with a thank you. I think I have really screwed the whole situation up royally, and that causes a pain within me that I don't even want to think about, let alone acknowledge.

I think the biggest shock this week was that I turned down sex. Yes, actual sex with a woman who was offering it to me on a plate right at my front door. But my brain and body are so fucked up with thoughts of Emma that the thought of even accepting her proposition didn't enter my head.

It was Tuesday night. Connie was still at the café, and I was home alone with my laptop, still working on a quote for a regular customer, when the doorbell went. Everyone who usually comes round here just walks straight in. I was only dressed in a pair of shorts, seeing as it was still steaming hot, but I didn't really think anything of it until I answered the door.

"I would have thought you'd have at least text to let me know you were back, not just let me find out from seeing my brother with his face rearranged," she purrs as she steps up to me.

"Danni." I move my face to the side so she kisses my cheek, not my lips.

"Oh, I see, you're gonna play it like that, are you? Make me work for it," she says seductively, smoothing down her long blonde hair that now comes to her waist.

The changes in her were obvious from the moment my eyes landed on her. She has always been into the fake tan, nails and eyelashes, but it seems that since I've been away she's taken it to a new level. Her lips are fuller, and I swear she couldn't frown even if I paid her a million pounds to do so, with the amount of what I presume is Botox that has been injected into her face. That isn't the most obvious change, though. Danni never really had what I would call my ideal figure. She's always been too slim for my liking. She's aware of it, and often made jokes about her boobs and arse being too small for me, but I didn't think that it actually bothered her. Looking at her now, I can't help but wonder if all the times she made those comments she was being more serious than she let on, because staring back at me now is a pair of overly large fake tits. They look way too big for her slender frame, and way too pert to ever be considered real. I may have a passion for a nice, large handful, but for me, they have got to be real. I don't want a handful of silicone.

"I'm not playing at anything. If I wanted to see you, I would have contacted you. Look, I'm sorta in the middle of something, so..." I trail off, hoping she'll get the message.

"I'm sure I could convince you otherwise," she says in a low voice as she once again steps toward me and starts running her fingers down my pecs, making me very aware of the fact that I should have put on a t-shirt before answering the door.

"I don't think so, Danni."

"Oh, come on, Ruben. You know how good we can be. I've missed it. No one else around here compares to you," she goes on, trying to big me up. It won't work, though. I have no interest at all.

"Yeah, it was good, but I'm done. You'll have to go and find yourself another playmate."

She sticks her already full bottom lip out in a pout and moves her hands up to cup her tits. "Surely you want to give these bad boys a go? Bigger is better, right?"

"Danni, I've already said I'm busy. Thanks for stopping by, but I need to get on."

She clearly doesn't get that I'm totally serious, because what she does next shocks me. Now, Danni has never been backwards in coming forwards. She does exactly what she wants and will trample over anyone who gets in her way, but I was not expecting this.

She lets go of her tits, but instead of dropping her arms like I expected, she pulls her strapless top down so it hangs around her waist and just goes back to palming her now very naked tits, stood on my front doorstep, in full view of my parents' house. I bet my dad's fucking loving it, if he happens to be by a window.

"Come on, Ruben. You know you want a taste of these. I can see it in your eyes."

I watch as she pinches her nipples and lets out a little groan that I'm presuming I'm meant to find sexy, along with her parted glistening lips and closed eyes. Unfortunately for her, it has the opposite effect. In the past, it probably would have worked wonders, but she doesn't realise that I've changed. To be honest, I hadn't realised either, but standing here, looking at her make a fool of herself, all I want to do is shut the door on her.

She continues with her little show and mutters things that I should be listening to, I guess, but I completely zone out, thinking about how Emma would never do anything like this. I think about her sweet and innocent demeanour that has her blushing even at compliments. I think about how I would never let anyone see her in any form of undress if she were mine. However, I have no qualms about letting Danni embarrass herself.

I watch as Connie walks up the driveway and smile to myself when I see her chin drop to the floor at the sight in front of her.

"Wow, Ru, I thought you put the rubbish out this morning," she comments as she comes to stand slightly behind Danni.

"That's rich after what you've been up to with my brother," Danni snarls as she looks Connie up and down, making no attempt to cover herself up.

"Fancy putting some clothes on? It's obvious he's not interested."

"That isn't up to you to decide," Danni states viciously.

"She's right, I'm not interested. It's time you left."

She stares at me for a few seconds, I guess to try to figure out if I'm actually being serious or not. After a huff, she covers herself back up, spins around and, as smoothly as she can with her high heels on our gravel, flounces back to her car.

"Wow," Connie says next to me as we both stand and watch in disbelief. "Those boobs look ridiculous on her."

"I'm proud of you, Ru," she comments as we enter the kitchen.

"What for?"

"The old you would have had her in bed in a flash. You like Emma more than you're willing to let on, don't you?"

"What... what are you talking about?" I ask, trying to sound shocked by her question.

"Oh, don't try that with me. I can tell by the way you are around her, how you look at her. And don't even get me started on how you've been acting this week since she stopped talking to you. I know you, big brother, I see it all. If you do anything to hurt her, though, I will go through with my promise of cutting your tiny dick off with blunt scissors while you're sleeping. I love you dearly, but she's too good for you. Too innocent for your man whore ways."

"What are you talking about? I don't like her. I don't like anyone. You know I'm not interested in a relationship." I try to plead my case, but it's clear I'm not doing anything to convince her—not that I really thought I sounded convincing in the first place.

"Whatever you say, big brother," she says with a wink before disappearing into her room.

Fin and I have spent the morning working on a project I've had going on for a few years now. One day, it's going to be my home, but there's still a lot to do.

"What the fuck is up with you today? You're all snappy and agitated."

He's not wrong, and I can't help it. It's just that I know Emma is currently sat around my parents' pool in the swimming costume I picked out the other day. I'm itching to be there, but I promised Connie we would give them most of the day alone before joining them. She had to convince Emma that I wouldn't be there to even get her in the costume in the first place, so she doesn't want her bolting too soon if we show up. I wasn't surprised to receive a text saying she had a fight on her hands. I didn't think

Emma would put it on without one. It will be fucking worth it later when I get to see her, though.

"It's just hot, is all."

Fin raises an eyebrow at me in question. "Right, so it has nothing to do with Emma, then. I know you're dying to get back to your parents' place to see her. It's written all over your face."

I'm not sure when exactly everyone started to be able to read me like a book, but it's really starting to piss me off. Can I have no secrets?

"Only a week till your parents' party now, dude. You're running out of time to do the deed!"

"Fuck off, Fin. It's not like that," I say, then instantly regret it.

"So, what's it like then?" In response, I throw my screwdriver at him. "Ohhhh, you like her," he croons. "Ruben and Emma sitting in a tree, k-i-s-s-i-n-g," he sings, wrapping his arms around himself and rubbing his hands up and down his back, imitating what I want to do to her.

"FUCK. OFF."

"Oh, touched a sore spot, have I?"

"How about you go and carry on in the loft?" I snap.

"Ouch, and to think I was going to offer to help you out."

It's a couple of hours later before I decide it's late enough to head back and find the girls. The anticipation is killing me. I'm not sure if I've ever been this excited before. It's hot as hell out, but I don't think that's why my heart is racing and my palms are sweating. We make quick work of showering and changing into our swim shorts. Fin tried to convince me to just change and head over, but there was no way I was turning up smelling like I did, even if I was just going to jump straight in the pool. He got a huge kick out of this and has been teasing me ever since.

"Come on, lover boy, let's go," he calls from the front door.

"Yeah, I'm coming, hang on."

"You were the one chomping at the bit to get there. What's the hold up?"

I find what I'm looking for and walk toward him. His wicked smile tells me he's down with my plan. In my hand are two super soakers. They just need filling with cold water to make our arrival go with a bang! I'm well aware that it could go horribly wrong, but I'm willing to take the risk in the hope a fun little water fight could ensue.

When we get to my parents' pool, Emma and Connie are laid out on the sunbeds. Emma is lying on her front, and I can see from here that her costume is undone. I can't see Connie very well, but I can see that her legs are bent up. I give Fin a nod and we quickly move toward them, unleashing our super soakers on our oblivious victims. I head straight to Emma, and Fin continues on to get Connie.

"ARGH!" both of them scream at the same time, while Fin and I laugh hysterically.

I watch as Emma jumps up off the sun lounger as fast as she can to get away from the freezing cold water. She must realise at the last minute that there's nothing holding the top half of her costume up, and her hands fly up to her tits to keep them covered.

"You fucking dickheads," I hear Connie shout from behind me.

"For fuck's sake, Ruben. You scared the shit out of me."

Her chest is rising and falling at a million miles a second, and her eyes are still wide and startled. Add that to the nice flush she's acquired from her day in the sun, and she's looking incredible.

"Here, let me," I say, putting my water pistol down on her sun lounger. She looks hesitant as I move toward her, but, to my relief, she allows me to take hold of the straps of her halterneck and tie them around her neck. I then move behind her so I can do up the strap that goes across the back. "You look stunning in that, Em," I whisper in her ear when I'm behind her. I love that my breath against her neck causes goosebumps to break out across her skin, and I'm even more delighted that she actually flinches when my hands touch the bare skin of her back whilst fastening her into her costume.

I'm distracted by another squeal from Connie and my temper surfaces the minute I lock eyes on her. Fin is still squirting her with water, but he is aiming and staring right at her naked tits.

"For fuck's sake, Connie. Put your fucking tits away. I don't need to look at them, and Fin sure as fuck shouldn't be," I shout angrily.

"Oh calm down, you've both seen enough boobs in your lifetimes. They're nothing new."

Fin just stands there, looking like the cat that got the cream, which continues to piss me off.

"That may be true," I say, silently seething that my past with women has once again been brought up in front of Emma, "but I don't want to look at yours, and I don't want him looking at them, either."

"Oh for Christ's sake, you prude," she whinges before turning and reaching for her top, revealing her barely covered arse for Fin to stare at instead. For fuck's sake!

"The only pair I want to be looking at are yours," I whisper cheekily in Emma's ear. I'm expecting her to hit me for the comment, but instead she just flushes and begins to walk away.

She's not getting away from me that easily. I take a step forward, wrap my arms around her waist and pull her with me into the pool. She shrieks in surprise as we fall, but it's soon cut off once we go under.

She's spluttering and trying to rub the water out of her face when we both surface. I turn her in my arms so I can look at her. She's still panting, probably from a lack of oxygen and lungs full of pool water.

"You can let go of me now," she says, trying to wriggle away from me, but all she achieves is rubbing her sexy curves against my body, making my dick twitch in my shorts. I loosen my grip slightly, but only so it won't be as obvious if my dick goes full mast. From what I know of Emma, that's a sure-fire way to freak her out.

"I haven't seen you all week, and I'm hoping you might forgive me for last weekend." I do my best puppy dog eyes at her to try to convince her.

"There's nothing to forgive, Ruben. It was an accident, I know that."

"So why have you ignored me all week, if you don't hate me?"

"I told you that I can't do this," she says, trying to get away again, but I hold tight. "I needed to not be around you."

"You said *needed*, past tense, so does that mean you can be around me now?"

She just stares at me. I watch as her eyes roam around my face while she thinks. "I don't think it's the best idea."

"Well, I think it's a fucking awesome idea, especially with you wearing that little red number."

"See, this is my problem. You need to stop that."

"Why, is it turning you on?" I ask, dropping my voice to a low growl.

I get a slap around the shoulder. "Ruben," she warns, moving with enough force that she breaks my hold on her. "I'm not the kind of girl you think I am, so just stop it." With that said, she swims to the other end of the pool to try to get away from me. Ha, if only it was going to be that easy for her. I'll do everything I can to show her that the kind of girl she thinks I want couldn't be further from the truth.

"I know exactly what kind of girl you are, Emma." *A perfect one.* I don't say that bit aloud, though. I don't want to sound like a complete sap.

Emma

I knew Connie was lying earlier when she said it would be just us two. I just knew he wouldn't be able to resist coming to torture me.

God, the way he looked at me and the things he said to me in those first few moments had me doubting everything. He's so fucking smooth, he knows just what to say to get a girl to react to him. But then I guess that comes with years of being a player and chatting up every girl that comes your way. Damn my stupid body for its reaction to him and his perfect one. I mean, seriously, why did the first guy that showed any interest in me have to look like a fucking god? It would be so much easier if it were a fat, smelly guy.

I watch from the safe seat on my sun lounger as he pulls said body out of the pool. Thankfully, I have dark sunglasses on, so I'm hoping he doesn't know that I'm watching all the water run down his bronzed skin and over the lines of his muscles until they meet the waistband of his shorts. Ruben, Fin and Connie have spent the last thirty minutes messing about in the pool while I sat and watched from the sidelines where I escaped after Ruben's earlier flirting. I got out of the pool as quickly as I could to get away from him, covered my thighs and arse with my wrap, and pretended to ignore them all while my body defied my brain with its reaction to everything Ruben did. It was like my eyes were glued to him, even though my brain was screaming at me to stop, to stop getting myself in any deeper than I already am with my feelings for him. I remind myself over and over again that I will end up getting hurt. Why would the ultimate player change his ways for someone like me?

"Come and help me grab some more drinks, Em," he says as he walks off toward the bar.

We make another pitcher of Pimm's and he grabs a couple of beers for himself and Fin. It's not until we're walking back toward the pool that he speaks. "Why have you covered yourself up in that?"

"I... uh... don't like my thighs." *They're the complete opposite of your muscular ones*, I think to myself.

"You have amazing legs, Emma. There's nothing wrong with any part of your body. In fact, as far as I can tell, it's all pretty perfect." I feel his eyes running all over my back as he says this. I don't need to turn around to see if I'm right. I just grunt a non-committal response at him and pour myself and Connie a fresh drink.

We spend a couple of hours enjoying the last of the sun while drinking and chatting. It doesn't escape my notice that this pitcher of Pimm's is way stronger than the first couple Connie and I made, and I do worry that Ruben may have done it on purpose to get me drunk. The more I have of it, though, the less I worry about his motives and just enjoy an afternoon with friends. It's been a long time since I've spent a carefree day like this. I thought I'd relaxed since moving here and starting my new life, but today has shown me that I've still been clinging onto a part of the old, depressed me. I will be forever grateful to the three people sat around me for helping pull me from that, even though they're totally unaware.

Hannah would have loved this, I think to myself, but surprisingly it's not a sad thought. I'm so glad I've managed to turn a corner and be able to be happy when I think about her, and not just be unbelievably sad that she's no longer here. I know that she'll be looking down on me now, smiling that I have at last moved on with my life. I also can't help thinking that if she was here, she would be encouraging me all the way with Ruben, no matter what is likely to happen somewhere down the road. Although shy, she was also up for doing what she wanted and making the most of opportunities thrown her way.

"Hey, you okay?" Ruben asks quietly, pulling from my thoughts.

"Yeah, sorry."

"S'okay. Here," he says, handing me a fresh drink.

"Thank you."

When we all came to sit down, the boys dragged a couple more loungers over to lie on. I look over to where Connie and Fin are lying next to each other, engrossed in whatever conversation they're having, I can't help but notice that Fin hasn't taken his eyes off Connie since the moment he arrived earlier, and I'm sure there was something a little more than friendly going on under the water earlier when Ruben was distracted.

"Are you sure you're okay? You look a million miles away," he asks, coming to sit on the end of my lounger. I tuck my legs up to give him space, but he grabs them and pulls them down on his lap. I'm weirdly comforted by his touch after my previous thoughts. It makes me feel all warm inside to think that I now have people who care how I am outside of my family.

"Yeah, I'm fine, just lost in my own thoughts."

I choke slightly on my drink when I feel his hands start to massage my calves. I cough and splutter a little before I realise he hasn't stopped, and that it feels amazing. I quickly finish my drink before lying back and enjoying the feeling of Ruben's hands on me.

I panic a little when I feel his hands start to go higher, but the alcohol running through my veins calms my nerves a little, and I let him continue because it feels too good for words.

"We're going to the Jacuzzi, as that's the only place left in the sun. You two coming?" Connie asks, looking down over us with a smile on her face before she turns and skips after Fin, who is already lowering his body into the water.

"You coming?" Ruben asks, unfortunately removing his hands from me and getting up.

I jump up after him and look down at the wrap covering my thighs. I look back up at him and he has his eyebrow raised in question. All the Pimm's must make me brave, because without even thinking, I untie it and throw it on the sun lounger. The smile that lights up Ruben's face warms my heart.

"Confidence suits you, Em."

His compliment makes me blush as always, but I try to take it seriously because it did actually feel good not to worry about my body for once. Maybe his constant compliments about my body are getting through to me. As I start to head toward the Jacuzzi, I jump slightly when Ruben places his hand in the small of my back, which is only partially covered by fabric. When his thumb caresses my skin, I feel my temperature increase another notch. He has some weird effect on me, this man.

He gets in the water first, then offers me his hand to help me up. It's all going really well until my fuzzed-up brain miscalculates the width of the step and I go flying forward into Ruben's chest. I fall with such force that he stumbles back and ends up sitting with me straddling him and holding on to the edge of the pool either side of his head. Somehow, during the whole thing, his hands manage to find their way to my arse, and my boobs are practically in his face.

I look down at him to find him staring straight at them with his bottom lip clamped between his teeth.

"Hey, look, Ruben's in his favourite place—between a pair of tits!" Fin shouts, but he's soon reprimanded by Connie and everything goes silent behind me.

I continue watching Ruben with amazement. As he swallows, I see all the muscles work in his neck and it causes something in me to want to put my lips there. He lets go of his lip and runs his tongue over it. I feel his hands squeeze my arse and he pulls me up higher on his lap. I suck in a breath when I feel something hit my thigh.

FUCK!

I panic and go to move, but he holds on to me tightly and his eyes dart straight up to mine. His eyes are dark, even darker than usual, but weirdly, the gold is shining brightly, giving them a really naughty glint that shows exactly what he's thinking. He squeezes my arse again, and I feel him roll his hips underneath me slightly, causing me to suck in another breath because he managed to move me up further with his arse squeeze and he is now pressing right against my core. The sensation that floods my body is like nothing I have ever felt before.

Thank fuck for all the Pimm's I've had today, because if I wasn't slightly drunk right now, I would be running for the hills. I suddenly hear Hannah's voice in my head telling me to enjoy myself, and it instantly calms me.

Giggling behind me distracts us both from whatever is going on between us, and Ruben loosens his hold on me, allowing me to move to the side and him to sit up properly.

He leans over to whisper in my ear, "I'm sorry, you just—"

"It's okay," I say, cutting him off.

"Really?"

"Yeah, really."

"Good. I don't want to scare you off again, but you have no idea how badly I want you right now." As he says this, he shifts to his side slightly so he can focus on me and, I guess, block Connie and Fin from his line of sight.

Heat instantly fills my face from his comment. I know that he's just as tipsy as I am, so I rationalise that it's probably just the alcohol talking... until I feel his hand run up my thigh slowly, stopping on my waist, and he slides me over into his body. Once again, I feel his length against my thigh.

"Ruben," I warn, but it falls on deaf ears.

He leans forward until he's running the tip of his nose around my ear. "Fuck, I wish we were alone right now," he whispers roughly.

His words make me look up to the other couple in the pool, and what I see shocks the hell out of me because there's only one thing that could be going on over there, and I'm instantly aware that I need to keep Ruben's attention away from them or this day could really go to shit. Fin is leant over Connie, a little like Ruben is to me. The difference is that Connie has her head back against the tiles with her eyes shut, her lips are parted with a small smile on her face, and I can see from here how fast she's breathing. I've read enough sex scenes to know exactly what's going on, and where Fin's hand currently is.

I focus my attention back on Ruben and let them have some privacy—as much as they *can* have in this situation.

Ruben moves his lips down and starts placing small little kisses on my neck. Goosebumps prick my skin. My nipples tighten, and a tingling floods my body and heads straight between my legs.

At the same time his lips hit the top of my chest, his hands come up to the tie around my neck and start tugging.

"What are you doing?" I ask in panic. He's not undressing me, not here. Not anywhere.

"Shhh... you'll get... tan lines," he says between kisses and nips to my skin.

He's right, I guess; I'm right in the sun, but I'm not convinced by his excuse. If he thinks he's getting a look at any more of me than he already has today, then he needs to think again.

When he's dropped the straps of my costume, he pulls back slightly so he can look down at my boobs—not that he can see them with the height of the water. I guess he likes what he sees, because I hear a low growl come from him.

"Fuck, your tits are awesome, Emma."

I feel his hand start to creep up from my waist and I start to panic, until I hear Connie moan rather loudly. Ruben doesn't seem to notice, but it's only a matter of time. I need to do something to keep his attention. I know that I'm seriously going to regret this, but I can't allow him to know what's going on behind him.

Without a second thought, I grab his hand and, to his utter shock, if his bulging eyes are anything to go by, I place it straight over my right boob. Not much is being covered now he's undone my top, and the heat of his skin burns into me. I hear some more whimpering from Connie, and I know it's now or never. I lean forward and place my lips against his. It takes him a second to do anything, but when he does, he lifts his other hand and threads his fingers through my hair at the back of my head and holds so tightly it almost hurts. He groans loudly as I open my lips for him, and our tongues touch for the first time. This groan is perfectly timed, because it comes at exactly the same time Connie moans Fin's name loudly.

I know I'm doing this for Connie and Fin's sake, but shit me if it doesn't feel fucking insane. I already knew having his hands on me was incredible, but kissing him is out of this world. Every time his tongue caresses mine, another bolt of electricity shoots down my body, causing the throb between my legs to become almost unbearable. When he also pinches my nipple between his fingers, I feel like my body is going to shatter into a million pieces.

Ruben eventually pulls back from our kiss and rests his forehead against mine. He looks straight into my eyes when I open them, and it's like he can read every one of my thoughts.

"It's never going to be enough with you, is it?"

I have no idea what he means, and I'm too buzzed from the mixture of alcohol and Ruben to really care.

"Woohoo, get in there, dude!" Fin shouts helpfully from the other side of the Jacuzzi.

I'm mortified that they just watched that. I lean forward and bury my head in Ruben's neck to hide my red face, wondering why I'm the one embarrassed from just a kiss after what they had been up to.

"Ignore him; he's a dick," Ruben whispers to me, then adds, "That was incredible, babe."

"I think it's time we go and start getting ready," Connie announces not long later. I'm seriously grateful, because it means I can get away from Fin's smug smile. I have no idea if it's caused by his own accomplishment earlier or mine and Ruben's kiss, but I have no intention of finding out.

CHAPTER EIGHT

Emma

"What the fuck was that?" Connie asks as we enter her bedroom.

"Me? You want to know what *I* was up to? That's rich, you little slut!" She does have the decency to look a little sheepish. "I was trying to distract your brother from killing Fin when he saw what the two of you were up to!"

"Oh. Was it that obvious?"

"You're kidding, right?" She just shrugs at me. "Not only did it look bloody obvious, but do you have any idea how loud you were?"

"Uh..."

"Loud, Connie. You were loud! Kissing him was the only way I could think that might not result in another fight. Do you go out of your way to try to wind him up, or is it just a natural talent?" I ask with a laugh.

"You'll be surprised to hear that I hardly do anything to piss him off. This week has been a one-off. I didn't sleep with Elliot to get to Ru; he was just here when Ru and Fin weren't and filled a hole, if you know what I mean."

"Ugh, Con!"

"And Fin... well, he's just Fin, ya know?"

"Uh... no not really. You've never said anything about him, but it's been obvious to me since he came back that there's something there. Care to share?"

"Not really, it's old news. We just have this pull, and as much as I know Ru hates it, sometimes I'm just not strong enough to leave him alone."

"You're kidding, you're seriously not going to explain?"

"I will, just not now. We've got just over an hour before I want to head out for food, drinks, and dancing. I don't want to ruin our night with that."

"Fine," I concede, but I will be finding out about them soon.

"Sooo... Miss Morrison, how was that kiss, then? It looked pretty hot from where I was sitting."

"I'm surprised you noticed," I mutter as I slump down on Connie's bed and put my head in my hands. She comes over and sits down next to me, gently pulling my hands away.

"I know we haven't really talked about Ru that much, but you do like him, right?"

I stare at her for a few seconds while I think about what I want to say. "I guess, but—"

"No buts, Em. If you like him, then go for it. Let go and enjoy yourself for once. From what you've said about your past, I'm guessing that hasn't happened often."

"No, it hasn't," I reply sadly. "But he isn't what I want, Con. He's a player. I don't want to be fucked and chucked, so to speak. Plus, he's your brother. That could make things seriously awkward around here. I won't lose you because something stupid happens with him."

"Aw, Em, you're not going to lose me. I'm gonna ask you a question. You don't need to answer if you don't want to, but I've got to ask."

Oh God, I dread what's coming next.

"Have you been with a guy before?"

I look up at her from under my lashes and gently shake my head.

"I thought as much. So, is that why you're so against anything happening?"

"Yes, no, I don't know. I think more than anything I just don't want to be hurt, and I know that he'll end up doing that, whether he means to or not," I admit, feeling stupid.

"Wow, you really have fallen for him, haven't you?"

I throw myself back on her bed with a growl. "This is so fucked up," I groan.

"I promise I won't tell him anything you just told me."

I look up at her, shocked. "I didn't think you would, but thank you."

"I know I've said it before, but I will cause him some serious pain if he hurts you, Em. He's different with you than with anyone I've seen him with before. He really seems to like you. You might want to give him the benefit of the doubt." I raise my eyebrow at her in question. "I'm serious. I know my brother."

Our conversation doesn't make me feel any more relaxed about the situation with Ruben, and it doesn't help that I can still feel him touching and kissing me. My skin is still sensitive from his touch and my lips still swollen from his kiss. I let the aroma of my raspberry shampoo soothe me as the warm water washes the chlorine from my skin. Just thinking back to our kiss earlier has my whole body humming for him. I'm suddenly having thoughts like, *I wish he was here with me now*, and *I want his hands on me again*. What the fuck?

I don't think things like that.

I run my hands over my body, soothing my skin with my moisturising coconut shower gel and notice how hot my skin is to the touch. Whether that's from the sun or Ruben, I have no idea. There's still a low thud between my legs, and my nipples are still peaked. *For fuck's sake, get a grip, girl.*

I try giving myself a pep talk, but I jump out of my skin when there's a knock at the door. My first thought is that it's Ruben and he somehow heard my thought about him joining me, but I shake the stupid thought from my head.

"Can I come in? I'm dying for a pee," Connie shouts.

"Yeah."

She relieves herself while I finish in the shower, wrap myself in a towel and step out of the bath.

"They haven't come in yet. I bet they're talking about you out there."

"Connie, don't."

"Sorry, but it's totally true. I've left your dress hanging on the front of the wardrobe. There will be no arguments about you wearing it, thank you very much," she instructs before beginning to remove her bikini.

I shut the bathroom door behind me and begin to head toward Connie's bedroom when his voice makes me stop dead. The front door opens and Ruben and Fin come strolling in with all their tanned perfection on display and water droplets still running down their skin. They look like a couple of models after a photo shoot. I watch as Ruben lifts his hand and runs his fingers through his long hair to get it out of his face. He's halfway through when he sees me gawping at him. The smile he gives me in response would melt the towel right off me if he had the power. I watch as he leisurely runs his eyes up and down my just-about-covered body, and the gold within them starts to sparkle again.

When he's finished, he walks straight up to me and puts his hand on my cheek before leaning in and whispering, "You're beautiful," in my ear. He then brushes his lips against mine gently, but doesn't push for any more.

He leaves me standing there like a statue as he and Fin head upstairs to get ready for our night out. I raise my hand and touch my cheek where he just did. *God, I'm sad*, I think, when my brain comes back to me.

I rush into Connie's room in case he comes back down, and the first thing I see is the dress hanging where she said it would be.

It's royal blue, and the top half looks just like the top of my swimming costume. It's halterneck and has cups for my boobs that will not allow me to wear a bra because of how low the front is, and it looks like it also has no back. It's loose-fitting from there down, which I'm grateful for, but it looks shorter than something I would usually wear. I continue to look down and see that there's a pair of silver-heeled sandals and a clutch to finish the look off.

The whole look is lovely. I'm just not sure how lovely it will look on me.

"Fuck it," I say to myself, before applying some of my favourite coconut moisturiser and pulling on the lace pair of Brazilian knickers I brought with me for tonight. I forgo the matching bra because there's no way I can wear it under the dress. Once I've soaked up the moisturiser, I unzip the dress and slide it on. The back is almost as low as the costume, and it has a matching strap across the back like Connie said it did. I'm grateful, because it gives the cups a little more support. I hate feeling like my boobs aren't contained properly.

I hate to say it, but the dress feels really good. It's loose and hangs smoothly over my stomach and arse, and down low enough to cover what I hate of my legs. I look in Connie's full-length mirror and actually smile at myself. It seems that Ruben is having a good effect on me with all his compliments. I wonder what he'll think of this dress on me?

I'm shaking that thought from my head when Connie comes in wrapped in a towel and clutching a chilled bottle of prosecco and two glasses in hand.

"Wow, Em, that looks even better than I thought it would. The colour really suits you, too. It really brings out your eyes."

"Thanks."

"You're not going to argue about wearing it?" she asks incredulously.

"No, I actually really like it. It shows more skin than I'm used to, and I can't wear a bra, but I think it actually looks good."

Connie comes bounding up to me and throws her arms around me, squeezing tight.

"I'm so proud of you. Ruben is going to trip over himself when he sees you later."

Almost an hour later and I'm standing back in front of the mirror, looking at the finished package. Connie spent ages curling my hair and doing my make-up. I have soft waves hanging around my shoulders. She wanted to put it up, but I refused because I thought it would make me feel even more naked with the open back. I have grey, smoky eyes, and dark lips. I don't think I have ever looked at myself in a mirror and been actually pleased with what I saw until now. I seriously owe Connie, because somehow she's performed a miracle.

"How did you do this?" I ask her as I turn from side to side, looking at myself.

"I didn't do anything other than enhance what's already there, Em. How many times do I have to tell you that you're beautiful?"

I feel myself tear up a little when I think that I would fit it better with Hannah and her stunning good looks instead of looking like the frumpy fat twin like this. We would have looked great together with our matching eyes and lips but opposite everything else. Dressed up like this, I can actually see more of her in me as well, instead of just those eyes and lips, and it brings a great deal of comfort to me in that moment that she's still with me, even though she isn't here in person.

"Are you okay? You look like you're about to burst into tears," Connie asks, looking concerned

"Yeah, I'm fine. Just a little overwhelmed." I turn to look at her and my breath catches a little. "Shit, Con, you look awesome." She has on a skintight black cat suit that's cut down to her bellybutton at the front and completely open at the back. Her blonde and red bob has been straightened and messed up. It looks great with her dark make-up. Suddenly, I feel like I've been knocked down a peg or two again.

Ruben

I haven't been able to think about anything else but Emma's lips since I moved mine away from hers earlier. Fin keeps talking to me, but fuck if I know what he's going on about. My head, heart and dick are still in the Jacuzzi with my hands all over her.

"Stop looking so fucking happy. Yeah, so she kissed you, and it was hot, but it doesn't mean she's gonna let you bang her."

"Shut the fuck up, Fin."

"Oh, is someone feeling a little frustrated, or was there more going on under the water that we couldn't see?" he says with a chuckle that makes me want to punch him.

"No, nothing else happened. Not that I would tell you if it did. Emma's not one of our normal hook-ups. She deserves more than how we usually treat women," I say, thinking of how we often share experiences of the night before. I will not be telling anyone about anything that happens between Emma and me. I might sound like a right pussy saying it, but that is strictly between us. She's too precious to share. Yep, huge pussy!

"Good God, she has you wrapped around her little finger, hasn't she?"

This continues on and off while we get ready for our night out, but I start to ignore his piss taking. I'm well aware of what a U-turn I've made with Emma. I know I've never felt anything for a girl, and that all I wanted was a quick shag, and now suddenly I have this girl who's turning my world on its axis with how much she's fucking with my head. I hate to admit it, but it's actually a nice change to be going after something I want for more than just a night.

We're both in the kitchen with beers waiting for the girls to appear sometime later because, as predicted, they're running late. It took me all of ten minutes to get dressed and run a little gunk through my hair. I really need to get it cut; it's starting to piss me off, being so long. I'm not in Australia any more. I went to find myself, but something I now need to do all over again.

A pair of clicking heels gets our attention and we both look up to see Connie heading our way, swaying a little with what looks like an empty wine bottle in her hand.

I need to start trying to ignore what my sister chooses to wear, because it only ever pisses me off. Tonight, she's showing off all her curves, and way too much cleavage and back in a skintight all-in-one thing. I roll my eyes at her and she smirks back at me, knowing exactly what I'm thinking. I'm sure she does it just to torture me.

"Where is she?" I ask, suddenly panicked that she might have done a runner again.

"Just coming. Calm yourself down, Ru," she laughs, before walking past me.

I keep my eyes trained on Connie's bedroom door until she appears. The sight of her when she does takes my fucking breath away. God, she's stunning, and I want her all to myself. Does that make me a greedy bastard? Fuck yeah, but I don't care. This woman standing here, looking unsure of herself is mine; she just doesn't know it yet.

She stops and stares back at me. I don't know why—I look like a tramp compared to her in my grey trousers and blue shirt that's a couple of shades darker than her dress. Coincidence? Um... no!

"The taxi's here. Will you two snap out of it? We need to go before I starve to death," Connie helpfully offers from the front door.

Emma goes to move, but in true Emma fashion she trips over her own feet and falls forward. I bolt toward her before I even realise I've moved and grab her around the waist.

"Shit," she curses and brushes her hair out of her face.

I hold on to her for a few seconds to make sure she has her balance. "Okay?"

"Yeah. Just a little too much booze on an empty stomach. Sorry for falling on you... again."

"Fall on me any day," I offer, as I brush a remaining strand of hair away from her eyes. "You're the most beautiful thing I have ever seen, Emma. You look absolutely stunning. I think I did a good job picking this dress, don't you?" I say, looking down at her tits. God, how badly do I just want to take her upstairs for the night and not go out where others can see her?

"Thank you," she says shyly, "you look good, too. Shall we go?"

"After you," I say, edging her forward and placing my hand on her naked back, just because I can. After all, I wouldn't want her falling again.

The four of us go to a Thai restaurant Connie chose in Cheltenham. The food is great and soaks up some of the alcohol we'd consumed earlier in the day, which is a relief. I'm not sure how long we would all last after the amount we'd had, combined with all the sun.

Connie drags us to a cocktail bar before we eventually end up in a club for some dancing.

After sitting opposite Emma at the restaurant and then again the cocktail bar, I was more than ready to get a little closer to her in that sexy little dress, but apparently fate has different plans. We aren't in the club five minutes before Connie bumps into a group of friends from school. We all start dancing as a group, but it's not long before two of the guys take a shine to Connie and Emma and concentrate their attention on them. Fin is more than happy to entertain the two females—no surprise there—and I'm left on the sidelines, watching them all enjoy themselves. Even Emma seems relaxed and happy as she dances with this stranger, which surprises me.

I eventually have enough of their jolliness and my patheticness and head over to the bar to drown my sorrows. I shouldn't be so depressed about not getting close to Emma. I should just man up like I usually would and cut in, but something is stopping me. I'm not sure if I don't want to come across like I'm jealous, which I am of course, or whether I'm actually enjoying watching her have fun, even if it isn't with me.

I down a couple of shots of Jack at the bar before I see her heading toward the toilets. Alone. I drain the last glass on the bar in front of me before getting up off the stool and following her out of the main room of the club.

I follow her until she's just in front of the disabled toilet. I step up behind her and she squeals as I grab her around the waist and pull her into the little room.

"Shhh... it's Ruben," I whisper in her ear as the lights flicker on with our entrance.

"Ruben what are you—" I don't let her finish her question. Instead, I show her exactly what I'm doing by backing her up against the wall and crashing my lips down on hers.

I touch my tongue to her lips, ready to convince her to open up for me, but she does instantly and she makes a sexy little noise in the back of her throat when our tongues collide. I lift my hands to hold on to her cheeks and tilt her head to the side slightly so I can deepen the kiss. I just can't get enough.

There's no finesse to this. I'm so desperate for her after the state she left me in earlier. I explore every inch of her mouth and start to run my hands over her sexy curves. When I get to the bottom of her dress, I hitch her leg up around my waist and slowly run my hand up her thigh until I'm palming her arse. I can't help the noise I make when I discover her high-cut lace underwear. I bet they look fucking awesome on her.

It's not long before her hands start to wander as well. I was worried that I'd ambushed her and she wouldn't want this, but she's giving as good as she's getting. She must be having problems dealing with the sparks that flew between us earlier as well. Her hands run down my neck and onto my chest, but she's obviously unhappy with the fabric covering me, because I feel her start to undo my shirt until she can touch skin.

"Fuck, Emma," I groan as she runs her hands down over my stomach. I drag my lips from hers and start kissing across her jaw and down her neck. While I kiss and suck her skin, I grab her other thigh and lift her off the ground. She instantly wraps her legs around my waist. This lines us up perfectly, and I roll my hips, causing my throbbing dick to rub against her pussy. Her head falls back against the wall with a thud. Fuck, she's so responsive to me. What will she be like when I get her naked? The thought gets me even more fired up, if that's at all possible. I pin her to the wall with my hips, grab her tits with my hands and begin kissing and nipping the skin gently.

"Jesus, Ruben," she pants as I suck hard on a bit of skin I've just uncovered by pulling her dress to the side slightly.

"I need you so badly," I say, going back to kissing up her neck. "I need to be inside you. I need to hear you scream my name. But you're too good for this. We can't do it here." It wouldn't be the first time I'd banged a girl in the toilets of a club, but that sure as hell isn't happening with Emma. She deserves the works: wine, candles, romantic music—the lot. "Come home with me, Em, please."

It's like my words are a bucket of cold water thrown over her. Her body stiffens beneath mine and her hands instantly lift off my chest.

"What... what's wrong?" I'm almost scared to ask.

"Put me down, please," she says coldly.

I do as she asks and take a step back from her. Her chest is rising and falling rapidly, she has red marks from my lips all over her neck and chest, and her lipstick is all over the place. She looks fucking hot. She pulls the top of her dress so it's covering her properly before smoothing down the skirt. It doesn't escape my attention that she hasn't looked at me since I put her down, keeping her eyes downcast.

"I'm sorry; this can't happen," she says in the same cold, distant voice, before she takes off. She flips the lock on the door and practically runs.

I desperately want to chase her, but I'm also aware that I'm standing here, half dressed with a raging hard-on and lipstick covering my face.

I quickly go about sorting myself out so I can go after her and try to find out what the problem is. She was into it. She was with me all the way. What happened to make her stop so suddenly?

CHAPTER NINE

Emma

What the fuck have I just done?

What the fuck am I doing?

I've got all these questions flying at a mile a minute through my mind as I run as fast as I can through the club in these heels.

"Emma," someone calls, but I keep my head down and keep going. I need to get away before he comes after me. He's going to want answers, and I'm not sure I've got any. I'm a mess, and a huge fuck up. I mean, what woman in their right mind runs out on Ruben Foster? Ruben Fucking Sex God Foster. I just left him in the disabled toilet after I half stripped him. He told me that I was too good to be doing that in a toilet and asked to take me home, and I just ran like the hounds of hell were snapping at my heels. What the actual fuck is wrong with me?

"Emma, wait. Are you okay?"

When the owner of the voice appears in my vision, I see that it's the guy I was dancing with earlier, and he looks seriously concerned. Well, to be fair, who wouldn't be? I can only guess that my lipstick is smeared all over my face and God knows what kind of marks Ruben has caused on my neck and chest. I must look like a right hot mess.

"Shit, what happened?" he asks, looking me over, I guess to check for injuries.

"I'm fine, I'm fine," I say, trying to convince him. "I just need to get out of here. TAXI!" I shout when I get to the curb outside the club and see one pulling up.

"I'll come with you, make sure you get home all right."

"NO!" I shout. "Sorry. I didn't mean to shout. Honestly, I'm fine. Thanks for your concern, but I really need to go." I jump in the taxi, give the driver my address and sit back. It's then that I see Ruben come running out of the club, looking panicked. I slouch down in my seat and pray he hasn't seen me.

When we get to my cottage, I pay the driver before jumping out and heading straight to my back garden to find the spare key I have hidden in one of those fake pebble things. I pay no attention to my surroundings—my only focus is getting inside my house and locking myself in away from Ruben, who I know is going to turn up very soon.

I'm embarrassed. I'm mortified, and I'm still seriously turned on. I can't get the image of what we were doing out of my head. It's like it's on repeat, as are the feelings that are still surging around my body. They won't leave me, either.

I shove the key in the door and quickly get myself inside. I smile to myself as I lock all the deadbolts my dad insisted on, but it only lasts a second because the thought of my dad—any of my family, in fact—bursts the dam that I was holding. The first sob erupts as I slide my back down the door. I put my head in my hands and let the tears flow. I let out all the frustration, tension and embarrassment that he has caused within me.

"Em, is that you?" I hear shouted from the living room, and I scream bloody murder. I grab the first thing I can get my hands on, which, usefully, is my fabric owl doorstop. It may be filled with rice to make it heavy, but it ain't gonna do fuck all to protect me from a burglar.

I go to stand up and have the owl in both hands ready to swing at whoever it is. It completely escapes my attention in my panic that the intruder knows my name.

"Shit, Em, what's wrong?" he says as he enters the kitchen and sees what a mess I am.

One look at his face and I drop the owl and run full force into his body. He has to take a step back to steady himself but soon wraps his arms around me.

"Shhh... it's okay, Sis, I've got you."

I'm only there for a minute or two before the pounding on the door starts.

"Emma, open the door, please." It sounds quite a polite request, but I can hear the panic and possible anger in his tone.

Dec goes to move toward the door, making me panic. "No!" I say between sobs.

"Uh... are you sure that's the right thing to do?" he asks, but continues to hold me as Ruben carries on knocking the door and shouting for me to answer.

"I'm sorry, Em. I thought you were with me. I didn't mean to freak you out. I'm sorry. Please let me in so we can talk about it."

Dec pulls back from me and I sheepishly look up at him. He raises an eyebrow in question and I let out a breath; there's no way I'm going to get away with not explaining all this to him.

"Do I need to go out and beat the shit out of this guy for hurting you?" he asks all protectively, which makes me laugh, but also makes my tears fall again.

"No. Come on," I say, taking his hand and dragging him into the living room.

"So you just ran out on him after all that?" Dec asks, looking both proud and shocked by my explanation of what happened.

"Pretty much, yeah."

"Why? It sounded like it would have ended well," he says with a wink.

I often forget that my annoying little brother is no longer a child and has grown into a fully grown player. From the stories I've heard, I'd say he's had more women than I've had hot dinners.

"I should've known you would side with him. You're just as bad as each other."

Dec looks a little offended by my comment but doesn't say anything about it. "So, you don't want to be with him then, even though you almost shagged him in the toilets?"

"I didn't almost shag him in the toilets. I told you, he said we needed to stop."

"Yeah, he said that, not you! I'm sorry, Em, I don't get the issue. How do you go from getting hot and steamy with this guy to running home and crying in my arms?"

"He's bad news, Dec. He's a player and he'll end up breaking my heart if I let him."

"Oh my God. You've fallen for him, haven't you?"

I just flush red and look away from my little brother. I'm aware of how guilty I look, but I can't help it.

"Wow, I never thought I'd see the day," he says with a smile. "You, who have always said you don't want a man, have fallen head over heels for one. Why are you running from him if you want him?"

"He'll break my heart. I just know he will. He doesn't do relationships, and I have no intention on being a one-night stand. After all the heartache I've had losing Hannah, a broken heart is the last thing I want to deal with."

Throughout our conversation, Ruben has continued knocking the door and shouting through for me to answer. It's not happening; I can't face him.

"You don't know that's what's going to happen, though. He seems pretty persistent for a guy you say only wants a quick shag. There's no way I'd go to this much effort. If a girl did to me what you just did to him, then I wouldn't be chasing her. I'd find a replacement. I'm sure the club was full of willing women."

I hate to admit it, but Dec does have a point. Why bother chasing me?

"What was that noise?" I ask when I hear a weird kind of purr come from the front door.

"Oh, it's your house-warming present. I completely forgot with your dramatic arrival."

I watch as he gets up and goes in the direction of the noise. A few seconds later, he comes back with a black case hanging from his arm.

"I thought it was about time you got what you've always wanted, now you have your own house. Say hello to Kia," he says, placing the pet carrier down on the coffee table in front of me.

I glance in through the black meshing and see a pair of green feline eyes looking back at me. My eyes fill back up with tears as we look at each other. I've wanted a cat for as long as I can remember, but Hannah was allergic. I spent a lot of years with an imaginary one when I was younger. I've had the name picked out for forever, and she had to be black and white. I don't remember why—probably from *Postman Pat* or something!

"I don't like the thought of you being alone," Dec adds, making me cry harder. I can't lie, the first thing I thought about when I bought this place was getting one, but with all the decorating and everything I hadn't really got around to it.

"Oh God, those are happy tears, right?" Dec asks, looking slightly panicked.

"Yeah, they are. Thank you so much, Dec. I love her," I say, leaning forward, unzipping the carrier and getting the tiny thing curled up on my lap.

"So how come you're up here during the summer? I thought you'd be too busy with your business." My little brother is always up to something.

He's currently studying for a degree in business down in Exeter, but at the same time he's started his own surfing company on one of the more unknown beaches. From what I've seen on Facebook so far, it seems to be taking off.

"Lilly hasn't been very well, so I had to come to see her."

"What? She hasn't said anything to me," I say, sounding a little put out. Things have been a little strained between us since Hannah's death. I couldn't help it, though; Lilly just looks so much like Hannah that it hurt like hell to look at her for quite a while after the accident. We've never spoken about it, but I know Lilly knew. That being said, I'm hurt that she's been so ill that Dec came all the way from Cornwall to be with her and she couldn't answer when I called and texted her over the last couple of weeks. "I guess that's why she's been AWOL, then. I was starting to get worried."

"She's just had a bad flu. She hasn't really been out of bed, so don't be offended that she hasn't been in touch." Something about the way Dec says that doesn't sit quite right with me, but I don't question it. "She's starting to improve, so maybe try again in a few days."

"I wish I knew you were coming. I would have sorted out a bed for you." My spare room is still full of boxes, most of which are rammed with books. I really need to get out and find a bookcase for them all. "You can sleep with me," I offer, but don't really mean it. I hate sleeping with other people. The only person I've ever shared a bed with is Hannah, and Dec knows this.

"I appreciate the offer, Em, but I'm okay sleeping on the sofa. I'm only staying the night, I really need to get back tomorrow. I don't trust the guys alone with the business."

After setting up Kia's food and water bowl and installing her litter tray in the bathroom, we turn in for the night. Dec to the sofa, once I've found him a pillow and blanket, and Kia and myself up to bed. She gets instructions from me about using the litter tray if she needs to and not the bed. She purrs at me as I talk to her, and I can't help but smile at her sweet little face.

Even though we went to sleep in the early hours, I give in and get up at seven. I might be an early riser, but that isn't the issue this morning. The problem is that every time I shut my eyes, he's there. His golden eyes won't leave me, and I keep waking up all hot and sweaty after dreaming about our rendezvous in the club toilets.

I'm still unsure how I feel about the whole thing. Part of me feels like a right tramp for doing that in the toilets, but another part of me seriously regrets running away. If I'd just agreed and let him take me home...

My mind wanders again as I visit the bathroom to start the day. I love that the minute I get out of bed, I hear small paws following me. We've only been together a few hours, but already she makes me feel much more content in my own home, and less alone.

I don't need to look into my living room to know that Dec is still asleep. I could hear his snoring when I was halfway down the stairs.

I get the coffee machine going as soon as I step foot in the kitchen. Being the daughter of a barista, only the best coffee will do. The first thing Mum bought all of us as we moved out was a smaller version of the coffee machines she has in Cocoa's, her coffee shop. Mum always said her kids were too good to drink cheap instant coffee, and I'm always grateful for that, but never more so than this morning when I'm exhausted and slightly hungover.

The smell of the beans instantly perks me up as I tidy the kitchen. I check Kia isn't about to dart for freedom before I unlock the back door to put the rubbish in the wheelie bin. I just step out of the door when a figure slumped in one of my garden chairs scares the shit out of me. I scream at the top of my voice and my heart pounds in my chest. I hold the rubbish bag to my chest in defence as I begin to step back.

When my panic starts to fade and I actually look at the person sat there, I realise it's Ruben, and he looks awful. His usually bright eyes are dark and sullen, and they have dark rings around them. He's still wearing the same clothes as last night, and his once crisp shirt is now rumpled and creased.

Our eyes connect and hold for a few seconds before I drop my arms and the rubbish bag in defeat. As I do this, I watch his eyes lower to take in my body. The moment I see the beginning of a smile tug at the corners of his lips, I seriously regret my choice of nightwear: his t-shirt!

"Emma, is everything okay?" Dec shouts as he comes running through the kitchen to stand behind me.

Ruben is instantly out of his chair and walking toward us. Gone is his tired and weary look, and in its place is a pumped-up guy ready to fight.

"Here we go," I mutter quietly to myself.

I look back and forth between the two of them staring at each other like they're going to kill each other.

I'm suddenly pushed to the side as Ruben launches himself at Dec and holds him around the throat up against my kitchen wall.

"Ruben, don't you fucking dare," I shout as I start pulling at his shirt. I've learnt my lesson from last time, so I stand well back.

I can see how he would get the wrong idea about what's going on here, with Dec in nothing but his boxers, obviously having just woken up, looking at the pillow crease on his cheek and his bed hair. "Ru, you've got it wrong. Don't do it, please."

"It's okay, Em. If he cares about you then he'll see it. And if not, I'm pretty sure I can take him."

I look at Dec, completely confused by his words until he winks at me. He means our eyes. If Ruben really cares and has paid attention, then he'll see the resemblance between us and back off.

I look back at Ruben and beg him with my eyes. He looks back and forth between us a few times before I see the penny drop. He slowly lets go of Dec and steps back.

"You're Declan," he states. Then, in case he's wrong, he adds, "Right?"

"Yeah. And I'm guessing you're Ruben, seeing as you've spent all night by my sister's back door. That's a bit much, don't you think?"

"I just wanted to talk to her," Ruben replies, like I'm not right here.

"Didn't you get the message when she left you high and dry last night and then refused to answer the door that you banged on for hours?"

Kia comes bravely to the back door and I scoop her up in my arms while I continue to watch what's going on in front of me.

"She can't just ignore me after... that."

"Hello." I wave at them. "*She* is stood right here and can speak for herself."

They both turn to look at me and wait for me to say more. I suddenly regret saying anything at all, because now Ruben wants answers I still don't have for him. I take a deep breath and say the only thing I can think of that's going to put an end to this situation. "Ruben... yesterday was a... mistake. I'm sorry, I just got drunk and carried away. It won't be happening again, so I suggest you leave."

"Come on, Em. You don't mean that."

"I do," I say as strongly as I can.

"No, you don't. I could tell that isn't how you felt, alcohol or not."

"You need to leave," Dec growls. "She's told you what she wants. You need to listen to her."

"But," he questions, looking between us, and I step aside so he can pass me and head home. Eventually, he gets the message and slowly starts heading through my front garden with his head down.

"You okay?" Dec asks as he puts his arm around my shoulder and pulls me to him. I nod into his chest, but I don't think I'm being truthful.

I didn't want him to go.

Ruben

I begged.

I practically begged for her to talk to me. And in front of her brother.

I sat there all night hoping she would cave and talk to me, even that she would feel sorry for me and at least let me in. I didn't know she was inside telling her brother all about what happened with me. No wonder he didn't seem to like me very much. If Connie had told me that story about some guy, I wouldn't be too impressed either.

"There you are. I just got off the phone to Emma. I'm sorry it didn't work out, Ru. When you both disappeared, I presumed... well, it doesn't matter."

I just look at her, grab a carton of orange juice from the fridge and head straight up to my bedroom. I need a shower and sleep, and hopefully at some point during those, I will forget everything about the last twenty-four hours.

I can't stop fucking thinking about it. About her. What the fuck is wrong with me? Why can't I put her behind me as a failed hook-up and move on to the next hot woman I find? Why am I comparing every woman I see to her, and why are none of them anywhere close?

I spend the rest of Sunday afternoon, after I get a little bit of sleep, helping Connie sort out a delivery at the coffee shop. Somehow, she managed to order double the amount she normally does and couldn't move it all herself as well as serve customers. I hated seeing the sympathy in her eyes every time she looked at me. I much prefer the look of distaste I get after spending night after night with different women.

I'd forgotten that we'd agreed to go to our parents' to have dinner tonight. Connie helpfully reminded me as we locked up the coffee shop. The last thing I need is my mum on my case.

I try really hard to be my normal self so that Mum and Dad don't notice my funny mood straight away, but I don't do a very good job, because we've only just finished passing around the jug of gravy before our dad asks what is wrong.

"The girl he wants turned him down. Repeatedly," Connie answers helpfully.

"Well, that must have been a novelty, Ruben," Dad says, laughing.

Mum keeps quiet about the whole thing, but I see her studying me, so I know she's going to add her two pence about the situation at some point.

An hour later, and Connie and Dad have disappeared to watch TV, leaving Mum and me alone in the kitchen, cleaning up after our dinner.

"What happened with Emma then, baby?"

I hate it when she calls me that. I'm twenty-bloody-seven years old now.

"How do you know it has anything to do with Emma?"

"Connie mentioned there was something between you two." Of course she bloody did, gossiping cow. "Connie is thrilled you've fallen for her."

"I haven't fallen for her, Mum."

"Really? So you're not sulking because she turned you down? I've never seen you sulk about a girl before. Normally you don't care less if they say yes or no to you. Not that many say no to my gorgeous boy," she adds with a wink, making me cringe. "Plus, I saw you the other day turning Danni away from your front door. She was so brazen as well. I was proud of you, baby."

Oh great, Mum watched Danni get her tits out.

"She's just different to the other girls. She deserves more."

"All girls deserve more than how you treat them, Ruben," she chastises, "but the fact that you've recognised that about Emma means you care more about her than the others. It would be so good to see you settle down, maybe make me some grandbabies."

"I don't think that's going to be happening anytime soon. She's barely talking to me at the best of times."

"She might be just as scared as you are, Ruben. Have you thought of that?"

"Scared? I don't think so, Mum. She doesn't think I'm good enough for her, and I can't say I don't agree."

"Don't be silly; any girl would be lucky to have you, baby."

"You have to say that, I'm your son!"

"No, I don't. From what Connie's told me, the feelings are mutual."

"I'm not so sure about that," I say sadly.

"If you like her, baby, you've got to show her how you feel. Fight for her."

"I thought I was," I mumble to myself, but Mum hears it and puts her arm around my shoulders.

Mum's advice rings in my ears all through the night and this morning. She's right, of course. I need to continue to show Emma how I feel if I want a chance with her. Giving up now would result in nothing happening. It's not like she's suddenly going to start chasing after me when she spends most of her time running away as fast as she can. She wants me, though. I can tell by the look in her eyes and by how she reacted to me on Saturday night. If she wasn't interested, she wouldn't have acted like she did.

Just one thought of Saturday night and my cock is as hard as fucking steel. Nothing I do relieves it properly. It's calling for her, and her only. If only she understood just quite how badly I want her. No, not want, need. How much I need her.

I found out from Connie last night that Emma isn't working today, so I decided to take the morning off, seeing as I have site meetings all afternoon and well into the evening, and instead I go for a run. I'm just hoping I can convince Emma to come with me.

When I get to her cottage, I knock on her back door, but after getting no answer, I check to see if it's unlocked. It is, so I peer around the door and shout for her, but again, there's no response. I'm not surprised, as I can hear music blaring from upstairs. I decide to go in search of her.

When I find her, I can't quite believe my eyes. I lean against the bathroom door frame and watch with amazement as she cleans the bath while singing and dancing along to Jason Derulo's 'Talk Dirty to Me'. She's scrubbing the tiles with a sponge in only a purple lace bra and knickers. This girl has turned me into a right perv, as I once again find myself watching her without her knowledge. She continues to wiggle her arse in time to the music, and I know I need to announce my presence.

"How I want to strip that lace from your body and make you scream my name," I answer, when she sings for me to talk dirty to her.

She screeches, like she does every time I make her jump. She turns around but must slip on a bit of cleaner in the bath, and I just about catch her before she crumples into a pile.

I lift her out and stand her on the shaggy bath mat. She instantly reaches for a towel to cover herself up.

"I don't think so," I growl, snatching it from her hands and throwing it across the bathroom. "Never hide this body from me, Emma."

"Wha-what are you doing here?"

"Well, I came to see if you wanted to go for a run, but I wasn't expecting to find this," I say, as I skim my knuckles down the side of her breast, over the indent of her waist and down to her hip. I watch her eyes glaze over slightly and my semi turns to a full-on hard-on when I see her nipples pebble under the lace of her bra at my touch.

"Fuck, you're unbelievable. Your body is like fucking heaven, somewhere I want to go and never leave." I watch as her heart rate increases with my words, but she says nothing. She just looks back at me with wide eyes. I know I've caught her off guard, and I'm realising that seems to work best with her. If I give her too much thinking time, she takes off running.

Her hair is pulled up in a clip, so I take the opportunity to place my lips to her exposed neck. The smell of her mixed with raspberry and coconut hits me instantly, and it makes my mouth water for a taste of her. I let my tongue sneak out and gently caress her soft skin. Her head rolls to the side and I feel her moan vibrate against my lips.

I step into her body. She must be able to feel my erection pressing into her belly, but she doesn't do anything. She's still frozen to the spot. I lift my hands slowly up from her hips, back up over her waist and grab on to her tits. I rub my thumbs back and forth over her peaked nipples and she moans again, making me lose my mind.

I grab on to her arse, back her up against her vanity unit and lift her up onto it. Her legs wrap around my waist and she holds tightly. My cock fits perfectly against her hot little pussy, barely contained by a small strip of lace. I continue kissing her neck and make my way around to the other side while I run my hands up her back and undo her bra. The thought of getting her nipples in my mouth has my cock weeping for her. I slowly start to pull the fabric away from her body before I get that feeling of déjà vu.

Her hands snap up to keep the cups over her tits and she leans back away from me.

"Get out," she says, so softly between pants that I almost miss it.

"Em, don't do this again. I need you so badly," I say, rubbing myself against her. "I promise you it will be amazing. I'll make you feel so good."

"No."

I stand back slightly to give her some space. After a second, she moves her arm so she can cover both tits, then pushes me back farther before jumping off the side and running to her bedroom. She slams the door, and I hear her thud back against it.

"Emma, what are you doing? Come out."

"Just leave, please," she says, but it sounds like she's holding in tears.

"No, I want to talk to you. I want to know what's stopping you. I know you like me, Em. I know you want this."

"You don't... you don't want me. I'm too much of a m-mess. G-go find some random girl to hook up with like you usually do and leave me alone."

"I don't want to hook up with a random girl. I want you."

"I'm sorry, Ruben. It's just not going to happen."

After a few seconds, I give up. It's not until I'm at the bottom of the stairs that I hear her start to sob. I desperately want to go back up and comfort her, but I know I'm not welcome. I want to know what's going on with her. She's so up for it, and then it's like a switch is flipped and she goes cold. What's making her stop, and how can I convince her that whatever it is, is all in her head? I want her so badly, but I can only hold out for so long. Mum told me to fight for her, and I have, but I can't help but feel like I keep hitting a brick wall, and something tells me I'm not going to break it down. How is it the only girl I've ever wanted has to be the most complicated one I've ever met?

CHAPTER TEN

Emma

I hate this little voice in my head that keeps telling me he's going to hurt me. That he will get what he wants, then leave me high and dry. I'm not too scared to admit to myself that I now like him way more than I should. I can't do anything that doesn't involve thoughts of him. I can't sleep without dreaming about his dark, golden eyes and how it feels when he kisses me. I want to slap myself around the face for feeling like this about a guy. Things were so much easier when I'd convinced myself that I didn't want a relationship, and that I was fine being single forever. I am well aware that I'm acting like one of those annoying characters I read about and want to scream at to get a grip—the guy likes you, go for it. But it's easier said than done when it's not your life and your heart on the line. This is my life. My life, that I would like to live without any more drama and heartache. I've had more than enough of that.

After spending all day writing with Kia curled up on my lap for company, I decide that it's time I manned up and went to talk to Ruben. I need to apologise for my actions the last few times we have been together, but I also think it's time I explain what my problem is. At least then he'll understand me a little better. The thought of talking about Hannah makes my heart beat a little too fast with panic, so I decide to waste a little more time and go for a run that will end up at his place.

Unfortunately, I'm at his front door faster than I was hoping for. I grab the handle while talking a deep breath, and I walk in.

"Ruben?" I shout as I enter.

"Hey, Em. He's not here. He's not home from work yet."

I let out a huge breath at the knowledge that I might be able to put this conversation off longer.

"Are you okay? You look like you've seen a ghost."

"Yeah, fine. Just a little light-headed from jogging in the heat, I think." I feel awful lying to Connie, but I can't cope with having the conversation I need to have once, let alone twice. She pours me a cold glass of water and places it down on the breakfast bar.

"So…" she starts. "Have you come to have a repeat performance of Saturday night?"

"No, that was a mistake. It won't be happening again."

"But…"

"No. I'm serious, Connie."

"But you both really like each other, what's the harm?"

"I'm not interested, okay?" I say, a little more harshly than intended.

"Okay."

Thankfully, Connie changes the subject to stories of her regulars in the coffee shop. I refuse her offer of dinner and I head off to finish my run. Now I've missed my chance at seeing Ruben, I don't want to hang around and wait for him to come home from work.

Feeling adventurous, I take a slightly different route through the fields to get home. I jog up a small hill toward a barn that looks like it's being converted. There's a bench in the field next to it, so I stop to catch my breath and to enjoy the view that goes on for miles over the valley below. It's gorgeous with the sun starting to descend and the sky turning a bright shade of red. Whoever owns that barn will get to enjoy some serious views when it's complete. From what I can see, the gable end is made up entirely of glass. It's the perfect writing spot.

I sit there for about ten minutes with everything about Ruben still rolling around my head, as well as all the things I need to say to him. I get up and head off when I start to get this weird feeling come over me that I'm being watched.

I spend the whole next day at work. I'm so busy that it almost distracts me from my impending conversation with Ruben. I decide that I'm going to see him as soon as I've finished work, seeing as I'll most likely end up being here late. I may have cut my hours down to three days a week at the office, but they're always three very long days.

"Hey," Connie says when I walk into her living room later that evening. She looks awkward and uncomfortable, which is really weird because Connie is always chilled out, no matter what's happening around her. "Shall we go and have a drink outside? It's such a lovely evening," she says, getting up and practically dragging me toward the back door.

"Uh... yeah, sure."

And then I hear it. A loud, female groan from upstairs.

"Shit," Connie curses under her breath and looks back at me with wide eyes.

"Is that—" I don't finish my question, because as more noises start to filter down from upstairs, it's damn obvious what's going on up there.

It's like someone has stabbed a knife through my heart. I didn't quite appreciate how much it would hurt to know he's with someone else. That's what I wanted though, right? I've told him multiple times to move on and find someone else. He's only doing what I told him to do, and yet it feels like my heart is bleeding and I'm about to lose the contents of my stomach.

"Emma," Connie whispers sympathetically.

She barely gets my name out before we cringe at a high-pitched scream, followed by Ruben's name shouted very enthusiastically. I can't stop it this time. I run to the bathroom, fall on my knees and heave until my stomach is empty. Connie is instantly behind me, rubbing my back.

When I'm done, I sit back against the bath and put my forehead on my knees.

"I'm so sorry," Connie whispers as she puts her arm around my shoulders in comfort. "If I knew you were coming, I wouldn't have let you."

"It's not your fault. And it's not his, either. He's only doing what I've told him to do. I just didn't expect—" I can't finish that thought. I don't even really know how to.

We've just escaped the confines of the bathroom and Connie is grabbing me a drink before I leave to get rid of the putrid taste in my mouth, when we hear the clicking of heels against the stairs. We both turn toward the noise and watch as she appears in our line of sight. I instantly feel sick again. She's tall with platinum blonde hair, and her make-up looks almost perfect, apart from the smeared red lipstick from her earlier activities. She's wearing a long mac that she's still doing up as she walks toward us, giving us a shot of her waxed nakedness and the garter and stockings she's wearing beneath.

My stomach churns at the sight of her perfection. I feel just like I used to when standing next to Hannah and Molly. Gone is the slightly more confident woman Connie and Ruben have brought out of me in the last few weeks. I crawl further under my rock the longer I look at her.

"Connie," the beautiful stranger says, as she walks through the kitchen toward the front door.

"Danni," she sneers.

Danni? Danni as in Elliot's sister who Ruben turns to on a regular basis? Of course she looks like that; why would I expect anything else?

"Been back to the Botox doctor, I see," Connie quips.

Well, that would explain her face. It makes me feel a little better knowing that what I'm seeing isn't natural. Only slightly, though.

Danni tries to frown and snarl at Connie's comment, but with the amount of Botox filling her face, she doesn't get very far. Instead, she flicks her hair over her shoulder and flounces out the front door. Seconds later, we hear a shout and loud bang from upstairs. God knows what he's doing now. All I know is that I cannot look at him. I need to get away from him as soon as possible.

"I should go," I say, heading the same direction as Danni.

"Wait, Em. Are you okay? Shall I come with you?"

"No. I'm fine, honestly. It's fine. This is as it should be." I try to make myself sound convincing, but I'm well aware that I fall very short of the mark. Connie's raised eyebrows tell me she doesn't believe a word of it.

I manage to convince her that I am in fact okay and take myself off home before Ruben shows his face. Connie was less than impressed with his actions, so I can only imagine what's going to kick off between them once I leave.

I don't care.

I don't care.

I don't care.

I repeat this mantra as I shower and change into my pyjamas. After feeding Kia, I grab my Kindle and get cuddled up in bed. If there's even a chance that he's going to come after me, I want to be as far away as possible in both distance and mental capacity. Lost in a book is exactly where I need to be right now.

Until my phone rings. When I see that it's Molly. I have to answer in case it's time for Sprout's arrival.

Ruben

I spent all day working after I found Emma in her bathroom wearing that bloody lace underwear. I tried everything, I still *am* trying everything, to get that image out of my head. After I finished everything I could think to do in the office, I headed out to what will one day be my home to keep myself busy. Hopefully, it will keep my mind distracted for long enough that an hour might actually pass by without me getting a hard-on. It's getting ridiculous.

I walk past the wall of windows and a figure sat on the bench in the next field catches my eye. I instantly know that it's her. The buzz that races through my body when she's near is never wrong. She's sat, staring into space, deep in thought. I desperately want to go over and try to talk to her. To try to find out what's eating at her, because it's clear watching her that she's fighting with something. I stand and watch her for a good ten minutes before she looks around, gets up and starts jogging off. She looks like a pro now. I'm really proud of how far she's come since that first day I found her, barely able to control her breathing. I work for a little longer, then I head home when it starts getting dark.

After getting another grilling for what I've done to Emma from Connie on Tuesday night after I finish work, I jump in the shower before dinner.

I'm just walking out of the en suite when a figure in my bedroom makes my heart skip a beat. For a fleeting second, I think it's Emma, but when my brain functions properly I realise that there's fake blonde hair and brown eyes looking back at me. My heart sinks and I'm just about to tell her to leave when she opens her coat and lets it drop to the floor.

She is stood in fire engine red lingerie. The bra is cupless, showing me her large, albeit fake, tits. A garter belt is around her slim waist, holding up sheer stockings with lace tops. I skim down her legs until I see her black, leather, strappy hooker heels. When I look back up and see her smooth pussy that I know will be ready for me, all thoughts leave my head. Emma doesn't want me. She keeps telling me to go and shag someone who is up for it, and here that is on a plate. I may as well take what I need. I'm still horny as hell from yesterday morning. No matter how many times I have a wank, it isn't going away. Maybe this is just what I need.

I stride straight up to her, grab on to her arse and push her back until she is up against the wall. There is no way we are doing this in my bed. The last woman that was on my bed was Emma. I am not ruining that memory with this trashy one. My lips instantly find hers, and I kiss her with all the passion that has built up in me from wanting Emma. I feel her hands go to the towel that is around my waist and it gets ripped from my body before she grabs on to my cock. I'm not completely ready for her, seeing as she isn't who I really want, but after a bit of encouragement on her part, I'm ready to go. I lean over to grab a condom and roll it on.

Danni goes to say something, but I return to kissing her, because I don't think I can bear to hear the sound of her high-pitched voice. I return my hands to her arse and lift her, before plunging into her in one swift move. She pulls her mouth from mine as it falls back and she lets out a loud moan that has me cringing.

Now, I'm not proud of myself. I'm usually a great lover, but this is about one thing. For me, this is about releasing my pent-up frustration over Emma. It has nothing to do with Danni, other than the fact she is the willing woman who is here right now. I have no intention of making this good for her. I know what I want, what I need from this, and I'm going to get it. If it was anyone else, I might feel guilty, but she uses me just as much as I use her, so I feel less of an arsehole.

I haven't had sex for so long that it doesn't take much to get me on the edge of orgasm. Danni is moaning and groaning for England, but that doesn't surprise me; she's always been a loud one. I know she is faking it, though, and to be honest I don't care. I shove my face into her neck as I let go. Don't get me wrong, it feels good, but it doesn't consume me like I need it to. It almost feels empty, which is a little like how I feel on the inside, knowing what I have just done.

I let her legs drop, pull out of her and move as far away as I can. I throw her coat at her when I pass it. "Thanks, but I think you should leave."

"But—"

"No buts. You got what you came for," *Sort of*, I think as I head back into my en suite for another shower. I can't keep the smell of her on me a minute more than necessary.

I listen to her pull her coat on before she storms out of my room and down the stairs. I hear voices downstairs and I can only presume that her and Connie are throwing abuse at each other.

I spin around, slam the en suite door and punch the solid oak with as much strength as I can muster.

"FUCK!" I shout into the enclosed space.

What the fuck did I just do?

<hr>

"You fucking arsehole," Connie shouts at me. What I don't expect is the unopened can of Coke she was about to drink to come flying toward my head. I just about catch it before it makes impact and put it on the side.

"What the fuck?" I question as she comes over and starts punching me.

"I can't believe you fucking did that, you fucking dickhead," she shouts as she continues punching.

I grab her wrists to stop her. She's really angry. Her face is red and she's shaking. "What's wrong with you?"

"Emma was here, you dickhead. She heard the lot," she admits at a much lower volume. "She heard you fucking *her*."

"Fuck." I let go of Connie and perch myself on the edge of one of our bar stools.

"One moan from Barbie and she was running to the bathroom to throw up. You've fucking done it this time. I hope the plastic princess was worth it, because I think that could be it for Emma."

"ARGH," I shout into my hands as I scrub them over my face and pull my hair back tightly. "I'm going for a run."

"Don't you dare go and see her. There's no way she wants to see you anytime soon, trust me."

"I won't." I mean it. I won't go chasing after her this time. I know I've fucked up badly. I don't think there's anything I can do to convince her that she's the one I want now.

I run for miles, trying to figure my shit out. It doesn't help. I still hate myself for fucking Danni, and I still can't get Emma out of my head. The thought of what she felt when she heard me with Danni makes me feel sick. I was meant to be showing her I wanted her. I was meant to be fighting for her.

I end up outside Emma's house. No surprise there. I have no intention of knocking, or even seeing if she's in. I just stupidly thought that I might find out if she's okay by just being here.

Well, that was the intention, but as I stand in her front garden, it's obvious even from here with her open windows that she's crying.

And now I feel like even more of an arsehole.

CHAPTER ELEVEN

Emma

The moment I heard Molly's voice on the phone the other night, I burst into tears. Not just tears—full on ugly sobs. I felt so stupid at the time, and I still do now, about my reaction to Ruben sleeping with someone. He's not mine. I've told him time and time again that I don't want him. I should not be this gutted about losing him.

Losing him.

Ha, I never had him in the first place. We've had what, like, two kisses? I've fought against my feelings for him because I knew I'd get hurt, and look what's happened anyway. I'm the one crying into my pillow while he's losing himself in another woman.

I blink back my unwanted recurring tears as I shut down my computer. I promised Molly I'd go round and have dinner with her and Ryan tonight. She wants to try to cheer me up, and to be honest, I really need it. I need a friend, and I hate to say it, but I don't want to see Connie. Not yet. She just reminds me of him, and I can't bear the look of sympathy I know will be in her eyes.

I head home first so I can get changed. I look ridiculous in my boring work clothes now I've lost some weight. My black trouser suits hang off me. I need to go to town to get some new ones. I'm sure my colleagues think I'm weird enough as it is; I don't need to be walking around looking like I've borrowed my grandmother's wardrobe.

I've just turned the car off when my phone starts ringing. When I see it's Connie, I have to fight with myself to answer it. I know I shouldn't, and that she has no control over Ruben's actions, but I'm not liking her much at the moment.

"Hey, how are you?" It comes out sounding way too happy and high-pitched.

"Uh, fine. You?"

"Yeah great, I just finished work."

"I was hoping you could pop into the shop. I need a favour."

"Yeah sure, but I'm going to Molly's for dinner later so I can't stay long. Let me just get changed and I'll be there."

"Awesome, thank you."

Thirty minutes later, I've found somewhere to park and I'm walking into Connie's packed coffee shop.

"Wow, it's busy," I say when I eventually get to the counter.

"I know, a load of coaches came for a day trip and now there's a water leak at the entrance to the car park. No one can leave until they've fixed it. They've all been here for hours."

"Good for business, though. What do you need me to do?" I watch as she reaches below the counter and hands a phone over to me.

"This is Ruben's. He left it here earlier. It's been going crazy. Please could you drop it at the house?" She must see the reluctance on my face. "He won't be there. He'll still be at work, I'd imagine, but at least it'll be there when he gets back. Some of the phone calls are from big clients, and I don't want them waiting too long if it's important."

"As long as I only have to drop it off."

"Of course, I wouldn't put you in that position, Em."

"I know. Okay, have a good evening. I'll see you tomorrow, what time are you picking me up?" Connie has booked us both in to her usual hairdresser's. She insisted that it was time I did something with my locks, and seeing as Saturday is her parents' anniversary party that I haven't been able to get myself out of, it's the perfect opportunity.

"Five. See you tomorrow," she says as she starts serving her next customer.

I quickly head to her place with the intention of leaving the phone on the kitchen worktop and getting the hell out of there before I run into Ruben.

The house is in silence when I let myself in with the spare key. I breathe out a sigh of relief that he isn't here.

I go over to the kitchen worktop, but something tells me to take his phone up to his room. I have no idea where the little voice comes from, and I have even less idea why the hell I listen to it. He's not here, though, so I can put it on his unit and then leave. He'll find it faster that way, I rationalise to myself.

I start questioning my decision as soon as I begin ascending the stairs, but I carry on nonetheless. As I hit the top step, a noise starts buzzing in my ears as I think about what I'm about to do. I should not be entering Ruben's personal space without permission. He has no idea I'm even in his house, let alone about to go into his bedroom.

The door is ajar when I get there, so I slowly push it open. What I find inside is not what I was expecting at all, and it has my feet rooted to the spot.

Although my body is frozen, my eyes flick back and forth between the TV and the back of Ruben's head and shoulders in complete shock.

I've never watched porn. People might say that what I read and write is porn, but they're wrong—that's romance, not just meaningless fucking. I look down from the very graphic scene on the TV and back to what I can see of Ruben, which admittedly isn't a lot, but I can still tell what he's doing. As well as the back of his head and naked shoulders, I can also see the top of his naked knees where they're slightly bent. He's sat on the floor, leaning back against the bed, and the slight movement in his body gives him away instantly.

Suddenly, making me jump, he throws his head back on the bed and grunts loudly. He stays there for a few seconds while he catches his breath, I guess.

I must make a noise that I'm completely unaware of, because he turns his head, snaps his eyes to mine and holds them for a few seconds. It's almost like he thinks he's dreaming, that I can't possibly be standing there looking back at him.

It feels like hours that we're both stock-still, just staring at each other. My heart is racing in my chest, and I know that I really should be leaving. I've just seriously invaded his personal space and caught him doing something I'm sure he really didn't want a spectator for.

He eventually breaks eye contact with me and begins to move, but before I know what's going on, he is in front of me in his boxers. Luckily, he covered himself up before walking over here.

He reaches out, grabs my wrist and pulls me into the room before closing the door behind me. I step back away from him but soon bump against the door. He steps into me, but not before I notice that he has a serious bulge in his boxers already. *So much for needing recovery time*, I think, before I'm distracted when he presses the length of his body up against mine.

I suck in a breath as we continue to stare at each other. Even more heat rushes down between my legs, and I feel it start to throb in a way I've never felt before. I'm sure the quiet moans and groans that are still coming from Ruben's TV aren't helping the situation.

"You're going to run again, aren't you?" he growls in my ear.

All I can think about is kissing him and having his hands on me. This is totally at odds with how I felt a few minutes ago, never wanting to see him again after the other night, but being here with him changes everything. He's right, I should run, but that rational side of my brain isn't firing right because all I can hear is *let go, take what you want, what you need.*

I can't form any words, so I just shake my head at him and bite down on my lip nervously, because I have no idea what's going to happen if I stay. It could be the biggest mistake of my life. *Or it could be the best thing that has ever happened to me*, a voice says from somewhere deep inside me.

"You should. I'm not good enough for you. I've treated you so badly. You deserve better than me," he whispers, running the tip of his nose around my ear.

"I know," I manage to say back. My voice sounds all gravelly and weird when it comes out.

"Fuck, I need you," he says as he rubs his erection into my stomach. "I made a mistake yesterday. Jesus, I need you so bad. Only you."

I sense some sort of apology in those words for what he did the other night, but I can't be sure, and to be honest, I don't really care at that moment.

"Fuck it," he exclaims before his lips touch mine and I feel his tongue pass them in search of mine.

I repeat his two words and tilt my head to the side to accept his kiss. The groan he emits when our tongues touch spurs me on, and I lean into him more. His hands that were gently resting on my cheeks skim down my sides, and I feel him lift up the hem of my vest top so he can touch skin.

He continues to kiss me passionately while he rocks his hips back and forth into me. His hands caress the skin of my stomach. I'm aware that I should be self-conscious that he's touching a part of me I hate, but it's only a fleeting thought. Having his hands on me again just feels too good for me to care.

He pulls his lips from mine and starts to kiss down my neck. His breath, like mine, is coming out in fast pants. I guess his heart is racing too.

His hands slip my vest up and over my boobs, exposing my white lace bra. He crouches down so his face is right in front of them, before shoving it right in my cleavage. I feel his tongue lick and his teeth graze my sensitive skin while his hands squeeze my boobs and his fingers flick over my nipples, sending tingles all around my body.

My breath catches in my throat when I feel him pull the fabric of my bra cup down to expose my nipple. The cool air of his breath makes it pebble almost painfully, until I feel the incredible heat of his mouth wrap around it. The feeling is like nothing I've ever felt before. The electric shocks shoot out all around my body. I even feel it in my fingertips and toes. I slump back more against the door as my body tries to deal with the alien feelings he's creating.

Ruben continues to suck and tease my nipple with his tongue. I'm aware I'm panting like a dog, but I don't have a care in the world right now. I'm totally putty in his hands. If he's worried I'm going to run, he shouldn't be, because I don't have the power to walk away from what he's doing to me.

"ARGH," I shout involuntarily when he pinches my other nipple. At the same time, he sucks hard, and I swear he nips with his teeth.

"Fuck, Em, you're so hot. You have no idea how long I've been dying to do this for. I've needed my hands on you since that first day I saw you in the coffee shop. I've dreamt of how you'd taste, what your tits would feel like. You've been fucking killing me."

I can only whimper back at his words as his attention returns to my boobs.

I feel his hand run down my stomach, and I don't think anything of it until it slips under the waistband of my skirt.

"Ruben?" I question.

"Shhh. Trust me."

I don't get time to even think about a response, because I feel his fingers part me and he grazes my clit gently. My whole body flinches at the contact, making Ruben chuckle to himself.

Ruben

The feel of the lace of her knickers on my knuckles tells me that she's probably wearing a matching set. God, how I'd love to see if I'm right.

I feel a small nest of hair and I can't help but think what a nice change it is from all the perfectly preened and hairless women I've been with in the past. I gently part her and softly touch my fingertip to her little bundle of nerves. I look up, because I'm desperate to see her reaction. She's been so responsive to me so far that I can only imagine how she'll react to this, and I'm not disappointed. Her eyes are closed, her cheeks are flushed, and she's biting down hard on her bottom lip. The soft purr that comes from her almost makes me lose all control and throw her down on the bed. I need to remind myself that although I want to take as much as I can here, I also don't want to push her too hard. She isn't one of those girls. She needs to be treated properly, which is a little of a novelty. Being a gentleman doesn't come that easily to me.

I continue to tease her gently while I watch her in amazement. I love how she reacts to everything I do. Wow, fuck, hang on. I never say that word when I refer to anything about a woman. The thought makes my movement falter for a few seconds, long enough for her to open her eyes and look down at me. When our eyes lock, it's like someone has taken a sledgehammer to my chest. Fuck. Me.

I shake the weird thoughts and feelings away as I reach a little farther down so I can slide a finger inside her.

"Holy cow," she mutters, followed by another purr.

I bend my finger up until I hit that spot inside her. I hear her breath catch again and watch her mouth fall open before her pussy clamps my finger with a force I've never felt before. Her whole body locks up tight before it starts pulsing with her release. All I can do is watch her in complete amazement. It is by far the sexiest thing I have ever seen. I'm completely lost in her.

When she looks like she almost has her breathing back under control, I lean in for another kiss. I pull my finger from her and revel in the little aftershocks I can feel. I pull my hand free before pulling back from her. I keep eye contact while I lift my hand to my mouth and suck my fingers into my mouth. Holy shit, if that isn't the sweetest thing I have ever tasted. I knew I wanted a proper taste of her before, but I'm now drooling at the thought.

"Emma," I go to say something, although I have no idea what to say after that, but I'm stopped by the look of horror on her face. "What's wrong?"

"I've got to go," she says in a panic as she starts to sort out her clothing and hides her awesome tits from me.

"Emma," I warn, "Don't run."

"What?" she questions, looking confused. "I'm... uh... not running. I'm meant to be having dinner at a friend's house. I should be there now. Shit."

I stop her with a hand on her waist before she bolts from the room. "Wait. You're really not running this time?"

"I... um... I don't really know what I'm doing, Ruben," she says, looking flushed and panicked. "Thank you... for... that, but I need to go. Sorry," she says, looking slightly embarrassed as her eyes drop down to my crotch.

She surprises me by reaching up on her tiptoes and giving me a short but sweet kiss on the lips. By the time I open my eyes, she's already down the stairs, leaving me alone once again. But this time, I'm left with a little hope. I look down at my cock that's barely being contained by my boxers and let out a huge sigh.

There's no way we are leaving it like that tonight. I don't care that she's going out; I'll be there waiting for her when she gets back so we can... talk. I don't know what's changed for Emma, but I'm going to make the most of the opportunity while I can.

CHAPTER TWELVE

Emma

I can still feel the tingles within my body as I pull up at Molly's place thirty minutes later. I tried to get here as fast as I could but ended up getting stuck behind a grandad driver. It's only now I pull up that I realise I don't actually remember the majority of the journey. My head was still back in Ruben's bedroom.

Part of me can't believe it went that far, but the other part is shouting, *At fucking last!* And that part is right; it has been a long time coming. I was so angry with him after he was with Danni, but one look at him tonight and all that anger just disappeared. For the first time, I think I really let myself admit how much I liked him. I've been telling him to find another woman, but the pain of him actually doing that made me realise how much I didn't actually mean it. I think I knew that anyway, but it actually happening was like a slap in the face.

Molly is pulling the front door open before I'm out of the car. She has a scowl on her face as I head toward her.

"Where have you been? I've been worried sick," she chastises.

"Sorry, I was—"

"There's something different about you." I stand there as she runs her eyes all over me. "You little minx, you're late because you've been with him," she correctly guesses.

"What... I... uh—"

"Oh, don't even try to deny it. Your eyes are glassy, your lips are swollen and, if I'm not mistaken..." She reaches out and pulls the neck of my vest down slightly to reveal a very bright love bite. "See. I fucking knew it! Come on," she says as she grabs my hand. "You need to tell me everything."

"Is that really necessary, Molls?"

"Yep. I haven't been able to have hot passionate sex for what feels like years with Sprout here in the way, so I'm gonna live vicariously through you."

I'm relieved to find that it's only Abbi upstairs, and that Ryan and Jax have gone to the gym. It feels alien enough having this conversation as it is, I really don't need to have it in front of them as well.

I find it a little odd to say the least that Molly is so excited and so proud of me for having my first orgasm. Both her and Abbi make me explain the whole experience for them. In detail.

"You know, I wouldn't have minded if you'd cancelled," Molly says, after asking as many questions as possible about my time with Ruben. "You could have continued what you started."

"No, it's fine. I felt kinda awkward afterwards, so it was good to get out of there," I admit.

"Why was it awkward?"

"Oh good, more questions!" I quip back, earning me two sets of raised eyebrows. "I don't know, I guess it's just not what I'm used to. I had no idea what to say to him after that."

"I doubt he wanted you to say anything, Emma. He probably wanted, and still wants, you to repay the favour. You once again left him high and dry, and probably with the bluest balls known to man."

"Oh shit." I never thought about what I was supposed to do next. I wouldn't even know where to start. Molly and Abbi can both obviously see the panic wash over my face, because they start offering me advice and tips on what to do.

When I eventually leave later that evening, not only do I have the dress Molly wanted to lend me for Saturday night, but my head is also spinning with all the different things I can do to pleasure Ruben. Some of them are pretty straightforward; others I don't think I'll be trying anytime soon.

I'm not surprised to find Ruben sat on the deckchair by my back door when I get home. Something told me that I hadn't seen the last of him for the night, and I can't help the butterflies that erupt in my stomach at the sight of him in his grey jogging bottoms and fitted white t-shirt. My mouth goes dry as I look at him, so instead of saying something, I have to settle with smiling.

"Hey, babe," he says, as he gets himself up and walks right up to me before planting a kiss to my lips. When he pulls back, the smile on his face melts my heart.

"I guess you're coming in, then," I comment with a laugh.

"Damn right."

He follows me in after I unlock the door, but as soon as I hear the door shut behind me, I'm pulled to the side and pushed up against the kitchen worktop. Ruben's hands go straight into my hair, and his lips are on mine.

His kiss completely overwhelms and engulfs me. I have no idea how much time passes. It's not until Ruben jumps back, scaring the shit out of me, that we disconnect.

"Fuck, shit! I forgot you've got a cat," he says, panting and holding his hand to his chest.

I look down to see Kia weaving her way in and out of his legs, purring away gently. After a few more laps, she sits at his feet and looks at him until he leans down and picks her up.

"Introduce me," he demands, as he looks back at me with a sparkle in his eye.

"Kia, this is Ruben. Ruben this is Kia," I say with a laugh as I scratch her head, making her purr in his arms. "Dec bought her for me as a house-warming present."

Watching Ruben with the small kitten melts my heart. His hands are almost as big as her whole body. I continue to watch as he tickles her behind her ear. "You go sit down, and I'll get drinks." I stand and watch him leave with Kia still in his arms. I can't help but admire his arse as he walks away. He really is fine, this man. Thoughts of what the hell he's doing with me re-enter my head, but I manage to push my insecurities away while I pour us both a glass of water. I'm sure he'd prefer alcohol of some sorts, but I don't have any in the house. In the long run, this could be a good thing, because God knows what would happen if I got even slightly tipsy with him around, especially after earlier.

When I enter the room, I'm still filled with warm fuzzies as I watch Ruben throw a little fluffy mouse for Kia. He looks up at me when I place the drinks down on the coffee table.

"She knows she's a cat, not a dog, right?" he asks, as Kia comes back over and drops the mouse by his feet.

She eventually wears herself out and curls up on the top of the sofa by Ruben's head.

"Now she's asleep, I can do what I really want to do," he says, before turning and leaning over me so I have no choice but to lie back on the sofa.

"I've had the longest night, waiting for you to come back," he growls, before his lips are back on mine.

As he deepens the kiss, he pushes my long skirt up to my thighs so he can get his knees between my legs. He must feel me freeze slightly when his hands run over the skin on my thighs, because he whispers that he loves my legs. Damn him for knowing what I'm thinking.

When I feel his hands move around to grab my arse, I pull my lips away from his to put an end to the kiss. He isn't happy with this and tries to continue.

"Ru, wait."

He sits back and pouts at me, which makes me smile back at him. I run my eyes down his body. His chest is heaving with his heavy breathing, and it's clear where his thoughts are at by the tenting of his jogging bottoms. "What?"

I'm silent for too long while I think about how to word what I want to say.

"You do want this, don't you, Emma?"

I scramble to sit myself up a little and put my hands on his strong thighs. "Yeah... it's just..." I trail off.

"Good. As long as it's what you want, because I know that you are what I want. I've never done this before. I've never felt like this before."

I can't help the goofy smile that lights up my face at hearing him admit that to me. Embarrassingly, my eyes also tear up a little. We continue to stare at each other until I build up the courage to say what it is I need to say.

"I've never done this before either," I say, but I don't think he realises I mean something different to him. He's never been in a relationship and cared about a woman before, whereas I've never been with a man, full stop. I'm not ready to admit my complete innocence to him yet, though. "So we're going to do this differently. I am not going to fall straight into bed with you, Ruben. We're going to get to know each other, to build up to it. This needs to be as different as possible compared to what you've experienced before."

I can see he's disappointed by what he's hearing, but fair play to him, because he covers it very quickly.

"Okay, so we're what? Dating?"

"Yeah, I guess."

"Wow, this is a novelty!" he says with a cheeky smile. "I can do this though, right?" he asks as he leans forwards and kisses me again.

"Uh-huh," I mumble my agreement against his lips.

I eventually managed to get Ruben to leave just after midnight. He tried his hardest to get me to let him stay, but it wasn't happening. I meant what I said: we are doing this properly, for both our sakes. For mine, because this is totally unknown territory for me, and the only way I know how to deal with it is to take it one step at a time. And for him, because his normal is to just to jump into bed with a woman. That will not be happening here. He's going to have to work for it. I don't mean work for the right to sleep with me, I mean work to build my confidence so I'll feel like I can put myself out there like that. The thought that he's going to rip my heart to pieces is still at the forefront of my mind, but I do realise that I need to live a little.

I re-read my book the other night and it reminded me that I had written more or less one hundred thousand words about being able to move on from a tragedy and finding happiness and love again. And there I was, possibly running in the opposite direction from those things. I'm aware it's fiction and not a self-help guide, but the therapy I found in just writing it is enough for me to try to follow my own advice.

I went to bed after I locked the house up last night, but I couldn't sleep. My mind and body were buzzing from my time with Ruben, so I ended up writing long into the night. Molly told me last night that she'd gone ahead and planned my book release for eight weeks' time, so I don't have to wait too long to find out what people will really think of it... if anyone actually downloads it in the first place.

I have no idea what time I eventually gave in and went to bed, but I was up again and writing by eight this morning.

I'm on a serious roll. I've written over ten thousand words today, as well as editing what I did last night. I almost don't want to go out to the hairdresser's with Connie, but it'll be good to move about and stretch my muscles.

"Mum, are you sure you're going to be okay?" Connie asks Elizabeth, her mum, as she removes her apron and grabs her bag.

"Yes, baby. I've done this a million times, plus I've got Zoe here as well," she says, referring to Connie's weekend lady.

"Oh my God, you never told me this was the salon you went to," I exclaim as I follow Connie into Altered Images.

"EMMIE," I cringe at the nickname I now hate being screeched across the salon. Shane comes over and kisses me on both cheeks.

"Please don't call me that," I whisper in his ear when he hugs me.

"Sorry." He actually looks really guilty. He knows that was Hannah's nickname for me. "I've been dying to get my hands on your hair for months."

"How's my best customer?" he asks, addressing Connie, who is looking at the pair of us with a confused look on her face.

"You two know each other?"

"Yeah, we've known each other for years. I went to university with Shane's now husband."

***

"You have no idea how long I've been dying to do that," Shane repeats as he holds the mirror up to show me my finished look. My chestnut hair is now sun-kissed with golden highlights, and it's been layered throughout to give me more volume along with a side fringe, which even I can admit softens my face. I look over to Connie, who now has electric blue streaks in her slightly longer bob than when I originally met her.

Shane ends up convincing us to go out for a drink with him and Chris, as we are his last clients of the day. Connie is very excited about this, as she has heard so much about Chris that she's dying to meet him.

I'd texted Ruben and cancelled him coming over once I got back, because after only a few hours' sleep the night before, I was exhausted. He wasn't too thrilled in his response, but I remind him that I'll be spending all tomorrow night with him at his parents' party, and that seems to cheer him up slightly.

I'm surprised that Connie doesn't say anything about the two of us. I can only presume that Ruben hasn't told her, and for now, I'm happy for it to be just between the two of us. I'm not going to be able to keep it secret for very long, though. I don't think we'll get away with it at the party tomorrow.

***

Connie and her mum pick me up at ten AM the next morning, ready for a day at the spa in the hotel where the party is being held. I'm not really into the whole girly pampering thing. Mum drags me along with her sometimes, and it is relaxing, but it's not something I would choose to do.

We're sat in a relaxation room, laid out on chaise longues, when Connie gets called out to have her facial.

"It's so nice to meet you at last, Emma. I've heard so much about you," Elizabeth says, sipping her orange juice. I could tell from the moment I saw her that she was an amazing mother to her children. She has the same warmth that my mum has. I hadn't realised until that moment how much I missed my parents. They've been gone nearly four weeks on their cruise. I can't wait for them to come back next week. I feel like so much in my life has changed in the time they've been away. Honestly, I feel like a completely different person to the Emma they left behind.

"You too. Connie's always talking about you."

"It seems my kids are slightly taken with you. I can't thank you enough for what you've done for them," she says softly.

"Me? What have I done?"

"When Ruben and Fin left for Australia, I was so worried about Connie. All her old friends had moved away after university, and the only people she was really spending time with was the boys. She was so sad for those first few months, she pretty much shut herself away either at work or at home. She changed her look dramatically, had all her gorgeous hair cut off and started wearing a lot of black. But then one day, she came home with her old sparkle in her eye and told me all about this girl that helped out when she was run off her feet in the coffee shop. I was so relieved to see the old Connie back.

"Then there's Ruben. I never thought I'd see him have any interest in a woman, other than the one-night stands he's restricted himself to for years. I knew what happened between myself and Nigel affected him; I was worried it was going to stop him finding someone. But then I saw the look in his eyes one night when Connie mentioned your name, and I knew instantly that he had fallen for you. I was so thrilled," she says, grinning widely at me.

"I... uh..." I stutter, not sure how to respond. "I'm not sure he's fallen for me."

"He may not know it yet, my dear, but trust me. He is so like his father, and the look that passed over Ruben's face that day was the same one Nigel has on his face every time he looks at me. You're a very lucky lady, Emma. The Foster men love hard. I should warn you, it can be a little intense sometimes. They can be blinded by it and do stupid things. I know that you've already experienced some of that." I go to say something in response, but Elizabeth continues. "Ruben has broken some hearts over the years. I can't promise some of them won't try to get in the way of what you could have. I know Danni has already tried."

"I... wow," I say, while I rub my hands down my face and try to take in everything.

"I'm so glad you feel the same way about him," is the last thing she manages to get in before another customer comes into the room and puts a halt to our conversation.

Once we've been scrubbed, polished, waxed and painted from head to toe, we go up to our hotel rooms to get ready for the night ahead.

Connie is standing behind me in a matching white fluffy robe while she loosely curls my hair and pins bits of it up, ready for the party.

"Soooo..." she starts, and I have a feeling I know what's coming. "Are you ever going to tell me about what's happened with Ruben?"

"Sounds like you already know," I say, trying to hide my smile.

"I'm only presuming, because he suddenly stopped moping around like a bear with a sore head on Thursday night. I'm guessing that only you could change his sour mood quite so quickly."

I feel my face heat, and, as I look at my reflection, I see that the make-up Connie insisted on applying earlier is nowhere near covering my flush.

"I fucking knew it!" she squeals. "Come on, spill..."

"He was there when I took his phone to yours on Thursday night. We... uh... sorted stuff out."

"Eeeeeeek," she squeals again. "I'm so excited for you."

"He isn't going to be able to keep his hands off you tonight in that," Connie exclaims when I turn around after she's finished zipping me in. The dress Molly lent me was one she had early on in her pregnancy when she'd put some weight on, hence why it now fits me. Her usual clothes wouldn't be anywhere near my size. Saying that, it's still pretty tight and fits me like a second skin... a second skin covered in navy lace, cut fairly low across my breasts, and with a split that luckily stops just before the point of my thighs that I can't stand.

"Well, he's going to have to, because I've told him that if we are going to make something of this then it needs to be at my pace, not his."

"I think that's the right thing to do."

Ruben

I get more and more agitated the closer it gets to seeing Emma again, what with her cancelling on me last night and then having to spend all day today without her as she was at the spa with my mum and sister. I'm slowly going out of my mind.

Now I've had a real taste of her, I'm dying to pick up where we left off. I understand what she said about taking it slowly, but, fuck, I'm dying here. I've never had to go without sex before. If I wanted it, I simply went out and found a willing partner. God knows how long I'm going to have to wait until I see any action. She seemed pretty set on the idea, and I get the impression she's going to be very stubborn about it.

Fin and I have been working at my new place all day. I made the decision—some would say a stupid one—to change the floor plan of the ground floor slightly. I just can't get the image of Emma sat at a desk by those huge windows typing away on her laptop out of my head. I had to rejig the other spaces a little, but I think it will be worth it. I've also had to make sure there's plenty of space for the giant bookcase I'm going to make for all her books that she still has boxed up at her place.

I know it's crazy to have these thoughts about her living here with me, but I can't help it. I never thought this day would come. In the past, I've begged for it not to happen. I never wanted to feel so much for one woman that my entire life became about her and I lost myself like my dad did. I watched first-hand the pain she caused him not so long ago, and I swore there and then that I would never put myself in that situation. But here I am, redesigning my house for a woman I haven't even slept with yet. Hell, I barely even know her.

"I think you're right, you know. These few extra feet will make all the difference to the living space, and I don't think you'll miss it from your office space," Fin comments as we finish putting up the studwork for the interior walls. I haven't explained my real reasons for the change. I would be in for a world of pain and an endless amount of piss taking from him if I told the truth. Luckily, he agreed and didn't mind taking down and redoing some of the work we had previously done.

"Let's call it a day and head over to the hotel," I say when the last piece of wood is screwed in place. To be honest, it's still probably a little early, but I'm so desperate to see her that the pull of even being in the same building as her is making me twitchy.

"Whatever you want, dude. You do need to make yourself as pretty as possible as it's your last night to hook up with Emma. And just because we haven't spoken about it, doesn't mean I've forgotten."

Fuck, the thought of strutting my stuff down a catwalk in a tiny pair of shorts enters my head. There is no way that, even if I did sleep with Emma tonight, I would be sharing it with Fin. I guess I'm destined to make my modelling debut next weekend.

"Fuck off, Fin. That's all a load of bollocks and you know it. Grow up," I shout back to him as I head toward my truck.

"You're not getting out of it now. A bet's a bet, mate."

The thought of him making Emma a bet, or more so that I stupidly agreed to it weeks ago, has me gripping the steering wheel a little too hard.

Fin must notice my slightly aggressive driving. "Dude, calm down, we're not going to be late. You'll have plenty of time to do your hair!"

He might be my best friend, but, at this point, I have no issue wiping that smug fucking smile off his face.

Despite texting and calling Connie, she refused to tell me what room she and Emma were in, so it was either knock on every hotel door until I found them, or head down to the bar and have a drink with Fin and some of my cousins before they appeared.

I'm barely listening to a conversation about the approaching new football season when I hear a familiar laugh. When I look up, I can barely believe my eyes.

Emma and Connie are laughing as they walk up to the bar. She either hasn't noticed me or she's doing a good job of ignoring me. I watch her lace covered body as it sashays up to the barman. The dress fits her curves perfectly, and it reminds me that the woman I first met when I came back from Australia would never have worn that. Her confidence has really increased in the past few weeks. I like to think I've helped with that. Her hair is lighter and softens her features, along with the light make-up she's wearing. As I walk up behind them, I notice that her high heels give her enough extra height to make kissing her that much easier.

"Let me pay for those," I say, as I line the front of my body up with the back of hers. My dick starts to harden the moment it brushes against her arse. I grab on to Emma's hip and pull her tightly back against me, so she has to feel it.

"You look stunning, Emma," I whisper, placing a light kiss to the side of her neck. I have to ignore the whoop that comes from the table I just left. Fin is really enjoying this. I will get my own back one day when he meets someone that pulls the rug from under his feet.

"She does. I thought you might appreciate it," Connie says with a knowing wink. I guess Emma has filled her in then.

"*She* is right here!" Emma says with a laugh as she turns and places a brief kiss to my lips that, once again, has Fin hollering. "Thank you. Vodka and cranberry, please," she says, giving the barman her order.

It's not long before the other guests start arriving and filling up the function room my parents booked for the night. They both look like they're on Cloud Nine as they jump from guest to guest, greeting them and enjoying themselves.

Emma, Connie, Fin and I are sat at a table drinking, when Mr. and Mrs. Scott come in. The three of them must notice my silence and the look on my face, because they all stop their conversation and look in the same direction. I can almost hear the held breaths around the table as we wait to see if their darling children are going to follow them in. Thankfully, it seems they've both swerved this event. I really did not want to spend an evening in the same room as either of them. Mum was well aware of this, but seeing as the Scotts are good friends with my parents, they had to invite Danni and Elliot as well. I'm very grateful they didn't feel the need to attend.

"Here you go, kids," Dad says as he comes to our table with a tray of drinks. "Make sure you put yours on our tab."

"Thanks Dad," Connie says as she starts replacing the empty glasses cluttering our table with the full drinks Dad delivered. It seems being the kids of the celebrating couple means everyone buys us drinks. That goes for Emma and Fin as well.

"Come on, let's dance," Connie slurs a while later.

The DJ has spent the last hour playing some eighties classics that have had all the older generation in the room dancing away happily while we've been sat here cringing at the choices.

"Really, you want us to dance to this?" Fin asks, looking a little offended by the suggestion.

"Well, I'm drunk enough that it doesn't really matter," Emma chips in as she tries to stand.

I've been watching her get more and more tipsy as the time has passed. I can't complain, because it means that she's been more and more relaxed with me. She's sitting much closer than she was earlier, and I'm enjoying the sneaky little kisses she keeps allowing me to get away with. I'm dying to drag her off somewhere for a little alone time.

Emma

"Let's go and get a drink," I shout to Connie over the music. We've been dancing for half an hour, and I'm melting. The air conditioning isn't quite cutting it.

"Well, Ruben is handling himself better than I thought he would," Connie says as we wait for our drinks.

"What do you mean?"

"I thought he would have dragged you off somewhere by now. I mean, have you seen the way he's looking at you?"

I look over my shoulder to where he's talking to his uncle and see that Connie is right. He's paying no attention to what is being said, but he's staring right at me. I run my eyes down his body. He looks unbelievable tonight in slim fitting black trousers and a white shirt, with a loose tie hanging around his neck. I couldn't believe my eyes earlier when I first saw him in the room. I almost didn't recognise him. Gone is his long shaggy hair, at last. It's back like it is in the photo I'm obsessed with in the coffee shop. It's cut close to the sides of his head, then longer on top. He's then run something through it so it's pulled off his face. He looks like a bloody model, standing there with his hands casually resting in his pockets.

"Emma... Emma. Bloody hell, you're just as bad as each other."

"Sorry. Thanks," I say, taking my drink from her.

"Connie, there you are," a sweet little old lady says, walking up to her and propping herself up on a bar stool.

"Nan!" Connie exclaims and throws her arms around her tiny frame. "Do you want a wine?"

"Does a bear shit in the woods?" the little old lady responds, making me choke on my drink.

Connie orders her nan a white wine before introducing me to her.

"Nan, this is my friend Emma. Emma, this is my nan, Maggie. Watch her, she'll drink us both under the table!"

"So this is the wonderful Emma. I've heard so much about you, dear. And don't listen to her, she makes me sound like an alcoholic!"

"Nice to meet you," I say, politely deciding to ignore the alcoholic comment.

It turns out that Maggie is the coolest grandmother ever. She's the complete opposite of the ones I had. She doesn't mince her words and calls a spade a spade. It's really quite refreshing.

"I was so glad not to see the Scott children here," she says, after finishing her glass of wine. "Nothing but trouble, those two. God knows how Henry and Louise raised such devil children."

Connie and I exchange a look and attempt to change the subject to a safer topic that doesn't involve either her or Ruben's extra curricular activities with the Scott siblings. The reminder of Ruben being with her sends a little current of anger through my veins. I down the last of my drink before excusing myself to use the ladies' room.

I feel myself sway side to side a little as I head in the direction of the toilets. I tell myself that I need to slow down on the vodka and also to visit the buffet table when I return to soak some of it up. I don't drink often enough to suddenly start drinking on an empty stomach.

I get stuck behind a couple of slow moving older ladies on my way to the loos. I stop trying to overtake them, when I hear a familiar voice that sends tingles down my spine on the other side of the room divider that blocks the toilets' doors from view.

"You're really enjoying this, aren't you?" Ruben laughs.

"Oh man, you have no idea! Sooo... is tonight going to be the night, then? Are you going to bang Emma and win our bet, or will you be flaunting your stuff next weekend?"

A white noise fills my ears. I'm a bet? I'm a fucking bet?

I don't hear Ruben's response, but as I manage to get around the old women, I do hear Fin say that he should have a good chance because I'm drunk enough.

I stumble my way into the toilets and sit myself on the closed lid in one of the available cubicles. My heart is racing, my palms are sweating, and my eyes are stinging with unshed tears.

Everything that has happened with Ruben is because of a bet with Fin. That can't be right, can it?

Everything he's said about liking me, about never feeling like this before. Was it really all crap?

Was he just making it all up to get me into bed?

I've let myself fall for him, knowing that he was going to hurt me, and just look how right I was... although I thought it might be a little further down the line, not just a couple of days into whatever it is that we had.

Why did I have to let go and try to have a life? Because I've written a bloody book about moving on and thought it would be a good idea not to just hide behind my laptop? I think of the promise I made to Hannah about how I would move on and be happy, not just wallow in misery without her. Well, look where that's got me: heartbroken and hiding in the toilets of my friend's parents' party, trying not to break down.

My initial reaction as usual is to run, but Connie drove us here, and I've had way too much to drink to even think about driving. I could call myself a taxi, but I know it'll just cause a scene and Elizabeth and Nigel don't deserve that. They both look so happy celebrating, I'd never forgive myself for ruining their night. I just need to see the night out, and then I can run as far away from the lying shit as I possibly can. Well, as far as I can when I live in the same village and his sister is my best friend. Fuck!

I have no idea how long I sit there trying to get myself together, but eventually someone knocks on the door, asking if I'm okay.

"Yeah, just coming," I manage, but it comes out all high-pitched and squeaky. I take a deep breath and square my shoulders before unlocking the door and walking out with as much confidence as I can muster.

Luckily, Connie is still talking to her nan when I re-enter the function room. Both of them have another empty glass in front of them. Connie wasn't joking when she said her nan would drink us under the table. She looks like she's been sipping on water all night, not wine.

"Hey, could I have the room key, please?" I ask Connie when I get to them. I didn't have a bag to match my outfit, so she has control of the key and my money tonight.

"Uh, yeah," she says, opening her clutch and pulling it out. As she hands it to me, she looks up. "Are you okay?"

I swallow down my emotions. "Yeah, I'm just a little hot. I'd like to freshen up a little."

"Okaaaay, do you want me to come with you?" she asks, clearly seeing that I'm anything but okay.

I eventually manage to convince Connie that I can go alone. She doesn't look happy about it, but the barman putting another drink in front of her swayed her, thankfully.

I must spend way too long upstairs because, when I reappear, Ruben practically pounces on me. He wraps his arms around me from behind and whispers, "Where have you been? I was worried about you."

Thankfully, he can't see my face, because I don't think I'm a very good liar. "Sorry, I wasn't feeling great. I just needed a quiet few minutes." I try desperately hard to act normal, not like he's just ripped my heart out and is stomping on it in front of all these guests.

"You're okay now though, right?"

"Uh-huh," I mumble as I walk us toward Maggie. Connie is now on the dance floor, prancing around with a number of people, including Fin and her dad.

"Ruben, come on, I want to dance with my baby boy," Elizabeth says as she saunters over.

I sit on the bar stool opposite Maggie as Elizabeth drags Ruben off. He doesn't look very impressed to say the least.

"I never thought I'd see the day," Maggie says, taking another sip. I dread to think how many glasses she's had now; there are two more empties since I left.

"What's that?"

"The way Ruben looks at you, my dear. It's just like the way my Jimmy looked at me, God rest his soul. When Foster men are in love, it's written all over their faces."

I just stare at her with what I can only imagine is a blank expression on my face. After what I've heard tonight, she couldn't be further from the truth. I blink back the tears and order myself a double vodka and cranberry.

Maggie continues to tell me all about her late husband, Jimmy, as we sit and drink. Luckily, someone comes over and places a few bowls of crisps and nuts in front of us, which helps to soak up the stupid amount of vodka I've now consumed. I love the way Maggie still talks about her husband with as much love and passion as I'm sure she did when he was alive. I feel gutted for her that she has had to live for so many years without him after he died so young. She's right, though: she has three amazing sons and now daughters-in-law to look after her, and her grandkids to keep her on her toes. I can't help my eyes flicking over to the dance floor to make sure Ruben is still over there and being entertained by his family. It's easier to pretend everything is okay when he isn't next to me. He creates such a reaction in my body when he's close that it's hard to concentrate.

I watch as Connie goes up to the DJ. She must be fed up of the old-school classics her parents requested for the night. It's not long before the familiar beat of her favourite Taylor Swift song starts to fill the room. Looking at Connie, I would never have thought she was a huge pop music fan, but it just goes to prove you shouldn't judge a book by its cover. I continue watching as she grabs on to Fin and starts dancing to 'Shake it Off'.

My eyes lock with Ruben's just as Taylor starts singing the chorus, and I can't help but think how fitting it is.

He smiles and blows a kiss at me before a woman I don't recognise pulls him back toward her and starts dancing with him. I'd like to think she was a cousin, but something in the back of my mind screams that she's probably another in his long line of scorned women trying to have a shot with him. The way she's moving with him definitely doesn't scream cousin to me, anyway.

I try to do as Taylor says and shake it all off, at least until I'm alone and can deal with this all my own way.

A couple more songs play that don't register, but I continue to watch the dancing along with Maggie. I notice Connie and Fin move themselves so they're at the back of the group—I can only presume so they're away from Ruben, because their dancing isn't looking particularly innocent at this point. I wish she would tell me the history there; I'm dying to know.

I move my eyes briefly back to Ruben to see him heading toward the DJ with the woman still clinging to him. I watch as he says something to the DJ before she gets all excited and looks at him, doe-eyed. What the fuck has he done now?

She excitedly drags him back, and I wait patiently to see what's going to happen next. When the song ends, Ruben looks up and locks eyes with me. He tries to gesture for me to join him, but I shake my head and refuse. I'm not going anywhere near him. I can't promise I wouldn't cause him some bodily harm if I were that close to him.

The sound of One Direction comes out of the speakers, and I groan at the same time the woman beams from ear to ear at Ruben. I can only presume that she thinks his song choice, 'What Makes You Beautiful', was chosen for her.

"Aw, that is so romantic," Maggie comments. "Go dance with him, Emma."

"No, I don't think so," I say, much to her disappointment.

I see him go to move the woman away from him and he takes one step in my direction, but he's stopped by his mum and a couple of his aunties, who put him in the middle of them and start dancing around him.

If I wasn't so heartbroken and angry, I would laugh at the look on his face at being trapped by a circle of middle-aged women.

The room had started spinning for me a while ago, and I know I need to stop drinking before I do something I'm going to regret, but my main goal is numbing the pain he's caused. I finish my latest double vodka and cranberry when the beginning of a song starts that I could happily never hear again.

Couples start pairing off on the dance floor almost as fast as I scramble, in my highly intoxicated state, off the bar stool, ready to run.

"Emma?" I hear Maggie question over the buzzing filling my ears, but I pay no attention. My only thought is to get out of here before the pain engulfs me.

I can't take more than three steps before Adele's voice booms out the first line of 'Make You Feel My Love'. I feel my knees go weak as I'm instantly transported back in time to Hannah's funeral and the image of her coffin disappearing for the last time.

I must make it another two steps before I feel my legs completely give way. I brace myself for the impact.

Seconds or minutes go by. I have no idea, really, before I realise that the pain never came. I crack my eye open to see that I'm moving up a set of stairs in someone's arms. Adele's voice is getting quieter, and I've never been more grateful for the person taking me away from it in that moment. The memory of Hannah's funeral and having to say goodbye to her is still imprinted on my eyelids just from hearing that beautiful voice. I never would have agreed to play such a popular song, even though it was one of Hannah's favourites, if I knew it would affect me like this every time I heard it.

Going through a door cuts out the last of the sound and my brain can almost function again. I open my eyes properly and look up to see who saved me. It should come as no surprise that the person carrying me away from my worst nightmare is Ruben.

He looks down at me and must see that sheer panic in my eyes. "It's okay, babe, I've got you. You're okay," he repeats, placing a kiss to my forehead as his long legs eat up the remaining length of the corridor before he stops in front of a door.

I place my head on his shoulder and shut my eyes while he tries to figure out how to keep hold of me, get his key out of his pocket and unlock the door at the same time.

CHAPTER FOURTEEN

Ruben

Something's been off with Emma since she disappeared to her room earlier. Before that she was enjoying herself and having a laugh, but since she got back, the sparkle has gone from her eyes and she won't move from her spot at the bar with my nan. I'm dying to go over and be with her, but people keep pulling me back on to the dance floor. If it's not Connie or my mum, then it's this random woman that I've never met before. My mum has acknowledged her, so she is obviously meant to be at this party. She seems to have taken a bit of a liking to me, though, and won't leave my side. I, on the other hand, have no interest in her whatsoever. What I want is sitting at the bar getting plied with drinks by my nan. I really should warn Emma that she has no chance in hell of keeping up with her. My nan can drink any man under the table, let alone a woman that hardly drinks. God knows where she puts it all; she's a tiny woman.

Connie must get fed up of the music, because I see her go over to the DJ to make a request. When I hear Taylor Swift come over the speakers, I shouldn't really be surprised. After all, it is usually being blasted throughout our house. What does surprise me, though, is the look I receive off Emma during the chorus of the song. I'm hoping it's just the effect the alcohol is having on her, but I can't help the nagging feeling that she's trying to tell me something.

I have no idea where it comes from, but the thought hits me to say something back to her. To tell her how I feel. I heard this song on the radio earlier today, and I couldn't help but think of her. Unfortunately, the woman currently attached to my hip seems to think I requested One Direction's *What Makes You Beautiful* for her, and she's all smiles at me. I try getting away from her so I can make it very clear that the person it's for is Emma, but I don't manage it and instead get accosted by my mother and aunts.

I keep one eye on Emma as the songs go on. I also keep count of the drinks she's having. For someone who doesn't drink much, she is doing a good job of holding her own with my nan. Well, that is until she decides to get off the stool. The song has just changed, so I use it as my escape from all the women and head toward where she seems to be trying to run from the room like she's seen a ghost.

I catch up to her just as her knees give way and she starts going down. I quickly reach out to grab her and lift her up into my arms while continuing out of the room.

"Hey, is everything okay?" I whisper to her once we are out of the function room, but I get no response. It's obvious why when I look down, because it looks like she's passed out. I hold her a little tighter as we head up the stairs toward my room. Fin will have to find somewhere else to sleep tonight. I'm sure that won't be a challenge for him with all the women down there; maybe he can have the woman that was after me—she'll be lonely now, after all. Just his type!

I feel the weight of her head lift when we are almost at the top of the stairs, and when I look down at her all I can see is sheer panic on her face. What the hell just happened?

I reassure her that she is okay, and as I start trying to figure out how to unlock my hotel door with her in my arms, I feel her head rest back down and her breathing get instantly heavier.

When I eventually get us inside, I kick the door closed and lock it before walking over to the bed and laying her down.

"Emma, babe?" I question to see if she'll wake at all. "Can you wake up to help me get your dress off?"

I wait a few seconds but soon realise she's completely out of it and I'm on my own.

"This wasn't exactly what I had in mind for the end of our night, Em. Although getting you out of your dress was part of it." I say to myself as I slip her shoes off her feet.

The sight of her newly painted toenails makes me smile for some reason. They're bright red to match her fingers. It's not a colour I thought she would have gone for, but it looks unbelievably sexy on her. Next, I carefully sit her up and unzip the back of her dress. I slip the tiny straps down her shoulders and reveal my favourite assets covered in a black, lace, strapless bra. When Connie told me about Emma's love of lingerie a few weeks ago, I don't think I really appreciated quite how much she loved it. She always has the most stunning underwear on. I stand her up and gently tug the dress until it slips down her legs. Her knickers, of course, match her bra and are black lace shorts cut high across her arse. My dick is throbbing against the fabric of my boxers from just looking at her. She has the most amazing, curvy, sexy body I think I've ever seen. I can't wait to do as I wish with it.

I lower her down to sit on the bed so I can pull the pins out of her hair, and as it tumbles around her shoulders, I can't help but run my fingers through it. Fuck, I'm completely lost to this woman.

I pull the covers back and manage to get her underneath. She still shows no signs of waking up. I make quick work of undressing down to my boxers and slide into bed beside her. She has another think coming if she thinks I'm sleeping in the other single bed. I pull her body back so she's tucked nicely against the front of me. My dick lines itself up against her arse, and I have to really try to ignore its position and shut my mind off to fall asleep with her. It must work eventually, because the next thing I know, the door is being hammered on and I hear Fin shout when he realises I've locked it from the inside.

I gently remove myself from Emma and pull the door open a few inches. "You're gonna have to find somewhere else to sleep, Fin. Emma's passed out."

"Oh yeah!" he says with raised eyebrows.

"She's had way too much to drink. She was asleep before I even got her to the room."

"I seeeeeee," he slurs, obviously not too sober himself. "It's fine; I've already got plans, I just need my stuff."

I leave the door ajar as I head into the room and grab his bag for him before handing it over. "Have fun," I say with a laugh, before I go to shut the door.

"Oh, I intend to, don't worry. My dick's gonna see more action than yours tonight."

"Fuck off," I shout as he heads off down the corridor, thrusting his hips.

I squeeze myself back into bed. Emma seems to have moved since I've been gone, not leaving me much space. I manage to move her over so my arse isn't hanging over the edge of the mattress, and I fall asleep soon after with the sounds of her soft snores filling my ears.

Emma

I wake up covered in sweat. I don't think I've ever been so hot. I go to throw off the covers, but I can't work out why they won't move. I go to lift my head to see what the issue is, but as soon as I move, the room spins and it feels like my brain bangs against my skull. I take a deep breath in the hope that it eases the pain and the rolling of my stomach. It takes a few more seconds of lying still for my brain to realise that the reason I'm so hot is that I'm not alone in bed, and that I'm currently wrapped not only in the sheets but also a body. A body I'm hoping and praying is Ruben's. Because as bad as this could potentially be, it would be marginally better if it were him.

I go to move again so I can see what the hell I've done, when I feel a squeeze of my boob. My eyes pop open. It's skin on skin. Fuck, fuck, fuck.

I turn my head and look behind me slowly. I'm relieved to see that it is Ruben lying there. I can't help but stop for a second and take in his face in his sleep. He looks so peaceful and sexy. I feel the rest of my body wake up as I look at him, and I curse it to hell as the memory of what happened last night hits me.

I quickly jump out of bed. My intention was to get out of here without waking him up, but I think my movement was too fast for that. It's also not helped the turning over of my stomach.

I put one hand over my stomach while I lean against the wall with the other to try to let the dizzy, sick feeling subside.

"Emma, are you okay?" comes a sleepy, sexy, gravelly voice from behind me.

I look up at him to see his eyes zeroed in on my boobs. My strapless bra has twisted around and one of the cups is completely lowered to expose my bare nipple. As relieved as I am to realise I'm wearing something, I quickly move my hands up so I can cover myself before running to the bathroom to empty my stomach after it turns over again.

I sit back on my heels and wipe my mouth with some toilet roll when I think I'm done.

"Are you okay?"

I look up to see Ruben leaning against the door frame.

"Please leave me alone," I ask, but he doesn't move, so I reach out and shut the door on him. I feel like a bitch for doing it for all of two seconds before the memory of last night returns. He had a fucking bet to sleep with me. Anger instantly surges through me.

I sit back against the wall, trying to contain my tears. Tears of disbelief, hurt, embarrassment, and of knowing I was right. I should have listened to myself in the first place and stayed well away. The last thing I want is for him to hear me crying.

Once I'm confident I'm not going to puke again, I get up, turn the shower on and strip off what little I have on before stepping under the hot spray, hoping it will make me feel a little better. Plus, I feel like I can probably get away with letting a few tears escape without Ruben knowing while I'm in the shower.

When I eventually leave the bathroom a while later, I find Ruben lost in thought, sat on the edge of the bed, still in his boxers. I scan the room to find my dress so I don't have to stand here in last night's underwear with a towel wrapped around me. I don't see it, but what I do see is Ruben's shirt. I grab it off the floor, turn my back to him and cover myself up.

"Where are my dress and shoes?" I ask coldly.

"Em, come sit down."

"No. I need to go home. Where are my clothes?"

He briefly glances at the floor next to the other bed. I follow his gaze before moving to pick them up.

"What's the rush? We're booked in for breakfast soon. I'll go and get your stuff from your room and you can get ready," he says, getting up to put some clothes on.

"NO," I shout and he looks back at me, a little shocked. "No," I repeat, quieter this time. "I have the hangover from hell, and I can barely even look at you. I need to go home. Now," I say, trying to keep control, but my voice breaks on the last word.

"I haven't done anything. I got you up here when you passed out last night and looked after you. Nothing happened, Emma," he says, trying to plead his innocence. "I wouldn't take advantage like that. I thought you knew me better than that." He walks toward me but stops when I take a step back from him. Fear and confusion are written all over his face.

"And you had the perfect opportunity to do just that so you could win your bet," I say in a quiet voice.

I watch as the words settle into his head. It takes a few seconds for them to register, but when they do, his eyes go wide and he steps forward again.

"NO. Don't you fucking dare, you lying shit. I heard you with Fin last night. I was a bet, you arsehole. A fucking bet. You must have been laughing at my expense as I ate up all your words about how you felt about me and how beautiful I was. How fucking stupid am I? I knew I wasn't good enough for you. I mean, look at you, and then look at me. You are so out of my league it's laughable, really. I guess it should have been obvious that it wasn't for real from day one."

I go to continue to rant on, but Ruben stops me by putting his hands on my waist.

"Emma, stop. Please let me explain."

"There's no need. I heard everything I needed to hear last night. I need to leave, so please," I say as I try to push him away from me, "let me go."

Thankfully, he steps back, looking a little defeated. He lets me grab my stuff and head toward the door. I make quick work of getting out of the room and heading down the corridor.

I bang on my hotel room door, hoping that Connie is in there because I don't have any other way of getting my stuff.

I start to think it's empty, but after knocking for the third time, I hear some movement from inside. A few seconds later, she's pulling the door open slightly. Even that is enough to see that she's only wrapped in a sheet.

"Sorry, but I need to get my handbag."

"Uh," she stalls as she looks behind her, "sure, come in."

"Thanks. Could you do me a huge favour?"

"Of course, is everything okay? You look upset."

"Ruben will explain later, but right now I need to leave. Could you pack the rest of my stuff and drop it off to me later?"

"What has he done now?"

"Ask him. I need to go. Is that okay?"

"Yeah, of course, anything."

"Thank you." I grab my bag, give Connie a kiss on the cheek and leave the room. My plan is to get to reception and get a taxi home before Ruben decides he wants to talk to me. That plan fails as soon as I start walking down the corridor.

"Emma, wait."

I ignore him and continue to walk as fast as I can. I run down the stairs, but I can tell he's hot on my heels and there's no way I can outrun him.

A few members of staff and some customers look up at me as I enter reception. I suddenly realise that I'm dressed only in Ruben's shirt, with wet hair, no shoes, and I probably have make-up all down my face both from crying and the shower.

"Emma, for God's sake stop, will you?"

Ruben grabs my wrist and halts my journey toward the desk.

"Let me take you home and we can talk." It's only now I notice he has his bag in his hand.

"Leave me alone... please," I hate that I start to cry at that. And I hate it more that I start to cry harder when he puts his arms around my shoulder and starts to drag me out the front of the hotel. I let him because I don't want to cause a scene in reception.

I shrug him off as soon as we're out the door and storm ahead of him toward the car park.

"You probably don't want to hear how hot you look dressed only in my shirt, do you?" I hear from behind me.

I have to bite my tongue to stop me from responding. I do not have the energy to argue with him right now. I just want to get home, have a nice long bath, and try to forget about this whole disaster—or at least have some time to process my thoughts so I can have an intelligent conversation about this. Currently, I'll just end up an emotional mess if we get into it. I'm too hungover, tired, and emotional right now.

As soon as we're both in his truck, he starts trying to talk about it. "Emma, just hear me out, please. I can't cope with the silent treatment. It's not quite as bad as it sounds."

"Just take me home, please." I turn his radio on and crank the volume up to show him just how uninterested I am in what he has to say. I then shift in my seat so that I'm slightly turned away from him, and I look out the window at the passing fields.

We're about halfway home and I'm amazed that he's actually done as I asked and kept his mouth shut, when I think to check my phone.

CHAPTER FIFTEEN

Ruben

Her loud squeal scares the shit out of me.

"Sorry. My friend has had her baby. Please hurry, I need to get to the hospital."

"I'll take you home to get changed, then I'll drive you there."

"No fucking way. Just drop me off."

"Emma, don't be stupid. You had way too much to drink last night to be driving yet. No argument. You get changed, then I'll take you. Okay?"

She huffs out a breath and I can see that I've won this argument. "Fine."

She sits herself back so she's twisted away from me in defiance. It's seriously pissing me off that she's refusing to talk to me. I need to explain that although it was a bet, I never had any intention of following through with it. And even if we did sleep together before last night, Fin would not have been getting any of the details. She means too much to me to do that. I'm not going to force it on her, though. If she needs time, I'll give her time. She'll have to hear me out eventually, right?

We're not far from her house when a song I remember from last night starts playing on the radio. I don't think any more of it until Emma jumps forward and slams her hand against the front of the radio unit. She hits it again and again while begging for it to be turned off. I quickly mute it from the controls on the steering wheel. It suddenly hits me that it was the same Adele song that made her run from the room last night.

I glance over to her, my eyes wide in shock at her behaviour and see that she has silent tears streaming down her face, and she's shaking from head to toe.

"Em?"

"J... just g... g... get me h... home," she sobs.

"Okay." I put my foot down a little and place my hand on her thigh in support. I have no idea what the hell is going on, but anyone can see that she needs some right now.

T he minute she unlocks her house, she bolts upstairs, leaving only the sounds of her sobs in her wake. I feel completely lost and out of my depth here. I've never cared before if I've upset a woman. I usually just walk away and find another one, but it's eating me alive that I hurt her with my stupid, childish behaviour. Then there's whatever's going on with that song. I've never seen someone look as distraught as she did in the car earlier.

Feeling completely lost, I decide the best thing I can probably do at this point is make coffee and breakfast. I have no idea if she'll want it, but surely the gesture won't go amiss?

It takes me a while to figure out her complex coffee machine. I always knew I should have paid more attention at Connie's. I get there in the end, before taking a steaming mug along with a bowl of fresh fruit salad and yoghurt up to her bedroom for when she gets out of the bathroom. I've never been upstairs in her house before, but seeing as she walked in on me the other day, I think I've got a free pass. Upstairs looks just like downstairs: all pastel colours, soft, romantic, and feminine.

Kia is curled up asleep on Emma's bed, and I make sure to give her a tickle behind the ear before heading back downstairs. I can hear the shower running as I pass the bathroom, but it doesn't mask the sounds of Emma's continued sobs.

I put my hand on the handle. I'm just about to turn it when I remember how we ended up in this situation. She's not going to take well to me intruding on her, no matter how much I want to comfort her. I stand there a while longer, listening to her, before I turn and head back down to the kitchen.

It isn't that much time later before I hear her coming back down the stairs. Kia came to find me a while ago and has been sat up on my lap while

I had my own coffee and breakfast. She keeps giving me an evil eye; it's like she knows I've pissed her mum off.

"Thank you for the coffee and breakfast," Emma mumbles as she enters the kitchen. It doesn't escape my attention that she doesn't look at me.

"My pleasure. I thought it might help the hangover."

I look at her as she turns back from the sink, and I desperately want to go over and hug her. She's blow-dried her hair and it looks amazing, but her eyes are red from crying. The tear tracks are still obvious on her cheeks, and her full lips are turned down in sadness. She's dressed simply in a pair of loose fitting jeans and a vest top low enough just to show the swell of her tits. I try not to look at them; I don't think me checking her out will make her happy right now.

"I'm driving myself. I feel fine now," she says with her hands on her hips, trying to look determined.

"Em, I'm not letting you drive. You'll still be over the limit. I'd never forgive myself if something happened to you."

I see her eyes flash behind me to the hallway, and we both dart toward it at the same time. Luckily for me, I'm faster and get to her keys first. I hold them above my head, knowing she'll never be able to reach them.

"Ruben, for fuck's sake, stop being such a child."

"Just let me drive." As I say this, I throw her keys up onto the top kitchen cabinets. She looks up to where they landed, then back at me with a face full of anger.

"Just don't talk to me," she demands, heading toward the back door.

Emma

The journey to the hospital takes forever. I'm grateful that Ruben does as I asked and doesn't talk to me the entire journey. My head is still spinning from learning I'm nothing more than a bet to him, along with the emotions that are now simmering on the surface again from the memory of Hannah's funeral. I haven't heard that song in months. What kind of cruel joke is fate playing, making me listen to it twice in two days? Haven't I been through enough already?

"Thank you," I say to Ruben after clearing my throat when he pulls up at the barrier to the hospital car park. "Don't worry about parking, I'll get a taxi back."

"Like fuck you will."

"Ruben…" I say with a sigh, trying to gather my thoughts. "I appreciate you bringing me, but you don't need to stay. You have most definitely done enough. Please just go home."

He opens the window and pulls a ticket from the machine before the barrier rises to allow us to drive in.

"No," he says stubbornly. "I'll wait for you."

"Fucking pain the arse," I mutter under my breath, but I guess he heard it from the laugh he emits. "Fine. Stay here, I'll only be about thirty minutes." I jump out of the car and storm away from him. What the fuck is his problem?

"Oh my God," I whisper when I poke my head around the doorway to the room Molly and Ryan are currently in. It was not what I was expecting at all. There's no hospital bed or medical equipment that I can really see, just a sofa, a chair, what I guess is a birthing pool, and a little kitchenette area. But what really takes my breath away is the sight of Molly with a little bundle in her arms.

"Em, come in," Molly says when she looks up and sees me. For someone who's just given birth, she looks remarkably good and so unbelievably happy.

Ryan gets up so I can sit down next to Molly and the new arrival. Tears stream down my face when I take in the little face peeking out of the blankets.

"Emma, say hello to Lois Hannah Evans," Molly says with a beaming smile as she looks down at her daughter.

I reach out and run my knuckle over her cute little chubby cheek as I sob at her name choice.

"You don't mind, do you?" Molly asks, suddenly sounding a little unsure.

"Of course not. It's perfect, and she's gorgeous."

"Just like her mummy," Ryan pipes up from his chair.

It's then that Molly really looks up at me. "What's wrong?"

I wipe at my tears with the back of my hand before saying, "Sorry, just feeling a little emotional with her arrival."

"No, it's more than just this. You look like you've been crying for hours. What's happened?"

"It's nothing."

"Emma," she warns.

"It's not important right now. She is way more important."

I manage to get Molly to start talking about having Lois, and once she starts telling the story about how her waters broke on early Saturday morning through to her delivering Lois in the early hours of this morning, she completely forgets to nag me to tell her what's wrong. I'm grateful, because I'm not sure I'm up to talking about it yet. I know that she'll know exactly what I should do, but I just can't bear the pain of discussing it and admitting how stupid I was to get swept away by him.

I have no idea how much time passes while Molly and Ryan tell me all the details and I get my first cuddle with Lois. I don't think I've ever held such a little person before. It's really quite scary. Kids aren't something I've ever really thought about. That's the next step on from having a boyfriend and getting married, and those are two things I've tried to avoid until recently.

"Please talk to me, Em," Molly tries again when Ryan leaves the room to put some more money on for parking.

I bite my bottom lip to stop it from wobbling too much. When I feel like I can speak, I mumble, "It's Ruben. I was so stupid to think he actually wanted me."

Molly is quiet for a while before she whispers something that shocks me. "If that's true, why is he here and looking like his world's come to an end?"

I follow her gaze and see that she's right. Ruben is leant up against the door frame with a lost look on his face. He looks like he's miles away right now as he looks at me holding Lois.

"He insisted on driving me because I drank a little too much last night. I've told him to go and that I'd get a taxi, but he wouldn't take no for an answer," I whisper back.

"Those aren't the actions, and that isn't the look of someone who doesn't want you, Em."

Our whispering must have brought Ruben out of his daze, because he clears his throat to talk. "Sorry, but you said you'd be half an hour and it's been well over an hour, so I thought..." he tails off.

"Damn, sorry, I didn't want to stay too long. You two need to make the most of this time together," I say to Molly as I carefully hand her little bundle of joy back to her.

"I wouldn't have asked you to come if I didn't want you here," she replies reassuringly.

After I've given Molly a hug and kiss on the cheek, I go to leave the room, promising to see them again once they're home. I walk straight past Ruben, presuming he'll just follow after me. I hear him say his congratulations to Molly before his footsteps start getting closer and closer to me.

"Do you want kids, Em?" he asks when he catches me up.

My response is to turn and stare at him. I'm hoping the look in my eyes conveys that I still want to hear nothing from him, let alone talk about my possible future. My main focus currently is to get away from him and put this disaster behind me.

"Thanks for the lift," I say coldly when he pulls up outside my cottage.

"My pleasure. Please can I come in so we can talk? I need to explain everything to you."

"No, I don't want to hear it. I've heard enough. I suggest you just go home and leave me alone. I was stupid to think there could be something here. I knew you were going to hurt me, and that's exactly what you have done. Goodbye, Ruben."

He's quicker than I am and manages to grab my wrist before I'm out of the car. "Emma, please just hear me out."

"No, Ruben. How many times do I need to say it? I'm not interested in hearing what you have to say." I pull my wrist from his grasp and jump out of the car.

"This isn't over, Emma. Not by a long shot," he warns as I go to shut the door.

"As far as I'm concerned, it is. Goodbye."

I walk as quickly as I can to my gate so I can let myself in before I burst into tears. I lock the kitchen door behind me, and I have to say I'm surprised that Ruben hasn't followed me, despite what I just said. I hate that a part of me is disappointed he didn't listen to me and instead fought for what he says he wants. Well, that just shows how right I am.

My overnight bag was by my back door when I got here. Connie must have dropped it off, so I take it with me up to my bedroom where I throw myself on the bed and let go at last. I cry for what I've lost, mostly for Hannah, but also for what I allowed myself to believe I might have had with Ruben. I feel Kia come and snuggle up to me. The image of Ruben with her on his lap when I came down from getting ready earlier pops into my mind and I cry harder at how such a strong man can be so soft when it comes to a cat.

It's not long before I hear a knock on my back door. It makes me jump, but I ignore it. After a few minutes, the doorbell at the front door starts ringing, followed by Connie shouting my name.

"Emma, please open the door. I've spoken to Ruben. He's a dickhead. Fin, too. Please talk to me," she begs.

Her knocking and pleading with me to answer goes on for at least another twenty minutes before everything goes quiet, and at some point I must cry myself to sleep, because it's early evening the next time I look at the clock.

After my nap, I make a decision. I can't put up with Connie constantly trying to get me to talk. Although I know she only wants the best for me, her pestering me over the coming days isn't what I want. Even worse would be Ruben turning up to do the same, which I know will happen eventually. He said before he left that this isn't over, so I can only presume that he intends on making me listen to him somehow.

I start packing my suitcase, along with everything Kia will need for a few days. I have to drag the bar stool over to the kitchen cabinets when I eventually remember where the hell my car keys are. After making sure neither of the Foster siblings are camped outside my house like before, I load my car, lock up my house, and disappear from the place I now consider my home.

CHAPTER SIXTEEN

Ruben

"Ruben?" Connie calls out the minute I step through the front door. Brilliant, just what I want to deal with. I spent an hour driving round the village roads after I left Emma's, trying to decide the best thing to do. My heart told me to go back and demand that she hear me out, but my head knew that wasn't the most sensible thing to do and that I need to give her some time. Hopefully, in a couple of days she'll be ready to listen. I can't lose her over this.

It's already starting to drive me a little insane that the image of Emma with a newborn baby in her arms won't leave me. I've never had any thoughts about marriage, let alone babies, in my future, but it's like that image is haunting me, and it's only been a few hours.

"Yeah," I call back quietly, hoping she won't hear and I can sneak upstairs in peace.

"What the hell's happened with Emma? She told me you would explain," she demands when she appears from her room. She sits herself up on a stool at our breakfast bar and waits with her arms crossed in front of her chest.

"Fuck! Right, well... it's not actually as bad as it sounds," I start.

"That doesn't bode well."

I tell her the whole bloody story.

"YOU FUCKING ARSEHOLE!" Connie shouts at me when I've

finished explaining, before she jumps off her stool so she can get close enough to start slapping and punching me. "YOU MADE HER A FUCKING BET," she screams in my face. "A FUCKING BET!" she repeats at such a pitch I'm sure only dogs should be able to hear her.

I eventually grab her wrists and hold them in front of her to stop the attack. I realise as we stare at each other and I take in her red, angry face and out of breath state that Emma would have been much easier to deal with if she were angry like this. The quiet, closed off way she was unnerved me.

"Finished?" I ask Connie.

She huffs out a breath but nods so I let her go and watch as she gets herself back up on the bar stool.

"I warned you to treat her properly, Ru."

"I know, but I never took the bet seriously. I'd forgotten about it, to be honest. And I had no intention of telling Fin if I did sleep with her. She's not one of the usual girls we get with. She's more than that."

"Damn right she is. I just can't believe you would ever agree to it."

"It was the easiest way to get him to shut up. He decided it was a good idea and went on and on until I agreed. I knew it was stupid as soon as he said it."

"I don't blame her if she never forgives you for this. In fact, I think I'd be inclined to encourage her not to."

I just stare at her. I know I'm in the wrong, but I sorta hoped my sister would help me out here, tell Emma it was a mistake and how much I regretted it, all that kind of stuff, not just agree with her and tell her to run a mile.

"You're both as bad as each other. Fucking children," she mutters before she walks off back to her room. It's only seconds later that I hear her shouting familiar words to someone. I can only presume she got straight on the phone to Fin so she could give him her two pence on the situation and rip him a new one as well.

In the week that follows, I run the same route I know Emma does on the off chance of bumping into her. I stop by her house at least once a day, but she's never there. Her car is always gone. I make sure I spend every night working on my house in case she comes back to sit and think on the bench like before, but nothing. The flowers I've sent her haven't been delivered because there was no one to sign for them. Embarrassingly, I ended up picking them up myself and giving them to my mum, as they refused to give me a refund. All my phone calls go straight to voicemail, and my messages don't even get delivered, let alone read. That said, I have become quite good friends with the landlord of our local pub.

"Still nothing from Emma, baby?" Mum asks when she stops by the office with lunch for Dad and me.

I turn to look at her sadly before muttering a quiet, "No."

"Just give her time. She'll come around."

Connie helpfully filled Mum in on what I'd done, so not only did I have to deal with Connie's anger, but later on that evening I had Mum in our kitchen, reading me the Riot Act over my behaviour. She was so much worse than Connie, because she was so disappointed in me. I hated disappointing my parents.

I'm not the only one having no luck getting hold of Emma. Connie hasn't managed it either, which surprises me and makes me think she could be lying.

"Still nothing?" Connie asks when I go into the coffee shop on Thursday night.

"Nope. And still no evidence of life at her house. I'm getting worried about her."

"I'm convinced she's either at her parents' or Molly's. Problem is, I have no idea where either live, other than on the outskirts of Oxford, which isn't very helpful. I think we're just going to have to be patient. She'll come back when she's ready."

Connie's words don't make me feel any better. Waiting sucks.

The fashion show that Saturday evening was just about as mortifying as I imagined it would be. Connie and Fin came along for the sheer entertainment value, which made me even happier about it all.

Unfortunately, Fin wasn't lying about the tiny shorts I had to wear. I should have just walked down that fucking catwalk naked for all the good the white Lycra hot pants with gold sequins did.

Danni seemed more than happy with her choice of clothing for me and couldn't keep her eyes—or hands—off me. She soon got the idea as to what kind of mood I was in, though, and backed off a little after a while.

My mum was thrilled I was helping out, but even she looked a little embarrassed by my clothing. No mum should have to see that much of her adult son. Ever. I guess my only saving grace is that, since Emma has vanished without a trace, my dick isn't constantly on alert for her. That's about the only thing that could have made the whole evening worse.

That night, I do as I always do and send Emma a text about my day. Yes, I know, I'm a sad fucker. I know she isn't reading them, but I feel better at least trying to reach out. I even send her the godawful picture Connie felt the need to take earlier so she could forever remember my punishment. She called it karma; I just call it what it is: Danni being an epic bitch. The thought of her opening that picture and smiling fills me with a fake hope that she might forgive me one day.

It's not until the following Sunday that I get a phone call from Connie just after lunchtime saying she's just seen Emma. I instantly drop the tools at my house and head straight over to her cottage.

To my relief, her car is on the drive, but there's still no answer. I can, however, hear Kia purring on the other side of the back door. Presuming she's gone for a run, I take off on her usual route, but still I find nothing. I'm getting more and more frustrated with every day that passes that I can't talk to her. All I want is for the chance to explain, for her to hear me out.

There's still no answer when I get back to her house, so I pick up my car, drop it off at home and head to the place I've spent way too much time this week: the pub.

Emma

"Emma, angel?" The sound of my mum's voice shouting through the house causes fresh tears to fill my eyes. I've been waiting patiently for them to come home all day. I've cleaned their house from top to bottom over the past couple of days.

When I woke up from that sleep on Sunday afternoon, I knew there was only one place I wanted to be: at my parents' house. It's so calm and peaceful, just what I needed to get my head together.

"Mum," I sob when I get to the bottom of the stairs where both she and my dad are standing with suitcases around their feet.

"Oh, angel, what's wrong?"

"I've... missed... you," I say between sobs. I move over to my dad once I've had a long hug with my mum.

"Pete, could you take the cases up? I'll get the kettle on," Mum says, before grabbing my hand and taking me into the kitchen.

I sit myself down at the table and will my tears to stop. I'm just so relieved to see them after all this time.

A few minutes later, Mum has a teapot filled and a plate of biscuits ready in the middle of the table. Dad came in a second ago to grab his mug, then excused himself to his garden, obviously sensing we needed some girl time.

"Silly me," Mum suddenly says, "You probably don't want biscuits, do you? You look beautiful by the way, angel. Not that you didn't before, of course," she tags on. After everything that happened at the weekend, eating hasn't been my priority this week, which I know is naughty, but I just couldn't face it, so I've managed to drop a little more weight.

"Thank you." She just looks at me, her eyes gently probing me to explain. "I met someone," I eventually say.

"Oh, angel. Who is he?"

"It doesn't matter now, it's over." I go on to explain all, and to apologise for the fact that I've been living in their house for a few days.

"I'm so sorry it didn't work out, angel. I wish there was something I could do."

"Just let me hide out here for a while. I can't face him yet."

"I thought you would have learnt by now that hiding doesn't solve anything," Mum says, referring to all the other times I've run away and hidden when things have got hard in the past. I am aware this is a trait that I keep repeating, but I can't help it. It's my coping mechanism.

"Just a few more days, please."

"Okay, but then you've got to go home and face him. You're an adult now, Emma. You've got to deal with your problems head on."

"Thanks. Oh, I've got someone for you to meet," I say, before getting up and going to get Kia from my old bedroom.

I end up staying at Mum and Dad's for two weeks. They aren't happy about it, but they don't kick me out like I'm afraid they might. I still go to work, I write, and I spend time with Molly, Ryan, and little Lois. I'd told Molly I was staying at my parents' after I explained everything to her on the Monday night that we all visited. She said the exact same thing as Mum did about me not running away from my problems, but she did understand. She offered to go and rip his dick off once Lois had finished feeding, but I assured her that wasn't necessary.

If I'm honest with myself, the only reason I decide to go home is because I really don't want to spend my birthday—mine and Hannah's birthday—at my parents' house. I'm not sure what they're planning, if anything, but celebrating what was our day is far from what I want to be doing. At least no one knows it's my birthday at home, so I can hopefully let the day pass like any other. It doesn't escape my attention that I'm choosing to deal with one problem so I can run away from another. Bad habits die hard!

I drop my stuff and Kia at home before heading to the coffee shop to see Connie.

"Emma, oh my God, I've missed you," she says as she excitedly comes out from behind the counter, completely ignoring her customers, and throws her arms around me.

"Sorry, I just needed some time to myself," I say, hugging her back.

"I understand, don't worry." She scurries back behind the counter and serves the small queue she has before focusing her attention on me.

"Are you okay?"

"Yeah, I guess. I just felt so stupid for thinking it could have been something real, you know?"

"It was... *is* real, Em. He's a fucking mess. I know what he did was utterly stupid, but he really didn't intend on going through with it. He was always going to lose. You've got to listen to him. I told him I wouldn't help him with you, because I agree with you that he was an epic arsehole, so this is all I'm going to say on the matter. Just as much as he's my brother, you're my friend, and you need to make your own decision. I will warn you, though, that I will be letting him know I've seen you, so if you're home you can expect a visit soon. So... anyway... where have you been?"

I spend just over an hour with Connie, and we agree that she'll come to me for dinner later so we can catch up properly. I see her reach for her phone when I head home. I just hope I can get back before he appears.

I have every intention of answering the door, but when that knock comes, I'm more nervous than I can ever remember being. I'm sat at my desk, looking out over the garden, writing, and my body freezes as the sound resonates through the house. Kia, the little bitch, jumps off my lap and runs to the back door when she hears his voice. I can't help but smile when she starts purring at him and he starts having a conversation with her. That's the Ruben I know, the one I fell for; not the arsehole that had a bet with his mate that he could bed me.

I feel like a complete wimp when the knocking and shouting eventually stops. "You're going to have to deal with him eventually," I say out loud to myself.

I save what I've done not long later and head up for a shower before Connie gets here for dinner. Luckily, I stopped and did some shopping on the way from my parents', so I have some food in the house.

"Ruben said he came round but there was no answer," Connie drops in as I'm dishing up.

I turn to look at her before responding. She must see the answer written over my face.

"You chickened out, didn't you?"

"Yes. I had every intention of speaking to him, but the second I heard the knock I panicked."

"You know he's just gonna keep trying until you speak to him, don't you?"

"Yes, I know. So, how was the rest of your parents' party? I'm sorry I missed the end."

"I told you not to try to keep up with my nan; disaster waiting to happen, that is!" she says with a laugh, and I'm grateful to Ruben in that moment because he obviously hasn't said anything about my freak out to Adele, otherwise Connie would be questioning me.

"Oh my God, you wouldn't believe who turned up a little worse for wear after you disappeared," she says.

"Go on," I say, placing a plate of pasta in front of her.

"Elliot and Danni."

I groan.

"Danni came marching in, demanding to know where Ruben was. Elliot, bless him, looked totally embarrassed and out of place as he tried to take her home, but she wasn't having any of it and ended up dancing like a slut with any man she could find. Fin very quickly tried to get rid of Elliot when he sat down with me, but after a while, Elliot managed to convince Fin he was only there to look after his sister. She eventually disappeared. Unsurprisingly, so did one of my cousins..."

I guess that answers my question about who was in Connie's room that morning.

"I thought you were done with him, Con. Ruben will go crazy if he finds out."

"He's too wrapped up in you to notice what I'm doing these days. Don't sweat it."

No sooner had Connie left last night than the knocking started on both my front and back doors. I wasn't surprised, but I was done for the night. As soon as Connie left, I got in my pyjamas and jumped in bed with my Kindle, and I was not getting out for anything. I never thought I'd say it, but I am actually feeling a little sorry for Ruben. If what Connie has said is right and he is miserable, I really do need to get over myself and talk to him.

Although I wanted to sleep through this entire day so that I could pretend it doesn't exist, I was awake at the crack of dawn. The first thing I do is turn to the photo of Hannah and me on my bedside table and wish her a happy birthday. Tears instantly start streaming down my face as I think that, yet again, we can no longer enjoy the birthday traditions we had. Ice cream for breakfast, having our nails done so one fingernail had our age on, and a cheesecake with candles in instead of a normal cake. It had to be toffee. I remember one year us making Mum drive bloody miles to find one, as our local supermarket had run out and we point blank refused to have a different flavour or a cake like normal people.

I reach over and pull open the draw in my bedside table. I open up the box and pull out my locket. Mum and Dad had it done for me for the funeral. The front has a ruby in it, our birthstone, along with the inscription, 'Miracles come in pairs', and inside are two tiny photos of the two of us, one as kids and one as adults. It's my most cherished possession. I really should wear it more, but I'm equally as scared to lose it as I am for people to ask me about it.

I sit up after wiping my tears away and secure it around my neck. Today is our day. I'll be wearing it.

After spending a long time lost in my memories of years gone by, I get up and pull the tub of ice cream from the freezer. I try to smile as I do it, but it's hard. Really hard.

I decide it's time to turn my phone on once I've cleared the tub of Ben & Jerry's. Diet? What diet? The cookie dough was just too good. Once it's had time to start up, I stare at it in amazement as message after message from both Ruben and Connie come through. There are fifteen from Connie. I look at them all quickly and they basically all say the same, asking me to talk, let her know I'm okay. I instantly feel really guilty that I just left without a word. If she did that to me, I'd be a mess, worrying about her. I promise myself that I will make it up to her as soon as possible. She's been nothing but a great friend since the day we met. She deserves better than how I've treated her. What I can't quite cope with is the number of messages from Ruben... thirty-seven in total. Oh, and eight voicemails.

I open up the conversation and scroll to the first one. The first few are him just apologising and begging me to talk to him so he can explain. There are a few telling me how much of a dick he is for what he's done, but then he goes on to send me a message about his day. They're really quite sweet, and I can't help smiling as I read some of his comments. There isn't anything exciting, just work, spending time with his parents, Connie and Fin, but it's like he wanted me to still be involved. I actually laugh out loud when I get to a photo of him wearing, well, not a lot. Apparently, because he lost the bet, he had to model in a fashion show Danni had organised and she had him in a tiny pair of hot pants. They're awful, but at the same time bloody brilliant because it shows off his body perfectly. A wave of jealousy washes through me as I think about all the women that would have seen him dressed like that, and practically hanging off him for a chance. Danni especially. I notice the light reflecting off his skin, and the green-eyed monster really raises its ugly head at the thought of someone rubbing oil all over him. I bet there was a queue a mile long to get involved in that little activity.

I give myself a talking to and continue with the rest of the messages. Unfortunately, there aren't any more photos for me to ogle, just more updates about what he's been up to and asking for me to come home. When I get to the bottom, I can't help but think that maybe what Connie was saying about Ruben not taking the bet seriously and about him being a mess is actually true. I mean, why would he bother taking time out of his day to tell me what he had been up to otherwise? He must actually care, right?

I lift my hand up to the locket that is hanging around my neck. "What should I do, Han?"

CHAPTER SEVENTEEN

Ruben

"Ru, have you seen Emma today at all?" Connie asks immediately when I answer the phone.

"No, she's still ignoring me. Why?" I question, because I can tell by her tone that something's up.

"Her parents are here. They're saying that Emma told them she had plans with me for her birthday. I didn't even know it was her birthday today. They've tried to drop a present off for her at her house, but can't find her."

"Well, maybe she's at work or something. I'm sure it isn't anything serious."

"They've rang her work. She's not been in all day. I know it doesn't sound like much, but they're really worried because today is a big deal for her."

"Why? It's not like she's turning thirty or something!" I say with a laugh.

"Ru... did you... did you know she was a twin?"

"No, I know she has twin siblings."

"She's a twin as well. Well, she *was* a twin. She died last year, and Emma hasn't dealt with it very well, according to her parents. They're really worried that they can't find her, especially as she lied to them about spending the evening with me."

"Hang on, I'm coming now," I say, shoving my feet back in the shoes I'd just taken off when I'd got in from work. My heart is in my throat as I run toward my car.

I rush through the entrance to Connie's to find an almost empty coffee shop with Connie stood talking to a man and a woman who look to be the same age as our parents.

"Ruben," Connie calls when she sees me. "These are Emma's parents."

I give Emma's mum a kiss on the cheek and don't miss her blush at the gesture before shaking her dad's hand and introducing myself.

"We're so sorry to drag you both into this. I'm sure she's fine, but we just want to be sure. It's so unlike her to lie."

"It's no problem. We want to know she's okay as well."

"I can't believe that she didn't tell either of you about Hannah. I shouldn't be surprised, though. She never talks about it. I just thought that after writing that book she had begun to deal with it better," Susan says.

Connie and I both look at each other. I haven't read her book, but I know what it's about, and now it all makes sense.

"Oh my God, the book is almost real life?"

"Yeah. Anyway," Pete says, getting us back on track, "Ruben, do you know where she might be?"

I lean back against the counter for a few seconds while I think. She could be bloody anywhere. How should I know? And then it hits me.

"I have an idea. You three stay here and I'll let you know if I'm right." I turn around and head out into the rainy evening. I leave my car where I left it on the curb outside the coffee shop and just hope I don't get a ticket, before heading off in the direction I think she might be.

When I'm halfway there, I start to have second thoughts. It's chucking it down with rain and I'm soaked through. If I knew I was going to end up doing this, I would have changed from my work clothes. Running in a shirt, trousers and smart black shoes isn't really ideal! Why on earth did I think that Emma would come out here in this weather? I can only imagine what she's going through today, but I'm not sure even that would be enough to push her to sit in the middle of a field in the rain. I rub the back of my hand across my forehead to get rid of some of the water running in my eyes before continuing.

I can't believe my eyes when I get to the opposite end of the field. There, in the distance, made fuzzy by the rain, is Emma. Sat on the exact bench that sprung to mind earlier. I up my speed to get to her, and as I get closer to her I can see that she's curled up with what looks like a stuffed dog in her arms. She's soaking wet, shaking, and sobbing her heart out.

When I reach her, she hasn't even looked up, so I pick her up and sit down with her on my lap. I put my arms around her and hold her while she sobs. If I can do anything for her in this moment, it's to offer her some support and warmth. I pull my phone out of my pocket and shoot a quick text to Connie to let her and Emma's parents know she's safe.

Her sobs go on and on to the point that I don't think she's ever going to stop. I start to toy with the idea of carrying her home, when I feel her breathing start to get easier. She doesn't move, doesn't look up, just stays exactly where she is. I start to think she's fallen asleep, until I hear a very quiet, "I'm sorry," come from her.

"Shhh, it's okay. I've got you."

We sit in silence in the rain for quite a long time after that. I eventually realise that I need to explain something to her, and this is the perfect opportunity.

"Our parents were always so happy when we were growing up," I start quietly. "I used to see all my friends' parents splitting up and listening to stories of double holidays, two Christmases and weekends with Dad. I could never imagine that happening to my parents. They were so in love. My dad especially. He doted on my mum. He had her so high on this pedestal that no one could touch her. I was amazed by their relationship, and knew that I wanted that for myself one day. A wife that I would go to the ends of the earth for, a couple of kids, and a nice home.

"Then one day it all came crashing down and no one, especially my dad, saw it coming. He came home early from working on site to find Mum in the arms of another man. He went apeshit. From what I've heard, he was damn close to killing the guy. Dad really lost it after that. He thought he had the perfect woman, loved her more than life itself, yet she somehow managed to do that to him. He had been working long hours so they could do the house up and we could all have a holiday. He never thought in a million years that, while he was slogging his guts out, she was at home shagging someone else.

"He'd been working on doing up the barn that Connie and I now live in for a while. They were planning on having it as a holiday let, but as soon as he found out what was going on, he moved straight into it. He didn't want to leave properly because he didn't want to leave us, or so he said. I now think that even though she hurt him, he couldn't be away from her.

"I've never seen someone so broken. It was like he lost his personality and his ability to laugh. He was just existing. He'd go to work, come home, eat, sleep, and that was about it.

"I swore from then on that I wouldn't let a woman consume me the way my mum had my dad. He could see no wrong in her until she betrayed him in the most awful way. If he wasn't so blinded by what he thought was her perfection, then he might have seen it coming, might have had enough wits about it to see the signs.

"So once I was old enough, I started having one-night stands, and as far as I was concerned, that was all I wanted. A woman to spend a bit of time with, fill my needs, but then to leave when I was done with her." I cringe at my own words and how awful they sound out loud. "Fin was on board with the idea as well. He's always up for some fun. And that's how it's been... well... until I met you." Part of me wonders again if she's fallen asleep, but I continue nonetheless.

"From the moment I laid eyes on you, I knew you were different. You weren't one of those girls, and you shouldn't be treated like one. Fin caught me looking at a picture of you that Connie sent me when we were in Australia, and he must have been able to read me like a book, because he knew then and there. Then I met you in real life, and the connection I felt with you was like nothing I've ever experienced before. All of a sudden, everything I thought I wanted before vanished. The desire to be with different women went, and I just wanted to spend time with you. I didn't understand it—hell, I still don't understand it, but I know that I want to be with you. I want to make you smile and laugh. I want to do things for you that will make you happy. Whatever I do, I think about what you would think about it, how you would feel about it." I don't mention the house, because I think that might be a little much for her right now. Plus, I want it to be a surprise when it's finished.

"What I'm trying to say is... I... I think I'm falling for you, Emma. I'm so sorry about that stupid bet. It was never anything I took seriously. Fin suggested it, and to shut him up I went along with it. I want you to know that, even if something did happen between us, I never would have told him. You're not some kind of conquest to me that I would go shouting from the rooftops. Whatever, if anything, happens between us, then it's between us. I always would have been wearing those godawful hot pants." I smile to myself because I know she's seen the photo now. I checked her messages earlier, and they had been read at last. "I never wanted you to find out about it. It was stupid and childish. You mean so much to me, babe, I really don't want to lose you over something I stupidly agreed to without any thought. I really never intended on seeing it through." I don't really know what else to say to her. I already feel like I've bared my soul, and I have no idea if she's even awake and listening to me.

She stays still and quiet a while longer, then I feel her move in my arms and she looks up at me. Her eyes are bright red and look really sore from crying. She stares straight into my eyes as if she's trying to see something in them. I just look back and hold her a little tighter.

Eventually, I see her lips part, and she says, "I'm sorry about your parents. That must have been really hard." She then stops. I can see that she has more she wants to say, but she's holding herself back.

"Your parents came to the coffee shop looking for you, babe. They were really worried. I know the gist of what's going on with you today, and I'm so sorry, I really am. I would say I wish you'd told me, but I totally understand why you didn't. If, or when, you're ready to talk about it, then I'm here to listen."

She quirks the side of her lip up in a little smile, so I know she has acknowledged what I said. She shivers again in my arms, and I decide it's time we move.

"Do you want to go home?"

"Please." I go to sweep her up in my arms, but she stops me. "What are you doing?"

"Carrying you."

"Thank you, but I can walk."

"Okay," I say, but I put my arm around her and pull her into my side.

"Thank you, Ruben."

"No problem, babe. Whatever you need, I'm here."

We don't talk all the way back to Emma's cottage. She unlocks the door for us when we get there, and she doesn't even flinch when I hold her hand and tug her in the direction of her stairs. She reminds me of a little child when they're sad and just go along with anything to make life easier, because thinking or having an opinion is just too much to ask.

When we get to the top of the stairs, I turn us into the bathroom, put the toilet seat down and carefully sit her on it. I then turn and start running her a bath. I find a bottle of bubbles and pour a load in. She shivered the whole way home; a nice hot bath should do her the world of good.

I turn back to her. She's sat with her shoulders slumped and is staring at the very wet dog in her lap. I go over and lower myself so I'm sat on my haunches in front of her. I gently reach out and tuck a strand of her wet hair behind her ear, before taking the dog from her and placing it on the vanity unit.

"That was Hannah's," she whispers.

I thought as much, but didn't want to say anything about it until she did. "He's cute. Are you okay to get in the bath or do you want help?"

"I'm okay. Thank you." She looks up into my eyes, showing me how much she means it.

"Okay, well if you need me, shout, yeah? I'll just be downstairs." I give her cold cheek a kiss before leaving and pulling the door to. I wait on the landing to make sure she's okay, but I soon hear the sloshing of water. Once I'm happy she's settled, I head downstairs.

"Is she okay?" Connie asks as soon as she answers the phone. I don't even get a chance to say anything.

"Yeah, she's fine. Just sad. Can you do us a favour?"

"Of course, what do you need?"

I rattle off a list of things for her to do before phoning her parents with the number they left for me.

"Hello?" Susan questions when she answers.

"Hi, it's Ruben."

"Oh, Ruben, thank you so much for calling. Is she okay?"

"Yeah, she's fine. I'll look after her, don't worry."

"Thank you, it's so nice to know someone is taking care of her. Ruben, please don't be offended if she doesn't talk to you. She hardly talks about it, even to us. She really needs someone though, even if it's just to sit with her."

We chat for a while longer before I promise to get Emma to call her when she's up to it. Once I've hung up the phone, I have a rummage in Emma's fridge to see if I can find something to take her up to drink. Unfortunately, I don't find what I want, but it's only a few more minutes before I hear Connie knock the back door.

"Here you go," she says, off-loading the bags she's carrying.

"Thank you."

"I also picked up a toffee cheesecake. Her parents said it was her traditional birthday cake!" she says, shrugging her shoulders. "If she needs anything else, please let me know, yeah?"

"Of course," I say, giving her a kiss on the cheek.

"Oh, there's a bag of presents for her that her parents left as well."

Once she's gone, I rummage through the bags. She brought me a change of clothes, along with a couple of bottles of wine.

I strip out of my wet clothes and put on the fresh jogging bottoms and t-shirt I requested. I make another quick phone call before pouring her a glass of wine and heading upstairs with it.

"Emma, can I come in?"

It takes a while, but I eventually hear a quiet, "Yes," from the other side of the door. When I enter, I see that the amount of bubbles I poured in earlier was a little excessive, as she's lying chin-deep in them!

"I brought this for you. Do you need anything else?"

She thinks for a minute before saying, "No. Thank you, though."

"My pleasure. I'll be downstairs when you're ready. I've ordered dinner for us. I hope that's okay."

She nods at me, so I lean down and place a gentle kiss to her forehead before leaving her to it once again. It breaks my heart to leave her when she looks so broken.

Emma

It was my own fault. I never should've got the old photograph albums out. I started with the ones of us as kids, but by the time I got to us as teenagers and starting sixth form, I was a blubbering mess. I thought I'd got over the worst of the pain, but apparently not. Today, it was as bad as it's ever been. It got to the point where I just had to get away from them, so I grabbed Hannah's dog teddy and left, running. I didn't stop or even notice it was raining until I got to the top of the hill that had the bench on that overlooked that awesome barn.

Ruben is in the kitchen when I get downstairs, getting plates out for us. He must hear me coming because he turns the second I walk in the room and says, "I was just about to come and get you."

I ignore his comment completely and walk straight into him. His arms wrap around me and I breathe him in deep. I feel him kiss the top of my head and it sends tingles through my body.

"Thank you."

"You're welcome. Whatever you need, babe, I'm here."

We stay like that for a few more minutes, until my stomach growls so loudly that I feel his body shake with laughter.

"Go and sit down in the living room and I'll plate it up," he says with a smile.

"No…" I say in a panic, "I can't go in there."

"I've tidied them all up. Go on, I'll only be a minute."

I turn to look back at him, and I don't think I've ever been so grateful in my entire life. I walk straight back up to him, reach up on my tiptoes and give him a quick kiss to the lips before going to sit down.

As promised, he arrives a few minutes later with the Indian he ordered.

"How did you know this was my favourite?" I ask when he puts a plate with not only my favourite curry on in front of me, but also onion bhajis and a peshwari naan.

"I asked your mum when I spoke to her to let her know you were okay. I promised her you'd call when you're up for it, by the way."

I already have my mouth full of food, so I respond with a nod and a smile.

"Oh my God, that was so good," I say as I sip the last bit of my wine. I only allowed myself a few mouthfuls upstairs, because I knew I hadn't eaten anything all day and I'd be a drunken mess by the time I got out of the bath if I had it all.

"I've got pudding as well, but I think I need a breather before that."

My eyes fill with tears as the image of the toffee cheesecake with two candles flashes through my brain.

"Hey, it's okay," Ruben says softly as he moves the tray from my lap and places it down on the coffee table.

"I'm sorry. It's just... we had all these birthday traditions... and I miss them. I miss her." I try my best to keep it in, but the sob erupts from nowhere. Before I know what's happening, I'm back on Ruben's lap and in his arms.

Once I've calmed down, I start to talk. Not just because I owe it to him after everything he's done, but because I find, much to my own surprise, that I actually want to.

"We'd both just finished a shift at Mum's coffee shop and my car wouldn't start. Hannah offered for me to stay with her and Ryan at their flat, but I had work in the morning and really needed to get home. Instead, she offered to drive me. We were quite happily singing along to the Bridget Jones soundtrack she had on when it happened. Neither of us saw it coming, it happened so fast. I only really know what happened from what I was told later. Hannah pulled out of a junction and bang. There was a bone shattering noise as a car collided with us. The sound of crushing metal was awful. I remember spinning off down the road and feeling like I was dreaming before it all went black. I was only out for a few minutes, because the next thing I knew, I was in agony and looking at Hannah in the driver's seat and telling her it was going to be okay. Her side of the car was completely caved in from the impact, but she looked perfect from where I was sitting. I was expecting her to answer me. Tell me it was all a joke or something. But she didn't. My head was throbbing from where I guessed I hit it on the window, my arm was burning with pain, and so was the entire left hand side of my body. Somehow, I managed to reach my bag and pull out my phone to ring for help.

"It seemed to take forever, and I kept blacking out, but eventually I saw the blue flashing lights through all the broken glass, and the relief I felt in that moment was unreal. I continued talking to Hannah, but she never responded. I willed her to talk to me, to let me know she was okay, but she never did. I knew, though. I think, looking back, I knew from the first moment I came to. Something was different. Yes, the pain from my injuries was bad, but there was this indescribable pain inside me that could only mean one thing." I take a few deep breaths so I can continue.

"You don't have to do this if it's too hard," Ruben whispers.

"No, I need to. I was taken out of the car and put in an ambulance. I looked back, and that was the last time I saw her.

"After I'd been cleaned, stitched and bandaged up, Mum and Dad came into my hospital cubicle. "She's gone, hasn't she?" was the first thing I said. One look at their faces and I had it confirmed. I prayed I was wrong as I laid there, waiting for news, but I knew. I knew she was gone. It was like half of me had died, and I didn't know what to do with myself.

"I remember thinking that everyone must think I didn't care, because I wasn't crying like them. I was numb. I couldn't feel anything. I just shut down completely. The only time I felt something was when I looked at Lilly. I hated myself for it, but she just looked so much like Hannah that I didn't know what to do. I could tell that she understood instantly, and she distanced herself from me. Unfortunately, it has stayed that way. Lilly and I have grown further and further apart, and I hate it." I make a mental note to try to rectify that situation. I'm her big sister; I need to do something.

"I didn't do it intentionally, but I shut everyone out and basically ran away. I never went to see her at the morgue with the others. I had to be seriously convinced to even attend the funeral. I just wanted it all to go away so I could pretend none of it had happened. I haven't even been to her grave since that day. I haven't been able to face it."

"Do you want to go?"

I look up at him. I wasn't expecting that question.

"I... uh..."

"If you want to go, then I'll take you."

"What, now?"

"Yeah, if you want."

I rest my head back against his shoulder and think about his offer. Do I want to go? A lot of me says that I really don't want to, but there's a smaller part screaming that it is the right thing to do. It's our day; I should at least see her.

"Okay," I whisper.

An hour later, we're in the car park of the cemetery. It's still raining, but it's much lighter than earlier.

"You ready?" Ruben asks from the driver's seat of my car.

"Um…"

"You don't have to do this if you don't want to."

"No," I say with a new resolve. "I need to."

I open the door and step out into the night. The sun set about thirty minutes ago, and the graveyard's only light is the moonlight. It's actually really beautiful. I start moving toward where I know she is. I may have only been here on the day of the funeral, but I know her exact location. I know that Ruben is somewhere behind me, because I can hear his footsteps in the gravel. I don't look back, though; I'm scared that if I do I'll change my mind and run again.

I slow down when I can see her in the distance and will myself to continue. I breathe in a deep breath and let my legs take me to my sister.

I don't know what to do when I'm in front of her headstone. I read the words our parents chose to have engraved on the front again and again while I try to figure out what I want to do now I'm here. I look down at the bunches of fresh flowers that tell me everyone else has been here today, and I instantly feel bad for not thinking of getting any.

I look back just before I'm about to bolt, and the sight of Ruben standing in the shadows on the path roots me to the spot. Instead of running, I turn back to her.

"He's given me the strength to do this, Han. I really wish you could meet him. He makes me feel like me again." I think about what I've just said, and have to correct myself. "No, he makes me feel like a better me. He gives me this confidence that I've never had before. You'd be so proud. He makes me feel and act in the way you always wanted me to. He makes me feel beautiful and sexy, not just like a fat trollop." I smile to myself at the memory of her trying to convince me I was beautiful. "I'm so sorry I haven't been here before, Han. Happy birthday."

CHAPTER EIGHTEEN

Emma

When we got back to my place last night, Ruben surprised me with a toffee cheesecake with two candles in. I couldn't get over how sweet and thoughtful he'd been all evening.

We shared the rest of the bottle of wine before we went up to bed. I didn't even think about the fact that I'd have to share my bed with him. It all just seemed so right.

When he came up after cleaning downstairs, he stripped down to his boxers and slid in with me. He immediately pulled me into his body and tangled our legs together. His hand started out resting on my cheek as he looked into my eyes, before it slid around into the hair at the base of my neck so he could pull my lips toward him.

We kissed for what felt like hours. He kissed me with such passion and gentleness that it actually brought a tear to my eye. The heat was still there between us, but, unlike the other times we'd kissed, it wasn't driving it. He was ready for more—hell, I was ready for more—but neither of us made the final move.

When I eventually fell asleep, it was with my head on his chest, my arm around his waist, and my legs entwined with his. To my amazement, I had the most peaceful night ever.

I can't believe my eyes when I look at the clock the next morning. It's gone nine. I never sleep this late. I roll back over in search of Ruben, but his side of the bed is cold. Presuming he's downstairs, I jump out of bed and head down, but there is no sign of him or any of his things.

I'm a little disappointed that he isn't here, but he gave me so much last night that I'm not too bothered. Instead, I head up for a quick shower before sitting down in front of my laptop. My characters have taken over my brain this morning, and I need to get it all down.

It's only just gone ten and it's already roasting hot, so I open all the windows to try to get a breeze. I have to leave the back door shut because I'm not brave enough to let Kia out yet. I shouldn't be this hot, seeing as I'm only wearing a thin vest top and a pair of boy shorts. I slide my glasses on as I took my contacts out last night because my eyes were stinging after all the crying.

I'm totally lost in my story, but something in the garden catches my attention. I look up to see Ruben looking back at me. He's topless with sweat running down his chest. I watch him lift his hand to his head and run it though his hair to get it off his face. We stare at each other; I can feel my heart rate pick up just from that. I know I said I wasn't disappointed that he wasn't here when I woke up, but I am very happy that he's reappeared.

I watch as he takes a step forward, but as he does that, what I'm wearing catches my eye. I can't let him see me like this. I look like a complete nerd in my vest that has a hole in, shorts have Little Miss Naughty on, and my glasses. I look like a child, only curvier.

"Shit."

I stand up quickly, pushing the chair out behind me, before running out of the room and up the stairs.

As I root through a drawer to find something to cover up with, I'm aware that he's in the house. I only hope that he'll wait for me downstairs.

"Stop," he growls loudly from the doorway.

"I'll be down in a minute." I'm just about to shut the drawer when the t-shirt I've pulled out is ripped out of my hand and thrown on the floor.

When I look up at him, my breath catches at the gold blazing in his eyes.

"I... uh..."

He reaches out to grab my chin and tilts it up so he can lower his lips to mine. Gone is the gentle man from last night, and in his place is the demanding lover I've had experience of meeting before. He steps into my body and moves us back until my bum hits my chest of drawers.

"You're so fucking hot," he grates out as he kisses down my neck.

He reaches up and pulls my glasses off before fumbling about to place them on the unit behind me.

His hands reach up under my vest, and before I know what's happening, he has it up over my head and on the floor behind us. His hands go straight to my tits while his lips come back to mine.

"Ruben," I whisper when he moves his lips down to my nipples. It's even more intense than last time, if that's possible.

"Fucking love these tits," he mumbles as his lips trail across my sensitive skin.

He stands back up and looks down at me. I feel my cheeks get even redder with embarrassment. No one has ever looked at my body before. My hands instinctively go to cover my boobs, but as soon as Ruben sees the movement, he stops them.

"Don't you dare cover yourself from me. I've never seen anyone as perfect as you. I will not have you hiding from me."

His words send heat rushing through my body, and my hands instantly drop back to my sides.

I watch as he takes a step back before taking off his running shoes, placing his thumbs in the waistband of his shorts, and shoving them down his legs. My breath catches at the sight of him standing in front of me, naked. I've never seen a naked man in the flesh before. Well, apart from my dad, but we don't need to go there right now.

"Fuck," I whisper as I run my eyes down to his dick. It's huge and pointing right at me. I mean, I've nothing really to compare it to, but it looks pretty huge to me. I can't help but feel completely overwhelmed by what is potentially about to happen. I run my eyes down to his thick thighs, then all the way to his feet, before dragging them back up again. My chest is heaving, my palms are sweating, and I swear my knickers are soaking wet.

"Em, you look a bit like you've never seen a naked man before," he says with a wicked glint in his eye.

I swallow hard before pushing off the chest of drawers, stepping up to him and stretching up to kiss him again while running my hands up his chest and to his shoulders. We are not having this conversation right now.

His hands come to my arse and I wrap my legs around his waist when he lifts me. He walks us back toward the bed and drops me onto it before following, so he's on top of me. My hands go to hold on to his biceps as he fits himself between my legs and continues kissing me. His hands roam all over my body, slowly making me lose my mind. I feel him start grinding his hips and it makes his dick rub against my core.

"Oh, God," I moan when he presses harder, causing the sensation to be even more intense.

He suddenly sits up on his heels and looks down at me. I resist the urge to cover myself up this time and instead put my hands on his thighs. His eyes almost pop out of their sockets as he watches my boobs squish together between my arms.

After making sure he's given my boobs enough attention, he starts to move down the bed away from me and I panic.

"Where are you going?" I ask, sitting up so I'm resting back on my elbows.

His answer is to smile and wink at me before he grabs on to the sides of my shorts and slowly begins to slide them down my legs. Heat rushes toward my cheeks and between my legs, knowing I'm lying here completely bare for him. I watch him lay down on his front with his face right between my legs. He grabs my ankles and pushes them farther apart so he has enough space. My face burns with embarrassment as he continues to stare at me there.

I'm suddenly really nervous. I hold my breath as he moves his head forward, but the minute his tongue makes contact, all the air comes whooshing out of me in a rush and I fall back on the bed.

"Ruben," I pant as he ups the pressure on my clit. Fuck, I never imagined it would feel like this. Not that I really had any clue what it would feel like.

It's not long before I feel that same feeling I felt in his bedroom in my lower belly, and all my muscles tighten up. I feel his finger at my entrance, and the moment he gently presses it in, my body explodes. Everything goes blank for a couple of seconds and all I can focus on are the fireworks shooting around my body. I swear even the muscles in my toes are twitching.

When I feel like I belong in my own body again and open my eyes, Ruben is back sat between my thighs, looking down on me with a smirk on his face.

"You taste like heaven. I knew you would," he says, before bending over me and kissing the life out of me. If my knees weren't already weak, they would be after that kiss. I'm not sure about kissing him after what he's just done, but after a second I realise it's hot as hell and lose myself in him.

He eventually sits back and I see him grab a little square wrapper from the end of the bed. God knows when he got that out. He keeps eye contact with me while he rips it open. I have to pull my eyes away from his when he starts to roll it on. I'm just too intrigued not to watch.

Once he's got it on, he lines himself up, then bends forward and frames my face in his hands.

"This is nothing like I've been imagining for the last few weeks. It's so much better. You're incredible, Emma." He presses forward and I suck in a huge breath at the invasion. "Fuck, you're tight," he comments with a smile.

He moves again, and all my muscles tense at the sensation and pain. He sits back a little, and I can feel him looking down at me, even though my eyes are shut.

"Em?"

I turn my head away from him as I feel the mortification of the situation burn my face red. He soon reaches out and cups my cheek so he can move my face back. "Look at me," he says softly.

I pull my eyes open and stare into his dark yet golden ones. I will him not to say what I know is coming. I could live without ever having the conversation and admitting my naivety.

"Em, is there something I should know before we go any further?" I don't respond. I just look at him, begging for him not to ask. "Emma, you've done this before, right?" Again, I don't move. All the things I should be saying right now are running around my head, but nothing comes out.

"Fuck, you're a virgin," he whispers, but it shocks the hell out of me when a smile splits his face. I was sure he was going to be pissed. He leans forward again and kisses me passionately. "You. Are. Perfect," he says between kisses.

"Really, you're not annoyed?"

"Why would I be annoyed? I wish I knew, so I could've been more gentle." I just smile at him while my heart does a little somersault in my chest. "You ready?"

"Yeah," I say, nodding.

He does as he says he will, and he's so gentle with me. Yes, it hurts, but that soon disappears and it feels amazing. He kisses me the whole time and tells me how beautiful I am. My heart feels like it is going to burst any minute with how he's making me feel.

"Oh God, Ruben," I moan when he hits a part of me that has me panting.

"I want to feel you come on my cock, Emma," he says, kissing my neck. I never thought I'd like dirty talk, but I was wrong. Just hearing those words has me closer to exploding.

Ruben pumps his hips in and out of me a few more times, hitting the same spot, before I see stars as my body flinches around him.

Just as I'm coming back to earth, he groans into my neck before I feel his dick twitching inside me. The noise he makes is so erotic that it almost pushes me over the edge again.

Ruben

Once I come back to myself, I roll us both over to our sides and pull Emma as close to me as I possibly can while we catch our breaths. My heart is pounding and every muscle in my body is twitching and enjoying the release. It was a long time coming, and it completely consumed me.

I can't wipe the stupid smile off my face, no matter how much I try. It's a good job Emma is tucked against me and can't see, because I'm sure she'd think I'd lost the plot. That was so much more than I was expecting. God, I sound like a right pussy. I knew Emma was naïve from my experiences with her before, but never in a million years did I think she would be a virgin. I'm the only man she has ever been with, and that makes me feel like a fucking king. She must have had plenty of offers over the years. I mean, she is sexy as hell with her curves; how has she refused all the others? And why did she decide I was the one after all these years?

I do wish she had told me at the beginning so I could have taken it slower. I hate the thought of hurting her. She looked so embarrassed when I asked her; I don't think she was expecting me to be over the fucking moon about the news. She's mine, this girl, and I fully intend for her to only ever have me inside her body. She was made for me. Lying here like this, it's obvious that we fit perfectly together.

I think back over the last few minutes and can't help but get excited about the prospect of all the new things, new pleasures, I can introduce her to. The thought makes my body tingle with apprehension and my dick to twitch back to life.

When I feel her start to pull away, I'm surprised by the disappointment I feel. This cuddling after sex thing is a new experience for me. They'd usually be well on their way, if not already gone by this point.

She pulls back enough so she can look at me through her thick, dark lashes. Fuck me, she's the most beautiful thing I've ever seen with her bright blue eyes, still flushed cheeks and messed up hair.

"Was that... okay?" she asks nervously.

My face splits into a shit-eating grin. Is she fucking shitting me? Was that okay? Does she really need to ask?

"That was way more than okay, babe. That was fucking incredible." I lean forward and place a sweet kiss on her lips. "Are you okay? Did I hurt you?"

"A little, but then I forgot about that and it was... wow."

"I can work with wow."

"Where did you go this morning? I thought you'd left."

"Just for a run. I needed to burn off some steam. I also had to stop in at the office to organise not being there today." She looks really guilty all of a sudden. "Don't give me that look. I want to spend the day with you; work's not a problem." Truth is, I had to swing by my new place because our couple of plasterers are quiet this week so they're in there getting my walls ready. I don't want to tell her this yet, though, because I want to take her there when it's done to surprise her.

She still doesn't look convinced. "Come on—let's get showered, then I'm taking you out for lunch. We still need to celebrate your birthday properly. And if you're up for it, Connie said she would like to cook a meal for you later. Nothing big or extravagant, just a meal for the four of us."

I watch her think about it for a bit before she agrees. I can see that she's still struggling with yesterday. I can see the shadows in her eyes, but I'm proud that she's fighting it. I will not let her have another day like yesterday. She needs to be surrounded by people who love her, not left alone to wallow.

"You go first, then," she says as she rolls away from me and sits on the edge of the bed.

I get up and walk around to her. Her first instinct is to try to cover her body.

"Stop it," I growl while pulling her hands away from her tits. "Do not hide this body from me, Emma. It's perfect, and I want to look at it every chance I get." I watch her blush creep up her neck and onto her cheeks.

"Now, when I said let's get showered, I didn't mean separately. Come on." I grab her hands and pull her along behind me.

Once the water is hot, I give her one last tug so she's in the cubicle with me. It's not the biggest of showers, so it's a bit of a squeeze, but I don't mind being in a confined space with a wet Emma!

She's nervous and self-conscious to start with, but she soon relaxes.

"Turn around," I demand, once I've finished washing her hair.

She does as she's told, and I stand her out of the water before grabbing the bottle of coconut shower gel. I now know where her unique scent comes from, because her shampoo was raspberry. I pour a load on my hands and begin running them over her skin. The moment I make contact, I see her nipples pebble, and her mouth drops open when her eyes shut. I run my hands over every inch of her body, making sure I spend extra time on her tits and arse when I get there. I fucking love the feel of her curves and soft skin under my hands. Her breath catches when my fingers find the sensitive skin of her pussy. I tease her by gently running my fingers everywhere but where she wants them the most. Her breathing soon picks up speed, and I watch her chest rise and fall at a rapid pace as the bubbles slowly slide off her smooth skin.

I've been hard since before we got off the bed, but it's almost painful now. My dick is begging to be back inside her again. I can't push her, though. I want her to be able to walk—well, today at least. That could well be my mission in the near future when I know it isn't going to hurt her.

Her back and head thud back against the tiled wall when my fingers graze her clit. When I look up, her gorgeous blue hunger-filled eyes are staring back at me. I step closer into her before lifting her right leg up and around my hip. I continue to circle her clit with the pad of my finger, and it's not long before she loses the fight and closes her eyes so she can absorb the sensation. I carefully slide a finger inside her while keeping the pressure on her clit with my thumb. I feel her whole body start to quiver and soft purrs start falling from her the closer she gets.

"Come on, babe, let go. Let me hear you. I want to hear how good it feels when you come over my fingers."

Just like last time, my words send her over the edge. She's not as loud as I would like, but she comes with my name falling from her lips. I might be selfish, but I want her screaming my name over and over, so anyone who might be able to hear knows damn well that this woman is mine, and mine only.

When she's finished pulsing around my finger, I switch places to wash the bubbles off her skin, but not before leaning in and capturing her lips in a wet and dirty kiss.

Much to my delight, I watch as Emma grabs the shower gel and goes to do the same to me. My dick twitching at the thought of her running her hands all over me catches my eye as she puts the bottle back on the shelf. I can only hope she'll give it a little extra attention as my balls are already drawn up, ready for another release. It'll make smelling like coconut for the rest of the day worth it.

She keeps to safe territory for a long time, just focusing on my shoulders, chest and stomach, and as good as it feels, I need more. I lean into her and whisper, "You can touch everywhere. Trust me, it'll only feel good," in her ear.

I once again watch the blush creep over her cheeks, and I can't help but think the comment I made earlier about her never seeing a naked man before is true.

She gets a little more adventurous, but nowhere near what I'm after. I give her a couple more seconds before grabbing her wrist and bringing her hand up to my lips. I place a kiss to her knuckles, then her palm, before placing it on my chest and slowly guiding it downwards. I watch her watch our hands descend my body with a look of apprehension. Her eyes still hold the same heat they did earlier, so I have no worries that I'm doing something she doesn't want to. We've just moved over my belly button when she sucks her bottom lip in and holds it tightly with her teeth.

"Fuck, Em, you have no idea how much you turn me on." I suck in a breath after the last word, because I feel her small, soft hand touch my dick. I guide her to hold on to me and slowly move her hand up and down to guide her. Emma is tiny, but I never really realised how small, until seeing her hand wrapped around my dick. She's told me before that she hates being the black sheep in her tall, slender family, but I'd have to argue, because to me, her body is perfect. I love being able to completely engulf and surround her in every way.

I remove my hand and let her continue on her own. Her movement stills for a second, but she soon continues.

"Fuck, that feels so good," I groan when she tightens her hold slightly. "That's it, keep going."

"I want to make you feel good like you do me," she whispers so quietly I almost think I imagine it.

"You're doing that and more, babe. You don't need to worry about it not feeling good."

I lean back against the tiles and continue to watch as she gets more and more confident with her movements. Suddenly, she moves, and I have to blink a couple of times to make sure I'm seeing things right. There, on her knees in the shower, with water pouring over her body, is Emma with her hand still wrapped around my cock. She's staring at it like it's the most interesting thing in the world.

"Can..." she whispers, then shakes her head. "I just... I want to..." She sucks her lip back into her mouth and I can't help but groan.

"As long as it doesn't involve your teeth, you can do whatever you want, babe," I say, watching her study me.

I watch with amusement as she looks between my eyes and my dick like she's trying to make some big decision. Eventually, she lets out a big breath and I hold mine as she leans forward. Her tongue sneaks out a little and my cock jumps at the tiny amount of contact. My response must spur her on, because after another look up at me she leans forward again but sticks her tongue right out this time and properly licks the head while continuing to stroke me with her hand. My head falls back against the tiles with a loud thud, but I don't feel anything that isn't south of my waist. I have no blood left anywhere else.

I have to force my head to move so I can look at her when I feel her lips wrap around me. The sight of her there with my cock in her mouth is pure heaven, the most fucking erotic thing I've ever seen in my life.

Embarrassingly, it only takes her a few minutes of sucking me like a fucking pro before I'm coming.

"Em, I'm gonna…" I can't finish the sentence, because a loud groan makes its way up my throat as my cock twitches and I spray my load all over her tits. "Holy fucking shit." I lean down and rub my cum into her tits and around her nipples. If I could, I'd write my fucking name with it to mark her as mine forever.

I pull her up from the floor and immediately pull her into my body, her soft, sexy curves against my hardness. "How are you fucking real?" I whisper against her lips, before crashing mine down on them.

We quickly wash the remnants of my orgasm off us as the water starts to go cold. I sadly wrap her in a towel before grabbing another for myself. I leave her in the bathroom faffing around, announcing that I'll be choosing what she's going to be wearing today.

CHAPTER NINETEEN

Emma

I watch Ruben's back as he leaves, committing the image of his broad shoulders and slim waist with water droplets running down them to memory. Shame he's covered his arse and solid thighs with the towel. I shake the thoughts out of my head when he disappears from my view. *What the hell is a man like him doing with me?* I wonder for the hundredth time in the last couple of hours.

Ruben has managed to do something that I never thought would be possible. He's made me feel like I might actually be desirable and sexy, and confident. It's a weird feeling to have after a lifetime of feeling like a short, fat, brunette version of the rest of my family. But the things he says and the way he handles my body leave no doubt that he means every single thing. He treats me like I'm the most precious thing in the world to him, while telling me things I think I've been yearning to hear for years. It wouldn't have been right, hearing them from anyone else but him. Oh, and his dirty mouth—never would I have thought that I would love hearing those kinds of words, but good God they do things to me I never would have imagined.

For someone who never wanted a man, let alone all the sex stuff that went along with it, I'm suddenly very, very interested in what's to come. I could seriously do with some more of that, thank you very much. I lift my fingertips up to touch my lips, remembering how it felt with him in my mouth, how soft yet hard he was, how he tasted. If you'd asked me before if

I would willingly do that, then I would have pulled a face and said one million percent no. But there, in that moment in the shower, all I could think about was tasting him and making him feel as good as he'd made me feel.

I try to remind myself that this might not last. I mean, this is Ruben, player extraordinaire—why should he stick around for me when no others have kept his attention for very long? Why should I think I'm different? A little voice in my head whispers that it's because he's different, he treats me differently, but I shoo her off, trying not to get any hopes up.

I think about what his clothing choice for me might be while I moisturise and put on a little—and I mean a little—make-up. If I'm going out to lunch with the Sex God, then I should put in a little effort. In my head, I have an image of a very skinny pair of jeans and a low-cut top of some description. He has said over and over how much he loves my tits and arse, so I can only imagine that he would choose something that would show off both. The thought of wearing something like that in the house, let alone out in public, brings me out in a small sweat. Good job there's nothing like that in my wardrobe.

I breathe a small sigh of relief when I go into my bedroom and see the maxi dress I bought with Molly earlier in the summer laid out on the bed. Ruben is just buttoning up a dark pair of jeans, but he looks up when I enter, and I watch as his eyes eat up every inch of my towel-clad body.

"Why this dress?"

"Because you looked seriously hot in it. Your tits were out of this world. I could barely contain myself that night."

I think back to the night in question and recall his weird behaviour.

I walk over to grab some underwear and the cami top I bought to go underneath the dress to cover me up slightly. Ruben comes over to inspect my choices.

"You know, you have the most incredible collection of lingerie. I'm expecting to see each and every set on your sexy body at some point in the coming weeks and months, and I intend to also see every set on the floor. If you could add some suspenders at some point, I would die one very happy man," he whispers in my ear, sending goosebumps and tingles shooting around my body.

"I'll see what I can do," I reply, trying to sound confident.

I hover around in the hope that he'll leave me to get dressed, but to my horror, when he's done he just sits on the end of the bed, looking at me. "Well, what are you waiting for? We're going for lunch, not dinner."

"I... uh..."

"If you're waiting for me to leave so you can get dressed, you've got another think coming. Come on," he says, gesturing to the pile of clothes on the bed.

I huff out a breath and mutter a 'fine' under my breath before dropping the towel. I don't know what I was worried about, because the look that appears on his face before the towel even hits the floor is worth it. His eyes are flicking around my body at the rate of knots, like he doesn't know what to look at first. His hungry eyes watch my every movement as I slide my knickers up my legs then clasp my bra into place. He scares the shit out of me, when he grabs the cami top as I go to put it over my head.

"What are you doing?"

"You are not wearing that. No covering up."

"But the dress is really low and I feel like I'm hanging out."

"Good, even better for me then, seeing as I'll be sat opposite you, enjoying the view."

"But..."

"No buts," he says, balling up the small piece of fabric and throwing it across the room.

After a bit of grumbling, I pull the dress on and try my best to pull the fabric about to cover the girls, but it doesn't have much of an effect. Ruben's eyes, however, barely leave my chest while I finish getting ready. I get the feeling he's enjoying this way too much.

It's another hour before we get out of the house and into Ruben's giant truck that he must have picked up this morning. It's a black Mitsubishi Warrior with 'Foster and Son' written in white down the side. It suits him; it's strong and powerful just like he is.

He made me open my birthday presents from yesterday and ring my parents before we went out. I got a couple of bottles of perfume, along with some clothes vouchers and new earrings from my mum and dad. Lilly and Dec went with the standard Amazon gift card; they've learnt that they can never go wrong with one of those. Molly seriously surprised me, though, by booking tickets to a book signing for next weekend that we were talking about possibly going back to last year when the line-up was announced. But then with her accident and pregnancy, it got put on the back burner.

Not only had she booked us tickets, but also a hotel. The only problem is that she can't go, what with Lois only being a few weeks old. She suggested in her card to see if Connie could come with me. I just hope she can find someone to cover her at the coffee shop at late notice, because now I've got the tickets in my hand, there's no way that I'm not going. I can already feel my inner fangirl breaking free.

Ruben makes a fuss of me getting into his truck. I tell him it's not my first time, but he's still insistent on helping me up. I think it has more to do with him being able to put his hands on my arse than anything else.

He took us to a pub a couple of villages over. It was a really cute old village pub with low ceilings and huge fireplaces. I bet it's so cosy in the winter with roaring fires warming the place up.

After a gorgeous meal and two fairly large glasses of wine, I'm feeling pretty good about myself. I almost forget that I'm flashing everyone a good portion of my boobs, but every time I catch Ruben's eyes dropping to them, I remember, and I feel myself flush red. That said, when we first arrived and walked up to the bar to get a table, the young barman had a hard job looking anywhere else... until Ruben pulled me into his side and kissed me like we were on a movie set. The barman actually had to clear his throat to get our attention. Weirdly, he didn't even look at me after that—the message was obviously heard loud and clear. The seriously dirty look that Ruben gave him didn't go amiss, either. The thought of him being jealous made butterflies erupt in my stomach.

"Where are we going?" I ask as Ruben pulls off the main road and down a little track.

"Just making a pit stop," he says as he turns into a field, pulls up in the corner and cuts the engine.

I'm just about to ask what the hell he's doing when he reaches out, grabs my wrist and tugs me over to him. His hand goes to my waist and he moves me until I'm hovering millimetres from his lips.

"I couldn't wait any longer. Look what you do to me," he growls out as he grabs my hand and puts it to where his erection is straining against his jeans. "I've been hard for you for hours, and I can't wait any longer."

His fingers snake into my hair and he pulls my head forward gently until our lips touch. It starts out gentle, but as soon as our tongues touch, it changes. It's like he's trying to get even closer. Our tongues duel, our teeth clash, as we pour all our hunger for each other into the kiss. He pulls me so that I'm straddling his lap, and I can't help but grind down on him. The noises that come from him make liquid pool between my legs.

"Fuck, you're gonna kill me," he grates out as he peppers kisses down my neck until he's nipping the tops of my breasts. "And these, fuck me, these are fucking awesome," he says as he lifts his hands from my arse to slip the straps of my dress and bra off my shoulders. He pulls the cups of my bra down so that I'm fully exposed to him. The gold in his eyes catches the sunlight pouring through the window, making him look almost predatory as he stares at my naked breasts. He lifts his hand and grabs one before pinching the nipple, then leans forward and takes the other in his mouth. Lightning bolts head straight to my core, and I continue to grind against his hard cock.

"Ruben," I groan, joining the sounds of our pants in the car.

"You're fucking perfect. I fucking love your tits," he says between kisses and sucks that are driving me insane.

"More, Ru, I need more,"

"Fuck, me too."

And then I'm moving and I feel the breeze flow over my wet nipples, making them harden even more.

"Ruben, what are you doing?" I ask in panic when I open my eyes and realise I'm now topless, clinging onto Ruben in an open field anyone could walk or drive past. I sit up in his arms and crush my chest to his to try to hide my nakedness.

"I won't let anyone see those perfect tits, Em, don't worry. They're mine."

I shove my face in his neck to try to hide my mortification, but before I know it, I'm flying backwards and hitting something soft. I open my eyes and find that I'm laid on my back in the back of his truck.

The next thing I know, the door is shutting behind him and an almost naked Ruben is falling on top of me. I prop myself up on my elbows and watch as he settles himself between my legs. He doesn't waste a second, because as soon as he's down, he's lifting my dress up around my waist, pulling my knickers down my legs and throwing them in the footwell where I see his t-shirt and jeans already are.

"If this hurts at all, promise you'll tell me and I'll stop," he says after getting me ready with his fingers for a few minutes.

I nod at him, unable to say anything as I watch him pull his boxer briefs down enough to reveal his cock. I watch in awe as he rolls a condom on, then shifts forward slightly and lines himself up with my entrance. He looks up at me before very slowly pushing into me. It stings at first, but he goes so slow that it subsides quickly. I break eye contact with him so that I can watch where we're connected to see him disappearing inside me. I feel my muscles clench and the sight makes my whole body shudder.

"Fuck, babe. You okay?" he grates out like he's in pain.

I nod again, keeping my focus on where we're connected in the most intimate way.

"Thank fuck," he mutters, before he starts moving in and out of me slowly.

He leans down over me and forces me to lie back before taking my lips with his. His tongue starts mimicking what he's doing elsewhere to my body.

It's not long before I start to feel the tension building in my lower body. Ruben must be able to feel it, because he sits up straight and the change in angle makes sure he hits a spot inside me that almost makes my eyes cross over with pleasure.

"Oh God, yeah, there. Shit," I mutter—well, I think I say it quietly, but I really have no idea.

I feel Ruben's hands slide under my arse and he lifts me slightly while continuing his punishing rhythm with his hips. The truck must be rocking a good 'un; there'd be no mistaking what is going on in here to passers-by.

"Ohhhh, Ruben, yes, yes." He lifts a little higher and I tilt my hips. One more stroke of his skilled dick sends me over the edge. White light flashes behind my eyes, and it's like my body has a life of its own. I'm vaguely aware of me shouting his name out, but again, I have no idea of the volume. I'm just coming back to earth when I hear him growl as his own release hits him, and he twitches viciously inside me. He drops down onto my chest and our sweaty skin instantly sticks together. We stay there for a few minutes, catching our breaths.

A thought suddenly hits me, and it's out of my mouth before I have time to think. "Should I be worried that you keep condoms in your truck?"

He sits up and lifts an eyebrow as he looks back at me. "I've never fucked anyone in here before. It was just here for emergencies."

He drops his lips to mine and it pushes thoughts of how this truck is pretty new out of my mind. I really don't need to be thinking of his past conquests, especially when I can feel him getting hard again inside of me.

He pulls back and out of me after a few minutes and I feel a weird sense of loss.

"Are you okay?"

"Yeah, I'm brilliant," I respond with a wide smile. How could I not be all right after that?

"You just had this weird look on your face."

"I just sorta... missed you." A smile splits his face at my comment.

"I'm not going anywhere, babe, don't you worry."

He reaches down to grab his clothes before opening the door and hopping out. I feel a whoosh of summer breeze lick over my exposed, overheated skin, and I welcome the fresh air. The truck smells like sex and sweat. Not the horrible kind, though—the hot and sexy Ruben kind.

"Can I have my knickers, please?"

"No."

I decide it's probably going to be easier not to argue with him, so I right my dress before sliding my way out of the truck. Embarrassment floods my body when I see two women about our parents' age looking over at Ruben as he pulls his white t-shirt on.

"No doubt I'd be screaming too, love, if I was in the back of a car with him," one of the women shouts out to me before linking arms with her mate and disappearing into the next field with two dogs in tow.

A smile tugs at the corner of my lips, and the minute I look at the shocked look on Ruben's face, I can't help but burst into laughter. I think I finally understand what Molly has been going on about—a good man really can make you feel great.

Ruben

"I'll be two minutes," I say, jumping out of my truck and jogging toward the shop. Today has been the best day of my life by far, and I intend on having many, many more like this with Emma. She's incredible. She's so kind, loyal, funny and so fucking sexy. I never thought she would have been so innocent, but in just a few hours, I feel like I've brought out who she really is. Gone is that timid, shy little mouse I first met, and in her place is a passionate goddess, just as I was hoping for. She's like putty in my hands, and one touch from me turns her on to the same astronomical level that she does me. Just being near her makes me hard. I should not be walking around in public sporting a massive hard-on, but I can't help it. She's like a fucking drug that I need more than my next meal. Hell, more than my next breath.

I head straight to a section I'm fairly familiar with before paying and heading out to the car with a smile on my face at how embarrassed the young girl behind the desk looked, scanning my items through the till.

I pass the bag over to Emma and jump back behind the wheel.

"What's this?" she says, looking in the bag at the two biggest boxes of condoms I could buy. "Ruben!" she squeals, looking a little like the girl behind the till.

"What? That was the last one I had, and I'm presuming you aren't on anything, so we're gonna need them. All of them," I say with a wink in her direction as I start to reverse out of the space. "I plan on filling you with my kid one day, but maybe not just quite yet," I say, completely seriously. I look at her shocked face as I pull out onto the roundabout and can't help but smile. I'm completely serious; I've got her now. If she even thinks for one second that I'm going to let her go, she has another think coming. Over the past few years I didn't think marriage and kids was on the cards for me, but that all changed the moment I looked into her gorgeous blue eyes in the photo Connie sent me months ago.

She's mine, and I am not letting her go for anything.

"Whose car is that?" Emma asks as we pull up to my place, ready for dinner with Connie and Fin.

"Grrr, not fucking again," I growl as I jump from the car as soon as it's parked. I storm into the house, ready to rip his fucking head off. I should have done it properly last time to stop him coming back after her.

I'm abruptly stopped in my tracks when Fin blocks my path to Connie's bedroom.

"Get out of my fucking way," I growl at him.

"It's not what it looks like. I've already had words, but he came because he couldn't find something that he needs for a date tonight or something. Trust me, I would not just be sat here if something was going on."

"Bullshit. Connie, get the fuck out here now," I shout as I shove Fin out of the way and storm toward her room.

When I get there, she's handing him a box. "I'm pretty sure I haven't got anything else of yours," she says calmly, even though she knows I'm there.

"Thanks, Con," Elliot says, placing the box in the bag he's holding. "She'd kill me if I didn't turn up to this place dressed properly."

"No, problem. Ignore him on the way out!" she says sarcastically, and he turns to leave.

"Ruben," he says, as he stands tall in front of me, waiting for me to move.

"This better be the last fucking time I find you in my house."

"See you later, Con," are his parting words as he barges past me and out of the house.

I feel Emma place her hand on my shoulder, and it instantly calms me down. I take a breath and follow Connie out of her room and into the kitchen.

"Why the fuck was he here again? You better not still be fucking him. I swear to fucking God, Connie, if I find out you are—"

"Ruben," she interrupts, "get a fucking grip of yourself. He came to pick up some stuff he left here months ago. He's got a girlfriend, for fuck's sake. He's taking her out to some fancy pants restaurant tonight and he couldn't find his cufflinks. And when I say girlfriend, I mean a serious girlfriend. We haven't been together for ages, so calm your tits."

"So, who were you with—" Emma starts to question, but she's soon cut off by the death stare she receives in response from Connie.

Fin then changes the subject by asking Emma what she wants to drink. I'm glad of the change of direction, because I don't want to know anything about what Connie is up to. It'll only piss me off.

We had a great night once I cooled off from seeing Elliot in my house again. Thankfully, Emma was fine with celebrating her birthday, and there wasn't a hint of her sadness from the previous day. Connie made her a homemade cheesecake for pudding and put some candles in for her, and even that didn't dampen her spirits. I was worried it might push her over the edge again, but I've actually never seen her happier.

Connie looked almost as excited as Emma when she started explaining about the book signing next weekend. Personally, I don't quite get it, but anything that makes my girl smile and bounce around on her seat like that is fine with me. Connie has already sent a couple of messages out to see if she can get cover for the weekend.

"You really don't have to come. I can make an excuse for you," Emma calls out from the bathroom where she's getting ready to go to her parents' for Sunday dinner.

I've lost count of the number of times she's said this over the last few days. Every time she brings it up, my answer is the same. "No, I want to come and meet everyone properly." I never thought I'd be actually willing to meet a girl's parents, but I'm weirdly looking forward to it. I mean, I'm obviously in her parents' good books after finding her on Tuesday, and I'm sure they've already filled the rest of the family in. It doesn't hurt turning up as the good guy. Better than looking like the player who's going to break their little girl's heart, which is something I've heard before.

When we get to their house, I'm greeted with a huge, warm hug from Susan and a handshake and pat on the back from Pete. They're such a warm and loving couple. They remind me of my parents before it all went to hell. Yeah, they're back together and in love now, but I don't see it quite the same after everything that happened.

When we move into the living room, I'm greeted by a range of faces, some of which I recognise, and others that I can only guess who they are.

Molly is the first one up to give me a hug. I vaguely recognise her, but seeing as she has a baby in her arms it's not hard to work it out.

"Thank you," she whispers in my ear when she gives me a one-armed hug. "We haven't seen Emma look this happy for years." She does then have a slight change of tune and shocks the hell out of me by saying, "But if you hurt her, you'll have all of us to answer to." She pulls back with a sweet smile on her face and goes on to introduce everyone as if she never threatened me. Dec, who I've met before, is there, along with his twin Lilly, who looks so much like the photo Emma has by her bed of Hannah it's unreal, Molly's fiancé Ryan, and his sister Abbi and her husband Jax.

I leave their house feeling weirdly content. My family has been mostly great over the years, but it's always pretty much been just the four of us. All our grandparents were around for a few years, but all but my nan passed away before we were teenagers. But being surrounded by such a huge family and listening to them all chatter away like they're the most important people in the world made me think that maybe that's something I want for mine and Emma's future. I can just see my new house full of people we love, with a few kids running around, maybe a dog. The thought doesn't scare me as much as it would have done even a few weeks ago. I even held baby Lois this afternoon without freaking out. I think the look on Emma's face helped, though. Her eyes went all soft and a little watery as she looked from me to the little bundle of pink in my arms. I couldn't help but notice Molly and Susan have the same looks on their faces as well. I guess they were all having similar thoughts.

I drop Emma off at her house with the promise that I'll be back in a few hours. I need to sort out a couple of things at work for the morning. She tries to tell me to just sleep at home tonight, but that's not happening. I don't intend on spending any nights away from her, apart from next weekend, when she'll be sharing a room with Connie in Birmingham for this signing thing. Two nights without her sexy body cuddled into mine is quite enough.

"Hey, it's Mr. Pussy-Whipped himself," Fin sings when I walk into the kitchen of my place.

I'm not surprised to see Fin here without me. He and Connie are close friends, and I know that Fin doesn't like to spend too much time at home. He lives with his dad, who brought him up after his mum died when he was little. I'm not sure what the deal with his dad is, because he never talks about him, but I know things aren't great at home. I haven't been to his house or seen his dad for years. It's the only subject that's off the table when it comes to our conversations. I've tried to talk to him about it over the years, but I've always been shot down. Connie hasn't had much luck, either.

"Fuck off," I grunt at him as I walk past and head up to my bedroom to grab some stuff to take to Emma's.

"Sooo..." he starts as he follows me into my room. "You had a taste of her sweet, sweet lady bits yet?"

"Fuck. Off."

"Oh come on, you're not usually one to shy away from the details."

"I am this time," I say, getting more and more pissed off.

"Oh come on, dude, she's just another girl."

The fine line I was riding between pissed off and angry snaps. I turn and have Fin backed up against the wall before he has time to blink.

"Emma is not just another girl," I growl in his face.

He puts his hands up in surrender, "Okay, okay, sorry dude. Didn't realise you planned on marrying this one."

"Well, you'd better realise soon, then, because that is exactly what I intend to do, and if you want to be my best man you'd better start treating her with the respect she deserves." I step back when I've finished my little speech and give my arms and shoulders a shake to release the tension.

"Aw, little Ruben is all grown up," Fin teases.

"Yeah well, maybe it's time you did the same, mate. Because fucking a different woman every weekend gets a little old in the end. The only thing I'm going to say about it is that it's sooooo much fucking better with someone you care about."

His face lights up like a Cheshire cat at that comment. "Is that fucking right?"

I leave the house a while later. Fin is still grinning as I give Connie a kiss on the cheek. "Rich tea biscuits? I haven't seen you eat them since we were kids and Mum gave them to us when we were sick," I comment on Connie's choice of snack before leaving and heading to the office, then to my new house to check out the plastering.

CHAPTER TWENTY

Emma

I pull up at Ruben and Connie's place just after six, ready to pick Connie up and head to Birmingham for the signing tomorrow. I let myself in and almost trip over the tiny suitcase sat in the hallway. I presume she must have more in her room, because there's no way Connie has all her clothes in there, let alone the books she wants signed.

"Hey, babe. Good day?" Ruben asks, coming over to me when I enter the kitchen. He pulls me into him, then kisses me like he didn't only see me this morning. I'm panting and starting to break a sweat when he pulls back. I'm suddenly regretting saying we'd leave so soon; I could do with an hour or so with Ruben now he's got me all fired up.

I worked all this week after having the previous week off, not knowing how I was going to handle my birthday, so we haven't really seen much of each other with the late nights I've done. He's still insisted on sleeping at mine every night, though, and no matter what time I eventually stumbled through the door, he was sat there with Kia, waiting for me with dinner cooked. I could seriously get used to this domesticated couple thing we have going on. I thought I would miss my own space, but I've actually felt lonely the few hours I've spent home alone this week.

Everything since last Tuesday has been perfect. We just seem to work together so well. All my family love him. My mum rang me at work on Monday to make sure I knew how amazing they all thought he was at dinner the day before. She also mentioned, as I knew she would, the way he held and looked at Lois. My heart melted when Molly passed her to Ruben to hold. He looked like a giant compared to her, but he was so sweet and soft with her. I fell for him even harder in that moment. I may have already been considering my future with Ruben after his comment about filling me with his kid a few days before, but now my mum is getting her knitting needles out, ready for her first grandchild.

"Yeah, you?" I ask once I'm put down.

"Yeah. So... listen," he starts, and my stomach flips at the tone in his voice. Nothing good can come next.

"Connie's ill, she's got a stomach bug or something."

It wasn't what I thought was coming, but my stomach drops anyway. I've been so looking forward to spending this weekend with her. "Oh."

"I'm sorry, babe, I know how excited you've been."

"Yeah, it's okay though. If she's ill, she's ill." I go to plonk myself on one of the bar stools and try to keep the disappointment off my face.

"What are you doing?" Ruben asks, grabbing my hand and pulling me back up. "You want to get there before it's too late, don't you?"

"What... but—"

"I'm coming with you. You didn't think I'd let you miss it, did you? Now, let's go get your stuff out of your car and get going."

"You want to come to a book signing with me?" I ask in amazement.

"Well, I haven't really got any interest in the book signing, but I want to spend the weekend with you."

An ear to ear smile spreads across my face. How did I find this guy who is not only hot as hell, but is the sweetest person I've ever met? And for the millionth time, why does he want me?

I poke my head in on Connie to check on her before we leave. She's sat in her bed with the TV on, looking very grey. I make sure she's got everything she needs before we head out.

"What the hell is in here?" Ruben asks as he lifts one of my two cases from my car.

"Books, of course." The first thing I did when I got a chance was to check out which authors are going to be at this signing, and make sure I had copies ready for all the ones I wanted signing. It took me forever to go through my boxes to find the ones I already had.

"Right, silly me," he says with a laugh as he puts it into his truck.

"I managed to organise the upgrade you requested, Mr. Morrison," the woman behind reception at the hotel says when we get to the front of the line. As expected, there are people—well, women—everywhere. God knows how he's managed to get a room upgrade; I'd have thought they'd be fully booked.

I look up to Ruben in question, but he just shrugs at me and sorts out the paperwork before taking the room key and nodding over to the lift.

"What is she talking about?" I ask with a raised eyebrow.

"It's a surprise. Wait and see."

Well, I was seriously surprised. Ruben had managed to upgrade the twin room Molly booked for us to one of the hotel's suites. I'd only ever seen rooms like it on the TV. It was bloody massive, with a living room, bedroom, and ginormous bathroom.

"This must have cost you an arm and a leg," I scold.

"You're worth it, babe."

"I really don't think I am, but thank you, it's amazing."

I'm quickly pulled back into Ruben's chest and chastised for putting myself down. I'm annoyed about being told off like a child until he puts his lips to the sensitive spot under my ear and starts kissing. It's all forgotten then.

His hands skim up from my hips until they're squeezing my breasts. "I wish I had time to get you naked, but I want to take you for dinner first," he groans in my ear, making goosebumps prickle my skin.

He quickly pulls away from me, and I turn just in time to see him adjust himself in his jeans.

"Come on, we're not going anywhere fancy. That'll just waste time." He grabs my hand and pulls me like a rag doll out of the room and back into the lift.

We ended up at an American-style diner. Both of us had their signature burger, but because I felt so guilty about having it after being so good with my diet for so long, I changed the chips for a side salad. Having said that, I did nick a few off Ruben's plate, much to his disgust.

As soon as we were done eating—okay, as soon as I was done eating, because Ruben wolfed his down in mere minutes then spent the rest of the time hurrying me up—he dragged me out of there like the place was on fire and back up to our room.

"Drink?" he asks, walking over to the minibar in the living room.

"Yeah, but should we go down to the bar and get them? That stuff costs a fortune."

"Shut up, Em. Just go with the flow here, and do as you're told."

"Uh..." I'm not really sure what to say to that.

"Perfect. I'll sort drinks. There should be a couple of presents for you in the bathroom; why don't you go and have a look?"

"In the bathroom?" I question.

"Yep, off you go."

I look at him for a few seconds in question, but he turns his back to me and grabs a glass. I eventually move toward the bathroom, wondering what the hell could be in there.

I see two gift bags when I look around after shutting the door behind me. Seriously intrigued, I go straight over and look in. There's a shoebox in one, and the other has something wrapped in tissue paper. I think I'm starting to understand. My heart starts pounding as I think about how if I'm right, this is more of a present for him than it is for me.

I pull the package out, open it and just stare in amazement. There, laid out on the vanity unit, is a set of almost completely sheer white lingerie, complete with corset, suspender belt and stockings. Oh, and a pair of sky-high silver, glittery heels to go with it. I rest my hands on the basin and hang my head between my shoulders.

Does he really think I can do this? Just put it all on and walk out there like I'm some pin-up girl? That's not who I am. I'm an overweight, frumpy girl whose hips and arse are way too big for the rest of her body. I can't just put this on and saunter sexily out there like some goddess. An image of Danni from all those weeks ago with her sexy lingerie under her coat comes to mind. I could never look anything like she did. She looked like a bloody model. There wasn't an inch of flab or a stretch mark in sight.

I lift my head up to look at myself in the mirror. I stare at my reflection for a few seconds before I hear Ruben's voice.

"You okay, Em? You're very quiet in there."

"I... uh..." I have no idea how to answer that question. He hates it when I put myself down or say bad things about my body so I hold my tongue. "Yeah."

"Good, because I can't fucking wait to see you in that. Been picturing you in it all day."

Hearing him say that makes me feel a little better. I look over my shoulder into the full-length mirror and run my eyes up and down my body, reminding myself of what he says he loves, and I try to ignore my inner demons telling me he's wrong.

I take a deep breath and start stripping my clothes off. It's not until I'm naked that I think to check the sizes.

It takes me ages to do up all the hook and eyes that run down the front of the corset and to wrestle my boobs into a position so they don't look like they're trying to escape. The thong is tied with two ribbons at my hips—I presume for easy access once the suspender belt is on.

Once I'm done, I teeter over and look back in the full-length mirror. I'm actually pleasantly surprised by what I see. The corset ensures my belly is held in a nice smooth shape and gives me a tiny waist. I kinda of feel a little like a burlesque dancer with the curves I've got. I have to smile to myself, because never in a million years would I have thought to compare my body to theirs; I mean, they're seriously sexy and they ooze confidence. I've got the curves, all I now need is the confidence.

I run my hands through my hair to give it some extra volume before taking one final deep breath and carefully walking over to the door. Confidence might start with having shoes that I don't feel like I'm going to fall out of at any minute.

I close my hand around the doorknob, shut my eyes for a second, and let out a breath. Without giving it any more thought, I pull it open and step out from inside the bathroom. The first thing that hits me is the soft music playing in the room. The second thing is the six foot something male propped up against the headboard of the four poster bed, naked, stroking himself as he stares at me with a hunger in his eyes that I haven't witnessed before. It instantly chases away my nerves and the butterflies that had taken flight in my stomach. They're replaced by apprehension and excitement.

The movement of his hand stills as his eyes run over my body. I walk, I hope somewhat sexily, over to him and watch the muscles in his neck flex as he swallows. His reaction to me brings out my inner vixen, because when I spot my drink on the bedside table, I walk over to it, turn my back on him and take a sip—well, it's more like a huge gulp—for liquid courage.

I hear his intake of breath as I presume he takes in my practically naked arse. Once I've downed half my vodka cranberry, I look over my shoulder at him and smile. He's now sat up like he's about to lunge for me, and the twitching of his cock catches my eye.

I stand back and let my eyes run all over him like he just did to me. Fuck, he's hot. His dark hair is starting to flop forward onto his forehead where the product he uses is starting to lose its fight. The muscles in his neck and shoulders are tensed, and his toned chest is rising and falling at an impressive rate, causing his abs to flex with each breath. His cock is thick and pointing its glistening head straight at me. What I love the most, though, as I always have, are his thighs, and as he moves himself off the bed,

I watch the muscles ripple in them. I bite down on my bottom lip to stop myself from groaning at the sight.

"The picture I saw of that did not do it any justice. Fuck me, Emma, you look... Fuck!" He gives up his fight to find the right words. Instead, he threads his hands into my hair and pulls my lips to his.

I take a step forward and my body lines up perfectly with his. The heels mean I don't have to reach up. I run my hands up his chest and over his shoulders so I can pull him even closer.

While he kisses me, he moves us until my back bumps up against one of the bedposts.

"You're incredible," he mutters against my neck as he starts kissing and nipping at my skin.

He runs his tongue around the inside of my ear and sucks the lobe into his mouth, sending shivers racing around my body. He then surprises me by whispering in my ear. When I feel his breath, I think he's going to say something sweet again, but I'm so, so wrong. "Get on your knees."

I pull back in shock to look at him. His eyes are twinkling in the low light of the bedroom, and he has a wicked smile tugging at the corner of the lips. That, mixed with his words, sends an unexpected surge of heat to my core, and makes my corset suddenly feel too tight in the boob department.

I slowly begin to slide down the post. Ruben watches my every move until I'm kneeling in front of him. I know exactly what he wants, because it's bobbing in excitement in front of my face, but I ignore it instead, going for my favourite part of his body. I run my hands up and down the solid muscle of his thighs before leaning forward and kissing up and down. His hand tangles in my hair and he makes me laugh when he starts trying to move me to the side a little to where he wants me.

"Patience, Ruben," I say, looking up at him through my eyelashes while running my hands up the back of his legs and squeezing his tight arse. "Can't I enjoy other parts of your body as well?" He just groans in response and loosens his hold on my hair.

I stretch up and run a series of kisses across the skin of his lower stomach before placing my lips gently to the side of his dick. I sneak my tongue out when I get near the end, making him hiss through his teeth.

I grasp him in my hand and begin to tease the head of his cock with gentle licks of my tongue. I know I'm driving him crazy, and I bloody love it. The control I have over him right now is awesome. I'm pretty sure I could ask him to do anything and he'd say yes.

"Fuck, Em, you're killing me," he grunts as he leans forward and places his hands against the bedpost above me.

I decide to give in and slide him as far into my mouth as I can, sucking and licking intermittently. I lift up the hand that isn't full of him and cup his balls, slightly squeezing them.

"Shit."

I continue for a few more seconds before I feel his legs start to shake and he gives me his normal warning that he's close. I've always pulled away at this point the last few times I've done this, but he's made me feel a little adventurous tonight. So I continue sucking him harder and deeper until his cock twitches in my hand and I feel a warm liquid hit my tongue. I keep going until he's stopped and I've swallowed everything. I'm not gonna lie, it's not the best thing I've ever tasted, but the look on his face and the smile I'm getting when I look up at him makes it definitely worth it.

He leans down, picks me up, then resumes the kiss from earlier while his hands run wild around my body.

"Hold your hands together behind the post," he orders, and I do what I'm told without hesitation.

The action makes my chest stick out. My boobs were already straining against the fabric, but now they just look ridiculous. Ruben obviously doesn't agree, because he shoves his face into them. He pulls away just as quickly, though, and when I look, he's on his knees and reaching up to untie the bows on the sides of my thong.

He watches with amazement as the fabric floats to the floor. He lifts his gaze, then does exactly what I did to him: kisses and teases everywhere but where I want him. My clit is throbbing for him, but he refuses to go anywhere near it.

"Ruben, please," I moan.

"Torture, isn't it?" he comments with a wicked smile.

"Please. I need—" I'm cut off when he runs a finger through my folds.

"Fuck, Em, you're dripping."

"Need you," is all I can say when he nudges my legs farther apart with his shoulders and replaces his fingers with his tongue.

"Hands behind your back," he growls when I move them to hold his head against me. I move them and a little thrill goes through me at his demanding tone. I think I love this side of him.

When my orgasm tears through me, Ruben has to grab on to my waist because my knees begin to buckle and almost send me tumbling to the floor.

He barely gives me a second to recover before dishing out his next order.

"Turn around, bend over, and hold the bedpost."

I turn on shaky legs and do as he says until my arse is sticking up in the air.

"Oh, fuck, yes. That is one sweet fucking sight."

I hear foil rip, then in a few seconds, he's behind me. He grabs a handful of my hair and tugs so I have no choice but to turn back to look at him. "This isn't going to be soft and loving like those soppy romance novels you read, but trust me, it'll be fucking earth-shattering."

"I'm not sure what you think I read, but soft and loving isn't the half of it." I may be naïve with doing this stuff, but I'm certainly no stranger to reading about it.

"Fuck," he grunts, before I feel him line himself up with me, and in one quick thrust he's inside. I have to quickly stiffen my arms to stop me going head first into the post with the force of it.

He pulls back out, only to slam back into me. He hits a place so deep that I practically see stars. His grip on my hips is so tight I swear I'll have finger indents when he's finished.

He's relentless with his thrusts and, within minutes, my entire body is shaking as what I think the most intense orgasm he's given me yet is about to rip me into pieces.

"That's it, Emma, come on my cock. Let me feel that sweet pussy."

His hand snakes around my body until he's pinching my clit, hard.

"Fuck, RUBEN," I shout into our room as I lose control of my body.

When I come back to earth, Ruben is pulling out of me and helping me to stand up straight. He places one arm around my back and the other under my knees before scooping me up and sitting with me on his lap on the edge of the bed. He tucks me into his chest and rests his chin on top of my head. I slip my shoes off, stretch my toes out and curl into him. I completely zone out just listening to his heart beating under my ear. I'm so content and relaxed.

"You okay?" he eventually whispers.

"Uh-huh."

He moves back to lie down, but instead of lying down with him, I straddle his hips and place my hands on his chest.

"Are you sure you're okay? I wasn't too rough?"

"No, that was incredible." I look down to where he's already hard again. "I might need a longer recovery time than you, though," I say with a laugh.

"My dick doesn't seem to register when it's been used around you. It's always ready to go."

I lean forwards and place my lips down on his. I run my tongue along his full bottom lip before sucking it into my mouth. His tongue tangles with mine and we kiss like teenagers for ages. When his hands that were running up and down my back move to squeeze my arse, I can't help grinding down on his dick that's lined up nicely with me.

"Em," he warns into my mouth, but I ignore him and continue to rub against him. "Don't start something you can't finish," he says when I pull back a little.

"What if I have every intention of finishing?" I say as I lean over to the bedside table and grab a condom out of the box.

I shimmy down his thighs a bit, rip open the packet with my teeth and experience putting a condom on for the first time. When I look up, Ruben looks like he could come any minute just from watching me.

Ruben

I seriously wasn't expecting to have sex again tonight after that. I mean, I wasn't exactly gentle with her, but fuck if I don't want to do it again.

Once she's happy, she moves forward again and lifts up. I move my hands to her hips to help her. Her legs are pretty short, so she doesn't have much movement once she's straddling me. She continues to hold my dick until she has us lined up, then she slowly, ever so slowly, sinks down. We both let out low moans as she takes me all the way.

Our eyes lock and she continues to move at a seriously slow pace with my hands on her hips for support. The slow build-up is fucking killing me. I'm desperate to up the tempo, but I want her to have her time, be in charge for once. Hell, I don't give it over often, so she needs to make the most of it. Come to think of it, I don't think I've ever let a woman take control before.

I break eye contact with her and run my eyes down her body. I knew when I saw the lingerie set that she would look stunning in it, but fuck, I never thought it could look that good. She looks like a fucking pin-up girl with her insane curves. I was worried when she stayed in the bathroom for fucking ages that she wouldn't do it, but I had faith in my girl. Her confidence over the past few weeks has skyrocketed. She needs to realise that her body is perfect. I can't get enough of it. Speaking of looking at her body...

"This is wrong," I say quietly. I instantly realise it was the wrong thing to say, because she immediately stops moving and looks very worried. "No, no, that's very right," I say, trying to reassure her. I encourage her hips to move again before taking my hands away from her hips and up to the top clasp of her corset. "It's wrong that I can't see your tits bouncing while you ride me."

"Oh," is all she says.

I slowly unhook every clasp until I can pull it from her body and drop it onto the bed.

"Much fucking better." I grab them both in my hands and revel in their weight and softness. "Fucking perfect," I mutter as I sit up so I can take them in my mouth.

"Keep moving," I tell her when her movements still again. "Lean back on your hands," I instruct, and I'm so fucking glad I do, because the position makes her tits stick out even more, as well as giving her a better angle to get off on. I put some pressure on her clit with my thumb while playing with her nipples with the other, and in seconds she's contracting around me, pushing me closer to my own release. When she's finished and limp, I take over and thrust up into her a few times as I chase my orgasm. I'm just about to explode when Emma moans loudly again and throws her head back.

"Oh fuck, yeah," I groan out as we ride out our orgasms together.

After cleaning up, we both fall fast asleep, our bodies exhausted after our activities.

The next morning, I'm woken by Emma, who's like a little Duracell Bunny buzzing around the room in excitement. She spends ages sorting out the suitcase full of books, along with pens in every colour you could imagine for the authors to sign them with.

It feels like no time at all before we're walking into the function room where it's all happening. I'm following behind Emma, tugging her suitcase along with me and taking in the sight of all the crazy women wandering around and beginning to form queues in front of tables where I guess their favourite authors are. What I wasn't quite expecting was the huge banners that consist of different views of men's naked torsos, some with tattoos and some without. I've never paid attention to the type of books Emma reads, and I hadn't thought about it until the comment she made last night, but clearly I was wrong with my thoughts that she read slushy, girly romance novels, because the images that surround me suggest anything but. There's even one that catches my eye that has an image of a woman with not one but two men. I make a note to ask her about these books when I get her alone.

When we get a little farther into the room, I see that it isn't just images of half-naked men around this place—there are actually half-naked men hovering by stands and having their photos taken with some very overly friendly women. The men don't seem too bothered by the women having their hands all over them.

"Oh my God, there he is," some woman squeals behind us. "He's so fucking hot, I'd let him do anything he wanted to me."

"Ohhhh she's over there, quick, get in her queue," another shouts to a friend.

I look over to Emma, who just has a small smile on her face.

"Why do you look so composed compared to all these lot?" I say, gesturing to all the crazy women.

"I'm containing it because I want you to think I'm normal!"

"So really, you want to be shouting and running around like this lot?"

"Yeah, pretty much," she says, looking embarrassed. "You know how men love football players, or whatever sport they're in to, and would do anything to meet them? Well, that's how we all feel about meeting our favourite authors. It's like a once-in-a-lifetime chance. These women are a huge part of our lives. They touch us in ways others don't, and to get the chance to meet them for even a few seconds is out of this world."

"Emma," I say with a smile. "Go as crazy as you want. I'll be behind you with the suitcase."

"You won't think any less of me?" she asks with a cute look on her face.

"Oh, I'll totally think you're a little closer to joining the nuthouse, but I can see how much this means to you, so go do your thing."

"Thank you, thank you." She reaches up and places a kiss to the corner of my mouth before taking off and shouting back, "Come on then, this way."

CHAPTER TWENTY-ONE

Emma

Today has been AMAZING! I've seen loads of my favourite authors, got all the books signed that I brought with me, plus I've got a load of new ones to take home to add to my collection. Bless Ruben, he's followed me around lugging all these books with him for hours, and he hasn't complained once. He's been surrounded by fangirling, screaming women and half-naked men all day, and somehow he's managed to keep a smile on his face. I'm not sure I'd be able to do the same if he took me to some football convention or something.

The minute our hotel room door is shut, Ruben drops the suitcase and bags he's carrying and starts pulling his t-shirt over his head. I want to scold him for treating my books that way, but when he starts removing his jeans, I'm too busy staring to care much.

"What are you doing?"

"I'm fed up of you looking at other men. I want your eyes on me."

I can't help but smile at him, "Are you jealous?"

"No," he says, but I'm not convinced.

I walk over to him, reach up on my tiptoes, and wrap my arms around his neck. "Good, because you are by far the best-looking man I've seen all day, and you're all mine," I say, placing my lips against his.

To my disappointment, he pulls away before the kiss really gets started.

"Strip down to your underwear, then go sit behind that desk over there," he demands, and I'm not ashamed to say my knickers get a little damp knowing that demanding Ruben is back. He's hot!

I do as I'm told, sit down and wait to see what he's planning.

"Here, put these on. Oh, and let your hair down," he says, passing me my glasses.

"Okay."

"The sexy secretary look suits you, Em."

I can see from here how much he is enjoying this, because his boxer briefs are seriously tented.

"Now, I've got a book that needs signing," he says, hiding something behind his back. "I want to have the first one because I know that this time next year, the author is going to be at one of these things signing hundreds."

I'm totally confused until he comes over and places an actual paperback copy of my book in front of me.

"OH MY GOD!" I scream. "Where did you get this?"

I turn it over and over in my hands, looking at every detail, and flick through all the pages. It's so pretty. The cover is an image of a blonde girl resting her forehead against a guy's ripped chest. Her hair is like a curtain covering her face, so you can't see if she's happy or sad. I'd seen the cover on Molly's computer hundreds of times, but not in real life. I don't think I have ever been so excited in my life than in that moment holding my book. MY book!

"Molly gave it to me on Sunday. Obviously, I was meant to give it to Connie to bring with her," Ruben says, bringing me from my thoughts.

I look up at him through my tear-filled eyes. "Thank you."

"So, will you sign it for me?"

"Uh yeah, I guess."

He takes it out of my hands, opens the front cover and places it on the desk in front of me.

"What's your favourite colour?" he asks.

"Green, why?"

"So I can get the right colour pen," he says with a smile, as he roots through one of the bags from earlier.

When he hands it to me, our fingers brush, and a bolt of electricity shoots down my arm. I realise something in that moment when our eyes lock, and I make a possibly rash decision.

I take the cap off the pen as Ruben wanders over to make us both a drink. I quickly write what I need to before I change my mind.

Ruben

Okay, so today hasn't been that exciting for me, but I've loved watching Emma enjoy herself so much. I'd been thinking all day about how to get her to sign the copy of her book that Molly gave me last weekend. I've also been thinking that I should have found some time to read it this week, especially now I know what the content is likely to be.

I walk over to get us drinks, leaving her with the pen poised, ready to sign her first book.

When I come back over, the book is closed in front of her and she has a weird look on her face.

"What's wrong?"

"Nothing."

I place her drink in front of her and she immediately picks it up and drinks half of it. I want to warn her to take it slow, because I wasn't shy with the vodka, but I bite my tongue because a tipsy Emma can only work to my advantage for how the rest of the night might go.

I put my drink down and pick up the book to see what she wrote. I glance at her before I open the cover. She is biting her lip and looking very unsure of herself. I blow her a kiss as I open the cover.

I look down at her script, and it's like the world stops spinning.

Ruben,
I love you.
E R Morrison x

No wonder she was looking unsure of herself.

Fuck!

I have to clear my throat, "You... uh," I stutter like a fucking idiot.

When I look up, I see the tears that were in her eyes earlier are about to break free. She stands up and goes to turn toward the bedroom. Her movement breaks me from wherever it was I went, and I quickly step to the side and stop her with an arm around her waist. I pull her with a little too much force, because she crashes into my chest. She keeps her head down, so I lift her chin with my hand so I can see her. She's reluctant to move at first, but she doesn't have a choice. When her face tilts up, she has one tear rolling down her cheek. I lean forward and stop its tracks with my lips.

I keep hold of her chin while I whisper, "You love me?"

Her eyes break from mine and she looks at my shoulder.

"Em?" I say, gaining her eye contact again and this time a subtle nod of her head.

"Yeah, I do," she says, so quietly I almost have to make her repeat it.

"Good, because I fucking love you too," I say, before I lift her and walk us backwards until her back hits the wall. Her legs wrap around my waist and I begin showing her just how much I mean those words.

I'm not sure I can put my finger on the point at which I fell in love with her, but somewhere along the line, I did. I think I might have even started to fall that day we got caught in the rain and I piggybacked her home.

I told Emma that we could go out. I'd heard all the other women talking about them all going to a certain club, but much to my delight, she told me she'd rather stay in with me.

She went to run herself a bath after I finished showing her how much I love her, because she was complaining her legs and back were hurting from walking around all day. I used the time she was gone to make a call down for room service. I told them I'd pay double if they could get it here in the next fifteen minutes, and a whole thirteen minutes later, there was a knock at the door.

"Who's that?" Emma calls out from the bathroom.

"No one," I shout back before letting the guy at the door wheel in the cart with everything I ordered on. He has a smug look on his face the whole time. Yeah, I know it's a little cliché, but so what?

I put what I want right now on a tray and carry it into the bathroom. Emma is just sinking into the mammoth amount of bubbles in the giant freestanding bath that sits below a skylight showing the sunset overhead. I don't think it could be more romantic if we tried.

"Wow, that's impressive," Emma comments as I place the tray on the side and slide my boxer briefs off.

"I know," I say with a wink.

She looks over at me from the tray and her eyes go down to my dick. "Oh yeah, that too!" she says with a laugh.

If I hadn't already made her come three times tonight, I might be slightly concerned, but I don't have any issues with the size of anything down there.

I get myself sat at the opposite end of the bath before passing Emma a glass of champagne and balancing the plate of strawberries on the edge of the bath.

"Notorious womaniser Ruben Foster is having a bubble bath with champagne and strawberries; whoever thought that day would happen?" Emma jokes.

"Yeah, all right, laugh it up. I'm as shocked as the next man, but you see, when you fall in love with an amazing woman, you do things you never thought you were capable of.

"Aw." She raises her glass before saying, "To us."

"To you," I say as I clink my glass against hers.

<hr>

The rest of our stay was great. We got back to Emma's in the early afternoon the next day, after stopping off for lunch on the way home. We spent the day doing really domesticated couple-y things that I never thought I'd enjoy doing. We went food shopping together, and I mowed her small patch of grass while she put the shopping away and ran the hoover around.

We just sit down to dinner when there's a knock at the front door. I get up to get it, but Emma stops me, and I watch her arse as she walks off instead.

The minute I hear Emma say, "What do you want?" I'm up out of my chair and standing behind her in the doorway, looking at Danni, who has tears streaming down her face, along with a lot of black make-up.

"I just came to tell you both that I'm pregnant. And it's yours, Ruben," Danni says, waving a pregnancy test around.

Emma immediately stiffens in my arms and tries to shrug me off, but I just hold on to her tighter as Danni's words settle into my brain.

"Bullshit," I snap. "I used a condom the last time we... And don't try the whole 'it broke' crap because I took it off, and I know for damn sure that it fucking didn't."

Danni starts sobbing harder as both Emma and I just stare at her.

"No, you didn't, you liar."

"Yes, I did. When you came to my house all those weeks ago, I used a condom. I'm not likely to go anywhere near you without one, if I'm honest." I can't help being a prick. I'm angry now, really fucking angry.

Danni's head snaps up and she looks like she's been slapped. "That wasn't the last time we were together, you arsehole. The night of the fashion show ring any bells? Against the wall in the toilet of Elements, and then again over the sink?"

CHAPTER TWENTY-TWO

Emma

If I don't do something, I'm gonna be sick on my doormat.

"GET OUT," I scream at the top of my voice. Danni takes a step back, but Ruben doesn't move, so I turn to him and take in his shocked face as I do. "I said get out. Yes, you. Get out now," I say, as I start to attempt to push him toward the door.

"But, I didn't... Emma, I haven't... It's not mine, I swear."

"You would say that. Now get out of my house." As soon as he steps over the threshold, I slam the door on them and run toward the kitchen sink to empty my stomach.

I knew it was all going too well. There must be a catch when a man like Ruben Foster tells you he loves you. If I wasn't so wrapped up in him, I might have kept my wits about me long enough to see something like this coming. Okay, well not exactly this, but something to ruin it for me.

I panic when I hear the back door rattling once the shouting has stopped outside my front door, and I'm relieved that I locked it after Ruben finished doing the garden earlier.

"Emma, open the fucking door," he shouts, but I ignore him, instead walking to the living room and sitting down on the sofa with my head in the hands. "Emma, I swear I didn't do anything with her that night. She's lying. Emma, please."

"Go away," I sob. I have no idea whether he hears me or not, and I don't care. I just want it all to go away. I want to go back to twenty minutes ago when I think I was happier than I have ever been in my life, instead of being sat here now with my heart ripped to pieces. *Haven't you said from the beginning that he's going to break your heart?* the little person inside my head says, and I want to slap her into next week for being so fucking right.

"Emma, come on. I promise you that I spent all night with Fin. Yes, we went to the club, but I stayed with Fin. I don't think I even saw Danni there."

The image of Ruben and me in the toilets in the exact same club from Connie's birthday comes crashing back to me and makes me cry harder.

It takes forever, but eventually Ruben gives up when he realises that I have no intention of talking to him. As predicted, it's not long before my phone starts ringing and Connie's face lights up the screen. I turn it off and head up to bed.

My suitcase and bags full of books catches my eye in the doorway of my spare room, so once I get changed and settled into bed, I start hunting for the perfect bookcase for my living room to try to distract myself.

The next morning, although feeling like my heart has been run over by an articulated lorry, I decide it's time to sort out another relationship in my life. I know she works first thing in the mornings, so once I'm confident she'll be home, I jump in the car and head to Cheltenham.

I ring the buzzer when I get there and Taylor, her flatmate, lets me in.

"Hey, chica, it's been forever. You look amazing, how are you?"

"Thanks, Tay. I'm good." He looks at me with a raised eyebrow, because even I could tell from looking in the mirror this morning that I'd been crying most of the night. "Everything okay with you?"

"Always, darling, always." He holds the door open for me and I follow him into their flat. "Lilly, you have a visitor," he shouts down to her room.

"Do you want a coffee, Emma?" Taylor asks as he heads for the kitchen.

"Yes please."

Lilly appears fresh from the shower just as Taylor puts a mug down on the coffee table for both of us.

"I'll leave you to it," he says, before disappearing down to his bedroom.

"Are you okay, Emma? You look like you've been crying," Lilly says, looking concerned.

As always, when I look at her, my heart skips a beat. Yes, she looks a little skinnier and slightly more gaunt than I've seen her before, but it's not her fault she looks like Hannah, and the reason I'm here is to try to rectify the issue so we can try to be close again like we once were.

"I'll tell you about it in a minute," I say, blinking back the threatening tears. When she gets closer, I notice something I've not seen before. I reach out and move her hair out of the way. "Is that new?" I ask, referring to the scar above her eyebrow.

"Oh, yeah, Tay and I got drunk one night and I fell on the coffee table," she says, looking a little shifty.

"Right, okay. Anyway... I want to apologise to you."

Frown lines appear on Lilly's face as she looks back at me, confused. "Why, you haven't—" she starts, but I cut her off.

"Lil, you don't need to pretend like you haven't noticed the distance between us since Hannah died. I want to apologise for letting what I was dealing with get between us. You're my sister and I love you. I hate that we have grown apart because of my inability to move on. I know you know how much you look like her, and that's been hard for me. But that isn't your fault, and you shouldn't lose your sister because of it.

"I hate that you've been ill and I haven't been here for you, or you've felt like you haven't been able to reach out to me. I'm so sorry, Lils. Can you forgive me?"

"Oh, Emmie," she says, before pulling me toward her for a hug. I know she's been ill, but she's lost so much weight, she's skin and bones in my arms. "You don't have to apologise. I can't begin to imagine what you've been through; I cannot imagine my life without Dec. You've dealt with it in the best way you can. I can't be mad at you for that."

The tears are streaming down my face by the time she's finished. Lilly is so sweet and caring; I never should have thought she would think less of me because of this.

"And I didn't ring you when I was ill because I felt so rough and didn't want to pass it on to you, not because I didn't feel like I could ring you. It really knocked me for six and I basically hibernated. Dec only came because he could tell something was wrong and wouldn't take no for an answer. I was quite happy, locked away on my own."

"You're feeling better now though, yeah?"

"I'm not totally there, but yeah, I'm feeling much better. So, come on, tell me why you look like a panda," she says, steering the subject away from her.

I guess she's referring to the black bags under my eyes, so I go on to explain about my latest drama with Ruben.

"I'm sorry, but you believe her? She sounds batshit crazy, if you ask me," she says when I've finished.

"I'm not saying I believe her, but I'm not saying I believe him, either. After the bet thing, I don't think I'm wrong in questioning him."

"True, but that was one mistake, Em. Look at everything else he's done for you to prove how he feels. He wouldn't do all that if he didn't care. She sounds like the unreliable one here, if you were to ask me. You need to speak to him."

"I know, I know. I just need to figure out what I want to say and try to work out what I want, whatever the truth is."

"Em, you've already told me you love him. Would you really throw that all away?"

That question plagues me for the rest of my time with Lilly and all the way home. If Danni is pregnant with Ruben's child, would I really throw away everything I have with him?

I'm just taking my shoes off when there's a knock at my front door. I rush over to the window and peek out, thinking that it's Ruben, but the person I see there has me running to the door and flinging it open. I run at such speed at him that he has to take a step back. "Daddy," I say into his chest.

"Are you going to invite me in?" he says with a laugh, as I continue to hold on to him.

When I pull back, he directs me back into my house with his hands on my shoulders. He steers me until I'm in front of the sofa, then pushes down until I sit.

"Lilly rang. She thought you might need a chat."

That's all it takes for me to burst into tears again. I repeat the story again but to my dad this time, who sits and listens to the whole thing. I love that my dad cares enough to listen to my girly drama. Growing up, I didn't know anyone else whose father would do that. I've been a daddy's girl from day one, though, and I know he loves the bond the two of us have.

"You just need to follow what your heart tells you, angel. No relationship is straight forward, not even mine and your mother's. They take work, compromise, and sometimes they need fighting for. And it sounds to me like Ruben might just need you to fight for him right now, because no matter the outcome of this, I imagine he's worried he's going to lose you because of it. I've seen the way that boy looks at you, and there's no doubting his feelings."

I feel better after a long chat with my dad. I hadn't realised how much I'd missed him while he was away. After finding some dinner, I head to bed and sleep like a baby.

I spend the next day at work, and thankfully it takes my mind off everything that has happened. I was grateful when I turned my phone on to find a message from Connie, letting me know that she's told Ruben to give me some space and that she'll do the same, but letting me know she's there if I need anything. It must be hard for her, not getting in the middle of the stuff between us. I know she has loyalties to me as her friend, but ultimately Ruben is her brother, so she'll always be on his side, no matter what.

I didn't manage to leave the office until after six in the end. One of my regulars was having some issue with his tax that needed investigating. When I get home, there is an unexpected visitor stood at my front door, waiting for me.

"Hi, Elliot, do you want to come in?" I say when I get to him. I've never spoken to him. I've only ever seen him in passing or when he was getting beaten up by Ruben. Connie spent a lot of time with him, though, and despite Ruben's dislike of him, I trust Connie's judge of character. "Do you want coffee?"

"Uh, yeah, please," he says, shifting around on his feet, looking awkward.

"What can I do for you?"

Ruben

I promised Connie that I would give Emma some space to get her head around whatever the fuck it is that's going on. I'm trying not to be pissed off that Emma doesn't seem to believe that I never slept with Danni that night. I know I was pissed; the amount of alcohol I put away that night was about as stupid as the fucking hot pants I had to wear, but I know for a fact that I did not sleep with her. I was too cut up over Emma finding out about the stupid fucking bet I had with Fin and her running away to even look at another woman, let alone touch one.

Fin confirmed it for me by agreeing with my story about us propping the bar of the club up for the couple of hours we were there. Even he wasn't on the pull, which I remember thinking was weird. When I got so drunk I could barely sit on the stool, he practically carried me home.

It actually hurts that she believes Danni over me, after everything that I've done to prove to her what she means to me, yet at the first sight of trouble, she turns on me and runs. Again.

I keep telling myself she kinda does have a reason to doubt me after the whole bet fiasco, but I thought she'd forgiven me for that and believed it wasn't serious.

I told her I loved her this weekend, for fuck's sake. Does that not mean anything to her? Because it sure as fuck means a lot to me. I've never said it to anyone other than my family before, and I don't actually intend on ever saying it to anyone else, either. I just need to somehow come up with a way to prove that that baby isn't fucking mine.

"Here have a beer and try to cheer the fuck up," Fin says, throwing me a can. We've been at my new place all evening, getting the first coat of paint on the new plaster.

"Thanks."

"She'll soon realise that Danni is a lying bitch. Don't sweat it, man."

"Hmmm," I mumble back while refilling my roller.

We're interrupted when my phone starts ringing. I leave it to ring off as I have no interest in talking to anyone, and I don't need to look to know that it's not Emma. After mine rings a few times, it stops, but Fin's then starts.

"Con, what's up, girl?"

He goes quiet while he listens, then hangs up after, saying that we're going there now.

"Put your roller down. We need to go," Fin says, putting everything down and pulling his shirt back on.

"Go where?"

"Emma's. Connie just drove past and she saw Emma going in with Elliot. She doesn't think that anything—"

I don't let him continue what he was going to say, because I'm already halfway to my car shouting, "Come the fuck on, then," behind me to Fin.

Luckily, the front door is unlocked when I get there, so I swing it open and storm in. Voices come from the living room, so I head straight there. Both of their heads swing around at the intrusion, and their eyes go wide as I head straight to Elliot and pull him from the sofa by the scruff of his shirt. I shove him against the wall and hold him there with my forearm against his throat.

"What the fuck are you doing here?" I growl in his face.

"Ruben, let him go," Emma says behind me, but I ignore her. I want to know what this arsehole is doing here with my girl.

"I swear to God if you've laid a finger on her, I'm gonna fucking end you. Connie is one thing, but my fucking girl? You've got to be an even bigger prick than I thought."

"Ruben," Emma shouts louder. "Let him go. He's here to help you, you idiot."

"What?" I question, loosening my hold on Elliot's throat slightly when her words register in my anger-filled brain.

"He came to explain what he heard Danni talking about on the phone. Elliot, tell him."

"I... uh," he coughs, so I let my arm drop, but I don't leave his personal space or drop my guard. I don't trust this guy as far as I could throw him. "I heard Danni talking on the phone."

"And?"

"She was telling the person on the other end how she had told you that you're the father because she has no idea who the guy was that she hooked up with in the club that night. She knew you were wasted, so thought she could pull it off. I wanted Emma to know. I couldn't let my sister ruin what you two have."

"Why? Why would you suddenly help me out?"

"I'm not a complete dick, Ruben. If someone were playing the same shit with Amy and me, then I'd want to know about it. If you're half as serious about Emma as I am about Amy, then I couldn't just ignore it."

I step back from him in shock. "You heard her say that?"

"Yeah."

"Well, um, thanks, I guess," I say, in complete amazement.

I turn away from Elliot and face Emma, who is staring at me, but it's like she's a million miles away.

"I'm gonna go," Elliot says, before I hear his footsteps get quieter.

"Me too," Fin adds, following him out.

It's not until we hear the door shut that Emma speaks.

"I'm so sorry," she says very quietly.

We both stand and stare at each other. As desperate as I am to pull her to me and never let go, it still hurts that she didn't fight for me. Her first instinct wasn't to talk to me, to find out my side of the story. She just kicked me out and ignored me. I don't want to sound like a girl about this, but it's eating me.

She goes to step toward me, but I instinctively take a step back. The hurt look that enters her features breaks my heart, but I just can't forgive her yet.

"So am I," I whisper, before I turn and leave the house. Her cries almost make me change my mind, but I need to get out of there.

I go straight back to my house, put some loud music on, and continue where I left off with the painting. I don't want to think. I just want to do, and the music blaring in my ears almost lets me do just that.

I have no idea how much time passes, but I've almost got the whole of downstairs done when the music suddenly goes off. I turn to see what's going on to see my mum stood next to where the speaker is plugged into the wall.

She comes walking over to me, and looks like she's about to hug me, until she registers that I'm covered in speckles of paint.

"Connie sent me," she says, as an explanation for her sudden appearance. "This place is really coming on, baby. I'm so proud of you."

"Thanks," I mutter, knowing she isn't here to have a look around my new place. "Go on, say what you're really here to say."

"I'm not here to say anything. I'm here to listen. I can't tell you what to do, that's for you to figure out, but I think you already know what it is you're going to do."

"She just assumed the worst of me though, Mum," I say, presuming she already knows the whole damn story if Connie's been involved.

"I know, baby. I'm sorry to say it, but you have given her reason to doubt you in the past," she says with a cringe.

"Thanks, Mum."

"I'm sorry, but you know it's the truth. You should have known your past behaviour was going to come back and bite you in the arse at some point. You've broken too many hearts over the years for that not to happen. She was in shock. The last thing any woman wants is to find another woman at their front door telling them their man has got her pregnant."

"Don't you think I was in shock? I knew it wasn't true, though. I knew I didn't do what she was accusing me of, but Emma didn't give me a chance to explain. She just kicked me out."

"I know, but I also know that she probably regrets it. There's no telling what any of us would do in a situation like that. Emma's coping mechanism is to shut things out, you told me that yourself not so long ago, so why should you expect her to do anything else?"

"I guess."

"Go and sort it out with her, baby. I can't stand seeing you like this."

Mum left me to my painting not long after. I hate to say it, but she's right, as always. I intend to go back and talk to Emma. Just not quite yet.

I t's almost two AM by the time I decide I can't wait any more. I got home sometime after eleven, and after showering, I got in bed and tossed and turned for hours, fighting the need to go to her. Eventually, I jump out of bed, throw some clothes on and head out.

When I left earlier, I know it wasn't going to be for long so I nabbed the spare key Emma keeps in a bowl by the front door. So when I get there, I let myself in quietly and sneak up the stairs. Kia spots me instantly and starts purring at me from what I class as my side of the bed. I silently strip down and shoo her off. I slide under the covers and right up behind Emma, who is fast asleep. She won't be for long, if I have anything to do with it.

I lift her hair gently off her neck before I plant kisses along her exposed skin. When she starts humming in her sleep, I know she's starting to come to.

I skim my hands down her sides to discover that she's wearing a little nightie, which is unlike her. I'm not going to complain, though, because it gives me easier access. When my hands reach her hips, I discover that not only has her nightie ridden up around her waist, but she also isn't wearing any knickers. My already hard dick twitches in excitement. I reach behind me into the bedside table to grab a condom and suit up ready for her.

I move back and slide my hand around to her stomach then down to her pussy. Even in her sleep, she's ready for me. I slide my fingers in and out of her a few times to make sure she's ready. She moans my name and I feel her start to rock her hips back into me, giving me the access I need. I don't waste any time in sliding into her, and I begin a gentle rhythm while I hold her tightly to me.

I know the moment she wakes fully, because she stills slightly, before turning her head back toward me. I sit up on my elbow and look down to her so we can meet halfway.

"I'm sorry. I love you," I whisper, dropping my lips to hers.

"I love you, too," she mumbles against my lips.

She begins to turn, forcing me to pull out of her and lift up so she can lie on her back. I settle myself between her legs and make love to her just like she deserves.

CHAPTER TWENTY-THREE

Emma

As soon as Elliot explained what he'd heard, I instantly felt awful for the way I'd treated Ruben since Danni's appearance. He didn't deserve to just be kicked out. I should have heard him out, but it hurt too much and I wanted to get away from it all.

I thought the moment I heard her say she was pregnant with his child ripped my heart in two, but that was nothing compared to how I felt when he stepped away from me earlier after Elliot left and I apologised. Never in a million years did I expect him to just walk away from me. The pain that ripped through me when I heard the door slam shut was like nothing I'd felt before, and it was my fault. All this time, I'd been telling myself that he'd be the one to do something to hurt me, when it was my actions that ultimately led to this. If I'd just listened to him, believed him from the beginning, then this wouldn't have happened.

Once my sobbing decreased to a bearable level, I phoned Connie to make sure he was all right. She still sounded rough on the phone, but promised to find him and make sure he was okay.

I went to bed not long after and cried myself to sleep.

I would have thought that waking up to find someone else in my bed would have scared me, but I instantly knew it was him.

My body knew it was him.

I feel his cock stroke inside me, and I can't help the little noise I make.

He came back.

Ruben made love to me for hours, our bodies moving in sync as we showed our love for each other and put our apologies for the last few days into our actions instead of words.

I have no idea what time I eventually drifted off to sleep in the arms of the man I love, but when my alarm clock started the radio playing, I knew I wasn't ready to wake up. I pulled my arm from under the covers and went to hit the off button, when a new song started to play. My first reaction was to panic, but I looked over my shoulder to Ruben and that feeling instantly transformed.

After everything I've been through, this is exactly where I'm meant to be, and I feel her looking down at me and smiling.

Everything happens for a reason.

EPILOGUE

Emma

I've been awake since five AM.

I'm excited.

I'm scared.

I think I'm going to be sick.

My book went live on all platforms at midnight, and I'm sat at the breakfast bar with my trillionth coffee and my phone, which I keep refreshing like it's my lifeline. I've had a couple of reviews posted already by people the host company Molly found sent it out to. They're both 5* and I'm completely blown away by their comments and love for my story and characters, but I'm now greedy for more. I know that realistically I've got hours to wait, because most bloggers and readers are American, and they are mostly still fast asleep.

"How long have you been up?" Ruben asks when he appears, looking a sleepy, sexy mess a few hours later.

"Hours. I couldn't sleep."

"Aw, happy release day, babe," he says as he walks over to the coffee machine, giving me an awesome view of his arse.

It still amazes me that the godlike man currently wandering around my house in just his boxer briefs is all mine.

Things have been beyond perfect since the night he appeared in my bed in the middle of the night. Danni has thankfully gone back into hiding, and we've picked up where we left off. Well, almost. I have a new-found trust in Ruben since finding out the truth. Although him being with me still astounds me, I know that he loves me and that he doesn't want to be anywhere else. He makes sure to prove it to me as often as possible as well, which doesn't hurt.

After spending all morning attached to my phone, Ruben eventually manages to get me into the shower and makes me get dressed so he can take me out to lunch to celebrate. I want to go, I really do, but I'm so anxious about missing a review come in or for someone to comment or download my book. I don't think I've ever been this dizzy about something in my entire life. I think I could get addicted to this feeling.

"Babe, you need to relax. Your book is amazing, trust me. And the reviews will still be there when we finish," Ruben says, trying to reassure me when he sees my knee bouncing on the journey to the restaurant.

I couldn't believe it when he said he'd read it the night I kicked him out after Danni's announcement. He said he loved the idea that I was thinking about us when writing the sex scenes. I didn't want to burst his bubble by telling him that I wrote the whole thing long before I even met him, so I just nodded along. Plus, it's not completely untrue, because I do use him as inspiration in my current manuscript.

Ruben booked us a table at this fancy restaurant. The food was insane, although I wouldn't expect any less when the prices are so extortionate.

"Where are we going?" I ask when Ruben misses the turning to my house and continues.

"It's a surprise," he says, looking over at me and winking.

"Okay."

After a few more minutes, he pulls over by a gravel track. I've never been this side of the village. I think I've run through the fields, but that's about it.

I watch as he hops out and comes around to my side before opening the door and helping me out.

"What are we doing?"

"Stop asking questions and do as you're told."

I shut my mouth and watch as he pulls one of my scarves out from the glove box. "Wh—" I start to ask but stop when I see the look on his face.

He ties the scarf around my eyes and, after checking if I can see anything, he begins tugging me along with him.

We seem to be walking for ages, but it could just feel that way because

I'm in darkness. I know we're walking up a gravel track, because I can feel the stones under my feet. It's not very easy to walk on in heels—he could have warned me.

Eventually, he brings me to a stop.

"You ready?"

"Uh, I guess," I say, but I have no idea what I'm about to be facing.

He pulls the scarf away and, after blinking against the bright sunlight, I see that I'm in front of the barn conversion I've been admiring for months on my daily runs.

"Why are we here?"

"Come on." He grabs my hand and pulls me toward the front door.

I watch in horror as he opens the door and goes to walk inside.

"Ruben, you can't just walk... oh," I say, when the sight inside takes my breath away.

It's as I imagined it would be. The downstairs is a massive open plan room, but it's completely empty, apart from a huge bookcase next to the vast floor-to-ceiling windows. What really takes my breath away, though, is the number of roses of all colours filling the bare space.

"I don't understand. Why have you brought me here?" I say, walking into the room behind him.

"I wanted to show you our house," he says with a massive smile.

"Our house?" I repeat in disbelief.

"Yeah."

"But... but is it even for sale?" I ask, completely bemused by this situation.

"No, it's never been for sale. I'm the only one that's ever owned it. Well, other than my parents."

He must see the utter confusion on my face, because he goes on to explain.

"This field and barn was on their land. I bought it off them years ago, and I've been converting it ever since. I was planning on moving in when it was all done. But then I met you and discovered you loved it as much as me, so I got it to this point," he says, gesturing around, "And stopped, because I thought you might want some input on it as well."

"This is... yours? All of it?" I'm completely gobsmacked.

"Yeah," he says with a laugh, "All of it. Well, actually, it can be ours. I have a key here for you."

I watch as he reaches into his pocket and pulls out a key. He holds it out to me and when I hold my palm out, he gently places it down. I briefly look down at it, but something about Ruben makes me look up at him.

"What do you think?" he asks, nodding toward the key and making me look at it a little more closely this time.

My eyes go wide when I see what he's really asking, and when he sees that I see it, he drops down to the floor.

On one knee.

Oh my God!

"Emma. I never thought that a serious girlfriend, let alone marriage, was in my future, but that was only because I hadn't met you. Since the moment I looked into your eyes when I was in Australia, you captivated me, and I knew you were mine. You amaze me every day with your intelligence, creativity, kindness, strength and love. I never want to experience a time without you or those things in my life. Will you marry me?"

Tears are streaming down my face and my whole body is shaking at this very unexpected turn of events. Never in a million years did I see this coming. It's so soon. We haven't been together very long. But even knowing that, there is only ever going to be one answer.

Ruben can obviously see the thoughts running wild around my head, because he tries to reassure me, "I know it's too soon, but I know you're the one for me. We don't have to get married anytime soon; we can have a long engagement. I just wanted you wearing my ring and knowing that one day you'll have my name as well."

"It is too soon," I sob out, "but that doesn't matter to me. I love you, Ruben, of course I'll marry you." I just about finish what I have to say before he's up off the floor and I'm in his arms as he spins me around the room. When he puts me back on my feet, he takes the key he gave me earlier from my hand, unclips the engagement ring that was hanging from it, and slides it onto my finger. I look down through my tear-filled eyes at the simple but perfect solitaire diamond on a platinum band. It's perfect.

Once I've composed myself, Ruben asks if I want a tour. Does he even need to ask?

"This end is going to be the kitchen. I was thinking of units all around there, a breakfast bar here, as well as a dining table in that space over there, but if you think something different, then we can change it," he says enthusiastically.

We walk through the space that is going to be the living room and over to the bookcase. It's only now I realise there's a book on it. And, of course, that one book is the one I sighed for Ruben weeks ago at the book signing. If it's possible, my smile gets even wider looking at it.

"This bookcase is gorgeous," I say, running my hand across the smooth, chunky wooden shelves.

"I made it for you."

"Wow, it's stunning, Ruben. You could make a fortune selling these."

"Nah, that's a one-of-a-kind Foster special for my fiancée." Butterflies erupt in my belly at hearing him call me his fiancée. It's gonna take some getting used to. I'd barely got used to calling him my boyfriend.

The entire house is gorgeous, even half-finished. The master bedroom has the same floor-to-ceiling windows that the living room has, showcasing the view. Waking up to that will be amazing.

I'm looking over the countryside beyond when something catches my eye and a thought hits me. "A while ago, I was sat on that bench mid-run, and I felt like I was being watched. I was being watched, wasn't I?" I ask, but I really don't need to. I know the answer.

I look over my shoulder at Ruben, who is completely ignoring the view and staring straight at me. His lips quirk up at the sides, and it's all the confirmation I need.

"That's how you found me on my birthday," I state. I never really questioned how he knew where to find me, but it's all become clear now.

He shows me what will soon be our en suite and dressing room, before going around the other rooms upstairs.

"I thought this could be a nursery," Ruben says, when we're in the smallest of all the bedrooms next to the master.

"Whoa, one step at a time, Ru."

"I know, I'm just thinking ahead."

I love the look Ruben's had on his face the whole time we've been here. It's clear to see the pride oozing from him from what he has achieved here. He's full of it, bouncing from room to room and telling me about all the work that has gone into turning the once dilapidated barn into a stunning family home.

And I have to say, I totally share his vision. I really can see us here, starting a family. My stomach flips in anticipation at the thought. How my life has changed in only a few weeks.

When I put that offer on my cottage a few months ago, I did it with the intention of starting over, getting a new life for myself. Never in a million years did I think that I'd have that new life so quickly. Not only a new life, but new friends, and now a fiancé.

The thought of leaving my cottage saddens me, but at the same time, the excitement of being here with Ruben cancels it out. Plus, it's still gonna be a while before we can move in.

Those aren't all the surprises that are apparently planned for the day. Once Ruben has showed me every inch of our soon to be home, we head back to my cottage. I spend the entire journey staring at my hand in disbelief.

There are cars everywhere when we pull down my street. I recognise most of them, so it gives me a clue as to what I'm about to walk into.

We go around to the back door, but instead of going in, Ruben steers me to the garden, where all the people I'm expecting to see are in my garden with drinks in their hands.

My mum and dad come straight over to hug us both, before my mum demands to see my hand.

"You guys know?"

"Of course we do, angel. Ruben came to ask your dad's permission."

I look over at Ruben and I fall even more in love with him at his thoughtfulness. That would have made my dad's day, being able to give him permission to marry me.

Once we've said hello to everyone and accepted their congratulations, Molly thrusts a laptop in my face. With all the proposal and house excitement, I'd almost forgotten about my book. She hits refresh on the screen, and I see twenty-five reviews, and when we go into them, they are nearly all 5* with a few 4* thrown in. I'm trying desperately hard to hold back the tears as I read through what everyone has said about my book. I'm completely overwhelmed.

Today is turning out to be the best day ever.

Molly takes the laptop back just as Ruben walks over to me. "Babe, is there something you need to tell me?" he asks, looking a little pissed off.

"No, I don't think so."

"Okay, so how about you explain to me why I found this in the bathroom bin?" he asks, pulling a positive pregnancy test from his pocket.

"What? That's not mine."

"It's not? So why is it in your bathroom?"

"I've never peed on one of those in my life." I break eye contact with him and look around all our family members in my garden. One person stands out to me, and she's sat at the garden table, looking a little green and sipping on lemonade with Lilly. "Connie," I whisper to myself, forgetting that Ruben is in front of me.

"Connie?" he asks with wide eyes.

"I don't know anything, I swear, but she's been sick a lot lately."

Ruben instantly starts marching in her direction, and I have to run to catch up with him. "Ruben, don't," I warn as he gets closer to her.

"We need to talk," he growls at Connie, grabbing her arm and dragging her inside.

"What are you doing?" she shouts at him, but he ignores her and continues pulling her toward the living room.

He sits her down on the sofa, then stands in front of her with his hands on his hips. "So, is it you? Are you?"

"Am I what?" she asks, but I can see the guilt shining through her eyes when she glances at me, pleading for help.

I put my hand on Ruben's forearm in the hope of calming him down.

"Are. You. Pregnant. Connie?" he bites out.

Her eyes instantly fill with tears, and she nods as they spill over her cheeks.

"Who's the father?" he demands.

"Ruben, calm down, you're scaring her. I'm sure she'll tell us everything when she's ready."

"No, I want to know now. I want to know what fucking idiot has knocked her up. How could you be so fucking stupid, Con?"

Connie goes to say something, but she's interrupted.

"Con, baby, what's wrong?" Fin says softly around a mouthful of hotdog from the barbeque that my dad and Ruben's are manning in the garden.

Connie and I watch as Ruben looks between her and Fin with a shocked look on his face, before he starts shaking his head. Connie starts to cry harder, and Ruben has Fin pinned up against the wall and his fist in his face faster than either of us can move.

"RUBEN, NO," Connie screams, as she leaps from the sofa.

Find out Connie and Fin's history, as well as their future, in *Falling For Fin!* *Download Falling For Him: Part Two now!*

Keep reading for Falling for Daniel.

ACKNOWLEDGMENTS

I can't believe I'm at the end of my fourth book in this series already. These four characters have been floating around in my head for so long, it feels amazing to put them out there. I've felt really apprehensive about Emma, because I feel she is so different to Molly, Ryan and their gang. She lives a much quieter life, and I was worried she wouldn't be as entertaining. I really hope you have loved her and her self-conscious, shy ways.

As always, I want to thank my husband for supporting me through this and listening to me talk all things books without looking too bored! Of course, my gorgeous baby girl, thank you for allowing me to write while pregnant, and then to complete and get her ready for publishing once you arrived. You are the most amazing little person ever.

To Pam, again, for helping me with ideas and beta reading. I couldn't do this without your support. Thank you.

To Evelyn at Pinpoint Editing for proofreading and polishing her up for me.

To Colleen and her reviewers and promotional team at Itsy Bitsy Book Bits. Thank you for everything you do to support and promote me—oh, and for making me cry while reading your reviews. It blows me away that you are writing those things about something I have written. And finally, to my Angels, thank you so much for all of your kind words, reviews, support, post sharing, pimping, and general awesomeness. You guys make me believe that I can actually do this.

FALLING FOR DANIEL

FALLING SERIES NOVELLA

CHAPTER ONE

Beth

I saw him the moment I walked into the room. I didn't want to come to this party. Celebrating was the last thing I felt like doing after everything that had happened over the last few weeks. But here I was staring at what could be my next mistake. Well, next mistake if I allowed myself to go there. I was so done with men.

Unfortunately, my eyes don't get the message and are locked on to where he is crouched down in front of two little girls in their party dresses. I feel Liv unhook her arm from mine and move away, but I don't look over to see where she goes. It's like my eyes are glued to him.

I should have learnt my lesson. My choice in men has left me seriously burned, yet here I am, completely lost once again around the sexy, older man in front of me.

It's obvious he's talking to his daughters. At this very moment there is probably a woman shooting me death stares for ogling her husband but even that isn't enough to stop me.

I'm just about to drag my eyes away when he looks at me. He holds my eye contact for a second or two before leisurely running his eyes down the length of my body, as he slowly stands to his full height. And to think, I felt he looked powerful and sexy when he was crouched down. His solid body is wrapped in a perfectly cut black suit that fits him like a second skin. It must be tailored. I run my eyes down from his perfectly styled chocolate-brown hair, take in his facial features and continue my way down his thick neck to the crisp white shirt he has under his suit. My eyes continue their journey despite my brain telling me to stop and move away. This man screams trouble and that is the last thing I need right now.

Thankfully, Ryan walks over to him with a drink. It distracts him and allows me to go to where I can hear Abbi and Liv calling me. It felt like I was stood staring at that sexy stranger for ages but when neither Abbi or Liv comment I realise it probably wasn't as long as I thought.

I join in with their conversation but I can't focus. My mind is still fantasising about those dark eyes and strong shoulders.

"Beth, get those thoughts out of your head right now. Your taste in men has already caused enough drama," my brother, Caleb, whispers in my ear before handing me a drink. Okay, so maybe it was obvious to some people but then my baby brother was in full on protective mode after everything that had happened.

"What?" I ask, trying my best to look confused by his comment. He just raises an eyebrow at me to let me know he knows exactly what I'm doing.

The second I accept the glass of red wine from his hands I swallow a huge mouthful as I try to give myself a good talking to, because he is right. I do not need another man, especially one like that. The one I recently ran away from has caused enough pain and heartache to last me a lifetime. Never would be too soon to feel anything like that again. I can't lie; maybe a good rebound man is just what the doctor ordered to help me forget about the dick I left behind. But I don't think falling into bed with another guy who has the potential to break me is the best idea for a rebound.

I glance around the room in an attempt to find someone possibly more suitable for the job. Not that I have any intention of hooking up at this party, or anytime soon for that matter. I just need a reminder of what I should and definitely should not be looking for. As I look around I see no sign of Mr. Dark and Delicious, nor a very pissed off wife shooting daggers at me from her eyes. I let out a huge breath in relief as I take another big swig of my wine.

I'm placing my empty glass down on the kitchen worktop so I can open another bottle of red when my breath catches at a familiar feeling. A rush of breath caresses the skin of my back that my dress reveals.

"Tell me you came here alone tonight," a deep voice whispers in my ear. I go to turn toward him but two large hands clamp around my waist keeping me in place. "Don't move," he demands.

I open my mouth to respond but no sound comes out. I'm too focused on the burning sensation his hands are causing and the goosebumps that are still across my back where his breath tickles my skin. I feel alive. A kind of alive that I don't think I've ever felt before. This guy has said only a handful of words to me and hardly touched me, yet my body feels like it's singing. My mouth is dry, my nipples peaked and my knickers are growing damper with every second that passes. Has this guy got some special super power or something?

After a couple more seconds I manage to swallow before answering him. "I... uh... I came with my..." I feel his breath again across my neck and it makes me pause.

"With your..." he prompts.

"Brother," I whisper so quietly that I don't think he will have heard me.

"Good, because you're going to bring in the New Year screaming my name."

I choke on my own spit when his words settle into my brain. What the fuck? Who does this guy think he is, or more to the point who, or what, exactly does he think I am?

When I've come back to my senses enough to turn around he's gone. I feel my face heat as I think about his words and scan the room. I feel like something huge just happened, well my body seems to, yet everyone is drinking and celebrating as normal around me.

Three more glasses of wine and an hour later and I almost feel like I'm back on level ground again. My knees feel a little sturdier than they did an hour ago and the butterflies that have been fluttering around my stomach are starting to decrease. I've kept my back to the room and have really tried to focus on what Caleb, Abbi and Liv have been chatting about but it's been a real struggle. I missed them when we left for America ten years ago, Ryan especially. We all grew up on the same street in Liverpool; the five of us were pretty close. I never thought I'd move back to England. If you'd have asked me a couple of months ago I would have said never, but here I am. I'd made myself a great life over there. Well, I thought I had. Then one visit to the mall brought it all crashing down around me.

When I look up I notice that everyone has gone and I'm now stood in the corner of the living room alone. Great one, loser! I look up in panic and immediately lock eyes with Mr. Dark and Delicious. His powerful strides eat up the space between us and in only a second he is right there in front of me. I have to tip my head slightly to keep eye contact with him, even in these ridiculously high shoes. I know that I should look away, make my excuses and leave... but I can't. My eyes are fixed onto his. His smell enters my senses and I swear if I could only smell him for the rest of my life I'd be happy. He smells incredible—like man, and power, and sex. Fucking hell, this isn't good.

"We're going now," he says, as he presses me back into the wall and places one of his thighs between my legs. I embarrass myself when I think about how badly I want to grind against it. Shit, I'm not one of those girls. I don't jump on men whenever the mood takes me. This man though, fuck. He's got me thinking all sorts of weird shit. "You can say no, but I know you won't. I can read your body and it is screaming 'yes'."

My breath catches as he says this and my eyes dart back up to his. It's not until they do that I realise my gaze had drifted down to his lips when he was speaking.

"Your pupils dilate as you look at me, your cheeks and neck flush red," he continues, as he lifts his hand and runs his fingertips across my cheek and down my neck. "Your breasts are swollen and your nipples peaked, begging for my touch." His fingers travel lower and I flinch when he finds my nipple. I notice a small smile twitch at the corner of his lip when he finds it as he expected. I knew getting a dress that couldn't have a bra underneath was a bad idea, this wasn't quite the reason I had in mind though. "Your heart is racing and your breathing is getting heavier. He pauses, as he runs his eyes down my body. "And I know you're wet for me, Red."

My chin drops open at his final statement. No man has ever spoken to me like that before and I have no idea whether to be offended or embarrassed that I'm now even more turned on by this delicious stranger.

I feel my heart start to race the longer he looks at me. His face is deadly serious, as if he's currently negotiating a business deal. Other than the fact he's standing way too close, no one would have any idea that he was propositioning me. He's serious, focused and confident. I'd put money on the fact he does this kind of thing regularly.

"I..." I begin to speak. I know I should be saying no, this is such a bad idea. I'm not the kind of girl that goes off for a hot night of steamy sex with a stranger. I'm the girl that likes to cuddle in front of the TV and then go to bed to make love. Maybe that's where I went wrong though. Maybe if I was more like this then I wouldn't have made my past mistakes.

The longer I stand there trying to tell myself that this is wrong, that it's a bad idea, the more my body is screaming at me to just do as he says. Then when he reaches down to grab my hand every rational thought evaporates from my head. He pulls me so I'm flush against his chest, my softness to his hardness. He looks like he's seriously cut under that suit and I so badly want to know if I'm right.

His dark eyes bore into my grey ones almost as if he's daring me to back out. I may not be used to doing this kind of thing but I'm not one to shy away from a challenge. So I put what I hope is a somewhat sexy smirk on my face and lean slightly farther into him.

He nods his head once before stepping away, pulling me with him. I don't get a chance to stop and grab anything. Thankfully, my purse is hanging over my shoulder. Before I know what's happening, he's pulling me into a cab that's idling at the curb. Did I have a sign on me that I wasn't aware of that said easy or something, for this stranger to be so confident I'd go with him he had a cab waiting?

I turn to look at him and seeing the smirk on his face it's clear that he can read my thoughts.

He tells the driver his address and the sound of his deep, demanding voice does weird things to my insides.

The cab lurches forward as he sits back and places his hand on my thigh. The heat from his hand burns my skin all the way to his house.

No words have been spoken the entire journey and I've just about managed to talk myself out of it by the time we turn onto a street—I'm presuming near the centre of Oxford somewhere—with some seriously expensive houses on. Each one is sat back from the road hidden behind a variety of trees and bushes. Some houses can barely be seen at all. They are the kind of houses that everyone dreams about living in but in reality they never even get to step foot inside one. They are the kind of houses that people like my boss back in Chicago lived in. Rich, arrogant, pompous assholes.

Just as I'm thinking that, the cab comes to a stop. I almost laugh out loud. I guess it was obvious really that Mr. Dark and Delicious lives in one of these flash pads, of course he fucking does.

Daniel

I had no intention of pulling any of my sister's friends tonight. But I also had no intention of spending New Year's alone. I'd decided to attend her party for a couple of hours before heading to the club to find myself a New Year's partner.

Well, those were my intentions.

Until she walked in.

The fiery red of her dress caught my eye the second she stepped in the room. I was talking to my nieces but everything around me faded the second I looked up at her.

Her dark hair was curled and resting on her shoulders. Her dress was red lace. It exposed her neck and shoulders but was long-sleeved. It had a full skirt and stopped a few inches above her knees. Her legs—fuck me—her legs were incredible and finished off nicely with a pair of sky-high, glittery-black heels. She called to me like nothing I'd experienced before. I've been with my fair share of women but there was something about this one. It was almost like I knew her, but I knew I'd never met her before.

I can't lie. I know I'm an arsehole when it comes to women. Everyone tells me enough. 'Stop playing', 'find one to settle down with', 'have kids', and all that bullshit. I like my life as it is. Where's the rule book that says that just because you're speeding your way toward forty that you should have a little woman and a couple of kids at home?

I work hard and play even harder. I love my life. I do what I want; who I want and no one can tell me otherwise. Why would I want to change that?

I had no idea who she was. All I knew was that she wasn't part of our family so as far as my cock was concerned she was fair game. I didn't see her come with a guy—I knew I needed to check though. Although if she had a boyfriend and he'd let her out of his sight looking like that then he deserved for me to happen to her because she should be treated properly, not abandoned at a party by herself. Though if I had my way then I wouldn't be treating her properly either.

I knew she wanted me. It was clear in her eyes and body language when she first looked at me. Some women are good at hiding their thoughts; she was not one of them. My cock twitched. I could practically see her thoughts running through her head, none of which I objected to in the slightest. It looked like I wouldn't need a trip to the club after all.

I kept out of the way. I wanted my distance to pique her curiosity and hopefully her desire. And fuck me, it worked like a charm. She was putty in my hands when I did appear. The sight of the goosebumps displayed on the naked skin of her back called to me. I desperately wanted to run my tongue down her spine, feel her moans of pleasure as they rippled through her. Thankfully the chatter of the party and the squeals of children stopped me from doing just that.

As the taxi pulls to a stop outside my house, I watch her in amusement as she stares out of the window with her mouth open.

"You... you live here?"

I don't respond. I hand the driver some money and get out. I'm pretty sure it was a rhetorical question anyway. I stalk around to her side of the car and open the door for her. She's still sat there looking a little shell-shocked.

I reach in, grab her hand and pull her to me. I put my hand around her back and step us both backwards so I can close the car door. The taxi immediately pulls away but I don't release her. Instead I pull her tighter. Her soft curves line up with me perfectly.

I lean down and run my cheek against hers before whispering, "It's too late to back out now," in her ear.

She lets out a low, shaky breath before responding. "I don't back down from a challenge, D."

I lean back and look at her as she finishes her sentence by calling me the first initial of my name. Maybe she does know who I am.

I wait for a second to see if she is going to say anything else. She doesn't but she does look down at my lips. It's all the encouragement I need. I lower my head and place my lips to hers. I'm more restrained than I'd like to be— for now anyway.

For some unknown fucking reason I decide to try to be a bit of a gentleman. Fuck knows why, it's a first for me that's for sure. I usually have no further use for the women I pick up beyond a quick fuck, but she's different. I don't know what it is but something is telling me to be different with this one.

CHAPTER TWO

Beth

"Do you want a drink, Red?"

I'm sure drinking more, on top of what I've already had, isn't a good idea but I need something to settle my nerves. I don't think I really thought this through.

I'm stood in the middle of this dark and delicious stranger's house. Okay, so calling it a house is not really doing it much justice. It's huge, and modern, and everything most people want but can only dream of affording. The outside was rendered white with black window frames and doors. The only bit of colour was from the few flowers in the giant pot by the door. Inside isn't much different. It's mostly black and white, a pretty stereotypical bachelor pad really. There's a sprinkle of colourful touches here and there, which tells me a woman has had some input at some point. My mind flashes back to those two little girls at the party. Are they his, like I first believed? Surely not.

I realise that I never answered his question, but when I look up he's standing in front of me with a glass of red wine in his hand, looking amused.

"Go somewhere nice?"

"Uh..."

"Here, this will help," he says, passing the glass over to me. I take his advice and take a very unladylike gulp.

"This is expensive," I say appreciatively, once I've swallowed and savoured the taste.

"Only the best," he says, before pouring his tumbler full of golden liquid down his throat. I watch, enthralled as the muscles in his neck strain and flex with his swallow. The butterflies that hadn't really gone anywhere since being dragged from Ryan and Molly's house earlier, quadruple in quantity; my heart starts to pound so hard that I feel it in every bit of my body, mostly between my legs.

I watch as he runs his eyes down me again, it's just like before but slower. Like he's memorising everything about me. Thankfully, the wine gives me enough liquid courage to be able to stand there without squirming under his gaze like I would if I were sober.

"This is your last chance to back out, Red, because once I touch you, that's it."

My mouth instantly goes dry as I try to swallow down my nerves. What the hell am I doing? I've just been royally screwed over by what I thought was the love of my life and now I'm about to jump into bed with the first attractive man I've found since coming back to England. And it's obvious from a mile away that he's only in it for one thing. Not that I'm in this for anything more, mind you. It's just that I promised myself when my flight touched down a couple of weeks ago that I wouldn't go anywhere near a man for a long time, possibly ever, yet here I am.

"So what's it going to be?"

I look up at him before stepping forward and stretching so my lips meet his.

Fuck it, you only live once and this man is a fucking god so I'm getting my fill.

He takes the glass from me before his hand comes up to hold the back of my head and the move reminds me so much of *him* that I almost step away. *He* was always so sweet and loving with me, I guess that's why I fell so hard and so fast for him. What I need tonight is the opposite of that. Rough, hard sex.

Just as I'm about to pull away and put an end to this whole thing he moves. His hands run down my back. They stop on my ass and squeeze harshly as he lifts me with ease. Immediately I wrap my legs around his waist.

That's more like it.

I wrap my arms around his neck and return his kiss properly. My tongue dances with his, feuds with his, as we put into action how we've made each other feel for the last couple of hours.

I don't realise we're moving until I feel a door at my back. When I pull away from him and look around I see that not only have we moved but we've come upstairs and are about to enter his bedroom.

"Fuck that bed's huge," I say in shock because well… it is.

He looks over at the bed but doesn't answer me. Instead he sets me down on my feet and takes a step back. He once again runs his eyes over me. His attention makes me burn up.

"Turn," he demands and I immediately do as I'm told.

When I have my back to him, I feel his fingers touch the top of my back before running down over the couple of buttons that hold my dress together before slowly making their way down my bare skin. Goosebumps prick my skin and I shiver under his touch. When he gets to the bottom I hear him move. Seconds later, I feel a light touch where the back of my dress starts. It only takes a second to recognise that it's his tongue running back up my spine.

When he gets halfway I can't help the moan that falls from my lips. It sounds so erotic that I question whether it was me or not.

I always thought I'd had a good sex life with *him* but standing here in this moment, fully dressed with DD behind me is the most sensual I think I've ever felt.

When he reaches the top he sweeps my hair to the side and runs kisses around my neck. I have another flash of the gentleness I used to get from *him*. It's like DD knows what I'm thinking because I feel his hands at the top of my shoulders before the fabric is ripped from my body, literally.

I hear the two buttons that were holding the top of my dress together scatter across the floor at the same time I hear fabric ripping.

"What are you doing?" I ask in shock.

"Shh… I'll buy you a new one," he says, between kisses to my newly exposed skin.

"What if it was expensive?" It wasn't, it was thirty quid from New Look. I just can't help myself though. If it wasn't obvious from his tailored suit that he had money then it is from his house. An expensive dress would probably be a drop in the ocean for him.

"I'd buy you the most expensive one I could find." He turns me around as he says this. His eyes are almost black and filled with a hunger that has my clit throbbing.

Slowly, he moves his hands down my shoulders, taking my dress with them. He peels the lace off me as if he's opening a precious gift. I've never experienced anything like it.

Once my arms are free, the top of my dress falls away revealing my naked chest to him. He sucks in a breath as he looks down, making my nipples tighten that little bit more. He wets his lips and bites down on his bottom one. It's almost like he's trying to hold himself back.

I'm so lost to him that I don't notice him reach out again and tug the bottom of my dress so it pools around my feet.

I'm stood practically naked in front of this stunning man who is still dressed in his flashy suit and I don't even give my body a second thought. The fact that I've eaten everything I've been able to get my hands on since *he* fucked me over doesn't register. I chose that dress because it didn't cling to my slightly podgier than usual stomach. I should be self-conscious, but standing here under his heated gaze washes it away.

He doesn't need to say it with words, his eyes tell me exactly how he feels about my body and what he wants to do to me. A bolt of electricity shoots down my spine and straight for my clit. I almost reach down to try to ease it. Instead, I resort to squeezing my thighs together.

"What I want to fucking do to you," he grates out as he grabs my hand and pulls me to him, making me step away from my dress. He holds one hand up and motions for me to spin. I do as he suggests because I can't get enough of the way he's looking at me. It's almost like he's never seen a naked woman before. I almost laugh out loud at the thought because these smooth actions are not of an inexperienced man.

Other than his chest being pressed up against mine, he doesn't touch me as he moves me backwards toward the bed. When the back of my knees hit the mattress I have no choice but to sit down. He continues to lean over me, still not touching me until I'm laid back. Once I'm down he places a kiss to the side of my mouth before kissing a line down the centre of my chest and all the way to my belly button. When he gets there he stops and looks up at me. My breath catches at the look in his eyes. The look of a predatory, hungry male.

When his hands touch my skin a shudder runs through me. His hands grip the edges of my knickers and he slowly slides them down my legs and over my shoes before throwing them over his shoulder.

He grabs my knees and forces my legs apart before standing back up. He looks down at me for the longest time. My confidence starts to wane a little as the seconds tick by. I start to wonder what's wrong, why he's not doing anything. Aren't I what he wants?

Then all of a sudden he's moving. His jacket is pulled off and thrown across the room, followed by his tie and shirt.

My mouth goes dry as I look at his naked torso. I don't think I've ever seen anyone so well cut in real life. And those shoulders that I was admiring back at the party only look bigger, stronger, without the cover of clothing.

His hands go to the waistband of his trousers and I can see from here that he is already hard for me. He drops his trousers at the same time as he toes off his shoes. In the blink of an eye his boxers are gone as well and he's lowering himself to the floor in front of me.

I'm pissed off. He just spent a long time staring down at me, taking in whatever it was that he was so fascinated by yet I got no time at all.

All thoughts are soon forgotten though when I feel his breath and then his tongue against me. I moan something incoherent as my back arches off the bed.

Fuck he's good at this, I think, before I begin to fall. I fall deeper and deeper before I explode into a million pieces. I feel all the tension that I'd been walking around with for the last few weeks disappear, and for that alone I will be forever grateful to this gorgeous man.

My dark and delicious stranger.

Mr. DD.

Daniel

Why is this woman so different to all the other ones that have been here? What is it about her that is making me be less of a selfish arsehole when it comes to her pleasure? I pride myself in making sure they enjoy it but ultimately it's about me. I've only known this woman a couple of hours but I already can't imagine her leaving, whereas usually I can't wait to get them out of my space.

Her body is fucking insane. She has just the right amount of curves, enough to grab onto but not enough to wobble about too much.

I've always appreciated the female form but this one calls to me in a way no other has.

"Fuck," I groan, as I pull out of her and fall onto my side.

"Yeah," she agrees, panting next to me. Her hair is stuck to the sides of her face and her chest is heaving up and down. It's the most beautiful she's looked all evening. And that's saying something because her in that red dress, fuck. My cock stirs back to life just at the thought. I suddenly regret ripping the dress from her body. I should have fucked her in it first, bent her over the—

"Ready for round two already," she asks, sounding amused as she looks down at my once again hard cock.

"Like you wouldn't believe."

I grab onto her hips and lift her on top of me. She lets out a little squeal in surprise but allows me to manhandle her into position.

I'm knocked sideways when I look up at her. Her eyes are shining bright and her cheeks and chest are flushed red from her earlier release. I run my eyes down over her tits taking in her rose-pink nipples.

"Are you okay?" she asks.

If I'm honest, I don't know. This woman is having some weird effect on me.

"Yeah, top drawer," I say nodding in the direction of my stash.

"Fucking hell," she says in shock when she looks over. "Were you a boy scout by any chance?"

"Always be prepared, Red."

She goes to hand it to me as she moves back but I make no move to take it from her. Suddenly she looks a little unsure of herself. She bites down on her bottom lip and looks from my eyes, to my cock and back again.

"Go on."

Watching her delicate hands sliding the rubber on me has me racing toward another release already. I take a couple of deep breaths as she lifts herself up over me.

"Make the most of this, Red. It's the only chance you're going to get tonight to take control," I warn. I have plans for her and most of them do not involve her taking the lead. I glance around my room trying to decide where next. I'm soon distracted though; all thoughts leave my head as I feel her slide down onto me. I can't hold back the groan of pleasure at the feeling of being deep inside her. I swear no other woman felt quite this good.

<hr>

"I guess I should be off then," she says, as she swings her legs over the side of the bed and stands. I'm surprised she's able to walk after the amount of orgasms I've pulled out of her over the last couple of hours. I did as I was intending earlier and we've fucked on nearly every square inch of the room.

Her comment makes me panic.

Then acknowledging that panic makes me panic even more.

She should leave. She's served her purpose. I welcomed in the new year inside her banging body so why am I panicking that she's about to walk out?

"What, why?" I ask in a rush as she looks around for her clothes.

"Well, I'm not exactly used to this kind of situation, but I'm pretty sure now that we've done... that," she says, gesturing to the bed, "I'm meant to leave. If you could just call me a cab then I'll leave you in peace."

"Stay," I blurt out. Then I burst out laughing at the ridiculousness of this whole thing.

"What? Why are you laughing?"

"Well, one, because you look even more shocked than I feel when I just said that. And two, I have no idea, this is crazy." She raises an eyebrow at me, waiting for more of an explanation I guess. "Please... stay?"

She stands there looking at me, then around the room while she rocks back and forth on her heels as she tries to figure out what she wants to do.

"I... uh..." I pull the covers back showing her what the thought of her staying does to me. I fist my cock in my hand and watch her watch me. She's totally fascinated, or confused.

CHAPTER THREE

Beth

I shouldn't be doing this.

I need to run as far away from this man as possible. Yet I'm pretty sure that's not going to happen.

My skin is tingling, like I can still feel his hands on my body. And I can definitely feel where he's been inside me. There's no denying that I've had sex—and a lot of it—in the last couple of hours. I feel sore, gloriously sore. He's got skills, that man.

Standing there, I watch him while my head and my heart duel over what I should do. I know I should leave. I've just walked away from one disastrous relationship, the last thing I need is to fall head first into another. Not that this could be a relationship. I mean this guy is clearly a player of epic proportions. If his skills alone didn't prove that then the drawer full of condoms sure did.

"Red?" he questions, I presume to bring me out of my trance. He props himself up on his elbows and looks at me, an eyebrow rises, while he waits for my response.

He looks like sex personified lying there like that and my girly parts take the lead in the decision making.

"Okay," I say as I make my way over to him and settle myself back on the bed with my head on his chest. He stiffens for a few seconds before he relaxes into it and puts his arms around me. If his normal MO is to kick women out then this must be seriously weird for him. Well it's pretty weird for me too; I've never done the one-night stand thing. I don't even know his name.

We stay like that for a while before he rolls me off him and gets up. I watch him pad across the room to the en suite before he then leaves the room. I start to panic that he might have changed his mind but within minutes he's back, carrying a glass of red wine and what I guess is a glass of whisky.

"I need to tell people where I am, they'll be worrying otherwise," I say as he hands me the glass.

"I've got it covered, don't worry. I texted my sister to tell her."

"Your sister?" I ask because that could be anyone as far as I'm concerned.

"Molly. She's my little sister." He moves to the other side of the bed and sits himself down before raising his glass toward me. "Happy New Year, Red. I think we saw it in with style." I lift my glass and tap it against his. Gently mind you because I'm sure they are worth more than I would care to imagine.

"What's your name, D?

"Why do you call me D?"

"Hey, I asked a question first," I say with a pout. The look he gives me tells me he's not going to answer so I reluctantly tell him. "In my head I nicknamed you Mr. Dark and Delicious." It comes out as a whisper in the hope he won't hear. No such luck though because a smug smile tugs at the corners of his lips. I feel my face burn with embarrassment. "Why do you call me Red?" I'm pretty sure I know why but I want him to say it.

"Your dress, your drink," he says nodding toward my glass, "the streaks in your hair." He gently plays with a tendril hanging around my face as he says this. It's so soft and gentle, totally at odds to the last couple of hours we shared in this room.

His hand then sneaks around the back of my head before pulling me toward his lips. I go willingly. I don't know what it is about this man but it's like he has me under his spell.

When I wake the next morning it's with the sun pouring into the room and my head spinning slightly. I blink a couple of times against the brightness but also as I take in my unfamiliar surroundings. When the events of last night hit me I instantly start to panic.

What the utter fuck was I thinking? I spent the night with a man I've never met before. I not only had a one-night stand with him but I'm still here, in his bed, wrapped in his sheets. Sitting up straight, I clutch the sheets against my naked chest and look to the other side of the bed. I expect to see him but it's empty.

Relief rushes through me. Maybe I can get dressed and get out. That way we won't have to deal with the awkwardness that is bound to happen.

I'm just about to lift myself from the bed when the door opens. I hold the duvet up to my neck and cling onto it like my life depends on it, as I wait for him to say something. I'm expecting him to tell me to get my stuff together and leave. What I'm not expecting is for him to have two steaming mugs in his hands.

He walks over and places them on the bedside table before sitting himself down next to me. He scoots up until his back is against the headboard.

"Good morning, Red," he says in a gravelly voice, telling me that he hasn't been up that long. He's wearing only a tight pair of grey boxer briefs and his hair is all over the place.

"Uh... m-morning," I stutter out. I'm totally shocked. I really was expecting to get my marching orders. "Is... uh... this," I say, gesturing between us and the bed, "a normal thing for you to do?"

"No, Red. It most definitely is not. Here, I made coffee. I hope you take it white with no sugar." I look from him, to the mug he's holding out to me and back again. How did he know? "Lucky guess," he says, obviously guessing my question.

I try to relax but it's not very easy. I'm in a stranger's bed. I don't even know his name and I'm naked. This is so unlike anything I've experienced before. I can feel him looking at me and I don't need to glance his way to know he's smirking at my awkwardness. I can sense his amusement from here.

"So if this isn't the norm, why am I here?"

"That is a very good question. And I really do wish I had the answer but I don't. I just... like having you here," he says the last bit much quieter, like he's embarrassed to admit it. I love seeing his slightly more vulnerable side. Since meeting him I've only really seen the alpha male, the womaniser in him. I think I unknowingly knew there was more, that's why I'm here. That's why I agreed to go with him last night.

"So what number notch am I in your headboard then, D?" I ask, my mouth running at a much faster pace to my brain.

When I glance over at him I see him pale slightly. Not the reaction I was expecting.

"Enough to fill my time with before I found you."

"Ugh, cheesy line, D."

"What? That wasn't a line," he argues.

"Whatever. So go on then... how many?"

I watch the muscles in his neck ripple as he swallows and thinks of his answer. His mouth opens like he's about to say something but he changes his mind and snaps it shut. I raise my eyebrow at him urging him to continue. After a few more seconds he answers.

"A couple a week." He immediately lifts his mug to his lips and takes a sip.

"And how long exactly have you had this specific headboard?" I really don't know why I'm asking, I don't think I actually want to know but my mouth won't stop.

"About... three years-ish."

I quickly do the maths in my head before jumping off the bed. In the process I throw coffee all over the duvet cover that I'm still using to shield my body.

"THREE HUNDRED!" I squeal in shock.

"I said 'ish'."

I feel slightly sorry for him. He looks a little mortified, though to be fair I feel more disgusted in myself. I've been getting all these weird vibes from him thinking maybe I'm special. Fuck knows why I care about that though because I do not need another man.

Daniel

I've never really thought about the number of women I've been with like that. Hearing it out loud makes me realise quite how bad it is. I was being conservative when I told her it was a couple a week. Most weeks it's more than that, and it's not just been for three years. It's been... well... since I was old enough. I'm always getting grief off my brother, Steven, and from Molly. They think I'm too old to be doing what I'm doing. I've always ignored them and pushed their comments to the back of my mind.

I glance at her. She's stood at the edge of the bed holding the duvet around herself and looking between me and the bed.

"Come back to bed," I say, in my sexiest bedroom voice. But she stays put. "Fine, okay let's shower instead then. I've got a surprise for you afterwards."

"Okay," she says sceptically. She's had a really weird look on her face since I came back to the room. I have no clue what she's thinking. "I can shower by myself though."

"Be my guest," I say, pointing in the direction of the en suite. I'm disappointed, but I'm hoping to get a lot more time with her yet so no biggie.

I finish my coffee while I listen to the water running. Thoughts of her sexy curves with water pouring all over them has me reliving last night. Needless to say that by the time she emerges from the en suite my cock is well and truly ready for her again. Looking up to find her wrapped in my huge, white towel with damp skin doesn't help.

"Stop staring at me like that," she says, embarrassed.

"What, you look hot."

"Whatever. Where are my clothes then I'll get out of the way. I'd appreciate it if you could call me a cab, please."

"You're not going anywhere," I say as I get up from the bed and pull her toward me, making her squeal in surprise. "I've not had enough of you yet." I realised this while watching her sleep last night. After I'd practically fucked her into a coma she fell fast asleep. I've never let a woman stay over before. Never. But having her there next to me felt so right. I watched her for hours. It didn't take me long to realise that the few hours I'd had with her wasn't anywhere near enough to get her out of my system. I decided that having her to myself for the weekend should cover it. I fully intended on keeping her here. But then I went downstairs this morning to make coffee and found her handbag on the floor next to the sofa. I leant down to pick it up and found her passport poking out of the top and it gave me an idea. An amazing idea.

I continue watching her as she slides her underwear on and then holds up her dress in her hands, looking at the ripped fabric. I'm waiting for her to say something but she doesn't. Instead she turns away from me and marches up to my wardrobe. She looks inside before pulling out one of my shirts, slipping it on.

When she turns back to me, the sight makes my breath catch slightly. The shirt is massive on her; it almost comes down to her knees. She stands and rolls the arms up after doing up the buttons. Her face, although still with some of last night's make-up on, looks fresh and her hair is wet but curling up around her shoulders. The need to bend her over the chest of drawers behind her is high but I know we haven't got much time and I need to make sure she's on board with my plan.

Once she's sorted she just stands and looks at me, waiting for me to explain.

"We're going away for the weekend. Last night wasn't enough for me," I state.

"Oh, we are, are we?" she says, putting her hands on her hips and trying to look stern.

"Yep, it's all booked. Once I'm dressed we can go." I get up and head for the wardrobe.

"I can't go like this," she says in a panic. "I'm barely dressed."

"I think you look perfect."

"What? Wait..." she says, shaking her head and looking completely baffled. "You're taking me away for the weekend? You don't even know me, you don't know my name." Now that's not true because I looked inside her passport but I don't tell her that. "And I don't know you. You could be a murderer or something. Plus, I might be busy this weekend."

"I'm not a murderer," I state, pulling on a pair of dark jeans. "And are you busy this weekend?"

"Well, no. But that's not the point," she says in a rush.

"What is the point then?"

"That I barely know you. I've already spent the night in your bed. You should be kicking me out now, not taking me away for the weekend."

I love the confused look on her face. It's really endearing. I pull my jumper over my head and step up to her. I hold her chin in my fingers and tilt her head up to look at me.

"Last night wasn't enough for me, Red. I need more," I repeat. I stare her right in the eyes so she can see how serious I'm being about this.

"O-okay," she stutters, before I place my lips down on hers—a small reminder of how good last night was, and a promise of what's to come.

Once I've packed a few things, I grab her hand and pull her toward the garage. I press the button to raise the door and I hear her chuckle to herself.

I turn to look at her and wait for her to explain.

"I shouldn't have expected anything different really should I?" she asks as she looks between my Porsche Cayenne and my baby, my Mercedes SL Roadster.

I pop the boot on the Merc and throw my bag in before opening the passenger door for her, much to her shock.

"Why thank you, kind sir," she says in a posh English accent.

"My pleasure, ma'am."

Once we're on the road I ask one of the many questions I have about this intriguing woman.

"So are you a yank with a scouse accent or are you a scouse with a yank accent?" Since the second I heard her voice in Molly's kitchen I have been fascinated with her accent. It's so unbelievably sexy and I don't know each time she speaks if I'm going to get the American twang or the British. It's really captivating.

"I'm British. We moved to Chicago when I was sixteen, only came back recently." With that one sentence I feel her shut herself off from me, making me curious to know why she's here. I resist asking, I'll find out eventually.

"I'll wait here, you grab your stuff," I say when we pull up outside my sister's house. She insisted that we stop and get her case. I was more than happy to go with her wearing my shirt, she looks sexy as hell in it, but she wasn't having any of it.

It's only seconds after I've watched her enter the house that Molly is heading toward me. I should have guessed she wouldn't let this go.

"Beth says you're taking her away. What the fuck are you doing, Daniel? She's not just some piece of arse you can pick up and drop. She's one of Ryan's oldest friends. I swear to God if you mess this up, if you hurt her in any way then I won't think twice about setting Ryan on you. Brother or not, I won't have it. Understand?"

"Jesus, Molls, enough," I say, putting an end to her rant. "I just want to spend some more time with her." This is clearly the wrong thing to say because the look on Molly's face tells me that she doesn't really believe me. I guess I can't blame her. I've never made a secret about my lifestyle. "Is that so hard to believe?"

"Yeah, it is a little. Why her, Daniel? Out of all of them, what is it about her?" she asks, looking curious about what has caught my attention.

"Honestly, I have no idea. She's just... different, I guess."

"Oh my God," Molly says softly and she looks down at me.

"No, no, no, don't be going and getting any crazy ideas. I just need a little more time with her, that's all."

"Uh-huh, I'm sure that's what they all say," she says in amusement. "So where are you taking her?"

Thankfully as soon as I've answered, Beth emerges from the house, which puts a halt to Molly's questioning. Unfortunately, Beth got changed while she was inside and is now wearing jeans, boots and a thick jumper.

Yeah, she still looks good but it's not quite the same. She's removed what remained of last night's make-up and I am thrilled that she didn't feel the need to put any more on. She looks even more beautiful without it.

"Have fun you two," Molly says with a smirk, just before I put the window up.

"Could she look any more smug?" Beth says with a laugh as we pull away. "So where exactly are you taking me, mystery man?" I'm really glad that the dark clouds that descended over her when I asked her where she was from have lifted and she's back to being her bubbly self again.

"Surprise. Just sit back, relax, and enjoy the ride."

"You make that sound dirtier than it should," she mutters.

"Oh, I can make a lot of things dirty, Red, believe me." I don't miss her thighs squeezing together and her shifting on the seat when I say that.

CHAPTER FOUR

Beth

At some point I manage to nod off. Not surprising really seeing as I'd only had a couple of hours sleep last night.

I wake up completely disoriented and in a panic. I was dreaming about *him*, about who he really was and all the lies he'd told me. It takes me a good few seconds to register why I'm in a car and who with. My panic doesn't dissipate quickly as I begin to think about what the fuck I'm doing. I have no idea who this guy is, other than being Molly's brother. This does give me some confidence that he isn't planning to kill me in my sleep. But other than that, Mr. Dark and Delicious is an utter mystery. I don't know why I agreed to this. I mean it's crazy, right?

I've only just run away from a huge part of my life and now I'm doing what? Running again? I ran here in the hope that I could forget *him*. Obviously that didn't happen because no matter where I am in the world *he's* going to be inside my head. Then I meet Mr. D over there and I jump at the first chance to make me forget, to take me away from it all. I don't even know the guy's name, yet I'm fully aware that he's going to hurt my already broken heart.

"Hey, sleepyhead. Are you okay?" There's concern written all over his face.

"Yeah... why?" I ask sceptically.

"You were talking in your sleep."

Shit. I have absolutely no intention of telling this guy the reason I left America.

"W-what did I say?"

He pauses for a beat before answering, which makes my pulse pick up. Please don't let me have said anything about *him*. "It was nothing that made any sense," he says, but I'm not convinced it's the truth.

"Why are we at an airport?" I ask in shock when I look up.

"I'm taking you away for the weekend, remember?"

"Yeah, but I was thinking that we were going to a seaside resort or something."

He glances at me before saying, "Do I look like someone who goes to Blackpool often?"

I can't help myself and I burst out laughing because he does have a point. He seems to have more money than most people can dream of, of course he wouldn't go somewhere like that.

"So, where are we going?"

"It's a surprise. I saw your passport sticking out of your bag this morning and I called in a couple of favours."

I sit there in silence as I let what he said settle into my brain. Why is he using up his favours on me?

A thought suddenly hits me. "You know my name, don't you?"

"Yes," he admits. "I needed your details to book the tickets."

"Are you going to return the favour?"

"No."

"Have a wonderful time in Paris," the lady checking us in says. "The weather is meant to be beautiful so I hear."

I wait until we aren't in hearing distance before I freak out. "Paris! You're taking me to Paris?"

"Yes. That's okay, right?"

"What! Of course it's okay. I've always wanted to go to Paris—see the Eiffel Tower, The Louvre, the Champs-Elysees and the Arc de Triomphe. Oh my God." I think I might be hyperventilating a little. This guy, who has been nothing but incredible since the moment my eyes landed on him, is taking me to Paris. I'm not sure exactly what I did to deserve this but I am seriously glad I did it.

He stands still, smiling to himself as he watches me freak out.

"So you're happy?" he eventually asks.

"Oh... uh, yes! You know, I mean, yeah it's okay," I say, trying to play it cool.

"Good, come on then."

He grabs my hand and gently tugs so I have no choice but to follow him.

"We can't go in there," I say in a slight panic. "It's for first class passengers."

"I'm sure we can sneak in," he says, with a cheeky wink that melts my insides.

"Good afternoon," the posh looking guy at the entrance to the lounge says when we walk in.

"Good afternoon," Mr. D says as he hands our tickets over casually.

I'm ready to turn around and walk out. What I'm not expecting is for the guy to wish us a pleasant stay and onward journey and to wave us toward the fancy looking doors to whatever may be behind. Growing up we never went without; Dad had a good job, we always had money but this kind of luxury is definitely not something I'm used to.

Once we both have drinks and fancy little pastry things to eat, we take a seat on a huge sofa by the windows.

"See it's easy, it's all about confidence and looking like you belong." As he says this I see the corner of his lip twitch up in a smile.

"We've got first class tickets, haven't we?"

He doesn't answer; instead he takes the coffee from my hands and places it on the table in front of us before sucking my bottom lip into his mouth. His hand comes up to hold on to my neck as he leans in properly. I lose myself in his kiss. Everything I should be worrying about right now evaporates like it doesn't exist. The only thing I'm aware of is him, his lips and how he makes me feel.

It feels like I'm dreaming. I mean seriously, this isn't my life. Flying first class to Paris with a hot guy for a weekend of hopefully even hotter sex, doesn't happen to people like me. I didn't really think it happened in real life. I thought things like this were reserved for romance novels and films.

The flight goes by in the blink of an eye. I'm used to flying back and forth to Chicago so the couple of hours we're in the air feels like nothing. Especially, when it's filled with champagne and fancy nibbles. I've never been up this end of a plane before and I have to say that it's going to be hard the next time I have to fly economy.

"We're staying here?" I ask in complete awe of the building I'm about to be dragged into. "Wow, I thought the outside was impressive." I'm completely lost in my own world as I look around the ultra-modern interior of the hotel. I've never seen anything like it. There are funky glass light fittings hanging from the high ceilings, all the furniture is ultra-modern and sleek and everything is either black, grey or red.

I'm so away with the fairies that I don't see a very well dressed gentleman heading our way until he speaks. It's not the voice I was expecting.

"Daniel, how are you doing, mate? It's been too long."

I don't pay much attention to what he says; my brain is too busy focusing on the name he just said.

Daniel.

It suits him, and now it makes sense as to why he questioned me about calling him D.

"Edward," Daniel greets. "It's so good to see you. Business looks like it's doing well."

They chat back and forth for a few minutes. They each ask about the other's families telling me they know each other well. I look Edward up and down and decide he must be about the same age. He's nowhere near as captivating to look at as Daniel though. Not as refined.

"So, Daniel, tell me. Who's the lucky lady you've brought on a trip to the city of romance?"

"Edward, this is Beth."

"Bonjour, belle," he says in a deep and slow voice as he grabs my hand and raises it to his lips. I don't miss the glare on Daniel's face as he does this. It makes butterflies erupt in my stomach. No, Beth, stop it. This is only about the weekend and only about sex. Do not think any more into it and definitely do not start to fall for him.

"Nice you meet you," I say politely while pulling my hand from his a little too harshly. Why exactly I feel the need to step away from this guy because of Daniel's reaction I have no idea, but I do.

I watch as Edward looks back and forth between us with an amused expression on his face before looking to Daniel and saying, "Well, I never thought I'd see the day."

"Fous-toi," Daniel says harshly. Although when I look at him he's smiling, I can only presume what he said. Holy fucking shit, he can also speak French, I swear my ovaries are on the verge of exploding. This man is too good to be true; he must have some dark secret hidden at the back of his closet or something.

I stand back as he unlocks our hotel room door. He stands aside so I can enter first and my chin drops the second I step over the threshold.

"OH MY GOD!" I scream, as I run toward the window. The view is insane. It looks right out at the Eiffel Tower. "This view, oh my God, it's amazing."

"I was just thinking the exact same thing," he says in a weird voice that makes me turn around.

He's stood leaning back against the door staring right at me. My entire body heats under his gaze. "Why are you looking at me? Look out there, it's amazing."

"I'm more interested in what's in here," he says in a low voice as he slowly moves toward me. He pulls his jumper off just before he reaches me and drops it to the floor. With his clothes on he looks impressive but with them off it makes him look bigger, stronger, even more powerful. My mouth suddenly goes dry as he stalks closer.

His scent fills my nose and I almost groan. He smells unbelievably good. My eyes are locked onto his, it's like they are trying to tell me something but I can't make it out. My thoughts are being overtaken by my desire for this man—my dark and delicious stranger.

Eventually, his eyes break from mine in favour of my lips and in only seconds I feel his against the corner of my mouth. He gives me the lightest kiss, as if he's scared I'm going to disappear if he's too rough.

He doesn't pull back. Instead he stays completely still and mutters quietly, "What are you doing to me?" Well, I think that's what he says anyway. "Fuck," he says louder and I'm half expecting him to walk away, but he doesn't. His mouth slams against mine and he forces his tongue inside my mouth. He presses me back against the full-length window and continues to kiss me. He only pulls back as he lifts my jumper over my head.

I reach down for his belt buckle and button at the same time he goes for mine. It's not until I try to open his fly that I register that my hands are shaking. I'm forced to stop though when he's more successful and starts pulling denim down my thighs. He drops down to his knees to unzip my boots before pulling each one off followed by my jeans.

He looks up at me with an unreadable expression on his face. I suddenly worry that he's regretting this, regretting bringing me here, spending more time with me. That is until he stands. He seems even more powerful when I'm stood here in only my underwear. He towers over me and makes me feel tiny.

My bra and knickers are hastily abandoned and I'm stood with my back to the vast window for all of Paris to see.

"Turn around. Bend over. Hands against the glass," he demands and I don't have any choice but to do as I'm told.

I stare out at the Eiffel Tower as Daniel slowly slides inside me. We've only had sex a couple of times but that doesn't stop the urge I have to sigh with the familiarity of it.

He moves slowly for a few minutes, letting me get used to him. I watch the little dots that are people walking down the streets. I can see people in an office sat at their computers all the while I'm bent over at this window with this incredible man inside me.

This is unreal.

Daniel's hands slide up my back then around so they are cupping my tits. He pinches my nipples almost painfully hard. I don't even recognise the noise that comes from me as he does it.

"Can you see all those people down there?" he asks.

"Uh-huh."

"They have no idea that you're watching them as I fuck you. Does it turn you on that they could look up?"

I don't answer him with words. I can't, all I can do is feel. He's hitting this incredibly deep place inside me that I don't think has ever been touched before.

He must feel me getting close because he starts upping his tempo. My legs start shaking so much that he has to hold onto my hips to stop me crumpling to the floor.

"Come for me, Beth. Tell everyone how good I make you feel."

I do exactly as he says. I scream his name as loud as I can when I lose control. I'm still feeling the aftershocks zipping through my body when I hear a grunt from behind me and feel his cock twitching.

He slowly pulls out but thankfully he keeps hold of me. I'm expecting him to maybe take me over to the bed. What I don't expect is for him to lift me so my legs wrap around his waist and push me back against the window.

"You like that people could see, don't you, Red. You like that they could see you writhing as I fuck you?" he whispers in my ear. His voice is like pure sex making liquid flood my pussy.

Daniel

Fucking hell. This girl. I thought I'd gone crazy bringing her here. I knew what everyone would think—Molly, Edward—but I had to have more time with her. Last night was incredible but it pales in comparison to what just happened. There have been many women in my past but I think I can say that this topped any of them. Fucking Beth against this window with the view of Paris in front of us was something else.

It's only been a couple of minutes but I'm ready to go again and I sure as shit know that she is.

"Argh, Daniel," she groans as I lift, then lower her onto my cock. I fuck her like it could be the last chance I get. She throws her head back as she comes but I don't slow down, I want more. I need to feel her tight little pussy clamping down on me. I need it almost as much as I need to breathe.

"Again," I demand.

"I can't," she whimpers.

She's wrong of course and in a few more minutes she's coming again. It's more gentle this time, slower almost. I watch with fascination as it ripples through her whole body. She's flushed and has a sheen of sweat covering every inch of her skin. She looks fucking incredible.

I thrust into her a few more times before dropping my face to her neck to muffle a groan as I come inside her. Fuck, she's gonna kill me, this girl.

After a few seconds I take her weight in my arms and carry her to the bed. I take in the room on the way. It's the first time I've paid it any proper attention. I told Edward when I rang him earlier that I wanted the best room he had and he didn't let me down that's for sure. It's spectacular.

"What time is it?" Beth asks groggily when she comes to. She fell asleep almost as soon as I put her down on the bed. I didn't sleep though. I couldn't, my mind is all over the place. As much as a part of me is screaming, 'what the fuck are you doing?' the other half is shouting 'at fucking last, don't let her go'. And quite honestly I haven't got a fucking clue what I'm doing. I'm just doing what feels right. I knew last night that sending her on her way wasn't what I wanted and this morning I couldn't bring myself to take her back to Molly's knowing I might not get any more time with her.

"It's just gone six."

She groans as she rolls onto her back and throws an arm over her eyes.

"No, you need to get up, we've got dinner reservations."

"Seriously? You've worn me out."

"Yes, seriously. Now get up."

I watch as she pulls herself up and I run my eyes down the smooth naked skin of her back as the sheet falls away from her. I have to really fight with myself not to lean forward and run my lips up her spine.

She looks back at me nervously as she clutches the sheet to her chest.

"It's way too late to be shy now, Red."

She narrows her eyes at me and it makes me smile in return. What I really want to say and do to her must be written all over my face because she tells me no and that she needs a break before dropping the sheet and standing. She tries to look confident but I can see she's shy. I love it, it's so different to the women I usually spend time with.

"Shit," she suddenly says, looking panicked.

"What's wrong?"

"You didn't use a condom."

I know I didn't. I realised the second I plunged into her. It felt so good to be skin on skin, it's not something I've experienced before. I'm usually totally on top of wrapping up. One of my worst nightmares would be for one of the women I've slept with turning up on my door with a scan picture in their hands, or worse, a baby. No child deserves to be born after I've had a roll around in my bed with its mother. I've experienced first-hand how being an unplanned baby can affect a child. How my sister managed to grow up to be a fairly normal, well-rounded adult is beyond me after the way our parents treated her.

When I realised I'd gone in bare I didn't feel any of the panic I would have expected to. It just felt right. I had no idea if Beth was on birth control or anything but the moment felt right. Like it was meant to happen that way. I can't really explain it other than I didn't wrap up and I still didn't really care. Suddenly, everything I have ever worried about has vanished into thin air. This is different. *She* is different.

"I know," I say with a shrug and watch as her eyes almost pop out of her head at my flippant attitude.

"What if I'm not on birth control? What if I'm not clean? You don't even know me, Daniel!"

"Are you?"

"Well... yes, but that's not the point. You just went in regardless. "Unfortunately I had to get myself checked recently so I know I'm clean and I haven't stopped taking my pill so we should be safe there but as I said, that's not the point."

"You could have stopped me," I say, reminding her that it takes two.

She stares at me for a beat. I think the look is meant to tell me she's pissed off but she looks too cute. When she realises that all I'm going to do is smile at her she huffs out a breath and storms toward the bathroom.

"Fucking hell, this is massive," I hear her mutter as she takes in the colossal bathroom. Edward's done a bloody good job with this place, I think, as I start to rummage around in my case for some toiletries.

"What the hell am I supposed to wear? I've only got jeans and jumpers in my case. You ruined my only dress," she says with her hands on her hips while wearing only her black lace underwear. She looks incredible and I almost cancel our reservations in favour of spending the night inside her instead. "Do not look at me like that. You just had your way with me in the shower. I really need a break, and some food."

"Fine," I say because she's right, and I could really do with some food. If things go as I have planned we're going to need plenty of energy.

I sit myself down on the edge of the bed so I can watch before saying, "Check the wardrobe."

She looks at me for a few seconds as if questioning me, daring me to laugh or somehow show her I'm joking or something. I'm not, I'm deadly serious.

When I don't respond, she moves gingerly toward the wardrobe. As she slides the door open I hear her intake of breath and see her hand come up to cover her mouth. "Oh my God," I hear her mutter in shock.

"Daniel, what... I mean... it's... fuck."

"Don't you like it?"

"No, it's amazing. I love it, but it's too much. You shouldn't have done this."

"It's a replacement for the one I ruined."

"That one was thirty quid from New Look, this is..." she pauses as she leans in, "fucking hell, a lot more than that."

I get up from my seated position and walk over to her. I grab her hips and pull her flush against me. "It's for you. Now get dressed, we have reservations in thirty minutes." I give a quick kiss to the corner of her mouth before going to get dressed myself.

It takes me all of about ten minutes to pull my suit on and run some wax through my hair. I decide to forgo shaving in favour of giving Beth some extra sensation on her thighs later. I spend the rest of the time sat watching her tease, poke and pull at her hair. I have no idea why she bothered because she looked beautiful before she started.

Eventually, though she is finished, she slides the red lace up her body and asks me to do it up while holding her hair out of the way. I gladly agree.

I run my fingers up the exposed skin of her spine slowly as I reach for the two little buttons at the base of her neck. When they're done up, I run my hands down her sides until they are resting on her hips. I look over her shoulder into the full-length mirror she's stood in front of. "You look stunning, Red," I say in her ear. "Every man in this place is going to wish they were me tonight." Then just to prove a point I press my hard-on against her arse.

She holds my eye contact but doesn't say anything. I wish I could read her mind because I have no idea what is going through her head at the moment.

CHAPTER FIVE

Beth

Daniel takes my hand and together we walk out of our hotel room and down toward the restaurant. Just like everything in the hotel, it screams wealth. I feel really out of place. This is not the kind of restaurant I would usually eat, or spend any time in. If we went out for a meal when I was in Chicago it would be to the local steak place. Nothing like this.

As Daniel takes a step forward to speak to the maître d' I look down at myself wrapped in a designer lace gown.

How did I get here?

Three days ago I was moping around my childhood home trying to mend my broken heart and shattered life and now I'm here, in Paris, with this amazing man. I remind myself again that this is only a few days of sex and to not get attached to this guy. So he bought me an expensive designer dress. It doesn't mean anything. He was merely replacing the one he ruined. I smooth my hands down over my hips; the lace is like silk against my palms. The top of the dress is just like the one I had with long sleeves and a totally open back but the bottom is completely different. Gone is the full skirt that I used to cover my comfort eating podge. It's been replaced by a full-length, skintight skirt with a high slit up my left leg. I kinda feel like a movie star.

And I hate to say it but when he was stood behind me in the mirror earlier we made a very nice looking couple. He's way out of my league but standing there, with me in this dress and him in his perfectly tailored suit we looked good. Damn it, we looked more than good.

Innocently, my mind wanders to me in another colour gown, walking toward him. I give myself a mental slap on the face. What the fuck are you doing, Beth? You've barely known the guy two days and you're imagining a white fucking dress. Get a grip.

When I look up, I see both Daniel and the maître d' staring at me with amused faces. I mutter an apology and step up to Daniel before we're both shown to our table.

It really shouldn't be a surprise to me that we have the best table in the place. The view of Paris at night is stunning. I don't know where to look, out of the window at all the lights or at the guy sat opposite me who is still staring at me with a smile on his face.

"What?" I ask a little too harshly. I can't help it. I'm still annoyed with my idiotic thoughts earlier. "Sorry," I mutter when I realise what a selfish bitch I just sounded like. "It's just... all this is so not what I'm used to. I'm completely blown away. Thank you," I say as sincerely as I can because I really mean it. "I haven't been in a great place recently, but this... this is just what I needed."

"You are more than welcome."

I sit and watch in amazement as Daniel speaks to the waiter in French, ordering both wine and dinner for us. I have to fight off the bit of irritation I have for him not letting me choose my own food, but when I glance at the menu I feel grateful because I can't understand a word on it.

"You speak fluent French?" I ask when we're alone again.

"I wouldn't say fluent, but I'm pretty good."

"Pretty good," I mumble with a laugh. I can barely muster up a *bonjour* and here he is having a full on conversation with the waiter. Talk about feeling inadequate. "So..." I start hunting for a topic of conversation that hopefully won't make me feel so bad about myself. "Have you known Edward a long time?"

"Yeah, we went to school and university together, along with his now wife. She works in fashion and got a job out here a few years ago. He followed her and opened this place."

"It's amazing," I say looking around the restaurant again. "And that explains the dress."

He doesn't comment about how he organised the dress, instead he changes the subject. "What do you do, Red?"

Thoughts of my old life immediately put a dampener on my spirits. I swallow it down though and try to have a normal conversation about my job. "I was a PA for an asshole of a guy who has a massive real estate portfolio. Well, I was paid as his assistant but he spent most of his time in exotic countries with different women so I pretty much ran everything."

"Interesting," Daniel mutters to himself as he sips his wine.

"What? Why?"

"Do you need a job?"

"I... uh... yeah, I guess," I say knowing that I need to get my life back on track. Moping around with memories of what used to be isn't going to get me very far. "Why? Are you offering me one?"

"Yeah, if you want it." My chin drops open in shock at his words. As if bringing me to Paris for a few days wasn't enough he's now offering me a job.

"I don't even know what you do. Plus I might be a terrible assistant, you have no idea."

"I'm a good judge of character, Red. Plus if you were shit, the *asshole*," he says, using his best American accent, "wouldn't have left you to it."

"I guess. So what is it you do then?" I've been dying to know how he got all his money since the moment I stepped into his house.

"I'm the English version of your boss, although I'd hope less of an arsehole."

"You're in real estate?"

"Yeah, although it's not called that over here, yank. My brother and I run our family estate agents plus we have a house renovation and rental side that we started up a few years ago." He has another sip of his wine before saying. "I'm serious about the job. My assistant is about to go on maternity leave. She's already told me she's not coming back afterwards. I've interviewed so many people for the job but no one's been right. You though, I think you'd be perfect for me." The way he says this causes tingles to run down my spine. Surely it's just my overactive imagination that heard the words 'you'd be perfect for me' in a different context than work.

"We'll see," I mutter, because I'm not entirely sure it would be a good idea. Thankfully, he drops the subject. I'm worried he's going to ask more about my life in America but he doesn't. He keeps the conversation light as we enjoy the incredible food that arrives at our table.

"Sir, your taxi has just arrived," the concierge says.

"Merci," Daniel replies, as he takes my hand.

Twenty minutes later and I'm sat on a stool in a bar with another glass of gorgeous French red in my hand listening to a jazz band play on the stage. The room is filled with elegant couples, young and old, enjoying a romantic evening together. There is an elderly couple up on the dance floor. The way they still move together shows the fantastic relationship they must share. They must be seventy at least but they are still moving as if they are out on their first date. It warms my heart to see that some relationships do stand the test of time and that love can last and if anything, grow stronger.

I lift my hand to my eye to wipe a tear but I'm not as discreet as I hoped because Daniel immediately asks if I'm okay.

"Yeah, it's just those two," I say nodding to the couple I was watching. "Look how in love they are." As I say this, the song comes to an end stopping their dancing. We watch as the man leans forward and kisses his wife on the cheek. It's such a sweet moment and it reminds me of all the things I thought I had.

I'm pulled from my depressing thoughts when Daniel laces his fingers through mine and pulls me from the stool.

"What are you doing?" I ask in a panic.

He doesn't respond, he just continues moving until we are stood in the middle of the dance floor. He comes to a stop and pulls me against his chest. His arms come around me and his hands rest on my lower back.

I'm completely blown away. Again. This man who claims to only want a weekend of sex is now slow dancing with me in the most romantic venue I think I've ever been in. How exactly does he expect me to forget about him when this is all over? I can feel my heart breaking all over again and our time isn't over yet. The problem is my heart is already too weak to be broken again so soon.

I lean farther into him and take in his scent. I try my best to memorise this moment. How he smells, how he feels pressed up against me because something tells me that this is one of those moments. One of those moments that you'll remember forever, and forever wish you could be transported back to.

Dancing with Daniel is the most erotic foreplay I've ever experienced. The way his body feels rubbing against mine. His hands gently caressing anywhere that is safe to do so in public is driving me insane. Every time he moves his hips I feel his erection pressing into my stomach. I swear if something doesn't happen soon then I'm going to combust right here on the dance floor. My desire for this man is off the charts.

"We need to leave now," gets growled in my ear after another song or two.

"Uh-huh." I'm no longer capable of words. All my attention is focused on him and what I need from him.

Daniel places his hand on my lower back and guides me to the exit. The skin of his palm burns my skin and makes my heart thump that bit faster.

We are soon sliding into a taxi and racing back toward the hotel. Unlike the journey here, this time the lights of the city pass me by. All my focus is on the powerful man sat next to me and the dark and hungry look in his eyes.

I run my eyes down his suit clad body, appreciating every inch of perfection that is in front of me. When I get down to his thighs I can clearly see the outline of his erection straining against the fabric. It makes my mouth water for a taste of him.

I reach out my hand but it gets stopped an inch from its destination. He lifts it to my lips before placing kisses to each of my knuckles then sucks my fingertips into his mouth. I swallow down the noise that bubbles up my throat in the hope it doesn't alert the cab driver to what's happening in his back seat.

Daniel watches intently as I fidget and squirm in my seat, as I try to ease the tension between my legs. Nothing works though; nothing short of him will solve my problem. His eyes get darker the longer he stares at me and his hands start to clench into fists at his side where he's trying to restrain himself.

"Bonsoir, Monsieur, Madame," the concierge says hurriedly as Daniel pulls me through the front doors of the hotel. I manage to squeak out a good evening before we disappear into the elevator.

I can sense that Daniel's restraint has snapped and as the doors begin to close I feel him turn toward me. Unfortunately at the last minute someone sticks their hand between the closing doors and halts their progress. We both turn as two men step in with us.

I hear a weird grunting noise come from Daniel and I have to bite my lips to keep myself from laughing out loud.

The second the doors open on our floor Daniel takes me by the hand again and pulls me out past the two guys who were just about to step out. I shout an apology over my shoulder and I'm sure I hear one say "Don't worry love I'd be rushing too," but I could be mistaken.

The second our hotel room door has shut he's on me. I'm pushed back against the wall by the entire length of his body. His mouth descends on mine and his tongue forces its way in past my lips. Daniel's hands rush around my body like they don't know where to touch first. It might be amusing if I wasn't so desperate.

My hands follow suit and run up from his stomach to his chest under his jacket. When I get to his neck I start pulling at his tie before making light work of undoing his shirt buttons. Once I'm at the bottom I move to his fly.

"Too many clothes," I mutter when his lips move down onto my neck. His response is to bite down on my exposed collarbone. "Argh, fuck," I groan.

Then his mouth is gone but when I look down he's pulling my skirt up around my waist and wrapping his hands around my thighs. My legs immediately wrap around his waist and I feel his hardness pressing into me.

"Need," is the only word I get out because he must feel my desperation. He shifts me slightly until he has his cock in his hand. The tip is glistening, showing me he's just as ready as I am for this. Not a second after he's moved my knickers out of the way do I feel him sliding inside me. I was expecting it to be fast but he takes his time. His eyes close and all the muscles in his neck pull tight as the sensation takes over.

He stills when he's as far in as possible. He leans forward and places his face in the crook of my neck. His heavy breathing tickles across my sensitive skin, making my already hard nipples tighten that bit more.

"Daniel," I groan because as good as this feels, I need more, I need movement.

After another couple of seconds his hips start to move. He thrusts in and out gently a couple of times before he circles his hips, sending me over the edge. I was so worked up that one perfect touch was enough. My muscles clamp down around him as the climax rushes through my body.

"Fuck, yes," he shouts before slamming his lips down on mine for a hard and dirty kiss.

When he pulls back, I'm panting again as I feel my second orgasm building. I've had multiples before but the speed of this second one takes me by surprise.

Daniel slows his movements slightly as he reaches up behind my neck. I feel the fabric tighten and I panic. "No!" He looks up at me in shock. "Don't rip this one," I say to clarify.

He lets out a breath of relief before saying, "This one is too good to ruin," and gently undoes the buttons so he can pull the fabric around my waist.

His hands move to my tits the second the fabric drops. He squeezes and caresses them before pinching both of my nipples, hard. That one last bolt of pleasure sends me crashing into orgasm number two.

When I've come back to reality, Daniel's hands are on my hips again and he's thrusting into me with determination. His head returns to my neck just a second before his body stills as he comes inside me.

"Never going to be enough," he says quietly as his breathing starts to return to normal.

When he pulls back and looks at me my breath catches. The look in his eyes, I can't describe. His passion and hunger are still there but there is more, awe maybe. I'm not entirely sure.

Daniel breaks free of his trance after a couple of seconds and drops my legs back to the floor.

"Are you okay?" I ask, as I reach up to cup his cheek.

His response is to kiss me and push my dress from my hips. I'm more than happy with this but I feel like he's doing it to hide from me.

Daniel

I'm once again laid here watching her sleep. I've barely known her twenty-four hours, how is it possible to feel like I never want to let her go. I know hardly anything about her, yet at the same time I feel like I know everything I need to know.

I run my eyes over her again. It's like I'm worried that if I stop looking or shut my eyes, she's going to disappear. Her hair is damp from the shower we took earlier, her face free of any make-up. The blush of her cheeks and chest is still visible from her many, many orgasms of the last few hours and her lips swollen from my kisses.

My cock twitches.

This is insane. How does she have such an effect on me?

Eventually, I must drift off to sleep because I'm woken with a start when I hear a shout.

"No. No you can't do this to me. No. Stewart, no, this can't be true," I turn and watch as tears start to pour from her eyes. I get this feeling wash over me that I don't think I've ever experienced before when I see her tears. "No, no, no," she repeats until she's quiet again.

When I wake again the room is bright with winter sunshine. I reach over to find Beth but her side of the bed is empty and cold.

I prop myself up on my elbow and look across the room. I see her instantly. She's sat in the chair facing the sights Paris has to offer, wrapped in a blanket. She's fast asleep though. I wonder if whatever she was dreaming about eventually woke her. I want to seriously hurt this Stewart for whatever it is he has done to her. I've never felt anyone's pain before. Well that's not entirely true, I felt everything that our parents put Molly through but that was different, she's my sister.

I quickly make use of the bathroom before noticing the time. I've got stuff planned for today so we need to get going. I quietly place an order for room service breakfast before I crouch down next to Beth to wake her.

I reach my hand out and run it down the smooth skin of her cheek and onto her neck. Her eyes start to flicker behind her eyelids.

"Morning, Red," I say softly before reaching forward and placing a kiss to the corner of her mouth.

When I pull back her eyes are open. I can see storm clouds in her light grey eyes showing me that her dream still has its grips on her.

"Good morning," she replies, as a beautiful sleepy smile creeps across her lips. That smile does something to me. It's like there is some kind of force pulling me to her. I don't fight it; I lean in and place my lips to hers.

"I missed you," I sulk when I pull back.

"Sorry, I couldn't sleep so I came over to enjoy the Paris lights. I must have fallen asleep at some point."

"Why couldn't you sleep?" I ask, hoping she'll open up to me. I don't want to question her but I will find out what went on in America before we touch down on English soil again.

"No idea," she mumbles in reply as she sits herself up. I decide to leave it for now. I don't want to ruin the day, yet.

"I've ordered breakfast. It will be here soon then we've got loads to do."

"Have we?" she asks with a smile.

"Yep. I'm going to show you Paris." I swear my heart turns over as her face lights up with joy. She claps her hands together in delight before hurrying to the bathroom, giving me a great shot of her naked arse and swaying hips. My morning wood returns in the blink of an eye.

"Wh... what are you doing?" she squeals in fright as I step into the shower behind her.

"What, you think I was going to allow you to shower alone?" I run my hands around her until they are palming her breasts as I run kisses down her neck and across her shoulders. She doesn't respond to my question with words, instead she makes this amazing humming sound in her throat which makes me lose my mind.

The guy who was banging on the bathroom door while we were in the shower obviously got bored of waiting because when I finally opened it there was a trolley fully stocked with food abandoned just outside. Beth wasn't exactly quiet so I can only presume he was aware of what was keeping us.

CHAPTER SIX

Beth

I think it's safe to say that today has been the best day of my life. Once I managed to push last night's nightmare from my mind and focus on Daniel that is.

I don't know why I was so shocked to find that he'd followed me into the shower. If the look on his face when I woke wasn't enough of a clue then his hard cock should have been. I think that was probably the best shower I've ever had. Much better than the one yesterday, before dinner. I felt like we were still fumbling around each other a little then but after last night I feel like I've known him, or his body more like, forever. We both knew exactly what the other needed and how to work each other's bodies to find the ultimate pleasure. There's a lot to be said for hours of mindless hotel room fucking.

When the banging started on the bathroom door, I panicked, but Daniel soon put paid to that when he circled my clit with his talented fingers and pushed me over the edge. I cried out, not caring that there was someone stood just outside. How could I care when I was under this incredible man's touch?

When we eventually emerged, Daniel found the most amazing champagne breakfast waiting for us. I swear I'm going to need to diet for a month after all the gorgeous cold meats, bread, croissants, pain au chocolat, and other French delicacies. It was out of this world.

Since then Daniel has taken me to every place I wanted to see in Paris. Each was even more incredible than I could have imagined. I'm not going to forget this trip in a hurry.

"The view from up here is amazing," I say to Daniel, who is standing at my back with his arms wrapped around my waist.

"Uh-huh," he mumbles as he shoves his face into my neck and starts kissing instead of looking at the whole of Paris laid out before us.

We're on our last stop of the day, the Eiffel Tower. I thought the view from our hotel was good but this is something else.

"Daniel," I say, giving him a nudge with my elbow. "Why aren't you looking?"

"I am. I'm looking at you."

"That's not what I mean."

"I've seen it before, I prefer you."

"Just look out there for me."

"No, I'm good."

"Daniel," I say with an amused tone in my voice. "Are you scared of heights?"

"Don't be stupid, of course not."

"Okay, so you wouldn't mind coming over to the edge with me and looking down then?"

"Uh... sure."

I go to take a step forward and his arms clamp around me like steel. I turn around so I'm facing him and smile because I know I'm right. He's scared.

"Fine, okay. I don't like heights."

Now I've turned around it's even clearer that he's uncomfortable because his eyes are a little too wide and he has a bead of sweat along his hairline.

"Why did you come up if you don't like it?"

"Because you wanted to."

Everything inside me tumbles at his response. What am I doing? I ask myself for the millionth time. I can try to convince myself all I want that this weekend has just been about the sex but I think it's time I stopped lying to myself because I know that I like him more than I should. I didn't think it would be possible to feel anything for anyone ever again but somehow this dark and delicious stranger has crept in through the cracks in my heart and after only two days is putting it back together again. The only problem is that I'm pretty sure he's going to smash it to pieces when our time is up and we fly back in the morning. I try not to think about the inevitable because it will put a dampener on our remaining time together.

"You're so sweet," I say as I stretch up on my tiptoes to give the corner of his lips a kiss, copying his move.

"No one has ever called me sweet before," he replies, screwing up his face in disgust. "Sexy, hot, sex god, yes. Sweet, never."

"Well, Daniel, maybe you've never been sweet before but I can definitely say that you are."

"What about the other things I mentioned," he whispers in my ear before he bites down on my earlobe, making me squeal.

"I guess," I say with a shrug.

"You guess," he repeats. "You guess," he says again as he forcefully pushes me backwards against the railing and sucks hard on my neck.

"Okay, okay, you are."

"I am what?" he asks once he's detached his lips from me.

"A hot... sexy... sex god," I croak out as his hands start wandering and he looks at me with smouldering eyes.

"Good, I'm glad you think so."

"Did I have a choice?" I reply with a laugh.

When Daniel steps back from me, or more away from the edge he reveals a couple behind him. "Oh my God," I say with a gasp, bringing my hand up to my mouth and making him turn and look in the same direction.

Just a few feet away from us is a guy down on one knee holding out a little black box to a very shocked looking woman. We stand and watch in silence as tears start to stream down her face. The guy is saying something to her but we're too far away to hear properly. After a few more seconds the woman starts nodding her head and shouting 'yes' over and over again causing more tourists to turn and look their way. The guy slides the ring onto her finger before standing and sweeping her off her feet in a huge hug. Everyone who witnessed their little moment starts clapping and a few cheer.

When their lips touch I turn around to look over the city again to give them privacy to celebrate. Daniel once again comes to stand behind me but this time when I look back at him he is looking out to the distance completely lost in his own head.

"Penny for your thoughts," I say, hoping to bring him back.

He looks down at me for a long time before opening his mouth to say anything. "Do... do you ever want to get married?"

"Of course, one day. Doesn't everyone want that?"

"I didn't," he says, looking away from me.

"Oh," I say in the hope it'll prompt him to say more.

"I never wanted to be a burden on anyone. I watched what it was like for my mum and dad. He worked a lot, like I do, and although my mum loved the money it was clear that she wasn't happy. I don't know," he says as he takes a moment to gather his thoughts. "I just think that a marriage should be about two people, not two people and a business. I imagine that a husband's world should revolve around the woman he loves, his family, not his work. I've never thought I could give someone what they deserve. I wouldn't be able to give them everything because so much of my life is work, it wouldn't be fair."

My heart breaks for him. The reason he's lived the way he has for all these years is because he doesn't feel worthy of someone else. That makes me so sad.

"Daniel, I..." I begin to say but I'm relieved when he stops me because I had no idea where I was going with that statement.

"It's weird," he says but pauses again, making me think he's not going to continue. "Suddenly, I feel like I have more to give," his eyes come back down to mine, "like I might be able to be that person, that man who puts his wife first, her needs before his own."

I turn around so I'm facing him properly hoping he'll say more but he doesn't. He just lowers his head toward me until his lips are against mine. I have no idea if he was trying to say what I think he was but I'm not going to push him. I'm achingly aware that he hasn't asked me about what brought me back to England and I'm more than grateful. I'm worried that if I push him for more, then he'll do the same.

We walk along the river hand in hand, taking in all the buildings and people we pass. It might be January but in the sun it's fairly pleasant. I feel a tug at my arm as Daniel decides to stop on a sun covered bench. I follow him and sit myself down.

We sit in silence, watching the world go by for the longest time. I glance down at my hand and smile to myself. When we came down from the Eiffel Tower there was a guy selling key rings and other merchandise. I wasn't intending on buying anything—money is a little tight at the moment, something I'm achingly aware of every time Daniel spends money on me— so I went to step away after looking at everything. I didn't realise that Daniel wasn't with me as I strolled away lost in my own world until he caught up to me and placed a little metal Eiffel Tower into the palm of my hand. When I glanced up at him to say thank you he had a nervous look on his face. Anyone would think he was the one just handing over an engagement ring, not a key ring.

"Thank you, you didn't have to."

"Something to remember me by," he replies sadly. My heart drops at another reminder that our time together is coming closer to the end.

"Are you okay?" Daniel asks, pulling me from my earlier memory.

"Yeah, I'm fine." I squeeze the key ring a little tighter in my hand and will the tears that are stinging my eyes to disappear.

"Can I ask you something?"

"Sure."

"Will you tell me about why you came back... about Stewart?" he says cautiously.

My heart started to race the second I realised where this was going. My stomach turned over and I thought I was going to puke right there in the middle of Paris.

"I... uh..."

"You don't have to if it's too hard."

I have a sudden realisation that I want to tell him. I have no idea why, because for the last few weeks I'd have rather pulled my eyelashes out with a pair of tweezers than talk—or even think—about it. Not even my family knows the whole truth behind my running away.

I take a deep breath and look out at the river. "I met him about four years ago on a night out. I was out with friends; he was on a stag do. I was instantly attracted to him and I couldn't believe it when he seemed to be interested in me as well.

"We dated for quite a long time. I was still studying and didn't really have time for a full-blown relationship. Once things settled down and I had a job we started seeing each other more and more. To cut a long story short he bought an apartment in the city and I moved in with him.

"Things were amazing, although he wasn't always around because of his job. But when he was, it was incredible. I thought I'd found the one. I started thinking about weddings and kids because I was convinced they were on the cards for us.

"It was coming up to our anniversary and he was out of town for a long weekend so I planned to spend the Saturday at the mall to get his present. I'd chosen the watch I wanted and planned the inscription.

"The watch was the first thing I bought before I started wandering around the shops to fill the rest of my day, not wanting to return to an empty apartment. I'll always wonder now how long it would have taken me to find out if I had left.

"I sat down outside a coffee shop for lunch. I was waiting for it to be delivered when I saw someone who looked just like him. I told myself it couldn't be though, because he was in New York. I'd taken him to the airport myself the morning before. But as I watched and he got closer it became clearer to me that it was him, and he wasn't alone. Attached to his left hand was a woman. She was older than me, probably about the same age as him. Then trailing along behind them were three kids. I slouched down in my chair trying to hide behind the menu. Eventually, they walked right past me, totally oblivious that my world was falling apart around me. As they walked past they were so close it was almost impossible not to see the wedding bands on both of their fingers.

"After throwing up in the coffee shop toilets I went home, packed some stuff and got on the first flight home. My dad's work contract had finished in the summer so he, my mum and brother were already back in England."

"What an arsehole," is all Daniel says as he pulls me in for a hug. "Have you heard from him?" he eventually asks.

"No, but I haven't turned my phone on since taking off and I don't have any intention of doing so. He doesn't know where we live but he knows our names so it wouldn't be too hard for him to hunt me down, I guess."

"That scumbag didn't deserve you, Beth. You did the right thing."

I know in my heart that I did the right thing. But it doesn't mean that I haven't questioned it over the last few weeks. He was my entire life. I thought he was the one I was going to grow old with and all the rest of it. He broke me, utterly broke me.

"Thank you," I say quietly. "I didn't think I'd ever laugh again after it happened but you've brought me back to life. These past two days have been... Thank you," I repeat because I can't put into words what these two days have been like for me. Amazing, incredible, no word I can think of fully describes how wonderful they have been. How wonderful he has been. I decide to show him instead, I wrap my hand around the back of his neck and pull his lips to mine.

The second we step foot back in our hotel room my phone stops ringing on the bedside table.

"Can you pass my cell please?" I say to Daniel, as he's heading that way.

"Pass your what?" he asks with a smile.

"Ugh, my mobile," I say in my best English accent. "Shut up," I mutter with a smile on my face as I take it from him. When I look down and see six missed calls from Caleb I decide I should probably ring back. I've already ignored loads of texts from him. I know it's because he cares but I know what I'm doing. He doesn't need to worry about me.

"Hey, Ca, what's up?"

"Beth, what the hell are you playing at going to Paris with some stranger?"

"Ca, I'm twenty-six not six. I can do what the hell I want. Is that all you wanted, to give me grief, because if it is, can it wait until I'm back?"

"No, that's not all. I need to know when you're back because... well you need to come home and deal with stuff Beth, not keep running away." The way he says this makes my stomach knot.

"Why?"

"Just get your ass back home, Beth. You've got a life to sort out," he says sternly, which is very unlike my little brother.

"Fine, okay, I'll be back tomorrow."

After saying our goodbyes I drop my cell to the bed before sitting on the edge and putting my head in my hands. He's right, of course. I've got to sort myself out. I need a job to start with. Most of my earnings in America went into a joint account so I only have what little I had in savings and that isn't going to get me very far.

"Are you okay?" Daniel asks as he comes to sit next to me.

"Yeah. My brother was helpfully giving me a reality check." Daniel doesn't ask any more, he must sense that I don't want to talk so he just holds me.

Daniel

Our final night in Paris is a quiet one. After her revelation about her ex and then the short conversation with her brother, Beth isn't really in the mood for getting dressed up for a fancy meal. So instead we stay as we are and find a quiet local restaurant for dinner.

I really want to press her more about what she's planning on doing now. The desire to ask her to work for me again and move her life down to Oxford is on the tip of my tongue all evening. I know it would be selfish of me to ask and for once I'm trying to do the right thing and not just think of myself. She's got a lot to deal with when she gets back and I need to not get in the middle of it, as much as I may want to.

Much like the rest of the evening the sex we have when we get back to our room is much calmer. I hate to say it but it's like we're saying goodbye. We both knew our time was coming to an end and this was us grieving I guess you could say. Well, it was for me anyway. I desperately don't want to say goodbye to Beth, I don't want this to be over. And as much as it frightens me to admit it, I know it's the truth. I never thought I'd find anyone that I would say that about but I have and now I have to let her go. It's like a kick in the fucking balls.

<hr>

"Flight BA365 to London Gatwick is now boarding, please make your way to the gate."

"I guess that's our cue," I say to Beth. I'm trying desperately hard not to allow her to see that she's affected me, that I don't want this to be the end. I'm trying to be the man she thinks I am and the one I need to be to allow her to find her place again in England. Her sadness on the other hand is written all over her face. All morning she's looked like she's on the verge of tears. I can tell she's trying to fight it, but she's not winning.

She barely says a word the entire flight back to London and she's still eerily quiet on the long drive up to Liverpool to her parents' house.

"I'm so sorry," she says quietly when the SatNav tells us we're only thirty minutes away. "I've totally ruined our last day."

"Don't be silly. I know you've got a lot going on. It's okay." I try to sound as reassuring as possible because I do understand. It's not really how I'd planned our last few hours together but I do get it.

I didn't think the day could get any worse but I was wrong.

"Do you want to come in for coffee?" Beth asks when I pull up outside her parents' house.

"Sure," I say because the thought of turning around and driving back to Oxford now doesn't thrill me.

We both get out of the car and I grab her bags then follow her inside.

"Hey, I'm back," Beth calls out once we're in the hallway.

"Is this you?" I ask as I stop in front of a recent looking family photo. I know it's her, I could tell from a mile away but she's got long blonde hair.

"Yeah," she says sadly and pulls at a strand of her hair, "this is new."

"Oh," is all I get to say because someone coming to stand in the doorway at the end of the hallway stops us both in our tracks.

"St-Stewart?" Beth questions when she looks up.

"Beth, sweetness, I'm so sorry," he begins saying to her but my movement makes him look behind her. "Who the fuck are you?" he growls. His anger is instant.

"Daniel, you need to go. I'm sorry." Beth turns to look at me, her eyes pleading with me to do as she asks.

There are so many things I want to say in that moment but I don't. Am I right in not saying them, who knows? I step forward and place a soft kiss to her cheek.

"It's been a pleasure, Red," I whisper before stepping back and walking out of the house without a second glance. If I looked up at him I'd have wanted to lay the fucker out for what he did to her and I know that isn't going to help anyone, well other than make me feel better.

The drive home is horrendous. Not only do I feel like I've left something very important behind but the traffic is nose to tail for miles. I spend the entire journey thinking about what I should have said to her before I walked out.

It's late into the night when I eventually make it to my front door. I slam it closed behind me, throw my suitcase in the general direction of the stairs and head straight for a bottle of whisky.

Why does leaving her behind have to hurt so fucking much?

EPILOGUE

Daniel

How can knowing someone for only three days have such a huge impact on your life? Not an hour has gone by since leaving her in Liverpool six weeks ago where I haven't thought of her.

During the day it's innocent little things like her smile, the way her accent changed with her mood or what she was talking about. I'd see things that would remind me of the colour of her eyes or her hair.

Then at night those thoughts change. They turn to how it felt to have my lips on her, how it felt being inside her. Her sweet smell, her quiet moans of pleasure.

Damn it, she's ruined me. I can't even bring myself to look at another woman, let alone touch one. My body has had a taste of her and now she's all it wants. If only I could have her.

I shake my head and try to bring my focus back to all the paperwork that is covering every available surface of my office. My assistant left three weeks ago and I'm yet to find anyone suitable to replace her. I guess being rushed off my feet is a good thing really because it keeps my mind off of her.

"Fuck's sake, what now?" I ask myself when the doorbell sounds out around the house. If that's Molly again trying to stage an intervention I'm not going to be impressed. As much as she's enjoying seeing me pining after a woman for the first time in my life, she's also worried about me. It's not necessary though. As I keep telling her, I'm fine.

I drag my pathetic arse toward the front door thinking that I probably should have put a top on and not answer the door in only a pair of jogging bottoms but I don't really care enough to bother. Instead I pull the door open when I get there hoping I can convince whoever it is to leave as quickly as they arrived.

The second I lock eyes on my visitor though, all those thoughts go out of the window. Staring back at me is a pair of familiar grey eyes. I watch in amusement as her eyes drop to my chest.

"Red?"

"Can I come in?" she asks, making me realise I've been stood here blocking the doorway just staring at her.

"Of course, sorry."

I close the door behind her and watch as she drops her bag on the sideboard before turning to face me. It's awkward for a few seconds. I want to say something, to break the silence, but I'm speechless. I was not expecting this, her.

I think she's going to say something but instead she steps toward me, stretches up and places her lips against mine. I respond instantly, my fingers come up and weave into her hair and I tilt her head to the side so I can deepen our kiss. It's not until that moment that I realised how much I needed her.

I lift her into my arms and carry her upstairs to the place this all started. Well, not quite, because the first thing I did when I got back from Paris was to order a new bed. And I hoped this one would be for one woman only.

"I can't believe you're here," I say breathlessly, as I pull my face from the crook of her neck. I look down at her and take in her flushed cheeks and swollen lips. Fuck she's beautiful. "I didn't think I'd see you again," I admit.

I pull out of her and fall onto my side. I refuse to let her go though, now she's here she's not going anywhere for a really long time.

"I just needed some time to sort my head out."

"I thought maybe you'd gone b—" I start to say but get interrupted.

"No. I would never go back to him after what he did. I knew I didn't want him but seeing him there that day, having to tell you to leave, it all became clear. I knew I wanted you, but I needed to get everything sorted before I could come to you."

I smile down at her. It's like she's always been here. I guess in a way she has been. "I've missed you, Red."

"I've missed you, too. I need to ask you something."

"Go on," I prompt.

"Do you still need a PA?"

Relief washes through me. She's here to stay. I lean forward and kiss her with everything I've got, trying to put everything I feel, but am too scared to admit, into it.

"Is that a yes?" she says with a laugh when I pull back.

"When can you start?"

THE END

Want more of the Falling Series?
Get your copy of Falling For Him: Part Two!

ABOUT THE AUTHOR

Tracy Lorraine is a *USA Today* and *Wall Street Journal* bestselling new adult and contemporary romance author. Tracy has recently turned thirty and lives in a cute Cotswold village in England with her husband, baby girl and lovable but slightly crazy dog. Having always been a bookaholic with her head stuck in her Kindle, Tracy decided to try her hand at a story idea she dreamt up and hasn't looked back since.

Be the first to find out about new releases and offers. Sign up to my newsletter here.

If you want to know what I'm up to and see teasers and snippets of what I'm working on, then you need to be in my Facebook group. Join Tracy's Angels here.

Keep up to date with Tracy's books at
www.tracylorraine.com

ALSO BY TRACY LORRAINE

Falling Series

Falling for Ryan: Part One #1

Falling for Ryan: Part Two #2

Falling for Jax #3

Falling for Daniel (A Falling Series Novella)

Falling for Ruben #4

Falling for Fin #5

Falling for Lucas #6

Falling for Caleb #7

Falling for Declan #8

Falling For Liam #9

Forbidden Series

Falling for the Forbidden #1

Losing the Forbidden #2

Fighting for the Forbidden #3

Craving Redemption #4

Demanding Redemption #5

Avoiding Temptation #6

Chasing Temptation #7

Rebel Ink Series

Hate You #1

Trick You #2

Defy You #3

Play You #4

Inked (A Rebel Ink/Driven Crossover)

Rosewood High Series

<u>Thorn</u> #1

<u>Paine</u> #2

<u>Savage</u> #3

<u>Fierce</u> #4

<u>Hunter</u> #5

Faze (#6 Prequel)

<u>Fury</u> #6

<u>Legend</u> #7

<u>Maddison Kings University Series</u>

<u>TMYM: Prequel</u>

<u>TRYS</u> #1

<u>TDYW</u> #2

<u>TBYS</u> #3

<u>TVYC</u> #4

<u>TDYD</u> #5

<u>TDYR</u> #6

<u>TRYD</u> #7

<u>Knight's Ridge Empire Series</u>

<u>Wicked Summer Knight</u>: Prequel (Stella & Seb)

<u>Wicked Knight</u> #1 (Stella & Seb)

<u>Wicked Princess</u> #2 (Stella & Seb)

<u>Wicked Empire</u> #3 (Stella & Seb)

<u>Deviant Knight</u> #4 (Emmie & Theo)

<u>Deviant Princess</u> #5 (Emmie & Theo

<u>Deviant Reign</u> #6 (Emmie & Theo)

<u>One Reckless Knight</u> (Jodie & Toby)

<u>Reckless Knight</u> #7 (Jodie & Toby)

<u>Reckless Princess</u> #8 (Jodie & Toby)

<u>Reckless Dynasty</u> #9 (Jodie & Toby)

Dark Halloween Knight (Calli & Batman)

Dark Knight #10 (Calli & Batman)

Dark Princess #11 (Calli & Batman)

Dark Legacy #12 (Calli & Batman)

Corrupt Valentine Knight (Nico & Siren)

Ruined Series

Ruined Plans #1

Ruined by Lies #2

Ruined Promises #3

Never Forget Series

Never Forget Him #1

Never Forget Us #2

Everywhere & Nowhere #3

Chasing Series

Chasing Logan

The Cocktail Girls

His Manhattan

Her Kensington